Table of Contents

Book One – Sylvie

Book Two – Gizande

Book Three – Clara

About the Author

Originating from southern England, after leaving university, Chris became a teacher in Merseyside and Bristol, where he became politically radicalised by the inequality and poverty he saw. Returning north, he became a bus man and a shop steward in Yorkshire for five years. He was unemployed during the "Winter of Discontent" 1978-9 and then trained as a probation officer. He worked with young offenders back on Merseyside for six years, and then became a children's services manager in a Welsh social services department. In 1997, he confronted his employers over their failure to follow their own child protection procedure. He took early retirement and became a witness against them to the Waterhouse Tribunal on child abuse. It was at this time that he started to write *The Tomorrows That Sing.* He subsequently became active with Freedom to Care, the whistleblower support group, particularly campaigning against corruption in public services. He was manager in a small independent fostering agency and now represents children in the Courts. He and his wife have five adult children between them, and live near Wrexham, in North Wales, with their grandchild.

Foreword

This is my story. Although I had never led an unremarkable life, reading back over these events now, I can hardly believe they happened to me.
I asked Chris Clode to write it and gave him the freedom to tell the story how he felt best, only requiring him to change the names of all except my family.

Jim Briggs,
La Retraite,
Ariége,
France.

Chris Clode

SYLVIE
Book One of
The Tomorrows That Sing

Je fais une derniere fois mon examen de conscience. Il est positif j'irais dans la meme voie si j'avais a recommencer ma vie... Je vais préparer tout a l'heure des lendemains qui chantent.

For the last time I examine my conscience. I am positive that I would take the same route if I started my life over again... I prepare now for the tomorrows that sing.

Gabriel Peri, Member French National Assembly, last letter, 1941.

Chapter One

That October evening they came in out the gusty rain blowing up the estuary. They shook the wet off in the pub doorway and Jim laughed at the scamble they made across the street from their cars. He looked at Sylvie and caught a serious look shadowing her.

"Come on, let's inside," he urged her. The bar was empty, but for the t.v. booming out news about Beirut refugee camps, then pit closures. He watched her sit, unusually self-absorbed, in a remote corner and had to wake her to his presence with, "Sylvie? The usual?" She looked up to nod. Jim was surprised at her drawn look which he had not seen during the afternoon meeting. Not being her routine ironically cheerful self, he busied himself with trying to get the barman for the order.

But when he came back with the drinks, she was looking at a handwritten letter in her lap. Flatly she handed it to him when he sat down. Jim looked from the letter to her quizzically, but she was already looking away.

He read: spikey, careful writing. Clotted biro ink where the pen had paused, uncertain.

Dere miss

from Damian Toser, Flat 15, Ratcliffe House.

I hope you remember me. I came to see you in the Northlodge office about my housing benifit in sept. You helped me get it right. Thanks.

I hope you can help me agane. I want you to stop Mr Jefreys coming to see me. He says I have to let him see me because he is a trusty for Northlodge. He has been coming to see me a lot since the summer. At first he was just friendly and came with food and things becos I didnt have money. I thought he was doing this for Northlodge to help me. Then he begins to touch me and becos he give me food and things I let him but I didnt like it.

Jim stopped reading here and looked up at Sylvie. She stared away from him at the distant television. He looked at her a minute, not to find anything in looking, but to hold back a moment from the swirl in his brain the letter was pulling him into.

"This is Councillor Jeffreys, is it?" he asked to her turned away face, knowing the answer even before she nodded in reply. A pause before he pulled his eyes back to the page. *He said how he could help me becos he had friends and he said was I lonley and he put his hand on my leg when he said that. I let him do it and then he touched me high up and I was fritened and I let him do things to me and he gave me money and I did things to him. This happend more than one time. I didnt want to do it but he told me I would get in trouble if I told. I would lose the flat and not get any other. But I think now hes wrong and hes just trying to friten me so I do it with him again.*

Please help me. I dont want Mr Jefreys to come to my flat no more. I want you to help me but I dont want to get into trouble. So can you help me without telling you got this letter from me so Mr Jefreys cant get me out the flat.

Dont write to me here becos letters get nicked.

Damian.

Thank you.

Jim felt heavy as if he had taken on the turbulent confusion that lay behind the painfully, carefully chosen words of Damian's letter. And then his mind stumbled away from the patiently hurt words of the boy to the implications of knowing this about the senior councillor.

"You know he's likely to be next Deputy Leader of the Council? Jeffreys." Jim's voice croaked a little. He rinsed his dry throat with a swill of beer.

"So what? He's Housing Committee Chair now," she snapped. "So we do nothing about it?"

Jim's mind dawned that just reading that letter he was now part of it. Whatever it might turn out to be, he thought. "No." So many blind routes of circumstance led from where they sat now, he had no more to say then.

"No, what?"

He answered by passing the letter back to her. "What if it's not true?"

Sylvie looked at him, spiteful for a moment. "Typical man's remark."

Jim flushed. His meetings with Sylvie had always been light and friendly. He had seen her once angry at one of the housing working party meetings, but he had then acted angry alongside her. This was different territory. "Sorry... but they're very, very serious things he's saying in that letter."

"Well I believe him. I know Damian. And you know Jeffreys is a creep."

"Yes. But not this stuff." He looked at her defiant and troubled face and he blushed again, as a sexual flush went through him- and he wanted to hug her to get past the barrier of her challenge to him. He cast it off by looking down at the letter in her hand. "Well, tell me what you think."

"Of course it's true. And it fits with some other things. Maybe." She seemed to take a deep breath. "There's other things. With other boys.

And money around, too much of it. And there's the move-on flats, after they leave the first-step units like Ratcliffe House. There's something odd about the way the Board allocates those. I had a row with Hillingdon about it last week. Allocations don't seem to be based on need. I have to submit reports to the Board with recommendations, but the last couple of months some odd decisions have been made. Boys jumping the queue, getting move-ons before ones I recommend. And Jeffreys seems to be very active in it. With some other names. Unlikely people in touch with the office about plans for the boys. You know, local dignitaries?" She looked in Jim's face, searching. "I hope I can trust you, Jim. Not just me, but Damian too. I don't know what to do next." Then as an afterthought, "Damian's still got a social worker. I met him once, but I wasn't impressed. Bit old. Near retirement."

"Like me," Jim said, but immediately regretted the feeble attempt to lighten things. "Sorry. What office does he work from? Do you want me to talk to him about it?"

"What would you say?"

What indeed, Jim thought. Then it was his turn to take initiative. He searched his pockets and finally pulled out a large folded and crumpled envelope. He took out its contents, glanced at them and crushed them up into the ash tray. Then he split two sides of the envelope and opened it up into a large ragged sheet. "Got a pen?" Sylvie fished one out of her bag. "Right." He wrote Jeffreys' name page centre, Damian's off in one corner with a line linking the pair. "Give me another name and tell me about it. Hillingdon, who's he?"

Putting together the names on the tatty page gave Sylvie a way out of her anger. Jim linked together names with lines until the page looked like a drunken spider's web with about twenty names on it, boys, officials, local politicians, a policeman and two businessmen. They had to lower their voices when three men in overalls came in to drink noisily at the bar, but by then Jim and Sylvie had done all they could that night. It was gone seven and Jim had to get home to Jane. He was exhilarated with the work they had done together and smiled warmly at her across the table.

"What are you grinning at, Jim Briggs?" But she let herself smile in reply. "You know, thanks. I haven't known who to tell." She looked at him as if for the first time. Then, "Come on, Jim. We must split."

Outside, in the shelter of the doorway, before they crossed to their cars, she turned to him in the wet orange streetlight. "I know you're not sure you believe it all, but thanks, Jim. It helps me deal with it, even if I'm waiting for an idea what to do next." Unexpectedly, she leaned up and kissed his cheek and went out across the windy street, calling after her, "Call me at work."

He would. He would.

He phoned Sylvie at work as soon as he could late the following morning. "Hallo. Are you free to talk?"

"Who is that?" He felt wounded, then foolish that she had not recognised him. After last night's training run, he had felt much clearer about the route ahead and had thought Sylvie into the train of events he had scripted. It had felt close to her, but the voice on the line was wary, distant.

"Jim. Who did you think?"

"Oh. Hi." Flat, offering nothing, waiting for him to say more.

"Can you talk?"

"Yes." Pause. "What about?" Jim felt weakened by the unexpectedly hard work she was giving him.

"Come on, Sylvie. Last night."

She gave a short dry laugh. "That sounds bad." Pause again. "What, last night?"

She was playing some game. "You know what, last night. The letter."

"No, I certainly don't want to talk about it. Especially over a line from where you are calling."

"But I'm phoning from Social Services."

"Yes," she said, tersely. "That's precisely what I mean."

What? he thought. "Okay, but you did ask me. We need to meet to work out where we go from here." He waited for a reply. It was so silent. "Sylvie? You still there?"

"Yes. Well?"

"Why are you being so difficult? God, I'm having to drag every answer out of you." Wait. No answer."Okay. I need to meet you. Can we meet at the usual place? I think we have to decide what to do next. You must have had a reason for telling me that, showing me the letter. What about it? The usual place straight after work."

"Okay. If you wish." Brightly non-commital.

Jim was late. She was already there. Seeing her, pushed aside all the discomfort of the morning call.

As he came back with his beer, she said in a guarded waspish voice, "Right. Of course I gave you a hard time on the phone. For someone with all that political experience you're always talking about, you're pretty dim. Careless." She stopped him speaking. "You hear me out. We sat here yesterday and you did that chart on the envelope of all the people involved. Then you come on to me on the phone and want to talk to me about it, like it's the weather. Mentioning the letter. Dim? Or what?" She looked at him, sat back on the seat, cowed by her low sharp words. It flicked across his mind how this younger woman could turn him into a little boy. "Who are we talking about? The most important people in this city. Police, magistrates, big business, senior councillers. And that's just what we're guessing. Who knows what else is happening?"

"Okay," he said with the weary tone of the often-told-off. "Okay. You're right. It may be the tip of an iceberg. And I'm the captain of the Titanic," he smiled.

"Jim, you're the captain of nothing. We're nobodies. Probably disposable. I've thought about this a lot before telling you last night." Her face changed as she searched his for something to trust. "Don't let me down. Anything we decide to do about Damian's letter has got to take into account his safety. And the safety of some others we don't even know might be involved."

"And ourselves," Jim said softly, almost solemn. "Right. We need some rules about using phones, what we write down. Should we keep a file of stuff, like Damian's letter? Do we have anything else to go on? Any other documents? Do we tell anyone else?"

"Okay. One thing at a time." She pulled a pad from her bag, searched out a pen from the half-chaos of papers, documents and makeup. "We need a list of things." She wrote down in a column along the left edge of the page:

Phone,
Records,
Meetings,
Share info with who?

The barman idly watched the couple crouched intently round the little fancy table writing and talking indistinctly and he assumed adultery.

The next time they met at Sylvie's flat as their work started to involve too many documents to spread across a pub table. She had brought Northlodge files. The boys' histories in care and one on a pair of move-on flats at an unlikely Belgravia address in London, with a to-and-fro correpondence of complaints about what the boys were doing there. Closed down by the copy of a final letter from a Vice Squad officer to a neighbour, reassuring that the Police had no grounds for further enquiries into the matter. A further letter from the neighbour with more evidence of night visits by men to the boys, remained unanswered. And a letter of thanks to the Police from Jeffreys, on behalf of the Northlodge Board.

Jim was aware he had stayed on too late, and should be getting home. But could not leave the sheets of paper spread across the table, settee and floor of Sylvie's living room. He restlessly crossed and recrossed the room, eyes down, stepping carefully around the papers.

They had been silent and reflective together for a long moment, before she spoke in a low voice, "Now let's be careful about this. No jumping to conclusions. Sit down, Jim." She waited for him. "This could be completely out of hand. All this is based on one letter. I know I've told you that I've picked up some other stories, all except one about Jeffreys." Pause. "But it don't amount to a hill o' beans. Does it?"

Jim cleared his throat carefully. "But gut reaction, Sylvie? What's your gut reaction to all this?" He gestured to the carpet of paper. "You already felt it stank before you first showed me that letter from Damien. If you thought it was a one-off incident, you wouldn't have involved me."

"Recruited you, more like," Sylvie smiled at him. "I think I would have preferred you not to confirm my worst fears. I suppose I couldn't have judged you very well. You've spent your whole life with worst fears, haven't you, Jim?"

Oh, what he could tell her. The way all this was unravelling his own childhood inside him. "You could say that," was all he said. Wanting so much to share it with this young woman, with her businesslike warmth.

"Whatever my gut says, we need more. More information. Another lad to come forward as clearly as Damien has. Until then, it's just... well, a few bits of the jigsaw." She looked across to him. "And I don't want you going off the deep end with this. Particularly while we've got so little to go on, you must keep it to yourself."

"Don't lecture me."

"I certainly will. And it's past the time you should have been home." She leaned over and started to pull the nearest papers towards towards her. He got up to help, then took two mugs to the kitchen to rinse.

She sensed his reluctance to leave. "Come on, duty calls. Back to your wife."

His discomfort at the other whole of his life spilling into this separate part annoyed him. He collected his coat. At the door he wanted some intimate acknowledgement from Sylvie of this secret piece of his life. A kiss on the cheek as she had given that once. Or something less, but special.

"I'll be off," he said feebly.

She was curled over the papers earnestly. "See you," she said, without looking up.

"Yes. Next Tuesday."

"Fine."

He closed the front door too loudly and stood in the porch, waiting for a sound of her inside. Nothing. He set off home, feeling foolish and angry at whatever it was he felt.

Chapter Two

Having sifted through all the information they had on the papers in Sylvie's flat, Jim was convinced that they were at the edge of something. It was time to step out from the private, secretive conversations into doing, action of some sort. He wanted Sylvie to set up a meeting with Damian Toser. The three of them. To move beyond the paper. She was reluctant, anxious about stepping out from the safety of the close consensual meetings between the two of them. When he proposed this at their next meeting in her flat, she sifted through the files of paper they had created without answering for some time. As if she was seeking some clue to confirm her hesitation. Jim sat there across from her leaning forward, forearms on knees, watching her. Ready for go.

The four meetings since she had first shown him the letter, they had changed roles. She had added more documents from Northlodge and his caution, the reluctance to take the risk against Jeffreys, had been cleared away by the cumulative circumstantial evidence she had brought. He felt increasingly confident and his appetite for doing something grew with it. For Sylvie, though, the gathering force of her own arguments brought fear. She worked her brain through the implications of what they drew out on sheet after sheet of documents those evenings.

For Jim there was also the other force rising now from where it had been secretly stored so many years, secret even from himself. That sense of injustice to the child he had been making a fragmentary rediscovery of, these last weeks. His memories of the Institute he had been left in by his Aunt Mary had none of the cynical sexual exploitation implied by the stories they were trying to piece together. Some institutional violence dressed up as morality, yes. But what else? He felt something that was him, slept deep within. Within the self that had been rollcalled as Briggs, James, and had lived more privately as Jimmy, all those years ago. And through these meetings with this young woman, a restlessness stirred that seemed to be pushing aside not just these last unsatisfactory years of his life, but also that period he had always regarded with pride. Those years as shop steward in the Car Plant. That Heroic Age, as Mark had termed it before he died.

Sylvie agreed that a meeting had to take place but was indecisive about how and where. Jim suggested the Baltic Fleet and finally, Sylvie accepted the unarguable and agreed to ask Damien if he would meet them both in the pub one evening the following week. Jim felt exultant, despite Sylvie cautioning that Damian might refuse.

Two days later, Sylvie phoned Jim at work to say codedly that Damian had agreed to meet them at "the usual place" the following Wednesday. Sylvie insisted that it was used just this once.

"Okay," Jim said. "Cool down." He listened quizzically into the faint hiss of her breath in the earpiece, wondering at her insistence. "Just this once. As you say."

They agreed to Sylvie and Damien having a meal first before coming to the Baltic, to ease his suspicious caution before meeting Jim later. Subsequently, she would tell Jim that Damien had asked if he was anything to do with the police. If she had told him this before meeting the youth, they would have laughed together at the notion.

Jim arrived early at the pub. The same barman, a glaze of indifference over his interest in what he took to be an adulterous affair developing between this bloke and the younger woman he met here. Jim noticed nothing. Self-absorbed with the coming meeting, he sat in the corner of the empty, stale-smelling room.

An hour later, Sylvie had not arrived. Although there were other customers in the next bar, the barman covertly smirked at Jim being stood up. When he ordered his third beer, Jim felt there was something indefinably irritating in the way he was served.

He worried. All the worst possibilities of the still-tangled knot of names that they had struggled with. His mind on this, he became aware his eyes had started to smart with weeping. A moment of disbelief, then he turned half-away into the corner of the seat and smeared away the near-tears with his fingers. He looked down at the wet fingertips, trying to work out where it had come from. The feelings beyond his control that reduced him- Jim- to this. What's all this about? reprimanding the unruly emotions, and had just got himself under control again when Sylvie and Damien arrived.

"Sorry we're late," she said, smiling too brightly.

Jim stood up, Damien's thin height still overtopping him. "Damien? I'm Jim." He half put out his hand to the youth for shaking, but pulled back from the met mix of unease and aggression. "What would you like to drink?"

"Lager." Bluntly offered word.

"Usual?" to Sylvie. The barman's knowing superciliousness again, then back with the drinks. Crossing the room felt a long way, many steps, over to the woman and the boy sat close but separate in the draughty, ugly room.

Drinks on mats, not looking at Damien. A generally proferred, "Okay?" Jim sat and looked over to cue Sylvie to start.

"Damien asked me to say..."

She paused and Jim, an oblique glance towards Damien, murmured, "Shouldn't he say himself- shouldn't you say for yourself?"

Face to face with him, the boy's eyes above the thin jutted nose, defiant and shifty. Wanting to appeal to Sylvie, not letting himself be outstared by this man. Jim let him off and looked down at his own fingers resting round the chilled curve of the beer glass. Waiting to let Sylvie go on.

"Damien wanted to say he's agreed to meet you, Jim, because I asked. He doesn't really want anything to happen that's going to cause trouble." She looked across at Damien. "But he wants what happens with Mr. Jeffreys stopped."

"So do we, Damien," Jim said softly.

The boy breathed in, then out slowly, as if he had resolved something inside his mind. Jim waited for him to speak, but the youth's eyes stayed downcast to the drink before him on the table, untouched.

"What do you want us to do?" Jim prompted.

"Stop... to stop it," the boy growled, barely audible. A rasp to clear his throat, then firmly, "He makes me feel ugly," and his face twisted around the mouth and eyes to act the words.

Jim felt the clot of emotion rise in his gullet again. "We can get him- you somewhere else to live." Then turning, "Can't we,Sylvie?"

"We can. But that's not what Damien says he wants, is it?"

To speak, he seemed to summon up the breath from somewhere very deep, very tiredly. Old. "It isn't easy. I'd like to go... to get out. But I don't want to leave here, the town. I don't want to go to London. And if I stay around they'll know I told..."

Jim looked over at Sylvie for a clue, but she was looking at the youth just as quizzically. She reached her hand out on to his sleeve. "Who? Who's they?"

Damien, eyes down, reached for his glass for the first time, lifted it, drank and kept the rim to his mouth, faintly playing along it with his lips. "Who," he echoed, flatly.

"Yes. Who are you talking about?" Her hand lifted from his arm and waited.

"The others. The other lads." Jim felt the front of his brain screwed up with concentration, his attention locked onto the boy's face, damming back the turbulence of speculative fear filling the mind behind. Damien looked up, eyes catching Jim, then Sylvie, before rolling away as if on the brink of fainting. Her hand dropped again to steady him. "The others..."

Sylvie waited. Then, "What about the lads?"

He jerked up, hurriedly took another and careless slurp from the glass, put it down half off the damp coaster. "They all know about it. Where they come from they've done it before- with other blokes. I've never been in a kids' home like that sort, so I don't know. They do it and get money. Like tarts. They set me up. It was Finchy who got Mr. Jeffreys after me. I didn't know till later. He brought him to my room one night. It was dead late. Said Mr. Jeffreys was on one of his trusty visits. Well I didn't know. And that's when it all started." His eyes glittered. "And I want it to stop."

"Who's Finchy?" Jim asked, more to Sylvie than to the boy. "Is that Billy Finch, Damien?"

"Yeah. I heard later that he got money for setting me up. Then he threatened me not to tell. And he said he'd spread it about that I was bent if I tried to stop seeing Mr. Jeffreys. And I'd get kicked out of my room. And he'd tell everyone I got AIDS." Absent-mindedly, he moved his arm away from Sylvie's hand and drew a shape from the edge of a beer spill on the tabletop. "It's got to stop, but I'm real worried about you doing anything. Finchy and some of the others are dead hard, and I'm on my own there. They've been together in that private kids' home before, mostly. I was in the foster home before. I didn't know them."

"That's Whispering Pines, the private home," she interjected. But Jim ignored it, "How do you know Finch got money? Was it from Jeffreys?"

Damien looked at him. "He told me. He laughed at me because I did it with Mr. Jeffreys for nothing. And he waved these fivers in my face. When I said what did he have to do to get the money, what dirty things like, did he have to do, he hit me on the neck, right hard, then laughed and said the only thing he had to do was set it up between me and Mr. Jeffreys. I really got angry with him. But... what's the use?"

Jim stared at his gaunt face and had nothing to say. Sylvie waited too.

"I don't know if I want you to do anything. Maybe there's nothing... I don't know." He was almost crying. "What do you want anyway?" To both of them.

Jim felt himself shrivelling away from Damien, impotent to help, wanting to leave him and the drab pub. The youth was not the mirror into himself he had half hoped for. Impatient suddenly with all this, "What do you want, Damien?" his voice harsher than meant.

"I said. I just want him to stop. Coming in my room and doing it to me."

"Okay," said Sylvie. "Let's look at it. Let's look at the choices we've got."

"Oh, fuck off with your choices," he sneered. "I can get that stuff from my social worker." He turned his angry, hurt face at both of them. "Are you going to do anything, then? Or more fucking talk... choices!" He spat out a word so familiar, so meaningless to him. He fingered his glass, then mumbled, "I want to go. This isn't... I'm going back." He half stood, crouching uncertainly, leaning over the table. "Okay?"

"No, wait," Sylvie asked, but Jim was aware in himself a wish the scene was over, willing the boy to defy and leave the two adults together. Damien's eyes met his, wanting to be held back, but he read Jim and pushed upright, back from them.

"No. I'm off." To Sylvie, softer, "Tell me what you're going to do. You don't need me." He went.

After a pause, Jim said, "Well. What happened there?" Immediately, he realised his note was smart, almost smug. "He's in a real bad way," he added, in retreat.

"I'll tell you what happened there," Sylvie said waspishly. "We made a real mess of it... really insensitive."

"Maybe he's right. It's up to us to sort it out. To tell him what to do. He's too messed up to know what's best."

"No. If he doesn't start to do things for himself, he'll carry on depending on adults. And vulnerable to them exploiting him. Don't you see that? You and your trade union experience should have told you that. All your car factory stories. People have to stand up for themselves."

He gave a short hard laugh he knew was false. "My experience? My experience was of getting men to stand up and be counted and when all the talking, all the fine speeches were over, silly-bugger-me and a couple like me were left to carry out all those fine words. So, Sylvie, don't tell me about blokes standing on their own two feet." He drank, emphatically.

"Well, that's obviously how it happens in your men's world. Perhaps I see it differently as a woman. We do things differently."

"Oh. Of course. All that womanly wisdom." He regretted the sneer immediately, wished it never said. "Anyway, Damien lives in a man's world. All those lads in Northlodge. Finch and the others."

"Yes. Your world. Men. And boys." Sylvie's harsh words. Jim felt them enter, hurt. Somewhere he had been trying these weeks to understand why, how he had been different from- or the same as- Damien and the other boys he and Sylvie had been trying to extract from the shadows onto the sheets of paper spread across Sylvie's floor. He wanted to be back there now with her, intimately allied and privately united, close to each other. He looked at her and must have seemed woebegone. It would have to move on to other things now. He reminded himself of his previous resolve to move it all on. Action, of some sort.

"Okay, Sylvie. What now?"

"I'm worried about us holding this information from Damien ourselves. If it gets out to someone else, someone in Social Services, one of the child abuse people, and we've been holding on to the story... It could mean trouble, especially for you in the Department."

"So, who do we tell?"

"And we don't have his permission, Jim." Between them a silence.

"Does he have the right to stop us?"

"To stop us doing what?" Jim realised he was unclear about what they were going to stop. Jeffreys? Something bigger? Telling someone the things Damien had told them was not a separate, distinct act. It would not be the relief of passing on for someone else to deal with. It would be the start of an unraveling of the things he and Sylvie had been piecing together: an unraveling that could entangle them and others in its own revenge.

Chapter Three

They were unable to meet for two weeks, but after their difficult meeting with him, Jim and Sylvie had agreed they did not know enough about how to ensure Damien could be protected from the consequences of whatever next step they took. Sylvie suggested she contact the N.S.P.C.C. and tell them anonymously about the situation and hear what they suggested.

The call had not been helpful. She said she had felt as if they were quizzing her for harming boys herself. Jim tried to take a reasonable line, suggesting that the N.S.P.C.C.'s caution was right. How could they know who Sylvie was, or whom she was calling on behalf of? He argued that to get any advice, she would have to tell more.

She called Jim again back at his office that afternoon, all their cautionary rules aside. "They want names and details. Said I might be committing a criminal offence by not telling them or Social Services. That whoever I was, I couldn't guarantee that I could stop the harm happening."

Jim nodded to the mouthpiece, "I think they're right from where they are." No answer. "Don't you?"

"I don't know. Don't trust any of them. Seems to me anyone spending all their time doing that sort of work- you know, chasing child molesters... they've got to be pretty sick themselves. Or have some other motive." She shifted from reflective to brusque, "Look, we shouldn't be having this conversation over your phone line. I'll phone them back again. I'll have to decide how much to tell them."

"Okay. Be careful." He tried to get the right amount of sincerity and concern in his voice, "You know how to get hold of me, Sylvie." His words had quavered slightly but she could not see the faint blush he could feel.

"Yes, Jim. I know. Don't worry. Okay?" She rang off.

He had to go out for a meeting that afternoon and as he returned to the office, it was against the tide of staff leaving for home, the Principal Caretaker now in command of the building, standing in the foyer with a preposterously large bunch of keys slung and swung from his wrist. "Not long Mr. Briggs, will you?"

He looked at him, a difficult man Jim had failed to help when he himself had been Union Rep for the building several years earlier. "No. Just any messages left for me."

A cleaner was in the General Office when Jim went to his pigeonhole. "It's alright, I'm off in a minute."

There were two phone messages for him. One was Foley asking to see him whenever he came in. *Urgent* was scrawled across the top. The other was from Sylvie. It said: *Meeting tonight of Association as arranged. Usual place*. It made no sense.

He went through to his room across the corridor and closed the door behind. He phoned the Northlodge number. It rang for a long time.

Finally, a man's voice, "Northlodge Housing Association. Mr. Hillingdon here. Can I help you?"

"Is Sylvie still there?" Jim said abruptly, his voice shaped by what she had told him of her boss.

"Miss Cathcart, do you mean?" With an edge, "Who's calling?"

"Jim Briggs. Social Services."

"Ah." Some sort of unshared understanding in that pointed release of breath. "No. I'm afraid you've missed her. She had to leave early this afternoon. Personal reasons." A wait- for Jim to speak? "Can I help Mr. Briggs?"

"No." Too sharp, so he soothed with, "I was just phoning to check the details of a meeting she told me about. It's okay, I'll phone tomorrow. Thanks." He wanted to put the phone down, but knew Hillingdon had not finished.

"I could check for you. We keep a desk diary with details of all Miss Cathcart's appointments in it. Let me look." And he was gone, the sound of the handpiece being placed on the desk and his receding footsteps in Jim's ear. He felt trapped. Put down the phone and if needed, account for it as being cut off? A knock at the door and the Caretaker came in. "Will you be long, Mr. Briggs? My cleaner is asking if she can come in."

"No. I won't be long," tersely.

"Good." He was smiling, flatly. "Will you let her know when you're ready. She'll be next door." He went and his head reappeared, just as Jim heard the returning footsteps of Hillingdon in his ear. "Oh, and Mr. Foley is looking for you." His hand's acknowledgement of this turned into a curt wave of dismissal as he heard the phone at the other end picked up.

"Mr. Briggs?"

"Yes."

"Which meeting were you wanting the details of? I have Miss Cathcart's diary here."

"Ah." What? A stumble towards credibility in this conversation. "Just one minute. I'll check." He swiftly put the handpiece down and looked blankly at the tidied papers on his desk for an idea to end this. He went to the filing cabinet and looked petulantly through the Housing files for inspiration. There was a Working Party meeting due.

As he turned back to the desk, the door opened again. Foley. Looking impatient. Scowling. "So here you are. I've been trying to get you since three o'clock."

"Just a minute. Phone." He picked it up. "Hello? The next Working Party on Housing. Do you have the details of that?"

"I know that," Foley said. "Who are you speaking to?"

Jim put his forefinger to lips. He could hear Hillingdon turning the pages of the diary and turned his back on Foley to concentrate.

Over the phone, "Something here." He read to Jim time and place of a meeting he already had slotted in his mind, as a time and place he would be meeting Sylvie again.

"Thanks, very much."

"I'm glad we have been of assistance. However, as the Borough Council is responsible for convening and servicing the Working Party, I would have thought..." and let the incomplete sentence trail, deliberately.

"Yes. Okay. Goodbye."

Putting down the phone, he turned to face Foley. Who said, meaningfully, "I need to see you now, Briggs."

Oh. Briggs, not Jim. "I can't be long. I need to get home soon." Foley knew about Jane's illness.

"I hope we won't be. Come upstairs to my office," and turned and left.

Jim felt angry. Being treated like a bad child swilled with the anxiety about Sylvie left over from the phonecall. "Sod it!" he muttered aloud and followed the Assistant Director.

When he reached the top floor, Foley was standing looking out of the window at the wet lamplit streets. Jim looked at the back of his neck with a slight contempt; the Boss-with-his-back-turned trick does not faze an old timer with bosses like me, he thought wryly and turned to casually look over some finance graphs pinned on the wall until Foley was ready.

"Jim." He turned from the window slowly. "I had a call this afternoon from the Assistant Director, Children's Services." The full title was meant to give weight to whatever might follow. "Your name was mentioned." Jim held his returning gaze, hoping any rising unease was not showing. "It appears that the Department has received a telephone call from the National Society for the Protection of... from Cruelty to Children." He got the bloody name wrong, Jim grinned inside at the misfired pomposity of the man. "The N.S.P.C.C."

"Oh, yes?"

"Yes." Foley growled. "It is a serious issue." Pause for this to sink.

"It appears you have been meeting with a member of a voluntary organisation and a boy who is still on a Care Order to this Department. This boy has apparently revealed to you allegations of sexual interference by adults. Is this true?"

Jim's mind went into low gear, no panic now. "This happened two days ago, Mr. Foley. And I have only met the young man once. I was not aware that he was on a Care Order. I met him because of what I understood to be a housing issue." All said with the slow deliberation that ran together the truths and the half truths, indistinguishably. He waited, watching for signs of how much Foley knew.

"That's not good enough. You should know that the Departmental Procedure is that any concerns about children must be passed on to the Department's own specialist social workers." "I did not believe the young man to be a child." Foley paused. Jim's instinct told him that the man before him knew no more. To confirm this, Foley turned back to the window.

To cut this pause for thought, Jim suggested aimiably, "I can go then, Mr. Foley?"

"No!" Surprised. "No... We've – it's got to be sorted out, this."

"What?" Jim asked flatly.

"Why the Procedure hasn't been followed."

"What Procedure?"

From Foley's internalised building anger, Jim guessed he was thrashing about trying to regain and exert his ponderous Assistant Directorial control. "You were responsible for finding out the situation - the boy's age, the Care Order."

"I don't think that's fair." Jim held the moment, then, "You clearly don't know all the facts," face placid, but eyes challenging the other man.

"Neither did you. Clearly." Foley looked down and leaned forward staring at the blotter on the cleared desk. "Alright. I'll have a written report from you about what happened. By tomorrow, five o'clock?"

"Impossible." Jim needed time to check out with Sylvie. "Next Monday, at the earliest." Followed brazenly by, "I'll have it on your desk then, Mr. Foley. By lunchtime."

"By twelve o'clock, mind."

"Fine. Mr. Foley." And he left.

Looking back on the whole train of events that had gathered speed and accelerated through his life subsequently, Jim later realised that the results of Sylvie's N.S.P.C.C. call were what prevented any possibility of turning back from the brink of what they had discovered. At that point, the events themselves seemed to take over the levers of control. But as he went downstairs, leaving the outmanoeuvred Foley behind, he felt in control. He was eager to see Sylvie, tell her the tale and decide what to put in the report for Monday. But later. He had to get home to Jane.

He decided to combine one of his evening runs with a visit to Sylvie's, hoping she would be in. When he got to her door, she smiled at him, scanning his bare legs and shorts, as she let him in. "Well, this is a Jim I don't know. Never dreamed of."

She ushered him in promptly. He thought she looked preoccupied. On the coffee table were two tidy piles of documents beside the executive briefcase he had teased her about. She sat down straight away and took off the top document from the pile. "You know I waited for you at the Baltic, tonight."

He remembered the cryptic message she had left. "Oh. Sorry. I didn't understand." But he smiled quizzically at her, "Anyway, don't we get a cuppa first? It's sure to be a long meeting, from the look of the papers involved."

She smiled. "Sorry." Then, with a shift into theatrical formality, "Mr. Briggs, what would you like to drink?"

"Like I said. A cuppa."

She stood up and swirled out, as if suddenly aware of him, "One cup that cheers, coming up!"

He listened to the water run into the kettle, then called through, "You sound very cheerful."

"What?"

He got up and leaned at the kitchen doorway, looking at the stretched line of her back as she reached up for mugs and tea-caddy. "I said, you sounded cheerful."

She turned, surprised he was close. "Cheerful?" quizzing the word, before passing on. "I've picked up a lot more information from Northlodge. Hillingdon was away last week. I had a free run of his files. I used the pretext of doing some research on previous Northlodge residents and chased up the subsequent addresses of fourteen lads. Five had gone to the same Belgravia house in London- including Finch, all boys who had come from Whispering Pines and six of the others had gone to a single address two streets away. Belgravia?" She paused, turned back to the tea-making and restarted in a measured way, "But there was also some stuff that might be really heavy. I didn't know it, but Northlodge has been bought up. By a set of building companies. I never knew it- I didn't think it could happen under our constitution. They're the Association of Building Contractors and Employers. ABC. We're a voluntary housing charity, I thought. But Hillingdon has his name on letters setting up the deal. And

Jeffreys. And the other trustees. That's how we got the Belgravia houses. It was part of the deal." She turned again and offered him the mug of tea. As if she had awoken to him really there, she focussed and studied his face. "I haven't seen you for a bit. How've you been, Jim?"

He felt suddenly and unaccountably tired from what she was telling. From the light mood he had felt at seeing her again, from the excitement of sharing their secret agendas, a realisation that the intimacy of their work together, its privacy would from now on have to draw others in. To protect the boys. And to protect themselves? The petulance was a regret for a private and special relationship that, he told himself, was only like that in his own head. He pushed his wariness back and turned himself outward, simply saying, "Okay. I'm a bit cold."

She to put the kettle on and went to a drawer for a grey teeshirt. "Here, change into this."

As he took off his vest, he was shy of his bare top and as he pulled on hers, aware of its faint scent. Of her. "Thanks."

She returned with her tea. "Why would builders want a voluntary housing association for kids like us?"

"To get their hands on your property? For development."

She shook her head as she sat, "No. I thought that. But the agreement with ABC specifies that Northlodge continues to supply kids for the London houses."

"Supply?" he echoed, vaguely.

"Yes. That's the words they used. Supply. Like a commodity-that's part of the deal. It all adds up to something murky. I haven't been at all happy since those calls I made to the N.S.P.C.C. I didn't like the way I was treated. The man interrogated me.This new stuff just makes it worse."

"They told my Department, you know. The NSPCC. Foley had me in. That's why I've called in. But I don't think he knew much."

"Oh, dear. Shit. That means they... they know enough to make a link from me to you. Jim, I only told them who I was. Never named you. Or Damien."

Jim's guts turned slowly as he tried to put together the implications of what Sylvie had just said. "Wait a minute. You didn't mention me?"

"No. All I said was..." She paused to recreate the words in her mind. "I told him my name, who I worked for. Said I had discussed it with someone from Social Services, but gave no name." She looked wondering, at Jim. "So how did they make the link to you?"

"Or Damien. Foley knew a kid in Social Services care was involved. It didn't sound as if he was making a clever guess, out of the blue." Jim's voice rose, "How would they know that?"

Sylvie stood up and turned away fiercely. "What the hell's happening?" She swung back again. "You haven't spoken to anyone, have you?" she accused.

"No!" Jim felt hurt and indignant at her sudden trustlessness. "Come on, Sylvie," he almost pleaded, "don't you know me?"

"No. I don't know anyone." Then waspishly, "Especially not men."

"There's no answer to that. Is there?" His voice was tired. He did not want to stay. Although he knew they should try to talk the fears through, her sudden, sharp mood hurt him. For a moment his mind flitted to the wife, Jane, he would return to when he left this young woman and he welled for her, for himself, vaguely for what might have been. "I must go," he said quietly, then looked at her. "What do you mean, you don't know anyone?"

"Oh, I don't know. Nothing, probably." She sat down again, heavily. Sylvie looked at him slowly. "Jim, I don't know. I wish I'd never showed you that letter."

He felt tugged back to her, the profound anxiety of her eyes. "I'm sorry. But you were right to show me and not hold onto it all yourself." He suddenly felt sorrow for this young woman. "Where do we go from here?"

"Don't know. No idea."

"I suggest we sleep on it, Sylvie. It's too much to take on at once." He half moved his hand across the space between them. To reassure. "Let's meet Thursday evening. We need to plan what to do next. Our next moves."

She looked at the hand hung there hesitantly, without seeing it. Her voice sounded dreamed. "Yes.You're probably right."

He stood up to go. "Your tee shirt?"

She got up to see him out. "You'll need it. Bring it back when I see you. Washed, mind," and smiled.

In the unlit hall she whispered, "Jim, just put your arms round me for a moment. Please."

He froze, then turned awkwardly in the tight space. Her head was backlit, hair tousled gold from the livingroom light behind her, the expression on her face indistinct with shade, turned downwards. He put his arms tentatively out, his fingertips touching her shoulders and she immediately nuzzled her face into the tee shirt, more a child than his own daughter Tracey had ever been to him. He surged with confused emotion, eyes filled, his throat choked, daring to make no sound, the bone of her shoulders beneath his barely contacted fingers.

She eased apart after a time and looked up at him, inscutable in the half-light. "Thursday, then. Goodnight, Jim."

Running back through the night, he could not make sense of her childlike gesture or of his own half-fatherly, half-aroused feelings about it. With women, he had always depended on them, was emotionally led by them. Sylvie had made an emotional move tonight, but one that disconcerted him, unsure of what had happened.

Back home, he shoved her tee shirt at the back of his cupboard. Jane, unwell and on drugs again, was asleep. Jim lay awake into the early hours, trying to work out Foley, Damien and the N.S.P.C.C., but the vivid feel of her face drew his mind away, still as if pressed to his chest through the night.

Chapter Four

Away from Jane, he became more dependent on the private meetings he was having with Sylvie, with their mix of "boys business" and talk about themselves. For Jim anyway, the self he restrictively shared with this young woman. Copied from Hillingdon's files, she had brought a file with the minutes of child abuse meetings with Social Services about some of the boys. So he used his lunchtimes to try to build up his own understanding and find out something about child abuse. He borrowed a book from the Department's Training Library. There was only a short chapter at the end about sexual abuse; it was mostly a detailed outline of the history of physical abuse and child murder. The photographs, in garish colour, of wounds, burns and tears in the bright pink flesh of limbs and buttocks drew his eyes back again and again to their clinical horridness.

At least this was not Damian, he thought. Then reflected on that. Was either worst? For the first time he visualised the scene with the boy and Jeffries. Sat on the bed beside each other in one of those small Northlodge bedrooms, perhaps? What actually would Jeffreys do? How would he start? Jim knew the man, could hear the soft-spoken voice in his head. How would he first touch Damian?

Looking away from the savage double page of illustrations before him, he closed his eyes and forced his mind to move the elderly councillor's hand across Damian's groin. The boy frozen with the fear Jim had seen flit in his eyes when he met him in the pub. The fingers tugging at the zip? No. A preparatory, gentle massage first, testing Damian's passivity, consent. Then the clothing. The boy's sex aroused despite himself and the old man touching it...

Jim surged with disgust. He opened his eyes and stared back at the photographs to tear aside and stop the narrative in his brain. Disgust with Jeffreys. Revulsion at his own imagination. Worse? Both. Like the pictured cigarette burns on flesh, it was the powerful deliberateness of adults to children that measured the cruelty of both ways.

Jeffreys? Chairman of the Housing Committee. A Tory, but old-school paternalistic. A bit oily, over-courteous, but pretty much an ordinary man, Jim had not even had any particular dirt on- surprising in itself for someone on Housing. Until this. He remembered reading an account years ago of the Nuremberg Trials and how the writer was struck by the ordinariness of those who led almost commonplace domestic lives, said goodbye each morning to their families and went with their briefcases to work in the concentration camps, back for dinner in the evening. He had met Mrs. Jeffreys at a Housing Department function a couple of years earlier. He recollected she had made him laugh at some observation of hers about the gathering. A nice enough woman. Probably with grown up children now. Jim surprised himself by thinking, this is not political. Not party-political, anyway. It's about kids. He allowed himself to wonder what Jane or Tracey would say about his involvement in all this, but they were too remote. On this he trusted nobody but Sylvie.

Chapter Five

After the new year, at the winter's coldest, Jim started the first of the long Sunday runs that were part of the preparation for staying four hours on his feet during the Marathon he was entered for in the Spring. It was a gusty, bright morning. He set off slowly, reserving his pace, listening to his body's signals, as he was becoming used to its middle-aged aches and pains, growing back to strength, revived muscles clasping the loose flesh back to the bones. As he ran, he started to riffle his mind through the documentation he had been reading with Sylvie. But the relaxed easy pace began to tighten with welling anger. At first it seemed at the stupid papers, pretending to be important but saying nothing to him. Then confused, as a childish swelling of hurt invaded him. He wanted to fight. If it hadn't seemed foolish on the street, he would have boxed his way with his fists against the wind as he ran. The boy he had been, stood before him limp-armed and appealing to the adult self.

"Jimmy!" he hissed through clenched teeth. What do you want? He had closed his eyes to realise the image for a few seconds, then shocked by stumbling on the uneven pavement, he locked his stare to a yard ahead of his feet and ran on.

What does he want? A welling surge of loneliness, loss, wept through his flesh, then ebbed and drained away. Leaving harsh, single imprints of his boyhood that he turned like pages, as he moved his old body out of the town into the country lanes and his memories back down the hard echoes of the child's shoes in the dull light of underpowered, naked lightbulbs, along those corridors. Brown-and-cream brick walls. Khaki-green metal lockers that banged and squealed, however they were touched. The funk of carelessly cooked vegetables, pervasive everywhere, even from beneath the skin. The fear beneath at every corner, every corridor junction, of strangers, what unimagined sudden hurt might leap out, grinning older boys with gripped, painful fingers and the stink of cigarettes on their spat and sarcastic words.

Some Sunday afternoon, aimlessly walking with another small boy around the Institute's grounds, recovering from the long and monotonous morning of chapel. Summoned by two big boys into a greenhouse in the remote and overgrown kitchen garden. Demanded for money, then threatened, held against a bench to let hard hands thrust into pockets to find nothing, but leaving him with a quick, vengeful twist of the testicles, sobbingly painful, his pants pissed and shitted with terror. The other small boy ran off shocked, abandoning Jimmy to smuggle himself back and upstairs to the out-of-bounds washrooms, rinsing and scrubbing the clothes, pushing the muck down the plughole, wringing the wet out with all the tearful stength in his skinny arms and putting the cold, sodden cloth back onto his wounded body...

As he ran on, the pain of the past was tangible, enervating him, slowing him down, so he had to keep pushing back up to pace.

Rain outside a classroom, work completed in the exercise book, pencil put aside. Watchful of the master dozy at his desk, he pulled out a letter received that morning from Aunt Mary and reopened it under the desk. And the photo she had sent. Of his dad. In uniform, just joined up. Six months before he disappeared somewhere in France. From now, Jim could not visualise that picture, only the sudden looming presence of the master above the boy and the letter and photo grabbed away, confiscated for good. He had never dared tell his aunt and now, forty years on, he did not know what his father looked like. Just the faintest sense of him somewhere in the background of dim early childhood memories...

Only Mary was left who knew Jim's dad. Somehow, unlike other people, his family had just faded away, with nothing to mark their going. Jim an only child. Mother dead in his infancy, father gone soon after. Aunt Mary now an elderly spinster in an old people's nursing home outside Bradford. A card every Christmas, but Jim had not been to see her for ten years. Only after Tracey's birth did Mary play any active part in their lives. As temporary support to Jane, while Jim led the sit-in from inside the Plant. Disregarding him when he finally returned with, "Just like your father," leaving him hungry for what she meant. And now, an ageing man running down a winter lane, that sharp phrase from Mary and the confiscated photograph thirty-nine years ago were both thefts. Of who he was. So far past his best now, his prime, he knew he had never known who he was.

The following day, Jim was visited by Damien's social worker, Flynn. He was clearly uncomfortable with what he was doing. Jim watched him sitting across from the untidy desk, wary with a sense that the man had been sent on a mission by others.

"It's about Damien Toser."

"Oh, yes?" Jim tried to give a relaxed but guarded warning in his tone.

"He met you, I believe?"

"Yes. Some weeks ago." Non-commital.

"He discussed child abuse issues, I understand?"

"Yes. This has been explained to me by Mr. Foley."

"Ah," he sighed, as if with caught understanding. Jim waited, eyes fixed unblinkingly on Flynn, who sat for a long moment toying with the lock on his briefcase. "I have come to ask you what Damien said... disclosed to you."

"Is this part of a formal investigation? If so, I'm not sure Damien would agree to me giving away what he said in confidence to me."

"And to Sylvia Cathcart." Flynn flicked a sharp, testing glance at Jim.

Careful now, he paused to reply, "If Damien was going to give me permission to tell you what he told us" -a challenge back including Sylvie- "he would have told you in the first place. After all you are his social worker."

"You don't understand. Things are not always that simple."

"Why don't I understand? Because I'm not a social worker? Because I'm not what you would call a professional?" Under the cool words, he held back his ire.

"I have known Damien a long time. I have had his case for four years."

"And you didn't know the most important thing about the lad." Acid now. "I suggest you don't know Damien at all. He didn't want you to know that important bit."

Flynn again waspish, "What important bit?"

Jim could not hold a laugh and it came out sudden and hard. Flynn looked back at the lock on his case. "The bit someone's told you to come and ask me about, of course."

"Who?"

"Who what?"

"Who's told me to come and ask you?"

Jim was astonished at the bizarreness of the question. Then stopped. For the first time the other man was returning a sustained stare, watchful.

"I've got my ideas who sent you. But they're only my ideas."

"So are you saying that you refuse to tell me what Damien disclosed to you?"

"No."

"But you are. What conditions would let you tell me what Damien said?"

"Damien's own agreement."

"But Jim," – awkward familiarity – "you're a member of Social Services, even if you're not a social worker. You know you can't keep this to yourself. The Procedures say you have to pass on any disclosures of abuse."

"So Mr Foley has already told me. I've given him a report. And as far as I'm concerned that's the end of it. I've done my duty for the Department." Then Jim tossed a last question back, "You seen my report?"

Flynn hesitated, not knowing how to answer.

Giving a Yes to Jim. "So you have seen it. Then you'll have come from Mr. Foley." The fiddled lock again. "Well?"

"I assume you'll not cooperate with my enquiries?"

"Assume on, old mate," Jim grinned. He felt dangerous to this lazy, weasely man opposite him, who had failed to protect Damien from Jeffreys. "I've done with my cooperating now. Tell Foley that." And lobbed a last tester into Flynn's dicomforture, "And tell the N.S.P.C.C., as well."

The old social worker rose hastily and untidily from the chair, some papers sliding from a file onto the floor. Jim bent to help, but was urged off with, "No, no, it's alright." Then Flynn shambled off with inappropriate thanks.

Sat back in his chair, Jim stretched across the gap to the just-vacated chair with legs aching from the day before's run and felt more in control of this part of his life, the pursuit of nastiness, but less in control of his personal relationships, Jane, Tracey, his father- whoever that had been- Sylvie. More in control of his ageing body than he had for twenty years. Less control of who he was than he had ever had. It seemed in some indistict way, that Damien was asking the questions Jim had been too busy to ask about his own life. And to get to what was happening to Damien included finding the answers to himself. His mind went back to Aunt Mary and he was surprised at the urgent strength he had so suddenly felt yesterday about the old lady he had neglected, had been so marginal to his life for so long. Rather than a vague intention to see her, he would arrange for Tracey to look after Jane one Saturday or Sunday and go over to see Mary.

He also needed to tell Sylvie about Flynn's visit. He phoned her at Northlodge, but she was out.

As he put the telephone down, it rang beneath his fingers. It was swithchboard. He was asked to ring a number he recognised as Tracey's work.

To his surprise, she answered immediately. "Dad. It's Auntie Mary. She died yesterday afternoon."

He wanted to say "I know", calmly realising that while he had been running, Mary's death had telegraphed across the hills from Yorkshire and printed out in his mind as the urgent but now hopeless wish to visit that last relative. As Tracey was saying something about how the sequence of messages had come to her, Jim wondered how he could be so relaxed and matter-of-fact about such a supernatural message.

"Dad? Are you alright?"

He must have been lost in those thoughts. He the sceptic, prone to tease anyone who believed in ghosts, religion or mind-reading. "Yeah? Sorry, I was just thinking. About your aunt."

"She wasn't my aunt. She was my great-aunt."

"Yes. Sure." He would not share what he thought with this businesslike, precise young woman that was his daughter.

"Dad, what are you going to do about her? They said you were the only family she had left."

Jim dreamily considered that. The only family. The phrase in his head shocked him alert. Before it was too late, he had to get to Mary.

"Dad?"

"I've got to get to her. Before it's too late," he blurted.

"Dad. It is too late. She's died already. Yesterday." Her voice had a concern in it not usual to her father.

"No. I don't mean that." Jim became aware of Tracey and defensive, private of his thoughts. A false laugh and, "No. I don't mean literally, Tracey." What would his explanation be to her? "I mean to sort out Aunt Mary's things. Any possessions or business she may have left." Or photographs, he suddenly thought, a hope of retrieving his confiscated father. Immediately businesslike, "What did the people at the old people's home say? When's the funeral? Maybe I'll have to arrange it."

"I haven't spoken to them myself. They phoned home and spoke to Mum. She phoned me. She says they take too long to get hold of you at Social Services, so she asked me to call you. She's too tired to mess about with your switchboard." An implicit and oblique criticism of him? Jim wondered.

"Anyway, I've got their number. You'll have to go over to Bradford. I'll go home and stay with Mum for a couple of nights. It'll take a couple of days to sort out. At least, I expect."

Chapter Six

That afternoon, he was on the M62 heading towards the Pennine edge that marked the entry down from Yorkshire, where he had turned from boy to man. And turning, turned his back on it all, searching for a future elsewhere. He had phoned the home in Bradford to tell them he was coming over and then spoken to Foley to get permission for time off, to be reminded that it would have to come off his annual leave entitlement, as an aunt was not a close enough relative for him to qualify for compassionate leave. It had been Foley's false sense of apology for this that soured Jim.

He had left a message at Northlodge for Sylvie that he would call her later. He had gone home to Jane and waited with her until the Health Visitor came. It had been a relaxed hour between the two. Jane was comfortable and he sat on the settee end, rubbing the soles of her feet, which helped her. They talked about Mary and he realised that Jane seemed to actually know his aunt better than he did.

"That's because we're women. She was with me those weeks when Tracey was born. We talked a lot."

Jim felt jealous. Another part of his family stolen by others. Or had he just been careless all his life with those he should have been giving care and attention to? "I wish I'd visited her more. Especially in the last few years."

"You've always been too busy. One thing ends and you get involved in something else. Like this running. You've filled your life with things." She looked at him reflectively. "Now I'm not sure, but you used to be surrounded by people..." Her voice trailed off.

"Now? What's different now?"

"Now?" She watched him. "You're surrounded by emptiness."

She had looked away towards the window. He followed her gaze. He was unsurprised by her observation. "No." Outside the skeletal winter trees groaned against the grey February wind. "No. Memories. Surrounded by memories."

She had looked back at him, ready to ask what he meant, but Jim had shaken the moment off by putting her bare feet aside and taking the teacups out to the kitchen.

He lost himself in the heavy traffic coming into Bradford and arrived at the old people's home twenty minutes late. He was ushered into the Matron's office.

"Mr. Briggs. Come in. Please sit down."

She was a bit effusive, but sincere in her eyes. Jim watched them, alert to protect whatever was left of his Aunt Mary.

Tea was brought and she fussed with the pretty service. When Jim was perched uncomfortably with his cup and saucer at the edge of his seat, she introduced herself as Joyce Phillips and started to tell him about the circumstances of the death.

Aunt Mary had been declining for a year, increasingly immobile, but her mind as sharp as ever. The Matron spoke of her as if she had been someone special as she descibed the single-mindedness of the old lady. Central to her life had been several cardboard boxes of documents which she sorted and, as her fingers became increasingly knobbled with pain, got the help of a care assisstant, Helen, in cataloguing them and adding dictated commentaries to them.

"What was it all about? The documents?" Jim asked.

"A lot of it seemed to be about the Catholic Church. She was very religious. You probably know that." Vaguely, Jim thought. "It was mostly very detailed records of the religious experiences she had. Confessions, what penance she had to do, when she went to communion... all with dates, going back years. And religious dreams, I believe. All written down. Helen will tell you about it all. Mary trusted her and towards the end made her promise not to tell anyone else- even me- what they talked about. Mary was such a gem and she was obviously getting herself ready for the end, so I went along with her wishes. She was a very special person and Helen is a particularly good member of staff- sensitive and discreet." She looked at Jim. "It's a shame you weren't able to get over to see her more."

Jim looked down at his hands. No answer.

"I'll let you see Helen. I asked her to come in when I knew you were coming, Mr. Briggs." She rose. "I'll fetch her now."

Jim sat alone in the room, looking at the tepid tea, gaunt with the sense of another lost opportunity, another person he had missed the chance of knowing, another misunderstanding.

She returned with a plump, cheerful woman, younger than he had expected. He stood and received her brisk handshake. Joyce Phillips then led them to a bare room with two tubular chairs, several zimmer frames tidied into the corner and three cardboard boxes with lids, side-by-side in the middle of the floor. The Matron left them and Helen sat, offering Jim the other chair.

"I know this must seem odd, Mr Briggs, but your Aunt Mary was an unusual lady." She looked at him with an almost challenging openess.

"Can I call you Jim? She called you that and I'd find it difficult to think of you as Mr. Briggs."

"Yes. Sure." Jim was surprised at her candour, but more at the idea that he played any part in the conversations between the spinster aunt whom he had put aside and this young stranger.

"She talked about you a lot. About the time when you were a little boy and lived with her. After your mum had died. And your dad left."

"Not for long," he murmured.

"Pardon?"

"Not for long. I didn't live with her for long."

"Yes. I know. That was one of the things she found most difficult to come to think about. She prayed about that a lot. She prayed for you. Every day. She was a very religious lady… spiritual, if you know what I mean."

Jim sat motionless. Soundless. He tried to grasp what being prayed for every day felt like. What words had been used? Or maybe it was about feelings. Yes, feelings. He realised being prayed for was the same as being loved. The tide of loss surged back through him, welling into a thankfulness, a humility at being, unknown, the subject of Mary's attentive thoughts for so many years.

"Are you alright, Jim?"

"Yes. Surprised. Just surprised. You see, I didn't know her really. Lost contact."

"Well. Yes. She felt guilty about you. She never forgave herself for not keeping you as a little boy. But she knew it was too late when she realised what she'd done. Putting you in that place, that orphanage." Helen reflected. "And it was real odd. The one thing she didn't want was your forgiveness. It was like that was part of her penance. Staying unforgiven. So she didn't really want you to visit her. It was like she wanted the moment she realised her guilt- she wanted that moment frozen in time. She once said to me that was when she really had God revealed to her. I think she was religious before- like, a good catholic. But thinking about what she did to you changed her." The young woman sought some way of telling Jim the size of it. "You know we get a lot of old people in here who get religion. But Mary was different. I don't go to church, but she made me believe it... I could see it was true. For her."

Jim had nothing to say. He looked over to Helen with a half-smile of embarrassment.

She pointed, one-by-one, at the boxes before them. "And she kept it all written down. At the end, it was me writing it down for her after her hands'd gone. It got so important for her, it kept her going over the last months." Helen touched one of the boxes with her toe. "That one's all old photographs and old letters from years back. She used to like to get me to read them to her. Or get out the photos and hold them for her while she told me about them. You see, she couldn't close her fingers to hold them herself."

She nodded to the second. "That's all the religious stuff. Everything. She wanted me to write down every prayer and who she prayed for. Everything that happened when the priest used to come. All her confessions and the penances he gave her." She smiled at Jim. "A lot of that was about you."

She paused and looked down at the third box. Raising her gaze, she said quietly, "That's the one I don't know what to make of. They're all letters from France. In French. I know she didn't understand them, but they kept coming, for the last few years. I don't speak French, but I offered Mary to get them translated. She wouldn't have it. But she wouldn't throw them away. She made me put them away. Neat, in bundles of ten, like all the other things she kept. She was a right stickler for things being kept neat and tidy, just as she liked it. Nearly all of them she never even opened."

Jim reached out for something of Aunt Mary he recognised. "Yes, I remember that. Her tidiness." He reached over for the first box and slid it towards himself. He felt Helen watching as he lifted off the lid. There were bundles of envelopes, tied neatly with wool.

"The photographs are underneath," Helen said.

He carefully, almost reverentially lifted the bundles out to uncover the carpet of browned and faded prints on the floor of the box. A little boy, about three years old, looked back smiling and uncertain at Jim. At the perturbed and older man he had become.

Jim phoned from the Matron's office and booked a hotel in Bradford to stay the night. Then he closed the door and went back to the desk to phone Sylvie at home. He took a deep breath to try to disengage himself from Mary's strange world, back to what he had left behind.

The phone was picked up immediately, but no-one spoke.

"Sylvie?"

"She's not here." A harsh male voice that sounded a long way from the mouthpiece. And before Jim could speak, the call had been cut off. He looked for a moment at his own handpiece, before replacing it. Another man? He immediately rejected his unguarded jealous stab with an ever-so-reasonable but rather insecure, Why not? He went off to the hotel with the three boxes beside him on the passenger seat of his car.

It was what had once been called a commercial hotel; a t.v. lounge with a few men watching football, a game of cards round a table in the corner of the tiny bar. As soon as he had left his case in his room, he phoned home from the downstairs payphone first. Tracey answered and he told her his immediate plans. Then he called Sylvie, tentative and watchful. Of who would answer. And of being overheard by the inqisitive woman at reception.

"Hello?"

He was relieved to hear her. "It's Jim."

"Oh, Jim!" and her voice caught with sobs, then a wail and a bang as the phone was put down.

"Sylvie?" he called to the sound of her crying somewhere across the room. "Sylvie!"

She came back. "Oh, Jim. Where are you?"

"Bradford." He filled her uncomprehending silence with, "My Aunt Mary's died. I've had to come over to sort it out. Do you remember me saying about her? I'm the only relative." Then he felt foolish saying all that in the face of her distress. "What's wrong, Sylvie?"

"I've been robbed. Burgled. My stereo's gone. So have all my papers." She wept again. "All the child abuse stuff, the London papers, all my notes. The stuff from Hillingdon's files. Everything's gone." She snuffled, then, "It's them." With certainty. Finality.

Jim suddenly remembered his conversation with Flynn- what he had called to tell her. But that was swept away by the shock recall of his earlier call to her. The man's voice. "Was someone in your place earlier?"

"Of course there was. A burglar."

"No. I phoned and a man answered. He said you weren't in."

"It must've been him," she said, matter of fact. "What did you say?"

"Nothing. He hung up."

She was calmer, her voice dulled. "I don't know what to do now. I can't stay here. I'm frightened. I expect this phone's bugged- oh, I don't know, Jim..."

"I've got to stay over here. I'm sorry."

"Where are you?"

"Bradford. I told you."

"Where though in Bradford?"

"I'm staying in a hotel. Horton Lane I think it's in."

"Right, I'm coming over. Give me the phone number and I'll book a room. I can't stay here. And there's no one else I can talk to about this.

And Jim, I really need to talk to someone- you." He gave her the number. "Call me back in five minutes. The hotel can tell me how to get there. How long do you think it will take to get over?"

"You should make it by ten."

He had been sat in the bar for too long, re-reading tabloids, when she appeared wet and suddenly in the vestibule. He half rose, but she shook her head and turned away to the reception to book in.

Jim looked at her back as she spoke to the manager's wife and, her bending to fill in the register, he felt himself stir as her damp cotton slacks shaped to her body. He knew he was blushing and allowing himself to covertly if a little shamefully, to anticipate something tonight.

She came over to him. "I'm just going to put my things in my room and change out of these."

"Are you okay?"

"Better now that I'm away from that place." There was a shiver in her voice.

"Go on. I'll have a drink ready for you. The usual?"

She pursed her lips, considering. "No. I'll have a brandy. I'll only be ten minutes." She went off.

He bought the drinks and waited. He stared at the glasses, tense. His forefinger traced a series of wet links between the rings left by his earlier drinks. As Damian had. He realised that Mary had been pushed back into forgotteness. Mildly surprised at himself, he decided there would be time enough for that tomorrow at the funeral. This reminded him that he had not rung home since he had arrived in Yorkshire. Time enough for that, too. Now was for Sylvie. And him. Whatever that would add up to.

She returned in a red skirt and white, sheer blouse. Jim realised he had never before thought about her clothes. It felt delightful and a little dangerous tonight, he let him say to himself.

"Well, that was quick," he said, giving himself permission to look her up and down.

"A girl has to be ready for every eventuality." She smiled as she sat down. Jim sipped from the glass to let her speak, if she wished. "Let's not talk about it for a bit. I'm sure we'll get round to it sometime. But not yet." Her voice was matter-of-fact but her face edged with pleading.

"I'm sure we will."

"Tell me about your aunt," she switched brightly.

"Well, she's dead."

Sylvie threw her head with laughter and Jim followed her, hearing the unintended bathos of his tone.

"Oh... Jim... I'm sorry..." she finally said after a long minute. Men at the cards were looking at them. "It was just how you said it. So- I don't know. Like that's all there was to say. Like at the end of Bugs Bunny. That's all folks!" She giggled.

"It sure isn't all there is to say," he said and went on to tell her about Helen's story and the three boxes, their contents now spread across his bedcover upstairs. He realised that although he was fully attentive to Sylvie and she to him, the riddle of Mary and her boxes was now more important than Damien and the boys. Dimly, he was aware that what he had been seeking was not the truth about them, but the truth about himself. And Mary's boxes had suddenly emerged as the new route to who he was. As he had picked up Sylvie's call for help with Damien and everything that had started to unravel over the boys, he hoped she might follow him into whatever labyrinth the boxes may lead him.

"That's weird," she said when he ended telling of the unread, unopened letters from France. "I don't speak it, French. Not since school. Sorry I can't be of help there." She looked around the room. Some of the other guests were going off to bed now.

"Do you want another drink?"

"Mmm..." she considered and Jim felt taut to read the meaning of tonight in whatever answer she gave. "Yes. But not another brandy. I'll have a white wine and soda."

"Very posh," he joked, relieved at a postponement of whatever, and went to the bar. When he returned, she had her head down, hair shading her face. "Here you are," he said to try to get her to look up.

Without raising her eyes, she whispered, "Jim, it was awful," and her shoulders trembled. He sat a little closer to her, but tentative about invading the space of her grief. "It's awful carrying all this stuff about the boys around and having no one to dump on with it." She looked up at him. Her eyes were dry and hurt. "I'm sorry, Jim. You know what I mean. I don't dump on you. You're as much in it as I am. I don't dump on you, do I?" She looked down again. Then she reached across and tugged at a loose thread on his cuff button. She left her fingers lightly on his sleeve. "I suppose I'm dumping now, aren't I?"

"No," Jim protested softly. He wanted to take her hand, his body was so tight-strung with wanting to touch her. But he held back. "I'd expect you to come to me after what happened. Who else could you talk to about it?" He wanted a sign- a consent from her to touch, but she withdrew her hand almost absent-mindedly.

They sat close, but separate and silent. Jim would not lead with words, lest they be wrong. He felt a stranger to this woman, wanting that sign of intimacy. As their reflective silence lengthened, he felt like a boat adrift, her withdrawn hand a slipped mooring rope. He did not dare look to her, fearing the sight of a detachment in her his life could little afford.

"Jim..." Her voice was concerned. "Your face... What's wrong?"

He looked up at her, the pain naked in his face.

"Sylvie...I don't know. I think I'm lonely." He was embarrassed at the word, surprised at it. "I don't know... I once knew who I was. I thought I did. I understood what went on. Now I know nothing. I don't know if the whole world's changed. Or if I was fooling myself all those years." He looked away. "I'm sorry. You didn't come over here to Yorkshire to hear about me."

"Don't, Jim. Don't say that. It's not you for me or me for you. In all this, we've got to be for each other." She changed her tone to mockingly school-marm, "James. Give me your hand now. This minute!"

He half smiled at her and lay his hand, palm up, on the tabletop. She reached over and folded his fingers within hers. He almost wilted with the released rush of emotion.

"Oh, Sylvie."

"Jim. Jim, what is going on?"

"I don't know. It's everything. It's you here. It's my Aunt Mary. All the stuff about the boys. And I don't know what you're feeling, what you expect off me."

"Jim, I don't expect anything from you. Just your honest self. Someone in all this I can trust, that's all."

He felt made devious by his aroused sexual feelings and which carefully framed the next question. "What are you doing tomorrow?" Meaning, what happens tonight?

She answered it at face value. "I might not roll into work until lunchtime. Tell Hillingdon I'm sick in the morning. Don't know. I'll see tomorrow." Her tone hardened. "I certainly don't think I owe them anything. They're in it up to their necks. And if anyone is feeding info about me to that heavy mob who raided me today, Hillingdon probably knows about it." She looked at Jim firmly. "I don't want to talk about it tonight. I've decided. Okay."

"Okay by me." Gingerly now, "Well, what next?"

She looked at him, now aware, a sly smile delightedly brightening her face. "Well. Mr. Briggs, what next indeed? And tell me, how long has that been on your mind? Or on somewhere else?"

He let loose a grin. "And this is my cue to say, I don't know what you mean."

"Indignantly," she laughed. "You forgot to add, you say it indignantly."

"Well?"

"Well, what?"

"There's an unanswered question hanging around somewhere. I think it was, What's next?"

She was now reflective, seriously addressing the challenge of the moment astride them both. As she placed her second hand aroud the knot of their locked fingers, she said gently, "No. I don't think so, Jim. Not tonight. Thank you. But I don't want you to leave me just yet. I want to carry on talking, to be with you for a bit longer. But not that..."

He felt let down with great gentleness, with consideration and fondness and was relieved at the result. His warmth towards her grew.

"Thanks, Sylvie. You are something special."

She raised her eyebrows. "I know. That's why I've got you to look after me."

After a time of shared quietness, they started to resume murmured converstaion. The bar closed. The card game the other side of the room broke up. They were sat close, talking when the proprietor meaningfully called goodnight, leaving the pair only a last corner of light in the darkened hotel.

Chapter Seven

Unsure whether he dreamed it or was vaguely remembering it at the confused fringes of sleep, it was the time after Mary had returned to Yorkshire. Reasons not to go home, to avoid the smell of boiling nappies, the expression of tired pleasure on Jane's face, but mostly her tiredness asking for his relief from little Tracey's demands. A Labour Party meeting one night, he gave Linda, a young Party member a lift to her home, enjoying the feeling of slight sexual dangerousness from being in the dark car with her. He let her out and had already engaged gear to drive away when she leaned in the open passenger door, smiling.

"Well, are you coming in for a drink then?"

Jim, without a pause, switched off the engine and got out. She was already up the path unlocking the door. As he followed her into the darkened hallway, he whispered, "We won't wake anyone up, will we?"

She giggled, loud in the quiet, "I hope not, Jim. A sleeping burglar, perhaps? This is my flat." He could not see her face but he felt enticed by her. And by himself.

She unlocked another door, switched on the lights and ushered him in, a touch of her fingers on his sleeve. He stood stupid in the brightness of the room.

"Coffee, tea or alcohol?"

His mind fumbled with this, from the suddenness of the situation he found himself in…

…and seventeen years later, in a hotel room in Bradford, Jim sat up in bed, starkly awake, memories of dreamed Linda swirled away into the worn patterns of the carpet in the dark corners of the room. What! Something shook him with an urgent guilt for Jane.

He looked around him, confused where he was. Realising, he relaxed back on the rumpled pillows for a moment. He sat up. The burglars! If they did it to Sylvie's flat - Jane and Tracey. He had to phone home. He reached for his watch but knocked it onto the floor, banging his eyebrow painfully on the edge of the bedside cabinet before retrieving it. 2.15. Too late to call them?

He stumbled out of bed, to do something to calm the panic. He stubbed his toe and swore, limping to find the light. Blinded again. Into the corridor, he pulled his half-undone pyjama top round him against the cold draught, heading for the stairs.

Down in the vestibule, only a low nightlight threw shadows. There was a payphone in a paneled cubicle. Jim swore at his stupidity. He had brought no money down. He went upstairs, two at a time. Somewhere a toilet flushed. Back in his room, he searched his pockets till he realised that, for their last drink he had asked Sylvie for change, adding to the last of the coins to help the barman who had already totted up the till.

He sat on the bed edge. Sylvie's room: the next floor up. He had walked with her to it before she gave the briefest brush to his cheek with her lips and slipped behind the closed door.

He embarked again, this time with stealth.

He tapped the door, at first with inaudible caution. He scanned the corridor nervously and knocked this time harder. Ear to the door, no sound from inside.

Knock again. Something?

Again. Definite steps.

"Who is it?" blurred with doziness.

"Jim."

The door opened. She pushed hair away from her eyes. "What?"

"I need change. For the phone."

She looked at him dumbly for a moment, and then turned back into the dark room. He followed. "What time is it?" she asked in a querulous voice, rooting in her handbag.

"About two o'clock," he murmured.

She stood straight and turned. "What!"

"I'm phoning home. The burglary..." he trailed off with as much of an explanation as he could manage.

Suddenly, she was awake. "What burglary?" She stared at him.

"I had a dream, a nightmare." He grasped again the fear he had felt. "If they went through your place, they'll have a go at mine. Jane and Tracey..."

"You haven't phoned them? You're going to- at this time? Jim."

"I didn't think." He unexpectedly deflated. He steadied himself against the dressing table. His head swirled. He reached towards her, then felt the room tilt sideways, swept the outstretched hand back to steady himself, but it slid away from under him on the crocheted cloth and he tipped askew, crashing his ribs hard against the edge of the furniture.

Dazed, he heard, "Jim, are you alright?"

A wait before he said, quietly, "Right as rain," and laughed. His side jabbed with pain.

Sylvie giggled and sat on the bed. "What are you doing?"

"Shhh. There must be a song for this situation. Something about dancing." She snorted a laugh and came over to help him up. He sat on the dressing table edge, watching her cross to close the door. The hurt in his side had stopped him. From the panic about Jane and Tracey. It imposed a pause. He watched Sylvie, aware as she was of the effect of his gaze. The distant disloyalties with Linda shot across the present moment. And dismissed.

"Are you seriously going to phone home? At this time?"

He looked at her, thinking otherwise.

Sylvie continued, a barely detectable catch in her throat, "Whatever might have happened, it's too late now. Jim." He was uncertain whether his spoken name had been attached to her sentence or set apart as the start of something else. The emotional pressure in the room between them mounted in the unfilled silence. Her eyes were down for such an extended period, he felt pressed to speak. Anything.

Finally, she looked up at him, "Jim..." Her voice crumbled into sobbing. She threw her head upwards, closed eyes to the ceiling, her mouth broken with the sounds coming from it. Arms rigidly holding hands gripped to the bed edge.

Jim pushed himself up, stood with a twinge and crossed to her. At first she continued sobbing, her body loose in his arms. He just held her and, part by part, she began to quiet, brought her wet face to the comfort of his neck and her arms gently round his back. It was so important for him to just stand there holding, and to dam back the sexual longing that was almost making him wilt with its surge.

It seemed hours later that he was able to lay her down on the bed still in her dressing gown, pull the covers over her, turn out the light and gently climb in beside her. They were both chilled and held each other for warmth, faces close, breathing off each other. Her eyes were closed. She gave no sign of consent, so he just lay close and let his exhaustion wear off the edges of his alert watchfulness.

He was unsure whether he had slipped asleep, when he grew aware of her hand slowly pushing itself between his pyjama buttons to gently rub his chest. Above his heart.

He woke early. Sylvie's arm was cast back across the bed clothes above him, her body curled away. By slightly raising his head from the pillow, he could read 5.45 on the watch on her wrist. He would return to his room at six. He reached out and very softly laid his fingertips against the fine hairs of her forearm. She did not stir.

He looked up at the ceiling. The shadow of a repaired crack showed faintly through recent replastering.

"Sylvie," he said quietly, rubbing her forearm. Ever so slowly, he felt her turned back stir. She pulled herself slowly round to face him. She was smiling softly, still hazy with sleep. She slid her bare body up against him under the covers.

"Good morning," she said hoarsely. She looked at her watch.

"Time I was moving along. Soon."

She gave a little growl of complaint.

"I'll see you at breakfast," but he did not want to leave the warmth.

She pushed her arms round him "If you must..."

He felt he might never leave. So he gently disengaged from her, turned and looked for his pyjamas.

Back in his cold room, he ran a sinkful of tepid water. Then, to get ready for the day. But Mary's boxes…

He pulled them from under the bed. Opened the one he remembered had the religious records in it and unfolded the large sheet of lined and closely written paper on the top. Lists of dates, leading short entries describing the events of his Aunt Mary's spiritual journey. *…Selfish thoughts. Confessed. The young, modern priest. Absolved me, of course. Gave 20 Hail Marys on my own judgement anyway... Thinking of James. Gave £3 to a charity for victims of persecution. Later spoke to Sister Angela and she told me that many of the victims were Catholics persecuted for their faith. God directs us in our acts...*

Jim sat on the edge of the bed. Both deflated and panicked. The junction of events in his life at this moment seemed to be roaring inside his head, overwhelming him with the need to decide. To cut a way through the succession of half-articulated obscurities. Damien, Finch and the stack of documents awaiting him back home – or perhaps burgled like Sylvie's? And Sylvie, lying upstairs in the warmth he had left in her sheets? Who is she? Weeping as she had beneath him last night. Reaching some calm only when she fell far away into sleep. And Mary, waiting to be buried, now more alive to him than the distant, slightly irritating figure she had been, living.

He looked again at the paper in his hand. *Another letter from her. 10 now. God will forgive me.*

From her? He passed by the unknown of Mary's words. A different world to one he had ever been in? He pushed it away to face up full to the fears he was overhung with in this cold, dawn hotel.

He put the sheet of paper down and went to the window, pushing aside the curtain to look out on the still-dark street. A tough-looking black and white city dog ran between the pools of orange light on some mission. Too early to phone. He felt foolish and turned back into the room.

What's important? The boys? Sylvie? Jane, or maybe more, Tracey?

He looked down at Mary's boxes. And knew it was whatever she had left him that would lead him to himself. And that was what Jim wanted. The last few months, signs of who he might be had been randomly thrown up by events. Memories of his childhood too painful before now. But in fragments. Now the boxes on the floor at his feet. They were his Dead Sea Scrolls. The keys to a past history but awaiting translation from another tongue. It must be all here somehow. The "her" writing to Jim.

He looked at the box with the unopened letters in French. Letters from "her"?

He pulled off the lid. An old shoe box. He took out the top tied bundle of envelopes, slipping out the first one. It was postmarked late last year from *Foix*. He had no idea where that was, except presumably France. He turned it over and carefully tried to peel open the flap, but tore it. He slid out the letter. Mauve, flimsy paper. Unfolded it.

An address. *St. Paul de Luz.*

Then, *Chere Madame Brige...*

Brige? A misspelling? The envelope addressed to *Mlle Mary Brige.* He turned back to the letter and scanned the neat writing, slightly arty with flourishes on some words. But it was impenetrably French for him.

He replaced it in the envelope and back in the box. He lifted out all the other bundles, all the letters still sealed. And unread. But at the bottom there was a single unbundled and open envelope. This was marked *Carcassonne*, but four years ago. Again to *Mlle Brige.* Checking the bundles, it was the earliest letter of a series that were strictly monthly. He suddenly thought to look at the end of the letter he had opened. Signed *Suzanne.* He wished at that moment to leave for wherever St. Paul de Luz was- immediately after today's funeral- and find Suzanne, whatever the letters said. He thought of Sylvie upstairs, Jane and Tracey at home, and it was, for a moment, as if rushing off to France would protect them all from the present by discovering his own past.

He packed away the letters and stacked the boxes on the bed.

Only Joyce Phillips and Helen from the home joined Jim at Mary's burial with the indifferent priest, who sped through the Latin recitals over the coffin to get quicker out of the raw hilltop wind. And the two undertaker's assistants, lads in ill-fitting suits and cheap crombies. Jim felt nothing for the ritual. Mary was more alive than she had ever been. He had phoned home after clearing his room, giving away none of his fears. Tracey had answered. Nothing had happened and they simply talked of his excuses for not phoning the previous night.

Sylvie had returned home after a breakfast where both had been preoccupied with their own thoughts. He felt insensitive towards her in retrospect, but had a sense that each of them had sought something distant from each other in their bodies last night. He felt faintly surprised at his own matter-of-factness about him at nearly fifty bedding with such a younger, attractive woman. The difference between last night's anticipation and today's reflection. It was business between him and Sylvie and sleeping with her had sobered him of any sentimentality about the pair of them.

The assistants lowered the coffin lopsided and there was a moment when it looked as if Mary would reach her rest lying on her side. The priest looked distinctly irritated, but Jim could only wonder if the body inside was now untidy, carefully composed limbs askew against the artificial satin. The box hit the bottom with a harsh bash. Everyone was scowling at the lads, except Jim. He wanted to smile, and looked away across the other graves, some broken, some daubed with nicknames and football slogans.

Having only Mary as family, funerals were unfamiliar. Once or twice as Union Convenor at the Car Plant, he had attended a man's funeral, representing the Union. The man who had died in the Paint Shop. Jim had seen the black, melted flesh when he was called from the office. The burying had been angry, mourners incensed at the unnecessary death. There had been an attempt by some men to sing the Red Flag, but people had already started to disperse. The widow and Jim had turned and waited for the ragged anthem to finish, then he had given her a lift home.

Now, he cast a shower of cold, moist clay onto the coffin, thanked Mrs. Phillips and Helen and went back to his car. Sitting in it, looking out of the windscreen distorted by the slick of oncoming rain, he did not really feel Aunt Mary fitted into a feeling of loss. She had done everything she needed to do to let her nephew know the next step.

Chapter Eight

He hesitated to deal with Mary's boxes for several days, as if a shade fearful of what they might insist from him. When he finally went to the box of photos and letters, the house was quiet, Jane still away with Tracey. At the top of the box, the most recent pictures were of Mary and various residents and staff at the home where she died. He recognised Helen and the Matron. Sorting through, he found a school picture of Tracey, about fourteen years old. And one of Jane with a much younger Tracey on a windy beach. Formby, he remembered. A photo of a middle-aged couple stood against a barn wall, then another of them against the same wall of them with a younger woman, probably a daughter, sometime in the seventies from the flared cut of her trousers. Then some pictures of the couple younger, until one that triggered Jim's comprehension. The couple at the centre of a soberly dressed, formally arranged group on the steps of a building. Above the portico behind them was written *Le Mairie de St Paul de Luz.*

He looked back at the seventies photo, at the two women. He guessed one of them must be Suzanne. He stared closely at the grainy faces, hoping for one to answer him.

He went down through the prints, back into the past, the man getting younger, then in uniform for one photo. Then out of it, but with a group of men and two women all armed, but casually un-uniformed. French resistance? he guessed. He checked the face of one of the women. The same as the older against the stone wall, but now younger.

Further on the man was in uniform again, but different with a beret. What?

Then, shockingly, even younger, almost a boy, he stepped into Jim's own life. Stood, one arm round a young but recognisable Mary, the other arm round a young woman with a face blurred by moving as the shutter blinked. Jim stared at it. To confront the obvious identity of this man, he had first to deny it. He sorted back through the more recent photos first, like a pack of cards. Then back to Mary, the woman and the man. He looked again. Then back to the last uniformed picture.

The same image that teacher had swiped away from him, those years ago. His father. A flush swept through him at this recovery. A reconquest of that theft.

But then, with urgent understanding, he dealt back through them again. The couple against the wall. Jim's father... his Dad, he thought intimately, older than he had ever believed he'd been allowed to live... His dad alive in the 1970s...? Jim measured that against the events of his own life. Still alive when Jim was trying to recover from getting thrown out of the motor industry... Mary's secret? Part of the guilt Helen had spoken of?

He had been there. Across Europe. While Jim grew up, became himself. Got somewhere into the boundaries of middle age at least- then the shock... Perhaps he, Dad, was still alive- now, a few hundred miles away.

Jim's heart heaved. He felt faint. From where he was kneeling on the floor, he sat back on his haunches to steady his dizziness. But instead of images of his father, his mind filled with the cries of pain from his lost childhood. Behind his closed eyes, dark, cold stone so tangibly pressed against the skin of his body, the remembering adult shivered. With the chill and swell of sorrow in his throat…

The remembered child screamed in his ears, then sobbed the sound from his adult's body. Jim knew what had happened... A long summer weekend, housemasters away on holidays, the Institute had given over to young ineffectual teachers, the Matron away in her room quietly drinking herself into solitary feebleness, the Senior Monitors in charge. Of justice, law and punishment. James and a friend, his name now lost, were late for supper, in at the Back Steps, chattering over a wonderful day away up in the hills, hawks in the sky above, grouse surprised out of the moorland heather at their feet. A hand grasped James' shirt collar, tearing it, regrasping his ear and dragging him into the overheated Monitor's Mess, smelling of toast on the grate and a burnt milkpan. The small boys were interrogated, accused of awful acts together they did not understand, roughly shaken for their answers, pinched to confess, crowded round with faces scowling and leering, gargoyles now in the far memory.

Then a moment of gravity, a sense of sentence being passed, when the older boys seemed to hesitate at what they were about to do- then torn aside by a whoop of savagery and James and the other were harshly hustled and pulled out into the corridor, swept down the flight of stairs, their feet catching and tripping, into the basement of the Institution they never knew, beyond windows, where the wood floors became stone. To stop before a small plank door. Then rough hands tore at his clothes, shirt further ripped, trousers and underpants pulled away.

The Monitors pulled back to look at the two naked small boys. The door opened behind them and they were thrust into the darkness as the door closed on them. Stood on steps. The laughing grim voices faded away. Only each other's breathing, a long time in the dark. They touched inadvertently and flinched away from each other.

"I'm going down to see," James said.

"Don't leave me," half sobbed.

James reached out his hand and moved it in the dark until their fingers touched and gently entwined, leading the other boy down into the cellar.

By groping around with their unlinked hands, they found some empty potato sacks and lay together beneath them for warmth. The boy cried quietly for a long time until he slept, his head cradled in James' arms, leaving him staring into the blackness, not daring to move, in awe at the arousal of his sex for the first time out of the sleep of his childhood.

They were released the next morning by a single, guilty-looking Monitor, who looked away modestly as they put on their returned clothes. He had never known how the teachers had found out what had been done to the two of them. It had not seemed in anyone's interest to tell the story. James had been questioned as if he had done wrong himself. He tried to mention it in Confession, but was blocked by the Father's unresponsive silence beyond the grille. The other boy was taken away without warning from the Institution. There was no-one to take James away to…

Jim was at first curious why another of these memories had lain hidden forty years. Buried hurt. Part of a sense of not being done right to that had shaped his life. In this room, a sheaf of photographs barely held by the tips of his fingers, a moment of remote quiet took him, a felt interlude of disengaged musing at the odd coupling of events that had made Jim who he was.

But his eyes drawn down to the photos again woke him to the pain of being abandoned by this man. He looked at the almost-boy with Mary and the other woman… his mother with the blurred face? Dead soon after he was born, that he knew. Shuffling back through the prints, he came to the man perhaps ten years ago, against that stone wall. How could he not have sought Jim? And the younger woman was, he knew, Suzanne. And a relative of his.

Despite Mary having in a sense left Jim the fragments of a family, he was mainly overwhelmed by a sense of anger, a child without answers from the adults who had owed them to him. How could they- all of them- have left him now, so late in his life, so suddenly uncertain, so rudderless? He thought of the naked imprisonment by the Monitors, the bled buttocks from the master's cane, the testicles crushed by the bully, and found these acts less unjust than this neglectful abandonment by his family, the lies Mary must have had to tell over the years to Jim himself... But most of all, the way his father had walked out of his life into another one. In another country.

How could that have happened?

Unexpectedly, Damien Toser's face was before him, angry, hurt, and Jim closed his eyes to embrace it to him, not the gangling youth himself, but sharing his sense of mistrust, seeking the opportunity to use the unease and guilt of the adults around him for help. The time back to these dead relatives shrank for a moment to now, his eyes opening to an accusatory stare at the photograph.

How had it happened? Secrets. The truth he'd lived with, a dead father, a patriot even, dead on a Dunkirk beach, was a lie told by those he had believed, trusted. The truth was a stranger in another country. Set up in a new life, a new family, his son closed away in that false castle, heartless and cut from cold stone, bleakly scowling across the wet northern heathland. The shadows in the picture measuring the warmth across the old man's shoulders, he looked back up at his middle-aged child crouched above him.

Jim slowly dealt it back onto the pile. Suzanne now smiled up at him. Without shock, he was unsurprised at the realisation that she was probably his half-sister. A long moment, he looked at her. A half squint from the sun shafting from the left, made her almost wink at Jim. He smiled, then pulled out a sheet of paper from the old briefcase and folded it round the photo, carefully putting it back into the inside pocket of his jacket. Things to be done.

Finally, Sylvie agreed to meet him in the Baltic after work. He realised how he had changed towards their business since Bradford. Going through the documents had become a chore, just as it had become more difficult to focus his attention on his evening runs. He repeatedly caught himself thinking about Mary, his dad, Suzanne. He knew he had to try to reunite with what was left of the family he had lost, but also knew he had made commitments to his present. Strangely, he expected nothing more from Sylvie.

Before she came, he bought her half-pint and set it on the table across from his own. Something in her tone of voice when he had spoken to her over the phone put him into defensive distance as he waited for her.

She entered, a slight smile, but eyes turned away. She was carrying a small holdall, which she propped against the pub table. She sat opposite and cradled her glass with her hands. Jim watched the cuff of her blouse darken, soaking up from the beer-spilt table. He reached across, but she moved her wrist away, "No!" sharply.

He thought to say he was not trying to touch her, but just felt a weary shrug inside and stayed silent, waiting for her.

"Jim." She paused, not looking up. "I can't keep documents in my new flat." He looked at her, unsurprised, and detected her flit a quick glance at him, then instantly away. "The burglary... can't take the risk..." The words trailed off.

He had hoped that he could extricate himself now from the commitment to investigate. The tired inevitability of taking on duties relinquished by others. A lifetime of that, it had felt to him. He said flatly, "Well, that means, either I'm going to continue the work on my tod. Or you are going to have to come over to work on them at my house. Which I'm sure my missus will approve of." He indicated the holdall. "What's the bag for?"

She looked down at it. "It's what I've got left. Papers they didn't take."

"I thought you said that the lot went in the burglary."

"No."

"Look at me," Jim said, a harsh edge to his voice. She flicked a glance, then down to her drink. Not like the confident Sylvie. "Has someone got at you?"

"No. Yes, the burglary has."

"Meaning what?"

"It's what...what I think I know's happening. To the boys." He waited for her to continue, eyes still down to the glass. "It's all about blackmail," she started in a dulled voice. "One of those London houses is the same address as the ABC head office. It's all about setting up boys down in London with...I don't know. What they used to do to dodgy councillors to oil the wheels was take them out to a night club, get them a girl. Now, it's our boys. The kids probably get money out of it and ABC'll probably get the compliance of the great and the good to push through stuff through their committees with the use of a little blackmail. Photos of them with the boys? Hidden cameras? Who knows?"

All the weeks of piecing together fell in place for him. Gritted him with the sudden clarity of her defeated words. "So? Let's go for it. We've clearly got them worried. I've still got enough copies of some of the stuff you got from Northlodge."

She appealed to him, "You weren't burgled."

"So, what happens now? I carry on- on my own?" He felt the weariness of ill-usage, so familiar. "You have the contact with Damian. What happens now?"

"I don't know yet." Then she challenged his gaze briefly. "It was like being personally attacked. Like being groped. You don't know what it felt like."

"Well, I do know," he said with flat sourness. "In the seventies, when they were getting rid of me from the car plant. They robbed our house then. Took my union papers. Cut off the gas meter padlock and robbed that. And just to make it real authentic, they pissed on the landing carpet. So, don't tell me about violation. Bastards even got the Gas Board to try and prosecute me for the meter."

She toyed with her glass and smiled. "I suppose I should have expected a lecture from you straight out of the annals of working class struggle."

He looked across at her, as from a vast distance, recognising how much a stranger this young woman was, how alien to what he knew, but angering, he leaned harshly in towards her. "Don't you fucking patronise me."

The snarled words said, there was silence. Sylvie stared at him wide-eyed.

He looked down at his fingertips, pressed hard and bloodless against the brass table rim, surprised at his own venom. "Sorry. But I mean it. You come here and dump all this poisonous mess on me. What do you expect? What do you propose to do next?"

Her eyes glittered with unshed tears. "I don't know. Nothing seems right. I'm confused. I was really frightened by the burglary, Jim."

"Of course you were," he said softly. "Look, I care for you, Sylvie. You know that. But I can't do this on my own. I've got all sorts of other things to sort out in my life too. The results of my wife's latest medical tests are due back sometime this week. Who knows what that'll mean?" He took a mouthful of flat beer and paused. He looked over to the bar. The usual sullen barman had been replaced by a sulky barmaid. "I don't know why we drink here. The beer's rubbish."

"That's why. It means it's always empty."

He nodded, then said, "And there's something else. I got boxes of photos and letters left me by my aunt. I've got other family. People I never knew about." He looked away from her. "It's been a bit of a shock." Then he said flatly. "I've not told anyone else. Not even Jane. You're the first person." He realised this was perhaps the first time he had used his wife's name with Sylvie.

She smiled, hesitant, "That's really good. Isn't it? I mean, more family."

"Could be." He retreated back into himself. Then, back to business. "Well, what about the abuse stuff? What do you want done with that?"

"I want time. Give me time. Let me settle into the new place. Maybe it'll be okay after a bit. Just give me time. It's been a shock." This last, half-pleading.

"Let's see that bag, then. What papers did they leave? It might give us an idea of what they were after, seeing what they didn't bother with."

"Don't open it in here. You know what we said about being careful."

"Okay." For a moment, he remembered her warm body next to him that night. "It's okay, Sylvie. I want to do what's best for you too." He reached over and she let him rest his index finger on the back of her hand and gently explore the line of a pale blue vein.

Jane had returned home from Tracey's with the results of the medical tests she had been having and told Jim that some of them had been psychological tests. When she had questioned what was happening, she was told that they had to explore everything and they had sent her home with some anti-depressant pills to take.

"What! After all this, they're saying you're depressed?" Jim spoke astonishment, but was not deeply surprised. Since he had worked with so-called professionals in Social Services and watched them closely, he had become increasingly convinced that their art was all the smoke and mirrors of words to confuse and deceive the poor and the ill-educated. "So it's your fault. You've got to get yourself better. Is that what they're saying?"

She looked at him tiredly. Jim realised how old she now looked. "Well, Jim, maybe they're saying it's our fault. Maybe we just haven't been supporting each other. I don't know. I mean it's not been much fun in this marriage of ours, has it?"

"So you agree with them," he spoke quietly, realising he was treading into sensitive ground, where his inattention to family life over the years may justify the pointed finger of an onlooker, professional or not. "So, is it me? Is that what you think?"

"Well you've never been here. Ask Tracey. And even now she's left home, you always find something else to keep you out of the home. Like your running, now."

"I thought you agreed it was a good thing, getting me fit, giving up fags."

"Of course it is. But it's like everything, it takes over your life. For years, it's been like you're not living in the same place as me- or Tracey. Even when you're in the house, you're next door, doing papers or whatever."

"Only when you're asleep," he said, sounding slightly plaintive.

"Do you think about me? How often do you actually think about me?" Jim's silence answered. "God, how long since we've made love? Love? Huh!" she grunted. "No, Jim. Depression'll do me as a diagnosis. It tells me I've not got anything incurable. I don't know why I didn't wake up to it before. What it tells me is that it can be sorted out by us. Never mind blaming doctors, either I get better with you- and that means some changes in how you behave- or I get better without you." She sat firmly on the sofa, having said her piece. "And now you can make me a cup of tea. It can wash down this pill I'm due to take."

Although initially shocked by the void this conversation opened his eyes to in their marriage, he came to think more evenly about the real possibility of them separating. He thought again of Sylvie, remembering the unexpected kiss on the lips as they last parted outside the Baltic. True, she had been sombre and had not phoned him as promised. Perhaps he was being the fool. He had thrown everything to the winds since he had lifted the top off Mary's boxes. Pandora's boxes, he thought, remembering reading something about the tale. And the last thing released from the box had been Hope. Not much of a reader, outside of union policy and political books, he remembered being surprised at the savagery of the tale, Hope itself being the last delusion.

Mary's boxes as a delusion? No. The evidence, the photos. The camera does not lie. His father had lived into the 1970s. Was he fooling himself? Was he drawing conclusions that did not add up? He needed to talk to Sylvie. There was no one else. She would have to listen to what he wanted to talk about. For a change. They had spent the night together. There were feelings there. Maybe she needed him to take the initiative.

He planned to phone her the next day, and spent the evening working through papers she had given him. There were minutes of meetings about abuse he had only given a cursory look, but now he read them carefully and tried to understand what they meant behind the discreet professional jargon. Cross-referencing the names of the boys in the minutes to those on the list of boys living in the London flats, he began to make links, increasingly absorbed, working on them far into the early hours of the morning. So tired when he slid into bed, that there was only a moment of consciousness to reflect on the depths into which he was digging, a stumbled and uneasy fragment of memory about learning to read as a small boy from one of the priests, before dreamless sleep.

He phoned her the next morning from the office when he was sure he would not be disturbed. She answered it immediately.

"Oh, Jim!" Too brightly, he wondered, but pushed that aside.

"I'd like to take you out for a meal." Pause. "No strings attached. Just a way of thanking." He waited for a response. "Somewhere out of the area, where we can relax. And not have to drink the Baltic Fleet's wretched beer."

"Well, that's nice. A nice offer, Jim."

"Well, I thought so, too. Will you take it up, then?" There was a playfulness in tone they had not had since before Bradford.

"Well, it's difficult at present. There's a lot of change at work just now. I'm having to take work home most nights."

"Like me and those bloody files you gave me," he said lightly, and then lowered his voice. "You know they've been tampered with?" She did not answer. "They are photocopies of originals where stuff has been wiped out with correcting fluid and then typed over."

"No. It's probably just corrected typing errors."

"No, I don't think so, Sylvie. And there's links with other things we've got. Where did you get them from?"

"Jim, shut up. We shouldn't be having this conversation. Not over the phone. We've said this before."

"Well. We need to meet, then."

"Okay." Reluctant, but then with a probably false light note, "And I thought you wanted to take a girl out for the pleasure of her company."

"I do." But Jim did not take up the note. "To pick your brains as well. This is not easy at present. These things and the people involved are very big issues. I can't do it all on my own. I can draw conclusions, but I also need to test them out with someone- and that's got to be you. Honest, there's so much going on in my life too, that I could do with a bit of help too."

"I'm sorry, Jim. I know I always go on about my problems. I realised you were struggling a bit, last time we met. When's the next Housing meeting? Could we do something after that?"

"Don't know. Have to check my diary." He was disappointed, knowing the meeting they both attended was not due till the end of the month. He pulled the diary from his briefcase onto his knee and leafed through the pages. "Twenty-eighth. Can't you make it any earlier?"

"No. Sorry. I've explained. Okay?"

"Okay." He felt flat. The meeting was distant.

"See you then. We can decide where to go then. Okay?"

"Yes. But I'm not happy to wait with doing anything about this stuff. We can't just talk about it between ourselves. We'll have to decide to do something. The bloody stuff haunts me." He held the phone to his ear for a moment, but she said nothing, so he put it down, firmly. He wished his old friend Mark was still alive and who he had been before he went to London. He needed the old combination of cynical humour and daring suggestions that had been his friend's stamp of approval on whatever Jim next needed to do.

That thought of Mark wailed in his head two days later, when Jim was called up to Foley's office. He went in at first guardedly relaxed, wondering what trivial complaint the Assistant Director was going to raise this time. But Foley was not alone. Mrs. Patterson from Staffing was sat at the long conference table that ran along the left-hand wall. Foley stood near and awkward, as if Jim's knock had cut a conversation.

"What's this about? Why's she here?" eyes fixed on Foley, but nodding towards the woman.

Foley tried his serious-but-supportive tone. "Jim, take a seat. We need to talk over something with you." Jim clenched his mind. The bastards always want me sat down and comfortable before they shaft me.

"Before you or I say another word, what's she doing here? What is the status of this meeting?"

"Jim, something's been brought to my attention and I want us to sort it out before it gets serious." He gestured towards Patterson with a generous smile. "Susan is here to help advise us of the best way forward."

He had never heard her called "Susan" before. "Come on. I wasn't born yesterday. What is the status of this meeting?"

"Jim. Let's not get so heated." Foley looked as if he was going to step forward and touch him, perhaps try to put an arm round Jim's shoulders, but thought better of it. "Status? I don't know what you'd call it. Let's call it a pre-emptive meeting. Getting a plan to stop something worse happening."

"Well, Mr. Foley. What's the Departmental Procedure for a Pre-Emptive Meeting? Do I get to have my own representation at this Meeting? Like you have." Another nod towards Patterson, who looked down at the blank cover of the buff file before her.

Foley sighed, a touch theatrical, a touch the tired adult with the surly child. "Yes. If you insist. You may have your representation present, if you feel you have to. It's not in the spirit of what I was trying to sort out."

"Thank you," Jim said sweetly.

"It would be helpful if you could be back here within the hour." A meaningful pause. "I am under considerable pressure from elsewhere to get this problem resolved." And, as Jim turned to leave, "Please don't leave this building before I see again."

That bad, Jim thought going down the staircase fast to find a Union Steward to go back in with him. It was then he thought of Mark, missing for so long from his life. In the old days, he would have relished getting assertive with Foley. None of the Union reps were in the building, so Jim phoned the Office for the full-time Official, Henderson, a florid drinker with a grubby line in jokes, not a man he trusted. His secretary, Kathy, said he was in a meeting, but he was on the line almost immediately.

Chapter Nine

He would not have said so then, but now, the phone down and waiting for Henderson to arrive and return upstairs to see what Foley had waiting for him, Jim knew his low expectations of an outcome made him just the cynic Mark had eventually taken him for. Something he had said to Jim when they met after Mark returned from Barcelona. Jim at the tail end of being a working class hero, Mark the loud camarada de proletaria Inglesa, from dodging the Guardia Civil with his new found friends in the illegal trade unions in the last days of Franco's senility. What his old, dead friend still had then was a questioning, challenging and finally satirical force against the unjust and the obsolete. Sat in his office now, he knew Henderson would never offer the certitude Mark had had, the irrefutable faith that to challenge those on the top floor was right in itself. Like Jim himself, that was now out of fashion, even more so since the world had watched those miners marching back a year ago, behind their bands and banners, into the penury of their broken communities. The movement had now been given over to the Ronnie Hendersons to make what deals they could or would from the shrivelled percentages now available to them in the world of 1986.

Henderson's tone was lightweight, "Well, Jim, what's all this about?"

"If I knew that, Ronnie, I'd 've told you."

"What? Foley calls you right out of the blue?" He wheeled a chair over from the spare desk. "No hint at all?"

"No. Just calls it a pre-emptive meeting, so I ask him what the procedure is for that." Henderson grinned. "Yes, Ronnie, it's me they're talking to. Well, I wasn't going to let him list the charges without me having a witness, was I? So the answer is, I didn't give him a chance to try to oil himself round me. You know what Foley's like."

"So, how do you want me to handle it?"

"Just be my witness. The delightful Mrs. Patterson is present- or Susan, as Foley chummily calls her. I don't want to negotiate. Just see what he's saying, keep our lips buttoned and leave the room, before we decide how to respond."

"But, Jim. This might be something or nothing. You're the one who may be winding this up a bit formal." Jim just looked with a placid, acid certainty at the deal-doer opposite him, a recognisable and untrustworthy species from his own past. Henderson took the hint. "Okay," he continued, "but have you no idea what it's about?"

"Foley irritates me about all sorts. Last two times were about Christmas shopping for the disabled and then rapping my knuckles for some procedure detail about talking to one of the Northlodge Housing kids."

"What was that?"

Despite jerking awake to what was probably awaiting upstairs, Jim tried to retain a casual off-handedness. "Apparently the kid was an active child care case. Some social worker called Flynn."

"So, what happened?"

"Foley asked me to do a report. He seemed satisfied with that. Heard no more."

"No, Jim." Henderson looked serious. "I mean what happened with the kid?"

"I don't know. Flynn took it all over. I tell you, I've heard no more."

"Flynn took what over? What had happened with the kid?"

Jim sighed, a gesture to minimalise the story to the man opposite, but also the weight of the unspoken burden of all the secrets only he and Sylvie could guess at. Oh, Sylvie, where are you now? Part of this? Or not? "This kid told a woman from Northlodge Housing I have meetings with. He told her that one of the trustees had been interfering with him. I put it all in the report to Foley." He looked at the other man, wondering what he would have done with Damien Toser. "But apparently, I didn't do it exactly and procedurally correctly." A somewhat gigantic understatement, he thought, the pages of the files in the back bedroom at home flickering through his mind.

Henderson breathed out, punctuating the importance of what he had to say. "That's child abuse. Very serious stuff."

Jim snapped out a laugh. "It wasn't me abused the lad, Ronnie!"

"I should think not. I know that." He paused. "I think we should play it by ear. There may be a handle we can get hold of to defuse things with Foley in this meeting."

"No. Let's see what they've got to say and leave without saying anything, before deciding how we respond. We don't even know what it's about yet." When he had been Union rep. himself, Jim had seen Henderson at work. He knew that the way to control him was not to let him run off at the mouth while in with Management, too keen to please. He needed to be scripted with what Jim wanted before the next meeting.

With the tired shrug of the professional who knows best, but is not listened to, Ronnie said, "Okay. If you insist. It's your meeting."

But it was not. As soon as they knocked and entered, the

atmosphere had changed. Foley was sat now at the top of his conference table, Patterson beside him. Two chairs had been placed opposite for Jim and Henderson. A nonnegotiable seating arrangement. Foley looked down at the sheaf of papers under his spread fingers, not inviting them to sit, but not giving them an alternative with his downward gaze. He only looked up after they had sat. Well, I said I didn't want to negotiate, Jim thought, and they've taken me at my word. Gone into full formal procedure.

By the end of Foley's first sentence, Jim knew he was going to be suspended. It was the Toser business. Both shocked and not, he missed some of the detail of the allegations, but knew they would all be listed on his own copy of the sheet Foley was now reading from. Failed to follow procedures. Failed to co-operate with the social worker. Failed to provide evidence of abuse to the Department. General stuff, no dates. Jim had been in a similar place so often before. Himself, or on behalf of others. Next the conditions of suspension. No contact with other members of staff, unless they were acting as accredited Union Representatives. No contact with clients known to be receiving services from the Department (Huh! Cut me off from meeting any more kids, Jim thought). Keep the Personnel Department aware of any changes of address or any absences when not available for further proceedings. Full pay until further notice. Finally quoting Section and Paragraph of the Council Disciplinary Procedures.

"Any questions." Foley said, with a finality that did not invite any.

Henderson looked glumly at Jim, who answered, "None."

The official looked with a tight smile across the table. "You'll let us have a copy of the charges?"

"Here." Foley detached a stapled pair of sheets from the file and slid them across the polished table. He then looked pointedly down again at the papers before him. Meeting over. Rising to leave, Jim half-smiled, never having seen his boss so crisp and disciplined.

Out in the corridor, Henderson expelled his breath, "Well! Were you expecting that?"

Jim laughed. "Foley certainly did it with a style I'd never have expected."

"Not exactly a laughing matter, is it?"

"Depends how you see it. Get me a copy of those charges downstairs and I've got the afternoon off. On full pay!"

"Mad bastard. They always said you were."

"Who's they? Mad, yes, but bastard, no. We're all mad where I come from. Get me those copies. I'll be in the Stanley Arms, waiting for you. May even buy you a pint, Ronnie."

Henderson did not stay for a drink, just slipped in, left the brown envelope and told Jim to keep him informed of anything happening. Alone, Jim finished his beer and wandered to the car park. He felt heady and carefree. A first hint of winter breaking in the blustery brightness of the wet pavements. He could smell the sea sloshing against the promenade a few streets away. He still had some running kit and a pair of trainers in the car boot, so he drove down to the Shore Promenade, parked, changed into shorts and teeshirt and jogged into the wind beside the waves slapping against the seawall. A small coaster was rocking its way up the choppy estuary towards the open sea. Jim ran to try to keep level with it, but it gradually overhauled him and he eased back to trotting comfortably.

What would Jane say about the suspension? She would not be happy. But he had been suspended for a reason. He would have to tell her the story of the boys. At least, some of it. He knew he had been right. He had no alternative, especially after meeting Toser. Two workless men walked past, dogs on leads, staring at Jim. He realised he had been muttering his thoughts aloud. He turned back and, wind behind, pushed his pace again. Only two weeks to the Union Race, eight weeks to the Marathon. It struck him that the instruction not to meet other staff while suspended would also mean not running with other staff in the Race. Bollocks. That was part of his training. Let Foley make an issue of that one, if he could. Back at the car, he did his best to wipe the sweat off his face and torso with a towel, but left his shorts on and drove home.

Jane was making herself some lunch in the kitchen, when he entered.

"What's all this!" she said, looking at his bare legs.

"I've been suspended. Foley, this morning."

"What?" looking from his face and back to the legs, as if what Jim said and his dress were somehow connected. "Suspended? For what?"

"It's a long story." He looked to her for sympathy, but found only disbelief. "Can I just change, then I'll tell you?"

Her face hardened. "Go on. You do what you like." She turned back to the stove. "That'll be a change."

Ignoring this, he went up to the bedroom. He wanted to shower, but that would have to wait. He pulled together trousers, socks and underwear, quickly rinsed himself, dressed in the bathroom and came down.

She was sat on the sofa, a boiled egg and toast on her lap. "Go on then. What is it this time," she said flatly.

"Well. I was given evidence that some boys in one of the housing association flats, that they were being abused. Molested." He looked at her, expecting her attentive, but she was carefully beheading the top of the egg. "These kids are ones who've been in care, in children's homes and the flats are to try to move them on to living independent. Trying to settle them out in the world. Get them jobs. Or training." She took a spoonful of yolk, looked up at him expressionlessly, but said nothing. "Well, I met one of the boys and he told me what had happened to him. And it's not just him, there's lots of them." She still continued eating. How far to go in the telling? "It shouldn't be happening, should it?"

"No, Jim. It shouldn't. So why have they suspended you for it?" She looked steadily at him as if she already knew the answer, as if it was a story heard before. Maybe a hundred times.

"Well, they said I should have gone straight to the social worker. I shouldn't have met the kid."

"Are they right? Shouldn't you have?"

"Foley knew all about it," he said with defensive dismissiveness. "I did a report for him on it. Saw the social worker. He was hopeless. I think he's the problem. I think he's probably complained about me."

"Jim, what made you the expert about children being abused? What do you know about it?"

"I know what I was told. I heard it from the kid."

She tore off a piece of toast and wiped some yoke from the base of the eggcup. He waited for her to finish eating it. She looked at him, steady into his eyes. "You heard it from the kid. How do you know it's true? Kids in care are always telling lies. For some reason or other. What did he tell you?"

"It's not just that. There are other kids." He hesitated before pushing deeper. "I've seen other evidence. Files on the others."

She put her hand up, palm stopping him, penetrating, "Wait. You've seen files? Where from? What have you been up to?"

Jim stepped back to sit down in the armchair opposite her. A moment to consider how far to go with this. He owed Jane the truth, but how much did she need to know? To understand, but not to get tangled up with Sylvie and who she was. A step at a time. "I was given copies of some files. They are all kids who've gone from children's homes into these flats. There's things that don't add up. Things are wrong!" His anger rose at the half-truth he was telling her.

"Oh. Things are wrong, are they?" She put the plate of fragments aside. "Yes! Things are always wrong out there!" He rolled his eyes, trying to jeer at her. "Look at me, damn you, Jim." Then, word-by-word spelt out, "Look. At. Me." He stared up, her mouth spiteful, but her eyes swimming on the desperate edge of tears. "It's always out there, Jim, isn't it? Some crusade. It was the sit-in, when Tracey was born. It was going off on flying pickets for others when you'd been sacked and should've been looking for your own job, for Christ's sake! Tilting at windmills! And they're always someone else's." She let pleading briefly flit across her face, but hardened. "What is the point? Whatever I say to you, there's always a bigger, better cause for you to charge off after out there." She gestured out of the window, now distorted with blown rain. "And I'm not well. Maybe it's depression, maybe not. But a little consideration, a little time from you wouldn't go amiss. It might even help me get better." She sniffed and turned from him.

He spoke quietly. "How can you say that trying to get something done about those boys- and what's happening to them- how can you say that's wrong?"

He recoiled as she turned back on him, livid with rage. "Don't you dare try to blame me! Don't try to make me feel guilty about things I can't do anything about!" She paused, breathless. "Anyway, what difference has anything you've done made to anything? The unions- look what's happened to them. Every time, they get rid of you and none of your blessed mates raises a finger to save you. And now it's happening again. Just like the Car Plant." She stood, a tissue to her nose. "God, you're hopeless, Jim. No wonder Tracey left. Just leave me alone." As she went out, she stopped and looked at him, piteous for herself, for their life and- a little for him too, sat crouched, silent. With nothing to say.

After she had gone up to the bedroom, he sat for a long time, looking at the sofa's crushed cushions in the space she had left. He listened for sounds of her, but there were none. He felt numb. It was true. Nothing he had done had lasted. And now she wanted him to drop the boys' stuff. In some ways, it would be easy to. Sylvie seemed to have gone cold on it since the burglary. He felt his body shiver. But, at the end of the day, he almost whispered it aloud, you have to live with yourself. With your conscience. That's who I am. And it's too late to change now. But it did not feel comfortable to say that.

He thought of Suzanne, and whatever sort of person she might be. She had wanted to make contact with her English relatives, but for some reason Aunt Mary had not seemed to want it, while she carefully stored away these remote links with her lost and foreign brother. His father. Did Suzanne even know of his own existence? The half-brother, he tried to think of himself as. He would write. In English, which she would be able to get someone to translate.

It had taken him a painful hour to write his first attempt, trying to put it into clear and easy words for her, but when he re-read it, he saw it revealed too much. He did not know who Suzanne was or what she wanted. He crumpled the sheet up.

Again. Address only, then:

Dear Suzanne,

My name is James Briggs. I have been given some papers from a relative of mine, Mary Briggs. They include some letters from you. It is not clear what relationship you may have with Mary. I would be interested to hear from you. Please write to me at this address. He straightened out the crumpled sheet to retrieve the last phrase: *I do not know if you can read English. I am sure you will find someone to translate this for you.*

Yours Sincerely, James Briggs. No photo.

Jane knew nothing of this. Sylvie a little, but probably retained nothing of it in her own turmoil. Caution, Jim thought. Who knows what I may be setting loose with this letter? I assume much about what was in Mary's boxes. But it has only been guesswork. Or wishful thinking.

Chapter Ten

Henderson phoned the following day to tell Jim that the Disciplinary Hearing would be at the earliest in two weeks time, according to Foley. Sounded as if it might be more than that. Would whoever want the boys' story out there at all? Bury Jim. Bury his stories with him. Not bloody likely. They can dream on if they think they can dig that into a grave with me. Two weeks would take him up to the Union 10k Race. He would do it proud. And show them.

Over the fortnight, he trained harder than he ever had before. He started to go out in the morning, about 6.30, when the first paling of the eastern sky showed. He would be back before Jane rose, quietly shower, make their breakfast, then take a bundle of the documents and his diaries in a cardboard box down to the Library when it opened at nine. On one of the scarred, dark varnish tables in the Reading Room, he would start to work through, making fresh notes, cross-checking those already made for links, for explanations.

It did start to take some fragmentary shape. The minutes of the child abuse meetings often seemed to be formal records of difficult discussions. One of them, a boy anonymised to "R.D.", had been particularly mauled with correcting fluid. A discussion about the boy's abuser appeared to have had a three line section deleted, with the re-typing over the original slightly displaced above the level of the rest of the type. It read, *R.D. was at first reluctant to disclose the name of the alleged abuser. Dr. Phillips (R.D's G.P.) told the Conference that R.D. had named the abuser to him. The Chairperson cautioned Dr. Phillips not to repeat the name, as R.D. had subsequently withdrawn his original allegation when further questioned by Police.* The conclusion was that sexual abuse had probably taken place against R.D., but the identity of the abuser was not known and that as R.D. had moved his placement into supervised accommodation with Northlodge Housing, he was no longer at risk. His name was not placed on the At Risk Register.

This made Jim automatically doubt the other minutes. And the reason for the alterations. He thought about Sylvie, now excusing the correction fluid as typing errors. How different she would have been two months back, urgent then for the truth. Willing to take risks. Pushing Jim to take them. The burglary of her flat had driven her for cover. And Jane? Now, Jim should not bother. Someone else's windmills. The alternative? Nights awake with this on your conscience?

In his mind, he knew that he would be sacked. He knew Jane would not support him and doubted Sylvie. Henderson and the Union would just try a deal. He wondered whether he could steer the Disciplinary Hearing into telling the truth. Force them to at least face the allegations. If only with further of their lies

The Union Race was on the Sunday before Monday's Disciplinary. Jane and he had spoken little since his suspension, both recognising each other's intransigence on the issue of the boys. He knew from her that Tracey was completely intolerant of his stand at the expense of his job. She was coming round to take Jane out for a pub lunch, so Jim got out of the house earlier than he needed to get to the Race.

He sat parked near the Start and enjoyed the precision of his own preparation, methodically pinning his number to his running vest, pasting his nipples with vaseline against rubbing sore, taking off his zip-up jacket to slip on the vest. Which he had carefully printed with felt-tip marker across the back, "Suspended for Speaking Out!"

Twenty minutes to go and he got out into the wind, pinned his car keys into his shorts and warmed up jogging up the road with a scattering of others, self-conscious that he was probably breaching the terms of his Suspension, as well as the written taunt across his back. Ahead was a line a women runners across the road, gently trotting, chattering and laughing together. They all wore the same charity teeshirts with a variety of jogging bottoms, only one wearing shorts. He quickened slightly to run round them, looking across to see if he recognised- Sylvie!

"Sylvie?" She was three women away from him, laughing at the centre of the babble. "Sylvie!" Louder.

She turned, saw him. Shock. "Jim?" The other women looked at him. "What are you doing…?"

He went trivial, arm wide, eyes down to his bare, running legs, "What does it look like?" The women near him laughed and it cued Sylvie to join them, her eyes dissembling, discomforted. "I'm the runner. You never told me you did."

The woman next to him laughed loud. "We don't. You won't see us after a couple of miles!"

Another one half protested, "You speak for yourself!"

Jim moved across the road to Sylvie's shoulder, "What are you doing here?" She glanced nervously at him. "Can I speak to you? Alone?" This brought hooting and whistling from the others. "Now," he said, clenched.

"If you insist," she said, quiet but hard. "Sorry, girls. Join you in a minute." Then as an afterthought, "This is business not pleasure. I assure you." More laughter from them as she slowed to drop back next to Jim and the line moved away.

Mixed with anger and genuine inquiry, he said, "I thought this race was for Union members only. You don't even work for the Council."

She looked at him, hard and sharp in a way he had not seen in her before, "Neither do you, so I've heard."

"What do you mean? Where've you heard that? Not from me. I haven't spoken to you since I was suspended."

She looked away at the road ahead. "It's common knowledge." Pause. "Anyway I phoned your office and they told me."

"Told you what? That I was suspended?"

"Yes."

"They had no right to tell you that." Now angrier, "Anyway, if you knew that, why didn't you phone me? Find out what happened." With a slight snarl, "Even to find out how I was." They ran on, without her answer. "And of course, you know what I have been suspended for?"

"I'm sure you're going to tell me."

"Damien. Damien Toser. I've been suspended for talking to him." He ran ahead of her a few steps and called back over his shoulder, "Why do you think I've written this on the back of my shirt? That's it. Suspended for speaking out."

"I'm going on to join the girls," Sylvie said, starting to run past him.

He pulled up and grabbed her upper arm. "Just a minute!"

"Let go of me," she said plaintively. She looked ahead to the women, but they were jogging on talking together.

He let go of the arm gently. "I need some support. You owe me it. We were in all this together."

She looked down, then briefly glanced into his face and away again. "We can't speak here," and shrugged.

"You suggest. You say where. It's always me." He was irritated with the plaintive edge that crept into his voice.

"I don't know. We can't meet in the Baltic. Lots of public places aren't safe."

"Safe for who? You? Or me?" He reasserted himself, "Don't worry about me. I've got nothing to lose wherever we meet." Without forethought, he added menacingly, "But you may. If you don't meet me."

She turned and he was surprised at the scared look in her eyes. "What do you mean?"

Jim was lost for a moment to follow up the threat, when one of the women called Sylvie and started to run back towards the two of them confronted in the roadway. Jim said, hard, "Where? And when?"

She was panicky to end before her friend reached them.

"Tomorrow. You know where I live now."

"I know the address. I'll find it." He knew where her new flat was. When she had first told him the address, he had driven off route, past it, on the way to a Youth Training Committee. Even then, he had been tempted to drop in a friendly note. But Sylvie had been acting so frightened and paranoid, he had decided against it. "Seven, tomorrow." Not wait. He steered away from her and ran ahead, giving the friend a smile as he passed.

Back home after the race, the car of Tracey's boyfriend Alex was still outside the house. Jim had expected them to be out with Jane by now and collected his bag of kit to enter the house reluctantly. From the hallway, he called out, "Hi! It's me!" and went into the front room.

Tracey stood up as he entered. On the coffee table, there were stacks of his files. On top his diaries, one open, imminent to slide off onto the floor at Jim's feet. He instinctively reached down, closed it and placed it to the side. He looked at his daughter scowling at him, then over to Jane who looked exhausted and turned her eyes away.

"What's this?" He gestured to the files. He felt he should be righteously angry, but was defensive. He took in Alex, perched uneasily on the arm of the sofa Tracey had risen from. Turning back to Jane, "What's this? Why're they out here?"

"I got them out," Tracey said defiantly. "Mum told me about you being suspended. Because of this," pointing at the documents. "I told her I would look for them."

Jim felt an unblocked surge of anger, "Who gave you the right?"

He turned on Jane, but Tracey cut in, "Don't blame Mum. It wasn't her fault. I decided after she told me. She wouldn't have done anything about you, if it was left to her." She turned to Jane, "I'm sorry, Mum, but it's true." Back to her dad, "You just always get your own way with Mum. And look how ill she is!"

"What right do you think you have to tell us?" He turned back to Jane, "These were confidential." Then gesturing at Alex, "Has he seen them? Have you let him see what's in them?" Alex leaned away from Jim's anger, almost tumbling from his perch.

"What right?" Tracey said coldly. "Confidential? Confidential from who? Are you supposed to have these, Dad? And who is Sylvie?" Jim jarred at this, with Tracey in pursuit, "Go on, tell Mum who Sylvie is? She's never heard of her!"

Jim bent and placed his fingertips momentarily on the top file. Protectively. He looked across at Jane from his bowed position, pointedly to her and not at Tracey. "Yes. I will tell you about it. I can tell you how this all came about." He stood straight again, his post-race muscles aching.

"I would have told you before, but you just wrote it off as more… tilting at windmills, you called it. I will explain it to you." Turning to Tracey and Alex. "But I do not owe you- either of you- an explanation."

Alex looked faintly relieved. Tracey turned to her mother, "Well do you agree with that, Mum? Are you going to let him mess things up again?"

For the first time, Jane spoke. "Your dad does owe me an explanation." She sighed, "I'm not sure I'll want to hear it, though." She looked up again at her daughter, a long, reflectively affectionate smile. "Thanks, love. You've done the right thing for me, but I think this is between your dad and me. I don't think Alex and you… should be part of it."

Tracey looked back at her and Jim saw what he had missed seeing in his wife and daughter, the deep affection between two women- something that must have been gently growing while he had been elsewhere. "Mum, you'll let it happen again. He's lost his job. Again. You're always the one who has to pick up the pieces after Dad has gone off on one of these things- his crusades." She turned to Jim, eyes glittered with a realisation, "In fact, Dad, it's not always Mum only that carries the can for you. I did, too! It felt like being brought up in a single parent family most of the time. That's why I got out so early." She pushed Alex's knees aside to cross to beside her mum. Hand on her shoulder, like an old Victorian photographic plate of mother and daughter, "Mum's her own worst enemy with you. These papers aren't yours. You should hand them in. It's about criminal stuff, isn't it?"

"Yes, they are. And it's nothing to do with you."

"Well, what's it to do with you? And who's this Sylvie?"

"As I said," he led in patiently, "it has nothing to do with you. I will discuss it with your mum. It will get dealt with properly. That, I can tell you for certain," a twinge of doubt, verge of a lie nudged him when he said this.

"Oh, yes. Sure. But it's lost you your job." Then leaning forward, "And this Sylvie. Sounds like a tart's name."

"That, Tracey, is just being ignorant," he snapped. "But it's not going to get me into a discussion with you- and with Alex, about this. I've told you it's confidential."

She looked down at her mother, who shook her head. Tracey then turned to look out at the dullening sky, verging on rain, folding her arms to mark the end of her efforts.

After a loaded silence, Jane stood up. "Time for us to get going, if we're not going to be too late for lunch at the pub."

"I'll get the car started," and Alex was gone.

As she followed him, Tracey stopped and put her hand on Jim's arm, gazing questioningly. "Dad. I don't mean to get at you… but Mum… you need to look after her. All this stuff you get into- it makes her ill. And you. You may be running and keeping fit. But it doesn't do you any good. Another job gone. And these papers- they'll get you in trouble." Then, almost exasperatedly, "All this standing up for other people- but not for your family. Where's that leave your family?" She turned and followed Alex.

The car started outside and Jane looked out, speaking almost dreamily to Jim still turned away. "We will speak, Jim. I have no doubt. But I may ask Tracey if I can sleep on her divan for a few nights. I hope Alex won't mind. I doubt if they're sleeping together yet. Tracey would have told me, I think." She looked back at him. "Her divan's not comfortable, but probably less stressful." As she walked out, she murmured, "Good luck at the Disciplinary." Calling from the hall, "You do what you think you've got to do, Jim."

The door closed and a moment later the sound of the car pulling away. He sat heavily on the settee, sighed aloud and thought, What a mess, wondering how he had such an alien daughter, so foreign from her father's beliefs in what was important to her. It had been a long time since he had been comfortable with her.

He drew the curtains against the rain now spattering against the panes, switched on the light and sat before the files. He pulled the child abuse one to himself, then the notebook, tore a rear page from it and started to prepare notes for the Disciplinary tomorrow.

Jane phoned in the early evening to confirm she was staying with Tracey. "You'll let me know what the Disciplinary result is, won't you?"

"Why- will you still be at Tracey's?"

"I don't know. She wants me to stay. For a bit." He let her fill up the pause. "You'll be okay with that won't you?"

"What if I said no?"

"I wouldn't believe you." A dry laugh, "If you said it and it was true, it would only confirm it for me. That you only notice me when I'm not there."

What to reply to that? "If you say so. But we do need to talk. About things."

"Jim, we've needed to talk for years. About anything. Why so suddenly now?"

"Well, a lot's been happening lately. I should have talked to you about it, but you'd only say it was more of… well, what you did say."

"About this disciplinary business?" In Jim's mind, he had the image of Suzanne's photo- which Jane knew even less about. "Well, what did you expect me to say? You may lose your job and you've told me nothing about what you've been up to."

He decided- nothing about France, yet. "Well, I didn't want to worry you," he said feebly.

"Oh, yes. Thinking of me," said dismissively. "Well, now you can think of me not being there." Then reflective, but still sharp, "Strange that, Jim. I'm more real to you when I'm not with you, than when I am." He did not reply. "Phone me tomorrow. When you hear about the Disciplinary."

"Right. Okay."

The phone down, he thought about her remark. More real when I'm not with you. Like Aunt Mary. Like his dad, thinking about him now more as he believed him to have only recently passed beyond his touch. He could have met him, he resented. Maybe, grown up with him, if he had made contact early enough. What would that have been like- to grow up, a child in France? He tried to visualise what it might look like. Impossible.

And why had his dad not returned from France after the war? Of course. Suzanne's mother. He shocked. A step-mother? He had a brief urge to get out the photos again, but stayed still. The fact was that, as far as the evidence he had, he ceased to be an item in his father's life after 1940. And had only been a remote item in Aunt Mary's- however much she might have prayed for him. If ever there was proof that there is no God, it would be how he found the state of his life now, after all the energy Mary had apparently expended on praying for him!

Surprised at this surge of bitterness, he felt it ebb as he thought about Mary. Her distant and private attentiveness to him had been her way. At least attentive… Crouching forwards over his knees, he smeared the tears aside, sniffed back the running nose, then rubbed his temples and pushed his fingers back through his hair.

Oh, God. All this has got to lead somewhere. Something has to come clear. He thought of Sylvie and how promising that had seemed at first. Not the sex. He had not expected that- but the comradeship of working together on the grave evidence they were accumulating. Maybe it had been the sex that had wrecked things, rather than her burglary. But wrecked it now felt. Tomorrow, he would see whether she would be prepared to do anything to help him in the mess that meeting Damian had now got him into. If she would not make some sort of stand for him, she certainly would not do anything worth a spit for the boys.

By tomorrow night, it might be all too late for her to disown the issue. He would take the story of the files to the Disciplinary and it would depend what questions he might be asked. He could think of several for which the answer would be, "Sylvie Cathcart of Northlodge Housing."

Chapter Eleven

He had worked through the files in the front room, making notes until four in the morning, when he decided to get some sleep for the afternoon Hearing. He was woken by the sound of the phone ringing. Sleep-dazed, he scrambled downstairs to the hall.

"Yes?"

"Jim? Ronnie Henderson here. Glad I've caught you."

"Why? What's the time?"

"Woken you from your beauty sleep have I?" He even managed to make that sound salacious.

"Yes. I worked late to prepare for today."

"Well, that's what I called about. It's been postponed. Not sure why."

"When's it postponed to?" Jim was irritated. By his yet-to-wakeness. By the wasted time he had spent preparing for today. By Henderson's voice.

"No date yet. So you've got more time off at the firm's expense."

"Huh. Trust you to find a good side to this mess."

In a changed tone, Henderson inquired, "Mind if I ask you something, Jim?"

"What?"

"Were you at that race the Union organised yesterday?"

"Yes. And I didn't run very well."

"Um. That may be why they've postponed it. You do know, of course that going to the Race may be considered a breach of the Terms of your Suspension."

"Really?" Jim asked sarcastically.

"Well, you know what you're doing. You, of all people. Just remember, it won't make it any easier, when the Union has to defend you."

"Are you jumping ship on me already, Ronnie? Is that what you are saying?"

"Oh, yes. Very clever, Jim." His tone had hardened. "Don't think I don't know about your history. You've always set yourself up as some sort of martyr. Well, I don't call that sort of thing martyrdom. Just plain stupidity. If you want the Union to help, you've got to behave as if you're in the real world. All those principles that people like you parade round with aren't worth a fig. If they don't put food on the table."

Jim left a break before reply. "Have you finished, Ronnie? Finished lecturing? Just phone me when Foley gives you a date." And he put the phone down.

He looked at the front door mat. Three letters lay there. Two pieces of junk, the third with a foreign stamp. From France. He picked it up.

Sat back in the front room, his hands had become awkward and big-thumbed as he opened the letter, tearing the edge of it as he broke open the envelope. He unfolded it and smoothed it carefully out across the setee arm. Large slow writing.

My Dear James,

I was most excited to receive your letter.

I could not fully understand it, but my daughter who has English taught to her at school, she explained your words to me. She is writing this letter, as I speak to her my words in French. I speak some English from my Father, but I do not read or write. The letters to Mary in French, Jim thought.

I do not know you. Mary was the sister of my Father. I wrote to her after he died, but she did not reply. Perhaps she also had died. You say you are a relative of Mary. What relative can you be? Perhaps you are a cousin, my Father your Uncle? Oh. God, she does not suspect who I am! He! Jim furied, He told her nothing! A liar.

My Father spoke little of his family in England, only near the end of his life he spoke of Mary. Ah, dead, definitely. A slight, expected saddening before angering over the father he had never met- a liar, by omission, yet whom this stranger-woman knew. But knew not. *He said he had written to her, but Mary sent no response. Did she die many years ago? We are excited, me, my daughter and my husband, because we discover a new family with you. We want to know of you. How many years old than me? I am forty two years. My daughter is seventeen years. Do you have family in England? We would like to know.* Would he tell them, Tracey and Jane? Jim wondered. This felt private, his own piece of the Earth at last. Not to be shared. At least, not until Jim was sure. That this woman was to be trusted, safe, he stonewalled with scepticism against the tide of wishing to touch, embrace these strangers, that surged inside him.

We live in St. Paul de Luz, which is a village. My husband is chemist and works in pharmacy. I am a teacher of small children in the School. I specialise in Mathematics and Ecology. My daughter wishes to go to University to study Ecology. She is my daughter! (She is laughing while writing this!) A vivid picture, daughter dismissing fondly her mother's possessive declamation. Sun perhaps slanting across the stone wall in Mary's photos, even at this time of year in that southern climate.

Please write back to us and tell us more about you. We wish to know. We wish also that perhaps you can meet us. Is it possible that you come to visit us? We live in a most beautiful region of France. Perhaps if you visit with you and your family, you will have a beautiful time staying with us. We have many friends here and our friends are your friends also.

Please write soon. Goodbye and au revoir from your new family!

God bless you, Suzanne (and Maurice and Marie Claire).

A family. A puzzle. Unknown to them, Jim felt denied by his dead father. Who for decades had retained his silence in France over his prior life in England. Then, towards death, he wrote to Mary. Not to Jim, his son. Those letters were not in the boxes Mary had left him.

But now he was gone. Spilt milk Jim could not help crying out over, his eyes slipping off focus from the written sheet before him, coldly and angrily turned from its naïve warmth. Stolen. Far off, that man had lived his second life, as husband, father, grandfather, an old man warming his back in that southern sun.

He picked up the letter and gently rubbed the texture of the paper between thumb and forefinger. It felt uneven, yet silky-surfaced. Hand made? Ink written. He lifted it to smell. Perhaps a faint scent of pine, but probably his imagination. Yet caringly done. For him.

He needed to decide what he was doing about it, before he shared it with Jane and Tracey. It had been his father. And his father's lies. Needed sorting first. He would tell them in time, but he needed to check out first why forty years or more of silence had been decided by that man. His father, though now unreachable by death, was clasped in anger by his son, gripped to have every answer, every shred of evidence shaken from him. To know who he was. To know why. And, most, to know that there was some reason. For saying nothing to his son.

Chapter Twelve

When he arrived outside that night, he parked up the first turning past the dark Victorian house Sylvie now lived in. It was raining again and Jim stepped cautiously on the uneven, ill-lit paving stones, muddied from a house building site at the end of the road. Music from a pub over the back. Not an area he knew. Old houses carved by hardboard partitioning into poky flats, he guessed. Garden ends fenced off and sold for building little clusters of houses for first-time buyers. Probably where Tracey would mortgage her future. With Alex, if he lasted the course.

Jim had his briefcase filled with files, but he felt they were probably a pretext. Did Sylvie want to talk about those boys? Although he felt that something would have to be done, in his head he had left that to when he had the Disciplinary. His day in court, he thought of it as. Knowing what he would have liked tonight, he rang the bell marked *Cathcart* tentatively, uncertain.

Feet on the stairs and she opened the door, profiled against the low hallway light. "Upstairs." She turned and he followed up the worn carpet, eyes upwards at her moving self.

Inside her flat, she busied herself with tidying away some books and then a tray of meal things onto the kitchenette bar. "Not brilliant, I'm afraid. But it'll do till I get something better."

Taking in the faded, cheap brashness of the wallpaper, the worn furniture, he was saddened to compare the tidy comfort of her previous home. "I'm so sorry, Sylvie. The other place was nice."

"Yes," she said tersely. "What do you want to drink?"

"Tea's fine," answering with a feeble attempt at a sociable lilt that came out trivial. He sat, wet briefcase on lap, looking everywhere in the room but at her. The rattle of cups sounded irritable in the wordless room. He opened the case, started to pull out the bundle of files, then slid them back in.

She brought the tea in a cup and saucer and saw him looking at them. "No mugs. The bastards who burgled my flat made themselves cups-mugs of tea. So I binned them." He wanted to say sorry again, but saw she was not in the mood for that. Hard, tolerating him being here because she had no choice.

"Look, Sylvie. It wasn't my fault you were burgled."

"I know. But that doesn't help." Her face was drawn down with hurt. She curled into her chair. "It happened. It was awful." She glanced at him, then away, hardened again. "You, nor anybody else can do anything about it. It was vile. It will always be vile."

Jim drank, giving a moment to settle. "I know." Ready to go on, she cut him off.

"Yes. I know. It happened to you." Bitterly, "Don't tell me again."

He put his cup back on the saucer, so loud in the silence, rubbing the tips of his forefingers together, looking at them. Waiting for her. Knowing her anger to be a thin shell.

"Well, you wanted this meeting…"

"Yes. I did." He breathed in. "Yes. It's about the boys. But it's about other things. A lot has been happening." He at last looked over at her, her knees drawn up to her chin, watching him from behind them. "To both of us. Yes?" She answered nothing. "The boys has only been part of it for me. We do have to discuss that, I know. I've got an idea for that, anyway." He waited to let her take that up first, if she wanted. She just watched him, guarded and unresponsive. "You remember me telling you about the family I've got. The stuff left me by my Aunt Mary when she died." She barely nodded. "Well I wrote to them. They're French. It's my sister- half-sister. She's got a daughter and a husband. They wrote back." What had the writing said? More, what had it meant? To him. He looked over at her, still and holding him with a passive and expressionless gaze. Should he be telling her? Who else, then? What would it mean to Sylvie, crouched in that seat around her pain? "My father… he went to France. I don't know when… when I was little, maybe in the war." Spelling it out, the painful neglect of the story, made him measure the words, for the truth of them, for getting it right, precisely how it was. With a little- not too much- of how it felt. "He married again in France. Had this daughter. Her name is Suzanne. But she does not know. He never told her. She never knew about me. And he never tried to find me again…" He looked away. At a stack of books on a chair, a spine towards him read *Effective Management*, another *For Whom the Bell Tolls*. "I was left to be brought up in that dump in Yorkshire. Run by priests." He brought his knuckle to his lips, then pressed them to rein in the passion he felt. Mastering his emotion, he went on measured and deliberate, "It has left me without a childhood. I feel like I stopped years back. Before I can remember." He looked back at her, unable to conceal the fear and sorrow from his face. "That's why I've made such a mess of things. I've gone on behaving like a child. Doing what I want. Not listening to others. Not grown up really." If anything, she had retreated further behind the cover of her knees. "Did you know I have a daughter? Tracey."

She nodded, then spoke slightly hoarse, "I think you've mentioned her."

He nodded. "Well, I lost her." He turned his eyes from her. "She's become someone I don't like very much. Someone I don't even understand." He gave a dry snigger. "She doesn't agree with me doing anything about the boys. We rowed about it yesterday."

"You told her? About the boys?" Sylvie stared at him.

"I have to give some explanation to my family about being suspended from work. What do you expect?" he asked, almost pained that he had to spell it out. That she was so reserved, obdurate and cold. But he drew back from telling Sylvie of Tracey's ferrety questions about who she was. Or the discovered files stacked in the front room.

"Your wife too? What do they know about it?"

"What I've told them. Bits." He turned to her, shovelling over the detail with, "It'll all be out at my Disciplinary anyway. Either Foley's version. Or mine."

She sat up, confusion in her eyes. "Oh, no, Jim. You can't." She looked down. "You can't… you mustn't use them. It's not right. They've got nothing to do with… it's not the right place for dealing with it." She spread her fingers, palms upwards, as if it was beyond words. Beyond dispute.

"What?" His mouth open, part disbelief, part to give the effect of it. Then more decisively, "What?" He let it hang, really filling with astonishment at what she may be feeling her way to saying. "Let's get this clear. I may be losing my job because I've got evidence that boys in council care have been probably molested. That I've spoken to one of them. That it seems nobody wants to know. Nobody wants me to lift the stone to see what else is underneath." She looked away at her hands, still splayed, and folded them away. "And you say, I've got to say nothing. That they're right. And we are wrong." Sourly, he added, "Not we. Me. It seems that I'm on my own on this, now. Am I?"

She was flushed. Upset and off balance. "No, Jim. Oh, I don't know." She looked up at him anxiously, then looked back down at the fingers now knotted in knuckles. "I'm frightened. Since the burglary, I haven't known where I'm going. It was a big thing, you know." She sniffed, but he could not see her face curtained by hair.

Jim was dragged two ways. He needed to get her to understand and agree what his strategy was for the Disciplinary. A platform to spell out what they knew. It was such an obvious opportunity, that he could not comprehend her objection. Silence was the last option likely to protect those kids. He'd had too much silence in his own life. It might be good manners to say nothing to protect hurt feelings, but he knew that the feelings protected would be those of the adult and the powerful. The hurt would be the powerless, the kids… But the other need in him was to be touched and to touch. He looked at her rub her turned-away face with her sleeve-end and wanted to reach out. Comfort her to comfort himself. But he did not move. The bag on his lap, being sat across the room from her, required so much organisation, so much choreography without spontaneity. And the moment, fragile and ambivalent, would be blown away in bathos, even farce. So he sat still. Watching her, waiting for her to put more words into the room filled now with the sound of her three or four short and final snuffles.

She eyed him, half pained, with half a tentative smile, "Oh, Jim. We're both such a mess." Then pulled herself back within a seriousness. "I just don't think I can take it. Do you understand? An inquiry. If you start telling it all, then they could call me. I'd be a witness." She pleaded, "Jim. I just don't think I could take it. I couldn't give what it takes." She shrugged. "I'm in sort of shock, I suppose. I just need to look after myself." Then, more firmly, "I also need those around me to look after me, too." She pulled her hair from her face with her fingertips, tucking it behind her ears. "And I include you, Jim. You're one of those…" A question, the desire for his consent hung at the end of her words.

Briefly, he felt manipulated. He tucked away the size of what he was being asked to consent to. "Nothing has to happen yet, Sylvie. But it will have to happen some time. They've postponed the Disciplinary. Did you know it was supposed to happen this afternoon?" She shook her head, confusingly beginning to smile. "What?" he asked.

"Oh, Jim. You are a love." She shook her head, her smile brightening. "I really can depend on you, can't I?"

He knew this was what he had come for. Human warmth. An insecure island of it in the rocking ocean of turbulence he seemed to have been blown into lately. But he had to nudge back the insistence of the boys, the weight of their files laid across his lap, nudge them back into deeper storage. He lifted the bag onto the floor. Reached his hand awkwardly, hesitantly, across towards her chair, her hand reaching back to his and twining finger tips. He looked longer into her eyes looking back than he had ever done before. She broke the gaze, looked down, her fingers pulling him. Pulled again, he rose and crouched before her, looking up into her inclined face. She placed her hands, the full length of her fingers on his cheeks and looked at him, so close the detail of her face was half blurred out of focus. Gently, she moved in and kissed him just above the bridge of his nose. Slowly he lowered his head into the stretch of her skirt, feeling the movement of her diaphragm against his hair. He closed his eyes and breathed her in deeply, the perfume and the body, as she gently massaged the temple turned up to her. For a long time it seemed they remained together like that, the only movement the tips of her fingers barely rubbing over a few inches of his skin.

Without opening his eyes, he finally said, almost in a whisper, "I can stay the night. If you want."

"Good."

He woke late for him. Sunlight around the corner of the carelessly drawn curtain. He raised himself on his elbow to watch her. She was sleeping on her back, smiling, satisfied, he thought. It was 7.30, but he had nowhere to go today. Should he wake her up for work? He smiled and gently moved his hand down the bed to rest it on the soft hair above her sex.

"Sylvie," he whispered. She did not move. Very slowly, with infinite concentration, he carefully began to rub her, each stroke of his hand, pressing a fraction further between the warm, soft flesh. Her legs began to open, eyes still closed, still smiling, her head turning away from him on the pillow.

"Sylvie." She shook her head, but said nothing. "This is your wake-up call," he said softly.

Still turned away, she growled at him, "Oh, you are a bastard. I thought this was for sex. Not work," she grunted.

"Sylvie, my love, sex is fine with me. I don't have to go to work. But if you want sex, don't expect me to do a rush job for you before breakfast. It's a full morning or nothing. You know what a perfectionist I am about these things."

She sat up, the sheet falling away from her. "Oh, what a self-congratulatory shit you can be!" She covered her body again. "Just because I said you weren't bad for an old man between the sheets, I suppose."

"Now, now, don't get crabby. Those weren't actually the words you used."

"Don't!" she grinned. "Don't remind of what foolishness I may have spoken in the flush of passion." In a mocking accent, she cried, "Jim, you are no gentleman. I do declare. And before you say it- Sylvie, you are no lady, either. In bed with a man nearly twice your age."

"Hah! Another exaggeration."

She looked at the clock behind his shoulder. "Jeez! Twenty to eight! I've gotta go." She slipped from the bed. He watched every detail of her long back, the shoulder blades, the curved edge of a breast behind her arm, the shadow where the tops of her legs met her buttocks. "Bloody shared bathroom'll be full now! I'll have to wash in the kitchenette sink. Not very hygienic, but there you are." She pulled on her robe and saw him watching her. "Hey, stop staring!"

He just shrugged as she left the room and lay back into the bedding, staring at the ceiling. He felt the contentment and comfort of the night sliding away as he faced up to what had to be done and how, the intractables of the day. By the time she came back to rattle at the hangers in the old wardrobe, he was feeling restless and tense, worrying his thought into all the unanswered questions that swirled about inside. Watching her pulling on her knickers, turned away beneath the robe, he asked, "You never told me how you came to be in the Race on Sunday."

"You don't have a monopoly on keeping fit, you know, Jim. Fit though you are," she ended lightly.

"Yes. But you don't work for the Council. It was a Union race. Council staff."

She turned away, picked a bra from the chair, slid the robe off her shoulders, pulled the bra on, reached back and clipped it. She spun round in her underwear into a dancer's pose, arms up, wrists turned, leg bent, hips thrust forward. "There you are. A girl nearly ready for work." Then back to the wardrobe to pull out a dark trouser suit.

As she slipped into the trousers, he persisted, "How come you were in the Race? I never even knew you ran."

"Well, there you are. Lots about me you don't know." Buttoning a blouse, "Some girls I know. Entered with them." Back to him, tucking the blouse in, "Anyway. You weren't supposed to be there, either, if you were suspended." Pulled on the jacket, "So that makes two of us." She presented herself to him, "Da-da! Okay? The working girl ready to fight the fight in this male dominated world."

He had always seen her in more casual clothes. He thought she was dressed like Tracey, but said instead, "You look like you're going for an interview."

She looked down at her shoes. "No. Just another day at the office. Said I'd be in early." She went over to him and gave him the briefest brush of lips to his cheek, but- before beyond his reach- he laughed and clasped her wrist pulling her back down onto him. She thrashed away from him, suddenly venomous, "Don't you ever! Don't you ever do that to me! Do you hear?" She stepped back and shook her hair into place.

"I was only joking. Just a bit of playfulness."

"Well it wasn't funny to me. Sicko sort of man's joke. I don't play like that. Do you understand, Jim?"

"Obviously not." He relented, a trifle reluctant, "I'm sorry. Didn't mean to offend you. You know that. I wouldn't do that."

She measured him. "Okay. I'm going now. Just pull the door

closed with the latch off when you go."

He called after her as she crossed the living room, "When will I see you again?"

"Don't know. I'll call." The door banged after her.

Chapter Thirteen

He reached home about ten that morning. When he unloaded the shopping through the front door, on top of the post was a folded piece of paper. It was from Julian, one of the Departmental Shop Stewards when Jim held brief tenure of the Chair of the Stewards Committee. He wrote that he had heard of Jim's suspension and he and some of his colleagues wanted Jim to contact him to see if they could give any help. His work phone number was on the bottom. Jim carried the bags on into the kitchen, wondering if he actually wanted any help to keep the job, as it was marked for the chop anyway. Julian had been nice enough. Middle class comrade, with a touch of environmental friendliness, a touch of anti-discrimination, he thought. He would ring him, but he did not want to meet them at present.

What did he want to do at present? And it came up, just like a one way sign. France. Suzanne and her family. His family. His other family. He found his passport and checked it was still valid.

He phoned Julian and he was out of his office. He left a message, telling him he would be at home all afternoon, then phoned Henderson.

"Sorry about the postponement, Jim. But more time off on the firm's money, eh?"

"Yeah. Well, that's what I wanted to talk to you about. I've got another ten days of this year's leave to take. Before the end of March. I want to take it from a week today."

Silence from Henderson, then without lightness, "Foley won't be happy about that. It's probably the time when he wants the Hearing."

"Ah. So he can piss me about chopping and changing dates. But I can't return the favour." Then, more sternly, "I reckon if I'm going to get sacked, I might as well take my holiday while I'm being paid by them."

"Come on, Jim, you won't get sacked. This isn't gross misconduct-immediate dismissal territory. All you did was fluff the child abuse procedures. And with the best of intentions, I'll be arguing."

"Oh, yes? We'll see what they come up with on the day." He was not going to share with tricksy Henderson what he knew and how he intended to play the Hearing for the maximum impact. "It was with the best of intentions, but I don't think Foley sees it that way."

"Why? What do you know?"

"About what?"

"About what Foley's thinking. How do you think Foley sees it?"

"You know he's got the precious social worker lobby at his back. I stepped into their territory, they think, by talking to that lad Damien Toser.

And they've got plenty to hide. Flynn, Damien's social worker. A really shifty bastard when I met him. He knows stuff he should have dealt with."

"Whoa, Jim! This is all a bit melodramatic. We're not seeking a confrontation." He tried to lighten it with, "Foley isn't a car plant boss, you know."

"Don't come clever with me about my past. I've got nothing to be ashamed of about those days." He was angry- with Henderson, so many bad deals to his discredit, with the so-called professionals who had always resented Jim's presence in their Department, whispering that his post was an empty sinecure, a political gift by a couple of well placed Party admirers. And the whispering was never so vehement as when he gave voice to some of the abandoned on the estates whom it had always been easier to reject as rotten parents or alcoholics or both. "You know Foley's been squeezing my job. Soon it'll have so many functions taken from it, it'll disappear in a puff of smoke. Yes, I come from a different world to this lot. You know that's why I dropped out as a Steward. They couldn't stand me telling them as it is. They wanted me to give them therapy. Not leadership."

"Whoa…Wait a minute. Get off your high horse just a minute. I'm not having a political debate here. You phoned me, remember? Okay, I will ask about the holiday. But I can't guarantee what Foley'll say."

"Say what he likes. I'm taking the holiday. I'm not losing leave owed to me."

"You're pushing hard for some reason. Try to be a bit reasonable." A change to an exploratory tone, "By the way, I was told officially you turned up at that Union Race on Sunday. There's been a complaint to Management, I've been told. As a suspended member, technically you should not have been in contact with work colleagues. You know that."

"You said this before, Ronnie. I'd paid my entry weeks before. Anyway, it was the Union running the Race, not Foley. What are you trying to say? That the Union is going to act as the policeman for the employer and ban suspended members from the Union's own events?"

There was a chuckle from the phone, "You have a way with words, Jim. Have it your own way. Just letting you know. There's been a complaint."

"Fine. Well now you know what I want you to tell them, when they come to you. And they will."

"Okay, Jim." He was playing resigned. The message was that he will do what you ask- but don't say he didn't warn you of the consequences.

"Yes. And remember the holidays. Ten days." And he put the phone down.

Ten days… From next Tuesday. It had not been a plan, more like an affirmation grabbed out of the chaos, something to be done that almost felt as if it had been thrust upon him, an assertion not by him, but upon him. He would go to France. He would find that other family, not the one here in England that he seemed sullenly roped together with from past and ill-made choices. But the sister. His father's other child. Not choice, but blood. Perhaps with the shadow of the face of the father he had never known, imprinted in her features.

Yes, to drive across France to Suzanne. If things looked uncomfortable in St. Paul de Luz, he would not have to wait for booked trains or flights, but he could drive right out of there. Ferry, to book. Car insurance for abroad. Bank for francs.

Hungry, he went through to the kitchen to fry up an egg sandwich. The phone rang just as the egg just broke into the hot pan. Irritated, he pulled it off the ring, hoping for a short call.

It was Julian. "Glad I could get hold of you, Jim."

"I got your note. Left a message at your office."

"Yeah. What the hell's going on? We heard about this Disciplinary. Something about child abuse. There's rumours flying about all over the Department. I've been told this morning that they've instructed Personnel to prepare an advert for your job."

"What! Foley isn't wasting his time, is he. Who told you?"

"Someone I know in Personnel."

"That bloody Patterson woman was at my Suspension meeting. With Foley. Him and Personnel probably had it all tied up before I hit his carpet."

"But what's happened? To lead to this?" Julian asked.

"Hang on. Something on the stove." He turned off the gas and went back to the hall. Here was someone else to tell Toser's tale to. The first of many. To do with the story whatever he wished. Jim was not going to carry the can on his own on this one. If he went down the road, it would be because others did not do what they should about the information he gave them.

He told the lad's tale, the links between Northlodge and the Pines, the meeting with Flynn. He did not mention Sylvie's name, but just spoke of her as "a member of Northlodge staff I liase with for the Department." He did not mention the identity of Councillor Jeffreys, just of a trustee. Nor of the London flats. The way Jim told it was as the innocent, checking out with the professional that, out of his naivety, he may have done the right thing. "They're trying to say I shouldn't have spoken to the lad. He came to me. I did a report on it to Foley. What more could I have done?"

"Smells of stinking fish to me. What does Henderson make of it?"

"Oh, Christ! Don't make me weep. Henderson thinks I should play it sweet and low. Take what they give me. You know what an arsehole he is with management."

"Yes. Creepy-crawly." He paused, then, "We want to see if we can get together with you and plan how to give you a bit of support. You know, some of the other Stewards."

"Fine. All the support I can get. But I'm taking some holiday. I've told Henderson I'll be off for ten days from next Tuesday. Got to take it before the end of the month or I'll lose it." He thought, why am I pretending to Julian? I'm not telling him I know I'll probably be sacked. Play the optimist to keep him on the ball. Tell him it's a lost cause and he and the others might not bother. This way, some others may be shouting off about the story. It may even get into the local press. But he was too old a hand to put faith in that.

Julian laughed, "Good old Jim. Make bloody Foley wait for his Disciplinary!"

"Him wait?" Jim sneered. "The bastard cancelled me already. Did you know I was due to have my Hearing yesterday?"

"Why didn't Henderson inform the Stewards Committee? It's part of the agreement that the Official informs us."

Jim grunted a laugh. "Well, there you are. That's full-time Union Officials for you." Enough seeds planted, "Okay, Julian, I'll give you a call when I get back."

"Going anywhere nice?"

"France."

"Taking your family?"

"No. On my tod." There was another decision made without forethought. No Jane. No Tracey. Not taking my family, but finding them.

After Julian rang off, he sat in the front room to write to Suzanne. There was time for the letter to reach her, but probably not time for her to reply. He would have to give her his phone number. If it was impossible for him to come out, it would give her the chance to tell him. It felt risky. Not sure why. But it left him exposed to the unexpected voice at the end of the line. He was giving out a little control to her. To her, the intimate stranger. Letters are different. Reply when you want. No dialogue. You can even pull out by pretending the letter you do not wish to respond to never came. But the phone. Either leave it ringing till it stops. Or risk picking it up, ear exposed to the unexpected, mouth expected to respond.

The letter was simple, inviting no response:

Dear Suzanne,

I have some holiday. It was not expected. So I will come out to see you and your family for a few days. I will be arriving in St Paul de Luz on Thursday. I will go to the pharmacy to find your house. I will stay in a hotel if it inconvenient.

Only telephone me if it is impossible for me to come at the time.

I look forward to seeing you all very much,

Yours, Jim Briggs.

Altogether, a crept step towards more intimacy.

Chapter Fourteen

He went back to the front room that had become his base of operations the last five days. Files, books, the greasy plate from the last meal. This front room he felt he would be leaving soon. What would he remember of this room here, years hence? Paper greying round the light switches. Overdue for redecorating, as Jane had reminded him several times. An unloved house, inhabited by an unloved and unloving pair. He needed to talk to Jane.

He finally got an answer from Tracey's phone early Sunday evening.

"Hello," she said in that factual and ungiving tone she had already developed from her six months training as a receptionist.

"It's Dad."

"Hello, stranger."

Was that a joke or just smart? Jim thought how they always seemed to get it wrong between them, even in the most trivial conversation these days. "Hello, love. Is Mum there?"

"Well, yes, but she's gone to bed early."

"This soon?" His tone a touch accusatory, he lightened up, "What have you two been up to? To need such an early night to recover."

"Come on, Dad. You know Mum's been ill. All this tires her out. She keeps going for a bit. And then it's too much."

He paused. Difficult territory with Tracey, her Mum's illness, so he just gave a non-committal, "Okay," before going on, "Can you ask her to be sure to phone me at home tomorrow morning? I'll be in all morning, but I won't be around after lunch." He had left tomorrow, his last night before the journey, free, half unsure whether to contact Sylvie before he went away.

"Sure. If she's still asleep when I go to bed, I'll tell her in the morning before I go to work." A ghost of a snigger from her? "Some of us kids have to work. To keep you oldies."

"Oh, come on, that's not fair, Tracey."

"Joke, Dad. Just a joke. Don't get shitty about it now."

"Okay. Sorry." To end on a healed note, he asked, "How are you, love?"

"Fine. At work, the office supervisor has said my word processing skills are so good, they're putting me onto the next grade six months early. And they are going to revise my training plan. I'm doing brill. And I don't mind saying it myself."

Real enthusiasm in her voice. He paused to answer, but she added, "I just wish you'd sort things out with Mum. That's what… does my head in sometimes."

"We will. We will," he said, his optimism touched with weariness. "Just get Mum to phone. Tomorrow morning."

"Okay. I will. I'm not an air-brain, I'm efficient. As you know." And she put down the phone.

Jim held his in his hand for a suspended moment wondering if that was how other fathers and daughters talked. Then put it down himself.

He slept poorly that night, rising three times to urinate, and lying awake long times before drifting into patchy dreams, that he reawoke into, alive and startled, but unremembered. The mirror in the room where he had watched his boyface was real, something excited and shocking, but nameless. A stuck and clickering frame, without the context of the rest of the reel of film.

The far insistence of the phone down stairs drew him out of the ragged edges of his sleep. It was eight o'clock. Sluggish urgency got him to the phone, just as he realised it would only be Jane.

"Yes?"

"What's so urgent for an early morning call," she said.

"I didn't say early. I just said, morning."

"Oh, Tracey must have got it wrong," a whisper of acid in her tone. Oh, yes, Tracey never gets it wrong, Jim thought. "You sound like you're just awake", she continued. "Unusual for you."

"Yeah. Bad night."

"Worried about the Disciplinary?" There was a touch of the old care in the question.

"No. Yes." Share, but not too much. "You know. It's the waiting."

"Have you got a date?"

"No. Not yet. They seem to want to put it off. Maybe Foley will never have the guts," he added with false bravado.

"I doubt it, from what you've said about your relationship with him." She paused. "I'd like to be there with you, you know, Jim."

What? he thought and then spoke it, "You said I'd been a fool over all this, didn't you?"

"Why not? I think you have. It doesn't mean I don't support you. I don't have to agree with you to do that, do I? To give you support."

"No. I'm just surprised, that's all."

"Maybe all that shows is how far we've drifted apart over the last few years."

Jim did not want this phone call to go in this direction. With everything else, he could not deal now with repairing his marriage.

"Okay. The reason I asked you to phone is that I'm going off for a few days. I need a break. I need to clear my head. Before this bloody Disciplinary." There was silence from her. He re-ran what he had just said in his mind, checking how it sounded, what it told.

Finally, she said, "Are you leaving me?"

"No!" he cried, astonished she should ask him the question he was beginning to secretively ask himself. "No. I'm just taking a break. Like you going to Tracey. I don't know where. Somewhere quiet. Where I can get more running in. It's only another seven weeks to the Marathon and I want make a fist of it."

"So, I won't be able to get hold of you? Will you leave me a phone number?"

"I don't know where I'm going yet."

"Oh." A sad sound, dropped like a stone into the space of silence between them on the line.

"It'll only be a few days. I want to get my mind round what I'm going to say to Foley, too."

"All right," she said tiredly, "if that's what you want. I would like a phone number when you get there, though."

Tricksily, he avoided her request. "It's not what I want, it's what I need. Like you at Tracey."

"No comparison, Jim. You can get hold of me here, like this phone call now."

"I won't be long. Maybe we both need a break from each other."

"I won't ask you how many days you'll be away, because I can tell I won't get a straight answer out of you today." Then, more sharply, "I really resent you using all your clever negotiating skills on me to avoid answering questions. I can only guess what you'll be up to. And who with. So I'm not going to say I hope you enjoy yourself."

He could hear her hurt at the line's end. "If that's how you feel."

"Yes. It is. And you are being a dishonest shit!"

Yes, he was. But he knew he would hold the line for things that had become more important than his relationship with this other woman he could hear faintly breathing in his ear.

"How do you want me to answer that?" he asked flatly.

"I don't, Jim." And the phone clicked silent.

He sat back heavily on the bottom stair, part relieved, part hurt at his own sly fencing with her. He looked out through the frosted half-light above the front door, from where the early spring sunshine drew a pattern across the wallpaper and the coats hanging on the rack. Sad to see his and her waterproofs shoulders leaned together, a memory of a walk together across flat, empty and windblown sands, clung together against the gusts and laughing. But years ago, it seemed. He rubbed his eyes of the residual shadow of her image, stood and jogged upstairs to put on his running kit.

When he parked near Sylvie's flat that evening, he was unsure what he was doing it for. He had no contact with her since last Monday. His mind was stuffed with France, the technicalities of getting there, the nervy anticipation of what would meet him there. But there was a corner with Sylvie in it that niggled. He wanted the sex of a night with her again, but not the edginess of afterwards.

Before ringing the bell, he walked to the side of the house, where he could see the light on in her first floor window. He returned and rang the bell, the slightest sound of it upstairs in her flat. He waited. In the bath? He rang again, thumb this time and longer. He waited longer for no sound. Last time, long and patient with the forefinger. Nothing. He shrugged, part relieved, decks cleared for France, but before he returned to the car, he went back to check her window. Light now off. Avoiding me? Or am I not the only visitor? he thought.

Chapter Fifteen

He drove off the ferry soon after ten at night. The photo of Suzanne from Mary's box was taped beside the car radio beside his route through France. He thought of how he had got to this point, the sweeping together of diverse consequences, forcing him to grab choices from the swirl of events. No choice, not by him, but he had been the recipient of a choice from somewhere else.

Mark had once been the person Jim had been able to explore these things with, to confide in. Oh, Mark, what a fuck-up you made of your life, mate. He remembered that last visit. Probably about nine months before he died. 1979. Back end of winter. The pavements around his flat were piled with bags of stinking rubbish, big black binbags, split and spilt onto the pavement, boxes of empties, awaiting the end of the binmen's strike. The flat stank of stale tobacco and sour joss sticks. The walls were hung with rugs and pieces of oriental fabric. The sink was full of dirty plates.

"I'm sorry, Jim. Jennifer promised to clean up, but she must've forgot. I don't know where she's sodded off to." Mark had not risen to greet him when he had come in the half-open door. Jim had stood, dull with shock at the sight of his old friend, dulled to speechlessness. Mark was thin and dirty. Gaunt and pale faced, what could be seen from under the scrubby beard. Finally saying, "Sit down, mate, sit down." There were only cushions and the mattress. He then closed the door behind him. Mark lay across the mattress, wrapped in a scarlet robe with a black dragon embroidered from chest to shoulder. Jim awkwardly sat down across from him.

"How are you, Mark, mate? You don't look well."

"Some sort of fucking flu I can't shake off. The heating in this place in the winter… the fucking landlord's a criminal. A robber."

"Have you been to the doctor?"

"Oh, come on, Jim," Mark bordered on contempt. "Doctors! Why would I trust one of those? Just give me some concoction a drug multi-national was paying him to peddle."

"Well, I'm no expert, but you do look rough." Jim did not want an argument with the friend he saw so seldom. "What does Jennifer think? She's your girlfriend, eh?"

"She's only a kid. What would she know?" He grinned, "Strictly for lovin', not for adult advice." Then, more seriously, "She gets all her thoughts about the big, bad world from me. And in return, she gives me her free spirit."

"Can we go out somewhere for a drink, Mark?" He was uncomfortable, squatted on the cushion and, aware of the filled sink, Jim wanted an excuse to get out of this depressed, sour room, to a pub or a café with a drink and the atmosphere and company of others to dilute Mark's embitteredness. The taunting cynicism that Jim had found such an antidote to the humourlessness of life as a Union activist in the Plant, now seemed arid.

Mark scratched his stubbly cheek. "I'd rather wait for Jennifer. She won't be long. She never is." Mark looked over at Jim. "Tell me how you're doing, anyway. You said something about working in that bloody tanning factory. Well, you can't be there now. Or I'd have smelt you coming up the stairs. Remember how the lads there could only drink in the Cambridge Arms because no other pub'd tolerate that stink they brought in with them?"

"Of course I do. I had to drink there myself." They both laughed a little. "No, I'm long out of that now. I've got a bit of work with the Citizens' Advice Bureau. They got some money to help set up tenants associations. I help with that. The money's rubbish, but I know I've got a year's work there. Until the grant runs out. It may lead to something else. I'm getting too long in the tooth to be labouring."

"You, setting up tenants' associations? I thought you'd let Jane convince you to get a mortgage and buy a house?"

"Yes. So what? I still know about organising. You know that, Mark." His friend just gave him a wry smile and raised his eyebrows. "So, what do you do?" Jim asked, a touch angered. "What do you do to advance the condition of the working class?" and he gestured round the room.

"What do I do?" Mark gave a harsh chuckle. "Advance the condition of the working class? What's that mean? A new car? A holiday in Spain? A colour telly in every room?" He sat forward, hands on spread knees, like a disreputable and angry holyman. "What good is all that junk, if it's without love? Too knackered from shiftwork to fuck your wife. Bitching together about bills." He brought his hands together and knotted their fingers into a single fist. "That's what we missed out. That's what the Great Labour Movement forgot. Money without love. Like the song, can't buy me love. We all lost the whole trick. Lost our innocence." He spread his hands wordlessly and leaned back to recline again. "That's what I've learnt. Not theories, but I've found my innocence again. Found my childhood. Jennifer's given me this. It's not words. Or things. It's just finding yourself in another. Someone not yet spoilt by the system. And how that system fears us…" He lay his head back on the bolster that lay along the back of the mattress. Jim thought he looked exhausted.

"Who's us? You and Jennifer?"

"Yes. And others." He raised his head enough to focus on Jim. "Why? Does it matter? Names, old friend, names. The raw material of the secret policeman. A name is not an identity. I would still be Mark if I was a Jim. Or Maharishi."

"Is that what this's about? Transcendental meditation and that stuff?"

"A bit. But only a little bit. That's just a means to an end," and, as he lay back again, there was a knock on the door. "Open it. It'll be Jenny."

Jim stood and unlatched the door. A beautiful child stood there. She looked at him shy with surprise, then smiled, "You are Jim." He nodded, then, to his astonishment, she reached out and pulled his head down to kiss his cheek. She turned and said to Mark pertly, "You locked me out, babe."

"Not me, Jen. My friend here."

As she looked back at him, Jim was cowed by her steady, open gaze. She could not, surely, be more than fifteen, perhaps younger.

"Jim is impressed with you, my angel," Mark said, grinning at Jim's disconcerted face. She slipped down into Mark's arms and curled on the mattress, her head on his shoulder. He dipped his hand into her long, golden hair. "But first, my love, the dishes."

"Oh, no, babe. Not yet. Just a snuggle, first."

"Darling, we have a guest. I haven't even been able to offer him a drink."

"I'll help," Jim offered lamely.

"Thanks, Jim," Mark said. "I would be a better host, if I didn't feel so shit." Jennifer uncurled from him with an exaggerated pout and went over to the sink, leaning against the water heater, watching Jim unpack the chaotic jumble of crocks and cutlery onto the greasy metal drainer. He was very conscious of her gaze, but did not look at her. Equally, he was alive to Mark, behind him, a cynical presence pressing forward into whatever the evening ahead promised. And Jim did not want it. He was uncomfortable. He had expected to stay the night here, but there was only the mattress Mark was laid upon and the double bed across beneath the window and he did not relish lying listening to the sounds of Mark and Jennifer in bed together. Mark was no longer just the sarcastic sceptic of previous meetings with Jim, but he was hostile. And ill. Jim doubted that he could keep up a comfortable conversation into the night.

He turned to Jennifer, "Will you wash or dry?" and she laughed, the sounds tumbling from her, eyes sparkling, until her head dipped for air and the hair fell across her face.

Jim turned to Mark and shrugged overstatedly, "So funny?"

"It seems so," Mark murmured, half a smile at last.

After the dishes, Jim went out to get them all some pizzas and a carrier bag full of beer. Back, sat around the floor on mattress and cushions, he steered the conversation back to his and Mark's old days. Mark reluctantly joined in, probably because Jennifer became fascinated, asking for explanations of some of the shorthand detail about this remote and male world of mills and factories, then turning to Mark affectionately with, "But you never told me this, babe," caressing his tired face. Probably enough reward for Mark to tolerate re-entering a world he had clearly now put far behind him. It was an effort for Jim, who wanted to talk to his old mate, alone, without the distraction of the lovely girl- who seemed so used to being the centre of adult attention.

Eventually, Mark spoke less, his head nodded a couple of times and then, smiling to Jim, her finger to her lips for quiet, she gently moved the tired body fully on to the mattress. Went over to the bed, drew off a blanket and lay it gently over the sleeper, tucking in the edges around his thin body. As if she had been unaware, Jim watched her crouched, attentive and affectionate, looking down at Mark's sleeping face. Slowly, she seemed herself to awake from her meditation and slid back across the rug to where Jim sat.

"You will have to sleep in the bed," she whispered. "There is an eiderdown rolled up under it."

"Doesn't Mark need it? He's not well."

She smiled towards the sleeping figure. "I will keep him warm."

Jim looked at the profile of this child, but with no-one else to ask and no-one else to care for his friend, he said, "Mark looks very ill. He says he isn't seeing a doctor. What is he doing to get himself better?"

"He understands his body. He knows what to do."

"Does he?" Jim muttered gauntly, more to himself than her. Then, "What is he doing? He said this flu has been around for months, hasn't it?"

"He meditates." She looked at Jim defiantly. "We meditate together. He takes vitamins. And he calms the angry spirits in his blood with pot."

He wanted to laugh. At her childish seriousness. At the simplified version of Mark's words that she was reciting. But he reined himself in and looked at her, reassuring with a smile. "How did you meet Mark, Jennifer?"

"I was in a squat. With some other kids. Mark visited us. Do you know about Liberate London?" Jim shook his head. "Mark and some other guys run it. It helps squatters and finds places in squats for kids on the streets. Well the place we were in was really shit. Rain came in the roof and it kept blowing up the electricity whenever we got hooked up to a supply. It was getting real dangerous and some of the others were quitting and going off. There were two of us in the end. We had no place. Me and this boy Sam. Mark let us shack up with him. Till we found something else. Then Sam split. He didn't like the scene between me and Mark." She grinned, "He was jealous, like. Repressed," the last a footnote from Mark's vocabulary.

Jim reflected that Mark may have been doing more for housing the homeless than his own respectably grant-aided work back home. He did not even know if anybody squatted still back up north. He had been told by old Party members there had been some after the War to speed up rehousing those who had been bombed out. But he had supposed that homelessness had retreated back into Sally Army hostels these days.

He looked back at her. The scene between me and Mark. He turned her words over in his mind. "But where did you come from before that, Jennifer? You must have a family. Where are they?"

"Fuck knows. And fuck cares."

He wanted to ask her if she went to school. She could only be a few years older than Tracey. But he felt he already knew this. "What if Mark gets really ill. What will you do? If you do have to get a doctor, they'll start asking questions about you. They'll send you back where you came from. You know, before the squat."

She looked hard at him, not with hate, but with narrowed, watchful, hunted eyes. "There isn't a kids' home that can keep me in," she hissed. "Last time I got out of secure. And I said I wasn't ever going back."

Jim was confused by all the implications of what she had said. "You're on the run, then."

"Didn't Mark tell you? He said he had." She looked over at the figure across the room. "I've not been on the run, not since I've been with Mark. He looks after me." Then smiling brightly back at Jim, "And I look after him. Like I am now. But he wouldn't ever let me go back in one of them places. You don't know what they're like."

Oh yes I do, he thought, but restrained himself from speaking it.

"You really like Mark, don't you, Jim? He was a grouch to you tonight." She smiled up at him and familiarly put her arm through his. "Did you notice that he was nicer to you when you came back with the pizza? That's because I told him he was being a creep to you. There, you see. I may be a kid in age, but me and Mark, we're like this together," and she rubbed her two forefingers together. Then she looked archly at him, pulling away, leaving her delicate hand on his forearm. She flicked her hair back from her face. "Go on then, Jim. Tell me how old you think I am. I bet you get it wrong. They always do."

He thought too young, but said, "Fifteen?"

"Yah! Again!"

"Sixteen?" She giggled and shook her head. I do not want to play this game with this child, he thought, because I fear what I may learn of my old friend. "I don't know," he said glumly.

"Go on! Another guess."

"No."

"Go on. Mark says I have the wisdom of a woman," she sniggered, "but that won't help you."

"I don't know," he repeated.

"I'll tell you anyway," breaking into a loud laugh, so they both silenced and looked over at the sleeper.

Jim looked back at her and inwardly pleaded not to know, to go away from this sad place, in ignorance of what he was about to learn.

"Most kids lie about their age. Pretend they're older." She looked back over at Mark. "I used to, but he got me proud of it. Old head on young shoulders, he says. He says he's learnt things from me that older girls couldn't. He says all people are born wise, but it takes a special person to keep wise. Because the world beats it out of you. He says I've not let it be beaten out of me. That's why I'm not going back in care. I'm staying wise, like he says." She looked back from Mark and asked, "Do you believe that, Jim?"

"Believe what?" he asked, woken from the still trance woven by her words.

"That we're all born wise. Until they beat it out of us."

There was a truth there, in that room, from the mouth of that child, that he could not deny then. And that he had rubbed in his mind like a worry bead at moments of uncertainty in the last seven years since she spoke it. But his only answer to her then had been, "Probably." A false yawn and, "Time I got some sleep."

"Sure. Sleep comfortable. You've got the best bed."

Jim went over, found the eiderdown and was laying it across the bed, when he was suddenly aware that she was beside him. "You shocked me," he said, a shiver passing through him, either from the cold or her proximity.

"Thirteen," she said, grinning. "I was thirteen last week. Old head on young shoulders," then went back into the shadows beside Mark.

Jim remained leaning his knuckles into the bedding for some time. Thirteen. Last week. A few years older than Tracey. Young enough to be a couple of classes above in school. Oh, Mark, what have you done? And yet Jim himself could not deny the brightness and charm of this child. What Mark called her wisdom, was it that? Or had his friend just been seduced by her repetition back to him of his own words re-shaped in that pretty, half-knowing, half-innocent mouth?

Only taking off his shoes, shirt and jumper, Jim slid into the cold bed and lay awake. Lights from the street outside, streaked and flickered through the thin curtains onto the ceiling. Voices. Cars. He listened. And thought, later, he could hear whispers, movements and her giggle. He waited, almost breathless, as if not being heard made him invisible, more than that, immaterial, absent from that place, where the man who had been his only enduring friend, was putting his penis inside a girl the age of Jim's own child.

Much later, still sleepless, Jim had gathered his clothes together and crept past the couple to leave, but she was awake, her eyes bright in the dark. He hesitated, to explain. Her hand came from under the blanket and she waved the tips of her fingers at him then, blew a kiss, before snuggling back against the sleeping Mark.

Now, these years later in France, he was near enough to St. Paul de Luz to stop and move his navigations from the list of towns and road numbers taped to the dashboard next to Suzanne, to looking at the map book. He turned off the headlights and his eyes strained tiredly out at the dark. He was aware that he had pulled off the road within a steep gorge. He wound down the window for air. The sound of broken river water and only a narrow strip of stars above between the towering rock walls.

He pulled his head back in and switched on the inside light to see the map. It revealed the slum that two days on the road had made of the vehicle's interior. Abandoned food wrappings and empty soft drink cans covered the passenger's foot well. He was also aware that he was unshaven and had given himself only the most cursory wash in a Les Routiers truck stop twelve hours earlier. Changing into fresh underwear inside the squat toilet had only been funny in retrospect. It was too late tonight to confront Suzanne. And Maurice and Marie Claire. The pharmacy would be hours closed and his long, hard drive down from the ferry had got him here an evening early. After the next town, Larozelle, the route to them turned off this road onto a spiraling climb of hairpins, out of the gorge onto the uplands above and St. Paul. He would find a small hotel for tonight before the climb and tomorrow morning.

Larozelle's streets were but sporadically lit, until the square, with a war memorial, houses shuttered against the chill night and a low-lit bar. Above the bar were rooms. Jim checked out key French words first, before entering and starting to ask the patron behind the bar for une chambre. The man was watchful, under a mask of indifference. Jim reluctantly handed over his passport in exchange for filling out a bilingual form with his name and details. The patron folded that inside the passport and slipped it into a drawer beneath the counter. Jim did not ask about food, because only several male drinkers watched him and there was no evidence of a menu. He retrieved his bag from the car and, following the laggard, wide backside of his host, went straight up to the simple room, took the keys with a wordless nod and sat on the bed, then lowered himself back on the duvet. He felt the soft bedding start to stroke the tiredness from him. He rinsed his face with barely tepid water in the sink, went over to the window, pushed aside the curtain, but could only see an empty stretch of cobbles through the shutter slats. Sliding gingerly into the cold sheets, he curled up until he warmed a space enough to sleep in.

He woke slowly, only gradually conscious of where he was. He looked at his watch. It was eight and he had been in bed almost eleven hours. Aware of his hunger, he pursed his lips, pushed the bedding off and went over to the sink. This morning, the water scorched him.

Shaven, dressed, he went down to the bar and placed his bag on a table near the window. A dozen men were there, mostly in blue overalls, mostly drinking coffee. A woman served behind the bar, probably the patron's wife. Slowly, partly with words, partly with pointing and gesture, he got himself a milky coffee in a cup like a soup bowl and two crumbly croissants. He smiled at some of the other customers as he passed to his table and some smiled back. An old bus stood in the square with a card propped up inside the windscreen, listing St. Paul de Luz among its destinations. While he fed, he watched the bus slowly take on a few passengers, everyone taking time to talk with the driver. Its engine finally coughed to life and it rattled round the square and away.

He settled up his bill, retrieved his passport and went out to the car. Although there was a bright blue sky above, down on the square, it was still chilly in the shadow of the steep valley sides. Now, he was at last excited by the certainty that he would meet Suzanne, that she would offer the assurance of some certainty about their father, perhaps even an excuse for the man's silence that Jim could give at least a reluctant nod of assent to. But also, as important, he would meet her. A sister. Her daughter, his niece. Maurice, his brother-in-law. After so many years without family, a surfeit of them.

He found the road up out of the gorge and started to climb. As he wound up, he was climbing towards the light, but beside this dark, corkscrewed road, patches of snow survived in the shade. Already, the opposite wall of the valley was in the rising sun, then, further up, he could see to the west, the Pyrenees peaks, their snowcaps bright with the reflecting glitter of full daylight. Though still in shade himself, Jim wound down the window and could feel the beginnings of warmth in the air. A couple of lorries ground downwards in the opposite direction in low gear and he had to follow the old bus for a few bends before overtaking. Towards the top, his shoulders were aching from continually feeding the steering wheel through his hands, first on a left-hander, then a right, changing up and down the lower gears. The sheer scrubby rock started to become grass slopes and then, finally, small pastures, as he crested the rim of the gorge behind him and the sun blasted into his eyes from the east.

He pulled onto a rough verge, put on his sunglasses and looked across the brokenly rolling, lush plateau, specked with small rocky outcrops and several forest-skirted peaks patched with snow. From here, the only buildings visible were some ruined sheds several hundred yards away. St Paul, he thought, must be in a fold of the land ahead. Checking his map, it looked only a few kilometers or so along this road. He thought of his father, having travelled here surely so often, through this landscape so different from the Yorkshire he originally came from. Warm and welcoming in this early spring, but the wide fields of distant snow on the mountains set him wondering how grim it could be up here in the winter. What can have brought him here, to such a foreign place?

It was now just past nine. He would go on to St. Paul. He let a van pass and pulled out into the road, for a moment so preoccupied that he steered onto the left hand side, before veering back to the right. He drove on carefully, taking in the details of fields, livestock, a distant tractor on a lane, a farm almost fortified with rough stone walls, a lorry with a trailer of logs bouncing along the rolling road at speed towards Larozelle.

Preparing in his mind for his arrival, Jim realised that he did not know Suzanne or Maurice's surname. It was probably in some of the past letters to Mary in French, but Jim had written his two letters to *Suzanne* only. He realised what an impulsive and unconsidered decision it had been to come to this far place to meet strangers. But, above that, he knew it was right.

At the crest of one of the road's rises, St. Paul de Luz came into sight. Jim was surprised how small it seemed, stacked against the far side of the small valley. Perhaps forty buildings in all. He drove on again. A road sign confirmed he had arrived and he parked by the church. In the square were a bar, a mini-market and a bakers, the minimum requisites for French rural life, Jim realised. He needed to find Maurice, so he pulled out his phrase book. Pharmacy was pharmacie. He had already mastered ou est...

during this trip. Two men were stood in the shade, talking beside a car. He reckoned they were negotiating a sale, gestures restrained by hands thrust in pockets, weighing the resistance of the other.

Jim climbed from his car and sauntered over to them. They watched him approach.

"Ou est pharmacie?" he spelt out.

"Pharmacie?" said the man Jim took to be the vendor. Then shrugged. He spoke a string of words, saw Jim's blank look and stopped. "Americain?" he asked.

"Non. Anglais."

"Ah," as if all was explained. Then, the two words separate and distinct, "Pharmacie. Larozelle," pointing back the way Jim had come.

He realised he had got it wrong. He had assumed everything was in St. Paul. He leafed back through the phrase book, the men looking on impassively.

"École?" he asked.

The same man answered. "La," gesturing out of town to the east. "Un demi kilometre."

"Merci. Merci."

Both men were still watching him as he drove off. In the first dip of the road beyond the village, there was the school, modern and single storey, beside the road. He slowed, but as he drove on past, he could feel his heart hammer at his ribs. He kept the building in his rear view mirror, until a bend stole it from view.

Fool, he thought. Present yourself. Confront the moment. Get a grip, Jim. And with that, he pulled the car hard round in a u-turn that bumped him up onto the opposite verge and drove back to the school.

After he had explained awkwardly to the woman in the school office, lining up each French word from his phrase book, she finally, reluctantly, went, with a backward look that indicated continuing suspicion of him and for him not to move till her return. That wait. A faint breeze through the half-open window lazily stirred papers on the desk. The sound of childish voices down a corridor. Steps approaching, then receding. Then adult voices. And suddenly, she was there in the office, the secretary stood in the doorway, behind.

"Jim?"

Her face was squared with a gently pointed chin. Blue eyes. Light brown hair with some blonde tints. She was smiling at him. Who did she look like?

"Yes. Suzanne?"

"Yes," she said, coming forward, hand out to him. He came round the desk to her, awkward with what to do but, as their hands embraced, she reached up and brushed his cheeks with her lips, one, two, three times. He stood back unsteadily, her face rinsed to a blur by tears in his eyes.

"Oh, Suzanne," he almost whispered.

She looked up at him quizzically. "Jim?" Then, aware of the secretary, Suzanne said something to her, took Jim's arm and led him across the corridor outside and into a small room with a tube chair and a padded bench. She indicated the chair and sat herself on the bench. He realised she had the same shaped face, the same eyes, as Tracey. He looked away, downwards into the palms of his hands. He covered his mouth tentatively with his fingertips, looking back at that face, then covered his eyes, wiped them and drew the hands aside like drawn curtains. A bare functional room for this.

"Jim. You are not in good health?"

He looked at her, all the dreams, guesses and speculations of the last months, become flesh before him, unguessing who he was, sat opposite her now.

"Suzanne." Not to wait. To step forward, through those curtains of deceit and omission and distance, into this relationship with this woman. "Your father. He was my father." Her eyes did not move from his face. "You are my half-sister." She looked at Jim and ever-so-slowly, gently, nodded her head. To fill the silence and the steadiness of her gaze, he said, "Is that how you say it in French? Half-sister?"

Her voice was slightly husky now. "I had asked myself, after your letter. My father- our father, he said things that… did not make clear. Maurice said you are perhaps close family." She reached her hands across to his and folded them within hers. "Welcome, Jim. It is very good for you to join us."

"It has been very good to come here. Very, very good. To discover I have family." He smiled. A smile that flooded through him. He realised how tired he now was, how the tension of anticipation must have been holding him on guard for so long and now the guard was dropped.

"Frere Jim. Brother Jim. El germa Jim. So good." After a further moment, she stood up. "I must go. My little students wait for me. Come to the office. I will draw for you a plan of St. Paul and you will see where our house is. Marie-Claire is there. She was there today because we waited for you to come."

He followed her. The secretary watched while Suzanne precisely sketched out the directions. Nothing was said until she led Jim to his car outside. "She is difficult. The administrator. She disagrees with me. I am an ecolo- an ecologist. Her husband works for a construction company. She does not say it because I am director of the school. But she says she disagrees without words. You understand?" He nodded, aware that he was still grinning with pleasure. Holding on to the grin of a lifetime. She looked at him, squinting in the sunshine, or perhaps with the narrowed look of examination. "You are a serious man, Jim, yes? I think so. It is good to see you so happy. But you are tired. Marie-Claire will care for you. I will telephone to tell her you are coming. But you ask her to let you sleep. I will speak to her." She gave him a brief hug. "Then tonight we can talk. I think we will be talking until late. We have very much to tell each other."

"Yes," he said. Was there anything else to say now? She turned back into the school and he watched her go, then went to the car.

Chapter Sixteen

The house stood a little apart from the village, on the hillside above, an old cottage at its core, with rambling, improvised additions and sheds to the rear. Marie-Claire appeared at the door of the large, glassed in verandah, as he drove up. Unlike her mother, strong rather than delicate, darker hair, but the same blue eyes. She greeted him with, "My mother has told me. You are to eat. Then you are to sleep." A brief embrace and kissed cheeks again. She smiled. "And she also said, you are not to argue. Welcome, Jim. Uncle Jim, I think I must call you."

"No. Please. Jim is okay." And he smiled to himself, thinking, he certainly is. In this moment, with these new relationships damming off the turbulence of his other life in other places, he relaxed in the living room with a cup of hot chocolate, listening to the girl preparing food in the kitchen. There were books everywhere. Shelves-full, stacks on the floor, a pile on the low table before him. And photographs. Framed and crowded along the mantlepiece above the large fireplace, unframed and pinned to the edges of shelves, stuck in the edges of the frame of the large, ornate mirror. He thought he was too tired to get up and look more closely, but he rose to walk round this treasurehouse of who he was. Or who he was being turned into.

He had only had a few moments to look at the photos, before she had come from the kitchen, but his father had not been there. Suzanne, sometimes her mother and Marie-Claire, in guises and groups that he would wait for his new sister to interpret for him later. After the baguette and drink, Marie-Claire showed him to a room facing out over the village rooves, across the valley. He had expected not to sleep after the eleven hours of the previous night, but he felt himself slide down, relaxed; the last sound some tinkling bells in the fields, before dreamless motionlessness.

Suzanne woke him with a coffee and left him to get up and shower and dress. It was six o'clock when he came down. He found the family out in the verandah, drinking wine, facing the sun low over the Pyrenees. Maurice, with the broad, strong frame given to his daughter, welcomed him and filled the glass already waiting for Jim. Food would be later. Suzanne started to tell the story of Francis, their father, as the evening light warmed, died and chilled into the clear, starlit and moonless night. They all quietly listened, even the daughter's soft and unnecessary corrections to her mother's English dying away. As it darkened, with only the dim glow of lights from inside the house, Jim ceased to look at Suzanne's face and listened only to that voice, his eyes across the dark shapes of the landscape before him.

"Our father, he first came into France through the passes of the Pyrenees. He was one of the refugees crossing over to escape Franco at the end of their war in Spain. There were hundreds and thousands with him. He had been a soldier for the Republic, like many foreigners of the Left. He had stayed to the last moment. He had been there for two years. It was a time he never forgot, but he did not speak of. My mother said it changed his life. He ceased to be English. And he always waited for things to change in Spain. He lived to see Franco die and democracy return. He died in 1982. Here in this house. This was his home since after the war, when I was born."

Spain, Jim thought. He knew a little of that civil war, of old Party members who had volunteered and fought there in the International Brigades. Of meeting Mark fresh from Barcelona, in Franco's last days. But he said nothing to break the enchantment of this story, spoken by this woman, her face towards those same mountains from where his father had appeared to start his new life in this land.

"Of course, when he arrived in France, he was interned. Like all Republicans, he was feared here by the government. He was sent to Gurs. It was the camp they built for refugees, near Pau. Later it became the Vichy camp and they were sent to extermination by the Germans. Father escaped in April 1940, but before he could get to England, the Germans invaded France and he tried to go south. He ended here. There were many Spanish hiding here and in the mountains. Now they had the Nazis and Vichy on one side and Franco on the other. They could go nowhere. They hid. Some were bandits, I think, but many decide to fight again against fascism, now in France. Father said to me that he was Spanish by election. He said he was born a Spanish, but in the wrong country and there were years until he found his home. He found it and it was stolen from him, Mother used to say."

As if prompted by Jim's unvoiced inquiry, Suzanne turned to him and said, "She died also. More than a year ago. It had been her wish to return home to Spain after Franco, but Father said it is too late." A regret, that Jim would never know the woman who shared the rest of his parent's life. His father, born a Spanish, as Suzanne phrased it. Leaving Jim's own childhood and parentless self a thousand or so miles away.

"That was the beginning of the Resistance in this region. It was the Spanish. They had no guns, but they knew the passes in the Pyrenees. They guided escaped English airmen into Spain. In Spain there were many who could not fight Franco. The Spanish in France knew these people. Helping

English fliers back to England to carry on the fight against the Germans was their way of continuing the fight against fascism. But also, sometimes the Spanish in France continued to make difficulties for Franco. There were some attacks on fascist police in Spain. Sometimes guns were taken and carried over the mountains to use against the Vichy and the Nazis. So you see, they commenced to become Resistance."

Maurice said something to her. She turned to Jim, "Excuse me. I am not a good host. Do you wish to eat now?"

He realised he had only eaten a baguette since the morning, but he only wanted to hear her story, to turn his face back towards the serrated silhouette of the mountains and listen. "No. Please go on." She murmured to Maurice, who quietly left him with the two women on the verandah. As she resumed, there were faint sounds from the kitchen.

"Father was different. He was English and airmen who had escaped, they carried this information to England. An Englishman came by secret to this region to help the escape line into Spain. But also, some sabotage of railways here. He stayed with Father and they worked together. But at this time, many French people disagree with destroying railways. Some were friends of Vichy, they had been fascists or of the Right before the war. Others said it is wrong to participate in killing other French when the trains crash. Some say the English did not help the French sufficiently against the Germans and only commenced the fight when the Germans dropped bombs on English cities. Some of these people still live here. My father-" she stopped and he could feel her smile, rather than see it in the darkness. "Our father, he would say to me, in the street, he would indicate this person and say, now they say they were a hero of the Resistance, but not then. Not in the first days. Then there were few. Later, after the war finished, he said there were those who did not like Father and Mother, because they fought against the Germans and the Vichy from the first days. They were strangers from other countries, but they made the example for many other French who followed later. When De Gaulle spoke and made the call for Resistance. I teach it to the children. On June eighteen in 1940, the British radio gave his speech to us. De Gaulle was of the Right and made many mistakes later, but in this he was correct. Many French here said that Petain and Vichy was the government and De Gaulle was a traitor to leave France to the Germans. But, after the Liberation, all of them were of the Resistance." Adding with a cynical twist, "Naturellement."

She broke again from the remote place from where she was telling this story and Jim could faintly see her face turned towards him. "I am sorry for all this complicated politics. But this was our Father. He lived here and his whole life was made by the war. Everything that followed was shaped by the first year in this country." His whole life. Jim considered that and recognised it to be true. Whatever was right or wrong about his father's life, he realised it had belonged here, on this high plateau facing south, not back in Yorkshire. Jim himself had no real call on this man now. It was this family, this half-sister, these, he felt were inviting him into their life, against the father, her father, who had sealed Jim away in the cold and cruel halls of that dark building in the north.

"No. No problem. I am a man of the Left too," he said, taking up her way of saying it. "I understand politics. A little."

"We are both the children of our father. Always the struggle." She turned her face back into the night. "Father, he became important to the Resistance. The English always consulted with him about operations in this area. Many of the Spanish were his spies. They watched the movements of Germans and Vichy. It was information that Father gave to the English by the radio they gave him. Then, in 1942, the Germans ordered the Vichy that young men were to be taken to work in Germany. The Service du Travail Obligatoire, it was titled." She turned to Marie-Claire and said something.

The daughter said to Jim, "Obligatory Labour Service."

Suzanne continued, "It was for the war industries. Immediately, the hills were full of young men avoiding this. Many simply did not want to work and became thieves. But many were patriots and wanted to fight the enemy. Also, now that Hitler was attacking Russia, many communists left the towns to start fighting. But like the others, the communists were not with us at the beginning, only later. But at the Liberation, Father was a hero. The National Committee of Liberation wished for Father to be awarded the Legion d'Honneur. It is our most grand award. But there were enemies and they were jealous. Many of his heroic acts were misrepresented. Finally, he was recompensed with the Croix de Guerre, but of a low rank. We buried him with it. It was not his wish, for he always looked at it as a memory of how his acts had not been recognised in full. But my mother said it was the symbol of Father's courage. It was her decision." She stopped, still eyes into the dark. Jim believed she was thinking of her mother. After a moment, Marie-Claire murmured something to her and Suzanne nodded and the daughter quietly left. Suzanne then turned to him. "That was our Father. He did many things since the war, but those were the days that made him into the man I knew. What do you think?"

Jim was answerless to such a question. What did he think? About this man and the tale he had listened to? Or about his own father, missing all his life? They were certainly two different people. One born in northern Britain, the other reborn in Spain, to become a man and a father, in France.

"Did you guess such things? Did you know any of his history?"

"None." He felt sorrowed and vulnerable to say to her, "No. I was told another story."

She reached over and touched his shoulder. "I am sorry that you did not see him as he was. He was a good man. I think you will not believe so. He abandoned you, it seems." She squeezed the shoulder. "But now you have found us. New family. We believe very much in family here. It was the way of my mother. It is the Spanish way." She stood and rubbed her shoulders, as if tired from the burden of telling. "I think the dinner is ready now. Enter. It is meat. I do not think Father would have approved." And she gently guided him into the dining room, before he could ask what she meant.

During the meal, he told his own story. He spoke of Jane and Tracey, of what they did, the dates and ages, but not of how he had left things at home. He told them of his days in the Car Plant, as leader fifteen years ago. And of his present job, but not of the difficulties now. He told them of his running, which amused them. Maurice spoke no English and Marie-Claire quietly translated for him. Suzanne only asked her for occasional clarification.

Then, Marie-Claire and Maurice cleared away the plates, while Suzanne led Jim into the living room.

"I will show you the photographs of our father. It will assist you to picture him."

"I have seen some. Aunt Mary kept them and I saw them after she died. Did you send the photographs to her? With your letters?"

"No." She looked quizzically at him. "Were they old photographs from before his arrival in France?"

"No. You were in some of them." He recalled the shock of his first sight of them. "And your mother. I think some may have been in Spain. When he was fighting."

"That is bizarre." She looked away at the shelves of books and photos. "I did not know of Mary while my father was alive. It was my mother who told me of her. She said that Father had told her of Mary only a short time before he died. She said that there had been family disagreement, so Father had not maintained the relationship. But he had the address where Mary lived in his papers. My mother discovered it and asked me to write. You see, Mary was family. But she never replied." She looked at him. " Why?"

Jim slowly shook his head. “I don't know. It seems there have been many secrets in our family. Father. And Mary.”

“It is perhaps our generation that finds the truth,” she smiled, crossed the room, pulled several large binders from a shelf and dropped them on the table in front of him. “The history of our family,” she laughed.

“Perhaps,” Jim said looking at them, then up at her, with a wry half-grin. “Or the version of history the previous generation allowed us to see.”

“What? What do you mean to say?”

Jim indicated the binders, “Perhaps these are the photos they decided not to destroy. What they have allowed us to see.”

She laughed again, “Oh, Jim! You are the cynic.” Then she looked at him, seriously, intently. “But, of course. You are the cynic because you had your father stolen away. By us.” She sat beside him, attentive. “Your mother? Is she still alive?”

“She died soon after I was born.” She put her hand on his sleeve. “I was brought up by priests.”

“Oh. Jim. Forgive me.” Her eyes were tearful, but he could only feel the familiar feeling of loss he had been exploring these last months, so many years after the event. The familiarity with the feeling like a bruise, less the stab of loss he had felt but months ago, when the boys had led him to lift the stone that he had allowed to lay across his past for so long.

“Suzanne, There is nothing to forgive.” He patted the hand on his arm. “I feel better from knowing the truth. It is not knowing that is so painful. That is what keeps me awake at night.”

“Good.” She stood again. “Before we looks at the photographs, I will put a disc on the gramophone.” She went to a cabinet with glass doors, slid them back and pulled a box from the records stacked inside. “Perhaps this should have been buried with Father. For him it was the true recognition of the acts he had done against fascism.” She brought the box over and lay it carefully, almost reverentially, on top of the binders. She opened it and slid out a disc in its sleeve. “See.” She pointed at a faded signature with some other writing. “Casals. Pablo Casals. Do you know him?”

“No.”

“Ah, Jim. Another story. I am sorry, but I seem to have many stories for you to endure.”

He shook his head and smiled. “No. They help me understand Father,” realising with that last word how he was sharing that man he never knew with this woman. So recently a stranger herself.

She went over to the record turntable and, with devoted care, set the needle hissing into the edge of sound. She waited, her ear tuned to the loudspeaker, still, until the sounds of the cello, sombre but dancing, swelled and filled the room. She returned to sit by him. In a low voice, not to over-intrude on the music, she continued, "Pablo Casals was a great musician. Of the cello. This is him, playing at the time of the Civil War in Spain. He was also anti-fascist. A man of the people, poor from a village. He would not stay in the Spain of Franco. He was Catalan. From Barcelona." She listened a moment to the rising spiral of notes. "He came to this region. He lived in Prades, which is to the south. During the war, Father came to know him through the Spanish communities in the region. After the war, Pablo gave father a set of discs, which he signed." She translated from the empty sleeve, "To my comrade and patriot, Francisco Brige, with thanks, Pablo." She listened again to the music. "I only remember him once. My parents took me to the festival in Prades. I was little. I fell asleep during the concert. But afterwards he gave me flowers. I was embarrassed. Later, he left France and he went to live in Puerto Rico. Father was very proud of these discs. But he would only play them alone. Since he is dead, I play them often. I think I will wear them away with playing."

"Francisco Brige," Jim murmured. "So he changed his name, too?"

"Yes. It was part a joke, but also for keeping secret his origin. The name sounds like the word in French that means to have aspiration, yes?" He nodded. "But also, it still retains the appearance of Briggs. Which is your name, yes?"

"Yes, of course."

"After the war, when secrecy was no longer required, he had become the man with that name. There was no possibility of becoming Briggs again. Do you understand?"

He laughed, an edge harshly, "Yes, I do." He looked at Suzanne intensely. "Suzanne, whatever you tell me, for me he will never be the man you knew. For me, he left only lies- no, not lies… just a hole. He omitted himself from my life. Do you understand?"

"Yes. I think so." She looked away, a shadow of hurt in her face, then looked back at Jim. "But, do you still wish to see the photographs, then?"

"Yes. Tell me about your father."

He lay awake, long after the sounds of the others in the household had ceased. The pages she had turned in the binders, the photos now dealt themselves through his head, stacked, re-shuffled and dealt again, as he sorted through them to make sense of the story Suzanne had told him. Maurice and the girl soon went, leaving them together, Suzanne giving exact information for each picture, date, location and who looked back at them. He recognised some of them from Mary's boxes.

When she had finished and looked up at him, Jim had asked about the photos stuck about the room.

"Ah. That is now. These-" she patted the binder she had just closed- "these were our father's photographs. Those-" sweeping the room with her hand- "are our life after Father has died." She smiled. "At the weekend, on Saturday, we will show you our life today." She rose and placed the binders back on the shelves, carefully lifted and sleeved the record. "Tomorrow, you will be alone, I am sorry. Marie-Claire cannot stay at home from school for a second day. It would appear wrong for a school teacher's daughter." She looked a touch anxious, "You will be okay?"

"Yes. I will go for a run. After the driving, my body needs it."

"Oh, of course. Very good. Please use the house as you wish."

This had left him downstairs, the silent echoes of Casals' cello still faintly vibrating in the air of the room. Thinking of the boys. And the child he had been himself. He had stumbled across all that with Sylvie and it had whelmed within him, receding sometimes in the surge of events happening to him. But always rolling back up the beach of the present, dragging fragments of memories from his own past, then left like drying, bleached debris, deposited for beachcombing. In moments like now.

Mirrors!

Why had he not remembered that? Why hidden for so long?

In that mirror, his boy-self faced the middle-aged man he now was in the dark quiet of this room in France. Jim watched the scene play itself out on the screen of his retina...

The boy held the book, nervous and angry, his eyes fixed away from the page, away from the man looking up at him, to that picture of the white cottage framed within the enraged sky, hanging on the far wall of that over-heated room.

"Posture, James. Posture. You need to acquire posture to read aloud in a proper manner. How many times have I told you that?"

"Many times, Father," the boy almost whispered.

"Turn to the mirror, James. Watch yourself as you read it out." The priest placed his hands on Jimmy's waist as he turned. Not again, the boy pleaded within himself. Knotted with tension, fixated with the anxiety of his own mirrored eyes, the man's hands rested there behind him now. On the upper curve of his buttocks, motionless for a moment, before they slid round to rest above the buckle of the belt on Jimmy's shorts, an arm round either side, enclosed.

"Posture," the man murmured softly and he gently pulled Jimmy's shirt up from inside his trousers. "You must have posture, my little monkey," his hands under the shirt, rubbing up and down between the boy's knotted stomach and the cleft of his groin down into his clothes. "Strong…relaxed…" Angry at the response of his body, the swelled sex pushing at his pants, Jimmy held himself gripped with stillness. The man's hands stopped, rested a moment on the curve of his belly, as if hesitating at the next barrier.

"Posture, my little monkey," and the large fingers pulled the belt together to unsnip the snake that held it, plucked the top button open and slid the short trousers down over Jimmy's hips.

The boy looked down and said with quiet directness, "No." He watched the man's hands stop, only a thread of the charged air in the room between his fingertips and the boy's swollen underwear. "No," again, louder, confident with the noise of his voice challenging and breaking up the leaden hush. He caught a quick sight of his mirrored head tossed back with nervous defiance- and it reinforced his resolve. He stepped forwards, pushing aside the man's encircling arms. "No!" even louder, was all he could say.

He turned and looked at the father half-sprawled, his soutane part-unbuttoned, hairy legs splayed across the rug. Now getting the hold of himself, standing above the man, Jimmy bellowed, "Noooo!"

"James. Stop it, now. Cease this, now!"

Jimmy pulled his trousers back up round his body with defiance. The man was scrambling to his feet and the boy danced round behind the armchair and shouted, "No!" with defiance. "No-no-no-no-no!"

Now on his feet, the man stood there, both angry and anxious. Jimmy skipped from foot to foot, watching his next move. "No," the boy said, eyes narrowed, challenging the visible uncertainty of the adult. He re-snipped the belt-buckle, freeing his hands to rest fingertips on the chair back, the rest of his jigging body ready for action.

"James, stop this silliness," the voice wavering between plea and threat, moving round the furniture. "What on earth do you think was going to happen?"

"No!" The boy skipped away, keeping the heavy, ugly chair between them. "Nooo!" he shouted again and the man froze, his face dark with anger and fear. "NoNoNoNoNoNo!" and the boy's cheeks twitched with the urge to smile.

"James! Do you know the consequences…" and the father reached out a grasping hand.

"Don' touch me!" He eyed the door half-way across the room and the man caught that glance, checked his position and backed to cover Jimmy's escape route.

The boy shifted from foot to foot, eyes narrowed, his cunning armed with the certainty his anger, his contempt at this man gave him. He jigged over to the glass-fronted bookcase, pulled open the door and grasped the spine of a large embossed volume, danced back behind the chair and held the hefty book over his head.

The father was astonished, "Put that down- give it to me immediately!" He moved across the room, back to the chair.

Jimmy sidestepped to keep it between them. "No! Make me! Try and make me!"

"You, young man, are heading for serious trouble."

The boy stilled, his eyes rivetted to the face of the man. "Because I won't let you pull my willy?" he challenged.

The unexpected directness of this flustered, "What do you mean? Do not be ridiculous - nothing of the sort…"

His arms were tingling from the weight of the book. He rested it a moment on the chair's headrest and the man lunged to grab it, before Jimmy danced back and still holding the book, dashed for the door. His sweated hand slid on the brass handle, he looked back at the man, who was still one knee into the cushions, where he had left him. From his face, pleading, a touch fearing, the boy knew there would be no chase.

"Not just me! Other lads've told about you," Jimmy accused. Then, with a defiant thrust of chin and shoulders, "I won't tell, if you won't."

The father stared at him, gauging the boy, then nodded and Jimmy gently placed the book on the carpet by the skirting board. He turned, carefully tried the handle again, then unlocked the door and pulled it open into the cool, fresh air of the corridor, ran to the top of the staircase and leapt them three-at-a-time down both the flights, whistling like a falling bomb.

The whole incident had been blocked into a hidden recess of his memory all these years. To emerge now, in this strange house. Perhaps. Perhaps, now, at this moment, he had found something. Beneath the coarsely worked tiles of this farmhouse roof, the woman and her music, his sister, the story of his father, all this drew a line beneath the tumbled and knocked-about uncertainty of recent months, years maybe. Gave him a floor at last to plant his feet upon. And now, a place for these few days here, at least, a place to reflect from. To learn from the rediscovered father, opened up by Suzanne's words like a flower… and, that way, opening up himself.

Chapter Seventeen

He awoke to sunlight on the shutters and the sounds of the family getting ready for the day and music. He rose, slipped his trousers over the underwear he had slept in and went to the smell of coffee.

"Ah, Jim," she said and came over to greet him, arms to shoulders, lips to cheeks, then stood back to take him in with smiling eyes. "How is it? This first morning with a sister? Is it good?" She spoke loud over the strummed, stamping sound of flamenco music from the record player.

Jim nodded, dumb at the question.

She returned over to the oven with a laugh. "It is good for me to have a brother. And for our father to have a son."

Maurice entered with a metal can, placed it on the table and went to the stairs to call, "Marie-Claire!" An answer and noise from upstairs and he re-entered. He picked up the can, held it for Jim to see into and smiled, nodding.

"It is sheep milk?" Suzanne said.

"Goat milk, Maman," Marie-Claire corrected as she hurried into the room.

"Yes. We produce goats. In the houses at the rear. Would you wish goat milk with your coffee? To drink before you run." She quickly translated for Maurice, who nodded, clearly convinced of the milk's benefits.

"No. I always drink coffee black. Without milk."

"Will you drink coffee before your run?" Marie-Claire asked. "I think that water is preferable."

"No. Coffee's okay."

"But you will not eat first."

"No," Jim smiled at the young woman. "I think you should be my trainer."

She laughed and there was a flutter of translation for both her mother and father.

Suzanne brought Jim the small bowl of coffee and sat him at the table. "What will you be doing after your run?" He shrugged. "I will return from the school at three, during the afternoon. My lessons will be ended. You may use the house, all the rooms, if you desire," she gave an expansive gesture. "This is your home, you may believe. While you rest here, it is also yours."

"If I go out, do you have a key?" he asked.

"Why, a key?" she asked, looking to her daughter as if needing translation.

"To lock it up. For security."

She smiled, "No, Jim. You are from the city. We are not in the city. Security is not necessary. We have neighbours." She brought the coffee jug and hot, crumbly rolls for the others to the table. "If you wish," she said with a serious look at him, "if you wish you may find the tomb of our father. In the cemetery. If you wish."

"You seem hesitant. You seem to be suggesting it… with great reluctance."

She ghosted a smile. "You already understand your sister," translating for her husband. "All things about our father have a story. Perhaps it would be better for me to accompany you to the cemetery. After I return from the school?"

He grinned at her, aware that his choice of words was gathering the slightly stilted shape of hers as he put together phrases she was confident with. "I follow your advice, sister. You know about these things. You know the stories."

She laughed loud, "Oh, Jim! You are laughing at me. I will send you home to England immediately- where you can lock yourself into your house!" Another translation for Maurice caught Jim wondering what the husband made of him. Was he really as amiably consensual to this stranger's intrusion into his home as he appeared? Or had the three of them carefully prepared for the arrival of the stranger-brother and worked to Suzanne's lead, deciding what they made of Jim after he had gone back north? Maurice laughed at her telling anyway.

Maurice left first with Marie-Claire to take her to her college in Larozelle. Jim sat slowly sipping at the strong, gritty coffee in meditative comfort, as Suzanne tidied the kitchen up around him. She went off to fill a briefcase with what she needed for work and reappeared.

"Jim. It is necessary that you enjoy today. The weather is fine. During your run, enjoy the countryside. We say here, Le pays est beau- il est ouvert. In English, it is-"

"Stop," Jim said, raised hand in arrest "Wait. I know some of those words. From learning French in school. Many years ago." He paused to dig the words up from where they might be. "Pays. Land. The land is beautiful. It is open." He looked at her, seeking approval.

She laughed. "Completely correct. Perhaps expansive would be more correct for ouvert. But I am a little pedantic. Like a school teacher. And my big brother attempts to become a French man, he attempts so much. But it is more true in the French." She repeated it, as if to erase his jerky English version, "Le pays est beau- il est ouvert," kissed his forehead and went to leave.

"And will we eat meat again, to our father's disapproval?" he asked.

She smiled, "Yes, and- I have another story for you about that, also." They both laughed.

After his run up into the bright and windchilled forest, he had returned exultant and breathless to make himself a long bath. By the time Suzanne returned in the afternoon, he was still stretched on the sunlit living room carpet, reading life into the photographs of his father. She looked down over his shoulder at the page he had open.

"1952, I think. I was seven years old," she said.

"And I was sixteen. I had been working in a mill for two years."

She nodded, gravely, then said, "Do you wish to see the tomb now? The cemetery will be quiet now. The people are at work."

"Fine. Yes."

"We shall walk."

They did, but he thought her uncharacteristically quiet. He said nothing too.

The cemetery was on a rise beside the road in from Larozelle. He could not understand how he had missed it driving in yesterday. But why not? He had not been thinking of what she termed as tombs. The elaborate iron gate was half open. Many of the graves were ornate, decorated with carvings, statuettes, set with small glassed-in pictures of the dead. There were several larger mausoleums, sepulchres with family names carved above the gated entrances. She brought him to a simple headstone set close to the rear wall of the cemetery.

Francis Xavier Briggs.

1915-1982

Christ could be born a thousand times in Galilee

But all in vain until he is born in me.

Just that. All in English. Even returning to Briggs, Jim noted to himself.

"He was religious, then?" he asked.

"No. Not until the last days. My mother understood, but she was silent on this. It was a mystery to me. He did not speak to me of these things." She looked at Jim. "I thought I had known my father. Until the last days. Then he appeared as a man with secrets. But he shared them only with my mother." She looked back at the gravestone. "And this?" she gestured at it, the man's last words. "What does it mean? I do not know."

Jim looked back at the stone. "It is different for me, Suzanne. I am not so surprised. He has always been a mystery to me. I expect to make new discoveries about him every day. But for you, this must be different, more difficult."

"He became a changed man in the last years. More private. Perhaps it was fear of death. He went away from us." She sniffed, looked away from him and the grave, off towards the mountains. "He had always been a notable, a man of affairs, of political activity. A socialist. Not like Mitterand today. An old socialist. But the changes. He had visited the church on the feast days. Then, it was an obligation to be seen in the church. For men of affairs, particularly. But in the last years, he ceased to attend. He retreated to his room." She looked briefly back at Jim. "It is the room you sleep in. But we have changed it. After Mother died." Eyes away at the peaks again, "It became a private place. Like a monk's room. He read much. But it was the bible. Other books of mysticism. Only my mother entered in the last years, but she slept in a different room. She would do as he asked, but I do not think she approved. We lived in the village then, Maurice, I and Marie-Claire. He would sit at the table for meals when we visited. But he would only eat fruit and vegetables. Sometimes, a little fish." She smiled at him. "There, Jim, you have another story. The meat and the fish."

"Did he speak of these changes he had made?"

She shrugged, "Not to us. But it was as if the changes were made to him. Not him who was making the changes. Do you understand?"

Yes, that I understand, Jim thought, just giving her a profound and wordless nod. Perhaps knowing you have no control, but are controlled, is part of getting old. Awareness of the imminence of Death, the Great Controller himself? Were the remembered, better old days just those when you still had the illusion you were doing things that made a difference? Actions, driven by delusions? He felt bleak. About the past.

He looked at the woman beside, looking at the grave and reached out and touched her shoulder, saying, despite himself, "But think of the good days. Remember the music." And realised, as he said it, that the past of the man buried here was in some sense becoming Jim's own future. Unravelling the dead man's story was changing the living one.

She put her hand up and pressed his fingers into her flesh. "Ah, the music. Casals. You are correct. There was much good of our father. Perhaps there is a little we do not understand. Perhaps we do not have to know it. He has his own little secrecies. It is his right. But as a child you wish to know everything about your parent." She looked into Jim's face. "But the secret he made of you. That was not correct."

"I don't know. Not for me, but maybe for him." He looked away from her, caught for a moment by a dip of emotion deep within. "I am only learning to know him. Slowly."

"Come." She put her arm in his. "Let us go, my brother. I will tell you what we have planned for the weekend. For Saturday and for Sunday. We have spent too many hours talking of the past. Now we must talk of the future."

At the gate, she detached herself for them to pass through and Jim stopped for a moment to look back, but his father's grave was out of sight, behind the interposed screen of statuary on other graves.

She took his arm again. "Jim. We will be going to a celebration tomorrow. It is a celebration and a defiance- you understand?"

"I understand the word. Please explain."

"We are ecologists. Is that the word? We wish to preserve the land. We are anti-nuclear, anti-pesticide, yes?" He nodded, having nothing to offer on that subject. "In the mountains, fifty kilometres towards the west, there is a valley. It has a very ancient community there. They are peasants. They cultivate the land in an ecological manner. They bring in little into the valley from the exterior. They grow the crops from the seed. They make spirit from the grain. Their land is fertilised with the cattle and the goats. They make their own cheese, as we do."

He was surprised, "You make cheese?" Milk, so cheese too was logical. He was related to farmers, he smiled to himself.

"Oh, yes! We did not say? I will show you our goats. We are very proud of them. We have won prizes. We have learned much from the peasants. And the valley we will go to, they have the most ancient ways. They are pure ecologists. They even use the cattle for the plough in many parts because it is too inclined for a tractor. In other valleys near to them, these ancient skills have been lost. Some of those valleys are empty, the farms abandoned with only old people living there. The young people have been leaving for the cities for several generations. Many used to go to America. Before the war they returned with money back to the valleys, but no longer. The young people who leave do not return- except to visit their elderly relatives. It is a little like here. Many leave, few return."

She broke off, looking across the roofs of the village below them. "But the valley I spoke of is different. Many of the young continue to work on the land of their parents. Some leave, but often come back. And now the Government has the plan to build a hydro-electric plant in the valley. The fields and the villages will be covered with water. We oppose it. The families of the valley have opposed it. They have refused the money offered by the Government. Many have supported them. The judges have, of course, supported the Government. The Court has made a citation. They order the people to move. But it does not happen. The building of the engineers and the hydrologists has been occupied. We expect the gendarmarie to come next week to remove the occupiers. Tomorrow, in the night, we will close them in the building. There will be many people there in solidarity. Also from the Basques and the Catalans. Because it is in the plan of our Government to sell the hydro-electricity to Spain." She looked at him for his response, "You will come, of course?"

"Of course." Then, "Would Father have approved?"

"Oh, yes! Before the last days. Before he found religion. Then, I don't know. He ceased to leave the house. He may have approved, but I do not think he would have come for the actions."

"It has been many years for me, too. To be involved in an action." He wondered briefly, whether the boys added up to an action, as she called them. "I was never a Green, an ecologist. I have always lived in industrial areas." He thought how his running had for the first time in years, probably since childhood, taken him out and into contact with the natural world, alone, listening and hearing it. Teaching him to listen to himself. First, before listening to others.

"Yes. And manufacturing cars to pollute the planet," but she was smiling. "I only joke at you."

"It was a job. Just a job."

"And we did not understand these things then. This situation has made some problems for us. Marie-Claire wished to join the occupiers. Her boyfriend will become sealed in the building. She wished to be with him. But it will be dangerous. Maurice and I believe she is too young." She stopped to look at Jim. "What do you believe, Jim? Is she too young? Should we prohibit her, if we are supporting the occupation?"

Jim looked back at her. What do I believe? A problem with a daughter wanting to do such a thing? He wondered whether to speak to her about Tracey and her rebellion into conformity, but he only said feebly, "Well, it does sound dangerous."

"Yes. We think so, too."

"Has she obeyed you?"

"Obeyed? I do not know. She has said she will not participate. But she does not agree with us. She says we speak, but we do not do. She says her grandfather would have joined the occupation. I am not sure that is true. But I could not say that. She remembers him as I would wish to. A brave man, who had principles." She looked down, as if searching in the stones on the path. "She has a simple remembrance of him. Perhaps I will learn to have that myself, with time. Perhaps it is the difficulty always between fathers and daughters. As I became old enough to know him, I also had the wisdom to see that all things are not as simple as they seem when young. He died when Marie-Claire was sufficiently young."

"And she compares you and Maurice unfavourably to him?"

"Yes. That is true."

"What does she think of him not telling you that he had a son in England?"

"I do not know. I have not spoken to her since you told me. I think she will give her grandfather reasons for his actions. She will keep him as a hero to her memory."

Chapter Eighteen

The following day, driven by Maurice in the old Russian four-wheel drive, it was an hour and a half's drive in the afternoon to the valley. The hairpinned plunge back into the gorges, westward and then climbing out up the Pyreneean side on a narrow winding road into the foothills. Jim was sat in the back with Suzanne. He had been less willing to talk. The vehicle was noisy for conversation and his mind had been so stuffed with stories over the last two days, he welcomed the chance to look forward over Maurice's shoulder, idly watching the road and playing back in his mind all he had heard.

Climbed back into sunshine shot through the tumbled dark clouds, they crested a rise beside a ruined castle shoved across the skyline by a shattered knob of rock. Banners hung across the gaps in the fortifications and, as they turned downwards into the valley, placards were planted in the roadside turf, skipping regularly into sight through the windscreen. The trees fell away from the side of the road, cleared recently from the torn earth, as they came upon the gathering. Vehicles were parked, disorderly on the verges, along the roadside, across the field entrances.

"There it is!" Suzanne cried, pointing to the left, where a group of metal cabins were clustered on a gravelled stretch of land, the surrounding wire fence sagged and broken. To the side a scaffolding platform with loudspeakers, the bare metal bars pennanted with bunting, a group of musicians huddled in debate behind the microphones. Hung across the top, a large canvas strip lazily slapped in the breeze, titled in bold red letters, *Palais des Peuples*. Crowds were congregating in groups, before the stage, amongst the cars, beside the road. Their vehicle was crawling now, Marie-Claire leaning from her window calling out and greeting people.

As they left the car. Marie-Claire ran over to the cabins and went in. Jim followed Maurice and Suzanne. Their daughter reappeared with a dark, unshaven man so tall he had to stoop his thin frame coming through the cabin doorway. After the parents had embraced him, Suzanne introduced Jim briefly to Felipe, before she led them away from the gathering crowd around the stage. Joining her mother and the man, Marie-Claire brought her edge of anger to their animated conversation.

Jim looked across at Maurice, gave a smirk and a shrug, encompassing the three ahead with a turn of his palm, the other hand still pocketed. Jim nodded, then said indecisively, "Difficulties?"

"Difficile," Maurice nodded slowly. "Difficile, oui."

Jim nodded back, empty of what to say next, but wondering about the impotence of fathers with daughters. He sought to imagine if it would have been different had Tracey been a son. Too late now. Worthless to speculate.

Suzanne came back to Maurice. The parents had a short, tense exchange, before she turned to Jim, "I am sorry, Jim. I am truly sorry. We have the problem with Marie-Claire. She wishes to join the occupation," gesturing to the steel cabins.

"What does Felipe say?"

"He says she must do what she believes. Of course."

Jim looked across at Maurice, now both hands in pockets, his eyes on his daughter's back. "How will you stop her, Suzanne?"

She shrugged, "Maurice will speak to Felipe. Another time." She turned back to her husband and spoke to him again, then took Jim's arm, "Come we will leave Maurice to speak with them. I am become too emotioned. Marie-Claire and I fight then." Then, with an assertion of positivity, "Come. We will look at the village. The village the government wishes to drown."

By the time they returned up the hill to the gathering, the light was moving to dusk, accelerated by the turbulent clouds rolling forwards over the declining sun. The village had been closed and shuttered, already a sense of bereavement in the narrow, shadowed street. Set against Suzanne's confident talk of how the community was organised around the traditions tuned for the best from each season, the silence of the village spoke of other things for Jim.

Back at the gathering, the stage lights were lit and the rock band was tuning up. They found Maurice. Jim wandered over to the cabins. Standing aside from the busy entrances and exits at the door, he looked in. There were camp beds with sleeping bags, a large gas bottle cooker and boxes of provisions. Felipe came out, followed by Marie-Claire.

"Jim. You are alone?"

"No. Your parents are over there." He indicated, then asked, "Will you be staying. For the occupation?"

She looked at him shrewdly, "Do you think I should stay?"

Jim stopped. He looked back at the young woman and instinctively knew that she had already decided not to stay, so he was safe in then saying, "It is your choice. Either you join the occupation and anger your mother. Or you miss the occupation and please her?"

"Is that what you really think, my uncle?" the last added with a sour twist. "Perhaps the way to describe the choices is this. Either I join the occupation and make a defence of the beliefs all my family say they believe. Or I do not join the occupation and feel cowardly to leave the peasants here to the government engineers and constructors. Is that not a more true way of saying the situation?"

Jim was wondering how long he could hold her firm gaze, when her parents came up and Suzanne hugged her daughter, murmuring in her ear. Felipe stood aside and waited. Inscrutable. Maurice came forward and rubbed Marie-Claire's shoulder, reassuring, confirming that Jim had guessed right; the girl would not be staying.

Suzanne disengaged and turned to him, "She is not staying. Maurice spoke to her."

"I know."

As Marie-Claire walked off hand-to-hand with Felipe, she brushed past Jim, muttering in his ear, "Huh, old people."

"They will be saying au revoir to each other," Suzanne said.

The band started, thrashing into an angry, fast number. Jim and the family found a place to the side of the crowd, but too near to a set of amplifiers for conversation. Between music, Suzanne told Jim who the series of speakers were- the village mayor, a Senator, a woman from the Basque ETA movement, a Green activist, a feminist leader. As the sun went out behind the clouds, darkening dramatically before night, a wind stirred and started to tear at the branches and banners in gusts. As the first raindrops were spat and hoods were being pulled over heads, a large woman in black came on stage, pulled a box over to sit on, leaving the stool for an elegant other, not-there. She crouched over her guitar, head turned down into it, the audience curtained off from her intensity by her long, dark shaking hair. The guitar reverberated the scatter of her fingers on the strings, until she raised her head, face turned above the crowd, above the valley rim, into the heart of the torn clouds, into the first flash and rumble of thunder, she sang. It was plaintive, defiant, clearly spoke in a language Jim knew the meaning of, if not of the words. It cut through the noise and the crowd was stilled for her in the accelerating, squalling rain. Her voice rose strong and fierce at the end. The crowd was silent for a moment before applause, but she had already left the stage without acknowledgement.

A last speaker, one of the organisers, indicated the cabins and they surged over to them. Jim was at the back, but recognised the guttering flashes of a welding torch.

"What is happening?" he asked Suzanne.

"They are closing the doors. How do you say, with oxygen burning?"

"Welding," he said. "Is Felipe in there?"

"Yes."

"Where is Marie-Claire?"

"She says goodbye. To Felipe."

He wanted to ask how she could be so sure, but it would be an intrusion.

When the sealing was complete, there was a shout as the welder flashes stopped, just as a massive gout of light tore the dark clouds overhead, immediately smashing the air with the shattered and exploded throat of thunder. The crowd cringed a moment, slowly stood and, as the rain began to torrent, a voice from the stage- and there was the large woman in black, without guitar, dancing lightly, hair streaked with wet, singing a tripping melody. She sang three verses, each one chorused by the crowd, a little louder each time, clapping syncopating to the rhythm. Jim looked around and Suzanne and Maurice, arms round each other, were singing with the rest. There was a cheer at the end, but the woman had gone already and the crowd quickly started to disperse to their cars.

"We must find Marie-Claire. Here are the keys to the auto, Jim. Wait for us there."

He crossed the mud and let himself into the passenger seat. The rain drumming on the roof, he watched the stage lights go off and tarpaulins dragged across the equipment. They returned, the two women into the back. Despite the wet hair plastered to her cheeks, Jim could see Marie-Claire had been weeping. She pushed her mother away and curled with her face to the window, knuckles pressed together over her mouth, watching the cabins, as they joined the headlit stream of cars slowly creeping away.

Suzanne leaned forward, "Now you have real mountain weather, yes, Jim? The sun we have the days you have been here, is not normal for this season. What did you think of this- the occupation?"

"When will the police come?"

"Not tomorrow. It is Sunday. Monday, perhaps."

"What will they do?" he asked, aware of the girl's fierce, hurt face over her mother's shoulder.

"They will attack," Suzanne shrugged and fell back into her seat, face serious, turned to the dark window her side, as her daughter to the other. Jim looked at Maurice, but his eyes were ahead on the crawling stream of tail lights winding down into the valley.

That night, lying in his bed, he could hear the softest murmur of Suzanne and Maurice talking together, until he fell asleep himself.

Unusually for him, he remembered the fragments of a dream when he awoke in the early light. Among a crowd of boyish faces… looking up into the struts of a factory roof, tangling themselves alive into clawed roots… a bowl of cold and greasy water splashed across the front of his trousers… shouting at people in a street unaware of him there amongst them… He lay hot and troubled, unable to fill in the gaps, leaving him too flaccid, enervated to do anything but lie, limbs spread beneath the duvet, letting the cool and the calm ebb through him.

During the morning Maurice and Suzanne were raking out the straw from the sheds where the goats lived in the winter, before being released out into the meadows with the spring. The animals waited, bleating their objections crowded into an enclosure at the barn's rear. Jim became the couple's inexpert helper, holding the hose while they flushed and scrubbed the floors with disinfectant there and in the twin-deck milking parlour next door.

By the afternoon Marie-Claire had not appeared and Suzanne started to prepare food in the kitchen, while Jim went through her photos again. In the late afternoon, a car drew up and Suzanne led in a couple and introduced them as Roaul and Élise. They already knew he was the half-brother and spoke to him in difficult English of his father as an important man, a hero. Marie-Claire appeared at last and greeted the couple affectionately, relieving them of the stilted conversation with Jim. He sat back smiling, looking on and trying to give off just the balance of satisfaction listening to the conversation he could not understand, but sufficiently receded into his sofa, not to invite inclusion and translation.

Suzanne brought in a tray of bottles and glasses, just as another vehicle scraped up outside. She called for Maurice, who soon appeared, ushering in a woman. Greetings with the others, then she turned and came over to Jim.

"Ah, the brother. I am Gizande." He awkwardly half-raised his bottom from the cushions for his hand to be shaken, but she did not take it. "You have caused so much pleasure for this family." She turned to the others, then back to Jim. "For Suzanne, in particular, it has been finding a treasure."

He blushed slightly and said in surprise, "Yeah?"

She laughed lightly and summoned Suzanne from her drinks tray. "Ah, your brother is so English. He becomes red when I say he is your discovered treasure."

Suzanne smiled and smoothed his hair with a stroke of her fingers. "I will not have you embarrassing my brother. He is charming." Then turning to Jim, "It is true. An English gentle man. But of the people, not of the aristocracy. Is that not true, Jim?"

He laughed out loud, "Of course it is! And any other compliment you wish to give me."

The women giggled, then Suzanne said, "The drinks. Come. Serve yourselfs."

Jim caught himself watching Gizande's legs walking away in her skirt.

Oddly, and unlike the previous night just with the family, dinner was started by Gizande, with a short prayer, either in French or Spanish, he could not tell. This meal found him sat on what was the English language end of the large table, with Suzanne and Gizande, sometimes a few sentences in French, but always translated for Jim. Marie-Claire was sat with her father, Roaul and Élise at the other end, louder and laughing in French.

Gizande was a quite serious runner, a club member, more than a health jogger. Jim thought, Ah, those legs. They exchanged information on training distances run, events raced and Jim realised he was not in her league, although she offered to do a run with him, until she learnt he was leaving the day after tomorrow.

"Perhaps, another visit," she said chirpily.

They then moved on to the occupation in the valley. Jim was aware of Marie-Claire part-attentive to what her mother was now saying. They spoke together of a demonstration against the damming of the valley, planned to start in Spain and march through the Pyrenees into the valley itself.

Jim remembered the Basque speaker the night before. "Why from Spain? Why start the march there?"

"The connection with Spain?" Gizande said. "We are people of the Pyrenees, before we are French. Our comrades are in the mountains here and across the frontier, not in Paris. We share languages. Basque is spoken on both sides of the mountains. Just as here is Catalan. It is not always a language of Spain. And we share the problems of mountain people for whom decisions are made far way in capital cities on the plains. They do not understand us. We share the winters of our friends across the frontier. We do not share the eyes, the ears and the scent of Madrid and Paris."

No, Jim reflected, like the North and London. "I know that from life in England. Is it the same here? I live in the North. Even the weather on television only happens in London. Is that the same with Paris?"

Both women smiled with amused recognition. "Perhaps more even in France," Gizande acknowledged. "We have been a colony of the North. In France it is the North that bullies the South, the opposite from in England, yes?" Jim nodded. "We were broken. The Inquisition was invented to break the spirit and the beliefs of here. Of Languedoc and of these mountains. We had our own religion. Have you known of the Cathars?" Jim shook his head dumbly. "Ah, the old religion." She turned to Suzanne and spoke in French to her and, as this happened, Jim noticed Marie-Claire hold her hand up to stop the conversation her end of the table.

Gizande was halted by the listening silence in the room. She said something to all. Then turned to Jim, "I must speak this in French for the others," indicating the end of the table. "And for you in English. For this concerns your father," and she looked again, searchingly into Suzanne's eyes, then back at Jim. "I have learned this from my mother. It is the first time that Suzanne has known of this." Jim looked into his sister's anxious face. "I have waited to tell Suzanne this. For the correct moment. Your arrival, Jim, told me it was the time now, while you are here. It is correct that the both of you hear this together. Have patience, for I must tell this in two languages." She paused and started to tell first in French, then English. With a serene intensity, of how her grandfather, during the war brought faith to those hiding in these mountains. He was part of the fragile inheritance of the old Cathar beliefs, stretching back hundreds of years to before savage slaughter by Catholic knights drove it back, apparently into genocidal night. But actually surviving as the most feeble, guttering light in a few of the remotest valley ends, where narrow paths known only to locals, unlocked ways through the barred doors of the mountains into Spain. With the Catholic Church here at best compromised with the Vichy, untrusted by the partisans, the Cathar Perfects, as these holy men and women were known, netted in those who sought prayer in that darkest moment of war. The faith secreted for centuries was well fitted and in waiting for administering to the souls and spirits of those hidden in these hills.

"And your father," she said to both of them. "He found faith with my grandfather. During the war, he visited my grandfather's farm, for it was on the route for airmen escaping into Spain. My mother knew this for many years, but she only spoke when she knew I am a friend of Suzanne." A sentence of French, her hand to Suzanne's shoulder, she repeated it in English. "I have held this till now, for I sensed from speaking with you, that you were disappointed with your father in his last years."

"La ligne Marie-Claire," Suzanne said, then turned to Jim. "It was the name of the line of escape that my- our father organised during the war." She looked across at her daughter, "That is the origin of the name. He asked that she is named Marie-Claire."

Gizande nodded, then turned to Jim. “But you have had a different experience of your father. Suzanne understands now from your story. The man she knew of as Francisco was different from the man you call Francis. You have told her of a darker side, perhaps. He sought something away from the killing and he found it with my grandfather. The father of my mother. Your father was not simply a hero of the war. Like us all, he had an identity of the spirit outside the person he was in the world of affairs- of business and of war.” Looking steadily into him, she placed her hand on Jim's. He looked down at it- away from that gaze and surprised at the strength and coarseness of the skin of her palm resting on his own softened flesh. “You, Jim, came here to find the same thing here. I believe you have found it?”

It was a question. Hung over him, waiting to be answered before this audience, eyes on him, round this table, in this place far off from where he had learned to live. His eyes still lowered, not to meet others, he looked at the empty plate before him, the smears of sauce with small fragments of food, the broken crust of bread on the tablecloth beside. Waiting for an answer. “I don't know,” coming out as a whisper, he cleared his throat. “Perhaps. Perhaps I have to go from here first, in order to know what I may have found here. In this place.”

She pressed his hand before removing hers. “And then to return here again. To us.” Jim looked again at her to see what she meant, but could not hold her steady, firm eyes long enough to know.

Suzanne broke the locked intensity Gizande had drawn him into, with, “And you can bring your wife and daughter with you. Jane and Tracey?”

What? he thought, and almost a whinny of laughter went through him. What would they make of this? Especially Tracey. He looked up to answer, caught Gizande's knowing, private smile to him, and hesitated, before, with effort, the stilted words, “Oh, yes. I'm sure they would love to visit here.”

Chapter Nineteen

It was late when the guests left. Raoul and Élise left first. Marie-Claire went into the kitchen and then Suzanne and Maurice took Gizande out to collect her coat. Jim was alone at the table, part relief, part regret that she was going, perturbed by her, unable to dismiss it as a wayward sexual brush with another woman. He drank the last from his wine glass, listening to the conversation from the verandah, and had just placed the glass down, stroking its stem meditatively, when Gizande re-entered the room. She came round to him and leaned down to level with his eyes, gathering up his hands and enclosing them within her strong, rough edged and gentle palms.

"Jim. We will see you again. The circumstances, if you come alone or not. These are unimportant things." She kissed him briefly on the forehead, stood back, looking down at him. "You understand." It was a statement. She turned and went.

He sat there motionless, the sounds of her goodbyes, steps down to the car, engine alive and tyres on the gravel, in his ears, but unlistened to. What had that been?

He was still, when Suzanne re-entered. She sat across from him. Poured a glass of wine. "It is late, but I have no wish to sleep yet. Would you wish for more wine, Jim?"

He stirred himself, "Yes. Please."

"She is an extraordinary woman, is she not? She is like a sorceress. She can think your thoughts, before you can think them yourself." She shook her head, a smile darkening to a tired seriousness. "And our father. A religious. That gives an explanation for his last days perhaps. And the inscription on the tomb."

He looked over at his sister and for the first time felt the strength of being her older brother. "Yes, Suzanne. I understand that it is a shock for you. But for me, our father changes. With every new story, he becomes different. Something is added. He changes, like the weather. As Gizande said. Sometimes he is Francisco, sometimes Francis."

"I understand what you are saying. But I lived with him." She put her hand across the tablecloth towards him, "I am sorry, Jim. But it is different. I believed that I knew him. That the way of his old age was perhaps an illness."

"I know. I didn't live with him." Until now, and through other people's stories. Telling a new tale of a different man with every one. Is that what we are- what people say we are? After death, certainly, the body gone, we can only exist in the dust of tales told by others. Complete with the mistranslation of misunderstood motives, unable to answer back. As if from nowhere, he heard himself say, "But Gizande understands this."

"Oh, yes. She has this impression on people when they are met first with her." A short laugh, "I see that you were impressed."

Jim smiled. "What does she do? Her work?"

"You will find this unbelievable. She is a peasant. She has a farm inherited from her grandfather, by the Pyrenees."

"Ah, the hands," he said.

"Pardon?"

"Her hands. They were rough. I did not expect it," and he felt a slight, unpredicted flush.

"Yes. It is true. I understand. But to say she is a peasant does not give the true picture. She is one of the credentes. She spoke of the catharism. She and her family have the tradition of believers." She shook her head, "To the south you see signs on the road for tourists. The Cathar Bar. The Cathar Gas Station. It has become fashionable. The touristic identity. They use the word to sell the commodities. But when you meet Gizande or her family, you know they have understanding. It is the old religion. Even her children have it."

He wondered at her husband, but asked, "What is their belief?"

"Ah, Jim, you must not ask me." She smiled and sipped her wine. "It was our father, it seems, who understood. And I eat meat. The true cathars will only eat fish and plants. That is not true of Gizande. She will not eat meat, but she will eat eggs and food from milk. I am told that her grandfather was true cathar. A perfect. Perhaps our father was trying to reach the state of true cathar at the end of his life."

"But is it only food? She spoke of the world of the spirit." He tried to visualise the scene around the table, but an hour ago. He could see her and the listeners he had been part of, but the words could only creak from his own mouth, "She said- was it the identity of the spirit?" Without Gizande speaking them, they sounded fumbled from him.

"Jim. I do not know." Suzanne was upset. "It is not for me to explain the beliefs. I know only a little." She rocked her head from side to side.

"What is wrong?"

She drank from her glass more fully and he could see her turned down eyes were moist. Maurice quietly entered behind her and spoke softly, rubbing his hand, soothing the neck beneath her hair. Head tilted further down to allow her husband to massage there, she replied. Maurice nodded, looked across at Jim, smiled and left the room, going upstairs.

They stayed silent, her face declined, her brother looking on at her with fond concern.

Finally, she raised her face, wiped each eye with a knuckle edge and smiled bravely at him, "I am sorry for the tears."

Realisation stood within him. The certainty of knowing what this recent-sister felt, "I understand. You are upset about Father. You are learning things about him from strangers. Things you believe he should have told you himself. I know how you feel. This is the only father I have known."

"Yes. You understand." Then with a warm intensity, "It is so good that we have discovered you. You are part of the family. A true brother." She poured more wine in her glass and indicated his, "Let us make a toast." He reached over for the bottle. She raised her glass, "For the family Briggs! Salud! Santé!"

He laughed, "For the Brige family!"

But the gesture did not clear the room of her sadness, her child-like resentment that the past was not as she believed it had been left when she had buried her father.

"What of your mother?" he asked. "She knew about what was happening with your father."

"She was very Spanish. The word of the husband was the law for her in such things. She was a catholic. For the true catholics, the catharism is a heresy. But she obeyed my father's wishes. If he did not wish her to tell, she would not tell. Anyone. Perhaps she feared it being known that her husband had beliefs of heresy in his last years."

Not just in his last years, he thought. Gizande had told of the war. He did not speak this to Suzanne, but simply said, "It is a strange story."

"Yes. For such a socialist, to become a religious."

"Not just that. How we met. The whole thing."

She looked at her watch, "I must go to sleep. I have to work tomorrow." She stood, put her glass on the cabinet behind and started to fold the tablecloth, sweeping the crumbs into it. Jim lifted his glass to let her draw the cloth away. Finished, she stood with it gathered in her arms. "What will you be doing tomorrow, Jim?"

"I will run. I may go down to the village." He shrugged, "I don't know."

"It is your last day with us. Already I have become so familiar with having a brother in the house. Even so few days."

"Yes. Now I cannot remember not knowing you."

She laughed, "That is too much!"

"Maybe. But it's true."

She put the cloth down and came round the table. "Come," she indicated him to stand. "It may be many months before I see my brother again. I wish to hold the memory," and she clasped him strong and tight, her face turned into his chest. He lightly rested his fingers on her shoulder blades. With a last crush of embrace, she disengaged, smiling up at him, a little emotional, lips pursed. "It has been very good."

"For me too, Suzanne."

"Enough," she said, gathered up the cloth again and went out, dabbing her eyes with it. A moment later, she called, "Bon soir," from the bottom of the stairs, before he heard her going up them.

Chapter Twenty

He joined the family for breakfast again in the morning. Marie-Claire seemed brighter and Suzanne showed no signs of the unhappiness, the preoccupation of the night before. When they had gone, Jim dressed for a long run. He went back along the road towards Larozelle, turned north down a side road and followed it through a silent hamlet as it descended into a craggy gorge, leaving a last squat stone farm behind, running out of metalling into a rough track, winding between stunted conifers and gorse pushed through out of the rocky ground. The weather had returned to more sunshine, but broken with cloud. He welcomed the solitude to feed on all the things he had heard, seen, felt and tasted over the last four days.

It was late morning when he got back and, as he tried to sprint the last hundred yards into the driveway, he slowed to a watchful jog. Because there was a car parked before the house with a stout elderly man stood beside it leaned on a stick, watching Jim as he came up the drive. He walked the last few steps.

"Oui?" Jim asked tentative and still hard of breath. He saw a young man behind the car's wheel, watching.

"Are you the English brother?" The old man offered his hand.

"Half-brother. Of Suzanne. Of Madame Planisolles." Jim took the hand briefly and non-commitally. "Why do you ask? Who are you?"

"I am Monsieur Jacob. Theodor Jacob. I knew your father. In the war. And later."

Aware he was chilling with sweat, Jim shuffled his legs to make the point. "What can I do for you. I am getting cold."

"Of course, of course. I wished to speak with you. About your father." Jim wondered how many other people in this area knew about him, both being here with the family and who he was. Bush telegraph. "Perhaps we can speak another time."

"I go home to England tomorrow. Tomorrow morning," he added, to leave no doubt.

Jacob opened his hands, gestured powerlessness, "Well, it must be today."

Jim was irritated by the certainty of the man, but intrigued by what he may have to tell. "Okay. Okay. You will have to wait here, while I get changed." The man nodded and Jim trotted in, leaving the man climbing awkwardly back into the car next to the young driver. Showering, drying and pulling on clothes, Jim had an edge of panic, an edge of intriguement at what the old man would have to tell. He came down through the verandah and out onto the drive. The old man opened the car door and looked up.

"How did you know I was here?" Jim asked, trying to see across to the driver.

"Your car is parked there. The English number," Jacob pointed.

That was not what Jim meant, but he steered into asking, with a tone of defensive impatience, "What do you want to say about my father?"

The old man put out his stick and a foot onto the gravel. "It is difficult here to speak. Can we not speak inside the house?"

"I do not know you. It is not my house." He looked back at it, then back to the man, "We can sit on the verandah and talk," then indicating the driver, "And him?"

"My grandson. He can wait here, if you wish."

"Yes. Come," and he led the way up the steps. The old man followed slowly and Jim indicated a chair opposite and sat down himself. After the run, he wanted a drink, but, if so, he would have to offer one to the other and he did not want to be hospitable to a stranger whose message he had not yet heard. "Well. What have you to tell me?" he opened, quite curtly.

Theodor Jacob rested his hands on the knurled top of the stick, looking down at the rug a moment, then commenced, the sentences scrambled together, but unhurried, as if a long time waited to be said and time taken to be believed, "I wish to tell you of your father. He is a man there have been many stories about. Many have their memories of him, in the war, before that in Spain and afterwards. And these stories are different. Many of them disagree. The facts cannot be true of both stories because they say your father was in two places at one time. Or he was on two sides, in different armies."

Jim had the now-become-familiar feeling of doubt, of belief on hold. Francis or Francisco, this time? Brige or Briggs. But he showed nothing to this stranger, except refusing being the passive recipient, asked assertively, "But who are you? What were you to my father?"

"Ah, me?" he smiled, an edge mysterious. "I am the Jew who led the bombers to kill the French. That is what some say." He rubbed his hands round the top of the stick. "I was an official of the SNCF- you understand, the national railways in France. I was a senior official in Toulouse, but when the Vichy brought the laws against Jews, I understood that I had to hide. I am Jewish and my family were of the Left. I came south to here with my wife. Where it was known there were many bands of anti-fascists in the hills, the Spaniards from their war. I was able to assist with information for the partisans who were attacking the railways to disrupt the Occupation. This is how I knew your father. This is how later contact was made with me by the British Secret Service. They wanted me to come to England to assist them in information for the bombers to destroy the railways. Especially, to stop the Germans bringing up their armies to oppose the arrival of the armies of the Americans and the British in Normandy." A solemn pause. "It was a mistake. For me. When I was directing the partisans, I could say to them which train was with troops or war material and which train was just with civilians. After I went to England, I could not choose. The bombers were directed by the American and British officers. Many French people who were innocent were killed. The lives of the soldiers on the beaches were of much more value to them than the lives of those who were killed here by the bombs. I became guilty of the crime of others. Many thousands were killed. Even the cardinals of the Catholic Church asked for the bombing to stop." Matter of fact, sighing, "So I stopped assisting them. But it was too late for those French-dead already. The British then treated me very badly. My wife was with child. I had insisted that she accompany me, but they made difficulties for her when our son was born." He looked across at Jim and smiled, "The young man in the auto. He is the son of that boy, born to us in England." He again withdrew into the kaleidoscope of years, maybe proud for a moment of where an old man had reached and what he would leave behind him.

Jim wanted to bring him back to his own father and stirred his feet on the floor boards. Jacob continued nodding to himself, then with a vigorous shake of his head, returned to the room, eyes back on Jim, now held there, not hostile, but penetrating, wanting to know what his words were doing to the Englishman sat across from him, "That is how I met your father. Already there were stories, from some of the Spaniards. That he was not to be trusted. That he was not a true Republican. At one time, he had to go into hiding from a band of Spanish partisans who wished to kill him. They said he was Francoiste. That he was responsible for Luis Companys being returned to Spain to be killed by the fascists. But when he started to work for the British, they protected him. It is said that they assisted him in killing some of his enemies among the Spaniards. I was with him then. In the hills. There were men who died." A brief remembrance. "There were stories. When I returned from the war at the Liberation, some of his closest comrades were dead. Because of what I had seen when I had been with him in the hills, I believed some of those stories."

The old man's eyes waited for Jim. Shouldn't he feel indignant? But he couldn't. Too much doubt. Too many tales of his father, now to be without doubt. "Who was Luis Comp...?" the name half lost, he asked, seeking a fact from the other man, fearing another opinion.

"Ah. He had been the President of Catalunya. In the Republic. He escaped when Franco was victorious. As your father had, across the mountains," indicating the serrated backdrop to the west. "That story is perhaps not true. Companys was handed to Franco by the Germans. But the Spanish were suspicious of your father. That he had a place in the death."

Jim cleared his throat, then said, a touch indignant, a touch of caution, "You come here to tell me of my father's treachery, but all you can say is that people disagree about him, you doubt the truth of some of the stories yourself. Why have you come, Monsieur Jacob?"

"I tell you the stories from others, before I tell you what I know from myself." The old man was looking straight into Jim's eyes and forced the indignation into retreat, turning away to the landscape. "The communists were very active in this area in the Resistance. That would be natural. Many of the Spaniards were communists or from the Left. They wished to defeat Hitler, then to liberate Spain. It is not well known that, following the Liberation, after the Americans had also landed in Provence, there was a large attack by the Republican Spanish across the mountains against Franco. It was at the time I returned from England. Your father was a senior figure. Because of his work helping escapers across the frontier, he was the source of information about what was happening there. He told that the Spanish people were ready the rise up, with the attackers. It was a disaster. It was led by Tovar, a man I knew and loved. He was a hero of the Resistance and before, of the war in Spain. He was killed, and many others. Thousands. The Francoistes had cleared the population from the valleys the other side of the Pyrenees, so there was no assistance for our men. This, your father must have known before. And afterwards, we heard that many sympathetic with the Republicans had been betrayed to the Brigada Politica Social before and tortured. The Brigada was the secret police. They were in France during the Occupation. They were trained by the Gestapo." Jacob gazed at Jim, nodding slowly, then quietly said, "Many knew. Your father left here suddenly at the Liberation and lived in Paris for two years. Many wished to kill him. But the British and Americans protected him. He was useful. They did not want the war to commence again in Spain."

Jim's voice seemed to come from a remote place, somewhere distant from his stilled, listening body, "Why? Why did you need to tell me this?"

"Why would a man not wish to know this? About his own father." Jacob stretched out a leg, as if stiff from sitting too long. "He did many good things in the war, your father. He was important in this region. Many escaped across the mountains because of his assistance. But he did bad things too. He was involved in the eliminatation of many who did not please people in London. Afterwards, the government wished to salute him for his work in the war. He was to be given the Legion d'Honneur, but it was considered a scandal. Many objected. There was a petition from the members of the National Council of the Resistance. The Legion d'Honneur was withdrawn."

"I know." So different from Suzanne's story, a few nights ago, sat here, the same mountainscape view dark then with the mystery of the night. Now, the sun come from behind a cloud, shone like an interrogatory spotlight into Jim's face. Did she know Jacob and his stories? He shifted his chair to take his face back into the shadow. "You have told me stories from others. What did you see yourself?"

Jacob looked at Jim thoughtfully, then turned his eyes back to examine the knurls of his stick, tilting his head for a moment as if to read a detail from them. He put one hand down to his knee and rubbed it, then continued, "When the British asked me to come to England to direct them in the bombing of the railways, before I was taken away, we returned to Toulouse. Your father and myself. The British wanted the operating manual for the S.N.C.F. It is three large books with all the information that a senior official needs to run the railways in France. It had the situation of all the railway sheds, the repair facilities, the signal systems and the bridges and the tunnels. In order to get the books, we needed to make meeting again with my colleagues who worked previously with me. The leading figures in the Resistance in the railways there were communists. They did not trust the British. It was believed that the Air Force parachutages of weapons were arranged to go to groups of partisans who were not of the Left. So, the communists in Toulouse said they would give us assistance to enter the offices of S.N.C.F. if first the British dropped them weapons. It was very dangerous. I had to hide in the city, where I was known by the Vichy police and wait while the negotiations with London took place over the secret radio. I was alone for many hours while your father completed this. When he returned, he was very angry." Sharply, he asked Jim, "You remember the anger of your father? It was well known. It was said he never forgot an enemy."

The absurdity of the question was almost funny. "No. I never knew my father. I do not remember." Only the memories of others. The memories they say they have, an ever growing heap inside his head, unsorted and chaotic. Surely somewhere there is a truth about this man, Spanish, French or English, hero or treacherous avenger, Briggs or Brige. Suzanne's doubt about their father's last days, where she was present as a witness, gave him a doubt about what she truly knew about his life before she was born. Had he been a man always escaping his previous pasts? A liar about yesterday to those he met today? Jim looked shrewdly across to the old Jew and understood his need to unburden these stories to the son. A way of settling accounts. And Jim believed him. "Continue. Please."

"I had not understood. That you did not know your father. I am sorry," Jacob said with sympathy, but also with the acceptance and wisdom that painful things need to be said for life to be borne. That unturned stones and doubts wore away and weakened. Also, that he too had a further insight into the man he had hidden with in the city over forty years ago. "Yes. I understand now," and he resumed. "Your father was angry that the communists had made these demands. That they had forced them upon him. I believe he felt humiliated in the eyes of the British. That he was not with the authority that he had allowed London to believe. After we left Toulouse, the partisan group, every member were arrested by the Gestapo. They died in the camps." Jacob stopped, letting that resonate, while perhaps he remembered lost faces. "When I arrived in England, I was congratulated by the officers of the British Secret Service, because I was a friend of your father. I was told that your father was the guarantee that after the war this region would be sanitised of the Left. They believed I must be a man of the Right, because I was a colleague of your father. They showed me a list of names to ask me what I knew of them. That they were causing difficulties for the British and the Americans and they wished them to be eliminated from the Resistance. On the list, there were the group in Toulouse. I knew they were already in the prisons of the Gestapo." Jim listened to his own breathing, his heart, felt sweat on his forehead gather and creep down his chilled skin. "It was him. Certainly. I was never his friend, but at first I was admiring of his actions against the Vichy and the Nazis. When I returned from England after the Liberation, he was already in Paris, escaping from the revenge of the communists from Toulouse. He had many enemies. I was also one. Not at first. But later, when I learnt. He was fighting for different things. I must say, he was a dishonourable man. When he returned here from Paris, he was able to become a citizen of my country. And a figure of importance in the region. He was able to say that I had made mistakes when in London. That I had directed the bombers wrongly and that French families were killed. He was able to silence me, to steal my credibility." He pulled his stick back and set it between his legs, hands tight round it, ready to get to his feet. "Thank you for listening to me. It was not justice that happened then. But your father was not a believer in justice." With effort, he slowly raised himself. Jim looked up at him, still numb. "Perhaps you will not believe my story. It is for you to make the judgement. But I believe you needed to hear the story I had to tell. It is your right to have heard what I have said to you. Thank you."

"Monsieur Jacob." Jim rose. "Thank you. It cannot have been easy to tell the story again. It is painful."

"More painful for you. I have told these stories many times. It was not easy for you to hear such things." He put out his hand, "But you were a good listener. I hope you are able to make use in your own life of what I have said"

It was a strong shake, held a moment afterwards while the two men let their eyes lock to each other a last time, before the old man moved slowly towards the verandah door.

Jim had watched the old man laboriously lower himself into the car, assisted by his grandson, then drive off. The stories he had listened to had been true. To the teller. Just as Suzanne's had been. The truth based on the evidence available to that person, the evidence his father had been able to leave visible. He thought back to the boxes on the floor of the room in the nursing home. His aunt's bequeath of doubt to him. He went to the records and found the set of Casals. *Comrade and patriot*, the cellist's signature of gratitude. Another victim of the deceit of Francisco-Francis? Every variation of the truth about this father was being brought to him, forcing him to judge. When all the evidence was in. For he was sure that more stories were waiting somewhere to be told.

He put the records on the turntable, one after another, with the same delicacy Suzanne had shown and he listened.

He was still in the living room, the music now finished, when Suzanne returned from work. He watched her, measuring what to tell her about the visit by Jacob. She prepared coffee and joined him.

"My last evening with my new brother," she said with light reproach to him.

"I must go back. There are important things I have to deal with when I get back."

"I understand. But you must return. With your wife. Jane, is she? And your daughter."

Jim looked across at her, this sister, knelt on the floor, as she attended to pouring the coffee. Weighed up, he cleared his throat a little and said, "That is one of the things. We are not living together. We live separately." He was aware these words had formalised and taken forward the situation at home, beyond some threshold he could step back across.

Suzanne placed the coffee pot quietly back down on the tray. "I am sorry. But I am not surprised. You have spoken only a little of your family. It was an emptiness. I had remarked of this to Maurice." She looked at him inquiringly, "Do you wish to speak of this?"

Jim shook his head. "No. Not yet." He retreated from what he had said, "Nothing is certain. Jane is staying with our daughter for the time being. We have to decide. But I will let you know what happens."

"Much happens to you, Jim. You are a man with difficulties. That is evident. But you are a man with new family, also. We live many kilometres apart, but we will continue to communicate, yes? And perhaps we are able to visit you in England." She handed over the cup to him. "But not until you have made your arrangements with Jane, I think," and she smiled.

Wanting to say no more of this, he sipped without comment, then, "I had a visit today."

"Oh, yes?"

"Jacob. Theodore Jacob."

"He came here?" she was clouded with anger.

"He was here when I returned from my run."

"What did he say?"

He looked at her, cautious, deciding to recount what he had been told in exploratory morsels. "He wanted to tell me about our father in the war. They worked together. Against the Germans." He paused for her response.

"Oh, yes? And was that all that he was saying to you?" an edge of spite in her voice.

"He went to England, Jacob did. Do you know this?"

"Jim. I know the stories of this man and his family. Do you remember the administrator at the school. I told you she was opposed to our ecologism. She is from the family of Jacob. They are politically opposed to us. They are in construction. They will benefit from the barrage they wish to build in the valley. They are also cutting trees. Destroying the forests. How do you say?"

"Logging?" he offered.

"Logging. Yes. They have always opposed our father. Jacob, old Jacob, the man you met. He has reasons to hate the British. He hated that Father had success here in France." She sharply challenged, "Did you let him into the home?"

"No. Just on the verandah."

"Oh, Jim. You should not. He is an enemy. They are dangerous to us. I do not allow the administrator to know of any business of our family. They spy, because they are jealous." She gave her head a vigorous shake, "No. They should not come here. I am sorry. But you did not know."

"I told him nothing. He asked nothing. He just told his stories."

"Ah, but what stories?" she flashed sharply. "Did he tell you about his pension? About the circumcision of his son?"

"What? No," and he could not fail to grin at the sudden disjointed arrival of these in the conversation.

"Yes. It is absurd. It is a joke. Jacob believes he has been a joke of the English." She looked away at the pictures on the shelves. "No. He tells the stories that are suitable for their family and their friends. The stories that explain their hatred of English and of us, he does not tell these." She leaned back against the chair behind. "Did he tell you that he insisted that his wife accompany him to England?" Insisted? Jim supposed he had been told that and nodded. "When their son was born, the wife was given free hospital for the birth. But not for the circumcision. It was a military hospital, I have been told, and that they were not qualified to complete the operation. Jacob was told he must pay for this addition." Or subtraction, Jim thought. Are lifetime attitudes shaped on such absurdities? "He refused. It was the duty of the British, he said, and he would not further assist them with the bombing of the railways. Also, when he returned to France, after the war, he resumed his work with S.N.C.F. When he came to retire, he was told that his pension would not apply from the day he left his work and came to find our father here. To the day he returned to S.N.C.F. after the Liberation. It was more than four years. S.N.C.F. said they had no record of employment for those years. He wrote to the British Government, for them to pay the missing years of the pension. But they do not admit if a person has been in their employment with their Secret Service. It is a secret. It was an injustice for him, but he made an enemy of the whole English nation. My father also." She smiled over to him, "Our father. It was a jealousy. Because our father was English and in this region, I believe he came to represent all of the anger of Jacob about his time in England during the war."

Jim nodded, to avoid answering. It was a story, another one. But did this tale of long-fermented bitterness match the reflective old man he had sat with and listened to on the verandah? Perhaps. Perhaps he himself was too easily credulous. Had been for a lifetime. What are the motives of any of the story tellers about his father? Rather than assume that the dead man had left behind a carefully crafted evidence of deception, maybe it was the tellers, dismembering the corpse for their own ends. Finally, he said softly and without conviction, "I understand."

Suzanne looked at him, then started to put cups back on tray. "It is true." She went through to the kitchen. Jim remained, feeling disloyal to her. Wanting to go through, to say something reassuring to her, something that leaned against her shoulder to support this good woman, so generous towards him her stranger brother, so loyal towards their flawed father. But Jim did not have the words and remained sat, listening to the clearing of crockery, with more than a rattle of her irritation from the other room.

She returned, drying her hands in a cloth and he said, "Forgive me, Suzanne. I cannot help my doubts."

"What doubts?" she asked curtly, not looking at him, fussing at the bookshelves, then seeing the Casals still out of place. "Ah, so you have been listening to Pablo. Was he also wrong about our father? Was he deceived also?" She stacked the records together, not waiting for an answer, put them back in their box and returned them to the glass cabinet.

"I have been careful with them," he said purposelessly. Then he reluctantly rose, filling the space between them with that, if not words. To leave her tomorrow like this.

She turned to him, "No. You must not give me your doubts. You did not know him. I did. It was a privilege for me to be his daughter. There were enemies, yes." She flipped them away with a gesture. "There were the jealousies. Of course. He was a success. And he was from another land." She looked at her brother, eyes glittered almost with tears, almost rage. "You did not know him, Jim!"

He shook his head. "No. I didn't." He wanted to overcome being stuck where he was, across the room from her, the coffee table between, when the phone rang. She went out quickly. Deflated, he sat again. Her voice on the phone took on a pitch of alarm for a moment, then quietened, almost in defeat.

Returned after several minutes, she was pale. "That was Maurice. Marie-Claire has gone into the valley to join the occupation. To be with Felipe. She has not returned to the pharmacie. Maurice returns with her after he has finished his work. One of the students at her college, her friend, carried a message to Maurice." She shook her head. "Maurice has said to me that the Gendarmes have been in Larozelle and the C.R.S. have passed through in convoy towards the valley. He will attempt to find her. So dangerous."

Jim remembered the daughter's venom the night before and now read her contrasting brightness at this morning's breakfast as deceit. "What will you do?"

"I must stay here. I am pleased you are here, so I am not alone." It was inclusively said, but her mind was elsewhere already. He felt impotent what to say or do. She considered a moment, then went out to the phone again.

She was reluctant to prepare dinner, hoping Maurice would soon return. With Marie-Claire. So they sat, Jim doing most of the talking. Desultory conversation about the past. Maurice phoned again, a couple of hours later. The valley had been sealed off by the paramilitary police. He had tried to negotiate to reach his daughter, but they were letting nobody in. He was going to continue trying to negotiate with them. They ate bread with cheeses and drank wine. Together in the same room, but Suzanne apart with her anxiety.

It was dark when she woke him. He had fallen asleep in one of her preoccupied silences, unable to offer up any more distracting stories for her. She told him to go to bed. He had the long drive in the morning. There was no more news of her husband and daughter. He went upstairs.

Chapter Twenty-one

The dreams again. Boys' faces, shambled together with bits of half-pieced-together buildings overgrown with filthy roots, awaking with a sweat of shame. Voices. At first he was not sure if they were the tenuous shreds of the dream washed up onto this blurred edge of wakefulness. But no, they were distinct. He remembered Marie-Claire, slipped on trousers and went quietly down.

Suzanne was sat there with Gizande, who held her hands with the intensity he remembered from her himself. She wore the blue overalls he had seen men wear across rural France. He stood a moment, half in the room, unwilling to break their intimacy.

It was Gizande who broke it, turning to him, "Ah, Jim. Come." She beckoned him to sit.

Suzanne woke to him, "There is no news. Maurice has telephoned again. He is waiting with others, where the Gendarmes have blocked the road. He believes it will be more difficult for something bad to happen, if they remain there. Some are trying to reach the village through the fields. Perhaps we will hear news." She had spoken stiltedly and looked exhausted.

"I am sorry I fell asleep. And was not here with you," said to Suzanne, but it was an apology for them both.

"Sit, Jim," Gizande patted the seat next to her. He did. "We have examined the possibilities of what may happen," she continued. "We were talking of what may have to be done in the morning."

"Can I help?"

Gizande looked at him, for a long moment. "You have many things to do when you return home. It is best that you return to England in the morning." She watched his face. He looked back into her grey eyes, serious, certain, a shadow of knowing amusement. Before he turned away, rewoke that there was another in the room, Suzanne, and he was going to speak, but Gizande ended with, "Perhaps you may assist in other ways. In other times." He would ask what she meant, but withdrew from her insistent attention to him and did not speak. She returned to Suzanne and spoke in French.

It was Suzanne who said, "Perhaps I will prepare some coffee. Would you wish for some, Jim?"

Gizande gently shook her head, spoke to her, then turned to him. "I have told her she can now sleep. No more coffee. She can recover some strength for tomorrow. You also, Jim. I will wait here for the telephone."

Suzanne nodded, looked at the other woman, unlocked her hands and embraced her, eyes closed, murmuring something. Then she tiredly and unsteadily rose. "Bon soir, Jim. I will see you in the morning. Before you depart, yes?"

"Yes," He was uncertain whether to get up and hug her, but, preoccupied again, she was gone. He turned to Gizande, "How is she?"

"You can see. It is difficult. It causes much unquiet for her. Many pains for us, when we are dependent of the actions of others. Our families. They take from the quiet of your spirit and they ask you to enter into the disturbance of themselves. And it is most difficult when the other is away from you. When you are not able to sit with them. To watch. To speak into the eyes."

"As you do," he said quietly.

She laughed. "I make the attempt."

He smiled at her, "You make the attempt, as you say, very well."

"Perhaps as you see it. But you understand much of this yourself, Jim."

"What? Of your old religion?" It came out too light and he looked aside.

"No," she corrected him. "It is too easy to joke. You hide behind such trivialisation. Perhaps that is the English way." She took his jaw between finger and thumb and centred his face back onto hers. "You joke because you know it is so serious. You have difficulties. Suzanne tells me this. But there is something else. I see a big shadow in your eyes." She took her hand away.

He held himself on the brink a moment, withdrawn from her penetration, then his mind melted under this strong and intimate stranger's insistence, restraints swept away, broken out into a surge of relief, tears dragged up from deep inside by the first of a series of huge, slow sobs. Gasping for air, he sucked back into his lungs all the quiet calm of this room with her, greedy for the easement, the solace from her, from the certitude within her. As the choking weeps retreated, he was aware of her hands on his skull, at rest, awaiting, her voice hissing out his name, "Jim… Jim… Jim… Jim…" a mantra.

His gasps reduced to steady, profound inhalations, half-snivelled through his nose, her fingers moved down to rest on his ears, not silencing the room from him, but protective. "L'exorcisme," she undertoned. Turning his face up towards hers, "Tell me. Tell me, Jim."

He accepted her scrutiny, now unintimidated to those unwavering eyes. Hands returned to rest in her lap, she was waiting for him to speak. To decide. And he knew then. Certain, yet looking sideways at what he started to say, odd that he should be telling this woman, here in this place, he started to tell her about the boys. It was a factual account, all the information retrieved from a place in his mind he had not known he had stored it in such an orderly manner, ready for the Hearing to come, back home. She remained the calm listener. He told her of the memories of his own childhood, woken in him as bad dreams. Of Mark. And his child-lover. Of Sylvie. At last ended, with no more to tell, he awaited her, looking back long at him, and could only punctuate the silence with, "There you have it. For what it is worth."

"It is worth much. They are fortunate to have you, these boys."

"I'm sure they don't think about me that way. They have their rewards for what they let those men do to them. I am a threat to that. Even Damien walked out on us. And he wanted it to be stopped. He wanted the councillor to be stopped from… what he was doing."

"They will not understand, the boys. Not now. Perhaps some of them may understand. In the future. Perhaps they will never understand. But you must do this thing. And you must do it as it is right for you. Not for Sylvie. Not for your wife and your daughter. Suzanne does not know this, about the boys?"

"No." He reflected, a moment, "It did not seem relevant. Like it is to tell you, Gizande." It was the first time he had spoken her name to her and the whisper it made.

"I think that this affair of the boys has been the reason for difficulty between your wife and you, yes?" He nodded to this, not the whole story of him and Jane, but to speak now would be pedantic. "Your wife- Jane is she named? And your daughter. Their consolation, they have each other. You must do this. With the boys. In the gift to the boys of your support, you are making a gift back to the boy you have been. It is necessary for you to do it." Matter-of-fact and unnegotiable, the concern dealt with, but she saw his retained doubt about what he was returning to. Away from the security of here. "You will also understand about your father. As you said before, you have to go away to understand him."

"I met a man today. Theodore Jacob. He had new stories about my father. Do you know him?"

"Yes."

"Is he an honest man? Are his stories true?"

"Yes. They are true for him. But the truth is complicated. It is simple to know the truth. But it can be complicated to say the truth to people who do not wish to hear."

"Suzanne, she was angry with me for speaking with Jacob."

Gizande just nodded.

Looking at her, he wondered at what she said of truth. He wished to speak on, further into the night with this woman, but there was nothing more for him to say.

She rose. "You must now sleep. You have a very big journey to make in the morning. Very important. Come."

He stood and waited in her gaze. She reached his head down to her lips and kissed his forehead, the same place as before, but held there a moment longer, the least sexual but reassured and sisterly au revoir.

He woke into half-light, unaware at first of her. Sitting on the far edge of the duvet, a tray in her hands. Coffee, its savour filled his nostrils.

"You have slept well."

"I know. No dreams."

"I know. I came in to see. You were calm."

"Haven't you slept?"

"No. I wait near to the telephone. Maurice will make the call when there is news."

"How is Suzanne?"

"She sleeps. I will allow her to remain. She will need to be strong today, I think." He slid up onto his pillows, looked quizzically at her. "They will attack the occupation today. The Gendarmes have blocked the road into the valley so that they may terminate the action. It will happen today, I think."

"But you?" he asked. "You must return to your family."

"I will. Thank you for your concern," she laughed. "My mother will take the children to the bus for the school. It is enough that I am returned to my home in the evening." She offered the tray. "Here. Eat. You need strength for your journey." Coffee jug, croissants, some slices of rough brown bread, cuts of meats.

"You have a lucky husband," he smiled, also aware of the interrogative about this woman's life.

"No. No husband. I have his children. But no longer with him." Unusual for her, she looked away.

"I'm sorry," he muttered. "Not my business."

"No," she looked back at him. "No. Do not be sorry. All men are not gentle. Some try to relieve their pain by making pain for other people. For their women." Would Jane believe he did that, he wondered. To her? "Others know that the relief of your pain- from inside you, is best achieved by the relieving of the pain of others." She pondered the man before her. "Do you understand that, Jim? I think that perhaps you are beginning to." She began to smile at him. Long, warm and deep. Then she stood. "Eat.

Wash. When you have dressed yourself, you are ready to leave, I will have food prepared for you for your journey."

"What about Suzanne? I must say good bye."

She shook her head, "She has other things to do today. She must be strong. I will pass on your greetings to her. She will understand. And you will return, soon."

"Gizande," he called her back as she turned to leave.

"Yes. Jim."

"You keep saying that. So certain that I will return…"

"Yes," she said, neither a statement nor a question.

"How do you know?" And he felt himself smiling, the pleasure creeping through the muscles of his face.

"Because you wish to, Jim. You understand that." And she was gone.

When he came downstairs with his packed bag, she was on the phone. He had not heard it ring. She indicated a large brown paper bag to him on the kitchen table. He unrolled the top. His provisions for the journey. He stood, now his mind turned to the return. Strong with the inevitability of it and what he had to do. As certain that he would close the doors, as this trip to France had shown him that others would open them. And he would walk through.

He waited for her to finish.

"Maurice?" he asked.

"No. Another comrade of ours. Nothing is happening yet." She anticipated his anxiousness. "We will communicate. You will know what has happened to Marie-Claire. Be certain." She smiled, "Come now. You must go. No more talk. Until you come again. To tell us. Va! Terminar! Depart!" She gestured him out to the verandah. He went down into the cold dawn, unlocked the car boot, placing the bag there, then the food on the front passenger seat.

He looked back at her on the top step, the blue overalls luminescent in the first warmth of sunlight coming over the forests to the east, cutting shadows into her face, dark round the eyes, her hair shimmering in a breath of breeze. He could not climb to her there again. They looked across the yard at each other for a long moment. Then, saying no word, he climbed into the car and, in closing the door, was closing it on this episode. For the time being.

Chapter Twenty-two

It was three in the morning when he got home. The house was empty. There were some letters on the hall mat, so Jane was still away. He was so tired from the drive through the night across France, that he stepped over them and went straight upstairs.

He awoke, sour mouthed from undersleep. He lay dead-limbed for a time, staring flatly up at the ceiling with a dull anticipation that he was back here with things to be done. Finally, he slid from bed, deciding to try to get Sylvie first, before she went to work. Sat on the cold bottom step in the hall, the phone rang a long time, before it was answered. By one of the other tenants. He said he thought he'd heard her going out to work already. Jim insisted, so he went and rang her doorbell, came back to the phone and confirmed she was not in.

Jane next? That could wait while he made a mug of tea, a conveniently cowardly delay, he supposed. He had already filled the kettle and gathered what he needed, before he saw the note taped to the oven door. Small and neatly, privately folded, he knew it was from Jane. He peeled it away, unfolded and read:

Dear Jim,

I want a trial separation. The situation is obviously not working out for either of us. I am asking you to find somewhere this week and move out. Take what you need for the time being. We can agree to the details later. Tracey says that I can stay until then.

Jane. Then as an afterthought, *Tuesday.* The day he left France.

The kettle boiled and he mechanically made the tea, then sat at the table and re-read the note. Problems. And opportunities? This week would be a pain, with all the activity of looking for somewhere, a bedsit or flat at best, he supposed. When he had the Disciplinary to prepare for. And what he would do after they sacked him. A job. Then back to the note, staring back up at him from between his fingers holding it flat. How to feel about this? At this moment? Relief? Or what happens to him now, all his locks into the world, home, job, wife, coming apart at the same time?

"Fuck it!" he said aloud and went out to the hall to try Henderson's office, to see if he was in yet.

He was.

"Reporting for Disciplinary Duties," Jim mockingly started.

"Oh, very funny, Jim. We're still stuffed full of bravado about this, are we?"

"Confident, Ronnie. Confident."

"Death wish, I'd call it," the union man said without humour.

"Do I detect that my representative is already going to throw in the towel?"

"You can laugh, but Foley was furious when I told him you were off on your hols."

"Well, I hope you told him how furious we were when he cancelled the original date for the Hearing."

Jim heard Henderson accept the futility of trying to steer him, shifting to, "Well, I hope your holiday refreshed you. Because you haven't half made them angry. Whatever you've been up to with this kid from care, they're steaming."

"My holiday was fine," Jim ignored the rest.

"Anyway, you're getting A1 treatment for your Disciplinary. Foley and Anderson from Children and Families are hearing it."

"Get lost, Ronnie. I'm not having them. There's a conflict of interest there. They were talking to each other about this when it first surfaced. They've got real stuff at stake in all this…" how to sum it up? "…murkiness I've come across. No, not them. It's got to go straight to a Hearing by elected members. The full-time officers are too tainted by it."

Ronnie was silent, then, "Straight to councillors? Can you really justify that?"

"Yes. Definitely."

"Okay. I'll ask."

"Demand, Ronnie? How about demanding?" he said acidly.

Henderson ignored the taunt. "Are you going to tell me the whole story, Jim? What it is that's behind all this to work them up so?"

Jim pondered a moment, then, "I don't know it all myself. A kid comes out of the woodwork. Says he wants to talk to someone. He's being messed with by adults. He wants it to stop. I didn't know he was a care kid. I didn't even know he was a child. Not yet eighteen. Foley carpets me. I write him a report. The social worker comes to see me. Someone's obviously got at him. That's it. Haven't seen the kid since." As much as Henderson needed to know, he reckoned.

"They're talking about papers. About you having some papers. Confidential. What's that about?"

Jim went shifty, exploring what Ronnie might know. "What papers?"

"I don't know. Some confidential papers about kids in care. Foley phoned me yesterday about it. No details, but it was like new evidence against you."

Jim's mind scrambled over this and came hard up against the documents stolen from Sylvie's flat. So Foley knows about that. The chill question that came to him was, who then did the burglary? Under whose instructions? He remembered back to Sylvie's pleading with him not to use the Disciplinary to speak of the boys. What had been said to her? Must speak to her. Phone at work. For Henderson, he simply offered, "I was shown some stuff."

"Who by?"

"No one in the Department."

"What do you mean?"

"What I say. I've seen some documents about abuse. Minutes of meetings. That's all."

"Who from?" Jim could hear the frustration at the other end of the line. "Why couldn't you tell me this before?"

"Didn't seem relevant. It wasn't about Damien Toser, the kid we met."

"We?" Ronnie cut in. "Is that the Northlodge woman you told me about?"

Jim was annoyed that he could not quite recall the boundary between what he had told him and what he had omitted. The price of lying, he thought. So he just offered a non-committal, "Yes."

"Would she be someone called Cathcart?"

Jim stopped, now suddenly watchful of what he said. Frivolity cut out. How to work his way round this one without giving out too much. "Yes. That's her. Sylvia Cathcart. She represents Northlodge on the Housing Working Party. I stand in for Foley on it." He added, with relaxed casualness, "She came to me about it. About Damien." Then, creeping into what more Henderson knew, he proffered, "Why, what are they saying about her?"

"Oh, nothing. Just her name came up in another context, that's all."

Jim knew he would give too much away now if he pressed on about her, so he asked, "What are they saying about documents? That I've got them?" a note of false incredulity in his voice.

"Yes. Something like that. But they're being guarded. Won't tell me what." Then he asked reluctantly, "Are you telling me you haven't got any of these documents they're on about?"

"I don't know. Not till I see what documents they're talking about."

The tired voice at the other end of the line, "Come on, Jim. Be straight with me. You know what they're talking about. Did you keep any of the papers Cathcart showed you?" He paused, then, "You're being as difficult as Foley in telling me what this is all about. I expect that from him. But I'm supposed to be representing you."

"I don't take kindly to be compared with Foley."

"Oh, come on. You know what I mean. You go off on holiday leaving me with the impression that this is just about an error in carrying out the right procedure. But you knew there was more to it." Then pleading, "What do you want me to say? You're just side-stepping me, all the time."

Jim pacified him with, "I will look through what I've got here, Ronnie. I don't think I've got any of the stuff that Cathcart showed me, but I've got so much work stuff here, I'd have to check first." He did not want his union man an enemy at the Disciplinary, but he just wanted to be sure it went the way he was planning it to.

"When will you tell me? Foley's going to put pressure on me to agree a date for the Hearing as soon as he knows you're back."

"Okay." Jim calculated what it would take to sort through for what might be acceptable from the files in the back room. "How about tomorrow? Afternoon?"

Henderson, at the other end, consulting a diary. "Okay. It'll have to be late. Four o'clock okay?"

"Well, as you know. I've got time on my hands, Ronnie."

"Well, if you try to be a bit more co-operative, I can try to make sure that problem is sorted and get you back to work. With just a slap on the wrist."

Just a slap on the wrist? He smirked, before saying, "Fine, Ronnie. See you then. Four," and put the phone down.

He sat a moment, thinking what he could let Henderson see without letting too many cats out of too many bags too early. He retrieved the tepid tea from the kitchen and went through to the back room. The familiar routine of opening the cupboard, unstacking the running bag to get at the files, his diaries on top, to carry them through to the front room where he had the space to spread papers while working on them. Dumped on the coffee table, he started to sort through for the familiar pink folder he had placed the child abuse documents in. Not there. He returned to the back room, looked into the bottom of the cupboard to see if there were any files detached from the stack. Only more running clothing. Restraining anxiety, he returned to the front room and started to methodically take and open each file to check for the child abuse meeting minutes. He noticed that other things were missing. His own notes were still there. But his copy of the Council Child Abuse Procedures was gone too, as well as a file with documents on Disciplinaries and Grievance Procedure. But the pink file, that started to give him real panic. He returned again, uselessly to search the back room and back again to sort through the stack. He tried to remember whether he had done something different after that last night working on the files before he went to France. He had worked late, but thought he could remember putting things away in his routine way.

Would Jane have been in and done anything? But the missing files were so selective… his blood drained down in a whirlpool of accelerating panic. Selective. Taken by someone who knew what to take… like with Sylvie. And her burglary. He wished that she was here with him at this moment, a hand to hold in this fear… but the wish went. He knew the reality with her would be altogether more ambivalent, watchful with doubts.

Back to the stone-faced question of, Who would do this? Who would burgle? And for whom? For Foley? He could not believe that fool had the call on such resources. Bigger players? Jim felt small, even vulnerable at this moment. No one to talk to. No one to check this out with whom he could trust.

He went out into the hall to phone Jane, reckoning that Tracey would be off to work by now.

"Hello?" Jane's voice cautious.

"Me," he said, then the civility of, "How are you?"

She ignored this with the loaded, "Oh. So you're back. At last."

"I've only been away a few days. Just over a week."

"Yes," as if there was no "only" nor "few days" to go with a week. "Did you have a nice time?" A barbed comment from her, not requiring an answer.

"Yes. I mean it gave me time to think. About us," he lied, then, "And other things."

"Oh, yes. Other things," she said wanly. "You read my note?"

"Yes." He paused before saying, a touch too brusque and trite, "I agree."

"With what? The separation? Or that things aren't working out between us?"

"Both. I suppose." Inevitable, but he had not wanted to go here with her. Not now.

"Both? Well that was easy for you, wasn't it?" He could see her cynical smile.

"No. Of course not. But it was your decision. To separate."

"Was it? Someone had to make a decision of some sort. You know I'll want the house. I've put more cash into it anyway, with all those years you were in and out of work. And paid badly when you worked." He read her criticism, not of him as breadwinner, but of his beliefs.

"You said we'd sort out the details later," not now! he thought. "I'll find a place to rent. Sort some of my stuff out."

"It's final for you, isn't it?"

She waited for him. He knew what she meant, but asked, "What's final? What do you mean?"

"It's not a trial separation for you. It's a final one." She gave a short, humourless laugh, "I've given you your freedom. Because you were too cowardly to ask for it yourself." Then, as if bored with the conversation, "Now you can do whatever you like. With whoever you like. But now you won't have to hide it."

"Jane," he half-pleaded, a dishonest gesture. "That's not fair…"

"Isn't it?" Flat with disbelief.

Jim swerved away, into assertion with, "Look. Has any one being messing with my papers? You know the documents. I kept them in the cupboard in the back room."

"Oh, yes. I was going to tell you. We sorted them."

"What!" he cut in.

"Tracey and me. We sorted out the Council documents. You wouldn't do it yourself." Then dealing him a matter-of-fact chop on the back of his brain, "We sorted them out, the official stuff from yours, and Tracey took them down to the Department. Left your own papers at home." A moment before she added, "But then it sounds as if you already know that."

Jim held his voice, while his mind was galloping all over the place with this. "Who did she give the documents to?"

"You'll have to ask Tracey. A woman called Peters, I think."

"Patterson?" he inquired.

"Yes. That's it. Patterson."

"You gave my papers to Patterson?" Disbelievable. But utterly credible, this conversation with the woman he saw for a sudden trice back down the long, drab hallways of their lives together, as the young and righteous girl who had once taken his life in charge.

"You forget, Jim. That is my house, too. You can't keep stolen documents there, without implicating me, too. It's criminal. You shouldn't have them because you're not qualified to judge on that- on the abuse of children."

Jim raged at her, his words knotted with frustration, contempt, "Qualified? You? You're qualified as a teacher. That doesn't qualify you about child abuse!"

"I've had training," she calmly protested. "You forget. These days, we all have in-service training on what to do about children."

He pulled back from the fury he felt, swallowed it sourly back down his throat. The arguments of a social worker. Of people like Flynn, he thought bitterly. To judge and decide on the lives of others. "What do you know, anyway, about the documents I had?" he challenged.

"What do you? We read some of them. They were minutes of meetings about abuse. But did you see the evidence? Of what happened to the kids? What makes you think you can judge?"

"Oh, yes," he sneered. "But you and Tracey can. She's only seventeen, for fuck's sake!" He stopped, backed off again, then resumed, a grudged appeal for reasonableness. "There were other things. Links. You need to see the whole picture to make judgements." Then, feebly defiant, "Anyway, we- I did see the evidence. Met the lad. Interviewed him." Hardly that. From down the distance events seemed to have made since then, he remembered Damien's taut, angry face those few minutes in the Baltic. Jim knew he was right, just as he knew she could only see him as wrong. In this and, now, probably everything.

"On that foundation- your links," she mocked, "you risk your job. The best one you've had for years?"

"What's the choice? To let the abuse go on?"

He became aware that the passion was gone from both of their words. The flat reiteration of their differences. From different ends of that lengthening corridor. "You didn't know the abuse was happening. The words of a troubled boy. It was just speculations you worked up. With this Sylvie. Conspiracy fantasies." Then, "Getting off on them with each other, were you?"

Surprised at her coarseness, he said, "No!" Too rushed a denial to convince, shakily propped up with, "Of course not!" He paused to regroup. "She had this kid come to her. I was the person from Social Services she knew. Of course, she was going to come to me."

"Come to you, did she?" Jane's voice had a dulled dreaminess, before she gathered it up to finish, "Anyway. I don't want to argue. It's fruitless. Those documents are out of my house now. You argue with Social Services about it. And I want you out, too."

"I will," he said, the only fragment of consent he could offer.

"In a week." Not an offer, a statement.

"Okay. Do my best."

"Oh, by the way," she came back.

A guarded, "What?"

"She's eighteen. Tracey's eighteen now. You forgot her birthday."

And the phone clicked her departure.

He sat with it still in his hand, defeated. Then out aloud, angry, "Shit! Shit-shit-shit-shit!" Welcome back, he thought sourly. To the real world. Or was it?

He put the phone down. No run today. Call Julian, for what he could tell Jim was humming on the grapevine about his case. And try to get Sylvie at work.

Julian was genuinely welcoming when he got him, "Hi, Jim. How's it going? When did you get back?"

"Early hours, this morning."

"Not letting the grass grow, eh?"

"No. That's why I'm calling you. Wanted to know what you've heard. About my case."

"Hang about," and there was a pause, where Jim thought he heard the muffle of voices through hand held over mouthpiece. Then, "Look, Jim. I'm going to take this call on a different phone. It's like mayhem in here. Okay? Hang on a moment." He did, left to listen to distant voices, several clicks, then the voices cut off.

"Julian?"

"Yeah. Couldn't talk there. Flynn's in the office. Your friend. He's a bastard. Been mouthing off about you, you know."

"What's he been saying?"

"Oh, you had it coming to you. Can't breach Procedures. You know the style."

"What else have you heard? What's other people saying?"

"Well, the Stewards' Committee is behind you. One or two grumblers. As you'd expect. But Henderson's giving away nothing. You remember I told you that he'd never informed the Committee about your Disciplinary? I confronted him and you know what he said?" No need to answer. "That his hands were tied. He was under instruction by the Regional Officials on your case. And that took priority over our local agreement that Henderson tells us about all Departmental Disciplinaries that come to him. What do you make of that, Jim?"

A sense of the inevitability of what was being put into motion. And it's outcome. "Well, let's put it this way, Julian. The Regional Office was never exactly my nearest and dearest, was it?"

"No. Certainly wasn't," he was answered with a rueful humour. "Oh, the other thing. They've got an outsider in to cover your post. Remember how I said that Foley wasted no time in advertising it? Well, he well and truly fast-tracked it. Someone started in it Monday. I couldn't believe it! Foley's been running down your post, got nothing good to say about it. Then he gets someone in, before you can blink an eye and there's twenty social worker vacancies can't get filled, childcare cases unallocated. It's really pissed some people off!"

"Pisses me off, too. After all the contempt he had for what I did." Then, "Do we know who this outsider is?"

"No. I took it to Henderson, because I reckon that Foley's cut corners in the process to get someone in. Not enough chance for internal applicants. Henderson said the Procedure's been kept to and isn't bothered. Won't tell me if he knows who it is. And she hasn't been seen. Ensconsed in Foley's office, apparently. Oh, all we know is it's a woman." He paused, then, "And, yes. Eyebrows have been raised. Knowing Foley's reputation."

Jim felt angry. Betrayed by those he knew would betray him all along. The job he had made into something. And now, a decision taken that, Jim now gone, the post was so valuable, it went to the top of the list. Foley had his way. So Jim would have his.

"Foley just wanted me out," he said bleakly. "Whatever it took."

"Don't sound so defeated, Jim. That's not like you. The post's only temporarily filled."

"Yes. That's the truth."

"So what happens now, Jim?"

"I've spoken to Henderson this morning. He's going for a date for the Hearing from Foley." He had got what he sought from Julian and wanted to give no more away. What he brought to the Disciplinary must be unexpected. He still had his notes. The key documents had gone. But they knew that he had seen them. They would not underestimate that. "I'll get in contact when I know the date."

"Fine. You know where to get me."

And they rang off.

Next Sylvie. He rang Northlodge and asked for her.

"I'm very sorry. She doesn't work here any more. Can someone else help?" Without response, he dropped the phone rattling back into its cradle, as if it had scorched.

Sylvie. What have you done? The dulled realisation, the dismal, sombre knowledge of having been used. Echoing. Emptied of everything except the inevitability of what he would do next.

He picked up the phone and dialled the number of his own phone in his own office in Social Services. As it rang, he visioned the scarred desk, the dusty bright plastic trays stuffed with papers, the neon striplight, the notice board with a calendar and outdated Union handouts pinned to it. A band of tension wrapped around his skull, pressed above his brows.

"Hello. Sylvia Cathcart here." Sylvia now? So professional and bright.

"Jim, here. Jim Briggs," he added.

"What do you want?" her tone shifted to waspish.

"Well. I wouldn't mind my job back. Sylvi-a," he added, hanging on to the last letter- of her new name. She did not answer. "Well?" he said, after a wait.

Distant, her attempted precision flustered, she postured, "That has nothing to do with me."

"I think it does."

"Your Disciplinary will decide that."

"Oh. So Sylvia Cathcart knows about my Disciplinary, does she? Does she know the outcome of it? Yet."

"Don't be silly, Jim," at last a personal note, an appeal to him.

"Sylvie Cathcart used to think all this had something to do with her." Pause. "I once knew a Sylvie Cathcart. She cared about kids. The boys." No answer, but he caught a sense that she did not dare put down the phone on this. "Did you know that Sylvie?"

"Don't, Jim," a wobble in her throat.

He laughed harshly, then calculated a wait before, "We need to see each other. You don't get out of this mess damage-free, you know. You owe me. You've got the job. I need to see Damien again. I need from you everything you've got about the boys. You owe it to them too."

"Oh, Jim. Be reasonable. How can I-"

He cut into her, "Reasonable? Why? What would that get me?" He clenched each word out, "You. Owe. Me. If you want to get out of this, you need me to help you. Get it?" He added, "I'm not in a reasonable mood. Is that reasonable enough for you?"

"What can I do? Now?" Plaintive with consequences.

"I will see you. Tonight. If you've got anything else on, cancel it. I take priority. For once."

She said nothing, but then he could feel her resentment. "All right. Tonight. But…" She trailed off.

"Nine. I'll come round at nine." Late. Enough time to let her anxiousness work on her. And he put down the phone.

Chapter Twenty-three

Exhausted after the four calls, he had gone back to bed and drifted in and out of sleeps beset with anxiety, finally getting up and running himself a deep, long bath. It was two o'clock before he had gone back to the files and, using the notes in the diary, started to compose what he would say to the Disciplinary.

When he parked in the side street near Sylvie's flat, he sat out the few minutes before nine in the dark car, before he climbed out, locked it, smelt the wet spring night air and walked round to her door.

She opened it, shot him a look, and turned wordless to lead him in. She was wearing her dressing gown and stepped too precisely up the stairs. Drinking, he thought.

He stood in the doorway to the flat. Boxes, as before, but now more of them, with crockery wrapped in newspaper and the bookshelves cleared. "Moving again?" he asked.

"Yes," she said, watchful, but defiant to him.

Uncertain in this her territory, he closed the door quietly behind, but did not sit.

"Drink?" she said, as if his presence here was a demand for her unoffered hospitality. Like a sullen barmaid.

"Yes. Please."

She poured from an open wine bottle. He watched her, a little sad. She came to him with the glass and, "Why don't you sit?" He sat on the arm of the same worn chair she had sat in when he last visited. She saw him perched and waved her glass at him, "Sit. Sit."

"I am, thanks," but slipped down onto the cushions anyway.

She sat. "How was your trip? France, wasn't it?"

"Okay." A taste from the glass, then, "I didn't come here to talk about that."

"Oh, Jim…" feebly.

"Come on, Sylvie. What's been happening?"

"I applied for the job." My job, he thought, without anger. "It's only temporary. Look good on my c.v." She looked at him, watchful through the edge of her hair. "Better me looking after the shop, than any old person. Till you get back."

"Oh? Yes?"

She smiled at him, flicking her hair back. "How was your sister? It was your sister, wasn't it?"

Such a puny attempt to divert, he ignored it. "When were you interviewed for the job? It must've been before I went away." She scowled, attentive to her glass, lips playing along its edge, eyes downward. "Come on, Sylvie. When were you interviewed?" He already had a guess about this.

"I thought you came here to get my help," spitting out the last, "not to interrogate me!"

"I need to trust you," he said, but immediately regretted this appeal.

She leaned out of her chair, unsteadily towards him. "You can, Jim. You know you can." Her gown fell away, a teeshirt beneath showed her legs up to the dark of her sex. He looked, then up to hold her eyes. She looked down, grinned, "Oops!" and smiling back at him, carelessly pulled the gown together.

He shoved away the touch of feigned comedy in this and forced her to look away with, "But can I? Can I trust you?"

"Oh, Jim." Then, harshening, "What do you want me to say? That I shouldn't have taken the job? That I should've stayed here. And at Northlodge? With that leering Hillingdon?"

"You could've told me," his voice coming out too pleading.

"They approached me, you know," she justified. "I didn't chase your precious job. Phil Foley approached me."

Ah, so Phil, as she familiarised Foley, had approached her. He nodded. "Of course he did. What did you expect?"

"Anyway, you didn't care about it. You were always going on about how they didn't care about your work in Social Services. About what you were doing."

"So, what makes it different with you there? Sitting at my desk. Do you think they want you to make a good job of it?" He coldly ended, "Don't make me laugh. It was to shut us up about the boys. To get me out. To get you under their wing."

"I'm not under their wing," and she upped and shuffled to the kitchenette to refill her glass. "More?" she held up the bottle.

"No."

She stood drinking, her back to him, neither speaking for a moment. His eyes set clinically on her. When she turned, she had hold of her face in a serious expression. "Anyway, you shouldn't be here. You should be with Jane. Didn't you tell me she was ill?" An instant of calculation, then looking at her glass, "I feel bad about her. Us. It shouldn't've happened. Betrayed another woman. I'm sure she must guess."

The feminist option? Jim thought. Then a moment of self-pity welled, a wish for her warm flesh, so available for him if he wanted tonight, he was sure. But not offered for himself, he knew. No, he should not be here. Would not be here. But. So he said bluntly, "I'm not here for sex. I'm here about the boys."

"Who said anything about sex?" There was a primness, a sense of theatrical indignation from her, almost laughable.

He smiled briefly, despite himself, at this child-in-drink, still fond of whom she had been. Then, gravely, "I want you to get me in touch with Damien Toser again." She looked at him, hunted by him, gulped the glass again. He put his glass down. "Well?"

"I can't," and saying this, turned her eyes towards him pleading, a tear trickling down her cheek. Shuffling back towards him, to her chair. "Please, Jim." Snuffle. "I can't."

"Why not?"

"I don't know where he is." A weak deceit. "Not now." She wiped her nose with the back of her hand.

"No?" Eyes to eyes, he let the intermission work on her, the plea there crumbling inwards, as her face fell weeping behind the curtain of her hair. He pressed on, "Give me the last address he moved to. He moved from Northlodge didn't he? I'll work out the rest." Her face was in her hands, trying to stem back the sobs. Like the night with her in Bradford, the pain of now, but something also dragging in from somewhere else, her fingers rising up through the tangles of hair, pulling her head down onto her knees. Crouched and broken, her back heaving, ugly little cries from deep within.

To touch her? Or not. Or wait out the tears? He continued to sit watching. Her pain. From another place. About this, now. But about other things. Remote from her with his unwllingness, but also his inability to do anything about it.

It was a long time. The tide of weeping ebbed. Her breathing evened. She remained. Crouched and foetal, quiet at last. A halt, a discontinuity in time, then slowly, she unfolded. Sat up. Stared into the untidy room. Briefly across with dead eyes at Jim. Picked up her glass, pushed herself uncertainly onto her feet and weaved her way between boxes into her bedroom. He was still sat there, staring at the space she had filled on the chair, when she reappeared, picked up the open bottle and an unopened one with the corkscrew, and went back her arms cluttered. Not looking at Jim once. He remained where he was a long time. There was the clink of glass from nextdoor. Then quiet. He noticed the sounds outside. A car. A whoosh of wind in a nearby tree. Footsteps and a laugh.

Silent so long, he noiselessly stood and stepped carefully to the bedroom door. She was across the tumbled bedding, wrapped tight in the robe, head propped up on a pillow, glass resting between her breasts. She opened her eyes at him standing there.

"Hello." She spoke as if he had just appeared. A welcoming and childlike smile.

"Hello," was all he could say to that.

She patted the bed beside her, inviting him, the gesture reminding him. Of something? He hesitated, but then relented. On the edge, sat away from her. Her hand found his, but he left it limp within hers. She emptied her glass, put it aside and curled over towards him, drawing his hand to her, up against her warm face, where he could no longer see it beneath her fallen hair. Eyelashes against knuckles, perhaps nose then lips and, without showing her face from under the hair, a small voice, uncertain and hesitant, "I love you, Jim." A stillness. "I do."

"Sylvie. You lied to me."

His hand gripped against her face harder, "No, I didn't. I never lied to you."

"You lied. By the things you have not been telling me. Lied by omission." Then, "Sylvie, you're making some shit life decisions."

"No, Jim," starting tears again. "Jim, I love you." She half raised her head to look and, finding him looking down on her passive and disengaged, still waiting for truth from her, she rolled away, taking his hand gripped in hers with her. He was pulled down to lie against her back, heaving again with weeping, the hot tears on his clutched hand. Reluctantly, he rubbed her shoulder with his free hand to calm her. Gently, fingers across the silk robe, the knobs of bone beneath, her heaves of sorrow eased, she quieted.

They lay there for a time. Very slowly, she turned round, still holding his hand and curled up against him, face down, her hair against his shirt. She released the hand and he felt her fingers at his trousers, unclipped his belt and was tugging at the zip, before he reached past her and pulled her hands away.

"No, Sylvie. No," angry at his own arousal.

She pushed her hair slowly aside to look up at him and smile, both mischievous and uncertain. "Oh, yes," and her hands were at him again.

He pulled them away, "I said, no, Sylvie," pushing himself away, up on to his elbow at the edge of the bed.

She drew her gown back, drawn back like curtains opening her nakednaess, "Don't you love my body?" She tugged and slipped her teeshirt up above her breasts, "I've got a nice body. Haven't I, Jim?" From laying so close to him, her full length nudity foreshortened her body to child-size. He deliberately disengaged her fingers from the teeshirt and pulled it down over her, drawing the robe across her legs. With care and sadness.

She closed her eyes, reopened them for a last look at him, before rolling away again, to weep again, this time loud with distress and anger. Between each stuttering sob, a long, deep breath filled the shape of her back, to shudder it out, the body crumpling in upon itself. Again and again. It seemed for hours, Jim waiting there, watching, powerless, propped across the knotted sheets from her.

It was some time before he realised she was saying something. To herself? Or to him? He leaned across to her hoarse whispering… a few words at first, some half swallowed in gasping inhalations… "…called me a whore… not my fault… blamed me… was the child… how could my mother… told me I was a liar… accuse my father… because it was him… did it when she was out at work… my mother… never forgive… abortion at twelve…" She pushed her face upwards, out of her tangled, wet hair, towards the far corner of the room, unseeing, the half profile to Jim, its skin collapsed and ghastly with the grief, poxed with the discomposition of her spirit, she finally cried out, both question and protest, "How could she call me a whore?" And sank slowly into the bedclothes with, "I was only twelve…"

He stayed, uncomfortable, frozen with what he had watched, on the mattress edge, eyes on her body. Until, at last, the even movement of her back showed sleep. With immense delicacy, he rose, picked up the edge of the duvet and drew it slowly over her. As he did so, she snuggled into it, pulling it round her face, still eyes closed, but smiling.

He quietly went into the living room and sat. Listening for her breathing. Then, reassured by the faint sound, he pondered the night. Her pain. The family she had never really spoken of. The tears the night in Bradford. But then not spoken. Did he believe her? Probably. For the most part anyway. But whatever the cause, the result was the same. The treachery and cunning learnt to survive. And learning to live with the consequences. To herself of her actions, now against others.

He quietly poured himself a drink of orange from a carton in the fridge. The cold liquid rinsed his throat, a cleansing. He sat for a long time in that room. Sipping and thinking. Until he could no longer hear her breathing. He crept into the bedroom. She was now lying along the bed edge where he had been. Eyes closed, she waved a hand at him.

"I'm going now, Sylvie," he whispered. "Are you all right?"

Her hand paddled again, eyes still closed, "I'm all right," in the voice of a small girl.

Turning off all the lights, bar one above the kitchenette, a little light in at the bedroom door, he left, closing the flat door with infinite care.

He drove to the sea front, parking where he could faintly see the white of breakers at the edge of the throw from the street lights along the Promenade. He remembered something from the book on abuse he had read. One in every ten is a victim of child abuse. Thinking of Sylvie. Of Damien. Of himself. He asked himself, where were the other nine? Abuse was a thing he had never considered for himself. Had put away his own memories, in fact. But now it seemed to fill his life.

An old man walked a dog, his face, turned to scrutinise Jim's car, was lined with life. An old retired docker, maybe? He looked at his watch. One o'clock! Time to walk a dog? He smiled at the independence of it.

Perhaps abuse comes and seeks you out if you work in Social Services. Maybe the carers and the cared for are all victims. Both seeking the care of each other. He remembered something Gizande had said- was it about relieving your pain by relieving the pain of others? Maybe that's what social working is all about, he thought, victims seeking out other victims and easing their own pain by helping them. Wasted childhoods, past and present, sat across the interview desks from each other. How on earth did he get here, among them? he wondered ruefully. Maybe he had been drawn there, unknowingly. A place his life needed him to visit.

He wound down the window, to suck the sea air deep into his body. Well, it's a passage in his life all but closed. Bar the shouting. Sat here at this shore, he knew he was no longer lonely, that state of dependence on those not there, the impossible relationships, the unavailable warmth. His was solitude. Inner dependence to set him apart and see him through. The next week. And then?

Chapter Twenty-four

He could not sleep when he got back home. Away from her, away from her closeted and dark sorrow, he was angry. With her deceit. With her ambition and her abandonment of him, retreating from him behind her cloak of victimhood. She had gone. And left him without Damien, without her evidence. Now he wondered if she had ever been there. It all felt like a set-up.

He surrendered to wakefulness about five o'clock, with the first birdsong outside. He got up, rooted around for running kit, put it on, stretched his legs and went out into the cold morning. It was less than a month to the marathon. He should now be running his longest training runs, but he had slipped back with the disruptions in his life. His mind on Sylvie, rewinding that last scene interwoven with others, he ran onto minor roads, finally the lanes of that strange, flat area that led behind the marshes lining the estuary, some decayed looking farms, but mostly acres of coarse tufted grass drained by mud streams across towards the distant, dirty tide. Disturbed from undergrowth the other side of the rotten-posted wire fence, a cloud of small birds rose, gathered and curved away towards the river. He felt freed. By others' disloyalties. There was nothing he could not do. He would summon Sylvie as a witness. Force her to confront him. And herself.

The track ran up to a broken gate and, beyond it wound nowhere into the marshland flats. He turned to return, inattentive to his running, working his head through an agenda for his four o'clock meeting with Henderson.

The Union office was the top floor of the Council's Highways Department. Kathy, the administrator greeted him warmly, as usual. Asking after Jane, whom she had met at Union functions when he had been active. Ronnie was waiting and he went straight in.

"Well. We've got a date and you've got your Councillor Panel," Henderson smiled, as if it had all been his own idea. "It's next Wednesday. They'll tell me on Monday who's on the Panel."

"Not all Tories, mind," Jim growled with half a joke.

"No. Not all Tories. Then, I've heard some of your worst enemies are in your own Party."

"My own Party?" Jim mused aloud. Is that what it was? Then to Ronnie, "Probably."

"Anyway. Business. Have you got those documents you were going to show me?"

He had thought over his answer to this long through the day. He had not wanted to display the dissent in his own family. He had always been quite private about his home life, but he saw no alternative to blunt truth on this. They had the documents. They knew Tracey had brought them in. Henderson would have to know.

"No. Problem there, Ronnie," Jim started, already feeling foolish, his display of certainty to this man he scorned, now undermined. Henderson's eyebrows were raised, theatrically. "Jane did some clearing up while I was away. Found a stack of the Council documents and returned them. To Social Services." Then cutting across any evasion, "She doesn't agree with what I'm doing. This stand." He would have softened this with something about her thinking she was doing this for Jim's own good, but recoiled against anything confessional with this man.

"A row, then?" Ronnie explored.

"Could say so." Then asserted, "But I've got full notes on all the key documents. The stuff on the abuse. Detailed. Dates of meetings, names of some of the people there. Initials of the kids." He knew though, that it was nothing to the documents themselves.

After a moment looking down at his pad, Henderson eyed Jim uneasily. "You don't make it easy, do you Jim? None of this." He sat back, a display of the complacency that Jim needed him, but watchful. "You know that Foley and Anderson are going to be witnesses against you. And it'll be Gross Misconduct. They're going for Dismissal."

"Not surprised. It's too big. They need to get me as far away as possible from their files. And secrets." Then grunted, adding, "If they haven't shredded them already."

"I can't accept that. All this conspiracy stuff of yours."

"Okay. Let's call our own witnesses. First, Sylvia Cathcart- and you needn't be shifty with me about it. I know she's got my job. You knew that yesterday, when I phoned you, didn't you?" Henderson nodded. "Why didn't you tell me? I only had to phone my own extension in the Department and she bloody well answered, didn't she!"

The official looked cowed when he excused feebly, "It's part of a current application to management. How her appointment was handled."

"Well." Contempt. "Don't you think I deserved to know? After all, it was my job."

"You don't have a right to know. She's a Union member too." Then, as a tail end, "She's only temporary. Until you get back there."

"Christ, Ronnie! You don't believe that!" No response, so Jim continued, "Get her on the stand. She knows. She gave me the documents.

From the Northlodge files. She set up the meeting with Damien Toser. She was there- let's see what she's got to say about that!"

"Okay. Okay. Cool down. I'll ask. For her as a witness." As a man knowing the limited realities of what's achievable, he added, "I can only ask."

"You can bloody well do more that that! You can demand. Now she works for the Council."

"Okay. I said, okay."

"And. I want you to ask for Toser, too. He knows how the meeting happened. He came to us. For help. To stop the abuse."

Henderson hesitated, before saying, "I'll ask. But he's a kid. I've never known it happen. A child as a witness at a Disciplinary?"

"Well, ask. At least, it sets our stall out." Then, trying to include the man, "Doesn't it, Ronnie?"

"I don't know, Jim," relaxing now the hostility was over. "It's a mess. Look at it. I mean, if you were representing someone who came to you with this, how happy would you be? Documents missing. Witnesses they may be able to block. It's not exactly a copper-bottomed case, is it?"

"No," Jim laughed, "more like hairy-arsed, wouldn't you say?" Not sure where that had come from, he seriousced, "But it's important."

"So you say. You haven't really told me anything about it yet. Just bits. It's getting late. It's Friday. I told Kathy I'd need her to stay late. But there's a limit to how late. And we need to start getting something down on paper. Are you all right if she comes in and takes it down shorthand? Otherwise, it's me writing it down. Tortoise pace"

"Fine with that," Jim agreed. "She's a good woman. I trust her." And another person to hear the whole story. For her, beneath the professional discretion of her trade, with a young family, another witness to store the awful story herself. Henderson called her in and she smiled at Jim as she sat wordless, pen poised above paper.

When Kathy finally let him out into the street, it was past six o'clock. She smiled, with a special "Good luck, Jim," to him and he was liberated out into the weekend. The story now laid somewhere else. With others to do something about the boys. Even if just to live with their own silent inaction.

Tomorrow, he had to hunt for flats, so he bought the Chronicle. By the time he had called all the numbers ringed in biro down the small-ad columns of the property pages, he had four places to see on Saturday and he was stiff from sitting in the hall by the phone. They had always intended to move it into the front room. Another thing they had not got around to.

Saturday was an irritating day. The last flat was a small two room attic, sloping rooves, beams to walk your skull into and dark with tiny windows. The landlord was a large man, aggressively dismissive in his tone, as if he had spent too many wet Saturdays wasting his time with people like Jim. There was a reluctant dispute between them about when the tenancy commenced and Jim could be given the keys. The landlord finally and sourly handed over the keys, with Jim to start paying rent next week.

That evening, he phoned Tracey.

"It's Dad."

"I'll get Mum," she swiftly put the phone down. Before he could say anything else.

"Yes." Jane, no inquiry of what he wanted, just a flat acknowledgement that he was there.

"I've got a flat."

"Well done." Expressionlessness defied content.

"I can't move in till Thursday. At the earliest."

Pause. "Okay."

"I'll let you know what I take. From home"

"You can have the record player. I've bought my own." He wondered at the life she was leading now, over at Tracey's. Buying a new record player? The records and tapes at home were hers anyway. "You'll have to get your own telly," she continued.

"Okay." There was little enough that they had shared anyway the last few years, he thought. Few? Probably longer than that. Then he said, "My Disciplinary is on Wednesday. You said you'd like to come?" Hesitant, unsure of what having her there would mean. How it would shape what he would say. Or sat outside the Panel Room, waiting alongside Sylvie?

"I can't. I'm back at work."

So soon? he thought. "Where? I thought your post had gone."

"Education phoned me up. I've got a job at Headquarters. Developing practice. For the new National Curriculum."

"Okay," Jim said quietly, the withdrawn offer of support final. Of other things, too. Then, assertive himself, he ended with, "Okay. I'll call when I've got everything moved out," and, as he moved to put the phone down, he sensed a wordless appeal from her, across the distance of the call. Back to his ear, he listened, a moment of them both listening to the silence between them. Then the click at her end.

Chapter Twenty-five

He had returned from his run and was drying after showering, when Henderson called on Monday morning.

"Nice and early, Ronnie."

"What do want first? Good news or bad news?" Henderson asked, trying to pick up Jim's light tone.

"Well, that's a cheery start. Thanks. Would we agree, Ronnie, on which was which?"

"Okay. First. No Damien Toser as witness. As a child in care, too vulnerable. They tell me."

"No surprise there. But I'm sure I could get through to him, if I knew where he was."

"Don't even think about it. They'll be down on you like a ton of bricks."

"Maybe."

"Sylvia Cathcart." Jim alerted to him. "No go on that, either."

"Ah! That's crap!" Jim blew.

"Okay. So you say," Ronnie said to pacify. "Her legal advice is that as she didn't work for the Council when the alleged meeting with Toser took-"

"Alleged! Fucking alleged now, is it? The lying bitch!" His head gripped with the anger of it, yet the inevitability, too. Its predetermined inescapability.

"Are you gonna let me finish first, before you blow off?" A wait before continuing, "Her legal advice is that the Council has no right to call her as a witness to the Disciplinary, because she was not an employee at the time of the meeting."

"Shit!" Then, the heat gone, "Whose legal advice would that be? The Council's? Or the Union's?"

"It wasn't from me," Henderson edged with pleading.

"Which means it was the Union. Regional Office, I'd bet. I've heard they're taking an unhealthy interest in my case."

"Where've you heard that?"

With penetrating precision, Jim replied, "You are not the only ally I have in this- if that's what you are, Ronnie. I still have my sources of information. I know the social worker lobby doesn't like me, but some people still talk to me, you know."

"Anyway, do you want to hear the good news?"

"Not before you confirm. It's been Regional Office advising Sylvie Cathcart, has it?"

"I wouldn't know that." And added, woodenly, "And I'd be unable to tell you, even if I knew."

"I'll take that as a yes. Well, what's your good news? If that's what it is."

"You've got Tony Wood on your Panel. Not bad, eh?" Jim knew Tony from the Party. An old shop steward like he had been. In a chemicals plant. Not much active now but, when challenged in the right way, he could be depended upon to produce his old-time militant credentials.

"Could be worse," Jim grudged. "But Ronnie. Are you saying there's no chance of getting Cathcart on the stand?"

"No chance. That's what I'm told."

Taking his orders. From further up the Union machine, he knew, but said, beyond the hope, "I really need her evidence. She was there."

"Well, without those papers… you lost… you're going to have to convince the Panel by the sincerity of your tone. Tony Wood should be easy. But the other two? A Tory and a Social Democrat."

"Who's the Tory?" thinking, surely Jeffreys wouldn't have the brass neck to volunteer himself?

"Ferguson. New bloke. Don't know him."

Neither did Jim. He was feeling dulled by it all. It felt as if everything was being put in place by the other side to stifle him. He had expected this, anticipated this in a remote, amused and cerebral way. But the reality hurt. With the crude severance of relationships it entailed. Tracey. Jane. And now Sylvie. Most of all, though most expected.

Ronnie had been talking on about the arrangements for Wednesday morning and he had to ask him to repeat. Something in Jim's tone prompted Henderson to ask, "Are you okay, Jim?"

"Yes," his mind elsewhere. "See you Wednesday."

Immediately, he pressed the cradle and redialled.

"Hello. Social Services." Not her voice.

"Is Sylvie Cathcart there?"

"Who's calling?"

"Who are you? I dialled direct to her extension."

"I am taking Miss Cathcart's calls. Can I ask who's calling?"

"Tell her Jim Briggs."

The phone went onto hold in his ear. He tried to imagine what was happening. Someone to answer her calls? That was a very sudden enhancement of the job since he had left, he mused. Must be her friend

Foley. Phil, he remembered sourly. A twist of sexual betrayal surprised him. Leaving her options open. And her legs.

Then, back on the phone, "Miss Cathcart is not available."

He laughed, caught by where his mind had been. "Isn't she?" Then, expressionless, "Tell her to phone me. At her leisure. She knows my number." Adding, "Jim Briggs."

That night, he waited until eight o'clock, before driving round to her flat. As he rang the bell, one of the other residents came out.

"Who you looking for?"

"Sylvie. Sylvie Cathcart."

He gave a knowing grin, "You've had it there, mate. She's moved."

"Where to?"

He shrugged. "Got to go," he said, but stood at the half-open door, as if interested in what this middleaged and disappointed lover was going to do next. "Landlord'll know, s'pose. But if she didn't tell you, why should he?" It was a taunt.

Jim pushed past him up the stairs to her door and knocked with hard, controlled wrath.

"I told you. She's moved," the tenant called from downstairs.

Jim listened to the door. Silence. Of course.

A moment, head at rest on the flaked panelling, the image jumped to him of how many boxes of possessions she would have had to haul down to the street, watching she was not caught. Nomads both of them, he thought, as she headed further out loaded down with doubts, fears, ambitions. And he was finding a route out of it, a touch fearful, but a little lightened with every step. He smiled to himself, turned, ran down and out the door, past the laughing young man, into the street and away.

Wednesday morning, he decided to forgo his run. He rose early and took a long, reflective bath. He was dressing when he heard the post. Attention to tie knot. Slightly pink shirt, slashed by a red tie, his gesture against male and bureaucratic uniform. Dark suit jacket on, a brush of the hand for flecks and he went downstairs. One letter. From France. Suzanne's writing, he believed. He took it into the kitchen and lay it in the centre of the table, while he made a mug of tea, looking back at the envelope there, unable to stop himself smiling. Good for her! What timing. Just on the right day.

He sat and opened it carefully. A letter. Another envelope folded inside. And a book of matches. He picked this last up to examine. Three flags on the front, France, USA, Britain, with the slogan, *Chaque Francais est un soldat de la Liberation!* Turned over, there was a crude map of France with red rail lines and Paris marked. Inside was written *Derailler Les Trains Nazis,* with simple instructions how to derail a train using a wedge in the rail. He looked at the enclosed envelope. *JIM* written in erect, precise letters, nothing else.

He read Suzanne's.

My dear Jim, I am extremely shamed that I did not awake to say au revoir to you when you were departing. I do not have Marie-Claire to assist me in the writing of English for you. So I excuse me for this letter. Marie-Claire has become imprisoned by the government. The gendarmes entered the occupation with much violence. She has not harmed, but we have been told that Felipe is much injured. That he is within the hospital within the prison. Marie-Claire is within the prison at Toulouse. Maurice and me have been to visit her. She says to us that the spirit of the prisoners of the occupation is very good. We hear the singing of political songs from the prisoners when we made the visit. We have hope. It has been a great scandal that the gendarmes acted with such violence. Many have come to the valley to make protest. The gendarmes will not permit them up to the village, but these are so many crowds on the road that the construction vehicles have great difficulty in making the entrance and commencing the work to make the lake. Questions are also being asked in Paris of the politicians. I am unquiet for my daughter but much is being planned to ensure their freedom soon. I hope we will see you soon. I think so. The letter accompanying this from Gizande will explain.

Ah, Gizande, he warmed with that.

It was a very good time that you passed among us. I am thinking often of you and the difficulties you are confronting on your return to England. I have placed in the envelope also the matches. They were a rememberance from our father of the war and the Resistance. They are for you, for you should have something to remember that good man you never knew.

Maurice and me and Marie-Claire send our love.

To My Beloved Brother,

From Suzanne.

He went straight to Gizande's envelope and tore it open. Two sheets held together with a simple pin.

Jim. You may remember that I said a procession was planned from Spain through the high passes into the valley in order to protest against the destruction. The governments of Madrid and Paris have conspired to prohibit such a procession. The clarity of her steady gaze bore into his head as he read. *There have been discussions with the organisations for running. They are sympathetic to the cause of ecology. We have organised a running that will take us up into the hills close to the valley that is to be drowned. Many wish to join us who are not serious runners, but can perhaps run along the roads. It has become an ecological event, not a race. We hope that the strong will be able to help the weak.* He speculated which was he, never having run on serious hills, even less the Pyrenees? *It will be in five weekends from when I am writing this letter to you. You will come?*

I also remember that you will be going through much difficulty at the time you receive this letter. You have your strength. I know that you are only recently discovering it. In your past, you have permitted others to speak their words for you. I believe that the search for your father has made you strong. You have not found him yet. When you find him, you will find yourself. Suzanne has said to me how you listen to the music of Casals. He was a friend of our family also and he was wise in other things. You will see this from the words of his I have attached to this letter. You understand that I have seen this within you and know this to be true. You have joked at me sometimes because you may on occasion fear to find your own strength. Do not fear. Enjoy it. It is your gift.

Till we see you again, my love and my pride at having your acquaintance.

Gizande.

His fingertips quivering at the edge of the paper, he sat there hot and transfixed by her words. For a long time, eyes unseeing cast down on the page. Before he refocussed them and turned it over to the attached sheet. The typed page read:

you are a marvel.

every second we live is a new and unique moment of the universe that will never be again… and what do we teach our children? that two and two makes four, and that paris is the capital of france.

we should say to each of them: do you know what you are? you are a marvel. you are unique. in all the years that have passed, there has never been another child like you. your legs, your arms, your clever fingers, the way you move. you may become a shakespeare, a michelangelo, a beethoven. you have the capacity for anything. yes, you are a marvel. and when you grow up, can you then harm another who is, like you, a marvel?

we must all work to make the world worthy of its children.

pau casals

Written in her hand, below, *Bear these words with you.*

He reread it. Then he returned to the words of her letter again, savouring them, but shy with disbelief at this barely-known woman's words. Weak as at the moment of being faced squarely by her intuitive gaze. That much belief from someone else, must earn him so much for himself. That strong? Perhaps. Certainly, it was himself, alone, on this one. His own self. A stand on behalf of some boys- apart from Damien and Finch, only initials- he would give of his self this morning. The self he was becoming. From out of that frightened boy in an overheated room, all those years ago.

Chapter Twenty-six

He arrived early, expressionless at knowing he was being silently and covertly watched. By the Town Hall porter and, when he had found a seat outside the Members' Committee Room, by staff who recognised him, passing by along the corridor. His case on his knees containing only his four sheets of commentary prepared for this, the notebook and a pad.

Ronnie arrived just after Mrs. Patterson swept past into the Committee Room, document bundles clasped to her breasts, an office boy with a further box of files in her wake. Henderson sat beside Jim. "Just been given this by Patterson," handing a typed sheet over.

Headed, *Statement by Damien Ian Toser,* it read on:

1. I, Damien Ian Toser, of- the address had been deleted- *make the following Statement, which I believe to be true and I understand may be placed before a Meeting of the Borough Council Employment and Disciplinary Panel. This Statement was made of my own free will and at my own request. I have not recorded and am unable to recall the exact dates of these events.*

2. In late 1985, I was approached by Miss Sylvia Cathcart, Senior Housing Officer of Northlodge Community Housing Association. I was then living as a tenant in one of their properties, Ratcliffe House. Miss Cathcart said she had been asked by Mr. James Briggs, an Officer from the Social Services Department, to request that I meet him to discuss certain matters.

3. I was not informed by Miss Cathcart what these matters were and, when I asked her, she said that she herself was unable to tell me, as Mr. Briggs had told her he was unable to disclose this to her at this time. I was reluctant therefore to attend such a meeting with Mr. Briggs, where I would not be privy in advance to the intended subject and content of the proposed meeting. However, Miss Cathcart reassured me that she would accompany me to the meeting with Mr. Briggs to ensure that I would not be subject to inappropriate pressure or harassment, should that happen. As I have previously received good support from Miss Cathcart on other matters, I agreed to attend on the condition of her attendance with me.

4. The meeting took place in the Baltic Fleet Hotel, Windlass Street. Present were myself, Miss Cathcart and Mr. Briggs. He informed me that he had received reports that some residents were being subjected to abuse within Ratcliffe House. I replied that I was unaware of any such thing taking place. Being clearly not satisfied with my answers, he pressed me on this. I found his manner intimidatory and threatening. After a time, I told him that I intended to terminate the meeting and leave. He attempted to prevent this, but I insisted and left.

5. The following day Miss Cathcart apologised to me for the meeting and any upset it may have caused. I have had no communication with Mr. Briggs since.

It was signed and dated in that spiky and uncertain handwriting. Well, that was authentic, at least, Jim thought and handed it back to Ronnie, with distaste and the flat comment, "Lies. They got at him. Is he appearing as a witness?"

Henderson shook his head. "No. Same reasons they gave us. Too vulnerable."

"Well. It's worthless. Without us being allowed to cross-examine."

"We'll see." He paused. Jim could see that he was nervous. "How do you want to play this, Jim?"

"Straight."

"No. Come on. I mean, how do you want to run our side of things. Shall I cross-examine their witnesses? Do you want to sum up or shall I?"

Jim reflected. It was becoming such a patent fit-up, it was no longer about winning or losing. It was about what went on the record. Bearing witness. And preparing for an appeal. Going to an Industrial Tribunal, maybe. "I'll sum up," he said finally.

"I'll do the witnesses, then."

"Will you really, Ronnie?"

"What do you mean?"

"Will you really be able to do them? After all, it's well fixed in advance, this." He gazed at the other man. Recognising bits of whom he had once been. Ducking and diving for miniscule results from the edges of a system that continued grinding out huge and global injustices.

"Come on, Jim," Ronnie came back with joviality. "You- of all people- know the game! You keep in there fighting…" trailing off at Jim's continued and unblinking eyes.

"For what? You don't really believe I'll get my job back from this lot. Do you?" Wondering what he would do if- by bizarre mischance- he was to be offered it back.

"Are you saying you want to pack in? To resign?"

"No. I don't want to pack it in. I just doubt that any of this is about me getting my job or not."

Ronnie was still looking back, quizzical, unfathoming Jim's other language, when Patterson's office boy came up, handed Henderson a folded note and left quickly, a furtive glance at the pair. The Union official shook his head and passed it over. "Wood's not on the Panel. Been replaced by Sinclair. Do you know him?"

Jim had once been introduced to him. A new Labour councillor. A different breed. Self-assured and patronising. A barrister. They had not liked each other, instinctively. "Yes," he said simply.

"Not good. Too friendly with the other side. He'll steer things, being a legal man. See how the Social Democrat, Empson, goes on it. Him and Sinclair will probably go together." Jim listened to Ronnie's calculations. But said nothing.

When they were summoned in by Patterson, Sinclair greeted them with over-courteous restraint. Three long tables, one for the Panel, one for Patterson and her boy, one, facing her, for Jim and Ronnie. Three sides of a rectangle, the fourth, a small table and chair for witnesses.

Jim sat, arms resting on his unopened case, fingers gently locked across it. He watched, as if from afar, the self-importance of documentation passed out, tidied, sorted, murmured over. He lifted his arms to let Patterson's boy place a stapled bundle on the case, then lowered them to rest, without looking down. Aware that Ronnie was looking at him, uncomfortably.

"I think we all know why we are here today," Sinclair opened in his slight, fluty voice.

Nods. From everyone. Except Jim, his view drifted out of the full-length windows to the shadowy, indistinct play of light from the silver birches on the grass banking outside, in onto the grubby net curtains stirred by the warm, stale air of this room. Brought back to this particular reality by Patterson's silhouetted foreground to this, her head declined respectfully towards the Panel.

Her deference returned with, "Mrs. Patterson?" from Sinclair.

She stood and read to him from a sheet. The charges. Breach of Child Abuse Procedures. Inappropriate Intervention in the Case of a Child in Care. Failure to Properly Consult with his Line Manager. Failure to Disclose Sources of Allegations Concerning Acts that may be Criminal. Obtaining Access to and Secreting Confidential Documents outside the Responsibilities or Duties of the Post he holds. She ended with, "The Borough Council maintains that the matters before this Panel conform to Breaches of Contract by this Employee that constitute Gross Misconduct and may warrant the Immediate Termination of James Brigg's Contract of Employment and his Immediate Dismissal." She planted her fingers on top of her files, leaning over them a moment for effect, then looked up, straight at Jim, the certainty of her stance speaking for what could not be seen from the backlit sunlight. "We will be calling three witnesses. Mr. Foley, Assistant Director for Adult and Community Services in the Social Services Department. Mr. Anderson, Assistant Director for Children and Family Services in the Social Services Department. Mr. Flynn, who also works for Social Services and is a Qualified Social Worker." Another pause for impact. "He is the Social Worker Responsible for the Care of Damien

Toser, the Child in Care who is at the Centre of this Case." A dignified nod to the Panel and she sat down.

Sinclair looked over to Henderson. "We will be opposing this."

"Of course," Sinclair put in.

"We requested two witnesses. But we have been told that neither can attend." Can attend? Jim reacted. Denied them, more like.

Henderson retreated back onto his seat, as Patterson stood up to say, "The Borough carefully considered these requests and took external legal advice before deciding that the requests for the two witnesses to attend were not possible. In one case, the requested witness, Miss Cathcart was not an employee, at the time she was required to give evidence on."

"But she is now," Jim spoke expressionless, to no one in the room in particular. Patterson looked to Sinclair for guidance. For support.

"Pardon?" he asked, patient with the interruption.

"I said. She is an employee now." Only then did Jim look across at the Panel.

"We are aware of that. However, that does not instrumentally change the issue. We do not have the powers to summon her to this Panel. On an issue that does not involve her employment by this local authority." Turning away, "Pray continue, Mrs. Patterson."

"The other requested witness was Damien Toser. As the Panel Members will be aware, he was at the time a child in the Care of this Authority. It was decided, following consultation with Damien's social worker, that he would be too vulnerable to be exposed to cross-examination. The Panel will have the opportunity to hear from Mr. Flynn later in this Hearing." Then, smiling directly at Sinclair, "However, we have succeeded in gaining a Statement from Mr. Toser, which you all have before you in the bundle of papers."

Henderson was up on his feet. "Are we to understand that Toser is no longer a child in care? Is he a child, still?"

Patterson, still standing, said quietly, "I understand that Mr. Toser has recently had his birthday. He is eighteen."

"Therefore, now an adult," Ronnie challenged. "And able to speak for himself. Why were we not told this?"

"He is still a vulnerable adult. I am informed he still continues to receive support and services from the Social Services Department. Mr. Flynn will explain this."

Sinclair leaned across, first to one, then to the other of his fellow councillors, then said to Henderson, "The Panel Members are satisfied that every attempt has been made to secure the witnesses you requested and these matters would not be served by further delay." A whip of a glance at

Jim, before turning back to Patterson. The predictability of every step taken in this room had the shape of an ensemble script. Jim knew he no longer had a place here or time worth spending rehearsing these rituals. Watching for the imminence of judgement. How often had he been wheeled into a room similar to this? To hear the voice of modest reasonableness state the inevitable. As if there had been a choice on offer to anyone else in the room. Only Jim had made the choice here and, in choosing, debarred himself from any part in the decision.

Foley was called. Jim watched that posturing man from afar, him and the rest as if through smoked glass. He stood, reading from his Statement, assembling a picture of Jim as resistant to authority, a maverick, then deceitful, undermining the good intentions of himself and other Officers and the Statutory Requirements that the Department carried out on behalf of Central Government. For the Protection and Good Order of the Community they served. Jim finally as possibly subversive. Dangerous to the Vulnerable. All outlined in the most reasonable voice. A touch regretful that it had to come to this.

Henderson asked Foley about dates, scoring a point that one of the dates in his Statement could not be right, being a Sunday and the Department closed.

Then Anderson. Jim had never met him. New, youngish, ambitious. Remaining seated, confidently delivered from memory. The meeting with Toser brought to his attention by Flynn's Team Manager. The breaches of the Child Abuse Procedures cited precisely, page and paragraph number. The actions taken, contact with Foley, reports requested, then, turning to Jim, Anderson wrenched him from the disengaged place he had curled into, away from all this- "And a copy of Mr. Briggs Report was provided for me by Mr. Foley. It was quite inadequate. It did not address the question of the breaches he had made within the Child Abuse Procedures, which I understand from Mr. Foley, that Mr. Briggs was fully aware of." Then, heavy with import, he continued, "However, most grave was his complete failure to make any reference to the Confidential Documentation which was in his possession at the time. This Documentation included the Minutes of Child Protection Conferences and Mr. Briggs had no authority to have even had sight of those Minutes. Much less to secrete them in a place away from Council Premises. Namely, in his own home. It was only with the foresight of his wife and daughter that the Documents were returned to the Council's safekeeping." As he sat back, he murmured, "I understand this was done without Mr. Briggs' consent. While he was away."

Jim sat forward, with a loud, "Pardon? Can you speak up?"

Anderson was taken aback by this, smoothed the ruffles by seeking the attention of Sinclair, cleared his throat gently and repeated precisely, "I understand this was done without Mr. Briggs' consent. While he was away. On leave." Then looked back at Jim.

"Why do you think I kept copies of the documents at home?"

The room stopped. For a moment, even the wind in the birches outside seemed to still. He stopped breathing, poised, staring at the man, then repeated softly, as reasonable as they had been behaving, "Why do you think I kept copies of the documents at home?" And thought, they all know.

Patterson cut in, less confident, a defensive glance at Jim, "That is an unreasonable question. He is asking the witness to speculate on his own motives."

"True," said Sinclair, giving the word the weight of one who knows.

Given confidence, Patterson continued, "We need to know who is cross-examining the witnesses, Mr. Henderson or the- Mr. Briggs. It's a matter of Proper Procedure."

"Ah, yes," Jim mused, "proper procedure… like all this." Then, edged with contempt, "I thought it was about children," the last word spat out, a word they had stolen, along with the childhoods that went with them, he angered.

Anderson silenced Patterson with a raised hand and turned back to Jim. "The two things are inseparable, Mr. Briggs," then turning back to the Panel, "You and all of us here understand that."

Jim understood, in that moment, that for this man, it was not Jim or his actions that were at stake here. No, for Anderson, this performance was a career move. A scalp, my friend. Not the first probably, nor the last, of many. Nothing personal, but this was a young man on his way. No dialogue required. None possible.

Jim turned to Henderson, "Go on then, Ronnie. You ask him." Like Mrs. Patterson wants you to.

The Union official was clearly as discomforted by the mood of Jim, as the others in the room were. Except probably Anderson. Jim knew they understood each other. In a crude sort of manner. And so, always with awareness and sometimes a checking glance towards Jim, he answered Henderson's frail line of questioning on the exactitude of dates and document titles.

Flynn, finally. The ground prepared for him by his seniors. Jim, attentive again, pinned his eyes to the flabby nervousness of the social worker, uncertain in this setting. He half-sat, then rose again to read out his

Statement. Sinclair reassured with a smile. His tale was that Damien had come to him to complain about the meeting with Mr. Briggs. That Mr. Briggs had no right to ask him such things. And where did he get such information. That Mr. Briggs had made no attempt to contact him, the Social Worker Responsible. And, finally, that Mr. Briggs had behaved in hostile manner during the meeting he had subsequently had with him.

Can't disagree with the last, at least, Jim thought.

Patterson said, "No questions," smiling at Flynn.

Smiling with cold eyes at Sinclair, Jim pulled Ronnie back onto his seat, as he rose reluctantly to play his part. "Can I please ask permission of the Panel to question this witness myself?"

Sinclair's brief consultation with the two councillors, then a serious nod to Jim, who stood, a brief wave for Flynn to sit.

Eyes on the window, the silver birches dancing again. "Do you deny that at the beginning of our meeting, you said to me… I have come to ask you what Damien disclosed to you?"

"Yes." Pause. "I deny it. That I said it."

He pressed on, "Do you remember me saying to you, If Damien was going to give me permission to tell you what he told us, he would have told you his allegations in the first place, because you were his social worker?"

"Yes-" flustered, "No!"

"Yes, what?"

"No. I mean, no-"

"No, what?" Jim asked, now fiercening to this little man, the rest of the room quietly aghast.

"No. I don't remember."

"Don't remember? But it could have been said." Then, "Couldn't it, Mister Flynn?"

Flynn looked at Patterson, who rose tentatively, to be rescued with a "Yes, Mrs. Patterson?" from Sinclair.

Jim stayed on his feet, scowling across at her, taking in the whole room with his scorn.

"This line of questioning assumes that Damien Toser has made allegations. Which he has not, as is clear from his own Statement."

With clenched courtesy, Jim turned to the Panel. "I am questioning Mister Flynn about his Statement. Not about the one allegedly made by Mister Toser. It has already been made quite clear that I will not be able to question anyone on Mister Toser's Statement. Hasn't it?" The Panel waited and, Patterson back on her seat, he turned again to Flynn. "I was asking you about allegations made by Damien Toser. Mister Flynn."

Timidly exploratory, "I know of no allegations. He made no allegations to me."

"Of course not. That is entirely my point," and he sat down, eyes a moment resting on Flynn's anxiety, then down to his papers.

"I don't understand." Jim looked up. It was the puzzled face of the Social Democrat. "What is your point, Mr. Briggs?"

Patiently and personally to the councillor, "That Damien did not take his abuse to his social worker- Mr. Flynn, here- because he did not trust him to do anything about it."

"You have no proof of that," Patterson cut in.

Jim weighed her up. To the point of her discomforture. "But you have." Then repeated, as if from a far place, "But you have…" His eyes and ears were already outside the room in amongst the wind and light in the leaves, when he replied to their question, "No more questions."

Patterson's summing up had the components of being sure, being certain, with all the evidence stacked in the files before her. But her delivery, towards the Panel, was cautious, uncertain of the man across the room from her, both of his disengagement and of his sudden disruptive lunges back into the room, turning over the proceedings with the violence of turning over the tables they sat at. Low-key and eyes down to the papers before her, she stepped through the evidence, keeping shy of provocation. Or of triumph.

Jim waited a long moment before getting up and walking slowly step-by-step, reflectively across the room to the window. He lifted aside a corner of the dirty net and looked outside. To see that the birches were fluttering the sunlight as delightfully as he had guessed they would. Turning with tired reluctance back into the room, he spoke. "What is this really about? All this?" He gestured them all, but looked at none of them. "Protection. Yes, protection. Not of children from being mo-les-ted," and he lingered on the glutinous awfulness of the word. "No. Protection of the adults in this. There's the Great and the Good. And there's those who serve them. And ensure that they keep their place. Except here, in this tawdry little performance we are all part of in this room-" eyes turned down as he swept them with his gaze- "here, we are not talking about the very Great. Just the quite middle-sized really." Turning to the Panel, "A councillor. Or two. Like you." Sinclair restrained a protest from the Tory beside him. Letting Jim have his head. In the controlled enclosure of this room. "Who would be nothing. Would have nothing. Would not be able to do what they do. If it wasn't for the rest of us."

He walked back to his table and looked eyeless down at the unopened case, with the papers he had so carefully nurtured. For evidence.

Still closed up. Patterson's documents resting on top. Henderson kept his head bowed. Jim turned to the room, envisaging Damien, his hurt, his confusion, and mostly, his fear. "There are two sayings. Been going through my mind, about all this. The appalling silence of the Good. It's from Martin Luther King. Things happen, not because bad people do them. It's because good people let them. Get away with it. People like you. Maybe. Toleration of the crimes of others. I've wondered if that's what democracy has come to. Toleration of the crimes of others," he repeated reflectively.

Lost for a moment, he reawoke to the room. "The other one. The other saying. It's a quotation from someone who was in the death camps. During the Nazis. Don't know his name, but it starts, First they came for the Jews and I said nothing, because I was not a Jew… then it goes on… they came for communists… and trade unionists. And it ends with, Then they came for me- and there was no one left to speak for me." He felt immensely tired. Now that it was all over.

Sinclair said something indistinctly.

"What?" Jim asked remotely, looking down at the councillor.

"It was Niemoeller. The quote, it was Pastor Niemoeller," then Sinclair looked down at his hands before him.

Jim looked long at the top of the tilted head. That man understands. And understanding, knows the trick of pre-empting the wisdom wrought from pain. He turned away with disgust and spoke to a listener off in the far and empty corner of the room, "From little crimes. Like the one perpetrated here today. From such as this, do we learn to tolerate the big crimes." He turned back to the table and lifted the case, letting Patterson's papers slip aside, some onto the desk, some the floor. Working his thumb on the soft, worn leather of the case handle, he then picked it up and faced back to the window, a last look at the light outside, before saying, "Damien wanted to speak. But you silenced him." And, as he left the room, nobody spoke.

He felt remote. Certain. And immensely relaxed as he walked away down the corridor. Henderson was hurrying after him, so Jim waited.

"Is that it? Is that all you're going to say?"

"What else is there to say?" Then, "Put in an appeal. See if Regional Office'll wear it. And the Union lawyers."

"What about the Panel's decision?"

"You wait for it, Ronnie. That's what you're paid for." And walked off.

As he entered the great Town Hall vestibule, on his way out, Sylvie was leaning, back to him, on the Porter's counter, chatting lightly. He skimmed her body with his eyes, from the electric-blue suit, down the sheened stockings, to her high stilettos, a gold tab at each heel. He stood behind her, waiting. In the moment before she sensed him, he noted that her perfume had changed. She shook with shock as she saw him.

"Are you happy now?" Jim said, with a shake of his head.

"I don't know what you mean," she said, brazenly.

"Don't you." Maybe she didn't. Not the meaning behind what happened.

And he walked out into the gusting and sparkling spring brightness.

Chapter Twenty-seven

When he had escaped from the fusty and self-important glories of the Town Hall, he walked in the gardens of the square before it. It was lunchtime and sunny, but the blustery wind kept the benches empty of office girls. He wanted to talk about all this. To someone who would understand. Who would affirm. Gizande, were she but near. She knew. The meaning of his words this morning, as she had that other morning. A strange and almost tangible connection to her. All but a thousand miles away… But here? Now? Someone to listen to now? Julian was all he could come up with. A good enough man. He went to a phone box.

"Is Julian there?"

"No. He's out on visits."

"When will he be back?"

"Later. I'll check." A wait, then, "He's put down three o'clock."

"Can you ask him to call me? Tell him- James," no point in getting him into trouble, so this feeble attempt at anonymity. "I'll be at home. Thanks."

Not heard from Julian by four, Jim, now home, phoned.

"Julian?"

"Yeah. Sorry, I didn't phone. Just got back. Flynn's been in apparently. He's been going round crowing about his performance against you. How you had it coming to you. All that stuff. I've just tried to phone Henderson, so I can put up some facts from the Union side, there's so many rumours flying about. Did you get a result?"

A result? Probably. But not in Union terms. "No. I left before they gave their decision." Then, to liven it, "Flynn didn't look so bloody marvellous sat there this morning. He was shit scared!"

"Henderson wasn't in when I phoned. Only Kathy. And you know what a pro she is. Couldn't even get a hint from the tone of her voice."

"Maybe I'll phone her myself." He was reluctant at this moment to think about the inevitable. As if it would be put off by not hearing the words. For the moment, anyway. "Yeah. Well the reason I phoned was to ask you to come out for a drink. Tonight, if you're free. I just feel the need to talk it through with someone."

"I promised to take Trish out for a meal tonight. She's my partner."

Partner? Jim thought. He had only had a wife. And lovers. Maybe partnership was what would have worked for him. "Oh. Well," he said, disappointed.

"Tell you what. We could meet you for a drink before we go to eat. How about the Labour Club?"

"That'd be fine. What time?"

"About seven thirty. No, seven." Then, 2How did it go? The Disciplinary?"

Jim reflected on what to say for this man. "I said what I needed to. Okay, I think." Would Julian have understood? If he had read it in a book. But probably not if he had been there, in the room, listening to Jim. "I'll phone Kathy for the result. If it's come through. See you at seven. Okay?"

He dialled the Union office straight away. It was engaged and creeping towards five o'clock closedown before he got through to Kathy.

"Ah. Jim, at last. I expected you to call."

"I've been trying. I gather you've been busy."

"Yes. Lots of calls asking about you."

"Who from?"

There was a silence on the line. She was deciding if to break professional confidence, he thought. "Members of the Stewards' Committee. People who would not give their names." Then, unexpectedly, "I'm sorry, Jim. So sorry."

"That bad, is it, Kathy?"

"Oh, I thought you'd already know. I got the impression from Ronnie… he's out for the rest of the day."

"No. I don't know. Give it to me. What have they decided?"

"Gross Misconduct. Dismissal to take immediate effect."

"No surprise to me, Kathy. It's been coming at me like a train."

Tentative, unlike her, then she said, "There's something else. The Panel decided to pass the file on your Disciplinary over to the Police. To see if there were possible criminal charges." That was unexpected. And the shock hit him hard. He intook breath to calm himself. "It was the documents you had at your home. The ones your daughter brought in to the Department. It seems they are looking at possible theft."

"Okay," he said, as much to steady himself with controlling his voice, as spoken to Kathy. "Okay. Not expected, that."

She waited for him, then said, "Jim, I'm so sorry. What will you do now?"

"About me?"

"About you and about the boys."

"What can I do about the boys? I've got no evidence. Nobody wants to hear it. In fact they want to bury it. With me."

"But, Jim. It's such an awful story. There must be something that can be done."

"I don't even know where Damien lives. I know nothing. Sylvia Cathcart knows more that me. And she isn't going to say anything. She refused to be a witness."

"I know."

"I know you can't comment on another Union member. I don't expect it. But if anything could be done about the boys, it would be Sylvie," a slip back to the familiar, "who could do it. Ask her."

"It's awful," she said, letting a hopelessness out- this woman, so precise, usually so restrained.

No further to go with this, Jim said, "By the way, I'm moving. Tomorrow." He gave her the address. He knew she realised the implication but would not say it, so he said, "Yes. Jane and I are parting." A strange word to come to lips. "So any stuff from Ronnie'll have to go there."

"I understand," so restrained, yet with the implication that she had the whole picture of the crux his life was at, not just in the change of postal address. Then, "Keep in touch. Don't lose yourself."

"Oh, I won't. Don't worry about that." And he quietly put the phone down.

The Labour Club was mid-week quiet. Jim had become gradually a less-frequent visitor here over the years. This night, there was no one he knew. He went into an empty corner with his pint. The quiet strength he had felt as he walked out of the Disciplinary had now receded. He could tell the story of the morning to Julian. But what was the way to tell it? This evening, it felt more like seeking reassurance, the pride in what he had done now touched with timidity, anxiety. At the consequences. Faced alone. The Pyrenees seemed, at this moment, not just remote in geographical distance, but taken on the additional perspective of faraway time. Wreathed in myth, seen from this club room, this evening. In this town, beside its dirty and redundant river.

Entered with Julian, Trish looked at Jim direct, when she shook his hand. "Heard plenty about you from Julian."

Jim raised his eyebrows and Julian laughed, "All bad, I can assure you, Jim. Do you want a refill?" indicating the glass on the table.

"No. I should buy. I invited you here," but Julian dismissed this and went to the bar.

Jim turned to Trish, reluctant to small-talk, "What's he been saying?" smiling to her nevertheless.

"Oh, you're a man with a history. I knew that anyway."

A policewoman? he thought sourly. No, the hair too long and unruly. "How come?"

"I teach at the College. Modern History. I'm researching local trade union history. For my thesis." Then, smiling, "You do feature, Jim, you know." Part of Local History, he wondered. Past history, from this morning. He drank. "I should interview you some time. As a piece of oral history."

He laughed, some beer spat on the table, "Oh god! Sorry!" He wiped it away with the cardboard coaster. "A piece of oral history?" And he thought of his final words to the Panel, the quotes, the tired defiance of them and, sobered, said to her quietly, "I guess that's how the world sees me. Now."

"Oh, I didn't mean-"

"No, that's okay. No offence taken." Then, reflectively, half to himself, "Because the world's moved on, it doesn't make it a better place." And thought of Gizande's story of the old religion, locked away for centuries in the mountains, sustenance for the Liberation fighters in the darkest of times. Is that what he would become? A torch carrier, through the long night? But he was not sure what his message was. The words of it. He picked up Trish's inquiring look at him, just as the moment was broken by Julian bringing drinks.

"Here. Another pint, Jim. I'm sure you've earned it today."

"Have you heard what they decided- on me?"

"No. Couldn't get through to Ronnie. I told you."

"Dismissal," he said flatly.

"Yes, but that was just Foley having a go. You're going to appeal, aren't you?"

"I asked Ronnie. But I doubt that Regional Office'll support it." There was a quiet moment. They all drank. Then Jim said, with a try at lightening, "I'll tell you what happened." He was precise in the telling and the precision itself was humorless. His experience in these things lent his memory the facility of the exact words of the charges against him. The comedy that could be drawn from the story was absent. None of Foley's inflated self-regard, the feebleness of Ronnie. Just the story told. To be judged for itself. With an unexpected seriousness to the two with him at the table. When he reached the end, he hesitated and, almost modest in the presence of Luther King and Niemoeller, he referred to them without their words he had borrowed.

"What words? What were the quotes?" Trish asked.

"The appalling silence of the good. That's Martin Luther King. And the other one was, then they came for me and there was no one left to speak for me," he said flatly. Then almost apologetically to them, "They seemed the right thing to say. For the boys. But there's nothing I can do now."

"Why? The Panel's not the end of the road?" Julian asked, quietly, tentative.

"As well as Dismissal, the file's to be handed to the Police." Julian dipped to take a drink and, in that moment, it was confirmed for Jim that he would get sympathy, but little more, from others on the Shop Stewards Committee he had once chaired. "I will appeal against the decision," he added, without conviction.

"You must!" Julian said.

"What will you do about the boys?" Trish asked.

"Ah. You're not the first to ask me that. What do you think I should do?" he replied, unaccountably smiling.

"Have you no documentary evidence left?"

"Not that you'd know. My own notes, mostly. Just my word." He drank, then repeated, "What do you think I should do, then?" He looked at Julian, questioningly.

Who said, edgily, "Well, you have to follow up the appeal."

Jim's look into his eyes made the other man look away. "Of course." They both knew. About Henderson. About the Regional Office.

Trish turned to Julian. "You know that won't work, don't you?" Then, with almost disbelief, "Do you mean that your Union will do nothing? When Jim here, has tried to get something done about those boys? Are you seriously saying that?" Her voice rose.

Julian shushed her, "We don't want everyone here to know."

"Yes, we do!" she said sharply. And Jim laughed. She turned back to him, a touch angry at him too, "What's funny?"

"Nothing." Then tiredly spelt out, "It's just the gap in the Union. Between what it says it believes. And what it actually does. Championing public service and all that stuff, but, at the end of the day, the public doesn't have a say. It just reflects what goes on in the Council, I suppose. What's the new jargon? Mission Statements? Because what we say we do is up on the wall, therefore we must do it." He sipped, then added ironically, "How dare we argue? When it's there before your eyes. In black and white."

"That's true enough," Julian murmured.

Jim turned to him, but addressed her, "Ask him what the Shop Stewards Committee will do about it? He still works there."

"That's not fair, Jim. I've never even seen the evidence you have. How can I- we do anything?"

Trish turned on him, "You've got Jim's word about the documents. That's enough!"

"Yes," Jim smiled, teasing this couple to explore the paradoxes of his own situation. "You have my word, Julian. The word of Jim Briggs," he ended sardonically.

"That's not enough." Then, appealing, he said, "I'm sorry, Jim. But you know what I mean."

Oh, yes. I know what you mean, he confirmed to himself. But he also knew that his own possession of the documents had been an illusion in itself. An illusion that the outcome of being right was dependent on the production of evidential truth. Proof of it to others? A side issue, in a flawed world where evidence is denied. Witnesses are turned and bribed. And files are covertly shredded. From this, he produced for Julian, "Well, you must ask Sylvia Cathcart. She knows. She's one of your Social Services Union members, now."

"Yes. You're right. She must tell us what she knows."

"But I wouldn't put money on it," Jim added softly, then turned to Trish, "You see it's up to Julian- and the others, now. I've done what I can to bring it into the light. Tell me what I can do, and I will." Then, back to the other man, "But do you think anyone will really be keen to follow this up? I doubt it." An untidy slurp from his glass, wiping his chin, he said, "Anyway, I need a job now. Any ideas, Julian, mate?"

"Trish?" He warmed to being able to help Jim, to offer a crumb of support. "Didn't you say they're looking for someone in the Unemployed Workers' Centre? Fund raising, wasn't it?"

Something. Anything. To tide him over. Until what? Jim wondered.

"Yes. I'll ask. Is that the sort of thing you do, Jim?"

"Grants. Claiming for them. It's what I've been doing with groups for the last six years. You know, tenants, clubs, that sort of thing. It sounds that sort of territory."

"I'll ask," she said. "I'm on the Management Committee of the Centre. I don't think they've got anyone yet." Then, hesitantly, "It won't pay well. We haven't got much money. You understand."

"I'm cutting back on my lifestyle, anyway," he replied, then to Julian, "Oh. And I'm moving tomorrow. No phone yet. So, I'll have to call you. Until I have a number."

"God! Bad time to be moving house," she said with sympathy, but Jim decided it would serve nothing to get into explanations of his personal life here and said no more.

The moment hung between them all. Further conversation now would retrace tracks, so Jim let them off the hook with, "Haven't you got a restaurant table to get to?"

Julian looked at his watch, "Yes. I suppose so," wanting to go, yet reluctant to leave Jim here, alone.

"Don't worry. I've got to get back. Things to do for tomorrow."

Trish shook his hand, then held it a moment. "It's been good to meet you. I'll find out about the job. You keep in contact with Julian."

"Sure. I will."

He watched them cross to the doors. He felt a piece regretful that he would not be going home with someone warm to sleep next to- but, at what cost. He drained his glass and rose to leave.

As he reached the doors, a man hurried out behind him.

"Mr. Briggs?"

Jim stopped in the ill-lit half corridor to the exit. "Yes?"

"Jim Briggs, is it?" Another man came noisily through the toilet door behind them. "We can't speak here," and he indicated out to the car park.

He followed out into the evening light, watchful, cautious. The man's face was indistinct, back to the light. "What do you want?" Jim spoke, keeping his distance with a cold, even threatening tone.

"I couldn't help overhearing you and your friends talking. You are Jim Briggs, aren't you? Who works for Social Services?"

Yes. And no. A complex question that. Today of all days. So he opted for the simple untruth, "Yes."

"Oh, I'm so pleased to have met you."

"Who are you?"

"Fred Toser." Jim recoiled, but the man did not seem to notice. "I'm Damien's dad."

"What do you want?"

"I wanted to thank you," and he half-offered his hand, gone limp at Jim's lack of reciprocation. "Damien said how good you were. You and that Miss Cathcart. To meet him. It wasn't right, was it? What… was happening to him."

What did this man know? Was this a set-up? Jim asked himself, so again gave a non-committal, "No."

Toser at last felt Jim's remoteness, even suspicion. Retreating, he said, "I just wanted to pass on our thanks. From me and the wife," and finally withdrew his proffered hand into his overcoat pocket.

Was this man actually sincere? He tried to study the little man's face again. As he peered at him, Jim thought, Surely, yes. So he asked with restraint, "How is Damien?"

"Oh, he's moved away now. Down south. London. Seems to be doing fine. We don't hear from him much now. You know what kids are like!"

"London, eh?" Jim said, feeling immensely depressed at the crude and cruel predictability of it all.

"Anyway. Just wanted to say thanks, Mr. Briggs. The wife says that the help you gave him, helped Damien get away from this place. There's no prospects here, is there? A lad's got more of a chance in London, hasn't he?"

Chance of what? A life in the flat. With those visitors? But only said, "Yes."

"Must go, now. Left my drink on the bar. Goodbye, Mr. Briggs," indecisive a moment, as if the offer of his hand was worth reviving, then taking in Jim's silence and remoteness, smiled and went quickly back in.

Alone now in the car park, he felt chilled. At the late spring coolness, but mostly at the sense of power distantly and precisely exerted. In the savage certainty of silencing the whisper of their crimes. And the huge and looming sense of their continued right to feed their unspeakable appetites. With whom they wished.

Damien, he mouthed silently. And felt the boy's gaunt presence pass close by, crying out. Perhaps with laughter.

Chapter Twenty-eight

It was drizzling when he returned from the ten miles he ran the next day and he was cold and uncomfortable. In a hurry to change and shower himself warm again, he picked up the post- a window envelope, probably a bill, and what looked like a couple of junk items- and took them up to the bedroom with him. Showered and dressed in jeans and an old check shirt for moving, he tossed the junk aside and reluctantly opened the envelope. If it was a bill, he would leave it for her to pay. She had work and he did not. But it was not.

Headed: *Carter, Hill, Rodruiguez, Solicitors.* A Bradford address.

Dear Mr. Briggs,

Re: Estate of Mary Theresa Briggs

We are acting on behalf of the estate of the deceased Mary Theresa Briggs, your paternal aunt.

Would you please contact us at our office, as there are matters relating to the estate we wish to discuss with you.

We apologise for the length of time it has taken for us to send this letter to you, but we have had considerable difficulty finding your address and have written to you at the earliest opportunity.

We look forward to hearing from you.

Yours Sincerely,
scribbled indecipherable
Phillip Rodruiguez.

Aunt Mary, you won't lie down, will you? The woman he had treated with neglect and distance while she was alive. Now more alive for him, since he had stood and watched that shoddy, untidy funeral in a wet cemetery. Her "estate"? More letters and photos? he wondered. Maybe some money? He could certainly do with that, at present.

He made breakfast and phoned Bradford as soon as it was nine. When he asked if he could make an appointment to see Mr. Rodruiguez, at first he thought of driving up there today. With his boxes for the new flat in the car with him. When the woman came back on line, he decided tomorrow would do. Pace his life, from now on. Rodruiguez may not be available himself, but one of the other solicitors would see him. Okay.

Friday morning, from a phone box in the motorway services, he hesitated to Jane's "Hello," on the other end of the line, before giving, as flat as possible, "It's me."

"I knew it would be."

"I've moved. I've left my new address on the kitchen table. No phone yet. I'm in a call box."

"How will you do without your phone, Jim?"

Sarcasm? he thought, but turned it with, "I will. I've started to get used to letters again, anyway."

"What?"

"Doesn't matter." A denial of entry into his new world.

"What happened at the Disciplinary?"

"They sacked me." And before she might commiserate, "Are you pleased?"

"Of course not! That was unnecessary. That was nasty."

"And they've passed the case to the Police. Whether it was criminal- me having the files. Surely you'd agree with that, Jane?"

Pause, before she spelt out, "It doesn't matter whether I agree or not. You took the files. It's your fault. The consequences of your own actions, you know."

"Is it?" he reflected ironically. "That's how it is, is it?"

She was irritated, "This is silly. I don't want to go on talking about it."

"No. I suppose you wouldn't." Then, "Do you and Tracey talk about it? About taking the papers back to Social Services?"

"No. Why should we? She was right. I wasn't going to be part of you settling your old scores." She then full-stopped the conversation with, "Now. If you've anything else to say, useful."

"No. Not that you'd want to hear, Jane." But she might have, at one time. In that past.

"Well, let me know your phone number. When you've got one." Then relenting, softer, "And good luck. Wherever you're going." The warmth of their past, despite everything. The intimacy never totally lost, with the woman he had shared a child with. However uneven the sharing seemed now.

He said, his throat a moment filled with hurt. For what might have still been, "And good luck to you too, Jane." Listened to each other's breath. And now, in the car, headed for Yorkshire, Jim was unsure whose end of the line first clicked silent.

The solicitor's office was up the hill from the centre, near the markets, above a bakery shop. Sitting in reception, waiting, the smell of yeasted dough being baked filled his nostrils with an appetite for his missed breakfast. His stomach growled quietly to him, until a surprisingly young man, almost a youth, led him down a corridor. Into a windowless room. An old desk. Grey metal cabinets and boxes…

Now, it seemed hours later, sat there alone, with the letters disorganized on the desk before him, Jim looked down at them, the pages untidily released, greedy to reread them. In any order. Sat back from them. Remoting himself. With their distastefulness, their distance apart. Their historical length of time away. From him here, in this room insulated from the busy streets outside and the world beyond. He inhaled, but down here the bread could no longer be smelt. Only the letters, the smell of paper stored too long. And the one in Spanish. The only one he had to open and had resealed. But, when open, indecipherably opaque, apart from the author. His step mother, *Constancia Brige.* And that quote he had seen, carved in stone, in France. His fingers had a fumbled numbness as he tried now to sort them into chronological order. To read the tale told by his father as it was written, unfolded in this episodic and fragmentary correspondence with his sister. With the final, hesitantly hopeful letter to Jim himself. Left properly unopened by his aunt, these last ten years.

A sharp discomfort jabbed inside the knot of muscles at the base of his neck. The letters sorted into order, he started to read through them again with the deep tiredness of the inevitable truth that leaked from them into this bare room. He remembered the words of old Jacob, so reasonable, "Why would a man not wish to know this? About his own father." He imagined the walls of other rooms splashed with the blood of his father's betrayals, looked down and read:

Lourdes *June 10th, 1936.*

Dear Mary,

It has been such a right thing to come here after Bernadette passed away. We have helped with some of the cripples from the Parish and I have learnt I am fortunate besides their pains and difficulties. I have lost a wife but I have gained a son.

We have had another Father besides Father Patrick to support us. He is Father Jerome and he is a young man. He is very passionate in his Faith and his prayers are powerful. He prayed specially with me for Bernadette's soul and heard my Confession. He is from Manchester- but he has returned last month from working in Spain where he says terrible things are happening to the Church. He tells us that there is a Red Terror with the socialists and anarchists burning down the churches, convents and monasteries. Priests and nuns are being killed. And he speaks of worse things that I will not write to you. He told us to take the news of what is happening in Spain back to our own

churches at home, so that prayers can be given there for those who are suffering for the Faith. Will you please offer a prayer in Saint Theresa's for our fellow Catholics in Spain? Please do it for me.
I hope James is well.
I hope this letter reaches you. They tell me the post is so bad in France with the strikes, that I may reach home before this letter.
Kindest Regards,
Your brother, Francis.

A strict Catholic, then. Not just a routine attender at church. For the appearance of things, but a passionate believer. Then,

Burgos,
Spain.
August 27th,1936.

Dear Mary,

Father Patrick will already have told you what happened.
Father Jerome told us about the crimes against the Church and the Faithful in Spain and five of us decided to get into the country to help, when we heard that the Army rose up on behalf of the Faith against the terrors that the Republican socialists in the government were committing.

Do not be angry with Father Patrick. He tried to persuade us not to go- especially me, because of little James. But this is so important. Where do we stop the spread of communism and atheism? Christ has always required the Faithful to put aside the things of the world- even our dearest love for others- in order to fight for the way of God and against Evil- to fight for that Greater Love.

Now we are here, I am starting to see what has been happening. We were taken to see a church where everything had been robbed- even the Cross from the altar. This priest escaped but the Army marched in and imprisoned the socialists in the town to try them for their crimes. It is said that they had murdered some of the Faithful- so they will face death themselves from the court.

We have seen General Franco who leads the Army. He is a tubby little man but his speeches seem to really get the Spaniards excited- although of course I do not understand them. All the priests and bishops back him.

We are trying to become volunteers to help in some way. The only other one you know in our group is Tommy Cavanagh. They call us the Inglis, but they do not know what to do with us! They have shown us off to some newspapermen and to the German and Italian Ambassadors to prove that ordinary people like us- good Catholics from England, understand what the good Catholics from Spain are trying to do and what they are up against.

I will write again when I know what use they will make of us. And when we start doing some work, I will arrange to send you some money for James. I have spoken to the British Consul here and he has told me how to do it.

Give my love to James- as I know you will.
And please do not be too angry with me for doing the right thing.
Kindest Regards,
Your brother, Francis.

A fascist. The truth from this flimsy, ancient letter. More crude and unapologetic than anything Jacob could have told.

November 27th,1936.

Dear Mary,

It has been such a long time since I have written a letter to you and to James. I have waited until we knew what was happening.
At last it has been agreed that enough men who speak English have volunteered to serve the Church and General Franco that they have put us together into a Company to serve with the Army against the reds. They have to train us first and I am learning how to fire a rifle. It is not easy- like it looks in the pictures. I have a sore and bruised shoulder from it kicking back at me when I fire it.

We have been shown off to foreign journalists again. I was interviewed by one from the Daily Mail. I do not know if what I told him was printed. Did you hear about it in England?

Something boyish, almost child-like in this. In its keen innocence. And ignorance.

We have been told that we will be moving soon, so I still can not give you an address to write to me at. When I have one, I will write again and tell you. I miss you and home and I do want to hear news of James and you.
I must end now. More marching and saluting to do!
I will write to you soon.
Kindest Regards,
Your brother,
Francis.

Flushed with enthusiasm. As the young men pouring through France to volunteer for the Republic must have been. To fight against my father. Naming him thus felt remote. My father. A man who made choices Jim would never have taken. Except perhaps about his child. It shook Jim to think this. The two men, as fathers, each chose the world of events, of politics, to the neglect of their child. Francis with Jim. He with Tracey. Jim would have liked to think it was different for himself. He never took off for another country. But he knew. Remembering the young man he had been in Yorkshire, living in the bedsitter after the McGregors. Whether with child or not, such a crusade as Spain would have drawn him. But to fight on the other side.

March 22nd, 1937.

Dear Mary,

Post has not been possible. We have been in the front line in the trenches through the winter. We think of Spain as a hot country, but the winter is very cold. Always snow. Always cold. I think the English here have found it very difficult.

Jim remembered listening to the story of an old Party member who had been in Spain. Using dynamite to blast graves from the iron-hard frozen ground.

I am not permitted to tell you where we have been. But I can say the war has been going very well for us. You will have read this. I have been told that the best truth is in the Daily Mail. We have driven the reds from the South and it is said the North will soon be ours too.

I pray for you and for James. It is not possible for me to receive letters from England here. Please believe me when I say it is right what I do here.

Pray for me, as I pray for you and for my little soldier in Christ, my son, James.
Kindest Regards,
Your brother,
Francis.

His little soldier in Christ? Christ! So remote from the reality, it made him smile.

Perpignan, France
Jan. 28th, 1939.

Dear Mary and James

Just to tell you I am safe at last in France. I am trying to get back to England. Things are very chaotic here. I will write no more, because I fear the post being read. I hope you receive this. I hope to be home soon.

The commencement of deceit. Pieced together from that last, that confessional letter to the son he had never seen since an infant, this man had begun his long journey of treachery. Beyond, far beyond the adolescent fire of Faith that took him that first time across those mountains. The first of many secret passages through that serrated wall Jim had watched turn into night from that verandah. Sat there, in that dead man's house, with his unsuspecting daughter retelling the untruths she had been left with.

My prayers have been with you both and you have been always in my thoughts. When I return, you will understand why I have been unable to write.

Kindest Regards,
Your brother,
Francis.

Then, this greater war. The dark clouds swept down from the centre of the continent. For him to hide within.

France
May 31st, 1940.

Dear Mary,

This may be the last letter I can write for some time. You have not heard from me as I was made prisoner by the French. I will just say that they did not understand who I was. But all has gone well. I will explain when we meet again, whenever that will be.

With the war now come to France, I must remain here.
Again, I hope this reaches you. I am sending it across the mountains into Spain, as the post here is collapsing since the German invasion.
Give my love to James.
Always in my prayers.
Kindest Regards,
Your brother,
Francis.

Mary then must have thought him dead. The lie she later told Jim, of his father's death near to Dunkirk. A gentle lie, perhaps grown out of this long silence from her brother, to tell the son, already reading, boyishly awesome of the war. Yet her brother had forced her into reluctant collusion with his abandonment of his son. Her placing little James in the Institution, at only five. Jim remembered the bare room, tube chairs and zimmer frames, where the young woman in the nursing home had first given Jim the three cardboard boxes from Mary, the afternoon before the funeral. Where he learned of his aunt's daily prayers for him. He had tried to read Mary's long recording of the life of prayer she had left along with the photos and Suzanne's unopened letters, but found it dull, opaque, like reading the log of a mechanic. The numeration of prayer and penance, without the whispered words.

Paris
December 15th, 1944.

Dear Mary,

As you will know when you open this, I am alive and I have survived the war in France. I am unable to return to Britain at present. I will keep in contact with you, as I can. Pass on my best wishes to James.
I hope this reaches you for Christmas.
Kindest Regards,
Francis.

Just that, after a wartime of silence. Then nothing. Until the old man's letters. Trying to tidy way the guilt. And the letter from his wife. Whatever remote and dirty cupboards that might open up, he thought. The letter to Mary brief, unapologetic, remote from a sister he had irretrievably severed himself from over four decades.

St. Paul de Luz
7th June, 1976.

Dear Mary,

It has been many years since you have heard from me. I can only hope that this reaches you. If you are no longer at the old address, I hope that this will be passed on. I have been unable to return to Britain for many reasons. At first, it was because my duty to the country required that I remain in France. I am sure that nothing I could write to you would justify my actions over these years to you, particularly leaving James to be brought up by you. I know the necessity of the things I have done.

You will see I have enclosed a letter for James. As he has passed the time of his fortieth birthday, I believed that the time has come for him to understand what I have done. Over the years, I have made my life in this country. I owe it to him to let him know about me. Please pass on the enclosed letter to him.
Regards,
Your brother, Francis.

Yes. The letter was received. But never replied to. Mary remained silently unforgiving to her brother. And must have reached a point when she sealed him off, unforgiven, into their past. Both hers and that of young James. Now, the man of that boy, sat in this room, read her silence from the page of this father's letter. And Mary said to Jim, now you know why. You may discover your father. But it was not possible in my lifetime. And she had carefully stored away the letters in this office in Bradford, until the process she had set in motion with the gift of the three boxes, now ran its course to the end. In this bare room. And her spirit could finally take its sleep.

He tidied the letters to Mary aside. And, alone on the desk's other corner, the Spanish letter. Yet to be read. Before him, the letter to himself. The only letter typed. The only words to him from his father.

S. Paul de Luz
1st June, 1976.

My dear James,

A week before that last letter to Mary. Had this taken a week to write? Or had it taken a week for the man to write that clipped and unapologetic letter to her? Distilling the words clean of any sense of guilt to her?

I write this as the Father you have never met since you were an infant, before any possible memory of me. I was unable to return home to England because of the war, but I entrusted your upbringing to my sister, your Aunt Mary, and I know she will have brought you up as a good Catholic. As a man of Faith, I know you will understand your Father's actions when I explain them to you.

When your Mother died, I came to Lourdes in pilgrimage. At that time there was beginning in Spain a terrible war between Catholicism and the Communist Republic. I am sure you will have read of the Spanish Civil War. It was the beginning of the Cold War that still goes on today between Christianity and Communism. Spoken to me like a child, Jim thought.

I fought there, as other young men did. But I was captured by the Republican soldiers in 1938 and I was taken to their security headquarters. As I was an Englishman fighting in Spain, I was of great interest to them and I expected the worst. The Republic was losing the War and was desperate. I could expect only the worst treatment when I was taken to their Head of Intelligence, a man called Sastré. Soon, I discovered that he was working in secret for our side and was passing on information to Franco that was helping to end that terrible war. I was given the job of joining the soldiers of the Republic as they fled across the border into France before our victorious Army. I was to infiltrate their ranks because it was feared that the Communists would try to return in time and cross back into Spain to commence the war again. I was to make sure that the Spanish Government was aware in advance of any such plans.

With the refugees I crossed into France in January 1939 and, with them, I was imprisoned in a camp at Gurs, quite close to where I now live. I was there for a year. It was a terrible place, but being a prisoner there enabled me to gain the trust of the Communists and Republicans I was with and when I was able later to escape from there, I could assist the Spanish Government, even returning some of the criminal Republican politicians from France to face justice in Spain.

But you will remember that in 1940, also the Germans invaded France. That was a very difficult time. Because I was English, I was in danger of becoming a prisoner again, so I went to hide in the hills with other Spaniards who feared the Germans and the Vichy Government also. You must understand-

Must? Jim thought. Only too well. But my own understanding of you, Francis, not the one you would have wished on me.

You must understand that I have always fought for Christian Civilisation and nowhere and at no time was Christian Civilisation in Western Europe more threatened than in Spain, where General Franco defeated the threat, and in France, from the time when the Resistance was started by Communists, especially the Spanish refugees in this region. Still today, France has a very large Communist Party and we must remain vigilant. But I am now becoming an old man and must leave these things to men of your age. After a time with the Resistance, continuing to hide my real beliefs from them, I was contacted by the British Secret Service. They wished to get the Resistance to fight the Germans in a more efficient manner. But also, they looked ahead to the situation when the war would be over. The British and the Americans wished to ensure that Europe remained within Christian Civilisation. They had to fight the Germans, of necessity, but they also knew that the real enemy would only show its red colours after the war. I was their man in South West France to make sure that after the war Communism did not rule here. I had to do many difficult things, some of which remain on my conscience to this day.

Jacob's story. Whatever Gizande knows. What Suzanne does not even suspect. And would deny. *They were dark years. I had disguised myself so well as a member of the Resistance, that the local priests denied me Communion or Confession. They took me truly as a Red!*

After the war, of course, there were those who were suspicious of some of my actions. I was called to Paris and for two years worked there for the Americans, trying to keep the Communists out of the Governments. Since then, I have returned here. I was with the Consul for the British Government here for a period. Then I worked for the Regional Government, assisting the development of tourism here. I have been involved in the ski resorts that have now become so popular in these mountains in the winter. I live comfortably. I have my own property. I am now a citizen of France, although the British Government give me a small pension for the work I did for them during the war and after.

No mention of his new family, wife, daughter, grandchild.

If you can bring yourself to forgive your Father for his silence, I would wish that you write to me here. I can no longer return to Britain because of the work I did. All this can be explained when I write again to you.

The photographs I send you with this may tell more of my story than the words I write. I hope to hear from you soon,

Your Father,

Signed, *FXB,*

Then typed beneath, *Francis Xavier Briggs.*

No invitation to visit. No family. The liar he had watched this man emerging as. Since Mary's death. A thoroughly dishonest letter. An old man crafting the sketch of an honourable life, from forty years of lies. A letter sent, but never responded to, allowed Francis so many things. To be the only author of his life. To leave Jim as the son he believed him to be. James, grown to become another Good Catholic Man of Faith. An old man's wish to leave the reality at rest in another country. For others to live through the consequences of his actions. And his neglect.

Constancia's letter. Only one phrase understood. Stood proud from the impenetrable Spanish handwriting, in English, *Christ could be born a thousand times in Galilee But all in vain until he is born in me.* The words on that gravestone he had stood at, next to Suzanne. He could only guess at the context. He needed someone to help. He looked at his watch. He had been left alone with the letters only twenty minutes. In Real Time. Felt as an hour. He picked up his step-mother's letter and went out into the corridor.

The young solicitor was apologetic. "I am so sorry, Mr. Briggs. There has been a mistake. Apparently Mr. Rodruiguez gave instructions that he was to deal with you aunt's will personally. It was part of the terms. Because he speaks Spanish. He is in Court today. He will be back later this afternoon. Can you return after four o'clock?"

Of course. And he was back out in the cloud of cooked bread smells on the street. The letters left gathered back into their file again by the young man behind him in the office. A hot pie wrapped in paper from the shop, in Jim's hand, a dribble of gravy on his chin. He wandered back to the car park, munching. With almost a certainty in his heart. Only his step-mother's letter and he believed the whole tale would be told. He had nearly five hours, so he decided to drive out of the city. Into the hills around.

Chapter Twenty-nine

He drove over the bare tops and down into the valley where he had first come to be apprenticed after he left the Institution. Back down next to the canal, the mill where he had apprenticed had a sign, *To Let Industrial and Commercial Units Available.* A large padlock across the gates. Broken windows. Rampant weeds taken root along the gutters and roof line.

Back in the car he said to himself, Might as well. And started off to look for the Institution. Where it had been. Eyes to the narrow road that unwound him from the crowded valley bottoms, up again, turned from the crowded terraces… to the last still-inhabited farms, set back-to the unusable upperlands, coarse grass and heather in amongst the tumbled stones of abandoned fields. To the Rocks. That landmark of wind-shaped sandstone blocks, almost femininely carved into curves and flutings, and he knew he was near. The highpoint of the road, beside the outcrop, the descent beyond and swept too steeply round the shoulder of the hill, he was above the back of the place. Solitary, sprawled and ugly, set in these hills, just this road down to it, then dropped to the village beyond, hiding in the cleft of the downroad back into the valleys.

He slowed towards the gates. The Lodge *For Sale,* but a sign planted in the grass verge, *Metro Training Consortium PLC Lynthwaite Hall.* Lynthwaite Hall? A name now, but had never been known by. Beyond, down the drive, he could see it. He engaged low gear and turned in. A car park had been extended across what he remembered of the lawn. Crowded with cars, but his eyes were on the building before him, as he switched off the engine. The windows, trying to approximate his memory to the rooms behind them. The roof and the crudely elaborate chimneys. The steps up into the gothic arch of the entrance. Like a blackened, yawning mouth. Still indeterminately threatening.

He quietly left his car and approached. Tranced. Even the slight grate of contact, sole to stone of the worn step, remote. As of another person. Another time. But of this place. He found himself in the hall. The sound of voices clattering at a meal. An unattended reception desk. Where what had been once? Carpeted now. Only the shadows in the high vaulted ceilings familiar from then. He looked up the staircase.

Light from the upper landing window drew his eyes up and he was about to follow, when a voice at his shoulder, “Lunch is down there, sir.” Jim must have visibly shaken awake from where he was. The woman's curious eyes were on him, her hand still half-raised to indicate down the corridor, to the sounds of eating and chatter.

From somewhere, his voice came, "I've left something behind. Upstairs."

"Fine, sir." Then her eyes still on something in his face, she said, "Don't be long. The main course stops serving in seven minutes."

"No. Thanks." And he approached the staircase. Her left her behind him, a moment watching. Before hurrying off on her business.

The carpets softened his steps, dream-like, insulating his mind from the harsh noises of then, a hundred boys hurrying their daily duties across the hard, uncovered polished planks and stone slabs. At the last stair, a corridor stretched either way. Left or right? Right. Doors on either side, as he walked further away from the window above the staircase behind, darkening. Counting rooms. He stopped. A plastic plate on the door, *Seminar Room 3*. One step to reach the brass handle, cold to touch. Turned, pressed at it and, slightly resisitant to the tuft of the carpet, the door opened. And he found himself framed in that threshold, facing that fireplace. Now sealed. No mirror now above it. The walls a functional cream now. But still that room, here, he had arrived. Without being summoned.

He stepped in. And pushed the door closed behind his back. For privacy. Leaning against it, the feel of its heavy, carved panels against his shoulders. Half a dozen steps to the mantlepiece. And he faced that mirror. Turning, he visualised the white cottage and the coming storm, that painting on the wall opposite. His memory furnished the room, swept aside these stackable chairs, the table with the overhead projector. Put back in place the glass-fronted bookcases. The sofa. The long setee to the left.

He moved to that long and cushioned seat and sat on it. Closed his eyes. And brought back that night. Only a lamp on the corner table for light. The young father took the book from his fingers and placed an arm around the boy's shoulders.

"You are unhappy, James. Come here."

Guided to the seat. In the gentlest yet strong embrace. Pressed down to lie there, cheek to the cushions, the boy wished to sleep. To sleep away the last night. Locked in the cellar, with the other. A blanket was drawn over him. The light went out and he slipped away, dreamless but aware of the man still in the darkened room… Slipping back awake after how long. Aware. Then stark, but frozen in the night. The unseen hands already unbuttoned his shorts, slid them down, the boy lifting his body to let them pass. Then the underpants. Wordless. The man's strong hand on the boy's risen sex, his own hand taken and folded round the other's huge and coarse haired piece. Shockingly naked in the dark.

"Like this", and the man began to pull the boy's foreskin back and up. Painfully.

"Like this. To me," anger crept to the edge of his words, but the boy's hand rested limp on the throbbing and invisible monstrosity. The man started to whip at the boy's penis, quick and harsh.

"Like this! To me!" He tried to force the boy's hand into motion, but all he could feel was the hurt of the hard gripped handful of big fingers tearing at his own skin, crying out in agony, faster and faster driven, pumped with weeping pain, legs drawn up with it, then exploded, limbs thrown apart, as wet hot slime shot across his stomach.

"Do it like that! To me!" But the boy was limp. Snot in his nose, tears from his eyes. His hand fell away from the man's phallus and, for a moment, there was just the separateness in the room together. His despair. And the man's anger. Then appallingly, the tongue and lips slobbered across his belly, drooling and sucking up his spilled spunk. And, as he was kissed and the big tongue shoved aside his lips and teeth, the boy was rasped by the stubble and swallowed the man's taste filled with sour wine and his own semen. Then, as suddenly, the man was away. Stiff with fear, the boy listened to the slap-slap, continued long from the dark across the room, ceased with a half-cry/half-growl. With then, just breathing.

"Get out! I'll tell you when your next reading lesson is."

And James had hurriedly and untidily dressed in the dark. Shamed, as if caught out in some awful digression. By his Aunt Mary.

The hard seminar-room chair beneath him, Jim opened his eyes to let the light in. And knew where he was. Now. From that dark, where he had needed- so long and so blindly- to go. Into the bright light of this room, sanitised, made functional, with its clean paint and furniture. Tired, he closed his eyes again, but that other room had gone. Already. At last. His head was now filled with the sound of Casals. And with Gizande. And he was permitted to weep. Silent, bowed and with relief. The quiet tears drained gradually away and he left them there a long time, before smoothing the trickled salt away with fingertips.

The door opened and a man and a woman entered. They were giggling together, an intimate conspiracy and did not see the silent figure of Jim in his corner, for a moment. The woman's hand went up to touch the man's face and froze there. Stilled by her turned eyes onto Jim.

Who stood and, smiling despite himself, said, "Sorry. Wrong room." And left, past them, leaving them behind the re-closed door in Seminar Room 3, laughing to himself, down the corridor, two-steps-at-a-time down the stairs and outside, where now some groups of people were enjoying a moment in the sun after lunch, before going back inside.

Chapter Thirty

Rodruiguez came to the reception himself to lead Jim through to his office. The same file Jim had left with the young man this morning, lay on the desk.

"I must apologise for the error this morning. The appointment was made with you without my knowledge. It was a specific requirement in your Aunt's will that it should be me who acted for her and met with you. It was because of this letter from your Stepmother. The letter in Spanish." Then, with professional sympathy, "This all must have been quite a shock to you. Finding out about your Father's past, in this manner."

"No. I knew much of it. I've pieced it together. You know I've been to France. I've met my half-sister."

Rodruiguez's eyebrows raised. "Did you then meet your Stepmother?"

"No. She is dead. Two years ago, I think."

The solicitor nodded, opened the file and withdrew the letters, separating out the one from Constancia. He looked up at Jim again. "It was an unusual request from your Aunt. She came to us with it in 1983. She had specially sought out a solicitor who could understand Spanish. She wanted the letters deposited here, only to be given to you after her death. I am to assist you with understanding this letter's content. The one from your Stepmother."

"So Aunt Mary's never read this letter."

"No. I tried to convince her. But she was adamant. Although the letter is addressed to her, she insisted that it was first opened by you." What impenetrable and knotted motives had Mary had for the way she had closed down her affairs, Jim wondered. Yet, there was a deliberateness about everything she had done. In how she wanted things left. Perhaps the result of years of prayer. "She had taken so much trouble to find a Spanish-speaking lawyer. Your Aunt was, of course at this time, elderly, but she had contacted the Law Society to find me. She was too infirm to come here, so I visited her at her nursing home."

"Did she even know who the letter was from?"

"I believe so."

"But there was no mention of Constancia in those letters from my Father."

"I believe she knew. That your Father would have started a new life with someone, all those years away from Britain." He reflected, "I felt she was worried. There was an underlying anxiousness in her determination not to know what was in the letter. Also, that you did not receive the letters from your Father- even the one written to you in 1976- that you were not to see them till after her death. She would not be moved on this." Then, pulling the Spanish letter from its envelope, he said, "I have taken the liberty of reading this letter this afternoon. I wanted to be sure that I would be able to translate everything for you. We speak less Spanish at home now, than when I was younger." Then, more seriously, "It would perhaps have been better, if I had been able to convince your Aunt to read this. I could have written on her behalf back to your Stepmother. As it is there will be some problems about the property that I will have to take specialist advice on."

Property? Jim wanted the letter read. Entirely. Immediately. Yet. And yet. No more sudden shocks, please. He had reached a position about his father. Done the pain in getting here. And hesitated before this new voice, another witness to Francis.

"Shall I start?" Rodruiguez asked.

"Yes."

"*My dearest Maria, my name is Constancia. I have to write this in my own tongue. My daughter understands English, but, as you will see, I write to you of things I would not share with her about her father, your brother, Francisco. I hope you will be able to get assistance to understand this.*

"*I bring you the sad news that Francisco died a month ago. I am his widow. I have been ordering his papers. I knew of you and I also knew that he had sometimes written letters to you. He was sad that you never replied, but I am sure you had your good reasons for this. He spoke little about you and little about England, but I know from him that you are a woman of religion and of the Faith. I write to you as a Catholic mother to her Sister in Christ.*" He paused to check out Jim, then eyes back to the letter.

"*In his papers, I discovered the information that Francisco had a son by a previous marriage in England, before he came to Spain. This was unknown to me while he was alive. I can only express my shame that he abandoned his child, but I cannot say that this gave me great surprise. He is the father of our child, a daughter, Suzanne, and he has been a good father to her. But as a younger man, Francisco was cruel. He committed many crimes, of which I can not speak. Although done against enemies, some of them Communists and other enemies of the Church, many of these crimes were unspeakable and can never be forgiven. Even to me, he has acted with coldness and cruelty. In 1944, the Committee of Liberation in the Region where we live commenced an investigation into his actions and he left me and hid in Paris for two years. I was with child and alone. In his absence I was taken by those who believed Francisco was a sympathiser with the Nazis and I was imprisoned. I was released by the intervention of a British Officer. It was then a terrible winter in our part of France. Very cold, with no firewood in the towns and no food. We were given tickets to exchange for food, but there was none. Only in the blackmarket and I had no money. I believe I would have had more food if I had remained inside the prison with the German and the collaborationist prisoners. During all this time I heard no word from Francisco.*

"When he returned from Paris, Suzanne was but an infant. I had considered leaving him, but what could I do? I remained a citizen of Spain, which was then a difficulty for me in France and if I return to Spain, there were many enemies there too, because of Francisco's actions and betrayals there.

"So, we have remained together. But in the last years, he has taken on a madness. I believe that his conscience has been troubled for many years by the crimes he has committed in the Name of Christ. He has lied to me, as he has lied to the world and I have had to retain the secrets that I knew of to myself. He has therefore made a liar of me also, for I have not told our daughter, Suzanne, of the things I know about her father. His later madness was a heresy from this Region. He had received teaching from an old man during the War against the Germans, when he was hiding in the mountains. But only when an old man himself did Francisco begin to say to me that he believed the World was the creation of the Devil. That the Flesh was evil. He ceased to eat meat. He also had his gravestone made before he died, with the inscription on it in English-" Rodruiguez looked up, "Here it is in English," and, to Jim's nod, continued, "*Christ could be born a thousand times in Galilee But all in vain until he is born in me.*" Without looking up this time, the solicitor said, "Now, back into Spanish. *The priest would not have allowed it in the cemetery, if he had understood the words. I was told it was a saying from the old heresy of the Cathars. I know that you, Maria, as a good Catholic woman, would be as angry at this as I was. I wanted the stone removed after Francisco's death, but I knew that my daughter would object. All I was able to do was to have special prayers to be later said over the grave, to exorcise this bedevilment of sacred ground. I am sure you approve and that your brother's soul may rest a little more still now.*

"I have thought what to do for my Stepson to repair the neglect by his Father. Francisco left me a small property in the hills some distance from here. It is a small hill farm named La Retrait Parfaite, that he intended to make into a hotel for the skiing seasons. But he did not and I have done nothing with it. I would like the son to have it. Please pass the information on to him and I wish him to write to me. My daughter understands English and could help me understand any letters from you or from your Nephew.

I hope you are able to respond to this letter soon,
Your Sister in Christ,
Constancia Brige."

So Mary never knew this. Never opened the letter. Yet, she knew all, which was why she never read it. Just as Jim was unsurprised, without any shock at the Spanish woman's story, Mary, then towards the end of her own life, would have known that the envelope contained things she could guess about her brother. Why then, would she wish to take on the obligations of replying- or deciding not to reply? Being forced to face again her own responsibility for Jim's childhood and how she must have guessed it to be, visiting the quiet, unhappy boy in that grey fortress in the hills. Her own collusion in the boy's abandonment and explaining it to another. The letter had remained unopened, a measure of his aunt's sense of failure to him, but also her obligation that finally Jim should know everything, through her elaborate mechanism, sat here across the desk from a solicitor who speaks Spanish in Bradford. Jim smiled. For a woman who had done her best. Considering.

"You do not appear surprised at the story she tells," Rodruiguez said.

"No. It fits. With other things I have learnt about my father."

"The property she writes of." Jim had forgotten that. What a gift from the woman he would never meet. Her concern for him. "Would you wish us to continue acting for you about this? We do not even know the location of it."

"I think I know how to find it. I am sure my sister will be able to help me in that." Then, recognising the other man's concern, "Will there be problems about me inheriting it? I may have to come back to you for advice about that. You know, me being British, inheriting a property in France."

"You are welcome to use me. Of course. We are not specialists in that field, but if you come across problems, please contact me." Then, putting the enveloped letter back in the file, he added, with professional sympathy, "I think these letters leave you with much to think about. And decide. When you are clear what you wish to do, then may be the time. We could advise you, should you wish to sell the property."

Jim looked shrewdly at him and smiled. "I think you know I do not intend to do that, Mr. Rodruiguez."

Who shrugged, "Today, you do not feel that would be right, but perhaps tomorrow. Perhaps when you see the property, your views may change."

Jim realised that beneath the other man's professional distance, was a real interest in the story. And where it would go next. "No. Today, at least, I am sure I will not sell it." He stood. "Thanks, very much, Mr. Rodruiguez. For the way you've handled this… carried out my Aunt Mary's wishes."

"No, Mr. Briggs. It has been very unusual. A pleasure." He came round the desk and held out the file to Jim. "I hope you enjoy the Perfect Retreat."

"What?"

"That is the name of the farm. La Retrait Parfaite."

"Oh. Yes," taking the file. Then, "You are Spanish yourself, are you, Mr. Rodruiguez?"

"My father was. He came here after the War."

"Which war?"

He looked at Jim. Understanding something of him. "The Spanish Civil War."

"He fought in it?"

"Of course."

"For which side?"

"The Republic. Of course."

"Of course." And, for a moment, beyond the formal relationship, the two men grinned at each other.

Then, shepherding towards the office door, "I can arrange for a translation of your stepmother's letter to be typed and sent to you, if you wish."

"Yes. Please."

Outside, on the street, a moment's reluctance to part from this man, into the crowds beginning to go home. But he did.

Grid-locked into the late afternoon traffic, it was some time before he reached the Ring Road. He turned away from the option of the Motorway and headed a last time through the thread of dark stone villages strung across the tops, decreasingly frequent, the road thinned of traffic as it climbed up the back of the crested escarpment of rock. Before the descent down to the lowlands where he had made himself an adult. He remembered a reservoir from years ago, where he and Mark would rest their bikes after the long climb up the hill, heading home Sundays.

Now, again, he pulled across and parked in the gateway to the Water Board land. He climbed the gate and walked slowly along the retaining wall. To where the escarpment hung like a massive, stilled and breaking wave above the descent down to the west. Vehicles crawling diminutively on roads across this landscape.

Mary had, in her way, made a decision for him again. From her grave. In that subtle, certain and secret way she had been leading him to here and now. And how things had become for him. He would not be running the marathon in London, but he would return to France to see the property, to take part in Gizande's running. To run with her. And her belief in him. And in the old heresy, that justice may be earned, but will not be gifted.

He had lost one family. And found another. And with that, himself. Mary had closed that door. He visualised the open belief in Suzanne's face as she spoke of their father. And of Gizande and her knowing. Would he tell Suzanne what he had learned of their father? As he stood here looking down across towards the low and broken sun tearing its scarlet and pink light through the ripped clouds. A bird call poignantly behind him and he turned. The gathering and darkening clouds to the east were touched with mauve. He was moved by the beauty of it. And understood.

The boys? The one he had once been? The others? Damien, Finch? And what they would become? The Council? Sylvie. He knew they had done all that possibly could be done. To make him into whom he had now- at last- become. Himself.

He remembered something once read or heard. Truth so precious, it should be attended by a bodyguard of lies. No. He would not tell Suzanne. She has her truth about her father. And Jim has his own. About his.

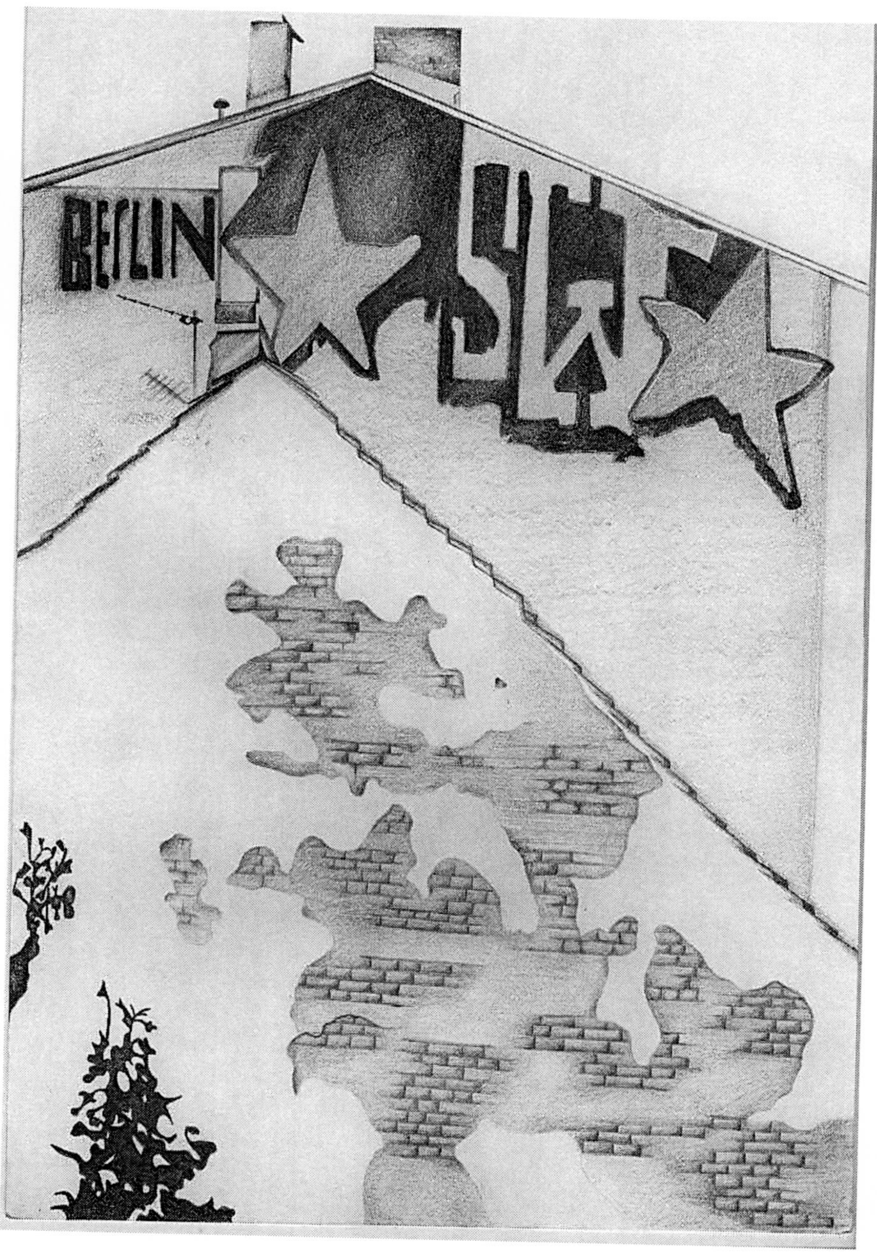
BERLIN

GIZANDE
Book Two of
The Tomorrows That Sing

Pére saint, Dieu juste des bons esprits toi qui jamais ne te trompas, ni ne mentis, ni n'erras, ni ne doutas, de peur que nous prenions la mort dans le monde du Dieu étranger- puisque nous ne sommes pas de ce monde et que le monde n'est pas de nous- donne nous a connaitre ce que tu connais et aimer ce que tu aimes...

Holy Father, just God of the good spirits, you who never misleads, nor lies, nor errs, nor doubts, fear takes hold of us that we will die in the world of the stranger God- since we are not of this world and this world is not of us- let us know that you recognise and love those who love you...

Cathar prayer, from 13th century Occitan text

Chapter One

3rd July, 1989

Dear Jim,

I hope you are well and also that the work on the farmhouse is progressing. Trish and I had hoped to visit you out there this summer, but her pregnancy has taken so much out of her that we're not sure and we won't make any immediate plans after the sproglet is born. Who knows what we can and can't do after that!

But I'm writing to you about other news. Do you remember Damien Toser? Too well. A feeling of foreboding just at the name. *Well, he has died.* Predictable that reading this had not surprised him. The youth's anger and vulnerability that night in the Baltic Fleet had been that fear...

It's happened in odd circumstances. The coroner has decided that he died of a drug overdose. But his Dad is kicking up all sorts of hell, saying that Damien was murdered and that it happened in Germany and not here as the coroner decided.

It's a very strange story and to cap it all, his dad asked for Social Service's file to be produced for the coroner's hearing. He was told the file was missing. Then one of the admin staff gets suspended for refusing to shred a set of files- including Damien's.

It all stinks of rotten fish and the reason I'm telling you is that you know more about this than anyone- well than anyone who's prepared to speak up. I know it's a long shot, but are you planning on making any visits to England soon? We could do with knowing what you know about all this. Even if you were willing to be a witness? A long shot, I know. But every one else either knows nothing or has clammed up about it.

Can you let us know as soon as possible if you can help? I know it's a long shot, especially the way the Union dumped on you in the past. But old comrades never die and all that.

Hope to hear from you soon.

scribbled signature

Julian, Trish (& sproglet!)

Superficially, it had not surprised him. As he felt it should have. But each time read since, it had extended its meaning. Increasingly less just about Damien, more a measure of where Jim now was. And wasn't. That boy, who had been so fiercely uncertain about himself, unknowingly drew Jim back from where he had retreated up into these remote hills, since rearriving in France. It had leaked all that other world back into the routines of slow labour to build something from the bulging walls and wet-rotten plaster of La Retrait Parfaite. Most days alone, mixing cement, but now with the words of Julian's letter, a penned rasping on the inside surface of his skull. As those edges of the heaved-up slabs of rock roughened at the skin of his fingers.

He had been alone up there that week the letter came, working slow and solitary through the long, late-summer days, rebuilding and mortaring where the stone lintel of an upper storey window had cracked with frost and tipped the wall above and the roof eave down into the yard. Without enough scaffolding as an economy, he had to lurch up the stairs inside with each enormous rock, teeth gritted and muscles spasmed with strain, to gently set it finally on the wet bed of mortar. With this and the eave above repaired, he would then start work across the wide shallow roof to replace and reset misaligned slates and seal them with bitumen. He had timetabled all this work to be done with before the weather turned in September. This had seemed the sum of his days since his second rearrival. Except those weeks when the shocking cold of last winter had prevented him even getting up the mountain to the place. But the letter brought another change, rewinding him back northwards to those litter-blown streets where he had left the major portion of a past life.

That first coming back to these mountains had been for Gizande's Running, a strange and wonderful event of several hundred jogging, walking up the valley paths into the mountains, groups coming through clefts in the grey rock ridges from Spain and Andorra to join the flags- Catalan, Basque, militant red, anarchist black, makeshift banners- singing, all threading back down into that to-be-drowned village, now again fenced off to contain a group of fearsome-looking visored paramilitary police. He had then also first seen the ruin of La Retrait, but the reality of living here had been harder than his first brief visits had let him deceive himself. The language. A slow learner, his ears were stupified by the clutter of words. At the simplest level, he still needed help to get everything more than a loaf of bread pointed at behind shop-counter glass. Especially getting building materials. Suzanne was never available weekdays except during school vacations. Gizande could only come with him to the bricolage when her own farm allowed her.

And the complexities. Of the taxes, for the building and for the land without building. And of the Permis form to allow him to "modificate" the farm. Jim had believed that he was just trying to make it habitable, but the previous summer Gizande warned him that he should invite the Mayor to look over the property before filling in the forms. He had arrived accompanied by a sour and sceptical official.

"Ha! L'anglais!" the Mayor had grinned, a firm handshake, a glint of contempt, then turned to talk swiftly in French to Gizande, ignoring Jim trailing them, while they went through the semi-ruined house and barn and the official silently made notes on a clipboard. Back out in the sun and feeling foolishly inadequate, Jim looked anxiously at her, while the Mayor and the official walked slowly from earshot.

Gizande had shrugged, "He says that the work you are wanting to be completed is not of minor modifications. You will require the Permis. He says what you wish to complete will change fundamentally the nature of the building. For this, you will need the Permis." Her eyes flitted to check out the Mayor who was coming back at them, beaming with malicious bonhomie. "I will explain it all, when he has gone," then spoke again in French.

The Mayor held out his hand for Jim's, but retained it, turning to Gizande to say in English, "Does our friend here comprehend about the matter of the frontier?" then turned that smile onto Jim, aware of the official's lizard eyes upon himself.

"No," she said, a touch tersely. Then, back into French.

Jim's hand was released, as if with faint dismissal and the Mayor spoke in English to Gizande, "He must know. But it will make no difference with the Permis." He glanced at the official, who nodded and they both turned to the car. At its door, the Mayor called "Au revoir," as if an afterthought.

As they disappeared down the track over the edge of the hill, Jim asked her, "Will we get it? The Permit?"

"Perhaps. He will make difficulties. He says that this land may be in Spain. He says that the true frontier is between here and the village. But I doubt it."

"You mean this is not in France!"

"France, Espagne, what does it matter? It's all Catalonia, both sides of the frontier!" Gesturing the ridge behind, "Spain commences there. But he still wants your Permis before you commence any more work." She had turned to leave herself. "I will assist you with the forms." Then stopped and smiled at him, "Do not allow yourself to become so anxieux." Then laughed, "It is all one now that Spain is within the Community European, but do not tell him that! He hates this because his family make wine and they fear the cheap wine from Spain." Now going, "Tell Suzanne. It may amuse her. Your father was an associate of the Mayor. Ask her."

He had. Sat across the kitchen table, while Suzanne prepared an evening meal.

"What did our father do up at La Retrait?"

"He had plans for a place for the skiers in the winter. He had hopes of the tourism."

"I found many bikes in the barn," Jim wondered. "Was that part of his plans?"

"I do not know of the bikes. Perhaps."

"They were very old and rusty. Corroded?" checking the word with her. "The Mayor also spoke of the farm being perhaps in Spain. Did you know this?"

Suzanne stopped, attentive. "No. Do you mean it is not within France?"

"Gizande told me that was what he had said. She also said he had been an associate of our father."

"Of Papa?" she was surprised. Jim reflected that the intimacy of her endearment for their father would be an absurdity from his own mouth. "No. That Mayor is a villain. It will all be falseness. I know of no relationship between our father and him."

And Jim found himself silent again about their father. As she firmly closed the door again to talking about Francis. After a pause, picking up Gizande's comments, he tried to lighten it with, "It won't matter anyway, it's all the European Community both sides of the border."

But Suzanne was not to be softened. "Ha! They try another way to steal our identity. More power to the cities."

"Our father was happy about it? About a united Europe?" he let himself explore her loyalty. To that father of hers. "It stops the Germans being at war with the French."

She looked sharply at him, "That was their problem- Berlin and Paris. Papa was forced to enter a war concerning their frontiers, not ours." And, finally to silence him, "What the Mayor says is nothing. Where is the border for the Catalans?" Again.

And the weather. The rain had come in thunderous torrents in autumn and spring, turning the track up the mountain from the road to the farm into a whitewater stream bed. And the winter cold. Frost shockingly chilled by gales down off the snowfields of the High Pyrenees behind him. In the village cemetery below, the gravedigger had dug half a dozen graves in the autumn, before the ground went iron hard, and Gizande told Jim the man had joked with her that one was probably reserved for l'anglais fou, the mad one, as he was being called. For trying to rebuild up where everyone else had abandoned life, decades since. For six weeks in January and February, unable to reach the place in snowdrifts, he went to help in Suzanne's school with English conversation for the oldest children. As late as early May, fishermen were still breaking ice on the higher lakes to get at their catches.

But mostly, it had been about him getting on with his own life. Some consolation on these summer days to rest his back against warm stone and scan downwards, beyond the closed huddle of that village beneath him, to the snout of the valley where it opened like a flower into the pastel farmlands of Catalonia. When it seemed what he was doing was given meaning. But much of it was alone. Suzanne and Maurice were busied with their lives. And Gizande. She had become remote, distant, even when she spent a day working with Jim on La Retrait. Speaking little and most of that practical, she laboured beside him, quiet and humourless. She had run with him several times that first summer of 1988, showing him tracks that wound up onto the ridges behind the farm, where the serrated blades of the main peaks stretched away to the northwest and unwound them with him back down into the pastures. But, too slow for her pace, the runs tailed off. He had eaten occasionally with her family at first. Sometimes, the mother there too, saying nothing to him. Only talking to her daughter in Catalan. And Gaillarde and Guillem, Gizande's daughter and son, serious and listening. But like their running together, this too had lapsed.

Some days he knew she understood what he was doing here. But other days, his own uncertainties would wall him in from those around, sealing himself off with the hard solitary labour of whatever it was he believed himself to be doing. Some warmer nights, he even spent up here in a sleeping bag, listening to the crickets and cicadas filling the silence and an occasional nocturnal animal moving through the undergrowth outside. Woken by the early woodpecker in the woods below. Coming out into the warming dawn. Like the lizard in the log pile. And scanning for vultures among the peaks behind.

But the letter. It let in the dark from that other place. Reminded him that he had not arrived here, so much as happened in a place on the escape from somewhere else. As his father had happened here, escaping over the mountains from whatever he had left behind in Spain. Returning home to his sister's house each twilight that week, he said nothing of it. She and Maurice did not ask about it, busy as they were with the preparations for the village's Bicentennial celebrations of the Revolution in a few days. Maybe he would have tentatively spoken of it with Gizande, but it was now the busy time on her small farm. So he had worked on building and the letter had worked on him, rubbing away at his undistracted brain, insisting on an answer to Julian. Re-engagement with that other world.

Gizande, it would have to be. He felt drawn to seek the permission of her wisdom- what to do about this.

The drive in the old Citroen van, down the repaired rocky track cut across the rough scrub that had reclaimed the farm's rock-strewn fields over the years. Through the narrow neck that dark blind village made of the valley, opening into patches of greener pastures, the road wound down to the fertile fields aside the river, flooded into green life every spring with the meltwater from the Pyreneean mountain snow. The same meltwater that higher up, tore up the track from La Retrait, down here irrigated this best land with the debris torn from his own earth. He sought to retrieve that calm of Gizande. Less her words, than the reflection of his doubt within the reassurance of that unearthly confidence she had shown in Jim when they had first met.

He found her in the steep garden, watering the flowers and vegetables. Her worn blue overall bodystill, encircled within the green, the yellow and the red of the lush slope at the back of her barn. Jim waited behind her while she swept the green plant tops with fine clouds of hosed spray rhythmically whiplashed by her wrist. Doubting that he could ever have such luxurious fruitfulness on his own hillside.

She knew him there, but neither spoke while she finished the task. Finally, without turning round, "Will you turn off the water? At the faucet. Please."

As he returned, she was rolling up the hose, walking back towards him, eyes to the task, still saying nothing. Until, "Bien," as she laid it neatly beneath the tap. Then, attention to him, "I was not expecting you, Jim."

"I was not expecting myself," he grinned.

She was a moment quizzical, "You have something to say?" But, those penetrating eyes into his face, "You have a trouble, eh?"

He did not answer, looked away. Had it always been so humourless between them? Then, as this was what he had come for, said tiredly, "Yes. I have a trouble."

"Come. We will go into the house," and she reached out, perhaps to brush his arm with invitation, but withdrew it, passing by him across the yard and into the back of the house, with its tall gaunt windows mirror-blinded by the sunset. Again, he wondered that she could live in such an externally ugly house. And be who she was.

He followed her through the storeroom, cluttered with tools, outdoor clothing, the chest freezer and the pedal-driven grinding stone. Up to the first floor. The kitchen. Dark, wood, bundles of dried herbs, onions and garlics hung from its beams. The smell of cooking. The shelves of ointments and oils.

"Sit." She turned away, "Will you stay? There is sufficient to eat. The children stay with their grandmother tonight."

"No. I have told Suzanne I will return."

"A glass of wine?"

"Yes." He held back from "please". Part of that discomfort with the platitudes of courtesy when in her presence. No need to fill silence with more than listening. Or waiting. Or with his own hesitations.

She brought the glasses over to where he sat at the heavy, worn table and sat near. But distant.

He looked up at her. "My problem," he smiled, a touch foolish. She said nothing. He edged away from the letter with, "I was unable to do more on the house today. So I came down here. To see you." Her silence invited him to go on. "I've done all I can do without help now. To get the new lintel in place. And then I can complete the broken roof."

She waited. He said no more, so she tilted her head inquiringly, "But, Jim. You knew I would not be possible to come to help this week. You understood, yes?"

"Oh, yes. You told me."

"So the lintel is not the problem. Yes?"

"No," both defeated and relieved. "No. I've had a letter." Her eyes rested on him. So he continued, "From England. From someone I worked with." He looked at the glass, elegant within his fingers, but put it down. "I have told you the story of when I was in England. What had happened. What I went back to. After I first came out and met Suzanne. When I first met you. The boys." He smiled to himself at his fragmentary sentences, then looked at her watching said, "When you first met me, you shook me."

"Quoi?" Cautiously, "I? Shake you?"

"No. It's an expression. A term of speech- of words- in English. You surprised me. Very much. You seemed to know so much about me."

"Non." She looked at him, then down, picking at a seam of the overalls. "I did not know about you. But I could see you. The boys. The crimes against them. They were in your face."

"You called it exorcism," he whispered.

"L'exorcisme," she echoed quietly. Then looked up at him.

He nodded slowly. To her. And to the awful fact that Julian had passed on to him and he now wanted Gizande to share the pain of. "Damien. You remember I told you of Damien Toser." She said nothing. Just the steady look. Awaiting Jim. "He is dead. They want me to come back. I'm the only person who knows about him. They are trying to destroy documents about him." He looked down, feeble at these broken bits of explanation he had offered her.

He wanted her to place her hand to his shoulder, to tilt his face up again to her, as she had once in the past. But she simply said, "Jim. What do you have to do?"

He felt irritated by the insistence of this story from a past he wanted shed. "What do I have to do? To rebuild La Retrait. To have a roof over my head by the winter. Somewhere to live. Not at Suzanne's." But healed the selfishness of this with, "Give her and Maurice their home back. So I have a home. Of my own."

She drank from her glass. "Can you do that if you don't answer the letter? A home is not walls. Not a roof reconstructed. That is only a building. A home is the spirit of who lives in it."

Jim looked round the kitchen. Inhaled the smells of the room. Of this home impregnated with Gizande herself. And brought his eyes back to her face, the generous breadth of her smile across the narrow jaw. "Then I must go? Back to England."

"Must you?" she asked, reflected back to him, the smile faded into expressionlessness.

Jim grinned, "I want you to tell me. But you won't."

"No." With seriousness. "You can only live here- only give your life to La Retrait when your spirit is no longer troubled by that past."

"Is your spirit never troubled, Gizande? You always seem so calm. Serene. Need to say so little."

She barely smiled. "Is that how I seem? Drink. The wine is fresh."

He looked down at the glass, but only stroked the stem. "Is it your catharisme?" He used the French word.

"I have my faith. It keeps me from too much in this world. Their world."

"Whose? Whose world?"

She sighed, as if restless. "You know, Jim. Why ask me for the answers you already possess?" An edge of frustration. At him. But a broader brush too, with a flick aside of her hand. "Those who win the prizes here. Those who celebrate the Revolution every July the fourteenth. Who stand and become saluted. My faith protects me from becoming one of them."

"Oh yes. July the fourteenth. Did Suzanne tell you? There's a row about where I am to sit at the dinner. Suzanne will be on the top table. But they don't know what to do with l'anglais fou."

"And you will attend?"

"For Suzanne. She wishes me to. It will probably be a laugh- amusing to see how they manage me," but his smile was despite how he felt.

"That is the prizes of their world. The place on the table for dinner."

He was silent a moment, as if caught out by her in a misbehaviour. "I would like to understand, Gizande? Tell me about it," he almost blurted, hungry for something of her assurance and calm. The certainty. "Tell me about your faith."

"I will. One day." She sipped and looked away. "I think I have told you. But you have not heared." Then back to him, "We will say another time. When you have returned after doing what the letter requires."

"So that's what you think I should do," he said seriously. A taste of defeatedness. By circumstances.

"I think that is what you think you should do, Jim. Yes?" She smiled and shook her head. "Why do you require someone else to tell you what to do, when you have decided already yourself?"

"I don't know. Maybe it's you. It's not just someone else, it's you. You seem to know what I should do." Then, almost childlike, "I wish you could come with me, Gizande."

Her face darkened. "No, Jim. I cannot. You know already what you should do. Is that not true? Is that not sufficient?" Then, almost a laugh, "How would you explain me to your friends? No. I have obligations here."

"Perhaps. I suppose so." But his sense was not that he had decided anything. He felt the last year, the work on the farm, slipping away from him. Wrenched back by decisions made in a part of his life he thought he had left behind. "Can you ever say no to your past?" he murmured, but she had already risen and gone round the table to the stove. Then, to her, "But you have belief. You seem to know- how to be guided. The beliefs I had, I have lost. I know what's wrong. But not what's right," almost plaintively. "What I should not be doing, but not what I should."

She turned. And for a moment studied him- as if for the first time. Softly she spoke, and he leaned his whole body, as if to hear, to be touched by her across the impossible distance of the room's breadth, "You commence to find the good, when you search for the evil. It is our belief. You will know."

"Will I? Why do I doubt it?"

"Ah, Jim," a smile, but also irritation in her voice. "You are a horse with the eyes-" searching the word- "bandés?"

"Bandaged?" he offered, then, "Blinkered."

"Yes," she nodded and, crossing the room back to him, "Jim... Jim. You live on the mountain, but you only see as if you are in the bottom of the valley." She sat again opposite him and at last took his hands in hers, her grey eyes into his and, for a moment he was confused by feelings of warmth and heat, shearing away from the surge and urge to be embraced with her. "You must not alone believe in the bad things of the world. The men who stand and become saluted. They need the fears of others so to exist. You will never become one of them. And we will never be those who salute them." Neither saluter nor saluted, but the warmth of her hands asked of him instead- ever to be embracing or embraced? Before he was shaken from this by her disengagement. Flurried by the intimacy she had prompted, she rose and, back across the wide room, at her cooking, she said without turning, "Drink. You must go soon. Your dinner at Suzanne."

Chapter Two

He had left her, dissatisfied. With her distance. He would think about it. Perhaps Suzanne would be able to listen after July the fourteenth. Last time she had worked up at the farm with Jim, Gizande had been there too. Suzanne had been angry. That the only space large enough for the celebratory dinner for the Revolution was her school hall and instructions had been handed down from the Ministry of Education about its use.

"They've stolen this Bicentenaire from us."

"Who?" Jim had asked.

"L'établissement. Paris."

Gizande, painting the barn door near to Jim, murmured in English, "They stole it long ago."

He looked up, but she carried on painting. Suzanne seemed not to have heard and continued, "Like the Liberation. Refusing Papa the Legion D'Honneur." Jim had noticed how she had reverted to this childish name for their father. Repossessing him from her half-brother's scepticism.

Gizande stepped back from her work and said to the door, "And like they did from us in 1968."

Suzanne heard this, looked surprised at the other woman and grunted, before setting off towards the farmhouse with a barrowload of sacks of cement.

Dipping her brush again and pausing it before the wet surface, Gizande spoke to it quietly, faintly smiling, "That is the cause why I will be in my fields on July the fourteenth. Not at the dinner table."

"Is this a cause of disagreement between you and Suzanne?"

"She is her father's daughter." Then looking at him, added, "Your sister."

"What do you mean?" Jim spoke quietly, an eye out for Suzanne's reappearance.

Back, eyes on her brush licking across the rough planks, she said flatly, "What would you wish it to mean, Jim?" further conversation discouraged.

Reflecting on this edge between the two women he had never suspected, he could make little sense of it. Gizande's touch of contempt for their father. A contempt Jim reluctantly shared, but would not speak of to Suzanne, his relationship with her distancing after a year with him still in the spare room of her home. Just as with Gizande. As if the freshness of his arrival had by now staled.

It seemed on that July the fourteenth, all the submerged tensions, all the unspoken histories, the unspent vendettas of Suzanne's village and its families troubled the air in that overheated school hall. As Suzanne had been up there since dawn with Marie Claire, Maurice walked with Jim to the school and helped him find his place, before he went to the top table. Most people had already arrived and were seated, conversing loudly and watchfully, voices lowering to comment on new arrivals. He recognised Raoul and Élise, the friends who had come to dinner several times. And, sat at a corner table, surrounded by family, old Theodor Jacob, that witness against Francis's heroism, a faint smile to greet Jim's arrival. The seven sat at Jim's allocated table went silent, watched him sit, then smiled at him.

"Bonjour," he nodded to the others. A farmer he had met. With presumably his wife. The garage mechanic where he had bought the Renault. His wife who worked part-time in the boulangerie. A couple he did not know. Their small girl stared at him. An empty seat next to him. A girl came with jugs on a tray, offering drinks. Jim indicated the jug with ice. Sazerac, he guessed, took a slice of lemon peel from a bowl on the table and rubbed it on the rim of his glass. Attentive to the cool drink, he watched the room around him beyond his table where the others resumed conversation.

Cold gazpacho soup was being served when the last guest at their table arrived. Jim knew him, Poux, the official at the Mairie who had come up that day with the Mayor. And with whom he had since had several difficult meetings. A man whose duty was to secure from you every nuance of doubt about your plans. Privy to that greater truth of governance, he always knew better. That there is always a greater good than what you plan for your own satisfaction.

He greeted the other couples round the table with precise courtesy, sat down and only then turned to Jim with, "Ah, Mister Brige. So surprised to see you here," in deliberately accented English. This man who had always spoken to him in French.

Jim grinned, too sudden with nerves, and realised what a long afternoon this would become. So he started to drink. Glass after glass of the wine from the bottles on the table. Silently and inward-centred at first, as the gazpacho was replaced by the salad, and then the chicken. The occasional glance at Suzanne, now with Maurice and Marie-Claire at the top table. The hall was becoming noisier as the courses passed, children restless and excited or complaining and bored, adult voices more emphatic with wine. And Poux, at Jim's elbow, more loudly and irritatingly pompous.

Getting drunker, Jim assumed an exaggerated listening pose towards Poux's lecture at the others. A fixed smile to his face, to provoke, rather than to hear the official he detested. Finally, Jim's pose was so intrusive, distracting the others round the table, that Poux turned at last.

"You find what I say of significance for you, Mister Brige?" he asked with an insultingly courteous smile.

"Oh! Yes!" boomed Jim. Then quieter, "Oh, yes. Especially when you speak to me in English."

Poux tilted his head and asked, "Pardon?" In French.

"When you speak in English." Aware of the eyes of the others on him, Jim said, "He never speaks to me in English." Some looked back at him vacant, some hostile as he spelt out with boorish precision. "I. Did. Not. Know. He spoke. English." Then struggling into French, "Je ne sais pas que il parle l'Anglais." Turned back to Poux, "I didn't, did I, Monsieur Poux?"

Poux shrugged, said nothing and smiled to the others for their toleration.

"Well?" Jim pressed.

"Monsieur Brige-"

"Briggs," Jim corrected tersely.

With another shrug Poux resumed, "Monsieur Briggs, I do not understand what you are asking."

"I am asking..." a pause to gather his sense. "I am asking why you never- never-ever- told me you spoke English." Then, in undertone, "You little shit."

Barely a hint that it had been heard, Poux said with the tired and rehearsed patience of the bureaucrat, "It was not necessary. The language of administration is Francais in this country. Not English." He turned to explain to the others in French.

Their looks from Poux to him angered and enfeebled Jim, blundering on, "But isn't it your responsibility- it's your duty to help- as much as you can... You should have told me you spoke English..."

Poux waited to see if Jim wanted to go further, then smiled, composed his hands on the tablecloth and said quietly, "To the contrary, Mister Briggs. It is your responsibility to speak in the language of the people you live within." Then, a wisp of triumph. "If I ever want to live in England- or in the United States of America, I will speak in English. As you see. But now," gesturing expansively round the tricolour-bedecked room, "as you see, we are in France." Leaning close, he then lowered his voice to a waspish murmur for Jim's hearing only, "Your father at least spoke to us in French. And would have respected the language on this day. Particularly. So, no more of this please, Mister Briggs."

Patronised, in the wrong and drunk, Jim pushed his chair back out of the other man's intimacy and snarled, "My father!" Poux recoiled with the others round the table. "You little shit! You- my father!" Then, as a ridiculous afterthought, to the others, pointing at Poux, "Vous! Petite merde! There! French for you!" Other tables round were rippled with quiet shock and Jim, crazy-eyed across the room, catching a look of surprised query from Suzanne, dragged his chair back threateningly close to Poux and growled, "Don't you dare… don't you dare talk about my father! What do you know?" Breathless, he stumbled on louder, "How can you compare him? What do you know about me? What do you know about what he's done?" And, feelings overwhelming him from inside, he asserted himself against the edge of tears, a rigid pointed finger in the other man's face, shook once for each word, "You. Know. Nothing." Then, in a mumbled fall, as he scraped the chair backwards to stand, "About me. And my father."

And stood, with nothing to stand for, but to queasily acknowledge the overlapping circles of eyes spreading with the silence. Till only the sound of a baby's cry and the continued far noise from the kitchens were left. And his sister's footsteps across the floor towards him.

Rescued, he sighed, "Ah, Suzanne," saw in her face and said softly to her, "Sorry," then, "I should not have come," meant to be an apology, blurted as half an accusation.

"No. You should not," as she took his arm and led him out across the watching room, out into the corridor, the voices resurging in the hall behind. She led him into that same room with the tubular chair and padded bench where they had their first close meeting three years earlier. Her tired, impatient, preoccupied face now shadowing that shape of Tracey's face. Even more so than that first coming together.

"I'm sorry." Now a felt welling of nausea.

"You have been a fool, Jim," both irritation and resignation.

He sat heavily on the chair. "Why did you sit me next to Poux?"

"Because he speaks English," she said, impatient with him.

"Yes, but I didn't know. All those times I'd met him."

She looked at him, uncomprehending a moment, before dismissing it with, "I must go now. There are speeches to be made. You must rest here. You have become too drunk. Maurice or Marie-Claire will come for you to take you home later. Rest here now." She went, closing the door quietly behind.

Relieved, he slumped back in the uncomfortable chair. The room still turned nauseously round him. Unable to think the complexity through the screen of booziness swilling about across the inner surface of his skull, he thought it was time to leave her home. He thought fondly, then fearfully of La Retrait. As the one place now- in the world- that owed him a roof. Sleep, he told himself. Till tomorrow. Another day. He slipped from the chair onto his knees on the floor, slid his shoulder down, to finally curl himself around that last thought in the corner of the room.

The sound of singing from the hall, of the Marseillaise, pulled him back to half-wakefulness. Mouth and head sour with the wine, he listened. Struck for the first time by the jolly pomposity of the tune. He pulled himself up to sit against the wall. Maybe he could not belong here either. No more than England. He slowly stood up and dusted off his trousers and jacket. And waited for whoever was to collect him. And take him home to Suzanne's.

Chapter Three

From the little room where her mother had hidden him away from view, Marie-Claire had collected Jim. She no longer lived with her parents. Since her brief spell in jail and Felipe's release some months later, she had gone to live with him in Toulouse, returning home seldom. Back at the house, he went straight upstairs, closed himself into his room and let them assume that he was sleeping off the wine. Which he did.

Later, floating to the surface of a dream, digging up a tree, its roots clutched around a mud-smeared pipe, following it subterraneanly, pushing up with it through slabs of rock into a dark barn, a woman in its shadows, indistinguishable, rain on his upward face as he left her through a hole in the roof, following the sound of birdsong, skywards and into the sunshine. And he woke, the evening sun through the window slanted across the mountains into his eyes. Leadenly, and sour from waking, he could hear Suzanne and Maurice returning. He lay his head back on the pillow, listening, anxious that she would come up and tell him off. Like a child. But she did not. Sliding his tongue round to seek wet in his bitter-tasted mouth, he pulled the bedding over his ears to keep out the distant sound of the family downstairs. Slipping back into sleep.

He woke with the earliest grey light, a few birds starting to chatter. He drew on clothes quietly, went downstairs, stepping past the stair he knew that creaked, taking a swig from the milk jug and putting two bread rolls in his pocket. He went out to the Renault, drew in his breath at the sound of it starting and drove off the farm. He worked particularly hard that day, intending it to be the last, leaving the roof repair to rip away the damp-rotted plaster on the inside walls, working with fierce bouts of energy chiselling and hammering it away, barrowing it off onto the spoil heap at the back of the barnyard. Door slammed on indecision, he would go tomorrow- if it suited Julian. Or even if not.

Back at Suzanne's, her car was on the drive and he remembered it was Saturday. Well, face her it was. With his behaviour yesterday. And with him leaving, back in Britain tomorrow. Probably as not-fully-disguised relief for her.

"Hello? Suzanne?"

She appeared from upstairs, arms full of laundry, including his own sheets.

"A letter has arrived. For you."

He looked over at the shelf where family members' letters were put. It was Julian's hand again. Now downstairs, she was looking at him but, when he met her flat look, she went off into the kitchen. He tore the envelope untidily, then went up to his bedroom to read it.

8th July, 1989

Dear Jim,

Me again.

You'll see how hard I've been working to get you back home for help with the Damien Toser case. My capitalistic brother has bought a holiday cottage in the Dordogne and he wants a cheap way to move some furniture etc out there. So, opportunist as you always said I was, I told him about you and that you said you now have a van and I'd ask you to do the job. Jim smiled at this. *From what I understand, you must pass by the Dordogne coming to and from the Channel.* True. Not far off route, anyway. *He would pay you, probably quite well. He says he wants it in before the winter because he plans to spend Christmas over there with his family. Leaving Trish and I to deal with the parents over the festivities- as if we won't have enough to do with the sproglet.*

So you can see that you can get paid for coming over & giving us the information only you can give to help Scadding- he's the admin member who's been suspended for not shredding the files. Do you remember him, Sid Scadding? I'd always thought he was quiet as a mouse, a management man, but he stood his ground. That was how Jim remembered him too, pedantic and bureaucratically precise. *And, confidentially, he's taken copies of the documents that were supposed to be shredded- the originals have probably been composted by now- but some of it's a bit difficult to see the links in the docs. With Toser. That's where you can help. Perhaps you can come over in August. Trish and I are taking our last chance for a sprogless week's holiday in Wales- close enough to get back to the hospital if things start happening early, I hope!*

Please let me know asap. We go on holiday on the 16th.

Jules. Trish and It.

He reread the last paragraph, wondering what documents they were. Even, if they were the ones burgled from Sylvie's flat? Now that would be a turn-up, he smiled. But the sombre shadow of Damien fell across his mind. The boy's corpse. Jim's anger crushed the sheet of paper into his clenched and whitening fist. Knowing himself to be a fortunate man. Able to choose to make his own mistakes. The sudden and surging memory of Damien's bitter sneer, "Oh, fuck off with your choices!" Pained and angry with the patronising false-care of the adults who were paid for it. And who went off shift from caring. But no other choice was on offer. Damien understood that. And, finally, by not speaking, the adults would take that as consent. And consent was only a step from being asked to put that consent in writing, as the dead boy had to Jim's Disciplinary.

But for Damien, somehow, it seemed that adult world had struck back. Awefully.

Jim unpicked the crumpled sheet, spread it back into legibility across his knee. At least two weeks before he could leave for the ferry. La Retrait had to be sealed at least sufficiently to keep out next winter's weather. Going to England would get him back here to the Pyrenees when? Unlikely before mid-September. Immediately all the parts fell into place. He would tell Suzanne. Take a grip at last.

That fortnight, he moved into La Retrait, camped out on the large ground floor kitchen/living room. He worked as he could never remember, driven by the imminence of his departure and the slightly more distant imminence of winter. He borrowed from Maurice a two-ring camping stove fed by a tube from a large gas bottle and set it up on the large table which, with its two unmatched chairs were the only pieces of furniture in the house. He worked the long days from dawn to sunset. As a temporary measure, he jacked up the broken lintel on the upstairs window with an arrangement of borrowed scaffolding poles, took some of the stone slates from a ruined outbuilding in the field behind and repaired the broken eave. The weather favoured him and, stripped to the waist, he moved across the shallow roof, slopping on bitumen to seal the stone slabs. The massive naked beams beneath seemed secure and he painted these too, finally sealing the upstairs by nailing heavy-duty polythene across the old window frame. Downstairs, after putting in a new window frame and glass there, he had cut up heather cleared from the yard and with a covering of blankets, made it into a rudimentary mattress for his sleeping bag in the driest corner of the room next to the old wood stove and oven. Then he set to finishing ripping off the rest of the old plaster, cementing up some of the largest crevices between the revealed and massive stonework, before starting a rough first layer of replastering.

The start of the second week, Gizande appeared. She had spoken to Suzanne or Maurice and there was concern in her eyes as Jim showed her round the work he had done.

"But can you live in her? In this building as it is now?"

"Is it any worse than the condition of the shepherds in the high pastures? In their cayolars, as you call them? Those huts at the tops of the valleys." She nodded and he smiled at her, feeling for some reason surer of himself with her from the ten days spent up here. "Didn't you tell me about the goodness of living up here? Wasn't it la terre chaude, down in the valleys, in Larozelle and the other towns? That the belief of the peasants was that down there was a morally inferior place?"

She looked at him, surprised, "Oui. Yes. Le monde du dieu étranger."

Jim laughed fondly at her, "Yes. The world of the stranger god. You see! I don't forget what you tell me, Gizande." Then resumed, "And it was up here, in la terre froide, up above all that, that's where moral grace is to be found. And right at the valley ends, up against the mountains themselves, beyond even the last shepherd's hut, where no one actually lives. That's where real divinity is to be found. Isn't that what you told me the peasants believe?"

She smiled and nodded slowly to him, "Yes. I said that. It was from the words of my grandfather."

"Well?" Jim gestured expansively round the half-plastered room. "This is it, isn't it? I'm living it. You won't get any higher up the valley than here, so I guess I won't get any nearer to moral purity. Being the good man," then he broke off into a long laugh, restrained by his smiling look of warmth towards her.

"Why do you laugh?"

"No, I'm sorry. It wasn't at you. I wasn't laughing at you." He walked over to the plaster and, closely examining it, rubbed his fingers over its rough edges. Reminded for a moment of the roughened skin of her palms, so long ago, his first visit to these mountains. Cradling his own face, so long ago. "No. Really," turning back into the room and her. "I just had to get it done enough for the winter. To keep the worst of the weather out. Before I leave for Britain next week."

"So. You will be going."

"Of course. You said that I should."

"No, Jim. That is not my memory of our conversation. It was something you knew you had to do. To return to speak for the dead boy."

"But you said…" What was it she said? Had she said it herself or had he? Had he been led by her to his own words? "You said I would not be able to make this a home. Unless I first went back to sort out- about the boys."

"So, that is true, is it not? Why are you making all this work, here," her opened arms embracing the room, "if not to be your home after your return. It is of no matter who said the words, if they are true. Yes?"

He smiled back at her, murmuring, "Oh, the wisdom of the woman."

"Pardon?"

Still smiling, he shook his head, "Gizande's wisdom." A moment when he urged to touch her for her warmth, even grasp her arm with a rough matey laugh, but held back and said quietly, "Your wise words."

"They are not my words. If you believe- in making this your home- if that is your belief, you will do what is needed for that to happen. You will do the building. You see- you do it now. And also, you will settle your heart so that you are able to return to a home. Here. And if that is what you do, they are not my words, they have transformed into your actions. Words are facile," using the French word. "They are an emptying of the lungs. Until the actions that may follow behind them. Only you make the words true. From your own actions, Jim."

He wanted to laugh with her. To reach a shared moment behind all the wise words. And the remoteness they seemed to place the person beyond. Whoever that person Gizande was. But he just smiled at her, with a sense inside of stoically accepting that she would continue to manage his distance from her. Perhaps for ever.

Turning away, he walked to the door, pushed it open and looked down the valley. His eyes smarted. The wind? Or her?

"I saw a pair of vultures quite low in the valley the other day," he said, out to the wide sky before him. "I've not seen them so far down before."

"They say there is a bear come into the valley," she had come close to his shoulder, but he held himself from turning, his eyes into hers, to that intimate and threatening proximity. "The vultures eat from the bones that are left from dead sheep. But I think it is foxes. It is only the sheep who have been born this year, the little ones. A bear has never been known so low in the valleys in this part of the Pyrenees."

A bear? Should he do something about it? Precautions?

As if he had spoken this, she said, "You should not be unquiet. Only keep the door shut at night. The farmers down in the valley wish for the excitement of a bear. Without the reality, I think."

He stepped from the doorway, so he could turn to her. With the space between them. "Foxes?"

She shrugged. "Perhaps you should have a gun. Up here." And seeing his perturbation, added, "When you return. For the winter here. When the animals become hungry." She turned back inside and he followed. Now wanting her gone, leaving the space for him to think of her. Without the problem of them being alone here. With the unspeakable thoughts about her, made foolish by both her presence and her remoteness.

"The stove," she said. "Does it function?"

"I don't know. I haven't tried it." He went over and gave it a doubtful and gentle kick.

"We will do that," she smiled at him, a quick unstiffening of the atmosphere in the room. "There is the wood in the yard. We will steal some of the dry bruyere for commencing the fire." To his quizzical look, she added, "From your bed."

"Ah! The heather."

And they set to it. Best for him when they were together but busy.

Chapter Four

As he drove away from the ferry, across the dark rolling road cut across the English night, he was travelling away from where he wanted to be. Work welldone on the farm in the last fortnight and the dawn display of beauty as he left, dovetailed his decision to leave into an unexpected, last minute and too-late-now certainty about the place. Two days ago, the trees afloat on wreaths of morning mist, he had sped away from the stood-proud plateau where Suzanne lived, winding down into the poor and dirty valley, the plunging road with faded slogans- "Volant!", "Allez!"- still from last year's Tour de France, early enough for the streets of Larozelle to be quiet, some overdue flags and streamers from Bastille Day limp in the twilight.

His hands on the wheel could still feel the rough cold rasp of the hundreds of stones and slabs he had shifted this summer. Work for himself that he had never done in his life before. The measured progress of raising walls and rooves. He wanted to be within them this winter. And firing the stove with her that day, taking him to the point of realising that living up there would be a real possibility. But a possible reality deferred by this. What he also now knew, as Gizande had confirmed, that he had to do this first. Turning his back on Damien would keep Jim awake at night. The poltergeist of worrying what he might have done.

For Suzanne, it was up to Jim. From her indifference, rather than any trust in her English brother, as she used to call him. But what held his mind now, the first sunlight from the east blindingly on the busying wet roads of the Midlands, were those strange moments with Gizande. Of unachieved imminence at the farm. And her words in her kitchen always with him, sometimes rephrasing his questions of himself into her accented and stilted English that threw a flash of insight by that crooked tilt of meaning. Episodes of conversation that told him to trust himself. As she strangely and reticently did.

Trish was in when he arrived. Filling the hallway, she was very laden with the impending child. "All this for a boy," she had said to Jim. "Look at me- I should be ashamed of myself!" Then hugged him awkwardly in greeting.

"When's it due?"

"Last week." She stroked her belly reflectively, "Too comfortable by half. The lazy bastard doesn't want to come out." She looked at Jim. "You must be exhausted. Do you want a tea?"

Yes, but he saw her propping herself tiredly against the sideboard. "No, it's okay."

She caught his look and smiled, “Don't worry about me, Jim. I'm better doing something. Stops me thinking about what's to come. If I sit down, I need a hoist to get me up again. I'm better standing and doing something.” She went through to the kitchen and he followed. “Julian won't be back till five. I may have to lie down for a bit this afternoon, but he's left you papers to look through. And I can tell you a bit about what's been going on.” She stopped preparing the tea and looked across. “It's awful. God alone knows where it will lead. It feels like the tip of the iceberg.” Then, unsmiling and serious, “We're both glad you decided to come back. But we wouldn't have blamed you if you didn't. To go raking into all this...” She looked back to putting milk in the cups. “...filth,” she said finally.

It needed no answer.

Across from him at the kitchen table, Trish leaned against the cooker. “In a strange way, all this makes us more determined about him,” pointing into her womb. “It's very animal. Hearing about what may have been done to those boys, it makes me fiercely protective of this little man inside me.” She mused, “I never thought I'd feel this about a boy. Always expected to have a girl. You know. Bring her up to be a woman who can deal with being in a man's world.” She smiled, “Sort of like an extension of a woman's right to choose. But it makes me feel that this one is more vulnerable. Needs the protection I- and Jules- can give him. I've been reading that male babies are vulnerable to all sorts of risks that girls aren't.” She shuddered, then pursed her lips, “In a weird sort of way, the Damien stuff confirms that.”

“He was strange.” Jim tried to revisualise him, but it was the flavour of his angry nerviness rather than his face that fixed in his mind. “Bitter, but sort of- I don't know- eager for us to help him. To get the abuse stopped.”

“Well, it has now. Certainly,” Trish said flatly. “Who was the us? You said us.”

“Oh. A woman called Sylvie Cathcart. Worked in the housing association where he lived.”

“I could be wrong, but I think Jules told me she's quite senior now in Social Services.”

He gave a sharp, humourless laugh, “That would figure. She got my job when I was sacked.”

“Oh. Sorry, Jim.”

“No. All that's gone. Best thing that could have happened. Though she nor the others didn't do it for my own good.”

She smiled distantly, "A farm in France now, eh? Sounds good," but he could see that her mind was inward on the discomfort of her body. She shifted laboriously again.

"Can I do anything, Trish?"

She shook her head, smiled again, vacantly, her eyes down to the swollen belly before her, totally engaged, he realised, with the other life inside uncoupling from her into being itself. Alert but powerless, his eyes on this other woman, a curiousness now for the missed birth of his own child, twenty years too late. Back here where home had been, he felt the urge to contact that child, Tracey. Unfamiliar and out of place as they had become to each other's lives.

But he detached himself from this with, "Look. You go and have a rest. Tell me where the papers are and I can look over them."

"You're a gent. But have you eaten? Are you hungry?"

"No. I ate somewhere in Cheshire. I'm fine."

"Well. Ironically enough, the papers are in his-" hand to her belly "- room. I'll show you." From the room, already decorated with animal wallpaper, cot and plastic mobile gently turning above it, he took the lidded cardboard box back into the living room.

"Well," she said, "I'll take your invitation and love you and leave you. See you later." He picked up the started mug of tea. "Make yourself another drink if you want."

Back in the lounge, he looked down onto the box, listening to the sounds of Trish. A door. Twice. Toilet flush. Another door and the flat was quiet.

Almost reverentially, he lifted off the lid. An elastic-banded bundle of Union correspondence about Scadding. He leafed through, without undoing them, then put them aside. More correspondence, replies from the Personnel Department. Later. That put aside too. Then two ring binders, a fat one of Disciplinary Procedures, a thinner of Procedures for the Storage of Confidential Documents. Interesting, but for later too. Copies from Scadding's own Personnel File. A glance at that showed he had been working for the Council back in its old Urban Borough identity since 1946. Forty three years. Revenge for loyal service, Jim shook his head sadly. Those joined the stack outside the box. As he looked further down into it. Finally, a large unsealed envelope which a felt tip pen had scrawled across "Scadding- Shredder Files."

Jim sat back into the sofa and, delicate with apprehension, drew the envelope from them. To lay on his lap. And there, on the top,

Disciplinary Proceedings: James Briggs

Statement by Damien Ian Toser. Jim read it through. With the afterknowledge of the boy's death. What had Damien been promised? Had he asked for the reward that had been offered? That they never intended to pay? Whoever They were. As low-level as Mrs. Patterson? As high as Chief Constables? Asking himself who would have been in on this, just sucked him into paranoid spirals of fruitless speculation. The Statement aside, there were papers from Damien's Departmental Child care file. Care Proceedings Court papers. Correspondence with a foster parent. A Police Caution for being Drunk and Disorderly when he was fifteen. A letter from his Dad, complaining about Flynn, the social worker. Fred Toser, that little man at dusk in the car park. Couldn't imagine him making murder accusations. How had Julian's letter put it? Kicking up all sorts of hell. It's what they can do to little people sometimes. Make heroism out of self-effacement. If pushed hard enough.

Further down, the turning back of the pages stopped. His fingers stilled by recognition. Sylvie's writing. A file of hers he had read. The one about the Belgravia move-on flats. The copy of the letters of complaint about men visiting and the Vice Squad reply. That had been burgled from her flat. Or not. And for the first time, the obvious about her. That maybe no burglary took place. No. Too many unaccountable things. Her distressed flight to him at Bradford. The man's voice on her phone when Jim had called? Does she know now what Scadding was refusing to shred? However senior she has now got herself in Social Services. But the significance over all woke in his mind. Her file was in with Damien's papers. Alongside his file. That alone made the connection. Sylvie and what she did or didn't know, what she did or didn't do, was insignificant. Jim let the air sigh out between his closed lips. And that was without accounting for the further possibility. Fred Toser's murder claim. And in Germany? It was the scale of it, the numbers and the seniority of those involved, to cover up such a thing.

Chapter Five

It was nearly seven when Julian got home. Looking tired, but keen. He came over to Jim, who was still surrounded by stacks of documents, his own cardboard box of them now next to Julian's on the carpet before him.

"Good to see you." Then, squeezing Jim's shoulder, "Glad you could make it over here, Not much of a swap. South of France for this sad old town, I'm afraid."

Measuring the man he had not seen for over two years, Jim simply said, "The job's got to be done." Emotionally pressed down by the weight of what he had been reading through all afternoon, he could not be infected by that joviality.

"Trishy? She resting?"

"Yes. Think so. She went for a rest soon after I came."

"Yes. She hasn't been finding it easy." Then, "I wish I could spend more time, but I'm trying to save up the rest of the year's leave for after the sproglet comes. I'm not sure that a week away in Wales was such a good idea. We spent most of the time worrying about what would happen if her waters broke while we were in remotest Snowdonia. But I had to get away from all this," a swept motion across the blanket of files and papers around Jim. "It's really starting to swallow up my Union time. And, of course, Management are putting an extra squeeze on me- on all stewards- that we don't go a dot beyond the time allowed by agreement for Union tasks." His grin resurfaced, looking down at the documents, "I hope you understand all this better than I can. Why on earth some of this stuff was even filed with Social Services, never mind being in a kid's Child Care file!" He stepped back. "I'll see if Trish wants a drink. Do you? Tea? Or a beer?"

"Beer'll be fine." Then, to the documents, "I'll clear up this lot."

Julian cooked the dinner, but Trish was too tired to join them. Jim was to sleep on the divan in the living room of the small flat. He had brought some running gear with him to try to keep fit while away from working on La Retrait, so he privately decided to take an early run each morning so that he could tidy himself out of sight from their living room before the couple appeared.

Julian had people for Jim to see. First there was Scadding. Of course. The administrator did not understand the significance of the documents he had protected. Only that he was being asked to take an action forbidden in a Procedure. Enough to transform the man into the stone wall he had become- to everyone's surprise, but his own, it seemed. Then there was Huntley, a local agency journalist, who was following the trial of a mentally handicapped youth for a string of indecent assaults on young boys. Julian had had one covert meeting with Huntley. As a care kid old enough to be planned for what next, the youth had links to Northlodge Housing. At this, Jim simply asked tersely, "And what's Sylvie Cathcart doing now? I see you have some of the documents she told me had been burgled from her flat. They're with the things Scadding was asked to shred."

Julian looked poleaxed. "What? Her? Burgled?"

"Yes. Didn't I tell you?"

"No. I knew you'd met Damien Toser with her. But that's all."

"And she got my job. While I was still suspended. Just that neat."

"Yeah..." Reflectively, "I remember something about that. Some excuse for her not to be called as your witness at the Disciplinary." Then, eyes seriously to Jim's, "You know what she is now, do you?"

"No. But I can see you're going to tell me."

"She's my boss. Head of Children's Services. Service Manager. Number Two to Anderson. And not even social work qualified. She's taken over all the day-to-day management of children's homes. Foster parents. Anderson's kept the Child Protection. There's talk about what she had to do to get there. From nothing. But Trish told me I shouldn't buy into all that sexist stuff. You know- who she's supposed to have slept with." Jim could not restrain the shadow of a cynical smile as he rephrased this as, Or fucked with. Placing her where she belonged, he thought. At last. But said nothing. "Well, the best bit- now you've told me about the documents- is that it was her orders that Scadding refused to obey. She'd been telling him to shred her own papers? Is that what you're saying?"

Smiling at the absurdity, the slapstick silliness of it, Jim replied, "I guess that's what I am saying." Then, "That would certainly make her very uncomfortable to know that I was back in town. Now." And, rubbing his hands exaggeratedly, "Sleepless night job for her. Of a different sort, I shouldn't wonder."

Julian smiled, "Not your favourite person, I gather. Not mine, either."

"How's she handling it? Isn't the job way above her league?"

"How does she handle it?" Julian reflected. "I'd say by a combination of charm. And bullshit. She picks up bits of jargon from others and talks it back of you. But if you look really hard at her- don't give her a smile to reassure her- you can see her get nervy. You know the sort. Likes to give out orders, make presentations- with the script already written- probably by someone else. Standing up with an overhead projector for cover. Won't get involved in a proper dialogue. Won't discuss a difficult child care case. Or what to do about a problem family. Just there to pass on the budget cuts coming down from Treasurer's." And he shrugged himself to a full stop.

Satisfied to hear her so vehemently condemned by this most unvehement of men, Jim chuckled, "I gather you really don't warm to her, either, Julian."

Julian's replying smile shrank to a serious look down into his opened palms. "The job's not worth it- if you can't help the kids we get have a decent life. Nothing complicated about it. The pay's rubbish, but if they let me do the job, it makes me the most privileged person in the world." He rolled his fingers up into fists and looked across, "You were never a social worker, Jim. I don't know if you got the same thing from your job. But it's often little things. Getting a DHSS grant for a mum who's always slagged off everything about Social Services. For years. And you're the first person to get her trust. And she actually smiles at you."

"I should say don't make my heart bleed, Julian. But I think I get it. I remember when I was in the car plant, there was a bloke who used to gamble away his pay on payday. And I negotiated with the men he'd lost his wages to- real card sharps they were. Got them to agree to pay him back most of it. He had a wife and- I don't remember how many kids. And the twat smiled at me with so much..." Jim searched for it, "thankfulness. Almost hero-worship. He told everyone what a fine shop steward I was." Then, with a coughed laugh, "Didn't stop him losing at cards the following week. A real pillock. But I think he got his mates to vote for me at Branch Elections."

"Yeah," yet Julian was not with Jim's recollection, still stirring his own discontents.

But the gloom of this discomforted Jim. He shifted himself to sit upright, leaned forward, hand on the papers on his lap, eyes down to them, lips bitten to a hard line. "Okay. But what to do about this? As well as Scadding and the journalist, can I see Fred Toser?"

"Is that the dad? If it's not in the files there, I wouldn't know where to find him now. Do you know him? "

"Met him once. Funnily enough, it was that night I met you and Trish in the Labour Club. He came up to me in the car park. As I was leaving."

"What did he say?"

Jim hesitated. Then, "He thanked me." But searching, he added, "He didn't know Damien had- you know, given a Statement against me." Finally, it came to him and he blurted, "London. Damien had gone to London."

Julian was looking quizzical, "What? When?"

"That's what Fred Toser told me. Damien had gone to London. I remember how sick it made me. He was happy about it. You know, his son making his way in the world, and all that." Then, picking up the London Vice Squad letter, Jim shook it emphatically, "But he didn't know about this. He didn't know what I knew about care kids suddenly going to London. And what happened to them."

"Come on Jim. Letters of one syllable for me. Please. What are you talking about?"

Putting the sheaf down on the other documents, "This." Then, woken from his memory of that night, "How much did I tell you about all this- that night with Trish?"

"Just about what happened in the Disciplinary. And that the Union wouldn't support an appeal. Against your sacking."

And Jim remembered his mild distrust of Julian, then. Measuring him now, across the cluttered table between them, Jim accepted that this man was his only way ahead with this. "Well you don't know the half of it, Julian, mate. Even less than that." He looked at his watch. "It's eight fifteen. Are you ready to make a long night of it?"

He stood, serious-faced, "I'll see if Trish is okay. I'll get some more beers."

"Not too much booze. Maybe strong coffees would be more like it."

"Okay," Julian grimaced.

"And remember." Terse and emphatic, Jim added, "Your boss Sylvia Cathcart knows all of this."

It was past midnight when Julian finally left Jim to tidy the papers back into their two boxes and make his bed. Trish had earlier joined them briefly, but she returned to bed leaving the two men, Julian listening, picking up points to be explained again, seizing cross-evidence between papers. After, Jim lay in the dark for a long time, wondering if Julian was tough enough for all this. Or whether that mattered. He knew he probably had a prejudice against the man- not really his style. Rueful about his own prejudices, he thought how he would not have a social worker's job like Julian's. At any price. Picking right and wrong out of that mess. A sort of toughness Julian had? And Jim did not.

He realised how unready for sleep he still felt. He got up found a bottle of beer in the kitchen, hoping the alcohol would help him sleep. Looking through drawers for the bottle opener, he found one full of old newspapers. Distracted, he pulled the top one out and started to leaf through it, surprised at some of the events in the world he was unaware of.

He went back to find the opener and took the stack of papers and the beer back to his bed. In France he had willingly lost touch with what went on outside the small circumscription of his world between La Retrait Parfaite, Suzanne's, Gizande's and sometimes, Larozelle. French-less in France, he did not read their newspapers and seldom watched the television. The last big event he remembered hearing about was the massacre of students in China. Last Spring. Now the old communist states seemed to be in turmoil. The Iron Curtain down in Hungary. Demonstrations and fights with the police in East Germany. Refugees coming west. He went on to read about domestic politics. Then sport. But it still seemed remote. Irrelevant to what was important in his life now. He was here for Damien's sake. Putting the boy's ghost to rest. Not some wider crusade. He was even unsure about getting involved with this other lad. The one with the mental handicap.

Get this done, if he could. Then get back to where he called home now. Because driving back into this town, with its shabby, surly buildings, its new rows of niggardly houses where the slums had been, with gardens as grudging as the yards and ginnels they replaced. Tides of litter already netted up against the fences. Convincing him that home had now become that other place.

Chapter Six

Two evenings later, they met Scadding in the Union Office. Jim remembered the small and tidy precision of the man. Sat when invited, hands tidily at rest along the crease of his trousers. But wary of Jim.

Julian opened things with studied casualness, "Well, I think you two know each other. From the old days, it almost seems now, Sid, with all the changes. Since Jim's left."

"Sydney," Scadding corrected. "With a Y. If you're writing it down."

"Right. Sydney." Avoiding looking at Jim, for fear that he might be captured by the amusement in his eyes. "I wanted you to meet because Jim knows a lot about the documents you-" a pause for the right terminology- "were not prepared to destroy. Jim's now explained what they were about. And that confirms- Sydney- that you were correct in not destroying them."

"I know that. Of course. None of the contents of a Child Care File should be destroyed for twenty five years. That has been a Departmental Instruction back to before the Social Services existed. In the old Welfare days." A touch of regret there?

"Well," Julian resumed, "it's your right to understand everything we can tell you about your case. When we get to Disciplinary- if Management still want to press ahead with that- we may have to introduce new evidence. And Jim here, has that evidence." Looking now at Jim, "How would you feel about us calling him as a witness?"

Jim now felt Scadding's eyes on him. As if they were both waiting for his answer. So he did, "That would be fine with me, you know. Sydney."

Scadding turned back to Julian. "How would having Mr. Briggs present be of assistance to my case?"

"Well, the seriousness of the documents that you were ordered to shred- to destroy- they were so serious that it might even have been a criminal offence to destroy them." Then, with affirmation, "It could be evidence in a criminal case."

The administrator completely stilled at this, his suspense signalling his gathering response. "But Julian. I was not aware of the significance of the documents at the time I was asked to destroy them. I made my decision purely in line with the Procedure. A very long-standing Instruction, I wish to emphasise." He turned, looked at Jim- inscrutable- then back to Julian, "It was not, nor should it ever be, my Responsibility to make a judgement about what document should be allocated for shredding. Documents in Child Care files are confidential. I do not read them. My staff's Responsibilities and mine as their Manager, are to ensure that such allocation for shredding is properly authorised and comes within the Rules we work to. And which the elected Councillors have decided are appropriate." He softly cleared his throat. "In this particular case, the authorisation was from a properly Senior Manager, but it was in conflict with the Council's Rules. It is my responsibility to ensure that these Rules are not broken. Even in error, by a Senior Manager." His voice risen, he finalised with, "It would be completely against the point of having Procedures and Responsibilities for documentation, if everyone was invited to have an opinion on what should be destroyed and what shouldn't."

Jim intervened, "Look, Sydney, irrespective of the rules and the Procedures, the destruction of the files- especially the one on Damien Toser- could be criminal. Destroying evidence of a crime. Even murder." Scadding's move to speak silenced by Jim's hand. "This is important. It's the same thing that they sacked me for. And the reason Sylvie-" suddenly correcting himself- "Cathcart wants them destroyed is that she is already involved in covering things up. Implicated, at least."

"Firstly, Mr. Briggs, I take exception at you linking your Disciplinary with my Suspension. I understand that it was exactly contrary to my circumstances. You were dismissed for having Confidential Documents in your possession, you had no right to. Your were, in fact, in breach of the same set of Procedures on Documentation, that I upheld. I see absolutely no similarity in our cases." Turning to Julian, "And I hope the Trade Union will not treat them as such. Any blurring of the boundaries between Mr. Briggs' actions and mine could only undermine the very Procedures I stood up for. And it would not, in my view assist my case in the slightest." He now frustrated Jim from interruption. "Secondly. I have of course heard of the allegations being made by Mr. Toser, Damien Toser's father. They are only allegations. And I understand that the Police will not be investigating them. Mr. Toser, as the father of a child who was placed in the Care of the Local Authority, is hardly the most objective person. Certainly not to play any part in guiding my actions." Then back to Julian, "Or the actions of those seeking to represent me."

In both anger and admiration of the precise and thought-through certainty of the man, Jim looked over at Julian. Who shrugged back. So Jim leaned forward, untidying the space round the little man who shifted slightly back, "Look, Scadding, this isn't about procedures. Councillors can change them to suit themselves to their hearts' content. At least one of them is implicated in this stuff. And the rest don't know what this is all about- except what's fed to them by the Chief Officers and the Directors." He pulled back and took an edge off his tone, flattening the awful words to let them speak for themselves. "This is about sex-crimes. It's about getting boys to have sex with important men. Moving them down into flats in London. Child prostitution. So that the wheels of industry can be oiled. Deals can be done with the kids as part of the price. Kids from this town. That your Council is supposed to protect." And, with finality, "Both Cathcart and Foley know about this. And Anderson, probably. That's what shredding Damien Toser's file was about."

Scadding's face was shrunken, eyes across to Julian for rescue, then, flashed back to Jim with anger and frightened indignation, he stood, unsteadily, "I don't have to listen to this! Not from you!" To Julian, "I am going. And I don't expect to have my case dragged into all this-" lost his precision- "nonsense! Political nonsense! That has nothing to do with my case."

As Scadding turned to leave, Jim stood and gripped his arm, thin and rigid with shock through the blazer sleeve. Face to face, Jim warned, pleaded, "You have to take sides- sometime you will!" Then lightly disengaged to let him go, out the door, sped steps clattering down the stairs of the empty dark building.

Jim sat back down. And to Julian's face of restrained alarm, shook his head and said, "The right thing for the wrong reason." Struggling for a comparison he could not find, settling for, "He could just as well do the wrong thing, for the same reason." Then growled, "Bloody procedures."

Trish went into hospital the following evening and Julian went with her. Jim tidied, washed up. He thought of Tracey. He had not spoken to her for nearly two years, not seen her for two and a half. She had not replied to his one feeble letter. He found her last phone number in the little notebook he kept and, his thumb rubbing meditatively to hold it open at the page, looked down at her name. Almost to the surprise of his thinking self, his hand moved towards the phone. Picked it up and dialled. A mistake. Redial, and then a ringing tone.

"Hello?" Not her. An unfamiliar woman.

"Sorry. I might've got the wrong number. Does a Tracey Briggs live there?"

"Ooo, no, love." Then a touch cautious, "Who's asking?"

"I'm... family." Then improvised, "Relative. Had an old number. And haven't been in touch. For years."

The woman seemed reassured, "No, love. She's not lived here for over a year. Fifteen months. They moved."

They? "Do you have a phone number?" Then thinking of his unanswered letter, "Or a forwarding address?"

"I used to, but I don't know if I've kept it. Just wait there, love. I'll have a look," and left the phone. He waited, now nervous about what he had started, but recognising that even with her address or her number, he could stop. Search no further, to hear her voice. But an obligation. Not to behave like his own father.

She came back, "You're in luck, love. A forwarding address. I never had a number. Here goes-"

"I'll just get a pen-" returned and wrote it untidily in the notebook. Surprised. Out of town now, down in that old walled city Jim associated with visits on days off, not with living in. Then, complete with the exactitude of the postcode, he thought, just like Tracey. He thanked her and put the phone down.

Directory Enquiries immediately matched name and address to a number. Again, he wrote it down. Then sat back. That was now as far as he could go without the real thing. A script? But, gone this far, he would make the call.

It rang a long time. So that he had begun to feel the relief of putting her off to another time, when it answered. Male. Curtly, "Who is it?" Not the voice of Alex, her old boyfriend, as he could recollect.

"Is Tracey there?" To Jim's ear, his own voice came back to him as almost fawning.

"Who is it?" now impatient.

"It's her Dad."

Surprised, "What? Mr. Briggs?"

"Yes."

"Right," said as if he would be watching what happened now, Jim heard him calling away from the mouthpiece, "Trace! It's your Dad... Yes, it is. Your Dad... Well, I don't know. But he says he is... Well you speak to him." Then, back to the phone, "Hang on a sec. She's coming."

A wait. Then her voice. Guardedly, "Hello."

"Hello, Tracey," almost gushing from him, pulling himself up with, "Who was that? Answered the phone?" Trying to sound chatty, not inquisitive.

She bypassed this with, "Where are you? Where are you calling from?"

"A friend's. I'm back in the country. For some business."

"From France? Why didn't you say you were coming?"

"Well, it was all a bit of a surprise. Last minute. Anyway, I've only just found your new address. You- I never knew you'd moved."

"You never asked." Then from flat to bitterness, "Not a word from you, since you up and left. To your new family."

"I wrote," he said, the familiar, feeble feeling from talking with her. Or being talked to.

"Too late. I'd moved."

Had the woman sent on his letter? He would not go there, so he tried to warm Tracey, "Well, whatever. Anyway, I'm here. Probably for a week or two. I'd like to see you."

"Have you spoken to Mum?"

Now why would he do that, he thought? And why should she ask? But he said simply, "No."

She shifted, remotely conversational, to, "What business are you over for?"

"I've got an offer. To do some furniture removals to France. To the Dordogne. So I'm looking into it." Sufficient truth included. And sufficient omitted. "But I do want to see you."

She seemed taken, a moment, by his sincerity, "Okay. What if you come down here. We could have a meal. You could meet Richard." Then, with a swipe, "You know. The man who answered the phone," but there was a hint of a smile in her voice. Then, unexpectedly, "I'd really like to see you, Dad."

Knocked speechless. For seconds. "Good. I'm glad."

"When, then?"

He guessed that Julian would not be making any appointments for him for the next few days. With the birth. So he said, "How about the evening after next?"

She suggested a restaurant. Neutral ground? And gave directions. And a time.

As he put the phone down, he felt it had not been warm by the standards of other families. But it was as good as it gets between him and his daughter.

He had not heard Julian come in during the night, so he rose quietly. Not to disturb him, in case. Jim pulled on top and shorts, doorkey pinned to them cold against his groin, knotted shoe laces and, feeling upbeat after a good night's sleep, set off running into the streets just starting to grumble into life. Steady, no rush, no race to train for, he set off up towards the long, wooded hill behind the town at an easy pace. With another jogger in the opposite direction, several early dog-walkers, he realised that the aloneness he often regretted, working away on that frontier mountainside, was probably real treasure. All his life, he had been crowded with the lives of others. Until this last two years. Running back, his calves and thighs unfamiliarly tightening, he kept proud posture back through the streets all the way to Julian's door. You never know who may be looking.

Julian was in the kitchen. Looking anxious. "The midwife sent me home at two. She told me to get some sleep and come back in this morning."

"Is it going okay?"

"Who knows? Do hospitals tell you when it isn't?" Shrugging, "Probably okay. But Trish looks in so much pain. And so tired."

"When are you going back?"

"As soon as I've had a bite now. Do you want some toast?"

"I'll shower first. If that's okay." But then, realising Julian was impatient to get back to the bedside, "No, okay. Now'll do. If you can bear eating in the same room as my sweat, I'll just pull on some jeans."

"What will you do today?" Julian asked as Jim came back in.

"If you give me his number, thought I'd try to meet this journalist. Huntley?"

"Oh. Yes. He was Trish's contact. Did some work with him about local history. For her teaching. He got her access to all the local papers' archives. He knew I was Social Services, so he contacted us when he picked up the story of the lad in Court. He just wanted some background stuff about how things happened with kids like that in care. Who was responsible. How old before Social Services drops them- that sort of thing." Jim could see it was an effort for him to reengage his mind from his wife to this. "We were already backing Scadding. And the pieces started to fall into place. Yeah. Go and see him. That makes sense. I might not be too much around for a day or two." Julian went over to his briefcase and copied out the phone number on the back of a supermarket till receipt. "He knows about you coming over here. Your history."

Chapter Seven

Huntley said to Jim, "Perfect timing. The lad's back in Court next week. Maybe you can explain some of this other stuff the Powers-That-Be wanted shredded." And they arranged to meet the following afternoon.

He was a stout, elderly man with thinning rolls of curls unkempt around the bald dome of his head. Like the shreds of a wig. His old-fashioned appearance tweaked by the half-moon glasses he looked over at Jim when they met in the pub. "Herbert Huntley. Gentleman of the Press," shaking Jim's hand. "To avoid the unseemly alliteration of all those aitches, I go by the name of Bert when in conversation."

Jim smiled, despite his surprise at the man. Who continued, "I will buy you a drink just this once. To give you a false first impression of my generosity. So that we can bond, as Julian's colleagues might say."

Returning with the beer, he looked steadily and a little ironically over at Jim. "Jim Briggs. Wrecker of the British Car Industry. Once. For our little town, for a time, a National Figure. Bestrid across our mean streets like a colossus. Bringing my fellow hacks from far-and-wide to marvel that the wonders of Rootes Motors and the British Motor Corporation could be brought to their knees from such a remote and grubby place."

"Very funny," wondering if this man had been sat here long enough to be drunk.

"No, Jim. True. That is how the feeble-brained of Fleet Street saw us. Up Here. They resent being ordered to come up and stay here. Away from their clubs and from the hotty-totty admiration of their little-girl office juniors. To have to expend too many nights in our unexceptional hotels. They never forgave you and the Comrades for that. Same with the Miners in eighty-five. Soon they won't have to leave their shiny new glass offices in the London Docklands. It will all be done by computer. Without a dirty thumbprint anywhere to be seen. All done by Government handouts, computer-to-computer." He supped from his glass, before continuing. Jim wondered what Julian and Trish thought about Huntley, but knew enough to know that any journalist with a listening ear needed to be nurtured. "But we know better, don't we, Jim?"

"Know better about what?"

"What happens in the Real World."

"Which real world would that be?"

Huntley laughed. "Why, the one that starts when you leave Watford. Heading North."

"I'd agree with you, Bert," the familiar term uncomfortable. "But I don't live here any more."

"Ah. Yes. The exile in France. The inheritor of a mountain estate, I understand. An unexpected turn in the tale of so proletarian soul as you, don't you think?"

"Hardly an estate. A ruined farm. On a bare hill. Nothing there, unless I put it there," surprised at his patience with the man's florid, ironic phrases.

The declamatory tone dropped, suddenly a quiet and intimate warmth to Huntley's voice, "No offence meant. If there is any justice in Creation, you have earned your reward, Jim."

"Well," coy with the praise. For a self that seemed to have long since deceased. "Thanks for that."

"As I said, I have studied your path. Unlike many in the trade union movement, you never seemed to take the easy route. Fight to a finish. You got out of union politics too early. You should have still been around in the Car Plant in '72 and '74, the first Miners' Strikes. When they brought Heath down."

"Huh! Easier said than done. You're only alive as long as the members let you be."

"So, at the finish, you find yourself abandoned by your erstwhile supporters?" Jim nodded slowly at this, thinking what an enormous understatement that was. "But I'd lost sight of you for years. After you were sacked from the Car Plant, you even stopped being seen in the Labour Club- one of the more detestable places I have to go in my trade. Didn't even know you were still in town. Then you turn up in Social Services, of all places! And leading an army of one on a Crusade against Child Molesters, for God's sake! But it was all over when I got to hear about it. And you'd left the country."

Beginning to get under protective concealment of this man's cloak of words, Jim started to warm to him. "Well. Here I am again. A bad penny to Them, you might say." Then, quieter, "And this is a real story. Shocking. Unbelievable, I suppose. But I've been carrying it about in my head for so long- over three years- that it's no longer unbelievable to me." Now intensely, reliving the moment, "Do you know, when I got the letter from Julian about Damien being dead- Damien Toser, I wasn't even surprised. Shocked, but not surprised."

"Well, Jim. Now that we've touched base, as the Yanks would say, perhaps we should get down to it. What we each know. And don't know."

"Okay, Bert. Fine. You tell me what you know. I'll fill in my bits. Then we see what we've got to find out."

The boy, Stephen Roberts, was eighteen. He had started to expose himself to children at a playground near the Northlodge unit where he lived. Then he had attacked two nine year old boys. One had escaped, but Roberts had forced the other to start to masturbate him by threatening him with a knife. They were interrupted by a passer by and Roberts ran off. There was no doubt about his guilt, but his solicitor had entered a plea at the last hearing of not guilty by diminished responsibility. When the magistrates reconvened, the issue of medical reports on Roberts would be decided. But Huntley picked up the seriousness of the story when he heard that Stephen Robert's Social Services file was missing and unlikely to be available for evidence in the trial. Through Trish, he had contacted Julian. Learnt about Sydney Scadding and had then really picked up the rotten odour of the story, as he put it.

"I'm unhappy about Scadding," Jim said. "A bit of a pen-pusher who might not last the course. Doing it for the wrong reasons. A procedure-wallah."

Huntley considered this, then, "No. I think you need to understand the man. Yes, his morals and his prejudices are distinctly of the old-fashioned variety. But they are the rock-solid and obstinate foundations to the position he has taken. Remember, he has everything to lose. He is due to retire in 1993. With full service with the Council since 1946. That's a lot of pension for him to put at risk. Especially for a careful man like him. But I do not think he had a moment's hesitation in challenging his Managers." He shook his head, "They don't make them like Sydney-with-a-Y Scadding any more. Do you know he was a Bevin Boy down the pits during the War? At fourteen he was taken off to Yorkshire to dig coal. For Victory. Then came back and started as an Office Junior- he called it Coolie Grade- and has been here ever since. I talked to him at some length. I must tell Julian that Trish should speak to him for her oral local history." Looking up at Jim, "By the way, how is she?"

"She went in last night." Jim shrugged, "Julian was anxious this morning. But it's his first. He wouldn't know what to expect," and his mind was checked by the feebleness of his own authority, based on his own absence from his daughter's birth, the crisp precision of her voice still in his ears from the phone call.

"Pass on my best wishes. I'll send her some flowers. What ward is she in?"

Jim realised he did not know and shrugged, "I'll ask Julian. And let you know."

Huntley rose, indicating the empty glasses, "Some additional lubricant and let your side of the story run."

"Just a shandy for me now. I'm driving."

"Oh dear, so am I. No matter."

He sat back and the wet-ringed table reminded him of those other meetings. The Baltic Fleet. And her. He should have been angry, but just felt tiredly wasted on her. And contempt.

Huntley back with the drinks. "I was thinking, Bert. To get a real idea of what we- I thought was going on, we need to sit down with the papers in front of us."

"Yes. The papers." He sat down, serious, "Yes, I meant to speak to you about that. You have documents with you?"

"Not here, now."

"But you have them?"

"Yes. That's what I was going to say. You need to see them to understand how I got to where I am about this. My conclusions."

"But where do you keep them?"

"At Julian's. With his stuff, because he doesn't trust one of the Union officials nosing around, if he kept it in the Union Office."

"You must move them. Or at least get copies made and kept in a secure place. With someone you can trust and whom the Powers-that-be here would have no idea is connected to you."

"Why?"

"There has been a forced entry into my office. Since I've been working on this. In fact the night after Julian took me to meet Scadding. Took nothing, but there was nothing there to take. Julian was not prepared to give me copies of anything at this stage. Because of the delicacy of his own position, if he handed over internal documents to the Press. And guess what? Somebody also ran off from the back of my house when I returned home late last week. So security would be a good idea. Especially now that Trish is no longer in the flat all day."

Jim felt gauntly again the revisitation of the seriousness of what he had reinvolved himself in. Not just an exercise in self-righteous indignation. But the shadow at his shoulder again. Of real and unfathomable personal risk. Reaching out towards him. And uttered, "This happened before." With Sylvie? Or had it?

Huntley was looking at him, curious, "What has? Burglary?"

"Yes. No." Too complicated to explain at this point. Save that for later with this man. Then the momentary anxiety swept away, by an inspiration. Rodruiguez. Who would know about him? Some correspondence about La Retrait after he had returned to France. But only that one meeting. And the complexity of that day's resolutions flooded into forethought- the letters from his father confirming the doubts planted by Jacob, the gift of the farm from Constancia, and that retrieval of the crude brutality that stripped raw the trusting childhood and had spat it as his own semen across his belly-

"Jim?" Huntley was looking with concern. At the haunting that must be showing in Jim's face.

"I've just thought," he said hesitantly, unwilling to let the hard-edged memorisation dissolve yet. Knowing that he had not the need to revisit that while away in the mountains. Cleansed of it. Satisfactorily sorted away and the door closed behind him on all that. The boy's decision then to refuse again, some way taking him to the threshold of the man he had been growing into. Whom he pulled himself back into now in this pub. Still chained somehow now in what he is doing, to what he learned then. "Yes, I just thought. I know somewhere. A solicitor-"

"Don't tell me any more. You know what blabbermouths we journalists are likely to be. As long as you think it's safe, I suggest you get copies there as soon as possible."

Then, the retrieved remembrance unwilling to fade, Jim mused, "Do you think there's more of it going on now?"

"More of what?"

"You know- adults having sex with kids."

"How should I know? I'm not a social worker. I'm a journalist. We're usually the last to know anything." Then he took up the question and regarded it, "More molestation by adults? No. I think kids are just getting better at speaking out." And then, at first lightly, "Now there's a project for Trish's oral history." Then serious, "But what pensioner would willingly say that about their childhood?"

Jim looked guardedly at the man, knowing not to speak of himself. And realising that Gizande was the only person he had ever told about- what to call it? Just that. The only person he had ever told. He now suddenly wanted to end this meeting with Huntley. To get out into the air, alone. To gather, sort and box away the emotional turbulence that filled his head now. Something important to say to himself. Without the blunder of being a fool to this man.

He remastered the task at hand, "We need another meeting, Bert. With the papers. I suggest at Julian's. But I'll ask him first. You know with Trish and the baby... I don't want to impose on them too much. There's enough going on for the pair of them."

"Fine. And in the mean time, put your mind to what I said. Get the documents safe. Young Mr. Roberts is back in court in two weeks time, so it would be fruitful for me to see the documents and gain your overview before then."

"Fine." And Jim was relieved to get out with a date next week to see Huntley again.

Outside, grit and rubbish swirled around the car park. But the wind felt cleansing. When he turned to go to the Citroen, Huntley was across the car park looking at him. Jim performed a cheery wave, watched him drive off in an opposite direction, climbed into the van, started it, pressed the Casals tape into the mouth of the player. Driving off slowly away from the pub, the vehicle filled with the vigorous cloud of the cello. Sounding down from the mountains. Out into the managed countryside southwards. Towards Tracey.

Chapter Eight

Over an hour early to meeting her. And Richard. Parking the van, he walked across the old bridge over the river, up stone steps and onto the city walls. There was warm, a humid drift of air from the west, where the watery sun was moving over the hazed hills of Wales. A few people walking in the opposite direction, mostly casually enjoying the views, some hurrying.

Anxiety brushed his mind for a moment with the picture of the two boxes of documents unattended in Julian's flat. He would have to phone Rodruiguez tomorrow. And drive up there again. He was distracted by some Japanese tourists being instructed in the history of the city by a hairy-legged man in a Roman legionnaire's uniform. His boomingly acted rhetoric translated into chicken-pecks of Japanese by their interpreter. Jim shook his head and passed on. Disbelief at doing a job like that. More incredible than Jim to become a farmer? He understood why they called him the mad Englishman down in the village. How, then, would he explain his now to Tracey? No, you had to be there to understand it. To be up on the top rim of that valley, looking down. To grasp what it meant. To let it take your breath away. The power of a daughter's approval, he smiled to himself, checked his watch and, bracing his shoulders for seeing her again-and being seen and summed up by those eyes- he set off to where they had arranged to meet.

She was on her own. Surprisingly, gave him a hug and kissed his cheek.

"We decided that it was best for me and you to meet together. Having Richard here, getting to know each other, would only get in the way between us. Catching up with all the time since we last saw each other." Then, perhaps seeing the uncertainty of her father at this unaccustomed warmth to him, she added, "I'm very happy now, Dad. With Richard."

He smiled, "Is this the real thing?"

"Probably. We've got no plans to marry, but we've known each other for nearly two years. Then I moved down here to his little house." There was an assured skittishness to her, somehow younger than the girl he had left behind. "Maybe you could come and see us there, before you leave. How long are you in the country?"

"Not sure, yet. Maybe a fortnight?"

Tentatively, then firmly, she threaded her arm with his and steered him across the paved street. Then looked up at him, "You look very fit. The life in France must suit you."

"Yes. I suppose it does." Then, seeking her opinion, "Strange isn't it?"

"What? What's strange?"

"Well, would you have expected your Dad to end up living out there? On a farm?"

She laughed, "I don't even remember you doing much in the garden. It was always Mum pushing the mower." But it was said with fond humour.

Prompting, hesitantly, "How is Mum?"

Serious now, "She's okay. Enjoying her work. We see her quite often. I told her you had called and we were meeting. She sends her best."

Relieved. That Jane did not want to meet. Why would she? "Tell me about Richard. What does he do?"

"He's in I.T. Manages the computer network for the Council. He started there soon after you had gone. That's how we met. Makes it quite convenient now as we commute together."

"So you work for the Council? Up there. My old hunting ground, eh?"

"I wouldn't call it that. Anyway, I work in Highways admin. Nothing to do with Social Services." Then, finalising it, "Thank you very much. Richard says they are a mess."

"So I've heard," he offered guardedly, doubting that she would know anything of what had brought him back.

She tugged his arm closer, "Tell me about yourself. About life in France."

But he could not shake off the old defensiveness to her, uncertain of this new open warmth from her. "Yes. I'm sorry you didn't get my letter. I did write you know. But when you didn't answer, thought you must still be angry with me. You know- breaking up with Mum."

"No. Well I was. At first. But it never really surprised me. It's almost like I could see it coming for years. I don't mean I knew it was going to happen, but when it did, all the signs were there from the past. Maybe not getting letters from you let me think about it." She shrugged and smiled at him, "I would've made contact with you soon, anyway. You weren't going to get away from me as easily as all that." Then, more reflectively, unwittingly beginning to smart his eyes with tears, "Maybe you have to grow up a bit to know what's valuable and what isn't. To stop being a kid and get your sensible head on." Finally, a smile again, "I wasn't going to lose my Dad. He wasn't going to get away with that!"

Looking away, Jim was silenced. Bewildered by the new territory opened up with this daughter of his. Defensively humble, even spellbound by it, not daring to look into her eyes for the emotion he may show. Expose to her. Ashamed of his own reluctance, at a loss what to say, they walked on silently for a dozen steps. Before he quietly came up with, "Like I lost mine," but was immediately mortified. By his own manipulativeness, against her open-heartedness. Wanted to swallow back the words.

"What?" She had not heard him. "Sorry, I didn't hear."

But he did not dare to invent what he had said. To be tricky with her. So he unwillingly said again, "Like I lost my father." Then, drew her into it with, "Your grandfather."

"Yes. Mum told me the story. It would make a great book. French Resistance hero and all that!" After a pause, "It's funny having so little on your side of the family. I can't remember much of Aunty Mary. But there's Gramp and Nan on Mum's side. And the cousins. Now I gather you've found me a proper aunty on your side."

"Well, she's my half-sister. Suzanne. But I suppose she's your aunt."

"We'll have to come out and meet everyone. See this old farm you're living in."

He laughed. Both at the farm as his home and at the nervous prospect of bringing together the chemistry of his past and present lives. He saw this off with, "It's still a bit of a ruin. I'm working on it, but I'm still living with Suzanne."

"I can't imagine you there," she smiled. But then, "Maybe I can."

"I'm not sure I can imagine myself there. Bit like a dream."

With a tease, she then said, "Parlez-vous Francais?"

A sheepish, "Non. Not very well."

Her long laugh made nearby pedestrians look. "Really, Dad! You should be ashamed of yourself!" Then, mischievous, "The restaurant's here. You can order in French." Remembering Suzanne's comments after his drunk at the Revolution Bicentennial may have shown in his face and Tracey pulled him up to look in his face. "I do love you, Dad, you know."

Do you? he thought. Did he love her back? From his past habit of penitence to the baby she had been. And he had then been too busy to know, as she grew.

Seeing his puzzlement, she said, "I've grown up. It's different now. Having you away made me realise that I didn't really know you. Who'd've guessed you would end up on a farm in France?"

"Not me, for a start," he joked.

Her seriousness brushed this aside, "And I thought I might not see you again. You'd be gone to your new family for good." Would she have cared two years ago? he reflected. Would he? How did he feel about it now?

He stumbled into speech, "Yes. France has changed everything."

Now blocking the restaurant's doorway, she led him to one side, this to be dealt with first. "Perhaps you needed to live abroad to sort your self out. To put all that campaigning and fighting for others behind you." He shrank the thought of Toser and Scadding from being spoken of to her. But she continued, "I've changed too. Richard, mainly. And the confidence I get from work. I'm doing really well there- though I'm not sure it's the sort of thing you'd be proud of."

"What do you mean?" he said in a feeble protest.

"Well I'm a supervisor. A sort of mini-boss, I suppose. Not your sort of ambition, would it be, Dad?"

He smiled wryly. "No. But you could call me my own boss now. For the first time ever. It feels odd sometimes. Without something to push against. To make the boundaries of what you're doing. Except the weather. That makes a lot of my decisions for me. Especially in the winter." Then, with real engagement, "You should see the winters. In those mountains."

And she smiled, shaking her head, "You're a different person, you know. You, on about the weather. I told Mum I didn't know what to expect. With you."

"Spoken to Mum," he echoed.

"Of course we've discussed it." Then, "Come on. Standing outside. Let's get in and get our table."

When they came out the sky was still edgy with the last light. It had been too noisy and crowded for intimacy. Suited to her happy, even bubbly mood, but not to his guarded exploration of his own conversational territory. What to say. And what could not. He told a sanitised version of Francis's story. One that Suzanne would have approved of. But, to the end of the meal, he had quietened, holding himself back from this unfamiliar daughter. She told him about life with Richard, described their home, but it tapered to ending the last dish, the wine and the coffee in a pool of reflective silence between them, within the noise about them.

Out, in the street, only some distant and raucous youths, he measured his words. Then spoke them. "The furniture removal was not the only thing- why I came back to Blighty," trying to lighten, trivialise.

She was serious, eyes ahead.

"I've been asked to be a witness for someone. Suspended from Social Services."

"Oh. Dad," defeat in her voice. "I knew it was too good to be true."

"You know I believe in standing up for people," both an appeal and an assertion, softly spoken, finally a plea for tolerance.

"I hope this won't affect Richard and I. As we both work for the Council."

"No. I shouldn't- it's nothing to do with you- with your work."

Tiredly, "Well don't tell me. Then I won't have to judge. Won't be involved." Then, looking at him, searching for sense from the shadow across her father's face, "It's like a drug for you, isn't it? Getting on your white charger." A dismissive grunt, "Must be heredity. Just like your dad. Running off to Spain. And leaving his baby for Aunty Mary to look after."

To place the baby in that orphanage, he thought. But that correction stayed un-spoke. Too complicatedly tangling with his own failures towards Tracey. And with Francis's own betrayals. She was waiting for an answer, but he shrugged and moved on a few steps. To take his face out of her line of vision, her probing gaze.

"And what a nice evening it had been, Dad. Until now." Coming up to him, to confront him again with her eyes, "Will this cause publicity? Will it make... a row?" But she turned away, idly looking into a lit shop window. "No. Don't tell me. You'll probably have to lie to me."

He was relieved. Again from telling the truth. To those who should trust him. So he could protect with the truth those who did not want his protection. A job to get over-and-done-with. But at what cost? Here in this darkening street, about to part from the daughter who, for the first time in years, had shown him warmth, had reached out to him. And he was about to leave her feeling spurned. That she had changed, but he was irredeemably the same.

"I do want to see you again, love," he offered. "Before I go back to France."

Her gaze still blanked at the window, her voice was hollow. Distant, "I don't know. I'll have to talk it over with Richard." Then harsher, but still turned away, "You do understand why I say that, do you, Dad?" He said nothing, guessing if she was on the edge of tears, but reached out his hand to her shoulder. She shrugged it off, stood still for a moment, then gathered her shoulders up, clenching them with resignation. "I must be going. Getting back."

"Where are you parked?" he asked, a tenuous restraint on their parting, an offer to walk her back.

"I'm not. I walked in. It's not far."

He knew he would not have permission to walk back with her to Richard. So he leant to kiss her cheek, but with only half a consent, she moved her face away, stepping back and unsteadying him. With a last inscrutable look that he remembered from past crossings with Tracey and, "Phone me," said flatly, she turned and walked off.

He watched her go. Trying to think forward and rehearse a future conversation with her, in a future time. When he would explain. Taking that meditation with him up on the city walls for a last walk round their fullest circumference, watching the lights in windows in the little brick terraces beneath and the last purple shreds of light to the west colouring the hills.

Chapter Nine

He woke, asweat from the dream, out of the subterranean muck, past the indistinguished woman, burst out into the sunshine - as the switched on light from the kitchen fell across his eyes. Jim sat up, shocked. Then reassured by the two boxes of papers still beside his bed. And the rattle of crockery. He lowered his feet to the carpet, scratched his head and dozily joined Julian.

"Sorry. Did I wake you?"

"It's okay," Jim murmured. "How's Trish?"

"Should happen tonight. Midwife says. And Trish agrees. Labour pains are getting more regular." He turned on the electric kettle. "Just came back to make a flask of coffee. Hospital drinks machine's broken. Do you want a drink?"

"Yeah. Fine."

Getting down another cup, Julian asked, "How did it go with Huntley?"

"Fine. I'm seeing him again with the documents-" then remembered- "He says we should take a copy of everything to keep somewhere away and safe. Did you know he's been broken in to?" Then, rubbing his face with his fingers to try to awaken his skin with some of the urgency of what he was saying, "Reckons it's all serious enough for somebody to want to steal the stuff."

"Do you think so?"

"I know a place. A solicitor. In Yorkshire. I think we should leave copies with him."

"If you think so. But... it's a lot to copy. I can't do it. Not now."

"Of course not. But it's got to be done. Should I ask Huntley to do it?"

"Would he?"

"I don't know. Can only ask." Jim realised that he would have to take over the task himself, with the brief, familiar feeling of both resentment and relief. Julian was too preoccupied, so he went to share it, "How's Trish doing?"

"Oh... I don't know. It's so strange watching the person you know so well- who you love- in such pain. She just goes away from me with it. Like her eyes don't see. Just looking inwards, at what's going on inside herself." Jim nodded, so aware he had never shared such a thing. And thought briefly of Tracey, still unsatisfactorily unbonded to him. From those first days of his absence at her birth. Emerging from his images,

Julian shook his head. "She won't take the pain killers. Of course." Then smiled, "That's Trish."

As Julian attended to making drinks, Jim thought of the imminent return of her with the baby. And him sleeping in their living room. Or not sleeping, wakeful with the child. A calculation. "I can move out, you know."

"Why?"

"With the baby. It's going to be pretty busy here," a faint and artificial smile. To cover his guardedness.

"No. I'm sure it will be okay."

"As long as you say," Jim trailed off, unconvinced. For the other man to remember this conversation. If the realities, rather than his good manners now, changed his mind.

After Julian had left with his thermos flask, Jim sat on at the kitchen table, awake and wondering at his enduring resentment at this good-enough man. His host. Who was doing everything right.

He went back to the divan. And eventual sleep, waking too late for an early run. After nine, he phoned Huntley. And, now sensitive to possible interference to phone lines, discussed the document copying in a coded and discursive way. At first the journalist was blank, then understanding, told him to bring them down to his office that afternoon. Jim's call to Rodruiguez clearly surprised the solicitor, despite the always-professional discretion of the voice on the phone. Jim remained indistinct about why he wanted an appointment, but was offered one the following morning. An early rise to drive over the Pennines, he thought. Into the sunrise, with luck.

Huntley was too busy and left Jim in the windowless backroom with the photocopier. As he copied sheet after sheet, he could hear snatches of phone calls and the rattle of the journalist's keyboard. For two and a half hours. After he had lugged the doubled weight of documents out into the Citroen, he reminded Huntley of next week's appointment. And Huntley swapped a reminder of the court date.

Julian's car was parked outside the flat. Conscious of its noticability, Jim parked the Citroen down the next sidestreet. He covered the plastic bags of copied papers with the blanket he used for sleep stops on long journeys, locked the doors and lurched, sweating up the staircase to the flat with the boxes.

Noisy with the key, he was let in by Julian, serious, "Born last night. Just after I left to come home to make that coffee. Trish is exhausted. We've called him Adam."

"Great?" but, looking at Julian's graveness, Jim could not keep a question out of his congratulation. So he quickly switched, "I've got the copying. Down in the van." Then the thought, "Do you think it'll be safe there tonight? I'm driving it up Yorkshire tomorrow. For safekeeping."

Julian's face, for a moment puzzled, disconnected from Jim's anxieties, then clued in, "I should think so. It's an old vehicle, isn't it? And the foreign plates would stand out if it was stolen."

Not feeling that Julian understood the depth of defensiveness the Toser case now needed, Jim just said, "Sure," unreassured. Then, putting down the boxes on the divan, he scrambled back towards the real centre of the other man's thoughts. "How are they? Trish and the baby?"

"Fine. But tired. I hope he stays tired for Trish's sake. They'll be in the hospital for a couple more days." Then at last a broad, tired smile and, "It's brilliant, you know."

"Yes. I know," he falsified, in order to reassure. Remembering how Mary had filled the gap he should have filled with Jane those first weeks of Tracey's life. The part of his own he most wished he could re-enact, from here, with what he knew now. He looked at the other man and, in this alone, he envied him. Though he barely conceived what it must feel to be there, grinning back at himself with this joy and proud awe written across Julian's face.

"Have you eaten?" Julian asked, still softly.

"No."

"I'll do us something."

Jim sat in the kitchen while the other man moved about opening fridge, getting plates. They ate silently. After eating, he went into the living room, leaving Julian to wash up.

"I'm knackered," he said to Jim from the kitchen doorway. "I'm going to kip."

Not daring to break the silence by either opening the bed up or turning on the t.v., however low the volume, he sat on. Thinking of what he had to do. After a long enough silence from next door, he wrote a note for them:

Julian, (+ Trish + Adam!)
Had to leave early for Yorkshire. See you teatime tonight.
Jim.

And gently let himself out and downstairs.

Chapter Ten

After a stop to sleep in the van in the motorway services, he had taken an expensive, greasy breakfast there and drove on up the escarpment across into Yorkshire, the rising sun in his eyes. Too early for his appointment in Bradford, he had parked and wandered round sour-smelling, part-decayed streets of old closed woollen mills. Then back into the centre, his nose cleansed of the city by the bread smells from the bakery next door as he entered Rodruiguez's office.

He was ushered by the receptionist into a meeting room, laid his bags of papers on the long polished table, then went to the window to scan the street below through the slats of the blind. Turning when Rodruiguez entered.

"Mr. Briggs," crossing, hand outstretched. "Please be seated," offering the table in its entirety. "I was so surprised to hear from you. And you seemed reluctant, if I may say, to speak of matters over the telephone."

Jim smiled and nodded.

"Are you progressing with La Retrait? Are you able to live in the house yet?"

"No, not yet. Perhaps by this winter part of it can be used." Then, how to broach it? "I have been a bit... delayed by the business I have had to come back for. To Britain."

"Ah, yes," the solicitor encouraged.

But Jim sidestepped, as yet, "The information about La Retrait that you sent me was very helpful."

"It was a most interesting piece of work for me. Out of the line of the matters I usually work on here."

"I can imagine. I have had a huge learning curve. Just getting through all the French systems. The permissions. But I have my sister and friends to help me. I have been very lucky."

"Yes. I contacted the French Consulate for advice and they were most helpful. Were you aware that a local official wrote to me just a few months ago? I had written to your Départment," said in French. "And it must have taken so many months for them to get back to me."

"What was it about?"

"An anomaly we had detected in two different copies of the deeds to the property. They were both sent to Mary. One from Constancia, your step mother. The other was sent on later, after she died. From her notaire- her solicitor. Yes, very interesting. Would you like to see the papers?"

"Sure."

"One moment," and Rodruiguez rose and went out.

Jim tidied his bags of documents off the immaculate table and stacked them away onto the chair next to him, before the lawyer returned with a handful of folded papers and glasses now perched on his nose. He came alongside Jim and unfolded the papers, one after the other, spreading them flat. Jim looked at them at first, unsure. Plans. Then read *La Retrait Parfaite* on the nearest one and the shape of the lane up to the farm and its cluster of buildings became clear. Looking to the other, it was titled *La Retraite des Parfaits,* with *Il Refugio* added below. The same features of the farm mapped, with some additional buildings in places where Jim now knew there were only ruinous tumbles of rock to mark where they had once been.

"It's the farm. But why are the names different?" he asked.

"We were not sure. Just a corruption of the original name over the years," and Rodruiguez pointed to the second map. "This was the original. 1893. The later map- the one attached to the letter to your aunt- is dated 1939. But the meaning of the original name?" He shrugged, "That I cannot say."

But a memory rose within Jim. That evening his first visit, alone speaking with Suzanne, after Gizande had left. Explaining the Catharisme to him, she had spoken of the Perfects. Les Parfaits. The way Francis had sought his private redemption, those last years of his life. He said aloud, "The Perfects. The Retreat of the Perfects." Then, addressing the other man's perplexity, "It's about the Cathar religion. It was a heresy in that part of France. The Perfects were sort of travelling preachers. They were wiped out by the Inquisition, centuries ago. But it survived. In just a few places. At the end of his life, my father seemed to have believed in it."

"But that was not the anomaly we wrote to France about. To the Départment about. This." Leaning across the 1893 map, Rodruiguez traced a dotted line that looped down between the farm and the track to the village. "This is the national frontier. Between Spain and France. And the earlier map placed your farm in Spain." Drawing the later map over it, "Now look. The frontier has moved. It is now behind the farm. We wrote to clarify this." He stood back from the table. "I judged it right not to tell you until we had an answer from France. As it was, the answer confirmed that the property was in France, so I felt there was no need to tell you. And would not have, had you not come here."

Oh, the Mayor and Poux, Jim remembered. Devious enough between the pair of them to know the truth. "Yes, I had heard something of this. A rumour, but the local Mayor seemed satisfied to sign my permits to rebuild the place, so I let it lie."

"Good. As we have. I discovered that frontiers are quite confusing round your area. There is a Spanish town there surrounded by France. An oversight from some treaty, apparently."

"Perhaps with everyone in the Common Market, it will make no difference," Jim said lightly. Then added, "Eventually."

"Perhaps," said Rodruiguez sceptically. Then, "However, enough of this. You did not come here for this, I assume. I will arrange for copies of both property plans to be sent on to you. Still at your half sister's address, Madame Planisolles?"

"Yes. Thanks." Jim paused to weigh how much to say, but, though trusting the man as he did, decided on the least needing to be known. And stated in as lawyerly language as he could muster, "I am involved as the witness in employment proceedings. Someone from the Local Authority I used to work for. I have documents and nowhere to store them. I am staying with friends and they are... in the process of moving house. So, for safekeeping, I have made copies. And here in your office seemed the obvious place for their- safe storage."

And he knew from the look in Rodruiguez's eyes that he probably did not believe a word Jim had said. But that, as a client, he would do everything legally possible to meet his wishes. "Of course, we have arrangements for the storage of clients' documents."

"Excuse me," asking Rodruiguez to step back from the chair he was leaning against. So Jim could draw out the two plastic bags and lay them on the table. "Not very tidily packed, I'm afraid."

"Fear not Mr. Briggs," he smiled. "We have to deal with worse than this, I expect." And he peered into one bag.

"What were you expecting to find?"

"Well recently, we had a will with associated documents that were- should I say, somewhat unnecessarily inclusive of generous traces of the bodily fluids of the deceased."

"Oh, god. Fond memorabilia!"

The solicitor smiled, then, "How long do you wish these to be stored?"

How long? For all this to be put behind him? "A few weeks. A couple of months, at most. Then send them on to me. When I instruct you." To the safekeeping of the safest place.

"Fine." Then stood formally, suggesting their business probably over. Jim stacked the bags on the table, as if to tidy. "We will deal with them. I will have them boxed." His hand offered, Jim took it. "I hope your business in England will not detain you too long. So that you are able to complete your renovations."

"I hope not, too." Bless you, Rodruiguez, for your discretions.

But released into more of the day left than he had expected, Jim stopped at a phone box and called Julian. No answer.

Stopping at a small shop for a meat pie, a pack of tarts, a bottle of milk and fruit, he then drove the Citroen up to that isolated reservoir. Parked as far along the track by the Water Board wall as he could. Taking in the breadth of the west stretching beneath, he waited through the afternoon for the sun to move towards setting, eating, then gathering his blanket about him as, hours later, the lights started to prick themselves out across the plain before him. Talking wordlessly to his father, long and uninterrupted, into the night.

Chapter Eleven

Back at the flat the following afternoon, it was Trish greeted him with, "Just the man! Julian's back in work and I need to waddle out to the shops. Just for half an hour. Can you look after Adam, while I'm out?" She smiled at the wordless consternation in Jim's face, "It's alright he's been fed. He should sleep now for a couple of hours. Here," and she led Jim quietly into the child's bedroom. To where the tiny boy lay, breathing softly onto the perfect little fingers, half-curled on the sheet as if to catch something. The last piece of a dream? Or life itself?

Jim could not help himself from smiling, but back in the living room, he whispered, "What if he wakes up? He doesn't know me. I'll terrify him."

"No. I don't think so. I'll only be half an hour- not that. I just need to get out. And I don't want to have to wake him. I'm sure he'll sleep." Then she went into the bedroom and came out with a pyjama top. "This is Julian's. If you have to pick him up, put this over your shoulder and put Adam up there. He'll know the smell of his Dad. Julian was up with him last night. Just gently rub his back while you walk around with him. Oh, and make sure you support his head." Smiling at Jim's doubtfulness, "You'll be fine. He should sleep on."

Then, finger to lips for silence, smiling brightly at him, she was gone.

Jim sat gently on the armchair, on its edge, alert not to make a sound. Then he stood to take off his jacket. Ambushed by her, he thought, without a chance to get his breath back as he had come in the door. After two bedless nights. But smiled despite himself, then crept to the child's bedroom door to listen. For the faintest sound of his breathing. Daring himself, pushed the door open and, step by step across the carpet, to the edge of the cot, hardly allowing his lungs to move, looked down again on the boy. At the unblemished translucence of the life there before him. As if from Tracey, with whom he had never had such a moment, he knew he must retrieve something. She had approached- then reproached him for seeming so much the same. Of his own father too, last night spent up on the escarpment with him, there were more quiet times to be had. As Tracey had said. White chargers. Just like his dad. Heredity.

And returning, that was where Trish found Jim, crouched, looking through the cot bars, still on watch with her child.

"What were you doing in here?"

"I thought-" then a lie, to cover the complications in his head, "I thought I heard him waking up."

She looked down at Adam. "No." Then studied Jim, calculating something about him? "Let's leave him to sleep." And he withdrew with her into the living room.

"Do you want a drink? Or some eats?"

"Only if you're doing something for yourself."

She scolded him, "Oh, stop being so modest about things. Julian told me you were worried about staying here. We invited you. And it was we- not just Julian. So chill out, as they say."

He smiled, released by her, "Okay. Okay, I'll have some breakfast, please."

"Right," purposefully. And he followed her through to the kitchen.

While eggs boiled, she washed up and he joined her to dry the plates. One slipped from her fingers and smashed shockingly loud into shards about her feet. "Damn!" as she bent to pick the pieces, Jim bringing over the plastic bin to her. "One of the problems, now. I'm so bloody preoccupied, whatever I do I haven't got my mind on it. I'm always off thinking about him," nodding out towards the child's bedroom.

And, as if on cue, Adam's cry into wakefulness. She rolled her eyes, smiled and went out. And Jim shovelled the rest of broken plate away, putting the bin back as Trish returned with the small thing squirming hungrily over her blouse. "Feeding, I'm afraid. Can you finish the eggs? And the toast?" She started to unbutton herself. To the boy's moist and moving mouth. And Jim busied himself away at the cooker, eyes modestly away. From the intimacy of her head curled down in absolute and awed concentration at the child's closed eyes, tiny fingers spread on her loose, full breast, to hold the dark pink nipple to his greedy lips.

As he brought the food to the table, she was buttoning herself up again. "Only a quickie. Here. Hold him a minute. While I make myself decent again." At his frozen hesitation, "Come on. He's not heavy," and she held the curved cradle of her arms out towards him. "Come on!"

Jim came round to her and half-knelt, arms awkwardly basketed. To receive Adam, eyes shut, fingers closed and fisted, Jim crouched for receiving the weight, the responsibility of the little moving body. And the mother's hands gently disengaged the child into Jim's held and absolute intensity, standing slowly back from her, his eyes fixed on the boy's face. Serious and reeling wild, with having this tiny person, completed in detail, the nails, the ear lobes, the threads of silken hair, all miniscule and moving against the man's chest. And who, if anyone, had held Jim thus? Then, sudden with the panic of realising the smell, the rough wool of the jacket was away from Mother, Adam whimpered. Coughed, then shouted tinily, limbs beginning to tread, to thrash- away from the man. Who looked over to Trish.

"Come on. I'm ready now. For the little bully. Wants to suck me dry again."

They ate together, she awkwardly and one-armed, with the child held against her ribs, Jim, watching the boy. And unable to stop himself from smiling.

"I said I'd meet Jules for lunch I was going to walk down to the Town Hall as it's a nice day. Take the pram. Use it as my zimmer frame to get some exercise back. Do you want to come with us?"

So they walked slowly down, she pushing the pram. Quietly amused at the couple with new child they must appear. Trish talking about the project she had when she got back to work. About women in the car industry. With Jim offering nothing. Except half-listening. Watching the streets they passed along, familiar with memories, eyes on the look-out for a known face. Steering round the broken stretches of unkempt paving.

"Not very child-friendly," she said, as it took two of them to lift and heave the pram up the Town Hall steps. "What if you had a wheel chair?"

"You'd have to go in the back," Jim said remembering the place. With anticipation. "There's a door at the back."

"Round by the dustbins, I shouldn't wonder."

And he laughed and nodded.

Then they were in. As he remembered it, the porter's counter, the staircase, the corridors off. But, like the adult returned to a place of childhood, smaller, dustier. Reduced. In both size and grandeur.

He sat with the pram, while she asked the porter for Julian. Sat back and watching. Trish returned. "They've called for him." Then grinning, "So. How does it feel? To be back on the battleground. Back in the bullring!"

He thought a bit, then, "Scruffier than I remember. Smaller? I don't know. What does it mean to me now?"

"Well, a lot of the secrets you want to get at are somewhere here. Somewhere buried in this building."

"I suppose so," but thought, more likely shredded. And composting out on the landfill site. Then summoning himself up to her tone, "Yes. You're right. The problem is, getting at the stuff. Scadding's a start. But he doesn't want anything to do with me."

"It'll happen," she said, in a way that made him look at her for her intensity. "Because you're here, Jim, it'll happen. I'm sure. Got that gut feeling. Trust me. I'm a new mum. We know about gut feelings."

He smiled at her, but he was distant from the certitude of her words. And her eyes upon him. Then the moment of stop between them was released by the sight of Julian crossing the polished floor towards them.

"Hiya, Jim," then a kiss for Trish before pushing his head into the pram for a loving look at his son.

"I've made sandwiches, Jules. Thought as it was nice, we could go down to the Prom. By the river."

"Lovely," and he took the pram handle to lead off, Trish beside him, Jim following, giving a last scan of the hallway. Jumped by a pair of eyes locked on him, from the mouth of one of the corridors. Foley, with another suited man Jim did not know, stared. Now fat, pushing up from the folds of his chins to piggify his face. Stopped by the sight. Of Jim. The other man looked enquiringly, said something that woke Foley. Who turned away a few steps, then stopped again. And across the large room, with his old boss staring, through two secretaries click-clacking out for their lunch, they held each other's gaze. Jim's heart beating out the long moment. Before Foley shook himself back into movement and flurried with his companion to the lift. Button-pressed and waiting to escape him, Jim irresolute if to walk across. And say what? Some cheap shot? Give away more than the secret his being back here had been? But, by then, the lift had come, they stepped in. And, out of sight behind the smooth closure of the doors, disappeared upwards. To something important.

Gathering himself together, he caught up with the others and helped them with the pram down the last few steps.

At the bottom, Julian turned to him, "Oh, by the way, Scadding's contacted me. He wants to meet you. On his own, he says."

From the address Julian had given him, he found Scadding's out where he would have expected it. In a line of 30s-built semi-detached, gardens neat with lawns or paving, too many cars for the street. So that Jim, after driving up and down, awkward in the big Citroen, had to park back on the main road.

Scadding's address was numbered 29b. Marked on a neat home-crafted sign pointing up a set of wooden stairs that climbed the side of the house. Jim double checked the front entrance. 29. So he went and climbed the stairs. Knocked and waiting, looked down into the garden.

Scadding was nervous, "Come in." Impatient, a glance out across the street, then hurried Jim out of sight and into a small living room. "Please be seated, Mr. Bnggs."

"Jim. Please."

"Jim," Scadding repeated, distant, as if with a touch of distaste. "Would you like a drink? Tea?"

"Milk. One sugar, please"

Left alone, he looked round the room, with the guarded aggression reserved for when not sure what would happen next. Neat. A small television. A roll-top desk with some reference books between carven wood bookends. Economic and loveless.

Scadding back with a small tray, offering tea. A china Royal Wedding mug. Jim picked it up and turned it to the two over-pink faces smiling at each other across the coat of arms. Simpering privilege, he thought knowingly.

Scadding sat opposite, erect and uncomfortable in his own home, his mug absentmindedly held aloft, unsipped. Jim drank and watched. He remembered what Huntley had told him about this little man and strove to imagine him as a boy coal miner, but just registered disbelief. Then, to break the silence, "Do you rent this place? It's unusual."

"Oh, no. I own it." Then, his voice withheld and discomforted, he began, "I want to understand. I never read those documents. My duty was just to prevent them being inappropriately destroyed." Uncomfortable with his hands, Scadding looked down at them. "However," paused with the difficulty of it, " since we met... and since the things you said about the-crimes, I decided that I had to read them. That I had another duty. Beyond that to the Council." Then, with a tangle of wonder and anger, "I never thought I would say that. It is a sorry pass when your duty as- as a citizen, diverges from your duty as an employee of the Local Authority." Something of the man's intensity held Jim's silent attention. A flowering respect for the stature of him. "I have given my life for this Council. I have done my duty. I have seen people work for me and move on to other things. And I have been proud of what they have done- allowing myself a little pride that I may have set an example that they have taken on to other places. I was trying to count the other day, how many people had worked for me, under my supervision since I started to work for the Council. And do you know, it has been thousands." He allowed himself a small reflective smile, before returned to his serious theme, "I call that service. I know that is not a fashionable term these days, but that has been my contribution. With all the changes in fashion that have gone through the Council over the years- all the new ideas that come and go, as often as we have had new Directors and now Chief Executives, as they've started to call them- during all those changes, it has been the responsibility of a few to remind staff- both those beneath us and those above- of some of the fundamentals. And

I count myself as being among those few." Then, with a trace of urgency to engage Jim, to get him to understand, "Like holding a line. Against all those who want to cut corners. Who want to rush things, in an ill-considered manner, without first thinking about whom we are employed to work for. I've worked for plenty of Senior Managers like that. All targets, or outcomes, whatever they like to call them, but really they just want to rush things. Knowing where they want to go, with no consideration of how to get there. That has been my responsibility. Pointing out the stages that have to gone through first."

Quiet for a moment, he resumed gravely, "It has not made me popular. And it has not gained me further promotion for many a year now. But I have accepted that. I have found myself in a post where I know everything that has to be done. New technology comes along, of course, and that has to be brought in. But even computers do not change the fundamentals of what we are here to do. They should just be helping us to do it better. More efficiently. The computer systems should be built around the fundamentals, reinforcing them, not replacing them." Jim thought of Tracey. And her Richard. Wondering if he had met Scadding. And how difficult this little man must sometimes have been.

"Please don't misunderstand me, Mr. Briggs. Jim. I do not see my working life as sacrifice. I have been paid well enough. I am not a complainer about things like that. I have always been a member of the Trade Union, but never active, you understand. You know that. And I'm sure we have very different views about that." A refreshment of tea, before a saddening continuation, "And I have the reward finally of a good pension when I retire. Or I would have had, before all this. Now, even that does not seem secure. If they discipline me, as they seem determined, I may lose my job. And the pension. They seem set on a course to find me guilty of gross misconduct. Me!" A cry, stood out sharp from the meditative restraint of all that had gone before.

"Gross misconduct!" shaking his head, lips clamped into a hard line, eyes glittering with anger or tears, he placed his free hand over his face. And spoke on through it, muffled, and untidy with pain, "And then reading those documents. It was awful! What does it mean? It was like the world turned upon its head. And those boys! And everything… the opposite of how... even the words... their meanings gone mad! Care! Children!" Dragging down the curtain of his fingertips from his eyes, he looked into Jim. Desperate with beseeching. "I want you to explain to me. What is happening? What we are doing."

This simple little man, sat in this room without trappings, confronted Jim with the stark core of the matter. With that sense of shockingness Jim himself no longer had. Worn down by the events of the intervening years. Rinsed out by too many launderings. Too many miniscule approximations by everyday life, to remain as startled as he had been then. Over three years ago. With Sylvie. By Damien. So even the boy's death had become more a word now in his head, than a feeling. Can you live alongside the pain of others, enduring it with them for so long, and it stay real to you? Compassion become loyalty, then duty. Until, droughted of the immediacy, even that withers. But for this man, duty was the lifeblood of his passion. Duty that for Jim, had been rules imposed by others. To be broken. What could he say now to him, this Sydney? Of sense and feeling?

Jim started to speak with quiet deliberation, watchful of the man, taking on the restraint, the precision of the language he took him to speak. "It should not have happened. And if it is going on now, it should not be happening. And must be stopped." A pause, to measure the next passage. "It was a cynical business deal. I don't believe it started out as that. Someone, at some time, learnt that some councillors liked to have sex with children." He stopped, Scadding's hands now pressed hard back into the skin of his cheeks, gaunt as a skull. Jim waited for response. None came, so he continued. "It became a way the builders could bribe councillors for contracts. They would set up flats and jobs for the young-" children or men? he hesitated to say, but settled for the casual vulnerability of- "for the kids leaving care. Then invite the councillors down. And the kids knew that they would get- rewards, on top of having flats and paid work in the centre of London. And, on top, the builders could probably exert some blackmail on the councillors." Then, letting this settle, he went on, "But none of this could happen without someone, quite a few people in the Council going along with it. There were some social workers. Their managers. And some Senior, even Chief Officers who must have known, even if just turning a blind eye to it." Finally, trying to draw the man closer to him, Jim smiled wanly, "That, Sydney, is what puts us on the same side. We would not turn blind eyes to what we saw. Of course, we did it in our different ways. But we were doing the same thing. Calling a halt to it, if we could."

Scadding slowly sat back in his chair, and, as if awaking from the words Jim had said to the person he actually was, slowly shook his head, "No. No. It was fundamentally different. You stole documents. I was saving them."

Jim's spirit slowly sank, searching for words to not get angry, "They were documents. Only documents. It is the people they are about that matters. The boys. And the things that are being done to them."

"They were not-" with almost sarcastic emphasis- "only

documents." Continuing with all the gravity of everything his life had taught him, "Documents are evidence. To everything we do. Even to who we are. They are essential. They define who we are. Your passport, your Health Card, your Driving Licence. You would not exist in the real world, if you did not have them. That is why it is so fundamental to respect the rules we have for handling them." Then, gathering the two mugs, Jim's still swilled with tepid tea, "That is the foundation of my case. They broke the rules. I kept to them."

"But you still have copies of those documents here in your home. What do the rules say about that?"

Terse and sharp, Scadding cut back, "That is different. Those are my evidence."

"As the documents I had were. Evidence. No difference. In fact, some of the documents you have here are the same ones I was disciplined for possessing."

He was now getting angry, losing the clear edge of his beliefs in this, "No. That was different. You stole the documents before. I only took the documents after the event. As my evidence for the Disciplinary."

"But, Sydney," Jim pleaded, defeatedly, "it doesn't matter about the order of when the documents were taken, or who did it! The kids were getting molested anyway, whatever happened to the documents." Then, a surge of fury, not at this man, but at the crude misery of it all, refusing to fade from his life, drawing back the renewal he kept reaching out for. "The crimes were going on anyway for Damien Toser, whatever lies were written in his files, whatever truth was left out by his social worker, Flynn. And now he's dead. Still almost a boy." A sudden memory grasped, "And they made him sign a document against me. Lies they made him put his name to. So what's the worth of that document, Sydney? Does it get the same protection from you as the truth?"

"Stop it! Stop it!" The shout shocked the tight confines of the room, the little man's knuckles gripped along the draylon rim of the chair, spilt cold tea splashed down the cushions from the cups hooked to his fingers. He looked down, then, angered at this accident too, turned his wrathful face at Jim again, "How dare you! In my house!" Then sneering, "Clever words, Mr. Briggs. Clever words. You try and twist round what I've done- into something else. You- just don't understand."

I do, Jim thought urgently, I do. But you just cannot hear me.

As Scadding turned to go out with the mugs, there was a knock on the door. He went through to the kitchen, put them down and returned. As he opened the door, Jim could hear a woman's voice, "Are you alright, Sydney?"

"Yes. Perfectly."

"I heard shouting. What were you shouting at? It was you, wasn't it?"

"Yes. I have someone here. Nothing to worry about."

And the door pushed open with a plump cheerful face finding Jim, "Oh, hello."

Jim nodded and, despite all, could only smile back, "Hello."

"Well Sydney, aren't you going to introduce me?"

"Mr. Briggs. Jim Briggs. This is June. Mrs. Scadding. My wife."

Then she entered, straight to the wet sofa "Oh, Sydney. What have you been up to?"

"Nothing. It was an accident."

"Well you can't just leave it dripping wet." Scadding was going to reply, but with a firm, "Here," she was past him into the kitchen and out again with a yellow cloth, vigorously rubbing at the stain. "Is this what all the shouting was about? Silly things. It's only tea. It'll come out. But Sydney, you may have to take off the cover and I'll put it through the wash. There," and she stood up, tilting her head to look at her work. Then at Jim, "I'm sorry if I've interrupted anything, Mr. Briggs. Lucky I came up, really." Holding out the cloth to her husband, she went to leave, then stopped, her finger poised, "Oh, yes, Sydney. Our Friday shopping. Can we start an hour earlier? There's a programme on the telly I don't want to miss. It's about the Royals." Then, giggling, "You know me!" she went to the door. "Oh. And so nice to have met you, Mr. Briggs."

Met? He watched Scadding's back as he closed the door behind her. Come from downstairs? Living separate, but shopping together? Her washing for him? Jim hardly dare ask. After the shouting.

Scadding rubbed his hand reflectively over the stain. "Well. I think you had better go now. We've said all there is to be said." Looking up, "And I don't want you having anything to do with my case. As I have said, you would prejudice what chances I may have of keeping my job."

Jim rose and, in a last attempt to placate, "Thanks for the chance to talk. Let's say we agree to differ. We don't agree, but we understand each other."

The little man looked back, blank with incomprehension for a moment, then, "If you say so." And stood back to let Jim to the door.

Scadding reached awkwardly past to unlock it. Out on the top of the staircase, Jim turned to offer a handshake, but the door was already closing behind him. Slowly he descended, thinking how frightening it must be to have such certainties twisted back as stabbings. Into the heart of Sydney's self. Certainties such as Jim had never experienced.

As he crunched down the gravel drive, Mrs. Scadding came out from the corner, jumping him with surprise.

"Mr. Briggs," she whispered. "Is Sydney all right? It's not like him to shout." Then, "I don't want to pry. But you understand."

Is Sydney alright? A bushwack of a question. Now and here. After tonight. "What do you mean?"

"I mean, is he all right? I worry about him, you know. Alone up there. It was his idea. Says I chatter too much. I always have." Jim sensed a self-deprecating smile in the shadows. "I have friends. But he never seems to have anyone. I could hear them going up the stairs at the side of the house, like I heard you tonight. I can't remember when he last had a visitor. Not that he would tell me. But I can hear, like I said. Nobody. Just his work, and he would not tell me about that anyway." Her eyes seeking answers across the dark, "Is he all right? Sydney?"

What to say? Does she even know if he is suspended? Would she understand why, if she knew? Finally, from somewhere, came Jim's answer. "I think he needs your help, Mrs. Scadding. He is a good man. But he needs to talk to someone."

Her hand reached out to him and softly grasped his wrist. "Oh thank you, Mr. Briggs. Thank you very, very much." And withdrew back into the shadows around the front door.

Chapter Twelve

The Courthouse foyer was crowded. Sullen youths filling the ashtrays with their stubends. Knowing solicitors talking down to their clients. The ushers, gowned and self-importantly loud in calling in the next accused. Brown greasy walls, torn fabric on the seat padding, dust on the sills, it was a place for those on a wait for the worst. But Jim was waiting for Huntley. He looked round to see if he could identify Stephen Roberts. Just a majority of young men, some with their young women, some with mates, trying to make the tawdry room their own, with bursts of laughter and the braggadocio of their forearm tattoos.

Another cluster of friends around an offender, noisily pushed out of the courtroom, with Huntley after them. "Jim. Our Mr. Roberts is up next. If all goes according to plan." Jim followed him back in and found a seat along the back, spaced apart from a dulled couple and an old man who seemed asleep. Huntley returned to a table behind the solicitors. The Court Clerk, back to the room, was talking up to the three magistrates up on their bench. Two lady Magistrates as pillars to the male Chairman. An elaborately carved dark-wood coat of arms added gravitas above their serious faces. There was a brief conferring, before the Chair, eyes over his spectacles, nodded, The Clerk returned to his desk, gave a signal, for the usher's booming voice out through the opened doorway, "Stephen Roberts."

In came the pink-faced boy, grinning round at the novelty of it all. A young woman in a denim jacket sat with him, with a solicitor hurrying in after, dropping his large bundle of documents with signal force on the table before him.

When he had sorted and extracted his papers, he looked up and the Chair said, a touch tiredly, "Yes, Mr. Dixon?"

Who stood. "In the matter of Stephen Roberts. Considering the papers, including having sight of the files provided on Mr. Roberts by the Social Services Department, I am requesting from the Court an adjournment to assess my client's fitness to plead. Mr. Roberts is a young man with a moderate mental handicap." All the Courtroom eyes to the beaming smile of the boy. "He has been in the care of the Social Services Department for eight years, since he was ten years of age. He was subject to an Educational Statement of Special Needs and consequently received his entire education within Special Schools." Dixon sat.

The Magistrates conferred, then the Chair to the Clerk, but loudly for the whole Court's hearing, "We will hear from Mr. Roberts. Please let him take the stand."

Roberts was cued to rise by the young woman and guided to the stand. Reaching there, with a different and elevated view of the Court, the smile dropped while he measured his new view of the world, then shyly, re-emerged.

"I think we will dispose of the oath at this stage," the Chair said, then waited for Stephen to turn round and become engaged. With the seriousness of the proceedings. When he did, it was with dumb unknowing, a nervous fear that looked back at the Chair, leaning forward, smiling, "Now, Stephen. Do you know why you are here?"

The boy nodded, relieved that he knew the answer to that one.

"Tell me... why are you here?"

The boy hesitated, looked down at the young woman, then back to the Chairman and the toothy grin returned, "Because I've been naughty." The voice was fluty, childlike.

The Court was transfixed by this moment, where this interrogation might lead. While the Chair considered the answer, "Hmm. Yes. Naughty." Then, "Who have you been naughty to?"

A rush of panic, he looked down to the young woman, to Dixon, the Clerk, then back into the eyes of the Chairman, who gave a reassuring smile. "I've been naughty... to Helen."

"Who is Helen?" perplexed

"I am, sir," but as the Chair looked into the Court for the source of the voice, the young woman tentatively stood. "Your Worship," she corrected herself.

"Sit down!" And she did, suddenly, to the lash of the Magistrate's angry voice. Then, caustically, "I am trying to examine Stephen's fitness to plead. Not yours, young lady."

The boy was confused by the exchange, upset to see Helen put down. On his account. Until the Chair's recovered smile calmed him. Looking at the boy, betraying to others in the Court his own hesitation over what the next question could be. The Chair's engaging smile went on, to the edge of shifting discomfort, until, "Have you been naughty to anyone else?"

"To Jed. I been naughty to Jed."

Now the Chair looked at the young woman for assistance, but her cowed head was down, looking at her hands, so she did not see.

Back to Stephen, "Who is Jed?"

"He's my friend." Then, an audible whisper, "My mate…"

"How have you been naughty to Jed?"

"I broke his jigsaw."

The people there audibly sucked in the last air from the stuffy Courtroom. As if this childlike confession was what they had been awaiting. Even the sleeper near Jim was now attentively leaned forward.

"Is Jed another... boy where you are staying?"

But the question confused Stephen, looking down to his Helen. Who now looked uncertainly back to the Chair.

Who sighed, "Well, young lady. Who is Jed?"

"He is the Officer-in Charge. Of the Pines Children's Home."

"And... jigsaws?" the Magistrate asked, defeatedly.

"Stephen loves doing jigsaws. But he gets jealous. If anyone can do them faster than him."

"Jigsaws?" the Chairman dully echoed. Then, turning the wider Court, shaking his head, finally looking at the back of the Clerk's head for inspiration. Until, with sudden and savage seriousness, back to the young woman, "Is this how he passes his time with you? Doing jigsaws? He stands remanded to the care of the local authority. For a most serious crime. For sexually assaulting young boys. And he does jigsaws?" He waited a moment, for the answer he knew would not be forthcoming from the young woman's declined head. Before resumption, "Have you anything... a programme of work... something to deal with his crimes? Something to lessen his risk of attacking other children?" No answer, so, "Well. Have you?" his voice booming about the walls of the room.

Her answer was inaudible.

"Please speak up," the Clerk said, matter-of-fact.

"No, Your Worship," and she hid her flushed face again.

The Chairman let the feebleness of this answer reverberate. Then turned to the solicitor, "Well, Mr. Dixon. Do you think your client understands why he is in the Court today?"

Dixon rose, looked at Stephen, then up at the Magistrates, "I have told Mr. Roberts. And I have explained the seriousness of the possible consequences of his offences-" correcting himself- "of his alleged offences. However. Whether he understands what has been said to him, is not for me to judge. The essence of my application today for an adjournment so that Mr. Roberts may be assessed for his fitness to plead has been exactly that, Your Worship." Pause for summary. For the winning point, "That the Court may see fit to seek the opinion of a specialist psychologist to report on my client's fitness to plead." And he sat.

The Magistrates consulted. The Clerk was invited to join the huddle of heads on the Bench. Then he turned to the Court, "The Court will rise." Jim rose with the others, as the Magistrates shuffled off, the women with their handbags, and left by a door at the back

Dixon started to speak to the Clerk. Helen went over to Stephen, still marooned in the dock. Huntley came over to Jim. "Well, well, well, the Pines," he murmured. "Whispering Pines."

"Wasn't that the place you were worried about? That lots of the kids who ended up in Northlodge were linked to?"

"Yes. It was private. But Social Services used it a lot."

"I'll check that, but I think it's run by the Council now. Must've been taken over some time."

"I'll ask Julian," Jim offered. "He should know that."

"Well. What do you make of it?" Huntley asked, almost a whisper. "The reason this took my interest was that I picked up from one of my police contacts that in Stephen's first statement to them, he had said that the sexual assaults he committed on the kids were what happened to him at the Pines. By adults. But he told it as if it was a game he was playing. The same game he played with adults back in the home." Then, even quieter, "And that the first statement was withdrawn. Disappeared. And another one appeared. Without Stephen being interviewed a second time. With no mention of the sex games back at the Pines." Nodding over his shoulder, he commented drily, "I would put money on it, that our young lady there from the home, Miss Helen, would have a story or two to tell. Given the right inducements."

"Maybe," Jim said doubtfully. "But will anyone speak? What inducement could be big enough? After all, even Damien was frightened off in the end."

Just then, the door at the back of the Courtroom opened, prompting the Clerk, "The Court will rise." All rose and bowed to the reentered Magistrates. The untidy noise of everyone reseating.

The Chairman. "Mr. Dixon." Who stood. "We are of the view to grant your application. That the Social Services Department arrange for a report to be prepared, at the earliest opportunity, by a qualified psychologist. And that the report should advise the Court of the fitness of the accused to plead," then, an eye towards the boy. "Guilty. Or not guilty." Then he nodded Dixon to sit down. "As to the place of remand for Mr. Roberts, we are concerned with what we have heard. You," nodding curtly to the young woman, "will convey to your Managers our dissatisfaction with what we have heard here today. It would be the Court's expectation that more would have been done to make it clear to this young man the gravity of his crimes- his alleged crimes." Then, sourly, "And in our opinion…, doing jigsaws is not the proper manner for this to happen." He waited for this to sink in. "And further, we expect Senior Managers in the Social Services Department to be able to justify the appropriateness of their choice of place for Mr. Roberts' remand. Therefore, we adjourn the case for one week, only, and we will be sending a letter to the Director of Social Services requesting him to attend, or one of his Senior Managers, in order to satisfy the Court that the arrangements for Mr. Roberts, while we await the psychologist's report, take sufficient note of the needs of public safety. Thank you."

The Clerk stood, "Case adjourned till next Friday. 10a.m."

Chapter Thirteen

That week he phoned Tracey three times before he found her in.

"Oh. Hello, Tracey."

"Dad." The flat marker to the start of a conversation she was not wanting to have. But had expected.

Bringing out a false cheerfulness in him, "I was phoning to check when we can meet again. Before I go back." Home, he added to himself.

She sighed. "It's not going to happen. While you're involved in this Social Services thing... there's no way. I talked to Richard about it. And he's adamant too." Then petulant, "It's not fair. To make us risk our jobs. Is it, Dad."

"I don't think that's what it would mean."

"How do you know? How do you know?" the repeat stressing the "you". "You're the last person to judge that. Your life's been full of unforeseen consequences. Just don't make our careers another one of them."

Stalled by this, by the thought-out preciseness of her judgement, he was stopped a moment, before he spoke, "I want to see you again. Before I go back. Even without Richard."

The phone only replied with her breathing, a sigh, then, "No. Not while this goes on. Dad, you can't just fly back into my life and trample around the way you did in the past and fly back out. We go on living here. And have to deal with the results."

"So, when will I see you again?" both plaintive and challenging.

"You tell me. When you can visit without any of this other baggage. Mum was right. There's always something more important than your family." The hardness of her voice began to fray with emotion, "I tried this time, you know. I really tried. To build bridges. That maybe I'd been too harsh with you as I grew up. I tried so hard the night we went out for that meal. And it went so well at first!" Her frustration burst into his ear, died away with. "Until you had to tell me. About you messing around with the Council still."

There was silence between them. Struggled inside with bad temper, at himself, at the situation, he was overwhelmed by the sound of sorrow and regret in her voice. And the platitudes he restrained from speaking.

"Well?" she asked, aridly.

"I'll probably be coming back to the UK more often. If this furniture moving thing comes off," he trailed with an audible lack of conviction. Feebly lying. Then, trying to push the responsibility to her, he offered, tentatively, "Or you could come out to France? With Richard? And see me there." But his mind was uncomfortable with Suzanne's ill-spirited tolerance of him. And what this crisply critical daughter would make of Gizande, his secret.

"Oh, yes. We could come out to France," dully echoed. Knowing, like him, another failure to deal with the here-and-now of their relationship. Another postponement. "Yes. Write to me when you are back there."

And? He wanted her to offer something more. Even if just for the future, a little final warmth to send him away with.

But it was left to his, "Okay," almost sorrowful, to end the conversation.

Except for her, "Bye, Dad," voice already receding from the receiver. Click. Silence, but for the hissing on the line.

And breaking his pattern of habit, he went out for a long run that evening, several morning runs having been lost. Returning quietly in the twilight to the flat, the two exhausted parents already asleep. With their child. Late into the night, awake on the divan, Jim's brain puckered with how he could have done things differently.

Chapter Fourteen

Friday. Back in Court again. Knowing the routine, Jim was there early this time and went to the bench at the back of the Courtroom, as soon as the usher unlocked. Huntley came in a few minutes later. "We'll see who the Social Services send along. To get barbecued by the Bench," then he slid to his table behind the solicitors.

The Clerk arrived and, after the curt rituals of obsequiousness as they entered, the same three Magistrates started to roll through the morning's business. Several fines for driving and for drunk and disorderly. And an assault that clearly was not as simple as expected, irritating the Chairman. Whom Jim guessed would have liked to send the unkempt young man down for a month or two, but had to bail him for a future appearance. Because papers were not ready, apologised a flinching young solicitor.

Then, "Stephen Roberts!"

And after a moment's noise from the open door to the waiting area outside, in came Stephen. Followed by a man with ponytailed hair. A smart younger man in an expensive-looking grey suit. And Sylvie Cathcart. With a chilled expressionless look of enduring a discomforting experience. But to Jim's eye, failing to conceal her edge of nerviness. He flushed inside at the sight of her. Anger. And regret. Eyes ahead, straight to her seat at the front, along with the boy and his other escorts, she did not see Jim. Who caught a swift nostalgic peep at her rear and thighs moving inside her glossed suit skirt. Dixon pursued them in, bundling his papers untidily onto his table.

The Chair scanned the row of new arrivals, then looked over his spectacles at the solicitor, "Well, Mr. Dixon. What have we here?"

Rising, still puffed, "Your Worships. Attending the Court today, we have representatives from the Social Services Department. In response to your letter."

"May we know whom we are dealing with?"

"Er, yes. Your Worship," leaning over and whispering to Sylvie, Jim intensely trying to catch sight of her half-turned face. "This is Sylvia Cathcart. She is the Children's Services Manager for the Department." Bent his ear to her whisper again, then rose, "She is the Senior Manager responsible for the Council's children's homes."

"Fine, Mr. Dixon. If we could not have the Director, I am sure-is it Miss Cathcart?"

"Ms.," Sylvie said.

"I am sure Miss" -hissed with emphasis- "Cathcart will be able to answer any pertinent question we may wish to put," the Chair ended doubtfully.

Dixon continued, "This is Geoffrey Dickinson," indicating the ponytail, "Officer-in-Charge of The Pines."

"Ah," the Chair sighed, "Mr. Robert's jigsaw friend." Then, with distaste, "Jed, if my memory serves me right." At this, the Courtroom prickled with expectation at what was to come.

Again, Dixon dipped to consult, rearing up with, "This is Mr. Finch. Mr. William Finch." Finch? The Northlodge bully? Billy Finch, had Damien called him? "Ms. Cathcart will explain his role. In due course."

"I hope she will," the Chairman tiredly rejoindered, with a lack of confidence in all those before him. "Right Mr. Dixon. First the matter of the psychologist's report. What can we learn about the progress there? If any."

"Could Ms. Cathcart please explain that, Your Worship?"

"Could she?" a vague echo. "Well, we had better have you on the stand, Miss Cathcart, hadn't we?"

She uncertainly got up and clicked across to the little boarded in dais. The Clerk approached, offering a bible. She looked at the offered book a moment, then took it uncertainly. "Do you swear, by Almighty God, that the evidence you give will be the truth, the whole truth and nothing but the truth, so help me God."

Not a chance, Jim thought sourly, but she answered, "I do." And turned to look across the Courtroom. Seeing him for the first time, she clenched her face as it drained white and taut. Her knuckles fastened hard to the rim of the dock. Her eyes swiftly swept away towards the Bench, before Jim had the chance to scrutinise them, to read the panic of their confrontation.

"Ms. Cathcart," Dixon started. But she did not respond. "Ms. Cathcart?" She turned to him, suddenly awake to where she was. What she was here to do. But could not resist a second glance to the back of the Court, to see if it could possibly be true, who was sitting there. Jim's face in that scowl back at her. Both the avenger and the redeemer. The price of her marketed conscience.

So that when she said, "Yes?" to Dixon, her voice was still whispy with aftershock.

Dixon glanced back to see what Sylvie had seen. And only saw the usual few in the public gallery, time on their hands with nothing better to do, or waiting for the next case, so turned back to her, "Can you outline to Their Worships what progress has been made with arranging for the psychological assessment of Stephen Roberts?" Who stuck his head up, a part to play, grinning at the first mention of his name this time, before dipping down again. All incomprehensible to him.

Sylvie cleared her throat. "We have agreed with a psychologist- who will carry out an assessment on Stephen Roberts- on whether he-" she fumbled for the words, "has the ability- the understanding to take part in the Court... process." Jim was staring relentlessly at her. Down into her, with the knowing he had of her. Sure his intensity, even across the room, could make the skin beneath her clothing crawl with discomfort. Sweat the perfume out of her pores.

Unimpressed, the Chair, looked away from her, "And, Mr. Dixon, how long will this take?"

Dixon looked quizzically at Sylvie, who mumbled, "He would be unable to start the assessment earlier than a month."

"A month?"

"One month," echoed Dixon, as if to tidy the information up.

"But what are we to understand from the phrase, unable to start earlier than a month. Presumably, that means a delay longer than a month, Mr. Dixon. Are we to suppose it could be two months? Or three?" And he sat back to glance at his fellow Magistrates, impatience on his face, before turning to Sylvie herself and growling, "Well, Miss Cathcart? Are we?"

She said nothing, motionless and pale, before nodding and saying something inaudible.

"What did you say? Mr. Dixon, please get your client to speak up."

"Ms. Cathcart, Your Worship, is not my client."

Irritated at the correction, the Chairman leaned out over the edge of the carved and pompous Bench, "Well, Miss Cathcart, I- we did not hear what you said."

Sylvie cleared her throat and replied hoarsely, "One month would be the earliest the psychologist could commence his assessment. Could meet Stephen."

Leaning back to his colleagues, the three Magistrates conferred. Then, "A month, if you must. But no interminable delays. We will not tolerate that." Damage done, he was ready to move on. "Well, Mr. Dixon, you said you would explain the presence of this other young man with us. Mr. Finch, was it not?"

"Yes, Your Worship."

"I trust this is relevant. To the case."

"Yes, Your Worship. It is in response to your concerns about the arrangements for Stephen Roberts' remand. Your letter to the Social

Services Department expressed- disquiet about the safety of the arrangements." Then, trying to recover some status for her, continued, "The Children's Services Manager will explain the new proposals for Stephen's remand."

Nodding to Sylvie, who looked to the Chair. Losing the moment she could have asserted herself, regained some lost territory here, Jim thought.

"Well? Miss Cathcart."

"We have assessed and approved Mr. Finch as a special remand carer for Mr. Roberts. The advantages of the new- the proposed new arrangements are that Mr. Finch would be the sole and full-time person responsible for the control of Stephen, while remanded. And Mr. Finch's property is sufficiently remote- in North Wales- it is away from children- who might be put at risk… by Stephen's presence."

"A carer, eh?" the word said with disfavour, before turning to Finch, "You look very young Mr. Finch, if you don't mind me observing. To be a carer." Jim could only see the back of the neatly haircutted head.

"Twenty one, Your Worship." Then, with a confident offer, "Would Your Worships like me to take the stand? So I can explain the planned arrangements for Stephen- for Mr. Roberts."

The smoothness with which the young man took on the climate of the room, caused the Chair a slight smile. For the first time. "That sounds like a helpful suggestion. A most helpful suggestion." And to Dixon first, then Sylvie, "At last," with a final brusque, "You may now stand down, Miss Cathcart."

She returned to her seat, eyes down and Finch comfortably replaced her. His narrow face with the right balance of confidence and reserve for the situation.

The Clerk moved to approach the stand, but the Chair interposed, "I don't think the oath will be necessary. In these circumstances." And turned to Finch, with a reassuring smile, "Please explain your plans. For the safekeeping of Mr. Roberts."

"As Ms. Cathcart outlined, I have a property in North Wales. It is a farm, where I live with my mother. I purchased it last year and it has needed a good deal of work to return it to a habitable and a productive state. Please don't misunderstand me, it is not a rural hovel," and smiled to the Chair, who was sat back, beginning at last to like what he was hearing. "The farmhouse has been restored, but there is much work to do on the outbuildings, the access road and, finally fencing and gating the fields. While I am off work, Stephen Roberts would live there with me and my family during his remand and would be working under my supervision and my instruction, doing useful tasks. I would also undertake to return him for any Court appearances or other appointments as necessary."

After a brief word to his colleagues, the Chair smiled, with a sharp glance at Sylvie and Dickinson, "Well, it sounds more useful than jigsaws." Some laughter in the Court, before, "But please tell me, Mr. Finch, are your employers satisfied with such a period of absence? And what experience have you in such work- for supervising a serious offender such as Mr. Roberts, here?"

"Your Worship, I have no direct experience working with offenders, except-" pause- "I have been responsible for managing large numbers of men, here and abroad, on building projects. I am employed by the Association of Builders and Construction Employers and Contractors." ABC! It hit Jim and he stared from Finch to the back of Sylvie's head. Oh, god, how could you, woman? "They are more than happy, as I am owed considerable leave from working abroad. I am the Labour Contracts Manager. If I may say, sir," getting almost intimate with them, "I have had to deal with men at least as dangerous as Stephen in other ways. And without the restraints provided by a Court such as this." A modest smile. Shared by the Chair.

Who turned to Dixon, "And Social Services have carried out all their checks, have they?"

Dixon rose, turned to defer to Sylvie, "I'm sure they have Your Worship." And Jim saw the back of her head nod.

The Clerk looked up to the Magistrates, expectantly, took his cue and, standing to call, "The Court will rise." And, as they all did- the door from the hallway opened noisily and the Clerk's and the Magistrates' eyes were on the man who entered. Damien's dad. Mr. Toser. Who stopped. And the ritual of retirement could resume.

As he sat back down, Jim looked along at the man, to check his memory of him. Then slid down the seat, up to him.

"Mr. Toser?"

"Yes?" Cautious at first, then recognition, "It's Mr. Briggs, isn't it?"

"Yes, that's right. You know I've been looking for you. I visited your old home the other evening."

"Ah. Yes, me and the wife moved from there. We could afford somewhere better. With the money Damien had been sending home." Sombre at the name of his dead son. Then, appealing, "You heard about him, did you? That he's dead. Murdered, he was."

"I heard. That's why I came back."

"Came back?"

With a brief, "I live away now." But back to Damien, Jim lowered his voice, "We need to meet. After this. Is this why you've come? The Stephen Roberts case?"

"No." He nodded into the Court, the backs of the row of heads in front. "I was tipped off that Finch was turning up here. Billy Finch. He knows more than anybody what happened to our Damien. He was his boss. Damien's boss." Then, scrutinising the group a second time, embittered, "Is that Cathcart here, as well? That fucking sly cow."

Jim hushed him with a hand on Toser's sleeve. "Later. Afterwards."

Huntley turned round and nodded to Jim. Who winked back, unsmiling. To denote, Okay. Knowing something had at last begun to unravel.

"The Court will rise," as the Magistrates filed back in.

"Mr. Dixon. We have considered the proposal from Mr. Finch to provide a safe place of remand for Stephen Roberts. Taking into consideration the considerable risk to children that Mr. Roberts represents and the quality of activity that had been provided in the children's home hitherto, we are prepared to accept the proposal." And the Chair scanned the row in front of him. Finch, Roberts, Dickinson, Cathcart, with Dixon hovered at the end in a gratifying pose. "However... However, we would place conditions on this arrangement." Looking gravely down on Sylvie, "The Social Services Department still has the responsibility to provide support and advice to Mr. Finch, should he require it. That does not mean waiting for him to call. Do you understand, Miss Cathcart?" Another cowed nod from her. "It means one of your staff regularly keeping contact themselves. Visiting to see that all is well. Whatever the costs in time and travel. Keeping active engagement, as I believe it is called. Because we consider this to be a most serious case." Then to Finch, "You understand. It is for your own benefit. They have overall responsibility for this, because of Stephen Robert's special needs. And his special risks."

"Yes. Thank you very much, Your Worships," Finch's voice as clear as a struck glass.

Back to Sylvie, chilled again, "We also hold Social Services responsible for ensuring that the report from the psychologist is completed and before this Court, as promptly as possible. At every adjournment in this case, we expect Social Services to be accountable. And that a Manager of at least your own seniority is present to give an account of the progress. Or the lack of it. Do you understand?"

Quietly, "Yes. Your Worship."

Suddenly and brusquely to the Clerk, "Adjourned for four weeks," stood followed by the silent women either side.

"Court will rise."

And, with them gone, the room seemed fumed with traces of the courteous and angry contempt of all that had just passed. The Social Services bench dared some restrained, murmured sounds.

But Jim was looking up at Toser, who was now standing. Grim face, the pulse under his jaw throbbing. His words, deliberate, all their fury clenched back, knifed into the Courtroom's moment of respite, "Shame on you, Billy Finch!" Who sat motionless. Still looking ahead at the vacated Bench. "Damien knew what you did to him. You knew what you did to him. God knows it too! Let your conscience- if you have one- be your judge!"

Suddenly, Stephen was up, twisted round, staggered and shrieked, "Damien!" He turned and hit Finch a blow, glanced off his cheek. And again, stretching louder, stabbing out from his crazed mouth, "Damien!" Finch was up and pinned Stephen's arms to his side, wrestling him back onto the seat, "Don't hurt Damien!" Before Dickinson clamped a hand over the cries of pain, and the two men forced the boy, locked almost motionless, bar the spasms of his shoulders, as he went down under them, full length on the seat.

The Clerk pushed away the others around the fallen and held boy, "All clear the Court! All clear the Court." And the usher rushed in at the noise. "Hold the boy, till the others are out." He started to flap his hand at Sylvie, Dixon and more vaguely at Huntley, at Jim, Toser, most of all Toser, and the others in the public gallery. To go. The usher moved threateningly towards them. Toser was already going, Huntley had gathered his pad up and was scribbling, moving slowly out, Jim waited. Dixon and Sylvie together past the front of the row he was in, but she could not resist. The determination of her averted face unlocked and, an instant of glance up into Jim's eyes showed a stripped-down terror in her face, stumbling as she accelerated through the doorway.

Outside, he saw her swerve out of the carpark in a large silver saloon. His arm on Toser's shoulder, "I want you to meet Bert Huntley. Do you know him?" As Huntley came down to them, shaking his head and grinning.

"No," but Toser was still agitated, waiting on the steps for Finch to appear.

"Bert," Jim said, the abbreviated name still somehow inappropriate for the man, "Meet Mr. Toser. Damien's father."

Huntley nodded, then to Jim, "What was all that about? Their plan to sweep it all under the carpet somewhat came apart at the seams.

Thanks to your intervention, Mr. Toser."

But he was impatient of them, of their good humour, "Thanks to me- nothing! Damien is dead- because of Billy Finch. And all those who did nothing- didn't listen to him."

"Mr. Toser, I'm Bill Huntley, freelance journalist. Do you want to tell me what you know? And I'll tell you what I know. And Mr. Briggs here."

But, after a brief scan of the two men, Toser was still waiting, eyes on the Court building door. For his quarry. "I want Finch," his gritted and understated venom giving stature to this otherwise modest, even ineffectual man.

"They will probably smuggle him with Stephen Roberts out the back door," Huntley explained. "But I can find out where he lives- where this farm of his is in North Wales."

"North Wales?"

"Yes, they said in the Court. That's where they're taking Roberts. Till the next Court." Huntley then tried a friendly arm round Toser's shoulders. "It looks like you could do with a drink. Do you want to join us?" with a checking look at Jim. "Look, we don't want to be hanging about outside here. Where everybody can see. Anyway, a fight with Finch here will do no good. He knows you'll be waiting. Let's get to see him when he doesn't expect it."

"Won't we lose him? He slippery as an eel, you know."

"Well, Mr Toser, tell us about him. You can't do this all on your own. We can help you find out what happened to Damien."

On the verge of tears, the man inhaled deeply to hold them back, then, turning for a last look at the Court entrance as it opened to let out two lawyers for lunch, exhaled in a sigh. With all the hopelessness and loss of his son. And Jim could see in the older man's face, the faithlessness and broken anger of Damien, that night in the Baltic Fleet.

Chapter Fifteen

That night, after Trish had gone to bed, Adam in the cot beside her, Jim and Julian sat on in the sitting room, quietly discussing where they were at. Itemising progress.

"First, there's nothing more I can do about Scadding. I've seen him twice now and he just doesn't see it. The big picture. He won't even think of me having anything to do with his Disciplinary. For him, it's all about documents, not about kids. You now know what I know about the documents and that's about all we can do there. When you get to the Hearing, the best route to go will be to cross examine Managers- especially Cathcart- why they were so concerned about shredding some of the stuff. And why papers about Cathcart's written notes were being kept in an old Child Care file, anyway." Then, shaking his head slowly, "But all this, round the Stephen Roberts case. This really seems to confirm some of the worst fears we had back before they sacked me. And by we, I mean Sylvie Cathcart and me. She knows all about it. I saw it in her eyes today. She was shitting herself, seeing me there today."

"Lucky, Stephen is eighteen," Julian observed. "He's an adult. If he'd been younger, it would all have gone through Juvenile Court. No public allowed in."

"That's probably started to pull their cover-up to pieces more than anything. Especially when Fred Toser burst in on us today. Now this is the bit we really have to piece together carefully. From what he says, Damien went down to work in London. I reckon that he was being pimped in that flat, for the benefit of ABC. And that's why he turned against me and that Witness Statement from him turned up at my Disciplinary. Anyway, at some stage Finch became his boss and, rather than just being rent boys, Damien started to go out to Germany with Finch. Don't fully understand what all this was about. Damien started to bring back presents from Berlin for his mum and dad. Fred believes that Damien and Billy Finch were doing some sort of work for ABC with British lads on building sites over there. But I think that's cloud-cuckoo land. They were only about nineteen or twenty apiece. Kids out of children's homes? Nah, something else. Don't know what that was about. Yet." Now Jim's face darkened. For the next passage. "How Damien died." He inhaled. Before commencing, "It's difficult to separate what's fact and what Fred would like to believe. To make the best of his son's death. Do we even really know why Damien ended up in care? I know the file says something about being picked up by the Police after getting kicked out by his parents. But there's nothing more than that. Some of what Fred Toser says may be to try to gloss over his guilt about getting Damien into the system that finally killed him. Anyway, he's convinced it was murder. But the weirdest thing is that he's also convinced that it happened in Berlin. The body was found here in a derelict house over here, as you know, but what hasn't come out is the date of death. Ten days before it was found." Holding back his nausea in telling it, as he had when Fred Toser had chillingly told it to Jim and Huntley round the pub table that day at lunch. "His face was barely recognisable. Rats had eaten it. So they established the time of death, before they identified the body. Cause of death was a heroin overdose. Injected. Damien's dad doesn't believe that. He doesn't believe Damien was a druggie. I'm not so sure. If he was in that rent boy world, it's probable he would have used drugs, wouldn't it?"

Julian shrugged, "Probably."

"But this thing he's got about Damien dying in Berlin," Jim shook his head. "Apparently on the day Damien died, he phoned home and spoke to Fred. He said he was coming home and had a ticket to fly back the following week. Said he was packing up the job in Germany, but had some things to clear up before he came back. Fred said he'd sounded so worried over the phone, he'd asked Damien if he was okay. I think that was unusual. That they didn't talk about those sorts of things, as father and son. You know, ask each other how they were feeling. Any way, Damien answered, I can't tell you now. I'll tell you when I get back. And put down the phone. Fred Toser puts a lot of meaning on that, as I s'pose you would. To the last words of your son. But he reckons that Damien was overheard. Or interrupted by someone. And then. The next thing is that Damien doesn't come home when he says. And his body's found. Having died some time shortly after the phone call." Jim sat up to unknot tension from his shoulders. "Somehow, he says, the body was smuggled back to the UK. And injected with heroin later. But the heroin wouldn't get round the body if it was later, would it?" Asked, as if to himself, barely aware of Julian. Beyond the haunted faces of father and son, stood in witness at the front of his brain. Wondering if he could have done better with Damien. The one time they met.

But Julian answered, "No. I don't think so. Not without the heart pumping the blood round. But they could have tied him up or knocked him out. Then injected him."

"Toser blames Finch for it. If not for actually murdering Damien, at least for not saving him. And then it's Finch who turns up, out of the blue. And fully approved by Social Services. To whisk off and out of sight, a pathetic, simple lad, who's said he's being buggered in a children's home by staff. And that really stinks."

Julian rubbed his eyes with his knuckles and looked up, bruised with it all, "And the people doing it were some of them my Union members."

"Dickinson? The Officer in Charge."

"Yes. He was on the Stewards' Committee the year before last." Then, offering a reasonableness, "We don't know he's actually one of the abusers."

"No. We don't. But think about it. Would he have been appointed if he wasn't up to his armpits in it? Stuff about the Pines was washing around when I was trying to get something done about Damien."

"I know. I know." Julian looked away, "It's all too big. For me in the Union at my level to deal with. I mean, the Branch doesn't have the means to deal with an investigation of this size. It's a Police matter."

"And don't you think the Police must be involved in sweeping this under the carpet too? Remember some of the names on that list I drew up. When I was working on it with Cathcart."

"And her involvement," Julian said, shaking his head. "I work for her."

"Well, if you work for her, who's working for the kids in that organisation of yours?" Jim's anger rooted about in the doubts he had about Julian, slinging down the challenge, "Well, I'll tell you what we're doing about it, Bert Huntley and me. We're going out to this place in Wales that Finch has got. Snoop around. See what your Department has approved. For poor little Stephen Roberts."

"That's not fair, Jim. And you know it! It was me that got you the address- at some risk!"

"Shhh," Jim pointed towards the bedroom door, then hissed, "Fair? Who said fair? This isn't about being reasonable, Julian. Fair to who? To Stephen? Or to the kids who might get attacked by the monster Social Services is going to make of him?" He wiped a fleck of spit from his mouth, "I might not be a social worker, but I know about this stuff. And what it can do," taking himself back to the flashbacked edge of memory. Still an almost physical snatch of pain at his groin, more than forty years later. Never gone entirely. Just managed into the background, until a moment like this. He hung his head and pushed his fingertips deep-pressed through the eyelids, to erase it from his eyeballs, sliding his hands back to squeeze the priest's angry voice from his ears, his contracted muscles almost retching to clench the slobbered tongue from off his belly. Head hanging finally, his fingers knotting his hands together through the hair at the nape of his neck.

Julian said nothing for a time, before, softly, "Are you alright, Jim?"

No answer.

"Jim…?"

Who slowly raised his head. With immense weariness. That of the child, forced to learn being a man. Before time. And that of the man, regretting the gone child, wanting to be away from this now and this then. Closing his eyes again to Julian. Bringing to mind Gizande, who trusted him, more than he trusted himself to do the right thing. Wishing the impossibility of her here now. His low voice almost a croak, Jim asked, "Well. Are you up for it? Coming out to see Finch's place with Huntley and me?"

"You know I can't do that. I'd just end up another suspension."

Jim knew that was probably true, but snorted, "Of course," knowing he would probably himself have gone on a trip like that. Just for the hell of it. And damn the consequences, as Tracey would have pointed out. But it was not recklessness that drove him, he knew.

"You can do that. You've got nothing to lose," Julian said defensively. Then, with more confidence, "That's why I asked you over here. You've got nothing to lose."

Haven't I? Jim wondered. Why did it seem that everyone had surer opinions about his life than he did himself? "Well, Huntley and I are going. We didn't tell Fred Toser we knew the address yet. He's a bit out of control with it all. But we're going to find Finch." But it sounded trivially adventurous. Forcing an amiable smile, he turned to Julian and, letting him down from his discomfort, said, "Come on it's late. Your family awaits you next door."

"Yeah. Good night." Then, "I'm sorry," waiting for something from Jim.

Sorry about what? Enough of a sorry for any of this? But released him with, "Yeah. Night."

After making up the divan as quietly as he had now learned, Jim lay awake outside the thin shaft of light from the kitchen that fell across one of the sofas and up the frontdoor and back across the ceiling. Thinking of Gizande was interrupted by the odd thought that Finch had been restoring a remote farmhouse. As Jim was. Or so Finch said. And just that oddity from nowhere, he took as a signal. Across the night, from that woman in her own gaunt farmhouse. That Jim was doing the right thing.

Chapter Sixteen

They went in Huntley's car. As they penetrated deeper into Wales, the drizzling clouds they left behind thickened until the first mountains were only gloomy shadows through the spray off the roads. Onto the climbing lanes, runnels of water were draining out of the fields, overflowing the ditches and turning the tarmac into brown and bubbling sheets of wet. They spoke little, Huntley peering through the screen, Jim with the map spread across his knees. They missed the place, Cartref, the first time, the broken-gated gap in the stone wall looking no more than another unkempt field. Huntley turned and they finally parked halfway onto a bank of mudded grass. They got out and surveyed the pair of sloppy ruts across the field towards the slate roof and chimney.

They had come dressed tidily and Huntley remarked, "Should have known better than to dress up for Wales."

Jim struck out first with, "Well, we're not going back now. Come this far." Avoiding the ooze of the ruts by taking the clinging wet onto his trouser bottoms from the grass between them. As they came to the crest of the field, below them was the farm. A litter of broken buildings with a large caravan parked among them.

"Not quite as complete as Mr. Finch would have Their Worships believe," Huntley remarked as he joined Jim. No vehicles.

"More your rural hovel, wouldn't you say?"

The journalist laughed, "Well it must be fine really. After all it has the stamp of approval of Social Services!" Then, "Well here we go. Keep to our story if Finch isn't there." And led off down the hill.

The caravan door was answered by a fortyish woman. "Yes? What?" defensively aggressive.

Huntley's beaming bonhomie, despite his bedraggled saturation, "You must be Billy's mum."

"Who's asking?" guarded, but interested.

"We work with him. For ABC. We were in the area for a meeting. He told us about his madcap idea of doing up a farm, so we came over to have a look. As we were in the area." Then added, hopefully, "Not much of a day to choose," nodding up into grey air.

"Billy's not here," a refusal of them, then taken back with, "Well you'd better come in out of the weather. Watch the step, mind," and at last a short smile as she stepped back into the caravan to let them in. Crowded together in the narrow corridor, the two men stamped some of the wet off their shoes and trousers, before Jim closed out the rain with the ill-fitting door.

"Come through," and they followed into the living room, wrapped around with windows onto the dismal tumbles of stones and weeds outside. "Cuppa tea?" They agreed and she took their coats. A tough woman able to charm when needed, Jim guessed. Confirmed by the way she crossed her legs when she sat back down across from them with their drinks.

Huntley opened with, "Thought Billy had got more done to the place than this. But then he's been working away a lot. Germany he was in last, wasn't he?"

"Who did you say you were?" she asked and Jim thought, we don't play this woman for a mug.

"Bertie Huntley. And this is James Briggs. We're also ABC managers," said with the relaxed and casual confidence of a good lie.

She seemed eased by this, "Well. Yes. Billy's off again. Without so much as a say-so. And I'm not right pleased, and all. He was to be here for the next few weeks. We had builders coming in, but I've had to put them off." She waved a hand at the outside, "And now this. A Welsh summer, I'll be bound."

"Has he said when he's coming back?" Jim asked, adding audaciously, turning to Huntley, "I'm sure he told me he would be back here. Did he say anything to you, last time you saw him?"

"No. But it happens, Mrs. Finch. Problems with a contract and they call you back with no notice. That's the way it is. Did he say where he was called back to? Was it Berlin again? Probably was. I heard that things are getting sticky out there. With the political situation and all that nonsense."

Edges of their seat, but trying not to show it, they waited for her answer, "Yes. Germany, anyway. He didn't say it was Berlin."

"Ah well," Huntley said, almost as if losing interest in the topic, "he'll be in contact soon, I've no doubt."

"Oh, I can phone him. No problem. But he should be back here. Getting the mess out there sorted out. Getting this place repaired." And ready for winter, Jim thought. Of La Retrait, too.

"Well, pass on our best wishes, when you next call him. We must be off. Just called in on the off chance. To see if he was in, Mrs. Finch."

And Jim smiled at her, "And thanks for the tea. Welcome, on a day like this."

"Sorry you came out of your way. And for the weather. And the mud," looking down at their shoes.

"That's all right." Huntley, jovially, "We'll give Billy hell when we next see him. Leaving his Mum out in the back of beyond. In weather like this."

They both shook her hand, but did not speak to each other till they were back in the car. Out of the drenching rain.

"I was so tempted to ask for his phone number. But there was something a bit smart about her."

"Yes," Jim agreed. "A bit sharp, although we lowered her defences. I don't think we'd have got away with asking for numbers."

"Well. We know he's not where he said he would be. What do we do with that precious jewel of intelligence? Write to the Magistrates? Ask for an interview with Miss Cathcart?"

"More important, where's Stephen? I'm worried about that. He's a liability to them. Just like Damien. And they're ruthless. As we know."

"Yes." The grimness of this settled between them. "But our best bet in finding Stephen, at present, is to find Finch. And I believe his mum, that he's in Germany. At least, as far as he's told her."

"Toser," Jim said. "Fred Toser. He'll have some numbers for Germany, from Damien. Get them off him and try them. But don't tell him too much yet. He's a loose cannon. I'll go and see him. He trusts me. Because he knows I helped Damien in the past."

"We can only try, Mr. Briggs. We can only try."

Fred Toser was out that evening, when Jim called. But he was welcomed in by Mrs. Toser- Edith- as soon as he gave his name. His reputation obviously held good in that household. She talked about Damien for some time, a Damien Jim did not recognise from his one meeting with the youth. A worldly success. Going places. London. Europe. The money sent home. The foreign gifts. Where next? Her identity for him, like the body on the mortuary slab. Cleansed as possible of the horrors of how he had died. And of whom he really had been.

So it was difficult for Jim to get to what he had come for. Numbers. Addresses. He had finally to firmly press the point. To quieten her, to explain the search for Finch. Without mentioning Stephen Roberts, of course. And her quietening became sombre silence. As he explained. Finally she rose, went to a cabinet, brought out a box. Delicately emptied it of an expensive watch, a tied bundle of letters and a small leather bound notebook. Which she opened.

"Here you are, Mr. Briggs. These are the phone numbers and addresses Damien gave us." Then, softly, "I'd like to keep the book. If you wouldn't mind copying them down?"

Jim did. Two Berlin addresses. Three numbers. He delicately handed back the book to her. And, with a few more words in a remorseful tone, he left her. The tidy house, in that ill-lit street. A vessel emptied of her son. And of the lost dreams he had borne.

The next morning, he went off to his appointment at Huntley's office. So they sat there, the phone between them, Huntley, with some German, to call the first number.

"Well, here goes." He buttoned out the numbers on the phone. And waited, watched by Jim. A long minute, before putting the phone back in its cradle. "No answer. Try the second." Phone up and dialling. Wait again. Then a jump in Huntley's face, into concentration. A quick sharp look at Jim, as if to tell him something- cut off with, "Guten tag. Ich heissen see Herbert Huntley," said with laboured precision. "Ja. lch bin Englander. Ah! Gut! Sie spreche Englisch?... Thank you. Can I speak to the manager? Der... er... Geschaftsfuhrer?" A laugh, nervous and courteous. "Danke. Thank you." Hand over the mouthpiece, he said to Jim, "I think it's an employment agency. For foreigners. Gast arbeiter something, he said." Then back to the phone, listening. "Oh, hello... Mr. Huntley. I know Mr. Finch- Billy Finch. I want to contact him… When?... Later today, you say?... Well just let him know I phoned. It's concerning Stephen Roberts... What? Wait!" Receiver back down again, he looked at Jim again, "Bastard cut me off. He spoke good English, too. It wasn't Finch."

"Was it Stephen's name that did it?"

"Just on cue with me saying it. And it sounds as if Finch is already out there, because he's due in this afternoon."

"And probably with Stephen." And the implication of that dropped heavily within Jim's abdomen. "Beyond our reach now."

"Well, I certainly don't have the expenses budget to go off to foreign climes to chase this story."

Reminding Jim that this was a story to the journalist. Just a story. But what to himself? One of Tracey's crusades? Going nowhere, anyway. Scadding turning him away. Finch back in Germany. "What if we inform the Council, formally? That Finch has taken Roberts out of the country. They'd have to do something"

"Would they? Where's the proof? A phone call to an job agency in Berlin? And we'd have to give over the phone numbers, letting them warn Finch, if they're in collusion with him. No, there must be something smarter we could do." A further thought, "They'd have to turn it over to the Police. And you believe their hands too are contaminated with this business, don't you?"

"Jesus," Jim hissed. "And they fucking criminalise the victims, like Stephen. And cosy up to the evil sods like Finch!" Turning savagely on Huntley, "What could you do that's smarter, eh?"

"I could see if there's a stringer out in Berlin who could follow it up. There're probably some journalists out there, even if they're German, who keep an eye on the Brits and US troops and diplomatic community out there. Who might at least have a look at the address. Trace the phone numbers for us. Specially with everything going on over there now."

"You sound really confident of that, Bert," Jim sneered, beginning to feel again left on his own with this. "Don't make me wait- or Stephen, god bless him- wherever he is- for what is only an outside chance of getting things moving on this. Stephen can't wait. It's... unimaginable- what may be happening to him now- at this minute! While we decide. And wait for some journalist you don't yet know, to choose to pick this up and do something. It would be quicker for me to get in my van and drive there."

"Go, if you wish. But I think the prospect of you doing that is at least as remote as me getting a German journalist to check out a couple of addresses for us."

Probably right, Jim thought. And him with nil Deutsch. Even less German than his pathetic French. But the anger still battered up from underneath the settling leaden weight of defeatedness. He would not let this lie, whatever it took. Chewing at his mind, as the rats had devoured Damien. "I'm not sure what next," Jim said vehemently, casting an incoherent challenge at Huntley. Or at the wider world. "But something will be done."

Getting up to go, it took Jim like a dream, "Some thing …" Turning to the journalist, "I'll think of something. I'll probably let you know."

Chapter Seventeen

So angry, Jim became aware he had been muttering aloud as he strode back to the flat. He turned off into backstreets of terraces, some of the last of the old Victorian housing stock that had not been swept away, the pavings glittered with sunshine after yesterday's rain. Heading for the riverside. To inhale its raw salt and ozone. There, he strode north along the Prom, past run-down and boarded-up hotels. Finally to where the promontory curved back, opening the prospect of the grey, sloppy, dirty sea washing the sunlight with its rag of waves. Always promising so much to the tired and pessimistic towns along its edge. Escape into a wider world. A kitbag-full of youthful optimism. Discovery. Now as empty to the skyline as the broken, rusting docklands behind him. With more empty supermarket trolleys sunk to the bottom of them, than ships with cargo floating on their oily surface. Leaning on the railings, out over the shred of stained and littered beach below him, he felt solitary. Foreign. Without a foreign language to his name, he thought. And not an idea of his own what to do next.

Turning from the ocean, he leaned back on his elbows, looking back at the remains of the seaside resort this part had been. A roofless bandstand. A slot machine Palace of Amusements, with a few truanting schoolkids playing them. A chippy. A closed pub. He chose the chippy. Not the best for keeping running-fit, he thought. But comfortingly warm, an insulation of fat to blanket him. He crossed over.

"Portion of fish and chips, please," to the teenage girl serving.

"Chips'll be ready in a couple of minutes." So he sat back on the sill of the front window, watching her stare idly out past him, almost wistful at what she must be thinking. Then stirring the fryers, before returning her eyes to the sea outside. That look, he thought.

A man came through from the back with a plastic vat full of white and freshly cut chips. Jim became aware of being looked at. "Jim Briggs, isn't it? From the Car Plant?"

He looked back at the man behind the counter, but the face said nothing to him, so he answered, "Yes." Then jokingly defensive, "So? Who's asking?"

"Oh, you probably wouldn't remember me." He went over, lifted a scoop of chips from the seething fryer, picked one and pinched it before throwing it back with the rest. "I wouldn't have been high and mighty enough for the likes of you, for you to remember. But I always voted for you in Branch Elections. Even when you lost and they threw you out."

Jim smiled, then offered vaguely, "That was a long time ago."

"Oh, yes. Got made redundant in '81. Unemployed till this. Never thought I'd end up here. Skilled man. Doing this," a dismissive swipe of his hand. "What're you up to now, then?"

"Just back here for some business."

"Business, eh?" uninterested. Then, "You know they say the P!ant will close completely next year? Work's gone to Spain. Now they're in the Common Market."

"No. Hadn't heard," not really wanting to talk about this. Dredge up that past. "As I say, live away now"

"Gone South, eh? Like plenty of 'em." Stirring the chips again, "You wouldn't get me giving up on the North." Then to the girl, "They'll be ready, love." He leaned across towards Jim, "You got out of the fight after the winnings had ended. After the 60s. When the lads started to lose everything. When they brought in Productivity and the Line speed-ups. When we really needed people to keep the flag flying, where were you?" He started to shovel out the hot chips, a fish dropped on top. "Salt and vinegar?"

Jim nodded, ready to go.

The man wrapped the food, but held back the package beneath his hand, "Where'd you say you live now?"

"France," he said quietly. Guiltily. So even the girl looked up at him from the till.

"That'll be a quid. Exactly." Jim paid. "Don't know what that is in francs." Then. Studying Jim's face, before sadly shaking his head, "South of France, eh?"

Sweeping the package to him and going, Jim mumbled, "See you."

Over his shoulder heard, "Oh, yes, Jim, see you too. Next time I'm down the Cote d'Azur. I'm the bloody Man Who Broke the Bank at Monte-Carlo!"

Trish put finger to lip for silence as he reentered the flat, signing that Adam was asleep in his room. He followed her into the kitchen, closing the door after him.

"The Police have come. About your van. They came this morning."

"What did they want?"

"Not sure. Wanted to know who owned it. Just sniffing around, I would've said, but for one thing."

"Go on, what?"

"How did they know the van had anything to do with us? You

park it in the street behind. I went out to check after they'd gone, because I hadn't realised you went out this morning without it."

Confused what she was saying, he offered, "The van's still there now. I saw it as I came in."

"Yes. I know. But I knocked at the flat downstairs. And the woman there said the Police hadn't asked her. She hadn't seen them. So what told them that your van had anything to do with this flat. So they came directly here."

"Maybe they spoke to somebody else. Some one might have seen me carrying stuff from the van up to the flat." He tried to lighten her concern, "There'll be enough curtain twitchers round here, won't there? With unemployment what it is, what else is there to do?" But it did not allay his own anxiety, his sense that all this was too big, getting too unmanageably complex for him. "What do you think they were here about? The Police"

"I don't know. It was like they knew more than they were letting on. The way they looked round the flat when they were here. Like it wasn't just about the van. That was a pretext, I'm sure."

He shrugged, "Not much I can do about it. What did they want to know about the van?"

"Just who owned it. I gave your name. I couldn't do anything else. And I'm sure they knew it was yours already. I said you were just a friend visiting. You lived in France."

"Well, that's true, isn't it?"

"Yes," smiling ruefully, "but it felt like telling a lie."

"Don't let the buggers get you down," and in saying that, felt properly got down himself. He looked over at Trish, before saying, "I don't know where all this stuff is going." He paused to assess what to say next. And Trish, who he was to say it to. "It's getting out of control. We think that Finch has taken the mentally handicapped lad, Stephen, to Germany-Berlin."

She was astonished. "Why?"

"He knows too much. Stephen does."

"But he's mentally handicapped."

"That's what makes him so dangerous. He can only tell the truth. Ask him a question and he'll answer it." Not like the rest of us non-handicapped folk, he thought. "I don't know what we can do about it. Normally, you'd tell the Police. But I doubt that they'd have Stephen's best interests at heart on this one. And what you told me about them snooping round might confirm that." For want of anything to add, he shrugged again. "I feel totally pissed off. About the whole thing," hoping for confirmation from her. Permission to retreat. Back to France, having done his honourable best, by even coming here.

But all she offered was, "There must be something we can do."

His mind turned away from her to Gizande. Knowing only that particular woman's permission would be enough. As Trish rose and turned her back to opening cupboards, drawers, fridge, wordlessly now preparing food, he closed his eyes to visualise the gaze of Gizande upon him here. He would phone her, he thought.

When Julian came in from work, he only added to Jim's feeling of hopelessness. He had been called in by Foley and quizzed about what Jim was doing with him. Julian had refused to discuss it as a private matter and Foley had lost his temper, shouting about breaches of the confidentiality of the Department's business. Although the Assistant Director had made a fool of himself, Julian was worried, as he would not have been before Adam's birth. In the mood he was already in, Jim just felt confirmed in the doubts he harboured about this social worker. As a bit of a dilletante in things trade union and political.

After dinner, Jim asked if he could make a long distance call to France. And, Adam asleep in their bedroom, they stayed in the kitchen, the living room phone left to Jim alone. Door closed behind him, hesitant before dialling. Chained to a trail of events here of others' making, he sought liberation from it all by Gizande. Consent for him to come home.

To business. He punched out the numbers.

"Oui?"

"Gizande. It's me, Jim"

A hesitation, "From England? You speak from England?"

"Yes. How are you?" Beneath the blandness, alert and listening. For what he could not see within her eyes.

"I?" A smile in her voice, "I am waiting for news from England."

He grinned into the mouthpiece in reply. Daring to hope, before addressing the seriousness. "News from England? The news is difficult. That's why I called you."

Just her silent listening.

"I wanted your advice."

"Oh. Yes." Inscrutably terse, that.

So he started with, "I will tell you all that has happened since I returned here," just the chronological facts, he thought, "and you tell me what you think."

"What I think," she echoed. Is that all she ever did, echo him back to himself? To let him listen better to himself.

"Okay? Is that okay? For you?"

"If that is okay for you, it is okay for me, also."

So, precisely, he began. Without humour, without asides, trying to restrain from his voice the rescue of talking to her again, the warmth of it in his throat. Scadding, Cathcart, the Court. Finch and Stephen. Fred Toser, the caravan and Mrs. Finch, Huntley and the Berlin calls. Leaving out Rodruiguez. And Tracey. Full-stopping it with. "So that's the problem."

"What is the problem?" she asked quietly. "Or is it correct to ask, which is the problem?"

Either or both, it's one big problematical mess, he thought, but said. "What to do next. If I can do anything."

"Jim, we have such a conversation many times. Cest vrai?"

"Oui. True. C'est vrai."

"What do you wish to do? Your true wish, from deep within your stomach."

Don't ask me that, the voice in his head said, but with his mouth spoke, "To get these crimes against the boys ended. At least, to get Stephen out of Finch's hands"

"So. You give yourself the answer."

"But easier said than done."

"Pardon?"

"It's easier to say that, than to do it," he translated for her.

"Why?"

Again at the point in such a conversation where he felt like a child, his voice slightly hardened, "Because how do I get to Berlin? If could get there, I speak even less German than I speak French. I know no-one there. Where do I start? How could I find where Stephen is? They're bound to be hiding him somewhere. Come on. Gizande, this is ridiculous!"

But she was laughing. Free, light and tinkling, as he had not heard since the night at Suzanne's when he first met her "Oh. Jim. You look for the problems before you ask for the solutions. Believe in yourself and you will find the way with the problem." She waited for him and he for her. "It is what I have known of you since we met. But there is more that you do not know. I know many people in Berlin. From the past, when I was a student." The heard smile again, "Was it not intended that we should know each other. To be friends."

So much meaning loaded on the last word. Almost to breaking point in his head and his heart. But all he could say was, "Oh Jesus."

She laughed again. "You amuse me very much. So solemn. You are surprised that I have had a life away from the Pyrenees? That I am not only the farm woman who smells of cows and goats?"

"No," he protested. She was never solely that. "No l just never knew, You never told me."

"You never asked. When I see you, you are often troubled with your own matters."

"I've never thought to ask. You seem such a private person. About yourself."

"Well. I am not now. I will tell you perhaps. When we next meet. What are your plans? Are you returning to France soon? Or will you now go to Berlin? And meet my friends."

"What? On my own?" She did not reply. "I have a job to do. I have to take some furniture to the Dordogne. I am being paid. By a friend."

"When will you do this?"

"I haven't thought of the date. On the way back home. When I leave here."

"What more do you stay in England for?"

"Nothing, really." She had drawn him to the point. Of departure. But a departure from here still with choices. Berlin? Really? "What do you propose?" back into that familiar slightly stilted way of words he assumed with her.

"I will meet you in Dordogne. With the information of Berlin. I will speak to my friends in Germany and explain. Much is happening there now."

He had seen some t.v. news. Demonstrations in the night. Police with batons. "Yes. I know. Doesn't that make it more difficult?"

"Well, we will learn from what my friends say."

He puzzled, "Are you coming with me? To Berlin?"

An instant of a break, before, "Me?" Then, "I will give you the assistance to go."

Was that a No? By not pressing the point, not asking the question again, he left it suspended between them. A possibility for him, that flooded him with a warm and thoughtless foolishness. "Shall I come home first, after the Dordogne?"

"I will preserve you from the additional driving, if you wish. You will have much driving already. I will meet you in the Dordogne and we will speak." A huskiness to her voice then? Or a blur on the long distance phone line? Was he reading something not there? Then, a businesslike recovery, "You will tell me when your have a date for taking of the furniture. I will meet you."

He pulled himself up. Again, it felt like she had freed him from a difficult decision. By making it for him, but not taking part in the doing.

"Why are you so sure I should carry on with all this... amateur detective work? Will it lead to... anywhere?"

Softly, gently now, almost a whisper, "Have you seen the mother of Stephen, the boy?"

"No?" What twist was this?

"If I was the mother of Stephen, I would wish you to carry on. It may carry little hope with it, but only you can follow Stephen. Is this not true?" After a wait for an answer out of his confused silence, "If he was your own child, would you not want a person such as you to continue to search? Until the last termination of hope? As the mother and father of Damien have believed in you."

Is that who he was? Did she really see him as that? He, who failed so surely and so repeatedly with his own child? He sighed, graphically, down the phone, "I suppose I'm all there is. For poor Stephen."

"Yes, Jim. You are. No one else has the interest."

"I really doubt myself on this one."

"Jim. I know. But I will assist you." Did he detect an uncertainty in her voice? Not about him, but about herself? "I will assist you to conquer the doubt. Speak to me again when you have a date for your arrival in the Dordogne."

"I will."

And her phone went down sharply, almost across his last words. A long moment before he delicately replaced his. Reflecting on the hurry she had ended it with.

Chapter Eighteen

He was late for her. The man at the Mairie who was supposed to give Jim the keys to the house where he was to deposit the furniture, had not been there and Jim had to drive him back after collecting the keys. Alone to unload the furniture through the narrow hallway and in a hurry, he had also pulled a muscle in his lower back, a discomfort that made him walk with caution over to the station café where he had arranged to meet her after. He felt tired and dirty.

She was at a table at the back of the room, deep in shadow from the hot slants of afternoon sun through the front windows. She put her book down and stood at his approach. But he brushed past her offered kiss to the cheek and embraced her, pulling her to him, within the full, enfolded wrap of his arms. Holding her, breathing in from the threads of her hair that fell across his face. And she allowed herself to be held, before, with a notification from the rub of her fingers to his shoulder, she slowly and gently pushed away. To look into his face. And he into hers, still alive to his arms around her, the shape of her ribs felt through the cotton of her shirt.

Her eyes, still so close, were looking over his face, still searching, "Jim?"

"Oh, I've missed you. So much, Gizande."

She smiled and delicately stood back, disengaging from his arms, but his hand left cupped round her elbow, holding her there. She smiled, "So, I see," taking his hand away, stepping back to sit down again.

Taking his eyes from her, he looked behind for his chair and sat down untidily. "So. What do you make of the story?" A little triumphant with what he had discovered, he then shifted uneasily to the awful plunging hole it left him with, "I daren't imagine what might be happening to Stephen, now." And, even in the warmth of the café, he gave a shudder. Stephen's fear greying the skin of his own face.

She nodded slowly to him.

"What does that nod mean?"

"Pardon? Quoi?" He imitated her and she gave a short laugh. Then, grave, "My... affirmative? It was to your face. Your air. You had the appearance in your face of your knowing. Of the boys. And of yourself."

My knowing of the boys, he turned her words around in his mind. And of himself. So that he knew what was coming next. "Yes. But it's what I don't know- what's happening now, that counts. What can I-?" then the slight daring of an oblique appeal to her, "What can we do about what is happening now? To Stephen, but to all the others they're… hurting," the weak well-manneredness to her of his last word, no match for the reality.

She was watching him, not for his words, but reflectively beyond them. So deep that it stopped him speaking. The silence of her beginning to both please and discomfort him in its steady persistence.

"Quoi?" he asked, the French word dropped as a lightener, but also as a signal of the resolution made to himself. To learn the language. And stop pretending he was a transient, now that he knew that there was truly nothing to take his life back to Britain.

From the profound place where she was, her voice emerged, huskily, from a distance, "When were you born?"

Why? "In 1936."

"No, not the year. The number of the day. And the month"

"March the 31st." Then, another try to pull her back towards him, "Just short of being an April Fool!"

Her face quizzed this, but reposed again, breathing out the words, "Ahh. Aries. Naturellement, le mouton. The ram"

"Astrology?" He had never believed in it. A trick to tell you that you could never change, born as you would always be. But with Gizande, as with the catharism, he could never be sure of his old certainties. So, "Tell me." He cleared his throat, "Tell me who I am."

The clatter and chatter of the room around them had receded, out beyond the encirclement of their mutual concentration. "Who is Jim." As if she was discovering the man before her for the first time, yet knew him through an age together. "You, Jim, are the firstborn of the Universe. The ram. To others you will appear to be confident. That you can do anything. But beneath the skin, you are less sure, less solid. Yes, you are brave, but you are easily disappointed." Jim nodded at the recognition of his mood at this moment. "You are like the first child- égoiste- how do you say?"

"Selfish?" he offered.

"No, that is not correct. You pass much time looking into yourself. This makes relations difficult with others. You need much reassuring." From the inner place where this was coming, she broke out briefly to him, "This is true, is it not, Jim?" His throat dry, by the time he had nodded, she had slid away again. "Justice. You have a very great belief in justice. You will go out and fight for others. It is Mars who rules you. The sign of le guerrier- how do you say?"

"War…? Fighter? Warrior?"

"Yes. It is warrior, I think" She touched the skin on her temple, as if to stroke out another thought, "You are also a sign of fire. Difficult to control. Touch it and you burn."

He considered. Then asked, "Is that me?"

"It is Aries. Is it you, Jim?" she asked back. In the way she had, of knowing his answer. "Ah, yes. I forget. The blue eyes. The handsome ram." And, reaching across to between his eyes to stroke a finger tip down from the bridge, "The nose of the ram." Smiling, her hands back and folded together on the table before her, "Remarquable. Éminent."

He glowed with it all. Boyish, also a little foolish. Light-headedly, he invited, "And you? What is your sign? Who are you?'

A sense of discomfort. Escape. From what she had started here. She tried to smile it away, "Non. Nooo, Jim"

But he would not have this and pressed her, still light with a returning grin, "No. You have all my inner secrets. What are yours?" but beneath the frivolous surface, his self waited, poised for the intimacy of this moment of learning. The essence of this woman, who took and gave back so much of himself. Of his own self.

Her acknowledgement of the rightness of his insistence was marked by her bowed head, eyes on her fingertips. A submission that what she had started had now passed over to his control. "Pisces," said almost confessionally. "Poisson. The fish. Water. Profound- the deep- and with dreams. The surface does not have the appearance of the depths. Fish see the world through emotions. Pisces. The last sign." And almost sighing with it, as if one of a failed family, "We have seen so much. We do not like the unpredictable. We work for others. We are the nurse." Then shrugged, "That is the fish." Looking up at him guardedly, through her brows. "As the world is new for the goat, so it is old for the fish." Then down to her hands again.

"Is that all? Nothing more?" No answer, still avoiding his eyes. "So what does the fish say about Berlin? It will say that I have to go?" Silence. "Of course it will. It always tells me to go. And pretends that I have told myself. So that I believe it." He shook his head and, easing back from his harshness, repeated, softly, "What does the fish say?" reaching across his fingers into her hair, to the line of her jaw, he gently tilted her face up. Her eyes were wet. Hunted. A single tear wandered onto the top of her cheek. His thumb reached across to trap it, balance the drop, held it. For examination, before, quiet with unsurprise, saying, "What is it, Gizande?" Knowing he had at last, for a moment, reached into something fundamental about her. Whatever it was.

But the moment was gone. She sat back, sniffed and brusquely wiped her eyes. Taking them off across the café. "You must have a drink. What do you wish for?"

But he was not to be deterred "Tell me, Gizande, what are you going to do about the boys?" Looking at her discomfort with this, "Are you just going to send me out to fire the bullets? When you know that me in Berlin would be worse than useless. Me! Who only survives in France because you and Suzanne speak the language for me." Dismissively challenging, "Me in German? Deutsch! I don't even know how to spell the word!"

She looked away again, anywhere away from his insistence. Finally resting back on her hands again. Folded so tight, they were squeezed bloodless. Finally, "I have thought about this also. Much thought." A wan smile to him, then away. "You know we Pisces, we are water. Do you not...? I fear that I throw my water upon your fire. Do you understand?" Head risen, she pushed her hair back behind her ears. Coming out from where she had retreated. A final wipe of her eyes, before, "I have thought much of this. The practical difficulties to do this have not been great. It is October. Much of the greatest activity on the farm is past. My mother will agree to look after the children, who are not little now, but nearly adults. They will go to the farm and look after the animals. None of this had been difficult to think of."

He sat back, still unsure of where this was going. But certain in his own mind that he would not go to Germany, unless she came with him. A farce- tilting at windmills, otherwise.

"But Berlin. It is a place in my past. My history. I lived there for two years. I had been very happy. But I returned to France." She appealed to him. For his understanding. "It is said, never return to a place you have left. My life would be different, if I had not made the return to France. But I am a person transformed now. By the years since then. My marriage. My children. My return to the land. The people that I know in Berlin... they are the people I lived with then. I have seen some of them when they have visited me in France. But I have never returned to Berlin."

She had paused to reflect, so he finished with, "You are fearful that it may show you... that your life since then has been a mistake. An error."

She nodded, dumbly, her lips clenched.

"Perhaps you need to lay the ghost. You need to bury the past. It was then. Things have moved on. You are different. It has made you a very unusual person. People know that. Suzanne knows that."

"Oh. Suzanne," she said, as if that was altogether another problem.

But he pressed on, "And Berlin's different. Look at all the events that have been happening in Germany this year. It has not stayed the same, just because you have not allowed your memory of it to move on." He shrugged, "Your friends? I don't know. But they will not be the same as when they visit you in France." A smile crept across his face, growing into the certainty of a grin, "Take this Gizande to Berlin. Not the Gizande who lived there all those years ago. She has gone. This Gizande needs to see if what she remembers is the same. And it won't be. And I need you." But, a step too far, backing off, "Your contacts. Your language." Finally, gravely, "And Stephen needs you. We may be the only hope of saving him. No-one else cares."

Said his piece. And said it well, he thought. He waited for her. Prompting her with, "So?" To which she still did not reply. Looking back at him with trapped eyes. "Look, we can drive back to your place. Pick up things you need. Clothes. It'll lose us a day. But then we can get off."

She closed her eyes, her shoulders shook. With a silent laugh? Or sobbing? But, when she looked up at him again, she was smiling. "Wait. Here." She rose and he watched her walk out of the café, turning in his seat to watch for what would happen next.

Back into view after a few minutes, she had a rucksack and a holdall. By the time she dropped them beside the table, they were both grinning at each other, her a little apologetically. He let her sit.

"I could not be sure, Jim. I came here by train, because I was not certain. It was difficult. To think again of the Berlin I lived in during the past."

He laughed, sudden and long, "Now, tell me. Let me guess. Did you buy a single ticket? Or a return, on the train?"

She looked puzzled

"Un billet... de chemin de fer… retour?" he struggled to grasp a few words of the language.

"Ah," and she smiled, a touch coy. "Non. It was a simple ticket. One way. No return." At his laugh, she protested, but still smiling, "Oh, no! It was not as you think! I was returning home by the train, if I decided."

He reached over to rest a hand on hers, "But you have decided not".

"Yes. I made the telephone call to my mother. She will attend to the farm." Then, pushing her chair back, "We must go- The time is important. Where is the van?"

"A hundred meters."

"Good. I will drive first. You will be tired. You must rest."

He stood and took the holdall, which chinked. As he lifted it, his back twinged and he put it down again. "Pulled my back- lifting out the furniture."

"Where is the injury?" He turned from her and rubbed across the spot. She touched it. "I have the oil for that. You must rub it in." She slung the rucksack onto her shoulders and picked up the holdall, "This is my medicines. Always they accompany me. They will keep us safe into Germany."

At the van, she sorted through the small bottles and phials in her bag and poured a few drops of pungent rosemary oil into his cupped palm. He rubbed it in under his shirt while she looked on critically.

As they then drove off into the evening of this last mild day of autumn, he asked and she began to tell him of her life. At first cautiously, with broken sequences of anecdotes, then, warmed to it and to his attentiveness, she told him of her childhood, the closeness to her grandfather, doing well in school, her medical ambitions taking her to University in Paris. And 1968, her ambitions to train severed in those nighttime streets on the Left Bank, the burning cars flickering beyond the barricades of torn-up cobbles, waiting for the next brutal, screaming charge of the riot police, retreating, chanting the taunt "CRS-SS", before diving off down backstreets into the dawn. Those long meetings in the lecture theatres, feeling the eyes of the world were upon them.

She broke off her narrative at one point, braking the van and, jumping down, disappeared into the field by the road, coming back with a green spiky bouquet.

"Rosemary," and she rubbed the needles of the plant to hold the heavy green perfume of it on her fingertips, fresh, balsamic and slightly woody to his nose. "It is your herb. For the Aries. Like the oil." She hung the large bunch swinging from windscreen mirror. And, as they drove off again, he reached up to crush some of the plant, releasing a gout of its smell into the van.

"Direction, L'Allemagne. To Germany," she called across to him. And started to tell of her flight from France after the collapse of the student movement, Jim watching her slight figure confident at the wheel, now speaking out towards the road ahead, as if a monologue- long overdue- to herself.

He was unaware of going to sleep. Only of waking to her hand across the dark cab, pulling repetitively at his arm. "Jim. Jim. Jim, we have crossed the Rhine. We are in Germany." He stirred awake, looked with bleary confusion out the window. In the headlights, a sign, Karlsruhe one way, Freiburg the other. Then back to her. "It is four hours. I have been driving for more than seven hours. I am tired. I have stopped to rest near Clermont Ferrand, but you did not wake. I have told by the telephone my friends Annaliese and Karla that we come."

He shook himself awake, "I'm sorry. I didn't realise… sorry." .

"No. You required the sleep. It is good. You are now strong to drive us into Germany. How is your back?"

He sat up to feel it. A bit stiff, but he said, "Fine. Okay."

"I will sleep now for some hours. Is it possible in the back?"

"It's a bit dirty. Here, I will show you." Getting a torch out of the glove compartment, he shone it over the back of the seats. She knelt up to look over.

"That will be enough. I have a sleeping bag. If I may use your blanket. To make it some more soft." They climbed out each side and went to the backdoors. As a huge lorry passed them onto the autobahn link road, blinding with its rows of lights, brushing them with its grinding hot cloud of fumes and noise. She pulled the sleeping bag out of the rucksack and together with the blanket, they both made a comfortable enough nest for her to sleep in, between the wheel arch and the back of the driver's seat.

He watched her climb in still clothed, curl herself into her cocoon. A last throw of torchlight on her face to check, he said, "You can only try it out. If you start to slide about, you can come up the front again."

"The autobahns are straight. You will not slide me about, Jim. I am certain of that."

Locking the back, he re-entered the cab, regretting her not here next to him. But aware that her presence in the vehicle changed everything. The possibilities were endless, but he dared not let his wishes harden into expectations. Just to have her with him. Whatever that meant to her.

Chapter Nineteen

It was between eight and nine that grey morning, concentrating to catch the right signs coming at him out of the murk to steer them north and east through the knotted autobahns round Frankfurt, that he put the Casals tape on. Volume down, the restrained figures of the cello danced around him in the cab. Her mood music, he began to reflect, as suite after suite asserted for his attention. The tranquility, the calm she imposed upon him. Through his own consent. Something perhaps about her and the old exiled cellist both living in those mountains. Something Jim himself would have to learn. To speak their French. Or even some of the Catalan she spoke among her family?

Out of the gathering morning traffic, he pulled off the road into a service area and parked among the towering lorries. He checked she was still asleep, only her tousled hair visible, and went to empty his bladder, stretching his tired legs into life. He brought back two coffees and quietly climbed back in.

As he settled, her voice from behind, "Good morning, Jim."

"Good morning, Gizande," grinning at himself for how good it sounded to say that. "Do you want a coffee?"

The sound of stirring, and her face appeared between the seats. Smiling, even a little disoriented. "Coffee? What is the time?" She took the cup.

"After eight. We are past Frankfurt. We are perhaps two or three hours from the border."

"We will be in Berlin tonight."

"You can continue sleeping. I'm okay with the driving."

"Take," she gave him back the cardboard coffee cup. Stuffing the sleeping bag onto the passenger seat, hoisted herself up to clamber through to the front. "We will be together. I will sleep, maybe. Maybe, no."

Looking at her, handing back the drink, "Are you pleased to have come?"

She sipped and considered. "I do not yet know." Looking out at the parked lorries. "It is perhaps a good thing. It was good to remember the past last night and tell it to you." Laughing, "Until you were asleep from the ennui of the story."

"I was tired."

"Jim. You must not always say sorry to me. Of course you were tired." Then, "You are an old man. Who needs his sleep," her eyes alight with the fun.

"You!" and he reached across to prod her. Smiling but watchful. Without the courage to turn it into an embrace. He sat back to his coffee. "Continue with your story. Continue from Paris. No, from when you left"

"Ah. My first time in Berlin." And, pausing to gather the trail of her tale together, she told it, her face mostly remote from him through the windscreen, to the end of the coffee, then back out onto the road, until the autobahn started to dip and climb between the tall dark forests closing in on either side, deep into Germany, towards the frontier.

1968. After the huge counter-demonstrations for De Gaulle, along the Champs Elysées, it was over for Gizande. The streets were back in the control of the Police. The professors sought revenge on the radicals, most of the students were back in the classrooms. But she was unable to. Those few weeks of glorious excitement had torn the conventional ambitions from inside her. She left her medical course, seeking out the energy of the Movement, wherever it was. She had gone to Frankfurt, joined a group that fought on through squatting, actions against big companies, street fights against neo-Nazis. She had met Andreas there and they had gone together to West Berlin. She had worked in a Left bookshop and had lived two years in that world of the SDS student activists, even some who went off into the shadowy Unterwelt, as she called it, of terrorism, whose names she read headlined later in the seventies. But Andreas was unstable. There were other women and then drugs. Trapped in the enclosed claustrophobia of the walled-in city, she missed the open air of her home and the guilt she owed her family by running away.

She returned to the Pyrenees and rediscovered her grandfather, his wisdom, his understanding of the natural healing provided by the plants around them and the distance with which he held the wider world through his quiet performance of the rituals of the old religion. But also, to satisfy her parents, she married. Yves, mechanic and garage owner. In the first pleasures of being back home that man was caught in the reflected rosy glow of it all. Her voice darkened. "He was brute. I did not at first see the ugliness in him. I was too charmed by the return to my country. But he loved his men in the bar more than he loved me. I was gross with Gaillarde." Pregnant, he thought, an imagined glimpse of the warm skin of her swelled belly- without breaking the taut thread of her telling. "For the good health of the child that was growing within me, I learned from my grandfather the food to nourish the best and the use of the oils to make my body calm. This was the true medicine, so different from my teaching to be a doctor in Paris. I become very interested in the ways of health through using what we are able to use from the plants about us." She brushed the bunch of herbs swinging from the mirror, "Like the rosemary. It is antiseptic. We use it in the kitchen to stop the rot of meat, yes? So also the oil is good for the system of nerves, to stimulate. And for the memory. I wrote also to Robert Tisserand. You have heard of him? No. He is the most famous in understanding oils in modern times." But her voice lowered again, "But it was a difference with Yves and me. He said that I was causing risk to the baby. Because I always chose the natural way first, before I went to the doctor. He ridiculed me as the witch. We fought. After the birth of Gaillarde, he was away from the house many evenings. And nights. He was in the bar, drinking. He loved to play the table football there, so I gave him the gift of a table football for the house. For him to return to me. But he brought his friends and their drunkenness to the home." She stopped, rerunning the scenes to herself, visible shadows in her face, before a crept smile and looking across to Jim, "I stopped this one night, by fixinq a door over the game. I took great care and fixed a door across the top with many screws. My vengeance, yes? It was of no more interest to the friends and he returned to drink with them in the bar after his work." She shrugged away the painful detail of it all, "It gave me the time to work on my understanding of the oils. I was with GuiIlem now." And out of the windscreen, to the road ahead, in general to the world, she said, "Why do we do such things? We have children for ourselves. Do we wish for the child himself? Or do we wish what it may do for us? To make things happen for us in the world. But the birth is the arrival of a stranger." She shook her head.

Jim was watchful, eager for the details leaking from the edge of her narrative. What she felt now. Knowing that the long disclosure to him from this most private of women, placed him somewhere in her life. But he said nothing. But for a sometimes glance at that proud and troubled profile, his eyes stayed on the back of the vehicle ahead.

The border was marked by joining the end of a creeping line of traffic. They had stopped at the last Rasthaus in West Germany to change money and now Jim was anxious with this different routine to the relaxed crossings of borders he had become used to since first come to Europe.

He looked covertly over to her, but she caught his glance, "It will be okay, Jim. I will speak with the guards and the officials. I understand the way of crossing the DDR to Berlin."

"Sure," he murmured, looking back to the vehicles ahead edging up to the grey cement passport office. An armed policeman in a cheap uniform was waving the lorries ahead to one side, chopping his arm at Jim to follow them. "Why're we being sent this way?" he asked her.

"We are van. Maybe the same as lorry."

Another policeman pointed to a space for him to park. Then

knocked on the window officiously and pointing back. "Komm. Die Passkontrolle."

"Passports," Gizande said and jumped down her side. After carefully locking the doors, Jim followed her, watchful. Stood behind her shoulder as she talked through the glass screen to the official. A cut-price metal badge of office in his lapel.

He looked at the activity around, lorries being checked, queues for getting passports stamped, a policeman with a surly black dog pulling against its lead. Until he realised that Gizande's tone of voice was argumentative. He moved next to her, "What's wrong?"

"They do not understand. That I am French. You are British. And the van is yours but it has a French enregistrement."

"But it's all legal. My documents are correct."

The man said something impatient. "We must wait. He must ask from his senior officer." She shrugged.

"But they've got our passports?" He was anxious, feeling pressed upon by the apparatus of coercion about them. Not knowing the rules of their game.

"Come," she guided his arm back towards the van, "we can only wait. It is the political situation. They are nervous."

But he felt surly, impotent, following her. Unlocking, they climbed back into the front seat. "Will they let us through?" He could only think of spy films he had seen. The man at the crossing point on his bike. Pedalling fast to cross before the sub machine gun started. Stupid, but the only language he had for this.

"Oh, yes. They will be difficult. They know that many from the DDR are coming now to the West across other borders, so they have to demonstrate to their masters that it is not here that there are problems. It is the weakness of others." She smiled tiredly. "It is the way with power. The powerful look for the little person to blame when the world does not go as they wish it. And the little person must prove that it is another little person who did wrong. Who must be chosen to be shot. It was the learning I had from my grandfather. This world we are in makes the little people choose each other for the punishment, the execution. That is how the powerful operate. He called the powerful Rex Mundi. The King of the World. This world of the Stranger God."

"So, what do we do about it?" Jim swept a dismissive hand out towards the exercise of power outside, the queues of traffic and people.

"It is between us. It is in the private time that close people pass between themselves. It is in the close time of two spirits. Without the public world. That is the world of the bullies. It is a world made to satisfy their ambition. Like your man- Finch, is it his name?" Jim nodded. "He lives in this dark world. It is the dark of this world against the light we can have inside us. Between those who are most close. That is the trust." Was she talking about the two of them together in this van? Or was she just remotely away with the memories of her grandfather? As if in answer, she turned to him, "That is what we do about it, Jim. We enter their world with the strength of the trust we have between us. The trust in each other. That is what they do not comprehend." And his mind quirked with the sudden memory of Scadding's wife reaching out to thank him in the dark, wondering if she had reconciled with that solitary angry man upstairs. An odd interruption to her continuation, "It has been the intimacy of those valleys where we live, the trust that the peasants had between themselves and against the world outside. That is why catharisme has continued during these many centuries. The Catholic Church could not terminate it because it could not understand it. They love to fill the church with gold and perfume. For the eyes to be always open at the beauty of the processions, the choirs. Because they fear the private world of the closed eyes. Where the real light will be found shining. They call it the sorcery and they burn it. They call the peasants, les gens rusés- what is that in English?"

"People...?" Jim asked himself. "Rusés? Ruse?" Then, smiling at his own inspiration, "Trick! Tricky. Sly," pleased that he felt he was beginning to grasp getting from one language to another.

"Yes. The sly people. It is the privateness of the peasants that they fear. Life is so difficult in the mountain valleys, that we must be sly. We must be clever with nature. That is why we not fight the battles with it. We must always make the compromise. We work together with the neighbours we trust. And we must work together with nature. Or we will be punished if we press too hard. Like the dams in our valleys. They will cause the crops to die, so that electricity and water will go to the cities. So they sell us chemicals to grow the plants faster. And to poison our earth."

"And here? How does that help us here?" he asked, wanting to hear something about himself.

"Do not become angry with the police here. We will go to Berlin. It is not important. You do not have to win a battle. It is their battle. Allow them to fight their battle between them. Without you."

He paused before saying, "And we have the power of our intimacy?" But the pause had let it slip back into an enquiry.

She looked across at him. Measuring. "Perhaps."

Chapter Twenty

Following the four hour wait for clearance at the border, it was late when they entered West Berlin. She was driving, with Jim trying to follow the street map by the streetlights. The city had changed in the near twenty years since she had been here, new roads, unfamiliar landmarks. They found the Kurfursten Damm, then a stretch of parkland, quieter streets and, a couple of missed turns, she drew them up outside *Foodi Cafébar.*

"Here?" he asked, allowing himself to slump with fatigue.

"Yes. This is the bar of Anna and Karla. Come." It was crowded, low lit and smelt well of food.

A woman in a black skirt and spiky tinted hair came from behind the bar, "Gizi!" embracing Gizande. Who stood back and said something in German, before they both looked at Jim. "Ah Mr. Friend-Jim," with a heavily ironic emphasis. "May I kiss Mr. Jim?' she asked Gizande.

"May Anna kiss you, Jim?'

He wanted to ask Gizande what she thought, but leaned forward for his cheek to be kissed. And pulled back from Anna's mischievous kiss on his lips.

."There," she said scanning him. "The Berlin Hello. Cheeks we are not interested in kissing. That is for the French!" and she laughed. "Come! A drink! I will call Karla from the kitchen. What will you drink, Friend-Jim?"

"A cognac? Please?"

"Of course" Then to Gizande in German, as she steered them to a table, at the back of the bar, made private by high backed settles.

While Anna went off for the drinks, Jim and Gizande looked across at each other.

"Okay?" she said.

"Gizi?" he smiled, the nickname so trivial. For her.

"Yes. Gizi. Here it is my identity. From the past."

He wondered if he could ever reclaim his boyhood Jimmy like that, then murmured, "But you will always be Gizande to me."

Too quiet for her to hear, "Pardon?"

But Anna was back with the drinks, smiling, with a tall thin woman, hair wrapped in a scarf, wiping her hands on a striped apron. Karla, with a calculated look at Jim, but kissing him on both cheeks this time. They were offered food, Karla went back to the kitchen and Anna back to the bar, coming back over to chat in German with Gizande when she could. With the warm food inside him, Jim's tiredness rose through his body. Another old friend of hers joined them and Jim dozily watched Gizande laugh and smile with him. Closed off by the language, he receded behind the curtain of more cognacs from Anna.

The gentle shake. Awake, with Anna's grinning face unfamiliar, confusingly too close, as he pushed himself upright on the seat. "Friend-Jim, the alcohol has sent you bye-byes," she said with a loud laugh. Just Gizande opposite now, a look of inquiry.

Jim stretched theatrically, "Yeeesss… I'm ready for sleep." And to Gizande, "You must be even more tired. She has driven for nine hours since yesterday."

"The bar is closing now," Anna said. "It is one o'clock. I will take you up to my rooms soon. I will show you where you will sleep. Okay?" And she went off behind the bar, clearing away the stacked glasses and wiping down the counter.

Jim watched her, avoiding Gizande for fear that his desire for her may show in his face, his hope that here in this place so distant from the restraints back home, that something may happen between them.

"Jim?"

He turned reluctantly to her, restraining his confusion.

"Are you... bien? I am sorry that there has been so much talking of German."

He shook his head and looked back at the bar. "No. I was tired. I am sorry I fell asleep."

And she said nothing more. The moment, if it had been one, now lost.

Upstairs with their bags into Anna's flat, over the bar. Gizande sat back on the futon Jim was to sleep on, her large woolen coat unbuttoned. Wide enough to envelop the pair of them, he thought. Again, with a sleeping bag in the living room, he was a tramp in the living space of other people. He asked Anna, "Can I borrow a key? I run early in the morning. So I can get back in after it."

She gave him a latch key and Gizande asked, "When will you go, Jim? I also have my shoes and clothes for running. We will see Berlin together. And we can talk of what we are to do to find Finch. And Stephen."

Flushed with this, the first time they would have run together for a year, he wanted to gush, but, Anna's quizzical and wry eye on him, he simply grunted, "About seven. Or eight," as if Gizande's offer had been an irritation.

"Only if you wish me to come and run with you, Jim?"

"Oh. Yes," the word almost held back with the strangulation of the contraries. Divulging it to her, but not to Anna.

Who laughed, "The runners! Together." And led Gizande off into the bedroom they were to share.

Left in the room, he sat on the edge of the futon for some time, before he slid his clothes off and pulled the sleeping bag up around him. He turned many times before sleep, trying to shift his confused thoughts behind him and to scoop a soft hole somewhere from the hardness of the mattress.

Gizande woke him. "Jim. Jim. It is coming to eight o'clock." She was wearing black tracksters and a zip top. Crouched over him, smiling.

"Oh, yes. Let me get ready."

She waited in the little kitchen, while he shook off his sleep and pulled on his running gear. Fussing whether to wear shorts or tracksters himself, for the look of it. Doubting that she had bothered about how she looked to him?

Outside it was a grey, still day, the traffic busy. They ran down across two canals, then alongside the park they had passed last night. Saying nothing, side-by-side, Jim trying to relax into the pace, the pulled back muscle a slight twinge. She led them off up a wide avenue and, coming out from under a railway bridge, it stretched away between the parkland to a tall ceremonial column. "We will run to the Wall," was all she said and he paced beside her, attentive to the closeness of her body, the rhythm of it, the sound of her breath, the slide of her legs back and forth, the lightness of her feet pattering the pavement. And it was hard work for him to keep relaxed, to work his own body with nonchalance to the pace she set.

"Okay?" she asked.

And he had to hold himself from panting before replying, "Yes," between his teeth.

She eased the pace anyway. They rounded the column and she pointed up the avenue ahead. "Brandenburger Gate." He looked ahead and it loomed dimly out of the dull light, so familiar a symbol. A few more paces and she said, "The Wall."

And they ran on together, drawing it up towards them, above the flat, crude wall that sealed it from them. Just before they turned, a huge memorial on their left, with an armoured tank jutted out above them. Two Soviet guards impassive, eyes fixed across the city.

"The Russian memorial?" he asked, she nodded. And, as they turned and put it behind him, he looked back at its brutal bulk, remembering an old man in the Labour Club he had once drank with, having it explained how it was the Russians who had beaten Hitler, not the Yanks. Jim had tolerated him good humouredly, until the old man explained how praiseworthy the invasion of Czechoslovakia had been. Then, Jim excused himself and left. Another 1968 event, like Gizande's Paris. Things that happened in other places that he did not have the arguments for. But behind them, receding now, that sense of history squatting so powerfully upon this city

Back at the flat they waited for each other to shower, then had rolls and coffee with Anna down in the empty bar, planning the day. First it had to be the Gast Arbeiter Agentur that Huntley had phoned. And see what happened from then. They decided to walk the twenty minutes, rather than try to repark the large Citroen. It was a shop front in a suburb near the airport. Young men waiting on plastic chairs to be interviewed, took an interest in the entrance of Gizande with Jim, the only woman in the room. They sat and waited too.

Jim was sure he could hear indistinct English spoken quietly between two of the waiters at the other end of the row of chairs, so he said over-loudly to Gizande, "I wonder how long we'll have to wait," catching the scowled recognition from the pair. So he called over to them, "Been waiting long?"

"Who's fuckin' asking?"

So Jim shrugged to her. Looking round, the room had all the appearance of a job agency. Multi-lingual notices about work permits. Health and safety notices. Cards pinned to a large board. He rose and wandered over to look at them. All in German, he could make nothing of them.

Turning, he jumped to find a man in a suit had come quietly to stand at his shoulder. "Ja? May I help you?"

"Yes." Indicating Gizande, "We're searching for someone." Pause. "A friend." Best to get the names out here. Before witnesses. "Mr. Finch. Billy Finch."

The man gave a suppressed twitch.

Then, "We are friends of Mr. Huntley. Who phoned from England last week."

Enough said, the man was visibly discomforted. He cleared his throat, "You will come?" indicating the door to inner offices. Jim nodded to Gizande who joined him and gave her hand a brief squeeze of comradeship.

Led into a tight office with thin walls and cheap furniture. A calendar advertising sports equipment.

Having sat, the man asked, "And who is this Mr. Finch?"

But Gizande leaned across and spoke in German. He replied uncertainly and she turned to Jim, "His name is Krommel. He is Under-Manager."

Jim nodded and continued, "We know that Mr. Finch visits this office. We wish to meet him."

Watchful of Gizande, Krommel replied to Jim, "Do you know Mr. Finch?"

"Yes. Of course. We are friends. From England."

"I do not know Mr. Finch." Then, shifting tack, "I do not know when he come."

"But he does come to this office."

"Maybe."

So, press the man. "We also have another friend you may know. Also English. Stephen Roberts."

During the long silence that followed, the tautening of his skin squeezed minute droplets of sweat to collect together down his face towards his chin. Krommel broke it with an angry scrape of pushing his chair back, "You must wait. Here." Clattering out, slamming the door, quivering the partitions.

Jim turned to her, "Well, we've certainly hit a spot."

"This now feels dangerous, Jim."

"Anna knows where we have gone."

"I do not want to bring trouble to her and Karla."

"We aren't. Just see what happens next."

So they sat silent for ten minutes, before another man came in, with a sense that Krommel was still hovering nervously somewhere out in the passageway.

"Phillip Klinsmaar," hand out to Jim, confident, polished.

"Jim Briggs."

Klinsmaar smiled at her and Jim introduced as, "Mademoiselle Gizande."

"I understand you wish an appointment to see Mr. Finch."

"Yes."

"We cannot be sure of when he arrives at this office. He is a very busy man. Can we make contact with you when we know that he is able to meet you?"

"We have a phone number," and Jim gave Anna's.

The other man slipped a pocket book from an inside pocket, slid a pen from it and wrote. "An address?"

Snuck that in, Jim thought, and replied, "That won't be necessary." Klinsmaar registered nothing, so Jim pressed hard with, "And Mr.

Roberts?"

"Ah. Mr. Roberts. We did have contact with him. But you will understand, there are so many young men coming from England to find work in Germany, that we lose contact with them. They move to other jobs, you understand. Or maybe they return to England and they do not tell us?"

Now, calculatedly, "Stephen Roberts did not come here for work. He was brought here."

Still smiling, his eyes chilled and fixed on Jim's, Klinsmaar spelt out, "We only deal with the work lives of the men who come to our office. You will understand that their lives when not at work are no concern of ours." Slapping the pocket book shut, "We will be in contact with you. About Mr. Finch." Stood now, "So good to have met you." Shaking hands, "I hope that you enjoy your stay in Berlin."

As they left, Krommel had been waiting to overhear in the corridor, as Jim had expected. Outside, Jim said to her, "What do you think?"

"I think the Klinsmaar is interested."

"Yes. I think he wants to know what we know." Then, cheerful and confident from the progress made, he said, "Let's walk to the city centre. We've got the rest of the morning. Back to Anna's for lunch. Then this afternoon, we can look out that other address that Damien's mum gave me."

"Yes. I agree. I will like to see Berlin. And how it has changed."

She put her arm through his, friendly, but no more, controlling his distance from her. Today, good enough for him. She spoke little, her eyes busy, measuring up the city, but being with her was also sufficient for him. Retaining little that went before his eyes, just the marvellousness of being with her in such a place.

Back at Anna's, Klinsmaar had already phoned. Finch would be in the office tomorrow morning. Nothing else said, Anna told them, not even a time for an appointment. Just the stated fact of Finch being there. But she laughed at the second address that Jim produced. It was over the Wall in East Berlin. They had only told her some of the story that had brought them here. Not Damien's death, so she laughed with, "Your friend's an Ossie! From DDR!" Then, cheerful as she was, continued, "Tonight we have a party for you, Gizi. Old friends. We close Foodi tonight and we have the party here in the bar. That will be good, Jim, yes?" smirking at him.

"Yes. I'm sure."

"Yes I'm sure," she mimicked "Oh. So English," and recruited

Gizande to laugh with her at him.

Chapter Twenty-one

The blind dropped down the front windows, a banner across the ceiling, *WILLKOMMEN GIZI WILLKOMMEN!* All the talk at the start of the party was the rumours of a huge demonstration going on that night over the Wall in the East. As he gathered from Gizande's brief translations, but most of the chatter was in German.

Despite his irritation with Anna, he moved over to the bar where she was queening it over the distribution of drink. To watch Gizande from afar, the length of her legs descending from the hem of the skirt he had not seen her in a long time, never having seen her so lightheartedly sociable. Making him feel gloomier for his exclusion behind the barrier of yet another foreign language. And his inability to be trivial and light in any language.

"Allo, Friend-Jim," beamed Anna. "What will you drink?"

"A lot. All the bottles you have."

"So. I do not think that is the drink of celebration." She looked knowingly over towards Gizande, "I think maybe the drunk of jealousy?"

Confused by her exactness, he protested feebly, "No. Jealousy? Why should I be jealous?"

She smirked and giggled, reaching over to tousle his hair, "Ah, our Jim, the English. Is he the gentleman also in his thoughts?" And her full, long laugh rattled round the bottles on the bar. "Come. Your drink. What will you have?"

"You choose." He joined her skittish, teasing play with no enthusiasm, looking away dully, around the filled noisy room.

She planted a filled glass at his elbow. "Vodka. With lemon. Sharp, to give you life!" He shrugged and drank. A bitter unsweetened citric taste. "You are not social tonight, I see. I introduce you to Helena."

"No, I'm fine," to steer away from any crude and teasing matchmaking.

She laughed, "No! She is not what you are thinking. She is an old lady. Very wise. She has lived through much. I think she will be sympathy with your mood, Jim." She came out from behind the bar, took his elbow and led him to the back of the room. He stood awkwardly behind her while she spoke in German to an elderly woman in a long blue silk evening dress, her chair turned out into the room for her legs to be elegantly crossed, filling the corner with the glistening drapes swept down to her ankles.

Anna, turned to him, "I have told her why you are here. To look for the boy."

He smiled uncertainly at the seated woman, now looking up at him through measuring eyes, "Yes, Mr. English man. I do speak your tongue. We Germans have had to learn the languages of those around us. We do not live on an island." Then, patting the chair next to her, "Please, be seated with me."

He sat, dumb what to say to her, so filling the space with a wider, fixed smile.

She turned to Anna, "Back to your bar. Your guests require you," dismissed with an imperial brush of her hand, turning to Jim. "I am Helena. Helena Clostermann-Sudhoff. You will see we Germans love long words, in our names too. Helena is sufficient for me."

He let his smile relax, "Jim will do for me."

She nodded to him. "Tell me, Jim, what is this search for the young boy? That brings you to our Germany at such a time."

He shook his head, at where to start, "It is a long story. He was abducted? Taken away against his will?" checking she understood the sense.

"I understand. I have lived here with the British soldiers and administrators for long enough to understand."

"I came here to find him. The English man who abducted him came here, we believe."

"He chose well. This city has been a place to lose your identity. This side of the Wall, not in the East. That is a small country. Everyone there knows everyone else. New people do not go there to live. And now we see the young people flee from the East. But here. In West Berlin, you can become who you wish. This is the theatre of freedom to show to the East. We put on our disguises to show how free we are to be any person we wish. Perhaps the only freedom we do not have is to be our selves, do you think, Jim? To be our true self?"

"I don't know that. I have only been in Berlin since yesterday."

"But I think your Englishman knows this. To bring the boy here to hide him."

"I will be seeing the Englishman tomorrow. Maybe I'll understand more then."

"Maybe. You say, maybe. Yes." And she looked away somewhere else. Somewhere far out of this room. Retrieved back to him with, "But this is not Germany, you must understand. Do you wish to see Germany, Jim?"

"Er, yes," stumbled by her turn of direction. "But I didn't come here to see it-"

"Yes," snappish in her interruption, "I understand. You came here to get the boy. But you may have to understand that all is not as it first appears here. This Berlin speaks to outsiders as they wish to hear. We hate the Wall. But we would hate for it to go. It makes the world easy to understand from here. We Germans have always had two directions to face. To the east, we have shown our angry face, always trying to keep the Slavs from coming into our lands. To the west, we showed our civilised face. Our art, our philosophers and, of course, our music. Hitler stole one face and left remaining just the angry one, towards both the west and the east. The Wall has been good for us. It has given us back our two faces. It has marked the line of division between them. And here, in this room, you see the west face." Her gesture made him look round at the noise over his shoulder, music now started, some guests were stacking chairs and tables away under Karla's supervision to make space for dancing. Gizande was talking intensely to a man with a beard, his own age. Turning Jim back, not wanting to see.

She continued, "Behind the Wall is the other face. The Stasi. The marching past of tanks and guns. But I think for the English, Germany is still just Hitler, yes? That our history stopped in 1945."

It was not an accusation, but, despite the resignation with which it was said, it required some riposte from him. "I think English history stopped after 1966. After that the Germans stopped us winning the World Cup at football again." A shadow of her bemusement at his triviality and he realised that this old lady was talking out her thoughts seriously, as if a lifetime's wisdom was just being born. And she needed a listener, so he tried to ease her to continue, "You must have seen much in your life. Have you always lived in Berlin?"

She smiled at him. Generously, though he had somehow missed the point. "No, Jim. I am in exile like you. My young days lay in the East. Now, behind the Wall," She placed her hand on his, her skin as fragile as tissue. "Now, I am too old for this," indicating the music and dance. "I must be going to my bed."

To recompense his failure at listening, he awkwardly offered, "Do you live far? I have a- vehicle," shearing away from offering this fine lady anything as crude as a van.

"No. I am very close. Anna or Karla will walk with me to my door."

"No, please let me. I will walk with you."

She smiled. And he felt he was forgiven the lost moments. "We must speak again. Please come to visit me before you leave Berlin."

"Of course."

She rose. He held the long fur-collared coat and slipped it over her. She held out her arm for his and they moved through the room, a few words of goodbye from her to Anna, the dancers, including the man and Gizande- giving Jim a curious look- falling back to let them past.

It was cold out in the street, the pavement slick with recent rain. She pulled her scarf over her hair and held onto him with her frail arm. They had nothing to say. It was only a hundred meters to her door, up the other side of the same street as Foodi. She took out her key and turned to him. "It has been good to speak with you, if just for a short time."

He felt pressed to say, "I'm sorry."

And she understood, "No, no. The circumstances were not correct for conversation. We must meet again. I say that not as the bourgeois English may say. It is with sincerity. Perhaps we can talk more easily when you have had a little more understanding of this country of ours. I hope we can help you to find your boy." And, astonishingly, she held out her hand for Jim. And he kissed it. Putting the key in the latch, she turned and absently remarked, "I do hope the police have not been brutal with the demonstrators tonight." A final smile to him and she was gone.

A beautiful lady, he thought, as he ambled back to face the rest of the evening.

Reentering the bar, tucked away in a dark corner to the right, Gizande was on the man's lap. Draped, Jim thought bitterly, her head laid on the man's shoulder, eyes closed. He went back to Helena's empty table and drank the rest of the glass he had left. Savagely between clenched teeth. He could only sometimes see Gizande through the dancing bodies, forced to look. The tears that began to wet his eyes, soured at his own crassness at first, as the long evening of vodka stretched out, embittered at her. For the betrayal of feeling he now knew he had no right to have. They danced again, bodies pressed together. Then they were not there.

Finally, weary with drink and disappointment, he went to Anna to ask her if she would let him upstairs into the flat. As she sent him upstairs, she patted his back, "You will be better in the morning, Jim. The world is clearer in the light, when the alcohol no longer makes fools of us all."

He turned to look at her, but the tease was no longer in her eyes. A gentle smile. Which he bent down from the stair and kissed, "Thanks, Anna."

"No problem," stroked his cheek and turned back to her party.

Upstairs, he went to the bedroom door, where Anna and Gizande had slept last night and listened. He pushed the door open slowly. The wide double bed was made and empty. Closing the door again, he sat on his futon, hollowed out with emptiness.

And, the light off, he thought of Gizande. Of her slight athletic grace. And of every conversation with her he could recall. Picking over these still when Anna came up much later, pretending to be asleep when she bent over him and murmured with concern, "Unglucklich Jim"

Her gone to her room and the flat quiet, he could still hear traffic on the wet streets. He wondered what the German word she had used meant.

When he got to the Agency office on his own, it was shut. He peered through the window into the unlit interior, but he had a sense of someone looking back at him. He knocked on the glass, "Hallo! Hallo!" He walked round the back. A Mercedes was parked by a locked back door. "Hallo! Hallo!" knocking again. He put his hand on the car's bonnet and it was still warm. "Come on, Finch! I know you're in there!" But nothing.

As he walked round the front, there was a youth in jeans looking in the front window as Jim had. "Closed." Without the German for it, Jim gave him the French, "Fermée."

"I can fuckin' see that for myself." Surly and watchful.

"Okay. Looking for work?"

He looked Jim up and down, with a roguish intimacy, "You offerin'?"

"Me? No?"

"You sure?" as the young man went into an emphatically casual lounge against the window.

"What work do you do?"

"On me cards it says Labourer. But I can turn me hand to anything. You want."

And Jim realised that he was being targetted with a crude proposal. Of course, so he remarked casually, "Do they only offer labouring jobs in here? Or other jobs... you can turn your hand to?"

But the sarcasm he turned the end of the sentence with, cut away the youth's plastered-on grin, "Who are yer? Some fuckin' grass? Who are yer?" threateningly squared up for aggression.

"Nobody," Jim put up a placatory hand. "Nobody. Just had an appointment here," thumbing towards the Agency. "But it looks like they forgot me. So, I'll be off." Finally, before walking away, most carefully casual and unsuggestive, "Good luck with getting work," the young man's eyes on his back, cautious not to hurry too fast.

When he got back to Foodi's, Anna was down in the bar, clearing up. "No run today, Jim?"

"No."

"Too much drinking, yes?"

He smiled and let himself upstairs.

Gizande was in the kitchen, sat before the debris of her breakfast. She looked up at him, both guarded and challenging, "You didn't wait for me."

"You were not here."

"I was here at eight, but you were gone."

"I wanted to reach the office by nine. When it opened." Then, pain beneath the anger, "Where were you? Who did you go off with last night?"

She scowled at him, then thought better of it. "Andreas."

"Your- the man you lived with, here in Berlin? Before."

She looked, trying to read into him, then away, as if showing too much of herself. "I was saying goodbye to him," she said tiredly.

"Or saying hello again," he sneered, surprised at the harshness of his own voice.

She remained staring at the crumbs across the plate and the table and, looking onto the top of her declined head, a domineering mood gripped him, a need to bully her. "Don't you want to know about my visit to the agency office? Or aren't you interested any more?"

"Do you wish me to be interested?" Still head down, she shook it, "You are too angry to be talked to."

"Well it was closed," with a finality, as if it proved it had all been her fault. Being here at the end of this cul de sac. Facing a wall as blind as the one they had run up to and turned away from yesterday.

She raised her face to him. A tear, run down the side of her nose to rest on the corner of her mouth. "What will you do now?"

Now? He thought. And when he was back in France, what? "Go home," he said, weighing the blame of it all upon her.

"But the other address? The other address of Damien?"

"That's in the East."

"We can go and see. It is possible to cross to the East. For one day you can get a Tagesvisum. A visa for a day." Then, hesitant for his response, "I can come with you? For speaking German." He considered, confused, so she gently pressed with, "You will need someone. To speak for you."

Always with someone else to speak for him. And alone with her over here. And angry with her.

"Why?" still as a flinty challenge to her, the word lashed the question at the both of them.

"Why?" she asked back, uncertain. "What is why? Because you need my language." Then, her eyes full onto his face, "For finding Stephen.

And Damien."

And his anger at her shrank. He looked back at her, both of them searching for a resolution, a settling back a little to how they had been, coming here. The comradeship and trust, even if without the intimacy he ached for. Yes, there was still the boys, he acknowledged.

"Yes. Okay," spoken still with a grudge.

She reached out and his arm went rigid to her touch. But she persisted, her fingers working through the cloth of the sleeve, insisting themselves on him. "We will go today," her voice hoarsened to a whisper. "The address of Damien is not much distance into the East. We will walk to the station that takes us across the Wall. The S-Bahn to Friedrichstrasse. I remember it. Then we will find the place." Taking him back into her care, an edge of his surly defensiveness still keeping her at bay for last night. And for Andreas.

Chapter Twenty-two

They walked wordless down the streets to the station. He, to register his sulky displeasure with her, she at the guarded distance he seemed to require. Their eyes narrowed against wafts of needling fine drizzle coming at them on a cold east wind, wavering the clanking from nearby rail yards. From the station, it was a couple of minutes train journey to Friedrichstrasse. She took his passport for the visas and, at the control, exchanged the West marks for a tired bundle of DDR notes, before descending into the street.

He was relieved that no particular attention was paid to them, "That seemed easy."

"It was easy. Sometimes the guards are easy, sometimes they are not." Then she stopped and, planting herself across the pavement, turned Jim to face her. "Jim. We are together on this. I see you are angry with me about last evening, about Andreas. You have not the reason for it. But for this, in the East, we need our confidence together. Our trust, one to the other, yes?" It was an appeal to him, but the strong hold of those grey eyes brooked no reticence.

"If you say so," then, immediately regretting the meagreness of this, "Gizande?"

"Yes?"

"I am confused about all this." He groped for something, looking at a passing workman curious at the couple they made there in the street. "I have feelings. It's about what happened to me as a kid, that I'm here. That brought me here. But I also wouldn't be here now, if it wasn't for you."

She smiled, "And I also would not be here, if it was not for you. So, we go together to this place to discover what we can, yes?" From her shoulder bag, she pulled the map she had borrowed from Anna. "It is close, the address of Damien." She pointed and he turned to look down a street of decayed tenements. "That direction."

Mid-afternoon and wet, it was quiet, even in the centre of this other city. While she routed them from the map out into a residential district, he looked up at the impoverished flats, some boarded up, some broken windows, one the cement facing rotted off to the girder ends beneath, stuck out corroded junk over the street.

A few blocks on, she brought them to the place. "It is this building. Number 27." She took his hand, "Ici, Jim," and led them down the damp and dirty passage. Out into the courtyard. Covering half of it, a tarpaulin had been stretched across a frame of scaffolding poles, above three Trabant cars in various states of disrepair. Two men looked up from under the bonnet of one and watched as Gizande approached with Jim.

She spoke to them, the men looked at each other, one replied and pointed up at the second floor landing. She turned to Jim, "It is here. He says it is empty."

The man spoke again, checked with the other, then continued.

"He says it has been empty since the Police came. The neighbours said there had been an argument and a fight. The Police were here the next day. And the Stasi."

She spoke with the man again.

"He says the neighbours have departed now. Many of the apartments are empty as the people leave. They go on holiday to Hungary and then cross into Austria, where the frontier has been opened. They leave for the West."

The man interrupted her with something else.

"He says the Police closed the flat. Put boards over the windows. This was five months ago."

"Can we get in now?" Jim asked.

She looked at him, surprised. "I will ask."

She and the man spoke again. His friend went off behind the Trabants and returned with a heavy screwdriver and a hammer.

"He will show us," and the tug of her hand to follow surprised Jim to realise their fingers had been relaxedly folded together all this time.

There were sacks of rubbish and splints of broken furniture stacked in the gloomy corners of the stairwell. Number 27 had rough planking screwed to the frame, tightly across the door, a notice pasted across them. With a check down to the courtyard, the man tore off the notice and started on the first screw, working steadily and methodically detaching plank after plank, stacking them against the wall. Then, the blade of the screwdriver rocked between the frame and the door. Four precise blows with the hammer split the wood to swing the door inwards. A corridor, three doors off it. The first room, just a bed with a stained mattress beneath a long mirror. The second room, blacked-out, disorienting at first with the other side of the one-way mirror looking back onto the bed. The third room, a kitchen, bare wires out of the wall where a cooker had been taken out.

"This is not an apartment," Gizande said. "What is this?"

"A place for questioning people? Interrogation?" Jim opened a wall cupboard. A dusty mug and two plates. The drawer below. A few pieces of cutlery rattled as he slid it out. Damien, were you here? He looked out of the window into the grey street. What had brought that bitter and defiant boy here? To die in this city, as Fred Toser insisted. To die here, in these rooms, he was certain now. The smell of a crime cleared away. Swept and bagged up the evidence, before sealing it off at the door.

"Quoi? What, Jim?" The grit of his thinking must show in his face.

He looked at her. The garage man was stood in the doorway, looking on. "This is where it happened. This is where they killed Damien."

He went back into the blacked-out room and tore the taped black plastic from the window. Against the sheet of glass that looked onto the bed, a table with a metal triangle bolted to it. He examined it. Then looked up at the man in the door, who was miming cranking a movie camera. Jim looked back at it and saw it for the tripod it was. He lowered his eye to look across it, through the one-way mirror, into the next room. How they must have seen what through the lens? Sex? Torture? He stood up, still staring through the glass at the bare room. A film of Damien? He sensed her behind him and reached back his hand. It was taken. An awkwardness of fingers, before she enclosed his into a soft fist.

"Ask him if he saw any of the men who came here."

The exchange in German behind him.

"Yes. They had trouble with their car. He assisted them. It was a Mercedes. He says there were also foreigners, who came here with them. He thinks Americans."

"Did they pay him?"

"Yes. In dollars. He has a phone number in West Berlin. For when the Mercedes was ready." She spoke in German again. "It was the Gast Arbeiter office."

"What were they doing over here?" He turned to her at last.

"I do not know, Jim. Only, we can speculate."

"Come on, Gizande." He felt shivered by the place. "Let's go back to the West"

And, not been three hours away from Foodi's, they were back there. With a bundle of unspendable Ostmarks.

Gizande and Jim sat talking it through in the back of the quiet-time afternoon bar.

Anna joined them, "It is the Agency you must go to again. You must be their ghosts. You must spook them."

"She's right," Jim conceded. "They could close this morning, because they knew when I was coming. They cannot close every morning. You're right, Anna. It's that Agency office that holds the secret of where Stephen is. Where we can find him."

"What are they doing in the Agency?" Anna asked.

"Getting young men jobs," Jim answered doubtfully

Gizande protested, "But that does not explique-"

"Explain," Jim inserted.

"Explain- that does not explain why there is the connection with Stephen, no?"

"If there is a connection," he said in a remote voice, his eyes on Gizande. Like his hand in her glove, he felt together again with her. Within that chaste and brotherly intimacy of her knowing. The possibilities of friendship alone between them stretched ahead, he wondered if such a love could ever be without the yearnings of his body. For hers, physically neat, but her face too bony for beauty. Except for those eyes. Anna forgotten, both women became uneasy with his staring silence at Gizande.

Who broke it with, "Yes, Jim?"

"Oh. Sorry... miles away."

Anna laughed at his shake awake, "Ha, Gizi! It is many years before that I have a man's eyes look upon me like that!"

"No," he protested, caught out. "I was thinking about Stephen," shamed by his own lie. "We will go back to the Agency tomorrow." Then a thought, "I will phone Julian tonight. My friend in England. And tell him what is happening." But from somewhere deep between his ears, almost surreally out of place and situation, the sound of Casals' cello wound its way, climbing up from within him with the same sense of melancholic hope that she, Gizande, invested in him. He wanted to speak of it to Gizande. Of this only music that had ever affected him like this, in his whole life. But with Anna present, instead he turned to her casually. "Helena was interesting." For Gizande, adding, "The old- elderly lady Anna introduced me to last night."

"Ah. Helena. Our book of history. She has more than eighty years. She was the wife of a Minister in the Government of the Weimar Republic. She has had a life of difficulties. Her husband was in Buchenwald, before the war. He was released, but the British returned him to the Russians. They returned him back into Buchenwald. There he died." She intook her breath. "She has terrible stories," shaking her head, as if to free it from the memories.

"I… No. Nothing." Jim hesitated, then, "I would like to see her again. It was impossible to speak properly, with the noise of the party." Gizande cut a look at him, but, no, he had not intended it to be a swipe at her. And Andreas.

"I have said I will help Anna in the kitchen tonight," she said. "So that Karla can have an evening to visit her friends."

He considered this, before deciding, "I will stay in the flat. I'm tired. I will go to bed early after I have phoned Julian. I can use your phone, Anna?"

"Naturlich."

It was a relief to have the evening on his own, upstairs, just the faint throb of music and the barely discernable clink of glassware from below. The strain of being with Gizande all the time, with that uncertainty of who she was to him rubbed away at him, even when he was unaware of it.

His phone call to Julian focused the two men on what to do when and if Stephen was found. They decided that Julian would ask for a meeting with Cathcart to inform her that the Union had concerns that Stephen had been taken out of the U.K. Leaving her and her bosses to confirm that or not. And, if confirmed, decide how to get Stephen home. They also agreed that Julian would call Huntley to suggest that he tries to place a story in the local press, asking if Stephen is missing. And finally, Jim remembered to ask after Trish and Adam, a gesture to the family he had left with so little ceremony.

He had got the Casals tape from the Renault and put it on Anna's tape deck while he prepared a simple dish of pasta. He dripped butter and melted cheese over the top, sat in the kitchen, eating slowly. Listening, to hear if the music matched the seizure it had made of him earlier. Reflecting that his life had been tone-deaf, until he listened to this in Suzanne's.

He was wiping his bowl clean with a knob of bread, when the phone rang. He waited. For Anna to pick it up downstairs. The ringing stopped and Jim went over to the sink, ran water into his bowl.

The door opened downstairs and footsteps. "Jim! Jim!" It was Gizande. "The telephone. There is an English for you."

Probably Julian phoning back. "Who is it?"

"He will not say, but he has your name. Anna is holding him for you."

Reached over to reject the music from the tape player. Then over to pick the phone up. "Hello? Okay, Anna. I'll take it."

"Mr. Briggs?" A touch of Northern, disguised?

"Yes. Who is it?"

"We have not met. My name is Finch." The pause the other end, calculated to let this sink in. "You met my mother, I believe."

"Billy Finch." Then, down to business, "Stephen Roberts' carer?"

"Yes. I thought you were in court that day."

Jim pressed harder, "Yes, with Mr. Toser, Damien's dad."

"You don't mess about, Mr. Briggs, do you?" humour in the voice, before the gentle wheedling of, "Can I call you Jim?"

A calculating manipulator, Jim thought, putting this together with the court performance he had already witnessed. "If you must."

"Well, is it cards on the table time, Jim?'

"You tell me."

"What will- satisfy you to go away and leave us alone?"

Jim measured the bluntness of this, letting Finch sweat a little. "What are you offering?"

"Perhaps we need to meet, Jim, to talk it all over."

He could feel the dangerousness in Finch's controlled relaxation of tone. "Well, I came to your office this morning, but it was closed."

"My staff had no authority to invite you back."

"You mean the nervous Herr Krommel? Or the smooth Klinsmaar-surely he knew what he was doing? Do you have the authority to invite me, Finch?" denying him the first name informality the other sought.

"Of course." Then, "What do I have to offer? We can discuss Stephen's future."

"Before I discuss it with the West Berlin Police?"

"West Berlin Police? That would get you nowhere, Jim."

So, it was confirmed. The East was used as a safe place for the disposal of embarrassments to Finch. And to whoever his masters were, sheltered behind ABC. "As well as Stephen, will Damien Toser's fate be allowed on the agenda too?"

"You can always ask the questions, Jim. Who knows whether I can supply the answers?"

"Okay. As you say, I can always ask the questions. And depends what answers I get, to decide what to do next. So, where? And when?" He nodded at Gizande, still watching him attentively from the top of the stairs.

"The Agency office tomorrow. I can ensure we will not be disturbed."

Jim heard the cold measurement in Finch's voice, and allowed himself a little fear. But burying this, answered, "Yes. Okay, fine. Nine o' clock tomorrow evening."

"Done. See you then." And. After a wait to hear the click his end, put the phone down himself. Turning to her, he said, "He's there. Finch is at the office now, I'm sure. Let's go there and get him now. While he's not expecting us. Not got some bloody welcome committee waiting for us."

She looked confused. For the first time ever, Jim thought. She said, "But I must be preparing the food in the kitchen. I must return for Anna."

"Please," he insisted. "Please, let's ask Anna if she can cover. Isn't that other friend in? The one who helped Karla with the party food. What was her name? Gudrun?"

"She is in the bar, drinking with friends."

"Well, explain to her. It's important. We have to catch Finch off his guard. Believe me."

When they reached the Agency, Jim parked the Citroen across the side alley, to stop any cars parked at the rear getting out. The office front was closed, but some light showed from a back room somewhere.

"Round the back," Jim hissed.

The silence of their rubber-soled trainers round to the rear door. No damned Mercedes, but a small Volkswagen. Quietly on the door handle and he was inside the building.

"Finch." No answer. Her breath close to his ear. "I've come early for our meeting."

The scrape of a chair. Jim tensed for what next. The door of a room opened and its sudden bar of light onto the corridor made him flinch.

But it was Krommel who appeared. Nervous, squinting into the dark, "Herr Finch. He is not here."

Jim stepped forward into the light and Krommel stepped back into the office. Jim followed him with Gizande, until they were all in the room. A different one from their first meeting, twice the size, with a computer one side of the wide desk, its screen lit with a list, a t.v. on top of a video the other side. They sat and Krommel went behind the desk. He looked at them, then, several strokes on the computer keyboard and the screen switched off.

Now, here without Finch, what? Try this, "I want you to call Herr Finch here immediately. Tell him Mr. Briggs has been advised that he should hand it all over to the West Berlin Police." Then, leaning forward threateningly. "Do you understand."

"Yes. I think so. Call Herr Finch. Mr. Briggs... but I do not think it will be possible. It is late. Mr. Finch is not close to here. He is not in Berlin."

True? Or covering for his boss? Jim scrutinised the anxious face before him, "Well, perhaps we will tell the West Berlin Police the story and they will hold you until Herr Finch arrives. Understand? Verstanden?" Then, turning with casual theatricality to Gizande, "Would you like to go off and get the Police here? While I wait here with Herr Krommel?" And made the point by dangling the Citroen keys. For her to take.

"Wait." Krommel stood. "I will phone. Wait some minutes."

With menace, Jim said, "Don't try to run off. Your car at the back is blocked off."

"No. Of course." And he went off.

As soon as he did, Jim leaned across the desk to press the switch on the computer, but nothing happened. Then saw, "There's something in the video." He pressed the Play button, turned the t.v. screen towards them and, after a few seconds, it came to life. Two boys bare-chested, in silent mid-kiss. Before turning towards the camera, as if to check for approval. Or instructions. Innocent fearfulness staring out. Then, both back to kissing again, this time with awkward embrace, their hands rubbing at each others' backs, as the camera's lens panned down in to the dark between their naked bellies, to where their purple-tipped penises crossed swords.

Behind him, Gizande, "It is the room! Look! It is the room! Of Damien's apartment!" And the edge of what the boys knelt upon, the edge of the grubby mattress's pattern was in frame.

A noise elsewhere in the office and Jim jabbed the Eject button. An age it seemed of the machine's clicks and clunks, before the tape box was pushed out. And Jim grabbed it, holding it up triumphant. At Krommel, just as he entered, astonished shock on his face.

"Nein! No!"

"Ja!" Jim snarled back. "Ja, mate. Now do as we tell you. Or this-" waggling the tape before his face- "is off to the Berlin Police."

"No," a pleading.

Brushed aside, "Did you phone Finch?"

"Yes. He said to me that you have broken the agreement he made with you. To meet tomorrow, this office. He will not be coming now."

"Well, if he won't come, you must take us to him."

The man looked uncomprehending.

"Do you understand?" Then, a lab of the finger, "You. Take us to Finch. Ja?" The jab now transferred to the video, "Or this. To the West Berlin Police. Verstanden?"

He nodded. Then, apologetically, "I understand, but not possible. Herr Finch is in DDR."

"That's okay. We have been to East Berlin. Take us to Herr Finch there."

"No. You do not understand. Herr Finch is not in Berlin. He is in East Deutschland. He is in Thuringerwald. Far from Berlin. It is not possible to travel there."

Jim turned to Gizande, "Where's that?"

"It is far away, I think." Then she turned to Krommel and questioned him in German. "It is near Erfurt. It is near where we crossed the DDR to Berlin. But very difficult for Westerners to go there."

"Well, Finch can." And to Krommel, "You take us to Herr Finch. Or the video to the Police." Adding, "And the computer."

"I cannot," with desperate crescendo, "Not possible."

Jim stood up and Krommel flinched- as if about to be hit. "Stay here!" he was ordered, then Jim ushered Gizande out into the corridor, closing the door.

"You were good, Jim. I have not seen you like so."

"All bluff," then to explain, but seriously, "Do we know anybody who knows East Germany? Any of Anna's friends?"

"Why?"

"If we can frighten Krommel enough to take us to Finch's little hideaway, we need someone with us who knows East Germany. Who knows that we are not getting-" a word for her to grasp? "- misguided."

"But we could not get the papers. The day visa we had today- it is not permissible to go out of East Berlin with it."

Pointing back at Krommel's door, "They know how to do it. They know how to get about. Bet Finch has got the guard at some crossing point working for him. Or false papers. Krommel will know how it's done. Do you know anyone?"

"Yes." He could not see her clearly in the dimness of the corridor, but felt her hesitation, "It will not please you." Pause. "Andreas."

"Oh, no! Not him," said with disbelief. "Of course, it had to be him!"

"Jim, please. You asked of me and I said. He is a member of the Communist Party in the West. He is able to travel. He is known in the East."

"A commie! A Stalinist?" almost laughing at her.

"No! Not Stalin. He is sympathetic to New Forum. He has travelled to the East to meet the opposition against the Stalinists. Against Honecker and Kreutz. He assists the opposition. It is dangerous now. But, if I explain, he may assist us."

"Do you- should I trust him?"

She reached out her hand to his arm, "You are correct. Andreas would wish to be my lover again, but I will not. But it is his wish for this that will keep us safe. He will be sure I am not harmed."

But keep me safe from harm too? Jim asked himself. Stuck in this tight corridor in the half light where he could not see every nuance of her face as she spoke of this other man, where there was no time, with Krommel in the office, maybe even now messing with the computer while they were out, destroying records. "Go on, then! Be it on your own head, if this goes wrong!" And angrily slammed the door open- on the furtive, hunted Krommel, eyes popped at him, his hands frozen from stuffing papers into a black document wallet. "Give me those!" grabbing it roughly from the man and slapping it into Gizande's hands. "See what this is he was poking away in his bag." Then, to Krommel, with all the fury of the trapped man he felt himself to be, Jim bellowed, "Sit. Down!" And the man slumped suddenly.

He looked round at her, flicking through the papers.

"Well? What are they?" barely able to be civil to her.

"Wait. I see." She finally reached the bottom, hesitating for a longer look at only a few of the documents on the way. She looked up at Jim, turned from his glowering face to Krommel and spoke in German. A dialogue, the German's eyes flicking back to Jim, who was still standing over the desk. "He says it is only documents needed for the journey in to the DDR. That appears to be so."

"Can he get the documents for us?"

"He says there is a crossing point where money is paid by the organisation to get across. But he says there is always a risk when you travel further. You cannot be certain that the Police or the Stasi in other parts of the DDR can be trusted."

Jim sneered, "So there are some Police in the East that Finch can't buy, eh!"

But Krommel did not understand and looked to Gizande for protection.

"Now, Gizande. Listen to me. We go to Anna's. We take this little worm with us. You phone your Andreas and see if he's willing to give us some of his time." Snidely inserting, "I'm sure he will. For you"

"Jim. This is foolish. You must not behave so. It will be dangerous, what we have to do. We must work together."

"Look, Gizande," trying to hold his voice hard, without an edge of pleading, "just make sure that Andreas does this for the right reasons. And not for you. As it is, I feel I've been dragged halfway across Europe under false pretences. On a fool's errand. So, come on, let's go." Then to Krommel, "You? Come with us. Now!" And unnecessarily, he reached over and wrenched the little man up with his lapel, jerked him at the doorway and tramped out, with Gizande following.

Chapter Twenty-three

Back at Foodi's, they were uncertain what to do with Krommel, now they had him. Jim was still sullen with Gizande and left it to her. As if it was her responsibility to decide now and that the inclusion of Andreas had taken everything out of his hands. So, terse with Jim, she went upstairs and phoned Andreas from the flat, while he sat downstairs in the bar with Krommel. Who wrote down the address where Finch was said to be. Hotel Jugend Sport, a name even Jim understood and cynically smiled at the uneasy hostage opposite him. He called over Anna.

"Our friend here says this is the place where we'll find the Englishman Finch. Now I read that as Hotel-Youth-Sport. Is that right?"

"Yes. That is right," she said seriously.

"Now, Anna, would I be wrong to read into that name the meaning of something other than athletic sport?" She looked at him quizzically, so he ploughed on, "It is called Youth-Sport. But what does that really mean, Anna?"

"I do not understand what you say, Jim."

"I mean- ask him- is this-" holding up the scrap of paper- "is where they take the kids to fuck them?" Krommel's face was deaf to the meaning of his words, but not blind to the contempt in Jim's face with which he said them.

Anna looked anxious, then firmly at Jim, "Come. Speak with me over here," indicating towards the bar counter.

"No. I won't let him," pointing sharply across the table, "run off. I won't give him the chance," knowing as he said it that his fury at the man was fake, a feeble swerve away from the complexity of her upstairs.

Anna spoke to Krommel and he replied at passionate and desperate length. Then to Jim, she said, "He will stay. He says that he wishes now to assist you. He has fears if the information you have is given to the Police, he will be deportation. He is from the Tschechoslovakei. He will not run off." Then, indicating the counter again, "Come."

He rose with studied weariness and followed her.

"Another drink?" she asked bluntly.

"Yes. A beer," adding, "Bitte," as a small joke. To himself.

When she brought the drink, she held it back from him. "Jim. You joke about the language. Other languages from English are humorous to you. It is a reason that Gizi finds difficulty with you. You live in her country, but always she has to speak with you in your language, English. It is the Imperialismus, yes? Teach the native your words, but do not learn their words, yes?"

"What? Me speaking English, this is about Gizande?" Both confused and watchful of what comes next. "Is this why you've called me over here to speak? Out of Krommel's earshot?"

"No. Yes. It is about Gizande. No. It is about you. "Then she softened her impatience with him, "It is clear to see, for everyone, that you have feelings for Gizi. That is true, yes?"

He did, but this was a confrontation by this woman with his privacies. He held her off with, "She has been a good friend to me." Adding, watchful for being caught out, "Yes. That's the way I care for her."

Anna shook her head, "That is what she would say of you. I do not know if the two of you are both blind to your own feelings. Or if it is some clever game you are both playing to hide your feelings from the other one." He held down his exaltation at this confirmation of Gizande's feelings for him, but retreated further into himself as she continued, "I think it is Gizi who is very injured. From her marriage to Yves. Also, before, with Andreas." He waited, on tenterhooks, for what she would say now about him. "She is in great difficulty. She has come here to Berlin with you to assist and it has come alive for her old feelings. She feels what her life would be if she had remained in Berlin. She talks with me every night together of these things." But Anna, does she speak to you of me? his voice bellowed silently inside his head. "She returned to France for pleasing her parents. They had wanted her as doctor, but she could never then please them. And it was confirmation for them when she leave Yves," Anna thrust her fingers back through the green-tinted spikes of her hair, "So you must have peace between you for this time in Germany. Gizi is hurt with thinking about her life. Also, it is difficult what you do, to search for the boy in the East. Her idea of using Andreas for assistance is good. She does not now love him, but he has still strong feeling for her. I think it will happen and he will come to assist. He is a man of justice, also."

"But a communist?" Jim explored with surliness.

"But not with Honecker and the others. Andreas is with New Forum. With the big demonstrations, now there is the opportunity of real Sozialismus in the East, not the Stalinismus of the Stasi-State. You will see. He has many friends in the opposition in the East to assist you, Jim." She smiled, "And perhaps you will assist Gizi. You will be there with her and so Andreas will always be a gentleman under your eyes."

"!f Gizande wants him to be," Jim said, a touch of bleakness in his words.

She reached over and patted the back of his hand, "Ah, Jim. You do have the feelings for Gizande. You are a good man and you understand not to hurt her. You must not become angry. She has told me. You must be working together in this difficult time." Then, with a scan of his face for the impact of what she said, "That is what I wish to say to you. Be tolerant to Gizande. It is a difficult time for her." And, an afterthought, "For the both of you, I think."

He could only nod to that.

He took his beer back to the table with Krommel and swallowed it down. Opposite the drinkless man.

And Andreas did come, of course. Late that night, the bar closed, Anna, Gizande and Jim had been sitting with Krommel for three hours. He, acting as if be was relieved to be with them and, away from the Agency office. They had already agreed to move his car from the office before Klinsmaar arrived to open up in the morning. And leave a note from Krommel that he had worked late and was ill when he left and not to expect him in that day. As most of the talk was in German, Jim had to accept the trust of the two women in the man.

Andreas knocked on the front window of the bar to be let in. A big man, greeting the women, exuding confidence, he enclosed Jim's hand within his and shook. "So. The English man. In search of monsters in this land of ours, but, this time, an English man in search of an English monster, I am told. The pimp of children. Mr. Finch." Turning to Gizande, "And I must thank you, also, for you have returned my Gizande to me. After so many years."

"You are a fool, Andreas," she said, in English for Jim's benefit, but without the force for his satisfaction.

"Of course, my Gizi." Looking back at Jim, "But a useful fool, who will come from his bed in the night for this adventure." He sat and took in Krommel with his eyes, "Krommel, ja?"

Who nodded. Then Andreas started to swiftly question him in German. Giving Krommel the briefest time to answer. After several minutes of this, including leafing through the document case, he spoke to Gizande, nodded to her reply and said to Jim, "It will not be easy. There is much confusion in East Germany now. There is a revolution happening, you know? We must pass close to Leipzig, where the movement against Honecker is the biggest. It may be difficult because the Police are nervous, but it may be more easy because they are too busy with the Revolution." He spoke to Gizande and Krommel in German again, then translated for Jim, "We will travel in my car. I am able to carry a DDR registration after we leave Berlin. Also, I have friends in Eisenach I will visit. It is near to where we go to find Finch. They are car workers."

"Ah! Jim was also a car worker. A leader in the trade union," Gizande said. Grasping at a straw to bring him together with this too-smooth operator, Jim thought.

Andreas looked at him. "Is this true. Jim?"

"Many years ago. Many, many years," unable to remember telling her of that far back.

Andreas nodded, then back into German for the others. "We must go quick, now. I wish to leave tonight. It will give us the surprise on Mr. Finch. The problem is papers. I have documents for travel in the East. Also Krommel has his papers. I can get us into East Berlin, no problem. But if we are stopped further on in DDR, it will he difficult for you and Gizande. Probably they will deport you to the West again. Perhaps lock you up for questions a few nights also. You wish to do this still?"

Jim shrugged, aware of Gizande's eyes on him. "Do I have any choice? If Finch could travel with the boy with a mental handicap, I'm sure we stand a chance."

"Ah, but Jim," the knowing shake of his head, "your Mr. Finch will have friends at the highest level to assist his travel. I have friends, but you have none." Then, an afterthought, "Have you asked Krommel if your boy is with Finch in this hotel?"

Kromrnel understood and nodded glumly. "Ja. Boy is with Finch. I am sure."

"Why? How do you know?" Jim asked harshly.

Krommel looked round for support and started to answer in German.

"English, damn you! I asked the question."

"It is the way with Finch. He takes the new boys to the hotel first with him."

"Why?" Jim's spat combined all the defensive aggression of being trapped before this audience watching him round the table. "What does he do with them?"

Krommel looked back at him, fearful.

"What does Finch do to them? After the video camera?" And Jim mimed the camera, just as the garage man had, in the flat that afternoon. Turning to Andreas, "Do you know about the video? Did she tell you?" still angry.

"Yes I told him," in a quiet voice. "But Jim, what reason is this for these questions?"

Then Andreas, "Do not frighten Krommel too much. We need his help."

Alliance with the devil, Jim thought, but said nothing more, a last glower across the table. Aware also that he was frightened himself of what they were about to do. And whether it was possible. And, most of all, now trusting none of the three he was to travel with.

Chapter Twenty-four

It was two in the morning when they set off in Andreas's worn black Mercedes, leaving Anna to tidy away Krommel's car. Sat in the back with him, Jim's eyes were on the back of Gizande's head in the passenger seat. Andreas crossed into East Berlin waved through at a checkpoint over a bridge, then took a lengthy series of turns through the backstreets of the city. Finally the streetlights became intermittent, they were out in the countryside night and it was raining. Krommel slept, or pretended to. Jim's own head slipped chin onto his chest several times, before he unslumped his body and shook himself awake, winding down the window slightly for a slit of damp cool wakefulness onto his face. Eyes out into the blank dark, buildings and signs only faint blurs at the edge of the car's speeding headlights. His temple against the cool glass, he could see just the suggestion of her profile in the glow from the dash board. Her and Andreas intermittently talking. Too dulled by it all, Jim could not summon up the energy to try to guess what they were saying. Leaving him to turn over again every conversation he could remember with her, rewritten with the dark foreboding he now felt about where he was going and who was with him.

He wound the window back up as they passed through an acrid chemical stink from some nearby plant. Signs for Leipzig passed. Later Weimar, and he thought of the elegant Helena, wondering what she would think of this odd expedition. Into enemy territory? No, into her country. But he returned again to Gizande, webbed up in his disappointments, wanting to speak with her, but not trusting himself.

Onto lesser roads now, they entered a small town, the fences of industrial plants first, then housing, finally into the old centre, cobbled streets turning uphill, past a battlemented wall and into barely lit streets. Andreas stopped the car and leaned back between the seats, "We stop here for short time I will see friend, before we continue." And he was out, crossed the road, knocked on a door and swiftly disappeared inside.

Leaving the three in the Mercedes, silence between them. Jim unable to speak what he wished to her in front of Krommel. Krommel saying nothing to provoke Jim's anger. And Gizande? Staring out at the wet street, her expression out of Jim's eyeline. He wanted to say something trivial, ask the time of her, despite his own watch, but as the silence stretched, it became more impossible to push words into the vacuum.

At last Andreas reappeared. He knocked at Krommel's window, who wound it down and they spoke together.

Back in the driver's seat, Jim asked, sharp from tension, "What was that about?"

"Was?"

"What did you say to Krommel? Don't I have the right to know?"

To Gizande, he said something, then to Jim, "So suspicious of us! I say we will go to the hotel and, if Finch is there, I will leave you to speak with him. I will bring Krommel here, where my friend will keep him. I then have meeting in Eisenach with friends of the opposition. I will return in afternoon, yes?"

"Why bring Krommel back here?"

"He fears Finch. But also, we have him for us if it goes wrong."

If it goes wrong? Jim thought. Anything could happen. Who knows what they may have set up for his arrival? "What do you mean? Leave me in the hotel?" Then, aware that no place had been specified for her in this, he added, looking at her, "On my own? Alone there?"

Andreas took the undercut of the words and said, "Gizande can come with me. Or with you. It is perhaps interesting for her to meet with the workers of the opposition, at this cross of history."

She said nothing for a long enough moment for Jim to feel abandoned, before she answered, "I will stay with Jim. Of course, he needs assistance with German, maybe." Said so conditionally, that he knew he had forced it upon her. A stale victory over Andreas.

So, barely as an apology, he replied quietly, "Thanks."

Andreas looked knowingly, from one to the other of the pair, then started the motor.

The hotel was up a winding bumpy road climbing out of a village through the tall trunked conifers. In a break, a castle showed, looking too ruined for the lit window Jim saw, at which a silhouetted figure stood motionless, looking down across the valley just emerging mistily from the night. He tried to twist his head to keep the figure in sight, but the forest closed it off again.

Krommel hissed something and Andreas let the car roll to a stop, engine off and silence. Ahead was a large dark building with outbuildings dimly clustered to the edge of the enclosing trees. They all sat watching it for a moment. In this early morning, only a dim light from the vestibule.

Andreas turned, "Now, Jim. What shall we do?"

Having reached the place, he was lost for anything else to say, "It's very early."

"It is a hotel. We can ask for zimmer- for rooms," Andreas grinned at Gizande.

Impatient of this, she turned, glanced at Jim, then to Krommel,

"What is best now? You know Finch. Will he come, if we ask for him?"

Krommel just shrugged, looked at Jim, then said, "I do not know."

"We will go in to ask for breakfast," she said, then for Krommel, "Fruhstuck, ja?"

"It's too early," Jim said. "Isn't it?"

Then Krommel said something in German and it engaged her with him in a serious conversation. Andreas listened and shook his head, while Krommel gave some long explanation. Finally, she turned to Jim, "It is a sporting centre for young athletes. They come to learn from the DDR coaches from all the countries in East Europe. Gymnastics and running."

Krommel interceded, "From Bulgarien, from Rumanien, from Polen."

She continued, "He says they will be waking the young people soon. They start the training for two hours before breakfast."

Jim looked past her at the building, wondering what was really going on for the kids in there, remembering the routines of his own childhood. He looked at his watch and, in the Institution as a boy, one of the fathers would have already stamped through the dormitory dragging off blankets a good half an hour ago. Now lined up and naked for showers, filing past the father supervising from his own bath, his back being soaped by his special boy.

Shaken awake from this, he said, "We just go in and ask for Finch." Then, to her, "Just you and me." To Andreas, "You wait here. With him," a contemptuous thumb at Krommel. "If things seem okay, we'll tell you. And you can go and drop him off with your friend. And go to your meeting." And, denying any delay, he pushed the car door open and stretched his tired legs out onto the roadside. "Coming?" to her.

She said something to Andreas, then was beside Jim. He took her arm and led her towards the glass vestibule doors, the bite of their shoes on gravel sounding loudly in the silence above the whispering of the trees. The doors were locked. They peered in at the empty reception, then Jim led off round the side. A yard for deliveries, there was a door propped open with a box. And voices.

They stood in the entrance of a scrubbed and disinfected corridor. "Hallo?" she called. "Hallo!"

The voices stopped.

"Hallo?" she called again.

At the end, in the half-light of a naked bulb above her, a large, aproned woman. Looked, saying nothing, scrutinised them. Gizande spoke to her, something about Finch and the woman disappeared without a word.

The pair stood there, looking down the corridor, waiting for several minutes, it seemed, before the sound of feet behind them in the yard. As they turned, two large men in tracksuits wordlessly shoved them both against each other into the corridor and the box was kicked away, the door slammed behind. Jim tried to turn to face them, but in the confines, she was in the way and the men's momentum pushed the two of them onwards. Stumbling out into a large kitchen. The aproned woman there and two other men in greasy white jackets. Now walking where they were being taken, Jim looked at Gizande, but her eyes were ahead. They caught at each other's hands and squeezed, both anxiety and reassurance. Another corridor and, steered into a small dining room, they turned and Jim watched the two large men who had herded them here watching back, one young, one in his forties, both with studied harshness of expression.

"Warten. Hier," the older barked.

Gizande nodded, then to Jim, "We wait here."

The men withdrew, closing the door after them.

"I am frightened," she said, but Jim put his finger to his lips, quietly rose and climbed onto a chair to see out of the single high window.

Returned to her, they sat and he whispered, "It looks out towards the front. You can just see the Mercedes parked there," relieved for the first time at Andreas's enduring presence outside, waiting to hear from them.

"What will happen now?" she asked.

"I only know what you know, Gizande," her name added with as much intimate reassurance as he could muster. "We wait to see if Finch comes. Or if this has been a..." but he trailed the bitterness of what he was to say into a slow shrug.

"Do you believe this- what we are doing?" her eyes appealed to him and it clicked with him that this was the first time she had been dependent on him.

But he could only offer his own doubts. "Do I believe in what we are doing?" he mused. "I believe that getting Stephen back- if we can- is right. I believe in finding out the truth about Damien's death- for his dad's sake. But do I believe we can do it? I don't know. I don't even know if coming here is going to help us." He looked at his fingers spread palm-down on the table, turned them over and studied them a moment, as if to guess if they were strong enough for what was coming. Whatever that would be. "But did we have any choice? We believed Krommel. I…" the pause to consider a waspish comment, before backing off it, "I trusted Andreas. To get us here."

"You did not trust Andreas," she said and slid her fingers onto his palm, which folded them to himself, his eyes smarting, cast down to look at his lap. "Jim. You were wrong to not believe in me, when I say that I am saying goodbye to Andreas. It is true."

What he would have said was severed- by the door banged open by Finch, slippered and bare-legged beneath a silk dressing gown. The older track-suited man behind him in the dim corridor light. Gizande turned to see Finch, releasing herself from Jim's hand.

"Jim. Jim Briggs," shaking his head and smiling coldly. "I never took you to be so adventurous. I suppose I should have guessed when you went and looked out my mum in her caravan. Did she moan on at you about her son? As usual." Jim said nothing, watchful until he had to reply. Then turning to Gizande, Finch asked, "And who have we here? The lady friend?"

"Madame Gizande Azéma," Jim answered, striving for best pronunciation. "She is a friend."

"I only said as much. Only a friend. I said no more," implying some conspiracy of silence between them against the truth. "Why is she here? For that matter, why are you here, Jim?"

"Why do you think?" balancing a true question with a covert challenge.

Finch leaned back against a table, as if considering his answer. "Mmm. Why do I think...? That would depend on your answer. You have come to me. Into my house, so to speak. Before I have an obligation to give of my hospitality, I ask you why you are here. Do you come as a friend? Or do you come as an enemy? An easy question."

Jim said quietly, "Yes. And no."

"To which question? Is it yes, as a friend? Or no, not a friend?"

"I don't know you, Finch. Becoming a friend or an enemy will depend," leaving it hanging there.

But Finch would not be manoeuvered, "Continue."

"The agenda is still on the table from our phone call last night."

Finch answered with one risen eyebrow, saying nothing.

So Jim continued, "The future of Stephen. A discussion about Damien." For the first time, he took his eyes off Finch and looked at her to say, okay.

Finch stood, as if weary with idle chatter, "You have travelled a long way in a short time. Are you hungry? Are your friends outside in the Merc? Will they join us?"

Krommel in the backseat would not yet be seen from the hotel in the twilight, Jim thought, but was it safe to send them on their way and stay here? "Our friends wait to see if we are- okay. Then they will go and they'll pick us up this evening."

"I will send someone to tell them you are okay."

"No!" Not that. "No. It must be one of us." Then, easing the edge in his voice with, "Why would they believe a stranger?"

Finch shrugged, as if now indifferent to it all. "The lady may go. Will she come back to keep you company?"

She spoke for the first time, "Yes. I will stay with Jim. I speak German for him."

"Ah, Jim and I will be speaking no German together, will we, Jim?" It needed no answer. "Return to keep him company, if you wish. After you have sent away your friends." He motioned to the silent figure in the door, "I will go to get dressed. When the lady returns, she can put her German to good use by ordering whatever you wish for breakfast. Das Fruhstuck, that is, Jim."

"Yes. I know," but Finch was already leaving, the other man closing the door after them

"I will go out to Andreas now," she said. "It must be before they see Krommel. I will tell Andreas to return before six hours, yes?"

Jim nodded, "Don't be long." For so many reasons.

After she went, he climbed on the chair again and watched her run across the yard to the car, bend down for a few moments, stood back as the Mercedes started and watched it back and turn, then roar off down the road. As she ran back, she saw Jim watching her from the window, and gave a fluttery wave of her fingers to him, which belied the seriousness of her face.

Chapter Twenty-five

"Andreas will return at six," she said.

"Well, we're not dependent on him now. Until he gets back, we're in the hands of Monsieur Finch, it appears. Assuming he comes back to us."

She ignored his caustic tone and simply asked, "Will we take the hospitality of the Fruhstuck?"

"Whatever they have to offer. It has been a long time since I- we've eaten."

"Okay. I will explore."

She returned with a tray. Slices of dark oily bread, cold meats and two plastic cups of sour-smelling coffee. "We will eat better when we return home," she said, but he grudged himself not to guess kindly about what she said.

They were just finishing when the door opened and two girls' faces, fresh and sweet poked round the door with irresolute daring. They looked a moment, then broke into nervous giggles to each other.

Gizande spoke to them smilingly in German, suddenly seriousing them. They looked at each other, before replying with slow consideration. Gizande beckoned them in and they shuffled, now with watchfulness into the room, against the wall, close to the door. Cheap, shiny shell-suits over their skinny bodies.

She spoke again to them and Jim asked, "Who are they? Where are they from?"

"They are from Bulgarie. They are gymnasts." She smiled reassuringly at them, but the girls remained cautious. She spoke again to them, but, before they could answer, there was a shout from down the corridor, the bark of the older man in the tracksuit, and the girls whipped out of sight, slamming the door behind them, the man's voice bellowing in pursuit off into the distance.

Jim looked at her and felt the uncertainties and fears of the day ahead in this building displace the jealous doubts about her. "I don't like this place at all. I fear what is happening to these children here," the sound of his voice hollowed deep from within his own childhood, his face letting itself slacken into supplication. For any reassurance she could give.

She seemed to be listening to the sounds of the building, voices, steps on the yard out side, a distant shriek, a collective laugh somewhere nearer, a routine of wakefulness being enforced on large numbers of children around them. Emerging to him, she nodded, "Yes," and would have said more, but the door opened and the aproned woman came in followed by the two young men in dirty white jackets, all three with trays which they carried over to the most distant table, passing the visitors' eyes ahead, as if they were not there. The rich spicy sweat from their platefuls of sausages filled the room.

Jim was astonished at the blatancy of it, "Do we have to sit silent, watching them eat, while all we've had is this crap!" indicating the plate before him.

She smiled, "Ah, Jim. It is the liberty of the chef to eat the best of the food."

The murmur of conversation from the turned away backs at the other table commenced.

"Where is Finch?"

"He will come," she said quietly. "He is too much interested by our arrival here, for him not to see us again. But he must appear to be… distant. Without interest. It is the preparation for the negotiation he will have with you."

Telling the truths he already knew, from his own past experience. But this, just another negotiation? Another wheeling-dealing to get a temporary advantage? He could not allow it to be that. To reduce this confrontation he wanted with Finch to just trickiness.

He shook this off by quietly saying to Gizande, "It's what I'm good at. Negotiation," but was unsure if the words sounded as confident as he intended.

It was half past eight when Finch collected them. The cooks had eaten and gone, leaving Jim and Gizande silent together, listening for cues from the sounds outside, waiting. Now in slacks, an open necked shirt and a blazer, Jim was struck by how old-fashioned-upper-class was the style Finch affected. Apart from a curt, "Come," he said nothing as he led them upstairs, through a carpeted hotel area, then into linoleum corridors like an old school. Into a large gym. Cavernous, underlit and cold. Bars up the walls, blue plastic mats on the floor, other equipment cluttered aside at the back wall. A group of girls, all in red track suits, obviously waiting for them under the supervision of a young woman also in red and the older man, the barker they had met earlier. There was a shuffle of anticipation from the girls. Jim tried to recognise the two girls who had come in the dining room and then chased off, but he could not. Uniform skinny fragility.

Finch switched to a generous benignity, turning to Jim and Gizande, his arms taking in the room and the girls, "We have something special for you this morning. Have you ever heard the songs of Bulgaria? No? Well, here," indicating two metal chairs for them. "Now," and he spoke in German to the young woman. She bowed and stepped forward, turned to the girls and stretched her arms, the young faces raised, shining with concentration. At first almost undetectable from their barely parted lips, a hum rose, lifted by the woman's rising hands, and swelled with the expanded lungs pushing open the mouths of white teeth, hardening into a harmony, harsh and loud, the note held in long, quavering certainty- cut dead with a chop of the woman's hand. A moment of breathless, shocked silence. Into which stepped one of the girls, with a delicate confidence, her pale face lifting dark unseeing eyes past the woman before her, up into the shadows in the roof. Her feet set heel-to-instep, like a ballet dancer, Jim thought her about to rise from the floor, less with a leap than floating, with the intensity wrapped within the bony little frame about to unroll itself. And it did with her voice, a single note shivered out, steel-hard and Jim, deaf to the foreign words, starkly heard her, calling out in her tongue, almost pressed back into the chair by the force of indictment against ancient wrongs, drawn from the body of this child, from the women of her people, mothers and grandmothers, the blood throbbing in the veins stood out on her skinny neck. A breath, she curled up again, less a song than a lament, each verse at once a descending stairwell of pained notes, but wrenching upwards finally into that single, held cry, defiant against inevitability. Three times her song fell and rose again, the last time reverberating in the deflated soundlessness she left in the empty space of the room. Stiff from his attentiveness, Jim was aware of sweat tickling at the side of his nose, despite the cold of the air faintly showing in his breath. The girl stepped back into line with the others and he looked at Gizande.

She turned to him and would have said something, but Finch stepped forward and started clapping the moment of trance out of the room. Turning to the seated couple, he thumbed back at what they had witnessed with, "They use the singing for breath control. Before they start their morning training, they sing a song or two." He grinned at Jim, then nodded to Gizande, "I thought it might be a nice start for you and your lady."

She murmured for Jim, "It was so beautiful."

But Finch cut in with, "Beautiful? Yes. But it's like all those Balkans, so much sorrow for the past, crying for lost causes, they've no energy for the present."

Jim wanted to get up and punch him, but he already recognised the deliberate off-the-cuff provocations that were part of Finch's style, part of his strategy of control. So he simply met the comment with, "Yes, it was beautiful," stood, stepped past Finch to the girls, who had been stirring awkwardly while the foreigners spoke and said to them, "Thank you. It has been an honour to hear you sing."

They looked at the woman conductor for a response and she gave a little bow and said something in answer that seemed to have the word "merci" at the end.

Finch was behind him now. "I think you want to talk now, okay?"

Jim turned and stepped back to find the other man so close. "Yes. Time we talked," said also across to Gizande, watching back, serious, even a little uncertain. Of what next.

Finch led them back into the carpeted hotel area, into a polished conference room. He offered them seats at the end of the large dark-wood elliptical table, while he walked over to the picture window and looked out into the forests. While his back was turned to them, Jim looked at Gizande and she was nervous.

He squared his mind up to the other man, as Finch turned round, "You want to hear about Damien, do you?"

Tempted to add Stephen's name, Jim held back from the obvious, letting what Finch said lead them where it will.

"He was local league, you know," he spoke in a disengaged, reflective way, slow steps along the carpet the other side of the table. "He didn't even know the First Division existed. He missed the opportunities that he could have got, too." Then, looking up at Jim, the hard measuring eyes, "How much do you know about us?"

"I know about Northlodge," Jim offered.

"Ha! Northlodge! Small beginnings. Yes, well that's it. Damien never got beyond the Northlodge mindset. After he agreed to make that Statement against you, he had to be offered something. So we let him run the local networks there. You know, getting him to recruit lads in the flats there and moving the best of them on to London."

Jim restrained his rising astonishment as the calculatedness of it all was spelt out. Worse scenarios than even he could have guessed at. But he heard himself ask, "Recruit?"

Finch swung a glittering attention to this, "Do you know as much as you pretend, Jim? Or are you just fishing?"

"I know about Whispering Pines. About the flats in London," with a casual knowingness swallowing back any doubt from his face.

"Well. So you got that far?" A pause. "Of course you did. That was why you had to be given the shove." He turned and started the long walk back towards the window. "Yes, we even got Damien a job with Northlodge. But it started to go wrong pretty quick. When Damien propositioned some of the boys, they started to beat up on him. Not the most seductive sort, our Damien. Bit of a wimp, really. Then a boy went to the Police and it started to get messy, with Damien likely to end up in court, charged as a perve. He did get arrested by the local fuzz and they pulled in Councillor Jeffreys too, and one of the residential workers at the Pines. It needed a bit of string pulling from our friends at the top - you know, the funny handshake brigade- to get them all released." From the far end of the room, he turned and grinned to Jim, "You know that at first, that stupid tosser Damien didn't even want to get released. We were having to get them bailed and then, when it died down, get the charges quietly dropped. But our Damien was too frightened, reckoning there would be a bunch of lads waiting to do him over when he walked out of the Police Station, stupid dickhead."

Then, a deference to Gizande, spiced with sarcasm, "Pardon, madame. Or madamoiselle, is it?" his eyes laughing from her to Jim. "No matter, Jim. No matter," before resuming. "So we had to shift him. London for a bit. Then out here, to Berlin, where we were just opening up the new operation, an offshoot of London. We had got the lads down in London good jobs on the building, to tide them over, until they started turning enough tricks to go full time. Or they got a sugar-daddy to set them up." At the window, again out into the dense darkness of the trees. "Berlin. This has been the big time. It all fitted together so well. We started to contract building workers out here from the UK- you know, Auf Weidersein, Pet, and all that. It was a legit front to the operation and lads started to go out from there, all over Europe. Supply a kid here and a kid there, then a little finger wag, naughty-naughty to a senior government minister, wave the video copy at them and it did wonders to wheel the oils on new contracts." Back into the room, he giggled at them. For the first time almost childish, Jim thought. The boy he really still was, so proud to talk his head off. Let him carry on. Whatever the price when he wakes up to what he's doing.

"So then we get a call from over the Wall. A new source of supply, they were offering. Gymnasts at first. There's nothing some of those parents in Bulgaria and Romania won't do to get their kids into a national sports team. They just hand them over to the coaches- and for the gymnasts, there's the extra. Eternal youth. They get the girls and drug them to delay their puberty. So, if you've a taste for a little girl, they keep the girl little. For a year or two, at least." Jim heard Gizande intake her breath sharply, then half cough, but, with Finch's eyes on him, he was not going to release him from his own fixed expressionlessness. Yet his head filled with the sound and sight of the frail singer in cold hall. "Then, when the drugs can't keep it up and they get too old for childhood and too big for gymnastics, send them back home with their medals. Or whatever. Those kids you saw today- how old do you think they are?"

Jim shrugged, and that distant, beautiful child in the dank room where Mark had been asleep, came intimately to mind. With her same question.

"Go on. How old?" Finch persisted.

"Twelve?" knowing it would be older.

"Thirteen, fourteen. A couple of fifteen year olds. And one seventeen- would you believe that?"

"The wonders of science," Jim said flatly, nausea restrained.

Finch laughed loud, looked at Jim and laughed again, "Oh, very droll. That's what they say, isn't it? Droll?" He shook his head, still smiling. "Well this is the future. Out here. Families can't afford to keep their kids in East Europe, so they'll sell them for any dream. Market forces. And anyway, children's homes like the one I was in will be a thing of the past back home, councils can't afford them. They're closing them down all over. Need to move farther afield. North Africa next. Now they really do know about the pleasures of the body. Yes," said with reflective appetite, "that's my dream. Winter in Africa, recruiting. Then summer in Europe, getting the kids to work the resorts." Now across the table from them, he leaned over, sneering into Jim's face, "Don't look so fucking shocked and puritanical. I know you'd fancy a try with a kid. I know. I know about the appetites of men, after all these years. Can't get them young and sweet enough, can we? Go on, deny it!"

Trembling with anger, pressing the vibration of his body out through his fingertips locked white and bloodless against the dark edge of the table, at last Jim growled out between clenched teeth, "You sad bastard."

But Finch danced back from him, taunting but dangerous, "Go on. Deny it. What about with her?" nodding to Gizande. "How do you like it with her? Dirty? Up the arse? Lots of licks? Go on, Jim! Let your fantasy go!" Now he was chattering and, all the measurement fallen away, he was dancing like an ugly monkey up and down along the carpet. "Go on! You and her together in a bed. With girls. How many? Or a boy? Can get that, too. Spice it up -"

"SHUT. YOUR. MOUTH!" The shrieked words from her were - each of them - a bellow from deep with the chasm her chest made of her slight body. Jim saw the muscles in her neck strung out, quivering, as Gizande stood, leaned forward on her hands, projecting fury and contempt. And then it was gone, in a moment she shuddered and shrank back into her seat, withered by the force of saying it, her hand scrabbling for Jim's and taking it gently but desperately, under the table into her lap.

Both stilled for a moment by her outburst, he looked across at Finch. Who said, with more caution than taunt, "Touched a raw nerve there, did we?"

Jim wanted to stand. To confront Finch at an even level. But he did not dare leave her hand from where it had curled, retreated within his own. "Less of the reasons Damien didn't fit with your business plans. That he wasn't very good at trading children. Tell us what you did with him. How you-" and he hesitated from the most damning accusation and stepped back to- "How he died."

All false smiles gone now, Finch was cold and intense, nothing to expect from either of them, "I bet you use all the words, don't you, Jim? Care. Abuse. Protection. What's the latest phrase? Community care, I've heard?" and he snorted. "It's all us exploiting kids to you, I suppose. But if they go through the system- go through the so-called care system, like I did- through those bloody children's so-called homes, where do they end up? They told us what they were giving us was care. But what they were really giving us was control- locking us up without the chance of a trial! Do you know the statistics? How many like me end up in prison? After the training they give us- social workers, care workers, the lot of them- all we know is about getting locked up. But it was different for me- I was given a chance. I was lucky. Got off the treadmill. Out of the statistics. Okay, I had to do a few nasty things for some dirty old men. But who was in control of that, me or them? I could get them to do what they like for me. We start making the choices. Best clothes, flats, jobs. They were shit-scared of me. I knew too much. Jeffreys and the others." He looked up the room to the window again. "Yeah, you'll be like the others. Speaking their rubbish, spouting their words. And it's all about telling kids like I was, what we shouldn't do. Never what was possible." He looked back at Jim challengingly, "I'm the real social worker here. Do you know that? I do the rescuing for the kids, not that lot back in the council offices. These kids here, from Bulgaria- what chances have they got in life? Shit countries, eating shit, shit work and an early grave. They aren't born with silver spoons. But we give them a chance to earn them. They've got no education, no chance. What they do have is their beauty. And we give them the chance to learn how to use it." He shrugged his blazer up on to his shoulders. "It worked for me, didn't it?"

The chance for Jim to cut in with, "Did it? You mean you wear a blazer now, and not a shellsuit."

"Dress for the client, my friend. Always dress dull in East Germany. The top guys in the Communist Party here, they're all tweed jackets and shotguns, you know. They wouldn't trust me if I dressed flash."

"And a nice grey suit for an English magistrates court?"

Finch laughed again, but watchfully, "Got it in one, Jim."

"But you're still steering clear of my questions about Damien."

"I told you. He couldn't hack it. Went on drugs. He was a liability, so we sent him back to UK. Where he o-deed. Pathetic."

But he waited for the first time, poised for Jim's answer. Which was quiet, unaccented and definite, "You know that's not true. He died in Berlin. ABC's friends back home sorted that one out, didn't they?"

"Crap. Melodramatic crap. You've got to have a martyr in all this, just to make your point that everyone comes to a bad end if they don't behave. Moral junk. Good behaviour? That would have been poverty for me. Damien had the chances. He decided not to take them." Then he turned a definite and defiant back to walk slowly to the window again, full-stopping what he had said with, "Then topped himself."

Wait. Both of them. For the other man to step into the silence that volumed now to fill the room. Looking at him, Jim remembered the window that day of the Disciplinary. So different for himself then, the shimmering light in the leaves, set against that roomful of deceit that had been behind his own turned shoulders. Finch looked on now outwards into these dark still and secretive forests. Hiding in them. Gizande tugged at his fingers for attention, but Jim briefly shook his head at her, aware that Finch could probably see them reflected in the glass before him, the lit room mirrored against the dark woods outside. Staring at the blazered shoulders, he could almost see the prickling discomfort of the other man's assumed indifference to the extenuated silence.

Almost oppressive enough to stifle, the soundlessness of the room made Jim breathe shallowly and silent. He stopped the miniscule movements of his hand on hers. Pressing their fixed watchfulness against the man at the other end of the room, almost pushing him physically up against the glass. So, when he turned, Finch thrust himself away from it, the print of his hands' condensed sweat a moment there before vanishing. His face sullen, angry, prematurely marked with doubt, pain and cruelty. Bruised darkly, but defiant with the cursedness, the inescapability of what he had done. Deeds marked for life. Eyes on them, then away, he swayed a moment, lurched, gathered himself back from the verge of disarray- and smiled at them. Garish over-brightness, denied by the darkness from deep within the sockets of his eyes.

Starting to walk back down the room, wooden-legged with control, he at last arrived opposite them, his hands steadied on a chair back. Which he drew away from the table and sat down. Face to face with them, at last. The sound of his breathing, before, "You want to know about Stephen."

A question? Jim refused it with, "So, that's it for Damien, is it? All you've got to say?"

"What do you want?" the words curled with contempt, an absolute challenge from so close across the table that Jim could smell cigarettes on the other man's breath. "An apology? A letter to his family? I don't do apology. I won't apologise for what I do. I sure won't apologise for the weakness of others. Either they keep up or not. That's the way of the world." He seemed to reflect on Jim for a moment, a whisp of a smile there, then gone, "I never ask for forgiveness for who I am. I don't do victim for myself and I don't do forgiveness for others, too. I will never ask you for forgiveness, so you never have to give it. It lets you keep your anger, Jim, and that's the fuel for energy! That's the thing that drives creativity. Anger. Forgiving is dull. So is being forgiven. It takes you nowhere." Then the smile hinted again, "So I won't apologise to you, for whatever you think I may've done to Damien. And that'll keep you up and running. You can use it now as the fuel to burn about Stephen. We can talk about that now. No point in turning over the past, is there? Nothing to be done about Damien, now, is there? Justice, as you'd call it, is wasted on the dead, isn't it?"

With sombre restraint, Jim said, "Not for his parents, it isn't," but knew it to be futile to carry on arguing the moral toss with this poisoned and poisoning young man

Confirmed by Finch's laugh, "What? Old man Toser? Ask him what he did to Damien to get him put into care in the first place, before you start knocking at my door for what went wrong with the lad. Bereavement? My arse! More like the old man's guilt!" He opened his palms on the table top, as if to show them empty. Of responsibility. Of any thing to say more on the subject. "So. Do you want to discuss Stephen? Or not."

Beneath the table, Jim released Gizande's hand- which Finch, missing nothing, faintly registered- and brought it up to lock fingers on the tabletop, his eyes down on this double fist. Before raising his eyes again to Finch's face, marking the page turned on from Damien. "Okay. Stephen. Do you have him?"

"I know where he is."

"Is he here? In the hotel?"

"He can be got here. Quickly."

"Why do you want to keep him?"

Feigning impatience, Finch asked crisply, "Are we getting into some moral discussion again, Jim? What we want now is to know what you have to offer to get Stephen off our hands. And for me to decide if it's enough to let you have him. Then, after that, if we have a deal, we have to work out how we can get him back to the UK. You do want to take him back to the UK, don't you? You are sure they'll want him back there- the so-called authorities, the Council and your blessed Social Services- are you? You know he's something of an embarrassment to them, don't you?"

"You mean the way Stephen can't stop telling the truth?"

Finch smiled at this, "You could say that, I suppose. One way of looking at our Stephen. He doesn't have enough up here-" tapping the side of his head- "to understand that the rules of the game don't involve a lot of truthfulness, do they, Jim?"

"That's the trouble, though, Billy," using his first name here for the first time. "Truth. Lies. They're all of a piece for you. Each of them, it's the least you can get away with, isn't it? How do I know you have got what you offer? You act as the big boy who can deliver, but really you're just a little inbetweener in all this. Your strings are pulled from London, aren't they?"

"Why ask me? You won't believe the answer," he replied flatly. "Because I'm all you've got, Jim. If you want Stephen, you'd better stop moralising and start speaking to me." He looked at his watch. "The morning's pretty well gone and we haven't started yet. Your friend is coming back this evening to pick you up." Finch stood and, looking away to the window, made himself remote from them, saying from afar, "You think about it. I'll arrange something for you to eat. I'll come back and then we can start talking business," his voice indifferent, tired. Jim was unsure if this was totally a pose, another trick of manner, or that tired pain from having seen and done too much in too short a time. Tempted to say something, to shift the balance before Finch left the room, Jim held back. Leaving his own last word an ambiguous and expressionless silence, still humming in the room after Finch had left, quietly closing the door behind.

After a moment, to her, "Well? What do you think of that?"

She unlocked his fist of fingers and took a hand into his. "Will he also kill Stephen?"

"He could do. Or get someone to kill for him."

"What will you say to him, Jim, when he returns?"

"There's something... something about him wanting to us to get Stephen off his hands. He introduced Stephen's name this morning. It's as if they made a mistake smuggling the boy over here. And we might be the way they can get themselves out of it. Do you understand?"

She looked over his face, anxious but searching for something reassuring to say. "Naturally, I understand. But I am uncertain if I can believe he will give us anything. This place, it is a factory for the manufacture of prostitute children. We are in a police state, without the authorisation." She squeezed his fingers, as if to draw from them for herself the shadow of bravado he had found for the negotiation, the joust with Finch. "What do you have to give to him?"

Her bleakness was infective. But something in the other man was appealing to Jim. Buried underneath the thin veneer of thought-through cynicism and contempt, there was a supplication buried there, Jim was certain. Inviting him to dig it out.

"A phone. I need a phone," he said suddenly.

"They will not permit you a phone, Jim."

"Maybe. I need Finch to get me to a phone." He looked at her, "He will let me phone if he wants me to."

"I do not understand. Who will you phone? It will be listened to."

"Dead right. It will be listened to. I've got to give Finch something to get him out of this and get him to release Stephen." He smiled at her, "You talked about trust. Now trust me. I think I know what makes Finch tick. The decision about Stephen needs to be taken out of his hands." She looked back at him, wanting to understand from his fragments, but confused. And with another "Trust me," he pulled up her hand, opened the palm and studied its roughness with the rub of his thumb. Before drawing it to his lips, closing his eyes and kissing it slow and long. Then, standing to look down on her, "I won't be long," he went out into the hotel to search for Finch.

Chapter Twenty-six

He went out to the hotel reception and banged the bell several times. Nothing. This part of the place was soundless, a façade to what went on in the uncarpeted corridors behind. So, after several long minutes, he set off down those corridors, looking for Finch. His first direction took him into an area they had not been in. This route was blocked off with rough ply sheeting and he could hear the sound of building work going on beyond it, the grind of a concrete mixer, the scrape of a shovel and the smell of the dust. He backtracked to reception, fruitlessly tried the bell again, then set off to explore another quadrant of the building. A section of offices. Soundless too, until the sound of typing from one. He tapped on the smoked glass and entered.

To the astonishment on the woman's face, Jim offered her a grin and, "Herr Finch?"

She did not seem to understand and her panic just wanted him out of her room. She squawked something at him and franticly waved her hands to shoo him out.

But he stood, still smiling, and repeated, "Herr Finch."

The woman said, "Nein," followed by a gabble of something else, almost in tears from her anxiety at him there.

Jim just shook his head, to indicate he was not moving until his request was answered. She picked up a phone, tapped out a number and spoke into it, never letting her eyes leave him. She put it down, leaving her fingertips resting on it as if ready to unholster it at the least false move by him, her eyes still fixed on him wide and worried. With nothing for Jim to do but to study her face back, broad, motherly, with tired eyes and tight coiffeured over-blonde hair.

When the door was pushed open roughly, it banged against Jim's shoulder blade and he lurched forward across her desk, momentarily face-to-face with her, breathing the same air, before he was yanked back outside from behind and slammed against the partition wall so hard it shook. Pain in his back and in his face now the barker in the tracksuit. Who gave a fierce and searching gaze, then shoved him forward down the corridor, Jim calling again over his shoulder, "Herr Finch?"

His arms both jerked so high up his back that Jim was forced forward into a shuffling head-down trot, the pain in his back locked into his twisted muscles, breathing through gritted teeth. Thinking, thuggish bastard, but sure it was the way to Finch. And a few wrenched turns later, a door was respectfully knocked at by the barker's big knuckles appearing over Jim's shoulder. Answered by Finch's voice and he was pushed inside.

Released, he slowly wound his arm to feel where the pain was in his back. Finch's face was angry. The door closed behind and Jim turned to look, but his escort had remained in the room, impassively threatening, his arms folded. Jim returned to Finch with, "I want to phone UK. It'll get the ball rolling about sorting out Stephen."

"You want to phone home?" Finch's mock disbelief then hardened to, "What makes you think you have the power to demand that."

"It's not a demand. It's common sense. To get the ball rolling."

Finch sat. Jim looked around for a chair, but there was none on offer.

"I begin to get your style, Jim. You're a rule-breaker- no, you break understandings- to try to keep the other person on the back foot all the time. Am I right?"

Genuinely exploring this, Jim said, "I don't know what you mean."

"You turn up at my mother's. You turn up in Berlin. You turn up at the office, I now hear, when we had agreed to meet the following evening- I want to know, by-the-by, what you've done with Krommel. Then I offer you lunch and discuss things afterwards and you come blundering into other parts of the hotel. As if you can do what you want. You're not in England now, you know."

"Sure." Looking at the face, Jim was certain there was a genuine invitation- beneath the shallow contempt- for him to come up with something. A willingness to listen. "I know we're not. But we need some people in England to help get you off the hook back there over Stephen. The way things are, if you want to return home, there are some questions floating around now that even your powerful friends back there couldn't stop being asked, aren't there?" He waited for Finch to reply. Whose watching silence, despite the curled lip, invited Jim to continue. To spell it out. "The local press have got hold of it and questions will continue to be asked. About who you are. How you got Stephen out the country. And why. And here in East Germany? And what happens if a journalist is sat in court when Stephen fails to turn up. For no good reason. He's due back there in a few days and it didn't strike me that the magistrates were very tolerant of the mess around Stephen. Get you tarred with the same brush as Social Services- as Sylvie Cathcart? What a juicy story that would make. Even the national press might be enticed to take a look at that one. Might cramp your style a bit about how you cross frontiers in future. Getting back to see your mum."

Finch looked down at a cheap biro his fingers were toying with and spoke with his eyes still down, "What makes you think you have the pull to get things done back home? To get me off the hook, as you put it."

"I have contacts in the Social Services Department who are not tainted by all this. Who could act as intermediaries. And start talking about how we can get Stephen back home," watching the seated man for the impact of the carefully chosen words.

Finch looked up, the contempt gone, replaced by a carefully expressionless scrutiny of Jim's own face, "Who?"

Requiring an honest answer, "Julian Radley."

"Julian? Sounds like a bloody social worker. Who's he?"

"He's chair of the Union Committee. And yes, he is also a bloody social worker. Who knows about Stephen." Then, following a pause for significance, "He also knows about Damien. The true story, that is."

"So." Finch looked down again at his fingers, still playing their automaton game with that pen, "What can this Julian do for me?"

"If I can speak to him. Tell him I know where Stephen is. And send him to talk to Cathcart. Or her bosses. I think they'd move heaven and earth to get Stephen quietly back home, don't you?"

"Maybe." Finch was searching for holes in the offer, "But, with Stephen back home, what guarantee could you give that the press wouldn't go mad with it anyway? Naming me and causing me all sorts of shit."

"Come on, you have your own contacts. We're only talking about some local press men on the story at present. I'm sure you could counter that. Maybe with you as Stephen's rescuer. Saving children across Europe from the terrible sex crimes that Stephen is supposed to be at risk of." Oh-so-tempted to rub in the irony of Finch in that role, Jim clamped himself back from speaking it. The obvious.

"Why should I trust you? I've got you- and your girlfriend- in my hands now. What do I need to start letting you talk to people back in England for?"

"So you hold us here. For how long? It's known where we are. People are coming back to pick us up. Friends in the West know where we are. How will you magic us away?" Then, calculatedly, "We're not Damien, you know. Dependent on you." Finally offering, "You can stay in the room while I phone. I've got no secrets."

A few more exploratory turns of the pen and he placed it firmly and finally down on the desk. "Okay. We'll give it a try." He turned and spoke to the barker, who left the room. Then he lifted the phone across the desk and planted in front of Jim, writing the international code down for him on an envelope.

It took several minutes before he got through to Trish's voice. At one point, Jim had to give the handpiece back to Finch to deal with the enquiries of a phone operator in German.

At last, carefully keeping his voice impersonal before the scrutiny of Finch, "Trish? It's Jim. Is Julian there?"

He was not, but she said she would phone him at work and get him to phone back. Jim gave her the number Finch counted out for him. After she had taken it down, Jim could sense that she knew he was not free to speak and there was a moment of silence between them, of mutual and anxious understanding, before he cut it off with, "Thanks, Trish. Make sure he calls," and put the phone down.

To Finch, he said, "That was Julian's wife. She will get him to phone here."

"How long?"

Jim shrugged, "I don't know." Then smiling, "You know you can never get a social worker when you need one."

"Very funny." He stood up, went outside and called the barker back in. "You will be taken back to the room where you were before. The conference room. I will organise lunch for you. If the call comes, you will be called." Further words to the barker and Jim had been humourlessly dismissed. Anxious not to miss Julian's call back, unsure if Finch would now play the game being offered, but mostly keen to be back with Gizande and discuss the risks and uncertainties with her, the taste of her palm to his lips suddenly given the space to be remembered.

She was still sat as he had left her, looking small and lonely the other side of the polished expanse of table.

"Oh, Jim," apprehensive, searching, as if she looked for visible wounds he brought back.

"It's okay. He let me phone England. Julian."

"What did he say?"

"Julian wasn't there. I spoke to his wife."

"No. What did Finch say?"

Jim considered that a moment. What had Finch said? "He's frightened. Underneath all that stuff, he's frightened. All that dark lord of the universe stuff - pah!"

"I do not understand," and looking at her, she really did not, he thought. Genuine fear in that face, as he had not seen there before, he felt regret for the harshness he had shown to her in the last two days.

Taking on her mood, he spoke gently to her, "He is not as strong as he acts. He has weakness. He wishes to go back to England, to his mother, perhaps. But he worries. He trusts no one."

"But he is bad. He is a bad man," adding, "Mauvais," as if her stiff English was not enough.

"Yes. He has been turned into that. But he is also frightened of what he has done."

She shook her head, "You can have no trust in this man."

"We can, if we have something he wants from us." Then he put his finger to his lips to denote no more speaking, pointing to indicate possibly listening ceiling and walls.

She patted the chair next to her, "Come, sit with me," her eyes following him as he came round to her. She spoke quietly, almost a whisper, "I was anxieux for you when you were away from the room. Ici, dangereux. Comprendes tu?"

Why French? he thought, but nodded to her, "Oui," translating, "Dangerous. I understand."

"And if it becomes five hours tonight and Andreas returns, will we leave, if you still do not have Stephen?"

He fed the dilemma back to her, "Will we? What do you think?"

"I do not know." For a moment silent, without the reassurance she had sought from him, she looked blankly at the panelled wall across the room. "It is so gross. So big. Can we change such things?" Turning back to him, "We cannot change the world. Is not Finch protected by people with great power?"

"Sometimes. But he knows that his own power comes without their loyalty to him. That's all the powerful ever give. They reward you with a little of their power for doing their work for them. It's all they've got to give, but they hate giving it and they're always looking for reasons to take it back again. Finch knows this. He knows they never give loyalty. Or trust. It's the rules of the game he's been learning. Les régles du jeu? Is that how you say it?"

And she smiled at him, despite herself. And looked at him deeply, her smile fading. She brushed his cheek with her knuckles, "I will not leave here without you. You understand that?"

He closed his eyes. Closing out the room and the reasons they were here, this postponement of undistracted attentiveness to her. Yes, this moment would not be forgotten. And opening them again to the light, she was still there, the same seriousness. In the same room, waiting for Finch to call.

To put it aside, he said, "Finch is arranging lunch for us."

"I wish that the food is better than in this morning," and she joined him, smiling, time to pass on and exchange the moment for trivia.

He shouted at the unseen listeners in the walls, "Do you hear us there? A decent lunch! Chef's portions, please!" putting his cupped hand to his ear for a reply, she also tilting her ear to hear. Then laughing together-

Cut short by the door tentatively opening and trays with covered plates and glasses appearing, followed by two of the gym girls.

Jim and Gizande resumed laughing, even more uncontrollably, looking at each other and back to the girls, stood now nervously half-in the doorway at the sight of these giggling foreigners.

"Too much!" Jim snorted, "It's too much! What timing!"

Gizande shook her head, her shoulders still shaken with it, "It is true. The walls do have the ears!"

Then, controlling themselves for their perturbed and confused young visitors, Jim turned to the girls. "Food? For us?" pointing at himself and Gizande. The girls still motionless, as if entranced by the foreigners, he continued ponderously, "Do. You. Speak English?"

The girls looked at each other, then one stepped forward, with same balletic precision as the singer in the hall this morning. "I. Spik. Angliski. Little."

He smiled to reassure, "Thank you. For the food."

After a look at each other again, they stepped forward to the table with the trays, placed them carefully down and stepped back, all in pretty unison. The speaker composed herself, then said, "Thank you also. Our pleasings."

Gizande slid her tray across, lifted the cover on the plate. Two long steaming sausages, each stuck out at either end from its small bread roll. "Thank you. Danke. Merci," bowing her head.

Jim pulled his food to him too. But the two girls were still standing there, watching, a little uneasy, their smiles gone.

Then the speaker stepped forward again, with the same formal steps. "We ask you. You can have us in family?" She paused. Jim pulled his hand away from the plate cover, but forgot it, left hesitant and still. With Gizande, he stared at the dark eyes struggling for the sense of what she was saying. "You," pointing at Gizande, "mama. You," to Jim, "papa. For us? We, family for you?" Turmoiled by the blank astonishment of the two adults, she pressed on, "We- we," indicating both girls. "You," pointing back and forth between Jim and Gizande. "We…" she looked at the other girl, fruitlessly for help, then turned back and said something, a tangle of s-sounds to Jim.

"What was that?" he asked Gizande.

She was frowning to understand, "I do not know. Perhaps it is Bulgarian word."

The girl finally brightened with inspiration, "Family. We, you, family?" Pointing again, to herself, the other girl, then to Gizande and to Jim.

It was on Gizande it first dawned. She leaned forward, as if getting closer would confirm what she was understanding, then turned to Jim, her hand clutching a wad of his jacket cloth. Her eyes swirled, liquid and urgent, "They wish us- the girls wish us to be their family. Their father and their mother."

But for Jim, it rose before him with another meaning. "They think we are married?" Was that how it seemed to them? To others? Paired together? Even in Finch's deliberately slutty mind and mouth?

But Gizande's attention was back on the girls. "Where is your family?" pointing from one to another girl. "Where, your mama, papa?"

As if it was an odd question, "In Bulgaria."

"You go back to Bulgaria? To mama, papa?"

"Neh!" The speaker shook her head and her companion seemed to understand and shook hers too, definitely, with finality. "Bulgaria bad. No go back." Then, as if to correct any misunderstanding, "No stop Deutschland. Bad. Like Bulgaria. Not like Bulgaria. More bad," shaking how bad it was out of her head. She stepped back to the other girl and embraced her, looking back, pleading, "You. We. Family. Please. Is possible?"

Gizande turned to Jim, "What shall we do?"

His head was stuffed with it all- the sudden wrench together by these girls of possibilities between him and this woman next to him he was addicted to being with, the impossibility of doing what the girls were asking, the wait for the call from Julian - the insistences of all these things was ready to explode crazily out of his skull. He looked back into Gizande's eyes, wanting to say whatever she wanted to hear. But finally only able to speak, "Don't know."

"How can we leave them? We know what will happen to them."

"How can we take them?"

"Speak with Finch. Ask him if we can take them."

Jim looked back at the girls, a momentary grasp that what he said of them may seal whatever future he may have with the woman beside him, good or bad. Then back to the grey eyes, reluctantly back to their scrutiny, "How can we? With Stephen as well? What happens back in France? Gizande, we can't just steal these children from their parents- however unhappy they may be to go home."

"Why not? Finch stole Stephen," but Jim knew she did not believe the desperation of her own arguments.

"You know it's not possible. With Stephen it's different. The authorities may cooperate with getting him back to England. What will the French authorities say to us? If we turn up with these two children?"

"But we know what is happening to them," her eyes swimming, then almost a sob, "Jim, we know," and she looked at the girls, snuffled, wiped her nose with the edge of her finger.

"If we tell Finch, they may get in trouble- be punished."

She looked back at him, tears now squeezed out onto her cheekbones, "Punished? How can they be punished by more than is happens to them now? What is more bad than what is being done to them now?" Her voice rose, almost keening the word, "Children!" Her eyes back to the girls, trying to smile to them, despite, repeating more quietly, "Children."

The girls were motionless, still entwined together, watching back.

From the desperation of being cornered by this confrontation, with the girls' pleas and with Gizande's grief, Jim began to search his jacket pockets with some sort of low-grade inspiration. They all watched him as he found a pen and the little notebook he kept for phone numbers. He tore out a page from the back and wrote *La Retrait Parfaite*, stopped, scribbled it out, then put the address of Gizande's farm.

He showed it to her, "Okay?"

"What reason for?" she asked, but then a defeated, "Okay."

Jim stood and went round the table to the girls. He crouched slightly to the speaker and handed her the scrap of paper, pointing to the address, then to himself, then Gizande, "Our home. We live," and pointed at the paper again.

"Ah. You family," holding up the paper, as if it were an awarded certificate. "We come. We, you, family."

Jim looked back over his shoulder at Gizande smiling tightly to the girls, and could only turn back to them and say, "Maybe."

The girl said, "We come. Family. Later," as if the problem was now overcome and, smiling, told her friend. Who disengaged herself, stepped forward and embraced Jim, her face buried in his jacket, her bony arms reaching round his ribs. Surprised, then overwhelmed, he closed his eyes. Enduring his betrayal of this child's trust. Gizande had come round the table and was hugging the other girl. The welcome by the girls, the farewell by the adults.

The girls stepped back and the speaker held up the paper again, "Thank you," folded it carefully and pocketed it. Then, standing formally, to Jim, "Good man." And to Gizande, "Good lady," both girls bowed their heads and with a last flash of their smiles, went to slip out the door.

"Wait!" It was Gizande. The girls stopped, looking at her. "What are your names?"

Incomprehension?

"Your-" pointing one to the other- "names. Me-" to herself- "Gizande. He-" to Jim- "Jim."

Realisation and a smile from the speaker. "I, Vanja. She, Julieta." She bowed again and the girls were gone.

Leaving them in the conference room, stood close together, each with their own thoughts about what had just happened. At last, restraining all the seething disquietude it left him with, Jim looked at her, but the smile she had drawn from herself for the girls was gone.

"What have we done, Jim?"

"What could we do? We have done all we can. What more…?" he trailed off.

"We have become liars to them."

"No. We could do nothing. We have done all we can. We put both them and us in danger. Remember, we joked about the walls listening. Maybe they have been. Heard everything."

"Do you think we have made danger for the girls?"

Another moment between them had passed, stolen by worries about others. So Jim walked back to his seat and lifted the cover on his sausages in rolls. Looking up at Gizande, who was still stood where they had been embraced by the girls, "We didn't make danger. As you said, what danger could be worse than what is already happening to them?" Then, a coarseness within him prompted spelling it out, "Rape. Prostitution. Forced drug-taking." And chewed off the end of his sausage, strongly aware that the anger he felt was not towards her, but the whining inside him asking for time to do what he wanted. To be selfish with himself. And mostly, to see if there was the possibility of sharing selfishness together, alone with her. However impossibly far into their futures that might be.

Chapter Twenty-seven

They had eaten silently together for several minutes, each with their own thoughts about the girls, when Finch reappeared.

"Your call from England." Then pronounced caustically, "Julian."

Jim had stood and taken a last swig of the thin beer from his glass, when Gizande spoke, "Mister Finch. We wish to speak to you. About the two girls who served the dinner for us."

Jim froze, looking at her calm certainty towards Finch. Then at him, who scowled, scribbling his eyebrows a moment, before an oily calm, "Yes? Madame Azéma?"

"They are unhappy." A moment as she decided how to go on, "They wish to leave."

"Oh, yes? And where would they like to leave to?"

Jim was unable to let her go on. "My phone call," he insisted to Finch.

Who put his hand up, without taking his eyes off her, "Madame Azéma?"

"They wish to come with us," but she could not keep an edge of the hopelessness of what she was asking out of her voice.

Finch turned to smile at Jim, "So. We are rescuing every child now, are we? A caravan of rescued children? A gypsy caravan, travelling its way across communist Europe!" He laughed, hard and false.

"My phone call," Jim repeated, trying to retrieve something.

"Oh, yes. Julian. Will he arrange for the little Balkan whores to go back to England, as well as simple Stephen?"

Jim filled up with disgust. At Finch, and at himself for wanting something from this evil young man. Knowing that he should strike out at Finch, for her sake, for the girls, summoning up a fury he did not feel. Just dull defeat at the unthreading of the deal he had half negotiated, its time ticking away.

His eyes met Gizande's and she must have read in them that he was not with her on this one. She shook her head and said to Finch, "Go. It is nothing. The phone."

Who said sharply to Jim, "Come."

And Jim followed, a glance back at her from the doorway, pleading for her understanding. But she was not looking.

Out in the hallway, Finch seized Jim's arm roughly and pushed him across the ever-empty reception, "Come on!"

"Let go! I'm coming," trying to wrench his arm free. But Finch still grasped, his face harsh and silent, leading fast down the corridor with long strides. Off the hotel carpets, onto linoleum, their shoes now grinding down the cold cement floors, somewhere beyond the limits of the inhabited parts of the building. Yanked round corners, Jim now let himself be led, for the sake of talking to Julian. But then they burst out of a pair of doors, into the yard at the back.

"The phone!" he exclaimed and tried to pull them both to a stop, but Finch careered on, Jim pulled staggering after him. Into a wooden outhouse that Finch kicked the door open. And stopped. Shutting the door, turning the light on dusty gym equipment awaiting repair. A vaulting horse with a plank off the side, two split medicine balls, a set of railings propped up behind, a heap of chairs variously broken.

Jim turned from this, "Where's the phone?"

But Finch was recklessly angry, all his smoothness now shed, "We had a deal! One phone call!"

"So?" keeping a defiance, "Where's the phone?"

Finch stepped up to Jim, filling him with his violence, little spits of anger on his face, "Fuck your phone! Fuck Julian!" He stepped back, eyeing Jim with contempt, "Do you know how risky this is? You're not in the fucking Home Counties now, me lad. People disappear in this country."

"Like Damien did?"

"Don't get fucking smart, mister." Then reconsidered, "Yes, if you like. Like Damien did. This-" pointing at the floor, the earth beneath it- "this is a fucking police state, if you haven't heard. You're here and I'm here, both of us, as guests of the Stasi. Ever heard of them?"

"Yes. They're your mates, aren't they?"

The anger risen again, "Don't fuck with me! If you want Stephen back, you've only got me."

"And who've you got, Billy?"

"Don't call me THAT!" he screamed the last word. He walked a few steps away, mastering himself, then turned back, "Your woman. Does she have any idea of how dangerous this place is? Those girls…" He studied Jim again, judging how to go on, "I'm just a middle man in all this. There's some very rough guys running this at the Bulgarian end. I'm not talking small-time criminals. I'm talking about guys with guns and with the protection of governments. And some of their men are here." Jim thought of the barker, thug in a track suit. "I don't mess with them. The girls are theirs."

"And what about the governments the other end? The ones that protect you in the West." Adding, for Damien's sake, "Let you carry corpses across borders."

"Button it about that. It's going nowhere." That curtly dismissed, Finch eased back with an exploratory question, "What did the girls say to you?"

Jim considered him before answering, "Couldn't really understand them. Their English was poor. What about my phone call?"

Finch ignored this, "Your Gizande seems to have understood them well enough."

Resentful of the sneer made in pairing them, Jim snapped, "She's not my Gizande."

"Well, whoever's Gizande she is- she seemed to understand them."

"Look. The phone call. Can't this wait?"

"What phone call?" Back to his creepiest, Jim thought. "You mean the one that was waiting for us? He'll be cut off by now. Haven't you heard about the phones here? There's only a handful of lines that go across the Iron Curtain, and the Stasi listen in to all of them. It took me a fair bit of work to get your Julian's call through. And you've blown it." He walked away, time for Jim to consider this, before slowly coming back. "I can get your Julian back on the line... probably. But, get this. If my Bulgarian friends find out that two of their little whores have been talking out of turn- and they find out I knew about it and didn't tell them...Then? It would certainly make things difficult for me. Even painful." A pause, "Know what I mean?"

"They just said they were unhappy. It was us that offered to take them with us."

"Us? Or just your lady?"

Jim said nothing, wondering how to reply. Remaining loyal to her, as well as credible. Or just let loose with the angered disgust at the man? But the pause was too long.

"There. Not exactly jumping to her defence, are you? It was crystal clear. Get this out of the way and we can get back to phoning Julian again, can't we?"

"What do you want me to say?"

"Oh, Jim," the performance of weariness. "You really don't get it, do you? You had the chance of getting Stephen. We could have done a deal. It suited us to get shot of him. He's not our material. Not bright, to say the least. He'll do anything we ask him to do, but... it's all a game to him. Not many punters go for wall-to-wall giggling with their sex. Yes?"

The image so visible of Stephen, the intolerable scum of it all, the slime of negotiating with this man, crawled nauseously up from Jim's belly, thickening his tongue with the taste of vomit, his body retching against it all. He staggered, as Finch swam before his eyes, clenched his throat muscles to hold it down, steadied himself and heard himself asking, as if from far away, "What will you do with him? If you don't let us take him."

"You answer that," in the cruelest voice.

Jim closed his eyes, drooped his shoulders with the faintness he felt, stepped back for support. Steadied against the cracked and dry leather of the vaulting horse.

"It's in your hands, Jim," spelt out coldly.

Raising his head, searching for air to breathe, up, beyond his reach, away from the stifling mustiness of the dust in his nostrils from old leather and wood, he was inhaling the recalled smell from his childhood of the cruelty of P.T. classes, the bellowed humiliations of the brutish ex-soldier who had drilled them. That however impossible the exercise, it was your stupidity to fail, again and again crashing and smashing your body to reach that point, the eternal hope for the "Well done," that was never spoken. And always, your own asinine fault it was never said.

"I have to know what the girls said, before you get your phone back."

And the enormous tiredness of not enough sleep- was it just last night, or how many stretching back it seemed? Like now, awake with his eyes closed against Finch, the doors blew open down a long corridor, all at once, to glimpse a slight figure at the far distance of the last doorway, uncertain in the dimness of the weak-bulbed and windowless half-light. Was it his young self, Jimmy? Or could it be Damien?

Eyes reopened, the lids peeled back from the eyeballs, Finch was still there. Cynically poised, but curious at the half-faint Jim was lurched awake from. Woken, to know that he could no longer. Consent to anything on offer from this slick and savage young man, vindictive and ruthless beyond his years. Jim pulled his steadying hand off the horse and stepped forward, but Finch was alert to the shift and started to dance back towards the door, eyes still on the swollen, surliness now clouding the older man's face. Who lunged, but only half-heartedly, stumbling free from the poisoned dialogue with this man.

"You fucking prat!" Finch whinnied, slipped the door open behind him slammed it and was gone.

Footsteps across the courtyard. Leaving Jim weak, enervated, stood amidst the broken rubbish of this place, feeling both released and defeated. Saving neither Stephen nor the girls, now was the time to save themselves. He looked at his watch. More than four hours before Andreas returned and they could get out of this place. He needed to be at least back with her.

"Fuck it!" his voice shocking the silent room. "Shit!" Angry at what he may have failed to do, but angrier that circumstance should have even dumped him here, in this dead-end of dilemmas, offering him only unreasonable choices.

Out of here! Find her. He pulled the door, but it was locked. Looking round, there was a window behind a tangle of broken chairs that tottered up towards the ceiling. Why had he been locked in? He began to panic for Gizande. He started to pull the chairs at the bottom of the heap away, but the metal legs were so twisted in amongst themselves that he threatened to bring the heap of them down on himself.

Back at the door, it looked weak enough, so he sought out a tool, something to lever it open with. Shifting junk aside showed a metal bar beneath, probably for weight-lifting, he supposed. He dragged the cold length of it out and weighed it in his hands. The first swing of it at the door only gave a skidding clunk against the wood. More carefully aiming at the joint of boarding to frame, he swung it this time twice, feeling its heaviness swing his whole upper body with it- until, a last wrench of a swing back, to slam the steel splintering deep into the wood. A split of light to the outside. He heaved the weight of the pole back again and forward, bursting the panelling. Putting it down, he pulled the door open, now confronting the open space of the yard and if he could remember the way back to the conference room. And Gizande.

Through the doorway opposite, he started to run up the corridors into the main building, from the noisy clatter of his shoes on the concrete, the slap of the linoleum, he had just reached the first stretch of quiet carpet, the reception vestibule visible ahead. Beyond, two girls in a group of men shouting, who spun round to see Jim, barely hesitate, driven on by the confused fury he was filled with. The barker and two other roughies, the girls Vanja and Julieta sobbing, beyond them Finch, his face nervous at last, backed away, lunging for him into the torrent of shouts, screams and oaths, Jim was pounded down, bloody-mouthed, fell amongst their feet, back curled against the hard thump of their shoes against him. Remembering to be relieved they wore trainers and not boots.

"Halten! Halten!" at last broke through the noise and the pain, Finch's voice. And they stopped. Just the sound of the girls crying and the sound of knocking on a door from somewhere. Relieved the kicking had stopped, the pain began to ebb back into the parts of his body. The blood in his mouth seemed to come from the back of his nose. The sharpest pain in the same lower back he had strained from shifting furniture in the

Dordogne.

"Auf!" from the barker, Jim's motionlessness earning him another warning kick, "Auf!"

Then Finch's voice, "They're telling you to get up."

Jim cautiously uncurled himself and looked up at the ring of faces above him. One of the girls, Vanja the speaker, was smiling between the shoulders of the men, her face fingermarked in red by a recent slap. He bent away from it, pushing up against the wall to unfold himself standing. The barker spoke to the two other Bulgars and one of them grabbed an arm each of the girls to push them off down the corridor, Vanja tilting her head back with a smile to Jim, "Good bye."

The knocking still on the distant door, Jim looked at Finch, "The conference room?"

"Out of my hands, now," Finch made the gesture of a powerless man. "You took it out of my hands, Jim. You asked for the impossible. I told you what these lads would be like if they thought you were messing with their girls. Nothing I can do now." A last look of rehearsed sympathy and sad regret for the foolish man he took Jim to be and he disappeared.

With Jim left to the Bulgarians, he sucked in his breath and bellowed, "GIZAAANNNDE!" Full-stopped by a punch below the ribs that buckled him, gasping, heaving for air, face pushed against his knees. Jerked upright, a man on each arm, they ran him away, stumbling off down the corridor, no answer to his cry, even the knocking stopped at the shock of Jim's voice in this silent building.

Chapter Twenty-eight

The whole period of his imprisonment could only be later recalled by Jim as some sort of unlikely and not entirely provable dream. In the telling, it took on a dubious heroism it had not actually had. He was first held in a locked and windowless storeroom by the Bulgars, somewhere near the gym, for he could hear the rhythmical noise of feet on a wooden floor and the harsh shouts of the trainers. When the door opened, it was two Volkspolizie, who marched him wordlessly out to an unmarked van. The van's closed back doors shut him into the seatless metal box, blind to the world outside and driven off. He had a fatalism to all this. After his fruitless charge down the corridor, action offered nothing. The unguessability of where he was going settled over him. Nothing for him to decide, nothing for him to do, but be driven wherever they took him. He just braced himself against the walls of the van to stop himself sliding round on the curving bumpy road down out of the forests. He guessed when the main roads were reached, straighter, with the occasional crunching pothole jabbing his pains. At least the flow of blood into his mouth seemed to have stopped and he spat out into a corner of the van to partly clear away the taste.

However much later, an uphill climb on the rhythmic discomfort of cobbles, before a stop and the remote sound of a brief exchange in German outside. The back doors opened, the two police dragged him out by his ankles and he saw they were inside a high dark building. Just that moment, before his head was stuffed into a rough cloth bag. A brief snap of shock at this, then his arms were held either side, not harshly, as if they knew the unresisting blankness that had overcome him and he let himself be led. Stone underfoot, dampness in his nostrils, the steps either side marched and, with only an occasional stumble, he matched their cadence. Footfalls ahead joined them, also in metronomic time and Jim started to swing to the rhythm of it, even a touch of delight at getting it right step-to-step, arms locked with his silent escorts. The sound of keys, door noise and the hood was stripped from him. Facing into the four-square, white-tiled, bright-lit cell, he passively let his jacket be slipped from his shoulders. A push in the back and the door crunched closed behind him. Before he could thank them.

Bed. Toilet. Walls. Sealed off from anything, he sat on the bed and rubbed his hand on the coarse texture of the blanket. The walls reflected only the blank, white electric light back at him in tile-by-tile portions. Saved the effort of speech, his head pulsed with the silence. As he knew he had not the language to speak to the police or whoever else here was now his guard, he also knew he had nothing to ask. Awaiting. Without guessing. It was all in the hands of others now. The closed and locked door relieved him of responsibility. For the first time in his life, or as far as he could remember, the dependence on unseen others gave him strength. The totality of his powerlessness. The meaninglessness of deciding anything now released him from the fear of getting it wrong.

Far up in the corner to the left, one of the tiles was cracked. Only one, and the cipher of it irritated him. The blemish made in the otherwise featureless box of light he sat in. Too far up to reach, it tried to shape a letter to him. To give a hint of meaning, get him guessing and it distracted him, so he turned his eyes away. But his mind ticked on at it… was it a T? Or an F, needing an extra cross to complete?… Or was it a J, his initial? He had to look back, but damned himself for it. Just a crack. Meaningless. So high up the wall, how had it cracked? When it was first put in, a lazy craftsman? Or had he no time to replace it. More probably. He looked down again, forcing his sightline no higher than the regularity of the wall before him, otherwise perfect and featureless floor-to-ceiling.

He lay back on the bed, carefully lifting his legs, so not to jab the pain in his back. But lying back, up in its corner, the imperfect tile faced him again. So he turned with a twist of discomfort to the wall and rested his eyes on the four tiles immediately in his face. And when his mind started to measure and compare the minute imperfections of the glaze tile-by-tile, the faintest ghosts in the grouting of the hand that laid them, he clamped his eyes closed again. Wanting sleep, which would not come. He looked for his watch, but it was gone from his wrist. In the kicking by the Bulgars? At first annoyed by it, he realised the loosening of this, released even from time. And it relieved him, slowing down his breathing, letting his eyes close themselves, he found himself a suspended place, comfortably enough at the edge of sleep, where wakeful consciousness began to blur, but not slipping far enough for the vivid cinema of dreams to start flickering across the insides of his skull.

So when the door opened, Jim sat up immediately- too quick to be comfortable for his back. To face a heavy built man in a tweed suit, red burn scar or birth mark running from his chins down into his tight shirt collar. Closed in the cell with him. From the remote and disengaged place where he sat, Jim watched the man circle the floor, eyes down, before he stopped, looked and said in a measured, almost bored tone, each question tipped with a querulous tail, "Brugge is your name, yes?"

"Briggs."

"What are you doing in the Deutsche Democratic Republic, Mister

Brigg?"

Answer the fact of it, simply. "I was visiting an Englishman." And taking on the ponderous precision of the man, added, "Mister Finch."

"Who gave you the authorisation to visit this Englishman?"

"No one," offered only as information, without apology.

The man considered this, as if an elaborate lie would have been more digestible. Took a turn of the cell, before, "Where did you enter our country?"

"Berlin."

"At which crossing point?"

"I don't know. There was a bridge."

"Who accompanied you here?"

Fruitless to lie, "Friends. Gizande- Madame Azéma. And Andreas." He left out Krommel.

"What is the complete name of Andreas?"

"I don't know."

He registered no surprise, but took another turn. "Where are these friends now?"

"Madame Azéma is-" hesitating, What was the time? Would Andreas have picked her up by now? "She was at the Hotel-" What was the name? He could only remember the English, "Hotel Youth Sport."

"What is that name?" for the first time, the harshened accent of the inquisitor.

"Hotel... Hotel Youth Sport?"

"Where is that?"

"I do not know. It is in the forest. The police know. They brought me here. From there." Does he really not know? Or a game? That Jim would once have played along with, but was too tired for now. So he just waited for the man.

Who nodded, continuing his circumnavigation of the floor. "The reason you were going to meet the English man, what was that?"

No easy answer to that one. "For business," he proffered.

"What was this business?"

Rape and murder, he thought, but offered, "Mister Finch is in the building industry. Construction."

But it was not enough for the man, who turned, stopped and fixed his eyes on Jim, as if he was now near to what he sought. But he only said, "Yes?" with sudden sharp penetration.

Jim was aware he was being forced over the line into deceit, despite the slumped reluctance of his spirit to play the game. He could only reiterate, "Mister Finch is in the building industry," starved of any inspiration.

"Is this only what you will divulge?"

Divulge? Where in his language travels had this man found the word? Said with the finality, as if Jim's lies were finally nailed. So, offering a bit more, "I was searching for a friend."

"What is the name of this friend?"

"Damien Toser?"

"This is an English name?" The man was now no longer circling and was not letting any detail of Jim's face out of his sight.

"Yes."

"Why would this Englishman also be in DDR?"

"He worked for Mister Finch."

"Do you also work for Mister Finch?"

"No." Firmly and definitely not.

"Why is Mister Finch also in DDR?"

Does the man know nothing? Or was Finch lying about the links with government people here? But it slipped away, trivial to how he felt now, only to shrug it off with, "I don't know." Maybe a lie, maybe not.

"Where is this Mister Finch?"

"He is at the Hotel."

"He is conducting his building industry in DDR?"

Another shrug, "I don't know."

"You say you come to meet Mister Finch for business. But also searching for friend. Which is the truth?"

"For the friend. For both."

"Where is your friend now?"

A pause, before Jim said, "He is dead."

This was too much for another immediate question, so the man walked another turn while he thought. Back at Jim, he asked, a weight to every word, "He is dead in DDR?"

"No." Confusion cluttered what he had wanted to be simple answers, "Yes. I do not know. He is in England now."

For the first time, the man was uncertain of what he was hearing, "He is in England? He is dead in England?"

"Yes. He is dead. In England."

"Why are you coming to DDR to find a friend, when he is already dead in England?" Asked not with any sense of having caught this Englishman out in a lie, the man was genuinely perplexed.

"To find the truth."

"The truth?"

"Yes. How my friend died," and he felt he had arrived at last at the point of giving this man a measure of the facts. Hoping that this would be enough to send him away. Let Jim curl back down on the hard bed again. But he doubted it, looking at the man's face, asking for more.

"Mister Finch knows about the dying of your friend?"

"I don't know."

"Have you asked him?"

"Yes."

"Why have you come to DDR for this? It is a question in England." Then, astonishing for Jim, "Are you not an English policeman yourself?"

"No!" arousing some momentary energy, that quickly drained.

"Did your friend die in DDR?"

"Perhaps. Some say yes. Some say no."

"What do you say?"

"I say yes. In Berlin, I think." Said without any sense that this would lead anywhere of use.

"What does Mister Finch say?"

Consider that one, before answering. "He says no." Did he say anything as crisp as that? He was not sure, but he was certain of the next, "Mister Finch is a liar."

Another turn round the room, then, almost casually offhand, "Are you not also a liar, Mister Brigg?"

Unsurprised at this, Jim considered it as a real question to be answered. But the ambiguities that had webbed themselves around him and his life allowed him only to reply, "Perhaps." Thinking, truth is not as simple as the policemen of the world would have it. Or as Jim himself would have once believed.

But the answer had been sufficient for the man. Who went to the door and knocked four times on it. It opened and he went out. Jim sat as he had been for several moments. Letting the tensions and the vibrations of the inquisition disperse from the room. Then he slowly lifted his legs again, turned to the wall, dragging the blanket across himself now as it had become colder, closed his eyes and tried to recapture that calm. Sat on the fence between the turbulence of sleep and the draining alertness of wakefulness.

Chapter Twenty-nine

When Gizande later asked him what he thought of in the cell, he could not exactly tell her. His waking mind was barely open. Or so it seemed. Ticking over at the barest register of thought, like the body of a hibernated mouse. It was where he hid himself in what seemed this deepest winter of his soul. So still on the bed that, even with just the cheap blanket about him, it sealed a gradual warmth about his body. Fear was somewhere in the room with him, hunting in the cold beyond the wrap of the blanket. But it remained formless, keeping its distance, unable to enter while he kept the doors of both sleep and sleeplessness closed and guarded. Later, in telling the story, he would try to calculate how long, but the eventlessness of lying there was unmarked for measuring.

Until he was taken to Klinsmaar.

Again, sat up at the first sound of the unlocking of the door.

The guard summoned, "Aus! Komm!"

Shrugging off the blanket, Jim got up, waited in the corridor while the cell was locked behind them and led off.

The room he was finally brought to was an office. Only the desk lamp was on, turned down to shine at the chair. Klinsmaar was leaned back against the desk front and there was someone else back in the shadows behind the desk.

"Please sit, Mr. Briggs," Klinsmaar's hand offering the chair, his voice harder than Jim could remember in Berlin.

He sat and tried to see the other face, but the light from the lamp was too immediate to see beyond.

"Where is Andreas?"

Surprised at this, Jim answered simply, "I don't know."

"Is he alone?"

"I don't know."

"When did you last see him?"

"This morning." Was it still the same day? So he added, "When we arrived at the Hotel."

"When will you see him again?"

"Tonight. At six o'clock." It must be past that now. "That was what was going to happen."

"Pardon?" an irritated edge at being diverted by uncertainty.

"I don't know the time. I suppose it's gone six now," more stated than asked.

"Will he be alone?"

"I don't know. He will have- Gizande with him, I suppose."

"Gizande? The woman you came to the office with?"

"Yes." Why did the man seem to know nothing of this?

"Where have they been?"

"Gizande was with me. Ask Finch. Andreas went away. I've already said I don't know where. He was coming back to collect us." He squinted up for what he could see of Klinsmaar's face in the half light and realised the man knew nothing of this.

"When did you meet with Mr. Finch?"

"This morning."

"Was he accompanied by another person?"

"Some Bulgarian trainers. Gym teachers. Coaches."

"Nobody else?"

How precise did he want it? The singing girls? The cooks? "Who do you mean?"

The silent figure shifted in his seat in the shadows and Jim glimpsed the red mark of skin going down inside the collar. Face-mark, he thought. And felt reassured.

Klinsmaar considered this question a moment, but opted for directness, "Have you seen Krommel?"

To tell all or not? He no longer understood the lies he was expected to keep, so, "Yes."

"When?"

"He was in the office. Last night."

"And after that? You have seen him after that?"

"Yes."

"Where?"

"He came with us." Then corrected, "We took him with us."

"Where did you take him to?"

"To the hotel. He knew the way. He waited outside." Then, to clarify, "I didn't drive. I was just a passenger," but on the saying, regretted it.

Klinsmaar responded to this, to Jim as himself for the first time, "So you were just the passenger, Mr. Briggs?" as if he had only been listening to his own questions up to then.

"Yes," feeling a slide towards deceit, "I did not drive."

"Ah, and I took you for one from der Runde Tisch?" And seeing Jim's incomprehension, "A knight from the table of your King Arthur?" Again, "But you do not understand, I see." Without explanation, he went on, "Was Krommel coming back with Andreas to meet you?"

"I don't know. I suppose so."

As Klinsmaar was shaping the next question, there was a knock on the door. He turned to the other man, who called, "Herein!"

From the corner of his eye, Jim could see a uniform. Who spoke in German to the Face-mark. Astonishment and what Jim took to be a request for some news to be repeated. Klinsmaar joined in the dialogue. Then looked down at Jim, "You must wait here for a few moments," spoke to Face-mark again and all three left the room.

Jim leaned over to shift the lamp's light out of his face, then sat back in the chair. Back into the inert and passive mood that had overcome him. Glad, for a few moments more, not to be the centre of anyone's attention. He closed his eyes. Waiting for someone to come for him, but hoping the wait would extend. Leaving him alone longer.

When it did end, it was only the uniform. Klinsmaar and the Face-mark had gone. But the guard was hurrying him, pushing him on several times, not the marching pace he had been earlier able to pick up along the corridors. He staggered a couple of times, even protesting once when the guard's push sent him shoulder-crashing into the wall. Back in the cell, even the door was slammed closed.

Before resuming the bed, he looked far up at the cracked tile and it was still there. He felt no hunger or thirst. Just the need for rest and retreat. The unyielding bed beneath him again, he lay down and pulled the blanket up round himself.

Klinsmaar came to the cell himself, alone, the second time. His smooth edges had been roughened by something. Maybe the news the guard had brought. He also circled the floor, as Jim's last interrogator had, but this was not the measured and reflective tread of Face-mark

Finally, he said, "You are in a dangerous situation, Mr. Briggs."

"Nothing I can do about it," Jim said flatly.

Not what the other man wanted to hear. Another irritated turn round the floor. "Have you the way of contacting Andreas- and Giz- the woman?"

Jim thought. But the question went nowhere. "At the hotel?" he offered. Then, "I can contact no one from here," indicating the box of white they were enclosed within together.

Klinsmaar took another tack, "You have things that you have taken from our office in Berlin."

Jim waited for him to clarify.

"There are papers. And a video tape," his eyes now sharp-set on the figure sat on the bed.

Jim's spirit sank. A real question. Needing a real answer. He shook his head before speaking. As if with regret. "Yes. We have the video. I know nothing of papers."

"Where is the video?"

"With friends. In Berlin." Then, an afterthought, "West Berlin."

"Hah! That bar?"

Foodi. How did he know that? But it needed no answer, so he sat continuing to watch Klinsmaar's expensive shoes working their nervousness out on the floor.

"Why did you steal the video recording?"

"Evidence," expressionlessly spoken.

Two circuits this time, until, "What will you want? For the return of the video?"

Another negotiation? Jim had little choice. But who was really the one who matters here? So he asked, "Why don't you ask Finch? He knows what we want?"

Another turn. "When did you last see Krommel?"

"Before we went into the hotel. I already told you."

"Why should I believe you?"

Puzzled at this, "Why should I lie?" There were things Klinsmaar was trying to dig for that Jim had not the least idea about.

"You lie because you do not understand the danger you are in. You are a prisoner of the DDR. You have heard of the Stasi?" Waiting for a response. Jim just continued to regard him back with passivity. "You think, because you are English, that nothing can touch you- that the great British Foreign Office will come to rescue you? They will not. You have entered DDR without permission. That is a crime in this country. Do you understand?"

Jim sighed, at having to repeat himself, "I did not lie."

Only a few feet away, but Klinsmaar was at the furthest corner of the room. Directly below the flawed tile. Examining Jim, "Ah. You have a belt for your trousers. In an English prison they take the belt from you, yes? And the laces from your shoes. Yes?"

Jim looked back, mildly quizzical at what was to come next.

"Do you understand why that is?"

You are going to tell me, he thought, but remained expressionless.

"As a prevention for the prisoner to take their own life." A pause for the weight of the next, "But you have been left with your belt, and your laces. Why is that?" Getting nothing back, Klinsmaar took a step forward. Threatening emphasis. "Evidence of how you will kill yourself."

Jim examined this and could only find absurdity. Smiling, despite himself.

"You smile! You do not believe in me?" Another step forward to impress, "That is how they will find you. With the belt round your neck. Dead in the cell." Then, oddly added, "Many will die like you now, in the days ahead."

The gravity of the words still ludicrous, Jim scanned the walls of the cell, then back to the man with, "But there's nowhere I can hang myself from," another smile, quickly switched off.

Klinsmaar showed disbelief at Jim's stupidity, "It is not you that will kill yourself. It is them," indicating the locked door. "They will do the hanging for you."

Should he really be worried? The smooth control of Klinsmaar when they had first met had now dissipated. Jim could no longer take the man seriously. "What do you want? I answer your questions. What more can I do?" Adding patiently, fragment-by-fragment of words, "You seem to want some sort of answers I can't give. I don't know where Krommel is. Or Andreas. And staying locked in here, I can't tell you any more. I can only tell you what arrangements we had made to meet. What happened when I wasn't there, I don't know." Now go away, he thought to himself, and take your threats with you. Jim just wanted to wrap himself in his blanket again. Finalising with, "Let me out, and maybe I can help you." If he could not rest undisturbed in this room, all he wanted was one where he could.

"The video tape," Klinsmaar taking another route. "You say that you discussed with Finch this?"

Regarding what the truth of this was, before answering, "Sort of. We started to talk about doing a deal." Why did he feel so locked into telling the truth to this man? He was just another one of the traffickers. Could they just delete him? Was the remoteness of it in the possibility of it happening, or just in the disengagement of his spirit?

"What deal?"

Summoning up the energy, "Finch has a boy. An English boy. We…" the right words? "…were arranging to get him back to England. It was a mistake… for the boy to be in Germany."

"So, what was Finch wanting in trade for this boy?"

From the acidity of the spat question, Jim began to realise that Klinsmaar was after something about Finch. He dragged his mind reluctantly to engage with this. To make an effort for his own liberation, perhaps. "We had only just started speaking about it. I was trying to make a phone call to England. To the people who want to arrange to get the boy back… home," this last word feebly inappropriate to cover whatever future Stephen might have.

"And, so?"

Jim shrugged, beneath it watching carefully now for Klinsmaar's response, "You know what the phones in this country are like. Kept getting cut off."

"Who are the people in England you talk to?"

"The Social Services. Someone in the Social Services authorities where the boy comes from," knowing who Julian exactly was, would not impress.

"They know you are here?"

"They know I am in this country. They know about the hotel. And Finch." Klinsmaar was now moving with a stiffer-legged edge of anxiety to his gait, so Jim pressed on, with assumed indifference, "They know about the set-up- the agency office. The flat in East Berlin. How the boys-" correcting himself for impact- "how the children are brought here." Finally chancing it with, "And the Bulgarian girls."

Klinsmaar spat a German word. At himself, or someone not in the room. Walked three steps up to the seatless toilet and looked down into it. As if seeking inspiration.

Then, decided, the strides back to the iron door and Klinsmaar hammered at it, turning with a brusque, "You will wait here, you understand?"

As if Jim had a choice, but he recognised the chink of possibility that some sort of release was buried in those words. Klinsmaar was gone through the door opened by the guard, who glanced in with a look of not unsympathetic curiosity, before crunching the metal home again.

Jim remained sat forward, as the other man had left him, waiting for the disturbances in the air of the room settle. He at last, lay down, turned to the wall, pulling the blanket folds close together over his eyes and slipping at last, notch by notch of losing consciousness, into deep sleep.

And the dream took him again…digging through the smeared mud at the roots that now clutched their suffocating bony grasps, dragging back from the stone slab of a door that offered opening to some hopefulness beyond, a slit of its light towards the woman hooded and shadowed in an unreachable corner of the great cold space of the room he wrenched himself free into, shot like a projectile upwards, high-speed down corridors, breathtaking last minute swerves at every corner, both chasing and chased by that cloud of threat, never quite discovered round every next racing zig or zag… his eyes wide awake and startled an inch from the white tile, his heart still galloping down the vertigo his mind had now fled. Shaken fragments of it in his head, he lay there, calming himself, trying to piece together meaning from them… Gizande? Probably.

He was unable to recapture the passive and stoical balance he had kept himself afloat on earlier. As if that sliver of hope he had read into Klinsmaar's last words had released him from that total and imprisoned dependence on others. Into the pendulum from expectation to despair. And back again. Examining for evidence in the most meaningless of dust.

And now, working on his expectations, he was hungry. Very hungry. And thirsty. His stomach shrunk in upon itself and his tongue rusty. Restless with it, he stood, walked over to the toilet. Looked down where Klinsmaar had, at the stained steel, walked to the door, wondered if to knock up the guard, thought better of it and walked back. Turned to check the cracked tile and the smile to himself may still have been on his lips, when the door was cranked open to let in Face-mark again.

Preferable as a person to Klinsmaar, but offering less hope? "Where is Klinsmaar?"

"He will not be returning."

Ask why? No. So, "I am hungry. Food. And drink."

"It will be arranged. Soon."

Really? Or just a postponement, to keep Jim engaged. "When? How soon?"

Obviously the prisoner's new assertiveness not expected, Face-mark took charge, "Sit!"

Jim stood a moment in confrontation, then went over to the bed. And sat on the edge, now alert with both his hunger and the change in climate this man's return had brought.

Stood still, Face-mark let the anger of the moment dissipate, measuring the prisoner with his eyes. Then slowly he slid his hand inside his jacket, freezing Jim to wonder if the banality of the gesture would produce a gun from an inside pocket. The hand hesitated, hid below the cloth, then slid itself out, an envelope between two fingers and a thumb.

"You are required to sign your name to this document," but even the borrowed language betrayed uncertainty. Or so he thought. "Do you speak Deutsch?"

"No." Obviously not.

He pondered a moment, then opened the unsealed envelope and pulled out several folded sheets. He peeled off the top copy, stepped up to Jim and held it before his eyes. Headed *Aussage*, it was all in German.

"What is it?" Jim asked.

"It is for your name to be signed."

"A confession?"

"No. Do you mean of crimes? No. No crimes," and he smiled down for the first time. "It is necessary for your release."

The suddenness of this parched Jim of words. "You will let me go?" Then, caution, to be crept upon by suspicion. "How do I know if I sign? That this is not a trick. To get me to sign for crimes, that I will then be kept here- as prisoner for?"

Face-mark pulled the paper away and studied the words himself, as if he had not thought of that. "You wish to return to your friends in Berlin, yes?"

A threat or an offer? Jim waited.

"I will take you to Berlin."

"To West Berlin?"

"Yes. To West Berlin."

Why? A trick? What about Gizande? Andreas? "I will not sign it until I am in Berlin, the West."

He considered this. "That is possible."

"What about my other friends? At the hotel?"

"I know nothing of them," a touch irritated. A prisoner daring to introduce such complications.

Jim backed off this, "Okay. You take me to West Berlin. I then sign," thinking he might come to a deal to solve the problems of the world within this white cell and no one would ever know the lies that had been told, he thought. Worth the try, whatever other games he may be contributing to.

"I will return. In a short time," turning to the door.

"Food?" Jim suggested. "And my jacket?" Passport and wallet.

"I will see what can be done," and he banged on the door for release.

Left back to the silence, it was retrospectively incredible. A deceit to soften him. To draw him out. Klinsmaar would probably return now, with his angered contempt. But to get to Berlin? Yet knew he had no alternative but try out the offer.

Chapter Thirty

He did return. An hour perhaps? With a guard carrying his jacket, with a clipboard for him to sign. This time a receipt, he supposed. He checked first that wallet and passport were still there, signed this and the guard left him alone with Face-mark. No watch.

"You've brought me no food."

"Later." He was agitated, nervous as he spoke, thinking of other things. "You are still my prisoner. Until we reach Berlin-"

"West. Berlin," Jim specified, almost as a question. To test how far this was going from words said in this room, translated to reality outside? Possible?

"Yes. Your name on the papers will be the finish. You can go then. To your friends." Adding the afterthought, "You will have your copy of the paper, also."

This is real? To give him time to think what next, Jim idly opened his wallet. All there, but the Deutschmarks were gone.

Defining the reality a little further, "What time do we leave?"

"I have some little preparations to make before."

"Can I have food? While I wait."

"I will see." An unimportance to him, he shifted to, "You will not speak to others, you understand? You will not speak anything to the other police." Severely, "You understand?"

"Yes. Can I speak to you?" doubtful what there would be to say, his head now filled with the expectations of a journey out of here and back into his life, that really seemed to be taking shape. He slid his arms into the jacket sleeves. Like buttoning his skin around himself again. A thought of Julian. What would he be thinking now? Stephen. Returning to Berlin without the boy. Lost him, as he had lost Damien too.

Face-mark had ignored Jim's last question. "I will ask for the guard. You will follow, as the prisoner. You will not speak to me, you understand? Say nothing. We will go to the car. Understand?" Then, a belated afterthought, "If you wish to speak to me, it will be after we have left. When we are alone in the car. You understand?" Then, again, looking at Jim curiously, as if seeing the person for the first time, "You have something you wish to say now? Before I call the guard."

Blank for a moment, about to shake his head, Jim relented, "Yes. What's your name?"

The man considered the question, before, "You have no need to know my name. You will know it in Berlin." Finally, with a hint of sly and private humour, "To you, I am the Ministry of State Security," full-stopping the dialogue by turning to knock on the metal door.

Face-mark you will stay, then.

Out in the cold, Jim's eyes took moments to accustomise to the sunlight. Face-mark was busy putting cardboard boxes into the boot of his large, old limousine. The courtyard was walled round with the shabby grandeur of the ancient barracks. Mesmerised by being outside his prison, Jim drifted over to a grass bank. Beyond, the stone fortifications jutted out over a city, a cluster of spires on an opposite hill like a handful of arrows, beneath, a wide square, crowds gathered, flags hanging from windows. Two policemen scanned the scene below with binoculars.

"Komm!" It was Face-mark. His guard? Or his rescuer? Nothing Jim could do, but be taken. Wherever. He wandered back to the car, now slumped on its suspension with the weight of boxes Face-mark was closing into the boot

He indicated two boxes still on the cobbles beside the car, "Inside. On the seats at the back."

Jim lifted one, heavier than he thought possible for its size, and dumped it on the seat. As he lifted the second, he felt the bottom of the box give, tried to rush it onto the seat too. But it split. Spilled brown-cover files around his feet. Frozen what to do next, he looked down at the one on top of the heap. Frayed thin card, with over-thumbed sheets of faded typing poking from inside. A sticker on the front read *Archivakte*, then some numbers.

"Heilige scheisse!" Face-mark was round beside him, angry for the first time, "Blodmann!" Then for Jim's benefit, hissed, "Idiot! Pick them up quick!"

Jim gathered them up, sheaf by sheaf of them and shovelled them into the footwell of the car's back seat. The other man was looking round the courtyard. Some policemen across the other side loading a lorry with black bin bags, paid no attention.

"Come! Now," closing the back door, indicating Jim to get in, he went round to the driver's seat. Jim sat silent while the car started. The other man was clearly rattled, ground the gearbox and jerked off too fast. A policeman by the lorry looked over, casually curious. Under the portcullised gateway, a guard with a machine gun slung across his large belly came out, glanced at the identity card Face-mark offered and with a nod. Let them go.

The narrow cobbled road beneath the fortifications, rising above them as they descended. The crowds in the square, a blur of happy faces, some maybe singing or chanting, were behind them as he accelerated the car away.

"What is happening?" Jim asked.

Without looking back, his eyes on the street ahead, "The fools are happy."

Jim felt further clarification was uninvited and looked out at the buildings in a run-down part they were now passing through. Dirty peeled plaster. An empty factory, weeds growing from its gutters. Then they were out into suburbs of stacked blocks of flats, before the country. And Jim started to dare himself that this man, for whatever reason he had, might deliver him back over the Wall.

After about an hour, the car stopped in a Rastplatz beside the road. Face-mark drove the car to the furthest end, away from several lorries, their drivers animated together. Jim watched him get out and walk round to open the back door. He tidied the broken files on the floor and covered them with a blanket.

When they set off again, Jim tentatively asked, "What were those? Can you tell me?"

Face-mark looked over at him, then back on the road, continuing to drive, until, "While you were our guest, Mr. Brigg, the world has changed. The fools have taken over our country. Stolen it."

"What do you mean?"

"You will see," said in a final snap shut.

And looking for signs, as they drove on, Jim started to wake to them. Cars with flags fluttering out their windows, a slogan fresh painted on a bridge over the road with a crowd of young people cheering the traffic beneath. Flurries of celebratory horn sounding from cars rushing the other way.

"What is happening?"

"That- those are the fools, Mr. Brigg!"

"What do you mean?"

"You will see most in Berlin." Then looking across, "The war is over."

"What war?"

"No. Not war. I say, the Wall is over. Down. Finished. Kaputt. You understand?"

Jim dwelt on this, a big impersonal idea a long way from where his mind had been. "How?" was all he could come up with.

Face-mark shrugged, "It is not important how. The Great Anti-Fascist Barrier is no more," he said bitterly.

"What will you do? You are-" holding back from the word Stasi, "you are State Security." Then, the files, "Those are police files? Where are you taking them?"

"Maybe they are police files. Maybe not. What trouble is it for you? You are going home to the West, ja? Why do you worry about that?" Eyes back on the road ahead, "Too many questions. You have your seat in the car. That is enough."

The signs showed Berlin closer now, but all was cryptic till they had crossed back through the suburbs. Long before the checkpoint was even in sight, they joined a long queue of mostly smoky Trabi cars. Hundreds were walking past towards the Wall, fewer returning, weighed down with bright carrier bags, cheering the drivers, waving bottles of beer, German flags at them. Face-mark wound up the window. Against the fumes, as well as to close out the celebratory scenes around them. When the Wall came in sight, there were silhouetted figures stood along the rim of it against the feeble afternoon sun. Border guards? No. For as they crept onwards, the guards were looking upwards, remonstrating at the young people stood or sat along the top of the Wall itself, hundreds of them, looking down into the East. Chanting, arguing, singing at the forlorn and serious men in uniform beneath them. Behind whose backs the whole of their city seemed to be emptying its population through the constricted neck of the border post buildings into the West.

"So it's gone. Anyone can cross?" Jim asked, not taking his eyes from the crowds, drinking in the freedom that had become his as well.

"It has gone," with regrets. "You also in the West will look back on this day with sorrow."

Looking at the man, "No. Why?"

"You will wish the frontiers again. We kept the East out of Europe. The Wall also was a wall against the Slavs. It only let across what you wanted in the West. Not the garbage."

"It's letting what you would call garbage now- isn't it?"

"That is the tragedy. For the world. We were part of your Europe too. Part of the civilisation of Europe. We stopped them from the East."

"Stopped who? You were under the Russians. Under their heel."

A youth, barely supported by a girl almost as drunk as him, hammered grinning on the roof of the car and lurched away, thumbs in the air.

"We were between the Russians and the West. The Wall, it was our idea. The idea of Ulbricht. We stopped the volkerwanderung. We stopped it."

"Volk- what? What's that?"

"The wandering of the people. The migration. From Asia," hissing the last word. "It was this destroyed Rome. Ended the civilisation."

"Ah. Volker… what was that?"

"Volkerwanderung," he repeated.

Folk wandering, would that be? Jim pondered, then said it, "Folk wandering. What beautiful words. That's what we need more of. Like these people here," and he indicated the panorama of joyousness around them, suddenly no longer an observer, but part of it. "We all become folk wanderers!"

And smiled on determinedly through Face-mark's curt, "Fool."

"Well, you are wandering to the West, too. Why not?" Immediately filled with the generosity of spirit surrounding them, Jim wound down the window, letting the uproar of sound break in around and between them, washing out the spite of the man next to him.

"Close the window! The stink of the Trabis."

Looking back at him a moment, Jim wound it back up with studied reluctance.

"When we are in the West, where will you be left?"

"I don't know. Where are you going? My friends are in the Wedding district."

Considered. "Too far," and rejected. "I will leave you by the Tiergarten. You know that?"

"No."

"It is near the zoo. You will find there the U-Bahn for Wedding. You understand?"

"Yes. The underground," but decided not to tell him of the theft of all the Marks from his wallet. By his fellow-policemen. He would walk. He thought it was close to where he and Gizande had run up the Brandenburg Gate that morning. An age ago, it seemed. Confirmed by the history he was sat jammed in the middle of. Near to release by this man with his carful of files, off to do some deal with the lives within them. The habit of a lifetime of buying and selling other people, probably.

Chapter Thirty-one

Jim had signed the four copies of the document on the roof of the car, but to his request for Face-mark's name, the man would only say, "Look. It is on the paper." Slamming the door with a grin through the window, before bumping down off the kerb and into the city traffic. Leaving Jim to look at the copy floating in the breeze in his hand, only able to guess from the crowding of German capital-lettered words which could have been the man's name. If any.

Anna would tell him and he set off to walk his way if he could find it, to Foodi. He was by the park he had run past with Gizande and started to retrace what he remembered of the way back. A sports centre, a bridge over railways, landmarks back. A wrong turning, a backtrack and he saw his old van parked distinctively far along the street, topping its blue roof above the cars parked around it. As he came up to the café, he saw the crowds inside, the banner across the inside of the windows, *WILLKOMMEN OSSIS WILLKOMMEN, OSSIS* taped over where *GIZI* had been written a few days ago. And under it, another strip of cotton pinned on, with *Wir Sind Das Volk!*

Jim entered and looked around at the noise, the crowd round the bar, empty glasses and spilled beer on every table. He started to move through, weaving a route between animated groups, the air thick with cheap tobacco.

"Jim! Ahhh, Jim!" Anna saw him before he saw her and she pushed through the crowd to crush him to her, closing his eyes against the spiked hair. And hugging her back, suddenly weak with it, sucking into himself the unqualified affection of her welcome.

"Oh, Anna," he rubbed his face slowly down into her shoulder. "Good to see you again."

She pushed him away, holding his shoulders to get a good look at him, both wry and fond, "Where have you been? We have all been so worried."

"I think I've been with the Stasi."

"You think! You mean you do not know?" And she laughed, "Only an Englishman could speak of the Stasi so!"

"I was in prison. But they did not hurt me." Then he smiled at her, feeling like a small boy home late, "But I am very hungry."

"The bastards starved you?"

"No, no," he reassured, thinking of nothing so crude done by Face-mark. "They just forgot to feed me."

Anna's eyes widened with astonished mirth and started a long laugh that shook through her body. Others stopped to watch her heaving and jellying backwards with it, looking from her to Jim to see what sort of joke his sombre figure could have resulted in what was happening to her. Finally whinnying herself out of the laughter, half-breathless, she spurted out in staccato gasps, "The Stasi- they forgot- to feed you!" looking around at the faces for validation of the absurdity of what Jim had said. But they were blank with incomprehension. "Ah! Ossis! They are from the DDR. They do not speak English." She pulled Jim's arm and he followed her to the bar. "Sit." Then, shouting through to the back, "Karla! We have a hungry Englishman to feed! Jim has returned. From the Stasi! They forgot to feed him!" laughing again at him.

Karla looked through from the kitchen, "Jim! You are okay?" Not waiting for an answer, "What will you eat? We have Schweinefleisch- what is that?"

"Pig-meat," Anna translated.

"Pork," Jim took it further. "That'd be fine."

"And potatoes?" Karla added.

"And everything, for Jim!" Anna gestured generously. Then, "A beer. A big beer," pulling a tall glassful for him. Customers were pressing round him at the bar and Anna shrugged, "I wish to talk and talk to you, but-" gesturing the room around them- "it is the thirsty Ossis. We give them free beer the first day after the Wall. They have great thirst for our Wessi beer! We will speak later. So much to say, Jim!"

And so much for him to ask. He sat on at the counter to drink that glass, but he was too weary for all the barging of other drinkers. For his second beer and for Karla's deep dish of pork stew, he sat at the corner of a table of increasingly drunk young men and women. He ate it quicker than the dish deserved, then returned to the bar.

"Anna!" catching her attention. "I'm tired. Can I have the key to the flat?"

"Of course. Naturellement," pulling it off her key-ring. Remembering, "Ah. Gizi. They are okay. They are still in DDR. They will make phone call tonight." Then, with that knowing grin, "She will be so surprised."

Content at that and too tired to say anything else, he just nodded, took the key and went upstairs, closing the door on the rowdy celebrations. Wishing he could be as sure of Gizande as her friend seemed to be in her coarse and confident way. But settled a little at least with the news that she was safe, even if it was safety with Andreas.

In the flat, he was restless. He wanted to talk, to have someone's undivided attention to his story- to have Anna hear what he had to say, explain the bits he could not, interpret some of the fragments of German nuggeted in the tale, to translate Face-mark's document… and also? No, for that, he knew he would have to wait for Gizande. To confirm the truth of it, to validate what they had witnessed, what Finch had said… and what was next to be done, if anything… only her. And Stephen. Had he ever been as close to- what to call it?- recapture?- as Finch had led them on to believe? And Krommel? Just another part of the grinder, chewing up the lives of those young people? He was out of the tiled cell, where there had been no choices to make. Just for twenty four hours, had it been? No watch.

He checked the kitchen clock.

That late?

Now, like the young and unaware Ossis celebrating down stairs, Jim was back in the world where choices pressed upon you, both the good and the bad. Realising that the temporary imprisonment of his body had also been the temporary liberation from a universe of dilemmas. Relief even from fear, when there had been nothing he could do about it.

He went into the bathroom and started to fill the bath, his head leaned into the clouds of steam. Cleansing, but unable to rinse away what he remembered, his memories. Those stripped children shuffling into line alongside him, comrades into the darkness that would never leave them. Marked by the crimes against them, like a tattooed number on the inside of their skulls. Shame and anger. The boys from Northlodge and Whispering Pines, the girls from Bulgaria, for whom Jim himself had impossible responsibilities. And Stephen, whom he had failed in this. Joining Jim himself, in the same naked inspection.

The cold stirred in, he climbed into the water and drew it soothingly up his body, a sheet of calm. He settled the enduring ache at the bottom of his back for comfort and lay still, the events since he had left France for England, so long ago it seemed, just short of three months. He would need to sort out getting some regular income when he returned. But too trivial and remote to be thinking about now.

Restless to stay long in there, he found that Anna had washed and pressed some of his clothes and neatly folded them back in his holdall. Fond of her for that thoughtfulness, dressing himself, thinking of that cheeky certainty she seemed to have about him and Gizande. Nobody who saw them together thought anything else. Except themselves. Should he be decisive with Gizande? How would that be done with a woman like that? No sweeping her away manfully, he thought ruefully.

He turned on the t.v. It was the Wall. Of course. Crowds around it, all over it, near the Brandenburg Gate. Would this last? Or would an eruption of tanks from out of those drab streets behind end it all? He looked closer, attentively. Young men were patiently chipping away at it with hammers, chisels, one even with a pickaxe, delicately working away at each weakness in the concrete. The camera shot flicked to the crowds still queuing at a checkpoint through to the West, more patiently it seemed and less celebratory than earlier in the day. It looked unstoppable, confirmed for Jim when the camera flicked back to the Wall and a group were cheering round a deep gash that had been cut through. Zooming in to see a chink of the spotlights from the other side glinting through to the West. So soon and so easy, Jim thought. Or had it taken the forty years of the DDR to reach this point? Or even longer, centuries for these people to get here? How long to learn to say No? The screen images blurred in front of him, as he remembered his own saying No, forty years ago. The refusal to tolerate another rape in that room. The event that had made him whom he had become. He knew that now. Just as, whatever happens in the lives of these young people chipping away at the cement now, or drinking downstairs in the bar, this would be their measure. A high point against which everything to come would be set against.

The phone rang. He stared at it, waiting for Anna to answer it downstairs. Gizande.

The door at the bottom of the stairs opened, flooding in the noise from the bar with full force. "Take the phone, Jim. It's for you," and she slammed the door closed.

As he put it to his ear, he heard the click downstairs.

"Hello. Jim?" It was Andreas. "Hello?"

"Where's Gizande?"

"She is in the car. We have Stephen. She is with him."

"Stephen?" in a ghost of a voice.

"Yes. We have him. Your Finch brought him out to us. He is totally drugged."

Who is? "Finch is?"

"No. Stephen. Finch says he is a crazy boy. Maybe they make him so."

Absorbing this, before awake to her, "Is Gizande okay? Is she safe?"

"Yes," not total certainty in that. "He is calm now. She hold him like a child. He likes that. But how long the drug last…? We do not know."

Summoning his imaginination to visualise this, he could not. "Where are you?"

"We are in Arnstadt, where my friend is. You remember we

stopped there before the hotel?"

"When will you be back?" thinking of the call he must make to Julian as soon as he was off this call.

"We will be leaving now. We will be in Berlin in the morning, early hours. Can you or Anna be awake for us? How easy is it to go through the Wall?"

"I think they are beginning to tear it down. Easy. The guards are not bothering to check anyone properly, there's just too many going through."

"No trouble from the Vopos? No shooting."

"No. They just seem to be standing there and watching."

"It will be easier to get to West Berlin in the middle of the night. There will be few people."

"Don't bet on it. They've been arriving here, at Foodi's all the time. I don't think anyone in Berlin has been sleeping."

A laugh at the end of the phone. "Crazy city. I love it!"

Irritated by this, by its untimely inappropriateness, Jim full-stopped it with waiting silence.

Andreas picked this up and said, "I must go. We must come home." Then, an afterthought, "Stephen will need a room to sleep in. Anna has only one bedroom. Will he use that?"

"I'll ask her," thinking, where will Gizande sleep? Before stuffing that away, both ashamed and reluctant of the absurd hope.

"Okay. See you in the morning. Early." And he was gone.

He put the phone down, went for the book from his jacket for Julian's number.

It rang at the other end for a long time. Late for them. Awaking Adam?

Finally Trish's voice, "Who is it?"

"Jim. Sorry it's so late."

"Oh, Jim. What time is it?"

He looked at his wrist, for the missing watch. "Don't know. Is Julian there?"

"He's in sleeping with Adam tonight. His shift. I'm sleeping on the divan. I was. He hasn't been sleeping-" finding it funny, adding, "Adam hasn't been sleeping, that is."

"So I can't speak to him?"

"No. Sorry."

"Can you take a message?"

"Sure. Wasn't Jules trying to get you at some East German number? They cut him off." Then, suddenly waking to where Jim was,

"What's it like out there? Are you still in the East? Have you heard about the Berlin Wall?"

"I'm in Berlin. Some friends are on their way from the East with Stephen. He sounds like he's a mess."

"What do you mean?"

What did he mean? Only Andreas's fragmentary account of things. "Not sure. But we need to know how Social Services are going to get him back. To England."

"Really? Will they do that?"

"I don't think they can afford not to."

The silence of her thinking, the other end of the line, then, "I'll wake Jules. See if I can do it without waking Adam. Can you hold on?"

"Yes." Adding, "I'm dead sorry about this, Trish," but she had already gone.

On the t.v., an overweight politician was making a speech. Jim turned the volume down.

A rattle as the phone was picked up, Julian's voice still disoriented from waking, "Jim? Where are you? Are you back in Berlin with Stephen?"

"No. Not yet. He's on his way. I've just spoken to friends who've got him," suddenly a jab of doubt about being totally dependent on Andreas for the truth. "They say they should be here in the early hours of the morning."

"How is he?"

"Who? Stephen?"

"Yes. Of course."

"He's drugged. Sedated."

"Why? What's wrong?"

"That's how- that's the state they were given him. By Finch- Billy Finch."

"Do you know what drug it is?"

"No bloody idea. But we're not looking forward to when he comes out of it."

"Why not?"

"Come on, Julian. Why would they sedate him if there wasn't some reason. Finch says Stephen is crazy."

"Crazy?"

"Yeah. I don't know what that means. But you've got to get someone out here to pick him up as soon as possible. Do Social Services know all this is happening?"

"As much as I knew yesterday. I got to see Cathcart. She wasn't happy about it, but Huntley's had an article in the paper about Stephen's case and they're all shitting themselves on the top floor, because they know he's due in court and that they won't be able to produce him."

He tried to imagine Sylvie's face as she had listened to Julian. Astonishment? Or steely hardness? "Does she know it's me that's involved in all this?"

"No. They may guess, I suppose. I just told her I'd tell her more when I got confirmation."

"Well, I guess this the confirmation."

"Do you think I should wait until you've actually got Stephen there? When it's definite."

"When we've got the body? No. Let her know now. We need to get him out of here as soon as possible. We've got a one bedroomed flat over a bar to keep him in and God knows how he'll be when he comes out of the drugs. Someone needs to fly over here and we'll get him to an airport."

"Has Stephen got a passport?"

"Christ! I don't know. Didn't ask. I'll phone you again when they get here and tell you. But don't wait till then to let someone know what's happening. They need to be getting things organised first thing tomorrow." Then, an inspiration, "Tell Cathcart- will you be speaking to her?"

"She told me to phone the out of hours number, who'll get her and she'll phone me back here."

"Well, you tell Sylvie Cathcart that it's Jim Briggs who's got Stephen and if they piss us about, I'll be phoning the papers in England from here. And not just Huntley, but the nationals would love this. Think what the Sun or the Daily Mail would make of this mess. Made by social workers, their favourite aunt sallies!"

"Steady on. I can't be threatening her. She's my boss."

"She may be yours, but she's never been mine. Tell her it's from me." Satisfied at having set this cat among those pigeons. "Come on. Enough of this chat. It's burning up valuable time. Have you got this number here?" Jim gave it, adding, "West Berlin. Don't know what the international code is. Get back to us as soon as you can. Hope you're going to charge the Council for all these international calls you're making on their behalf."

"No chance. I'll ring you back."

With the phone down, Jim smiled. He felt back, giving some steerage at last to events. He sat down again in front of the t.v., but his mind was away from the history being made on the screen. Getting back at Sylvie. The crudity of revenging hurt feelings.

He had half-dozed off when Anna at last came up from the bar and flopped into the armchair. "We have sent the Ossis home at last. We have been open, without stop, for forty hours. It is time for break."

"It must've been mad, here."

"It was. Like the whole city is crazy!" Then, remembering something, "Oh, yes. The British Police came here. The Army Police?"

"The Military Police? Red caps?"

"No. They were not in uniform."

"What did they want? What right have they got coming here?"

"Huh! You do not know! Here, we are still under the occupation. The British and the Americans- and the French- they can imprison us, if they wish. They can listen to our phones. One of your generals said he was the rightful successor to the Third Reich and our laws can not touch him."

Jim grinned, with disbelief.

"No! It is true, Jim!"

"Well, what did they want here?"

"I think they wanted that video recording. The dirty one of the boys you got from that man- was his name Krommel?"

"Yes," wondering what was happening to him. No mention of him from Andreas. "What about the video? Did they get it?"

"No," she smiled, too tired for the grin required. "Of course Anna had it hiding, in a safe place," and put her finger to her lips. "I will give it to you, before you go from Germany. But what has happened to you?"

Because he was not sure of the whys and the whos pushing him about in those two days in the East, he did not know how to start. Then remembered Face-mark's document. "Oh, I got given this," pulling the paper from his jacket. "It's from the bloke who rescued me from the prison," sounding far more dramatic then the memory of events.

She looked over it, then looked up at Jim, "It is-" then down at it again to check. "It is from an officer in the Stasi. He says he free you from prison."

"There. I told you that. Does it say why?"

"It says that you were in prison against the laws."

"Who is it to?"

"It is for the… attention? The attention of the senior officers of the Police in West Berlin and the officers of the armies of the Allied Powers. And this is your name written at the bottom?"

"Yes." Had he done something wrong, signing it? "It didn't seem anything wrong with putting my name to it."

"You mean you did not understand what you were putting your name on?" She shook her head.

"Was I wrong? What will he use it for?"

"I do not know. To prove he is a good Stasi?" and a short dismissive laugh.

"He also had files with him. Boxes of them."

"Ah! So, that is why. A clever man who understands the falling of the Wall. That it is the end of hiding behind it with their crimes. So he will buy himself out with files."

Feeling that he had partly colluded, Jim said, "Well, I wasn't going to get out of their prison any other way."

Anna looked up at him again from the paper and studied him, "No. This perhaps was the only way. It is like this always. If you sign anything for a policeman, you feel that he will use it for something else. That is true both sides of the Wall."

"What was his name?"

"Narbefleische. Gunther Narbefleische. Where did he go? When he left you."

Jim shrugged, "He just dropped me in the centre of the city. And I walked." Gunther. Where are you now? Doing a deal with other people's lives.

Then she remembered, "The phone call from Andreas. They will be here in the morning with the boy, yes?"

"Yes. We need to use your bedroom to let him sleep. He has been drugged."

"Will you really be able to get him back to England?"

"We have the authorities there planning it now," but he thought of the reality, Sylvie woken- sleeping next to whom, a savage inserted thought- her panic, all her slick charm frightened away. "I am waiting for a phone call. It will come soon, I hope."

Anna rose, heavy with her exhaustion. "Well, I will sleep on my bed, until they arrive. It will be the last time I sleep there for some days, I think."

"Sorry."

She laughed, "Oh, Jim. Always sorry." Then, "You should be sorry. Since you arrive in my home, all the trouble you bring with you. You bring here Krommel as a prisoner, the British Army search my rooms. I think it is you that bring the Wall down, also. Nobody thought that the Wall would be finished on the day you came to Berlin. Now, look," indicating the t.v. screen, "Phutt! It is all gone." And she laughed. "I will see you when they arrive with the boy. I hope it is a long journey, for my sleep. No. I joke. I will see you later."

Chapter Thirty-two

Andreas let them into the bar and through to the flat with Gizande's key, Jim presumed. He had been woken from dozing by the door downstairs. He sat numbed, waiting mostly to see her, but dimly aware that there would probably be no time together for the next few days.

Andreas appeared first, with a falsely light-hearted, "Hi!" to Jim.

Then Gizande, with her arm round Stephen, his mouth agape, eyes shooting around the room, then alighting on Jim and smiling broadly for a second, before flickering off, frightened. Jim stood up- to do something- turned to go to wake Anna, but she was already in the bedroom doorway in a robe, watching Stephen too.

"Gizande," Jim stepped towards her to help, but Stephen turned to him, the smile returned, reaching out arms. Jim stopped, backed off.

"Hilfe, Anna," Gizande said. "Jim, you stay back." Then to Anna again, "Schlafzimmer."

And the two men watched the women take the boy through.

Jim turned to Andreas, "He's no longer drugged?"

Andreas whistled softly through his teeth, "No. He is no longer drugged." Then turned away and continued, "No. He attacked me. He is dangerous, I think. But he does not speak."

"What's wrong with him?"

"What is wrong?" Andreas considered that, "He is- how do you say- mental defective?"

"Mental handicap. But he can speak. I have heard him."

"Yes. But he has also been sexually attacked too many times. No, attack is wrong. He has been exploited sexually by others. Many times." Jim remembered Finch. Stephen as wall-to-wall giggling? "He tries to attack in the trousers. He thinks that- all men wish to have him play with their penis. You understand? He is now mad with it." Nodding towards the bedroom, where Stephen's voice could be heard, crying out softly beneath Gizande's gentle cooing of his name, "Only Gizande can keep him quiet. She hugs him," smirking back knowingly at Jim.

The phone rang at that moment. Jim went for it, hesitated, then thought it would likely be Julian at this time of the morning. Whatever that was, still dark outside.

But he answered with, "Ja?" just in case.

"Jim?"

"Yeah."

"Cathcart's phoned back. They will start arranging for getting

Stephen back as soon as the offices open."

"He's just arrived. They've just brought him in."

"How is he?"

Jim looked over at Andreas, who was listening. "He's attacking men. Trying to get into their trousers, I'm told."

"What?" Julian's disbelief.

"Your lot needs to move quick. All we've got is a tiny flat here. We can contain him maybe, but that's all. Oh, and make sure they send women over to collect him. He doesn't attack them." Then, emphatically, "Now will you believe me, what they've done to these kids?"

"Jim, I always did. I always did believe you."

"Sorry." A miserly apology, Jim enlarged with, "No. I'm sorry. It's just… we've got the body, so-to-speak. And we need it shifted-" suddenly jerked to a halt by the image of Damien, his corpse smuggled away from this city. To be left in a derelict building, chewed by rats. "What will happen to Stephen, when he gets back?"

"Don't know." And the silence between them was heavily and mutually knowing. Before Julian covered it over with, "He'll go to court."

Jim wanted to know, but he knew that pressing hard on that would mean following the boy back to England. And another campaign, he knew he would not be fighting. He would have to turn his back on this one. And leave it to people he did not trust, while he went back to France. To sort out his own life.

"Has Stephen got his passport?"

"I don't know. I'll phone when I know. They're just settling him down, now."

"Who's with you?"

"A German guy. The woman who's flat it is." And Gizande? "A French woman, who came with me. To Berlin." Covering his reluctance to say more with, "The two women. They're settling him down. Like I said, it needs women to calm him. Okay? I won't be leaving this phone. I'll call you about the passport. And you ring me, when you hear anything."

When he turned from putting down the phone, Andreas was still looking at him, wryly.

"Well, Jim Briggs, I must be leaving now. I will leave you… with the French woman who came with you to Berlin. I have wasted much time on this," indicating the bedroom doorway. "There is much to do in Germany today. In the DDR, Stalinismus is ended. There is now the opportunity to build a true socialist society there." Switching to contempt with, "Maybe that is something that is forgotten by the English working classes, with their Maggie Thatcher?"

What to say to that? Just a feeble, "I'm no friend of Thatcher."

"Hah! It is the way of the British man. He likes to have orders from his women. In politics and in the bedroom- always the schoolmistress is best, yes?"

"No. That's stupid." From first defensiveness, Jim's jealousy yet debtedness to this man, turned, "Oh, just fuck off, will you."

Andreas just laughed. "I am fucking off at this moment, Englishman. This German guy is going out to…" a moment for the right words in a foreign language, "…the future. Now we are free of the past." He went to the door and turned, "We have no memories of old empires to keep us trapped in the past. Good bye, old chap," with a cheery wave and he was down the stairs.

Anna came out of the bedroom, some clothes under her arm, "Andreas has gone?"

Jim just nodded at the empty room. Then, "How is Stephen?" really meaning, how is Gizande?

"He is quiet now. Gizande is with him." She looked at Jim searchingly, as she said, "She must lie with him, to make him quiet. She must embrace him. It is the only way." Then back to business, from Jim's half-concealed childish hurt, "I will be going. For the night, I will go to Karla's. There is not much night remaining. But I will leave a sign in the window. Tomorrow, we are closed. Too tired." Before going, she said, "You will be okay, Jim?"

"Yes. I'll be okay," defeated tiredness in his voice.

He turned the t.v.'s sound down and just watched the silent images on the screen. It was some time of soundlessness in the flat before he dared creep to the ajar bedroom door and push it open to see in. She was asleep the other side of Stephen, both under the duvet. The boy was awake, his eyes bright in the half light from the living room. Staring at Jim, smiling uncertain, then beaming, he pushed the duvet back to display, bursting from his trouser front, his puce-tipped erection grasped in his hand. He jerked the foreskin back and forth a couple of invitational times, before he recognised the shock and disgust in Jim's face. Backing out of the doorway, pulling the door to behind him.

"Shit!" he swore quietly. At the mess he had always known the boy would be in. He had not shared nakedness with other males for many years. Not since team showers after football his early years at the Plant. He had once been offered the penis of another boy at the Institution. It was late at night in the dormitory and he had taken it and offered his own, as they crept into bed together and hugged each other afterwards for the warmth of it, warding off the loneliness. A matter-of-fact memory now turned on its head. What had Stephen been inviting him to do?

He went to the divan and started to open it up. There was a wail of pain from the bedroom. Then Gizande's soft and deep tones of reassurance. Quietly, Jim completed making the bed, slipping in still clothed. He lay listening, but the flat was quiet and the sound of traffic on the streets murmured him back into sleep.

Movement in the kitchen. Jim slid from the bed. Her back to him, she was waiting for the kettle to boil.

"Gizande," barely above a whisper.

She turned. "Jim. We have no time to speak."

We never do, he thought. Always the interruptions from the outside world. He tried to read from her face, but only tiredness was written there. "You look tired. Exhausted."

"You also." The kettle clicked itself off. "Do you wish a drink? It is only granulated coffee."

"Yes." He remained stood indecisively in the doorway, the table still between them, looking at her back. He wanted to go round to her, to close his body to hers, to wrap themselves together. She came to the table with the drinks and the moment was lost.

"Are they coming to take Stephen home?"

"Yes. I've spoken to Julian." Adding unnecessarily, "In England."

"When do they come for him?"

"I'm waiting for a call. A phone call. Does he have his passport?"

"Oh, yes. All the papers. All the formalities and the documents from Finch. He was frightened. It is the Wall. They have become used to hiding behind it."

"Yes. I think both sides. Finch used to hide both sides, when it suited him."

"Yes. Andreas says that for the West Berliners, as well as the East Germans, that the Wall is in the head also. If the Wall remains open, it will change the life for Anna and Karla also."

"And for Andreas?" suppressing the acidity he still felt. Thinking, perhaps he gets his identity from the Wall most of all.

"Oh, Andreas. He will always find a way to… make adventures from the situations."

Of others, Jim sneered to himself.

But she must have seen the shadow of it pass across his face. "You must not feel that way to Andreas. He has helped us. I know your feelings…" trailing this off, as Jim leaned forward, ready to, but funking from speaking, his head overcrowded with possibilities for making these moments alone with her decisive. But she closed the door on it with, "Now is not the time to talk of this. When Stephen is gone." Eased with the promise, "When he has gone, before we leave Berlin, we will have one last run, yes?" Smiling tiredly, moving away from that, "Anna said to me that you were in a Stasi prison?"

"Yes. For a night and a day. Or more? Did you hear me? When they arrested me? I shouted your name."

"Yes. I was very frightened. They had locked me in the room where we were. Finch came to let me out when Andreas returned. Did they hurt you?"

"No. Klinsmaar threatened me a bit. He was there. Do you remember him from the office?"

"Of course."

"What happened to Krommel?"

"Andreas let him go. He was returning to Prague. His home. He was frightened."

Krommel gone, with the evidence he represented? At first irritated by this, Jim allowed this information to release him a little. Nothing to be done about it. Let the case close itself through the actions of others? "What will we do, Gizande? We have the video. The tape of those boys."

"I do not know. I am too tired to think of such things. We must decide after Stephen has gone."

She drained her cup and looked into it reflectively.

"Gizande." His throat was constricted and his tongue parched, despite the drink.

She looked at him, saw, and the grey eyes looked away again.

"Gizande. Whatever happens… I know you know what… my feelings are," out in fragments of awkward truth.

She took her cup to the sink and, back still turned to him, she said, "I know. I have said. After."

He sat on in the kitchen, long after she had gone back to share her bed with Stephen.

Chapter Thirty-three

The next thirty hours or so, the inhabitants of the flat got into a cautious routine. Jim had laid sleepless on the divan after she had gone to bed, those grey eyes still open inside his head. When dawn came around the edges of the blind, he had folded up the bedding and crept down stairs to the silent bar. In Karla's kitchen, he made himself a sandwich with some salami and took it with a glass of apple juice to sit and look out of the window at the life on the street outside. A man in overalls came and knocked on the door to come in, but Jim waved him away, pointing at Anna's sign.

Julian phoned and it became the first of several that day, a running commentary of delays by the Social Services senior officers, of what he could imagine was panic in the corridors of the Town Hall. A sex offender in their care found in Berlin. And found by an ex-employee they had sacked two years earlier for investigating sexual abuse in their own services. He went upstairs once, but Stephen was angry and tearful to see him, howling Jim out of his sight, so a brief conversation with Gizande in the kitchen and he updated her with what was happening, agreeing to stay out of the boy's sight.

He turned on the t.v. in the bar and idly watched. Many of the images were now repeats, ones he already saw last night of the crowds round the crossing points, on top of the walls talking to the policemen, chipping at the Wall, now interspersed with politicians making speeches. He could see the spontaneity going out of the events, as the power-brokers moved in to do business over the ruins of the Wall. He wondered what deals Finch and Klinsmaar were trying to cobble together, and who with. And Face-mark.

Early afternoon Anna came in. She went up to the flat, came down and cooked omelettes, taking two back up for Gizande and Stephen, joining Jim back in the bar to eat with him. He was reluctant for the light chatter she offered, feeling gloomily trapped here by the delays enforced from another country, separated from Gizande, dependent for the next move on people he did not trust. Finally, it was dark again and Anna had gone, when the confirmation at last came. Early the next morning flight in from Heathrow via Hamburg. Julian said they had not yet decided who was coming to collect Stephen. Jim was to be at Arrivals with a sign, *Stephen Roberts* written on it. He had laughed at this, suggesting a carnation and a rolled copy of the Times instead.

He told Gizande. She had listened, but the tired colourlessness of her skin and the deadness in her eyes, told him that all the arrangements were left to him. Finally, he had quietly gone up to lie on the divan. Listening to her voice nextdoor, soothing Stephen through the night.

Although it was only a short journey to Tegel Airport, it had been an awful experience. Stephen's anxiety started to rise as soon as it was clear that arrangements were being made to leave. He shouted and snarled at Jim, clung weeping to Gizande. Anna arrived to help them down, her arms round the boy from the other side. Jim had the Citroen parked and running, double-parked outside the bar. They tried to settle Stephen and Gizande in the front, but the proximity of Jim set the boy off again. Anna got bedding from upstairs and made a cushioned corner of it in the back of the van. As he moved off into the traffic, the map of the city spread across the seat next to him, Stephen was cooing pathetically, "Loo… loo… loo," from behind him.

Jim missed the exit off the autobahn and had to do a detour to get back to it. By the time he had parked outside the airport terminal, the flight was already due in. "Back soon," was all he said over the back of his sat, then ran inside with his cardboard sign. From the screens, he found the gate number, controlled himself to a walk and went there to wait. The first passengers were coming through, businessmen with briefcases who knew what they were doing. Jim held the sign against himself, feeling faintly foolish for no particular reason.

It was Flynn he saw first. Disbelief at the provocation of it, the witness against him being sent for this. Then he saw her. God, Sylvie! In an over-shiny dark red suit, big gold buttons, the skirt tightening her walk. And a face like thunder to see him, he noted. Got given the job nobody else in the Department would take.

All he could say was, "Well, well," beaming at the pair of them, with the bizarre joke of how this scene had been cast.

"Where is he?" she asked sharply.

"In the van outside."

"Take us there," so keen to get this over, before it spilled into something else.

"Whoa. Hold your horses. This is not just an easy pick-up. Stephen needs careful handling. When's your flight back?"

"In about two hours," Flynn offered from behind her shoulder.

"I think you can leave the handling to us," she cut in.

"Oh, yes. The experts. You've handled it all pretty well so far, haven't you?" jokiness dipped into acidity.

"We did not come here for this," her discomfort shored up behind the arrogance of her office.

Thrusting his face towards hers, "I don't work for you, Sylvie Cathcart. We'll make sure this one is alive when he gets on the plane, shall we?" As he saw she knew what he meant, adding past her shoulder for Flynn's benefit, "Not make the same… mistake- as with Damien, shall we?" Then, back to her, "You'll listen to me about this. As we've had Stephen for the last two days, we know something about how to deal with him. Savvy?"

Aware that the scene in the middle of the concourse was attracting the attention of some of the bored passengers seated nearby, with a sheen of sweetness over her irritation, she offered, "Shall we sit down somewhere? If we've got to discuss it."

"Lead the way," Jim said.

They sat, lined along the seats, Flynn in Jim's eyeline, past Sylvie's face. He could smell her. More expensive than when he knew her. Her hair highlighted an impossible red. He could not be sure, but he felt that beneath her discomfort at being with him, she might not also be feeling a touch thrilled by the edginess of the situation. So he played with the idea, "I'm not discussing Stephen, while he's here," nodding to Flynn. "You know how I don't trust him."

She considered this a moment, then turned to the social worker and said, "Just wait- over there. Have a coffee- No." She looked back at Jim, then, "Stay within sight."

She's playing with it also, he thought, watching Flynn go off to look idly and inattentively at a nearby boutique. The lapdog, used to hiding bones.

"Well, I'm listening," she said with a perched impatience.

"Stephen won't let men go near him. Unless…" hesitating. How to put it? In her face with it?

"Unless, what?"

"Unless it's for sex." She was discomforted by his bluntness, unsure where this might lead. "He offers himself to the next new man he meets. Then shrieks and shouts if he's rejected." She said nothing. "Do you understand?"

"I was told he was under some sort of medication. To calm him."

"Medication?" Jim laughed bitterly. "Coshed with chemicals, more likely. By your blessed carer, Billy Finch. They wore off days ago."

Completely inappropriately, she turned on a smile at him, her voice softened, "Well what do you suggest…?" and he knew she did not know what to call him, tempted but not daring to use the intimate, Jim. To get him on side, in her feeble charm offensive. To throw a false and insecure bridge over all the dark waters of deceit that had flowed between them. Since.

"What do you think I should suggest?" Adding, tartly, "Sylvie?"

"I thought…you were going to say…"

"No. You don't know what I was going to say." He sighed and looked away, this game-playing between them too trivial and dirtied with the past. And the unguessable crimes she might be party to from now on. He nodded towards Flynn, "You'll have to keep him at a distance. He needs a woman to cuddle. That's the only thing that keeps him quiet."

"Who's with him now?" she asked sharply, looking at him.

Looking back, to get her meaning. Then, disbelief at her probing jealousy. Even now? "A woman," was all he would give, disgusted at her, without the pity he once felt that night she had slept herself drunk with the clinking bedful of empties. And yet pathetic here, overdressed and childishly sly. "You'll have to cuddle Stephen yourself on the flight back." Take him away, to release my Gizande, he thought. "We'll have to go get him. Time's moving on." He stood, then looked down at her, "What will happen to Stephen when he gets back?" She was uneasy, at him standing over her. "What will you do with him?"

"He must go to Court," she hedged.

"After that."

She stood, deciding to face out his probing, "He will be sentenced. It's not up to me- us."

"No," he sighed. "It never is, is it? It's as much what you don't do that hurts people…" Not support Damien, not be a witness at the Disciplinary. Not answer the door." It was not worth the time to go on at her. "Come on. I'll introduce you to him."

Sylvie called over Flynn and Jim led them out to the carpark. Through the back window they could see the boy curled like a monkey round Gizande's smaller body, his face pressed in between her breasts.

"Stand back," Jim said. Then to Flynn, "You, keep out of sight."

He pulled open the back door and Stephen shook into life, crunching up his legs defensively, eyes open with panic.

Jim pushed at Sylvie's back, "Go on."

She shook him off angrily.

"Go on. Get in there. With him." He looked at Gizande who was stroking Stephen's temple to calm him. "This is Sylvie," unsure how much he may have told her in the past about this woman in red, who was now eyeing up what to do next. "You're not dressed for the part, are you, Ms. Cathcart?" he grinned at her discomfort.

Defiant, without looking back to answer, she kicked off her high-heel shoes, hitched the tight skirt up her thighs and awkwardly clambered onto her knees in the back of the van, a fixed smile shone towards the boy. Jim could only see the tight backside and the revealed thighs, as she said softly, "Stephen… Stephen… Stephen." Beyond her, the boy was intrigued and watchful, then looked to Gizande. Who smiled too and gently disengaged from him, still stroking his head. "Stephen… Stephen," and Sylvie, now within touch of him, sat down, shifting to pull her rumpled skirt back down. An arm and its hand outstretched in offer to him, he sat watching her. Jim could now see Sylvie smiling and Gizande now rubbing her hand on his back, to move him forward with the softest of pressure. Watching through the window, entranced by the beauty of it, the two women leaned in upon the boy, their faces filled with considerate compassion. The most gentle passing of Stephen between them, one to another, until he was within the embrace of Sylvie, head on her shoulder, eyes closed. Jim looked at Gizande, sat back and separated, and she returned him a slight smile.

The boy and the woman lay against each other for some time, reassuring each other, before Jim said quietly, "Time, Sylvie."

Slowly she shifted round on the dirty floor, holding the boy's head to her shoulder gently, starting to slide them both awkwardly towards the back. Stephen woke and found himself looking straight into Jim's eyes, through the back window. Uncertain at first of what he was seeing, then he remembered. Jim ducked out of sight. There was a bang from inside the van and the boy's quavering cry, stretching itself out, wavering down into a rhythmical chant, "Er, er, er, er, er…," beseeching reassurance and comfort, with Sylvie's soft insistent repetition playing below it, "Stephen… Stephen… Stephen…"

At last, he saw Sylvie's legs, first one then the other, appear out of the van. Jim hurried to put the high heels upright for her, looked up, but she shook her head and leaned back in to gather the collapsed boy back to her. Jim gave the shoes over his shoulder to Flynn, without a look. Gradually, down onto the tarmac, she started to shuffle Stephen towards the terminal, leading the strange procession across the carpark, Jim following, Flynn in the rear, briefcase in one hand, pair of high-heeled shoes in the other.

As they entered the building, Jim remembered and ran back to the van. Gizande was still sat in the back the doors agape, recovering. "Oh, Gizande- won't be long now. The passport. Have you got it?"

She pulled a wrap of papers from under the seats behind her and he reached for them, taking her fingertips into his hand too, "You were wonderful. Brilliant!"

"She was also very good, too. Your Sylvie, yes?"

He supposed she was. Unexpectedly, skills he had not guessed at. Smiled crookedly and ran back to the others inside the terminal.

Flynn was just coming back to them with a shopping bag which he gave to Sylvie.

"Torn my tights. On your van," she said testily. Stephen still hugged to her, eyes cautiously hunting round him for threats.

Jim laughed and turned to Flynn, "Buying the boss's underwear now, are we? Here," handing him Stephen's documents. Then, back to her, "I don't know how you're going to change into them. You can't take Stephen into the ladies with you." Adding with unnecessary crudity, "Not even you," immediately regretting it.

She looked at him sharply, "I'll get them done. Whatever you may think." Then to Flynn, "Come on, we're going to be late. What desk do we book in at?" And, a last summing-up look at Jim, "Well. Goodbye. Now you can get back to France, can't you?" Setting off, barefoot and posed with pride. Jim watched the three of them go off into the crowds and had to acknowledge that, if nothing else, she had carried it all off with considerable style. Whatever that was worth.

Chapter Thirty-four

He almost danced back to the van. Relief he knew he should not feel, with perhaps the confused and damaged boy just entering another episode of unguessed-at pain. Back at the Citroen, she was sat now on the front passenger seat.

"What will happen to Stephen now?" she asked. She had been crying, he thought.

The mood of release evaporated. Getting him on the plane did not absolve his responsibility, she was reminding him. "I don't know. Be put back in a home- an institute. For others like him."

"Do you trust them?"

Of course not, but he said, almost pleading with her to put it behind them, "What else could we do?" But he could not look into the judgment of her eyes and let his own follow a huge jet lumbering off into the air above them.

"Nothing," she said quietly. But could not leave it alone, "They gave him to Finch. Will they give Stephen back to him again?"

"I don't know, Gizande." Adding, "Finch wouldn't take him back now." Finally looking at her, "I do not know. And I- we've done all we could. I will ask friends in England- Julian- to try to keep an eye out," but he knew he did not believe that. He started the van's ignition.

"What is, keep an eye out?"

"Try and... follow what's happening to Stephen," revving the engine and pulling away into the traffic, in order to slam the questions down. Angry. She gave him a last look, before listlessly staring into the traffic out of her window.

Back at the bar, it was still empty. So was the flat.

She simply said, "I go to sleep," went into the bedroom and closed the door after her. He stared at the closed door, then sat down and turned on the inevitable t.v. There was what looked like a trivial soap in German. He watched, half attentively trying to understand the gist of it. Then he switched channels. Came across a news programme. Pundits talking, in front of a backdrop of the Brandenburg Gate. He switched it off. All the excitement of what had been happening in this city was distant, remote to him. Somehow trivial to what was on his mind.

He got up and searched the flat for paper. He found a pad and, a last listen at her door, he went down into the bar. He sat in the window and started to write it all down. He tried to get the right words for a proper evidential statement. Trying to organise it into a chronological structure of words, pared of the feelings that went with them.

When the tapping came on the window, he did not at first connect it to himself, so absorbed was he. It was Helena. The same long fur-collared coat. He let her in.

"Ah, so. You have returned. Did you find your boy?"

"Yes." Moving on with, "So much has happened, since we met." Offering her a seat, "Please sit down."

She looked round the bar without sitting, "Where is Anna? Karla?"

"They have gone to sleep. They were opened for two days, without a break. For the Ossies."

"Ah. The Ossies. I may be an Ossi also."

"I don't understand…"

She nodded slowly, then looked up at him, "Will you get me a schnapps?"

"Yes. Of course." He went over behind the bar.

"I will come." She followed and sat herself delicately on a bar stool. "I do not like to sit by the window. People may see you, before you see them, if you sit by the window."

He looked over at his papers, on the far table, but Helena was waiting to be served. He searched through the bottles, found a likely one and offered it to her, "This one? Okay?"

She looked critically at the label, then waved it away with, "That will do."

He poured the drink, then looked out a bottle of Pilsner for himself.

She sipped, peered at the glass, then, "Yes. I will be leaving Berlin. I think the Wall is now finished. I will return to Weimar." Looking briefly and searchingly at Jim, before saying, "My husband died there."

Weimar? Buchenwald, hadn't Anna said? But what he spoke to Helena was, "I saw the sign for Weimar. When we were in the East. Looking for the boy."

"It will be different now. And it will be changing again, now. With the Wall finished." But she was disengaged from him. Probably also from the room and the city it was set within. Was she back there now, herself as she had been in the 1920s? And the early 30s, before Hitler. Jim knew how beautiful she must have been, back as the person she had once been. Before the terrible stories Anna had spoken of. He sat watching her, her own eyes deep within the small glass held within her hands.

Then, long enough for it to have become a stare, he looked away. He walked round the bar and went to collect the uncompleted papers from the table in the window and came back to her.

"Ah. I have interrupted you in your writing." It was not an inquisitiveness, but a comment.

"No. It's all right. I wanted to see you before we left."

"Ah. You go now. Soon?"

"Tomorrow." Then thinking of the uncertainties of Gizande, added, "Perhaps."

As if she knew, she asked, "And will Gizi go with you?"

"I think so. I go back to France."

"Of course. Of course," her words encompassing both his uncertainty and his destination.

"You told me we could speak…" What had she said that night, as he had conducted her back to her door? She was looking back at him, with quizzical amusement. "…when I understood Germany better."

"Do you understand Germany better?" a laugh still in her eyes.

That stopped him. Had he even been thinking about Germany? Had he ever thought of places like that? As places to understand. Like people. He doubted it. Places had just been where things happened. Thin walls as a backdrop to where things were done. To you and by you, with other people. Like a movie set. If his life had happened elsewhere, would it have been the place or the different people that drove him in a different direction? So what about France now? Finally, all he could say was, "I don't know."

She nodded slowly, still smiling to him, and put down the glass. "Germany. Ah, Germany. So difficult, so different in its parts. It is a country of three halfs, you understand. The North, the South and the East. There is no West. Then also, there is Berlin. It easier to think of it with simplicity. For you English, Germany is Hitler. For the French, it is their Occupation. But, you will find, we are a young nation. We always look for who we are. We are forced to examine our history. The world makes us. The Jews make us. We are not like the old countries. We do not have the comfort of their myths. We must look at the truth. We try not to, but we must look straight into our eyes. Like this!" and she jabbed her bony wrinkled fingers sharply back at her face, as if to blind herself of a lifetime of seeing. Then she sipped her drink again. "And now, with the Wall finished, we will look at our history again. The victims of what has happened will make us. You will see."

"Were you a victim?" out of his mouth before he could stop it.

"Me?" Her consideration of his face was a measurement of what answer this foreign man was worth. "A victim…? Yes. Because my life was taken from me by others. I was not permitted to live the life I dreamed of as a child- as a girl. But are we not all victims of that? Life is never as we would wish it. I did not wish to live in Berlin for so many years. You have come to Berlin because of others. You did not plan to chase this boy across Europe." She watched her old fingers precisely lift her drink. "I have lived many years…"

He watched her, lost again in contemplation of the glass. But he said nothing.

Then, re-emerged, she looked at him again, "You will return to Germany?"

He could not imagine so, but said, "Perhaps. For a holiday next time," he added implausibly.

She nodded, but her eyes were out on the street, "Ah. Here is Anna come."

Jim turned as Anna let herself in.

"Helena!" She embraced the old lady. Then, "Jim?" but returned to the other woman and they started to speak together in German. Jim looked on for a minute, then gathered the papers he had been writing. Anna broke off, "You are alright, Jim?" Then, the afterthought, "Did Stephen go back to England?"

"Yes." He held up the pen and paper. "Work to do. I'm okay," and went back to his window table to resume, the women's voices as background. Alternating from Anna's chatter to the measured responses of Helena.

After Helena had left, with just a thoughtful nod to Jim, Anna told him she had been unable to sleep at Karla's. The excitement of the last two days would not relax within her. She said many other Berliners were the same. Just walking the streets, embracing strangers, gathering to cheer and sing at the border crossing points, going to watch the Ossies, entrancement in their eyes, wandering round the stores on the Kudamm. So she had come home at last to try to sleep.

"Gizande is asleep in your bed."

Anna sat down opposite him. "How is it, with you and Gizi?"

Shy with her confrontation of it, he looked away down to the papers he had been writing on. "She is angry… I think."

"Angry? At you?"

He shrugged, "I don't know. You must ask her." Then, reconsidered, "No. Say nothing to her."

"When will you go home?"

"Tomorrow. I'll go tomorrow." Whatever. Too tired of the same questions he had been asking himself. And it came out, quietly and naturally, "I do love her, you know, Anna."

She reached across and rubbed her fingertips across the stubble on his cheeks, "I know, Jim. It is visible to the world."

"Does she know?" he asked hauntedly, the last question at the tail of a long and exhausted exploration.

"She does. But so much has happened to Gizi. She has been hurt. You know of her husband?"

He nodded.

"She… is hiding… from such a thing happening again. Perhaps… in time?"

"Perhaps." Escaping from the meagre hope of it, he looked down at the papers. "I am writing a statement. Of what has happened. With Stephen. And the other children."

"Ah. To put the horrible story away? By writing it down."

"No. When I have finished, can I make copies? Is there a shop near here with a photocopier?"

"A Xerox? Yes, it can be done."

"I want one copy to go to the police here- in Berlin- with the video. One copy will go to England. I will keep one."

"Why to the police in Berlin? You are going away. They would wish to question you."

"They will have my address in France. If it is so important, they can contact me there. I cannot wait in Berlin any longer. I have work to do on my farm." Strange to be saying that, but it was the simple truth of his life now.

"Why do you have to continue? Stephen is now on his way to home, yes?"

For Sylvie? At what point did a person like her so poison their beliefs with ambition, that other voices of protestation became a joke? "They need to be reminded that someone out there knows the truth."

"Who is they?" she asked.

He shrugged.

"Jim. You must end this at some time. You can not continue with this… hunting, for the rest of your life."

Inner relief to hear this, but all he could say was, "Maybe. Maybe not."

She stood. "I will go to bed. Gizi will have to make space for me. Will you sleep?"

"I'll finish this first."

It was getting dark and he had to put on a light in the bar to finish. Some people knocked on the door to come in, but he waved them away and went back to writing. Finally, he read it through and was satisfied. He stretched his tired body and rubbed the sore back. Home tomorrow. He would like now to have gone out into the city for its flavour, but he would not go alone, without the language. So he quietly let himself upstairs into the flat. There was no sound from the bedroom, its door slightly ajar now. He would not look, for the feelings seeing her there loosened in him. He switched off the lights and lay on the divan, without opening it out for fear of the noise it would make. It seemed hours that he looked up at the shaft of streetlight round the edge of the curtain, thrown across the ceiling. Speculating, sometimes hopeful, sometimes gloomy, about tomorrow.

The sound of Gizande in the kitchen woke him. Between the door and the frame, an opened slit let him see her back moving and removing itself. Reappearing with two mugs in the doorway, surprised to see him awake.

"Are we going running today?" he asked tentatively. "Before we go?"

She looked down at him, but from where he lay, he could not read her upside-down face, and he rolled over. "No. I do not wish to." But she waited for his response.

"No. Of course not," he replied, with both anger and defeat. He pushed himself up on his elbows. "Don't blame me, Gizande for what I can't change. If I had done nothing about Stephen- about Damien- you would not be judging me so harshly now."

Anna had appeared from the bedroom, looking grey-faced.

Jim sat up, "Good morning, Anna." He leaned over and pulled out clothing and trainers from his bag, "I'm going running." And went into the bathroom.

Only Anna was in the living room when he came out, her hands round the mug of coffee. "Gizande is running also. You wait."

What to turn his anger into now? He sat, flat with it, looked up at Anna and said, "Was it because of you? Did you ask her?"

"Yes, I asked." Then seeing the disappointment in his face, she added, "But she did not have to say yes, Jim."

Gizande reappeared, blue tracksters and a red waterproof. "We go, Jim? The last run?"

Forever? he thought, but she was already heading down the stairs, so he followed, Anna watching, arms folded.

Outside on the street, Gizande had already set off. When he caught up, he asked, "Which way?"

"To see the Wall," without looking at him. So he followed alongside her, the same route they had run before the East. Now in the still and early sunshine. Across the canals, past the park- where Face-mark had dropped him- then onto the avenue, and hundreds of people were walking the pavements. As they rounded the ceremonial column, stretching up toward the Brandenburg Gate, there were scores of vehicles parked in the roadway, trucks, vans, satellite dishes, antennae, technicians busied round television screens fed by banks of electronic boxes. She started to dodge, first off the pavement onto the roadway, then to weave through the vehicles parked carelessly, jumping over bundles of cables, round improvised open-air studios. It was tiring, changing pace, swerving direction to follow her. As they neared the Wall itself, the crowds were denser, there were television cameras on cranes.

"This is impossible, Gizande."

"Yes, you are right."

He glimpsed the Soviet memorial to their dead. West German police were arguing with some young people about a banner they held up against the monolithic stone. The two Soviet guards impassive as ever above the turmoil below. Jim touched her shoulder and pointed, "What's that? What's the banner say?"

She stopped, but could not see, slight amongst the moving crowds round them.

"Here." So daring, he afterwards could not believe himself, he stepped up behind her, put his arms round her waist and lifted her, his locked arms under her ribcage. He could not see her face, his own eyes closed and buried against her shoulder blade, his nostrils filled with smell of her exercised body, her sweat- so powerfully and suddenly her, he reeled with it, steadying his footing. A moment and he put her down to ground again. She turned to his. Flushed with exercise or what had just happened, she looked at him quizzically.

He looked back, and allowed himself a relaxed smile, before eventually asking, "What did it say? The banner?" Adding, "Did it also say, *Welcome, Gizi, Welcome*?"

She gave him a play punch to his shoulder, "No! It did not. It say, *Let the leadership parade before the people*." And, without warning, she turned to run back through the crowds, away from the Wall, Jim setting off to zig-zag after her. Finally past the densest, they were able to run together again, there was nothing for him to say. He was sure a thaw had been started. Over the second canal bridge on the way back, he began to accelerate steadily, feeling her surprise at his pace, matching him, dropping down into the gutter to avoid other pedestrians, dogs on leads yapping at them, he led her, feeling the strain of keeping the speed, beginning to punch the air ahead out of the way with the effort, his legs strung tight, commanded to race onwards, a hesitation at how many corners before they turned- before the street with Foodi in- and she captured him, alongside, then ahead, her own pounding body out the corner of his eye, holding himself there, hanging on, suddenly they were in the home street, the top of the van, the *Foodi* sign and he desperately lunged out into the street, sprinting up the clear space between the parked cars and the moving traffic, eyes only ahead- and dodged back onto the pavement to breast the invisible tape outside the bar first, Gizande crashing into his back, spinning, staggered laughing and panting away from each other.

He was bent over, hands on knees, gasping to her, "Life- in the old dog- yet!"

She weaved across the pavement to him and put her hand on his shoulder. Limp, resting, "The last time, Jim. No more winning!"

He stood and, still asmile, said, "Time for us to get ready. Home, today."

She took her hand away, "Yes," looked away from him. A cloud across the moment. "I will go for the shower." And he followed her in.

While she showered, Anna watched him folding his clothes into his bag. "Will you come again to Berlin?"

"I don't know. I would like to." Then, like asking a fortune teller, "Do you think I will return, Anna?"

But she only laughed, as if she knew what he meant. Shook her head at him and went back into her bedroom.

When Gizande came out of the shower, she was wearing the blue overalls he remembered from that first departure he had made from France. "Simple clothes. For a long journey," she answered his look.

After he had given Anna the copy of his statement, they had said goodbye to her on the street, and she and Gizande had spoken in German together as he loaded the van. He had recognised Andreas's name buried in the language. In the van, he had asked her, "Do you miss the life you had in Berlin?" Seeking out comparisons.

"Sometimes, it was easy. Sometimes, it was difficult. But, finally, it was not possible." Said with a deadened prohibition against talking of it further.

Chapter Thirty-five

Berlin long behind them, Jim finally drove them across the border out of East Germany in the early afternoon. They had spoken little. He had appeared to be concentrating on the route, simple as it had been, but his mind was on that lost moment of laughter together at the end of the run. Where had it gone? Where had she taken it? He had taken a few side swipes at her with his eyes, not to be seen seeing her. She was lolling her head against the window, looking out without seeing.

Just into the West side of the border, ahead, the traffic was slowing down, brake lights coming on along the dipping road ahead like embers. Slowed to a crawl, he joined the end of the jam, watching it in his mirror stack up behind him.

Jim looked over to Gizande, "Are you alright?"

She looked back at him. With an undefined unhappiness in her face. "Why do you ask me?"

He wanted to say, because he cared. But, instead, "Why, don't you want me to ask?"

She looked away, out the window, saying, "Games, Jim. No games please, Jim."

Quietly, he said, "I'm not playing games, Gizande."

She looked back at him, caught by the seriousness of his tone, but looked away again. "Later."

It was ten minutes before they passed the accident. It came up upon their right, marked by the flashing light of a police car just arrived. Everybody's eyes turned to the BMW. On its roof. The driver and the passenger still hanging in their straps, upside down, seen through the rose-red of windows washed with their blood. A moment and it was passed, debris of another car scattered along the side of the autobahn, and the traffic slowly started to pick up speed, the vision receding behind the busy and forgetting schedules the rest of the world still had to meet. Among the survivors, he thought. But, remembering Damien, Stephen and the Bulgarian girls- Julieta and Vanja, were they?- and also Sylvie, the cost of survival. For you and me, also, Gizande, the costs of our survivals, too.

After fuel at a Rasthof outside Frankfurt, she took over the driving. The silence between them endured. He had not the courage to fault by breaking it, so, in the darkening cab, he padded his jacket against the window and tried to doze. The evening traffic was heavy and every time the van had to slow down, he woke, looked at the head and tail lights ahead, looked at her profile with the lights running over it and turned his face back into his jacket.

It must have been past the rush hour, out onto the speedier roads towards France, when he woke to see her still sat straight, slightness and strength locked to the steering wheel, but tears glittering on her cheeks in the luminescence from the instrument panel.

"Gizande?"

Rigid at the sound of his voice, she said nothing.

"Gizande. What's wrong?"

The van rolled on.

"Gizande. Tell me. What is wrong?" now feeling a fearfulness at what she might answer, but needing to know all the same. The sign for services coming up, he said, "Pull off here. Pull off at the Rastplatz."

She said nothing, but at the next sign started to indicate, slid them off the autobahn and parked, hidden in among the lorries towering either side. Dark, so he could not see her face.

"What is wrong?" said into the shadows.

"If I say, please understand me. Please do not be angry with me." A child's plea.

"Of course not," a blank cheque that he could not guarantee? Would it be about Andreas? he thought with dread.

She started, her voice soft with pain, "It is the nights I spent with Stephen. They were terrible. He cry all the time. Not the loud shouting. Only quiet… cry, cry, cry. Never when you were there. He was frightened of you. You were Finch. A man. You understand?"

He nodded in the dark, then near a whisper, "Yes."

"I hug him. All the time I hug him. But still, cry, cry, cry. Then sometimes he becomes angry. Not to me, but it frighten me." She stopped. Not a pause, but a deliberate consideration about how to go on from here, that Jim could feel across the dark cab. "He tried to put my hand onto him. Many times. You understand?" He knew she was looking at him now. "On his penis. You understand?"

Silence. He could not add anything by replying.

"I was tired. I had not sleep for many days. The party. The night we drove into the DDR. The nights you were in prison- looking for you. Waiting. The night we drove back with Stephen to Berlin. I was very tired. Very, very tired. Then always with Stephen. And always he is asking for me to do this to him. No one else. I was alone with him. Anna had gone to Karla's. I could not have you- or any men in the room, because of Stephen's anger." Then wordless space ticked away, to become a chasm, stretched wide across the space between them. Before the simplicity of, "So I did it to him. And he slept."

His mouth shrivelled dry, he waited.

There was a sob in her voice, when she continued, "Not once. It was three times I did it to him. It made him sleep. Each time. I had to say something to Anna. The marks on the bedsheets. I told her that Stephen had done that to himself. Even Anna, I must say lies to." Her hand reached and found his in the darkness. Not gently, but scrabbling for him. "Do you think he will say to the people in England? Do you think he will tell the Social Services people?"

He restrained the anxious hand between both of his. "No," he croaked, cleared his throat and tried again, "No. He can't explain these things. He doesn't talk. They wouldn't believe him."

"That is worse." She tried to release her hand, but he held on. "He is without the power to speak. He is a child."

"Gizande. Did you do it for yourself? Or did you do it for Stephen?"

A lorry next to them suddenly choked and roared into life. Too loud for talk, they waited. It pulled slowly away, drawing away its curtain of shadow with it. Her face was now slippery with wet, teardrops collecting on her chin, looking towards him, snuffling her nose.

"I did it for me. I know I did it for me. To get me to sleep."

"And to get Stephen to sleep," he squeezed her hand.

"But, in my mind, I know." She pulled her hand finally free and tapped her temple fiercely with her finger, "I know, inside my head. It was for me that I did it. For me to sleep. I wanted it so much."

"No. Gizande, what are you saying? You are like Finch?" Then, almost inquisitive with the picture of it in his own imagination, he asked, "How were you with him? Were you gentle with him? Were you...?" Running out of imaginings.

She looked up at him with astonishment, "What do you say? Why…? If I am gentle with Stephen, that makes it okay?"

"No. But you were two very tired people. Two exhausted human beings. You found the way you could both sleep. It was that. Only that. It wasn't sex that you had with Stephen, was it? It was like giving him a sleeping pill, that got you both to sleep. Medicine."

She looked away and rubbed tears from the rim of her face with impatient knuckles.

"It was, wasn't it, Gizande?" Determined to get her assent.

"But… he could do nothing. He is the child. I am the adult." She turned fiercely to him, "Would it be acceptable for me to do the same with my own child? Tell me, Jim! Do you have the morality for that, also?"

"No, I don't," he said tiredly. "I am not talking of morality." What was he saying? he wondered. He groped for the meaning of it, "I'm saying… it was the spirit you did it in. It was not using him... not exploiting him. Do you understand?"

She banged her fingertip word-by-word into her stomach, "But I feel exploitative-" saying the word in French. "I have the feeling, whatever words you say, Jim."

"That's just the idea- in your head. You were not exploiting him. Not-" repeating her French- "exploitative. I don't believe-" grasping for words- "you would have that in you. Would you?"

"When I look at it, it was wrong. So very wrong."

"Was it? You both slept. Right and wrong actions are not black and white. It depends how they are done. And why."

"You do not believe that, Jim? That some people have forgiveness for - des faits mauvais - bad doings - actions? They do their crimes in a pleasing manner? No!"

He knew, but had not the words. "Gizande. Listen." Surprised himself, as the words came shunting each other out, "Acts are not out of books, right and wrong. I know- I've learnt, it can't be taught. Just like you can't pay people to do moral things- to act with ethics. You feel it- that's what belief's about!"

She looked at him and the gauntness in her face broke down into wretched sobs, covering her face with her hands, falling across the steering wheel, hidden in her hair. He leaned over to touch her tentatively on the shoulder, then slowly circle the tips of his fingers across her jerking back, rubbing in his reassurance with his palm, gradually slowing down the spasms of her distress, calming her.

"I will drive. You will sleep. You are still tired."

He waited till she raised her tired head and nodded, without looking at him. He walked round to the driver's door, while she slid over the other side. He climbed in, leaned over and adjusted the blanket round her. Her eyes closed, he dared not touch her face with a final stroke. Before driving off towards France.

Chapter Thirty-six

He entered France in the middle of the night. He was the vehicle's automatic pilot. Just wanting to get home. She slept on. Relief was already distancing what had happened to him. To them? The immediacy of what had been going to happen next, now the certitude of La Retrait at the end, what he had to do there, whether the snow was down yet, what he would be telling Suzanne. And Julian, a phone call there too. He started to frame it all in his head, as the story that he would be explaining. Bits inexplicable, probably. How did others keep their doors locked against what they knew, and go on living with themselves? The dream came to mind, the way he had last dreamed it, in the cell. Rushing down corridors of closed doors. But Sylvie… oh, Sylvie… you knew, you had looked Damien full in the face… And now? An odd-job woman. Conspiring for ambition, what are your dreams like now?

He looked over at Gizande's slept face, flickering in the accelerated lamplights along the autoroute. What are your dreams? Both smiling and wondering at her. Finally, mouthing the words, "My darling," soundlessly.

He stopped in services somewhere north of Lyons, in the still-black early morning. She had woken, asked where they were, then rolled herself back into sleep. He had tried to sleep there too for some time, slumped on the steering wheel, closed his eyes, but his brain was still sorting through the meanings of everything and it was cold. Eventually, he gave up, quietly locked her into the van and went over to the services for a coffee. An Arab woman with her head covered, serving. At a table, the only other customer, a big-bellied, shaven-headed man, a ring in his ear big enough to hang a curtain from. The quiet thoughtfulness of his tired lips and eyes belying the tattoos, the black vest bulged with muscles. Jim did not want to look at the man, uncertain of him, but his eyes kept returning there. The threatening bulk of him, the hurt tiredness of the face, just staring and picking at the roll in front of him in a defeated way. Too self-absorbed to notice Jim.

Eventually, the man rose, looked with a glance of blank sightlessness at Jim and slowly rolled out through the doors. Over to a lorry, heaving himself up into it. The engine rumbled into life and, as it pulled past the café windows, Jim could see him in the light, belly jammed against the steering wheel, sat proud and relaxed, all the doubt gone, a man in control, master of his juggernaut of Luxemburger cheese. To envy him the simplicity of his purpose now? Or sadden at that doubt the man had showed, sat at the table? Suddenly Tracey came to mind and all her face said to him was, "You didn't have to do it, Dad. You didn't have to do any of it."

He drank back the last of the cleansingly bitter coffee and walked out, towards the van, knowing why the woman asleep inside it was so important. She knew why he did have to do it. She understood the consequences of not doing, that to do nothing was also a choice made. As well as the costs of doing it. To live on with the mistake, more tolerable than living without the chance taken? The sleeplessness of, what if?

When she woke two hours later, she was watchful of him. His unexpected cheerfulness. He offered her music. Not the Casals Bach, but tuning for a radio station of trivia. Light-hearted pop, with plenty of bright French chatter between the tracks.

"Why are you now so happy, Jim?"

"Because! Because!" was all he would reply to her, humming on to the music.

She smiled and shrugged and, snuggled back under the blanket, her legs tucked up on the seat towards him and without looking at her, he knew she was watching him. He simply patted her ankle, then left his hand there. And she let it stay.

They swapped driving as the first full blast of Midi sunshine swept its way through the clouds to the east. He went to sleep at last. They stopped for breakfast and she laughed at Jim's ravenous appetite. They talked about the future for La Retrait, even drawing out plans for the outbuildings on a serviette. It was as though the more kilometres, the further they put behind that other world, distance gave them the permission to revive. Happy, but not serious, though in the far back recesses of his mind, Jim could not stop unfolding deeper feelings and wilder hopes. Just not letting them show anywhere in his face.

It was gone midnight, nearer one o'clock, he guessed, when they were close enough to home to decide.

"It is too late for you to go to Suzanne," she said, but, her turn to drive, she did not have to look at him, keeping her gaze on the road ahead.

His hopes were so constricted in his throat, he did not dare himself to say anything. Throughout the day, as they had drawn nearer, following the intermittent sun westward across the south of France, it had started to nag at him. After this, what?

So she continued, "We will wake them with the sound." Looking at last at him, seriously, "You must stay at my house tonight."

Whatever that meant, he thought, but said, quietly and with restraint, "Fine." Even though she probably could not see in the dark, he shifted his seat and pulled at his trousers to conceal his arousal.

She eventually pulled the van round behind the house, into the yard. There was a dusting of snow visible, before she turned off the engine and the lights, leaving them silent in the dark, a punctuation at the end of the tremendous journey. And before the immediacy of now.

"Come. We will get cold. I must start to bring heat to the house. You take the things from the van."

Little enough for him to bring in, he went through the dark storeroom, up the stairs to stand in the kitchen doorway, watching her riddling the stove of ash. Until it was alive, an electric fan heater was humming loudly in the corner.

"Come inside. Close the door, for the cold," she said, without turning.

He put the bags down, closed the door and stood warming his hands from the heater. "Anything I can do?"

"There is another heater in the bathroom. Also on the wall there is the tank for the hot water. You will have a bath. We will make it hot." Still not looking at him, but with humour in her voice, "I do not forget your back, Jim. I know it is still painful from the manner of your walking."

With all that had been happening, he had been shaping the way he sat and walked around the point of discomfort. She was right.

When he came back down, the stove was starting to roar with paper and wood. She was at the large table, chopping vegetables. "At this time, Gizande? What are you doing cooking a meal now?"

She stopped, looked at him, looked down at the shredded onions on the chopping board before her, and smiled back up at him. "I wish to cook for you. A meal, after the autoroute food. No more of the German wurst."

"You're crazy! No. Don't you have a tin of something? Just to put in a saucepan."

She went to the shelves behind her and studied them. And spoke to them, "I will prepare some food for later. Some food to clean all the meat from our bodies." Then she turned, her smile so shy, "It is our return. It must be parfait."

"Our perfect retreat. Our retrait parfaite, oui?" he laughed.

"Oh! Too many languages! Here," she held out a small net bag on a string. "Herbs. Aromatic, for your bath. Hang them in the water. They will bring you calm. There will be towels. Go, before the water is too much."

He carefully and slowly prepared for getting in the water. It slid its sheet of warmth over his tired body and he lay there for a long time it seemed, listening for the sounds of her downstairs. Dozing into the intimacy of hearing them. So it shocked him awake when the bathroom door opened. He pulled the flannel to cover himself and sit upright. Watching her.

She was carrying a tray. Glasses of wine and two large unlit candles. She smiled, then set the candles, one either side of the room and lit them, switching off the light. She pulled over the chair to beside the bath and placed the glasses there. Then, stepping back into the yellowing half light of the candles, she unbuttoned her overalls and stepped from them. Reaching back, she unclipped her bra, loosening her breasts, bent and peeled off her knickers. He was surprised at the broad muscularity of her nakedness. And the welcome of it as she gently pressed his shoulders forward, climbing behind him into the bath. A moment of awkwardness as she threaded her legs, one either side of him, resting her feet on his thighs, the flannel floating away. Finally, she delicately pulled him back onto her, feeling her body's wet enclosure round his back.

He twisted his head round to try to see her, "Gizande… oh–"

She silenced him with fingers over his lips, "Shhh…" And he kissed them, before they lighted on his temple and softly rubbed there, floating him back onto her shoulder. Rested there, wordless the pair of them, quiet at last. The wine forgotten.

However long, before she slowly slid out from behind him, padded wetly across the floor and shook a towel open. He watched her. Towelling each shoulder, lifting first one breast, then the other to wipe dry beneath, over her belly, between her legs and down each one's length. Another towel and she shook it open to hold it out for him. He pushed himself up and stood, aware but relaxed at the visibilty of his arousal, now. The most natural thing in the world. And stepped out to her vigorous rubbing of the towel across his skin, round his back, up and down his legs, gently between them. Before she finally stood back, to inspect. He leaned forward to kiss, but she only accepted the briefest touch between their lips.

Taking his hand, she led him first to one candle and blew it out, then to the other. A moment in complete darkness, before she opened the door. "Wine," was all she said and they each took a glass. Following her down the stairs, the stone chill to the foot, to a living room he had never entered before. Candles again, a well-burning open fire, duvets and cushions spread before it. Letting go of his hand she went over and knelt on a cushion, indicating the bed of duvets for him, "Lie there, Jim." Putting his glass down on the hearth. He lay on his back, looking up at her. She touched his shoulder to turn him on to his front, "The other way."

He lay with his chin at rest on his knuckles, her knelt and open thighs a few inches from him, his head filled with the smell of her. She leant over him and tipped some oil into her palm from a dish by the fire.

Then her hands started to press into his flesh, squeezing it, folding it, shaping it, unfolding the tiredness from deep within him, working from his shoulders, down his back, the spine itself. Now out of his sight, he felt her moulding his buttocks, down the back of his thighs, to his calves.

"Turn. To the back."

He rolled over, her upside-down face above him, hair hung either side, absolute concentration on what she was doing. As she moved down over his ribs, her nipples swung near enough for him to touch with his mouth, but not yet. As she finished flexing his feet, she put herself astride his legs, took a last palmful of oil and stroked it into his sex. Finally, bent across him, her hair falling across his belly, she gave it a dry, almost reflective kiss. Moved up and raised her self over him, her hand guiding him inside her, the lips of her body opening for him to enter, and, as he slid into her, he felt all the uncertainties, the failures and the last shreds of tiredness being drawn from his bones and the flesh that wrapped them.

Some time during that night, she said, "I have never had trust for passion. I have waited for certainty with you, Jim. That it was more than passion between us. I have had passion before. My husband. Also Andreas. I know you were hurt very much in Berlin. I was a fool. I wanted to return to being young, with Andreas. But I am not young. And it was not so good with Andreas then, also. But my husband, that was passion alone." She took Jim's hand by its fingertips and placed it on her clitoris, then moved it round the top of her thigh. "Do you feel, Jim? Do you feel the scar?"

A ragged line across the warm, moist flesh, "Yeah. I think so."

"That was my husband. He was brute. With the leg of a chair. He had broken it with his anger. Life was like that between us. I did not at first see the ugliness in his soul. I was too charmed by the return to my own country. It was the night when he found his table football, with the door fixed to the top- do you remember I tell you? I provoke and he becomes angry. I become mad with it. When he was angry, when he hit me, it was easier than the quiet times with him. When it was waiting for him to explode. It became so I preferred the exploding to the waiting." She retrieved his hand, put it to her lips. "He held me over the table and tried to rape me with the leg of the chair. It was sharp with broke wood." Dark now, with just the embers of the fire making a dull red light though her hair, he was unsure if she was smiling when she said, "It was when I was certain you were not that sort of man… but also that I would not be that sort of woman to you. Then I know."

"When did you know? What happened to make you certain?"

"So much. Perhaps what you say to me about Stephen. But long before that. Before Berlin. When I decide to accompany you to Berlin. It does not matter now. It is past. It has happened. We are together. Now it is what happens now. The future. The children. My mother. Your daughter?"

Tracey? Would her opinion count with him, any more than his would with her? Probably. But he said, "What will happen now? Tomorrow?"

"It is tomorrow now. It is dark, but it is the morning."

"What will you tell your family? Your mother? The children? Guillem does not like me much, I think."

She was silent and lay back to look upwards, her profile outlined in the rose firelight. Her nearest breast uncovered, he played his fingertip round the uneven dark disc of skin that framed the nipple. She smiled, "No," and removed his hand. "I can not think to answer your question if you are doing that." Then, "I will tell them. It is not immediate. During the winter they stay during the school days at my mother, because it is close to the road. For the bus to school, it does not come up near to here. What will you tell Suzanne?"

He thought about this. After July the fourteenth, his departure from his sister's home seemed even more overdue. Now near three months out of the country and no progress with La Retrait becoming habitable, he did not relish the anticipation of seeing her again. "I don't know. I will have to go on living with her and Maurice. If there is a little snow down here, there is probably a lot up at La Retrait and not much I can do before April. They won't come up there to put in the electricity till then, will they?"

Still staring upwards, "After I tell the children, you will live here. During the week, while they are at school. Then the weekend, you live at Suzanne and Maurice. When Guillem and Gaillarde are here."

He was greedy for life with her to begin, but cautious. "I will soon have no money. I must find work… something."

"For that you will need to speak French. You will help me on the farm. I will speak French with you. Oui, mon ami?" giving him the softest punch of her knuckles to his stubbled chin.

"Oui, if you say so. Mon amour," he smiled.

Chapter Thirty-seven

She told Jim that her announcement to her family had not gone well. Her mother had been contemptuous and angry at the news, he gathered. Guillem had said nothing, but would not look his mother in the eyes. Gaillarde had waited till she was alone with her mother and asked about the practicalities, where Jim would live, would her and her brother still keep their rooms at the farm? And had looked unconvinced at the answers Gizande had given. So Jim went back to Suzanne's for the time being, spending the day up at Gizande's working with her, speaking French and leaving after the evening meal. Except at weekends, when the children came home. Christmas would be with his sister, he supposed. But he said nothing to Suzanne, too hesitant about how his future with Gizande would happen to make plans about it.

A letter from Julian. Astonished that Sylvie had been sent over to collect Stephen and wrote to Jim that the boy had been sentenced a Probation Order by the Court on his return from Berlin, but had then disappeared somewhere into the adult care system. Now so removed from all that, and so entangled with relationships, Jim could only parcel that up and put it away in his mind. To be dealt with, maybe, some other more suitable time. Also with the letter from England was an insert from Julian's brother. A copy of a news sheet published for English people living in south west France, suggesting he advertise as a small haulier from England. *A growing market with the growing émigré population*, the brother had scribbled on the margin. Market? Jim had asked himself. Was that what he was now becoming, a small businessman? But he had written off to be advertised, both amused and excited by the prospect.

After a week at Christmas without seeing each other, Gizande was invited for a meal with Suzanne. Unwilling to phone Gizande and have one of the children answer, Jim did not have the chance to plan how to play it with his sister. And he was feeling increasingly uncertain how to respond, when Gizande's name came up in conversation, or when he was telling Suzanne what he had been doing day-by-day at the other farm. It was making him shifty and he caught his sister's eyes on him several times, watchful and measuring, certain she knew. Barely tolerable discomfort.

Gizande arrived, skirted and smart. After greeting Suzanne and Maurice, Jim kissed her on the cheek, pulling her body up against himself just for a second. As he let her go, his eyes to hers had said, we tell them. Tonight. Over drinks, conversation had drifted to the prospects of war in Iraq and, as Maurice wanted to be included in this, the language shifted beyond his crude and functional shopping French. Gizande, across the table from him, was aware of his eyes upon her, increasingly blatant to the other couple too.

It became so intrusive to the talk between the French, that finally Gizande stopped, looked back at him and asked, with an arch look, almost challenging him, "Oui, Jim? What do you wish to say?"

Caught out, he honked a surprised laugh and looked from her to Suzanne, "Nothing about Iraq. That's for sure!"

Gizande laughed herself, wiped her nose and the two of them giggled, snickering together. Before she turned to the hosts, "Pardon. We are sorry. But-"

Maurice said something.

"Pardon?" Jim accented in French.

Suzanne and Gizande started to speak to Jim at once, but Suzanne deferred. "That we have a relationship together. Maurice says it is evident to the world, you and me," Gizande told him, smiling.

"It is true, Jim?" Suzanne asked, seriously.

"Yes. Yes," ending with an emphatically satisfied look at Gizande, "Of course. Naturellement!"

"Then, what do you plan?"

He looked at his sister, waking to the serious business of her question. "Plan?"

"Yes. Your plan." Shaking her head, "You will be living together?" waving a finger one-to-another, almost with admonishment. "You will not continue like teen age lovers? You will have a house together?"

The light mood of a moment ago had been clouded by her seriousness. Maurice looked on at his wife and Jim glanced at Gizande, before hesitantly starting, "We've- Gizande has spoken to her family- it's too early- both the kids start to go to college next year. By then La Retrait will be ready too." He grinned at Suzanne without conviction, "Then we'll have a choice of two homes to go to."

But she was shaking her head at him. "No. That is too long time, Jim," her eyes hard set on him alone in the room. "You have lived here for more than one year. Soon, you will be here two years in my home. You must make a plan to go sooner." Her discomfort with saying at last long-held-back feelings, hardened and distanced the edge of her words as she went on, "You have much consideration for the family of Gizande. But you have little consideration for your own family- for me," pointing at herself. "You have abandoned your first family- your daughter and your wife in England." His mouth to protest- braked hard by her hand spread-fingered at him, "Yes. I know there were the reasons for the finish of your marriage. There are always reasons. But you have no respect for this family here. You go to England. You do not return, but you go off again to Berlin. Sometimes I have a phone call to know if you return. If our daughter- if Marie-Claire was still at home and she did this, I would be asking her also to find another place to live." Then, with an emphatic angering, "You do not respect my family. You bring your doubts about our- about my father here- into the home that was his. You listen to the tales told by his enemies. But, of course, you are always the English gentleman- you are the guest, so you can act in no other way. When you see it upset me to bring me these stories, you tell me them no more. Is it the English discretion, do you call it?" Her shaken head forbade an answer, "But I can not now speak of my father in your presence, without I see the doubt in your eyes. And I know, Jim, you continue to search for what you will call the truth- like a wild pig seeking the truffles." She brought her hand to the side of her face, as if slapped by an invisible other, and plunged her look down to the floor before her. "And every time you return, I am fearful. What other story have you been told by an enemy? And I do not know, because now your politeness makes you silent- but your eyes… they are still impolite with the doubts in your heart." She stood suddenly, as if remembering something urgent elsewhere, then looked down at Jim, discomforted at the casual disarrangement of his limbs around the chair he sat in, gone rigid-stiff with listening to her. "You have his farm to live in. A gift. Why do you need to go on asking questions from the dead man who left it for you?"

And she was gone, into the kitchen. With the sound of her weeping.

Maurice followed, leaving Jim and Gizande looking after them, at the gap left in the doorway by their goings.

Then at each other and Gizande said, "You must come to stay with me on the farm. We must tell the children it is to be so. They must accept that it is so."

And Jim nodded, too confused with how this had suddenly turned around, to feel any joy about it.

Later Jim would reflect on the bizarre play that his dead father had again made with the life of the son he had left behind. And who had arrived in search, that few years too late. Francis had forced Gizande's hand, so-to-speak. She went after New Year to speak first with her mother, for if Gaillarde or Guillem did not wish to share the home with their mother's new lover, Gizande wanted to ask their grandmother if she would let them live there. Gizande returned from this meeting, cold with anger. Cruel things had been said, but she would not share them with Jim. She then asked the children to dinner with Jim. But Guillem had refused to come, staying down at his grandmother's and finally phoning the following night to say that he was going to live with his father and the new girlfriend. Only Gaillarde had come to the dinner, looking at Jim with a calculated and critical archness, as if challenging him to see her off the family property. Enfeebling Jim's attempts to be nice in English. She had already decided, anyway, to live with her grandmother and her attendance at the dinner was so that the two adults were in no doubt of her disapproval of their liason.

So the couple had got their way and the empty house. But it felt unsatisfactory. With Gizande veering between anger at her mother and her ex-husband and tears at the ease with which her children had deserted her. And Jim just felt the selfishness of that disruption his own satisfaction had caused. It became too the source of malicious gossip in the village and the shops. One day, in the agricultural suppliers with her, a big, rough man had said something to Gizande that caused the other farmers there to roar with laughter. She spat venom back at them and dragged Jim after her out of the store. Jim asked her what had been said, but she would not tell till they reached home. There, she said, "He hopes to hear from his farm the sound of my bed. With you. And if he does not hear this, he will come up to show you… how to pleasure me. I did not tell you, for you may have laughed also. With the other men."

"Gizande- no! It was a gross and childish thing for him to say." And she embraced him, as if the doubts spoken by her, were really her appeal to be reassured, comforted again by him.

Yves, the children's father had also come up to the farm one night, to argue with Gizande about money from her to pay for Guillem living with him. Afterwards, she had said that Yves had claimed Jim should pay because there were rumours that the Englishman had plenty of money. Like his English father before him. Why else would a younger woman like her sleep with an older man, but for money? So he should pay for his pleasures by paying for the children to live elsewhere. All Yves had for Jim was to say, as he left empty-handed, "Piece of English shit!" Probably the only English he knew.

But gradually, reluctantly, the world moved on and, as Jim did not go away, as indeed he appeared more often on his own on errands, beginning to speak in improving French, maybe l'anglais fou was going to stay. Was worth a smile from the shopkeepers, if just for the trade he brought.

As soon as the worst of the snow thawed to make it passable, they went up to La Retrait. A pane of glass had been broken downstairs, but otherwise, Jim's temporary and rushed work the summer before had survived. They planned to clear the shrubs in the fields directly around the farm to open it up as pasture. This first summer, Gizande would bring her own goats and sheep up to graze it. In time, maybe it would be worth renting for farmers down in the valley to bring their herds up for the fresh and juicy mountainside summer pasture it could become. The advertisement in the émigré newsheet had also brought him work and three times that summer before they returned to Berlin, he had driven to England and brought back a van-load of furniture to make real the dream of another wealthy English family in the rusticated romanticism of rural France. All the jobs had been based in the south of England, so he had neither the opportunity, nor the wish to return to his old home town. In fact this work was so rewarding that he and Gizande discussed possibly getting a loan to replace the tired and over-travelled Citroen. La Retrait electrified and completed in a simple crude manner and still unfurnished, Jim started to rebuild a tumbled barn at the back to become a garage and storeroom.

And there was the training for Berlin. Ever since Anna had sent them two entry forms for the Berlin Marathon- due to run thousands of runners through the Brandenburg Gate into the East at the end of September, three days before German Reunification. Gizande had said they would enjoy celebrating the fall of the Wall this second time around and every evening available, they set out along one of the tracks from her farm, running through the fields by the valley streams setting the dogs going in every twilit farmyard they passed. Or, if they had been working up at La Retrait, from there winding out of the meadows, up through the scree, to end up careful-footedly jogging along a knife-edge ridge, backs to the deepening cobalt behind them, faces down towards the closing, bloodied eye of the sun to the west. Before homewards, the race together to the finish, driving back to her farm, bathing each other and cooking, drinking and talking in the kitchen. Together there, into the night until later than they should have. They still talked between themselves in English, she being better in his language than he would ever be in hers, but out in the villages and towns, at the markets, Jim was increasingly confident in getting what he wanted in French, whatever the twisted faces at his accent.

Julian and Trish came over with Adam to stay for two days in April, passing through on a driving holiday into northern Spain, but as Gizande's fortieth birthday had recently passed, they were persuaded to stay for the belated party Suzanne and Maurice threw for it. For Jim, it felt like half a reconciliation between the two parts of his life. The coming together, edge-to-edge of the geographies of his two continents. And the return of some cautious warmth also between him and his sister. Gizande and Trish got on well together. Julian told him that Stephen was known to be in some specialist psychiatric unit for people with mental handicap, better at least than the prison system. Sylvie was still the Manager, but curtaining herself off from her staff with schedules of important meetings in preparation for the reorganisation of the Department. Scadding had been sacked and the Union was waiting to see if he wanted to appeal against it. By the time the couple left, Jim had to reluctantly admit he had been wrong. Julian and Trish looked like becoming long-term friends, both to himself and Gizande.

And then, four weeks before they were due to be leaving for Berlin, she came back up from a trip to Larozelle to him at La Retrait, with the news that she was pregnant. She had told him that she believed she might be prematurely menopausal, so they had several times not used contraception. Jim was dumbfounded at the news at first and said nothing, unsure from how she had told it, whether she was happy or not about it.

"Well. What do you think, Jim?" she asked, scrutinising him. " Are you able to be a father?"

"Of course!"

"And are you happy for it to happen?"

Watchful of her, "If you are, Gizande, I am."

She laughed and flung her body round him, pulling herself from the floor to crush him to her, "Oh, you English fool! I am so happy!" she mumbled into his ear. She dropped to the floor again and leaned back to look him in the face, "I am as happy as any time in my life. This child-" taking his hand and placing it beneath her jersey, on the warm skin of her belly, "Yes. This child will be born into a happy home. It is a gift to us, after we believed it was not possible."

He closed his eyes to concentrate on exploring his fingers across her flesh, as if already searching for signs of new life there already. Then looked at her, "Gizande, it is the most beautiful… thing."

"Doctor Rameau said to me that I am able to run in Berlin, but I must reduce the training. And I am not to run too hard in the race. Maybe you will have the opportunity to finish quicker than me for the second time, Jim, eh?" grinning up at him.

They went to bed together early and lay late into the night, her hand across the back of his, at rest on her stomach, talking quietly about the child to come. And the life they planned for it.

Chapter Thirty-eight

As her mother refused to help, Gizande had to pay a neighbouring farmer to come in to feed and water the animals and generally keep a watchful eye on the farm, while they were away. They left on the Tuesday, taking the secret of their baby with them. It was a beautiful mild September, with milky sunshine softening the landscapes and misting the forested hills as they entered Germany. They sat in the van, taking turns driving, talking about their future often through mouthfuls of the fruit, feeding them for the marathon. Parked off the big roads up what little lane they could find, it was cool those nights, but they were able to leave their sleeping bags unzipped far enough to sleep face-to-face, their hands on each other's bodies. Each of the mornings, an easy run together for twenty minutes before setting off again.

In Berlin, the *Foodi* sign out side the bar had changed to *Fast Foodi* and the banner, the same one that had welcomed *Gizi*, then the *Ossis*, overwritten now to read, *WILLKOMMEN OSSIS und WESSIES! Wir Sind Ein Volk!*

"Wasn't that different?" Jim asked. "Doesn't it say something else, now?"

"Yes. It welcomes people from the East and the West."

"But the other bit- at the bottom?"

"I think last year it say, *We are the people.* Now it say, *We are one people… We are one nation.*"

"And *Fast Foodi*, too?"

Anna had seen them from inside and leapt out across the pavement, shouting, "Gizi!" embracing her friend. Then turned to Jim, smiling impishly, "There! You English. I know that you get it together." Wagging her finger at him with admonishment, she turned back to Gizande, "I said to him last year. I knew it would happen between you two."

"Did you really, Anna?" Jim asked sceptically.

"Yes," with finality. Changing the subject, she pulled Gizande round to face Foodi's. "What do you think? A change, yes?"

"Yes. Now the end of Wessies and Ossies? Is it good in the new Berlin now?"

Anna put an arm through each of theirs and led them inside, "You will see. You will see. Andreas-" she stopped them and gave Jim a calculatedly teasing look, "I can speak of Andreas now, without a problem, yes, Jim?"

He half-smiled and shook his head at her.

"Okay. Andreas is angry. He shout at me about the banner. He does not wish the Reunification. He wanted true Socialism in the DDR. But DDR is kaputt. He is angry with the people for wanting one Deutschland. Angry with das Volk for voting for ein Volk," indicating the banner above them. "Yes? Come," drawing them inside. "The new Foodi. For us, business is good. The area here becomes better, with more young people. Here, it is okay."

The interior seemed to have more glass, more plastic and more strip light. It was half-crowded, a more youthful set than Jim remembered from last year.

Gizande asked, "Is Karla here?"

Anna went to the bar, "You want a drink?" Then, from behind the counter, "No. Karla has gone. Fast Foodi is not for her. She move to the old East of the city. She is opening a new restaurant. Near Alexanderplatz. For the businessmen who now go there from the West- to buy up the industries. Now I have boys from the East to work in my kitchen!" She laughed, "Everything change!" Then to Jim, "Helena also she has gone."

He was disappointed, "I'd hoped to see her. Where's she gone?"

"She went home. To Weimar. But she could not live there, in the East. She now lives in Nurnberg. She help with refugee children. At her age!" She shook her head. "Beers? Or can you not drink so near to your race?"

"Drink, yes," Jim answered. "But drunk, no."

"We have a supper for runners here on Saturday night." She pushed over to them a glass each of beer. "Big plates of pasta ready for the race. You will be here. I give you my folding bed for your stay." Then, to Gizande, "You will be comfortable there?"

"Yes. Ja, naturlicht."

Back to the world of divans again, Jim thought. But shared, at last. He took her hand beneath the cover of the counter and folded the familiar roughness of her fingers within his.

"I'd like to see the East," he said. "Before it goes for ever, next week- if you understand."

"There is nothing to see," Anna said dismissively. "And it is dangerous, now."

"Why?" Gizande asked.

"It is safe to stay here, in Wedding. Over there, there are many crazies now. That is why I think Karla is mad. To go over there. If you go there, be careful. And not at night."

"Why?"

"There is no order there. It is between DDR and Deutschland, not any country, you understand? There are gangsters there. And gangs of racist boys. And they have made an amnesty for prisoners, but with the politicos they have liberated many rapists and murderers. It is dangerous. Also Russian soldiers, they run away from their army and they take their guns with them- to join the gangsters with their AK47s. It is bad, bad, bad, over there. It is of no surprise that Helena go back to live in the West, in Nurnberg. And also, you will see the Poles. Strasse 17 Juni is like a dirty Turkish market. The Poles are living in buses there and are selling rubbish, the rubbish of their poverty." Then, she gave a cynical laugh, "Now that the Wall is down, also their foxes bring across from the East the Tollwut-" turning to Gizande, "what is that in English? The illness of dogs?"

"Rabies?" Jim suggested.

"Yes. I think so. Very dangerous. It kills a person if the dog bites, yes?"

Jim nodded, seeing something of the irritated bourgeois Wessi that she had not been last year. Only the hair was still a little spiky. "So you also aren't happy with the Wall being down?"

Anna pondered this, then, "No. The Wall had to come down. But it was too quick. It has permitted bad things to happen, before the government comes in from the West." Then, reflectively, "And, yes, it has changed the Berlin I have lived in. My Berlin will never be again. We lived from the Wall. We get tax money for all the things to make West Berlin look good- to make the Ossis who look over the Wall with jealousy. It was good for us- the theatres, the concerts- Andreas say that we were just the whore for capitalism. But, maybe whore was okay? It was fun, but now I think Berlin will become big city, serious with government, and important buildings. It will become so serious- without the jokes or the danger of how it has been." With a brusque rub of the counter top with a cloth, as punctuation, she finished with, "Maybe it is just that people do not like to change."

"Not when the past has been so good," Gizande said, and Jim thought of the cheerful crowds who had queued to cross through the Wall last year. And the fragile optimism of their hopes. Had the change they had sought been as good as they had hoped for?

"Maybe, also, I am becoming old," Anna said, with self-mockery. "I am sure becoming too boring," she grinned. "Complain, complain, complain." Then clinking their glasses with hers, "Gesundheit!" the three of them drank. "What about you guys?" Then repeated, almost salaciously, "What. About. You guys!" reaching over to rub their shoulders fondly.

"We will be having a baby," Gizande said, with quiet and watchful shyness.

"No! No!" and Anna broke into laughter. "And I say I am too old! Never too old!" Turning to Jim with a roguish look, "Never too old, Jim! Ha!" She came round the bar and embraced Gizande, speaking in German to her. Gizande replied and Anna turned to hug Jim, "A baby in the Spring. A Fruhling baby- ein kleines Kind- a little baby to keep you warm in the winter night. And to be born in the spring. Fruhling!"

Hit by the truth of it, Jim turned to Gizande, "Fruhling? Is that Spring? There's a name for it. Boy or girl. Fruhling."

Later, in the flat above the bar, when they were together alone again, Gizande said to him, "That was inspiration, Jim. Fruhling."

"It was natural. It was given to us. Isn't that how it felt?"

She smiled at first, then shaded into seriousness, "It is how everything between us has felt. That it was given to us. If we had the belief to take it."

"Perhaps." He worked his mind back over how things had happened. "It is hard to believe in that too deeply. For me, anyway."

"Why?"

"I have never believed in fate. I always believed you do things for yourself… to make things happen for you in the world. But… it's been different for me the last two or three years. It always seems to be something to do with my father. Do you understand?" But she looked quizzically uncomprehending. "I would not have come to France, without finding out about him. We would never have met without some letters from him that my Aunt Mary had kept. And held back from me till she died." He shrugged with the frustration of it, the dependence of events on that liar of a man, reaching out still from his grave in Suzanne's village. "That man guiding my life for the good? That's not possible to believe."

"Maybe… maybe, it is not as simple as that you say. Maybe it is not between you and your father. It is only a mechanism, the letters that bring you to France. So that we meet," shaping her fingers softly and seriously from the lobe of his ear to his jaw, before letting go.

"That's fate you're talking about," he replied. "But how could it through such a man? Do you believe he was as bad as he seems? What did your grandfather say about him? They knew each other, didn't they? In the war? And afterwards?"

"Your father was spoken of little in our family. I know he was known. But he was not to be talked of. I think that the stories my family had of him in the war were also the stories that were not heroic. People do not know what side he was fighting. Perhaps he just fight for himself. That is why I do not participate in the discussions between you and Suzanne. Her family have the story of your father being the hero of the Resistance."

"But you do not believe it?"

"I think that a mythology has been created after the war. It has become a war of heroes and monsters. But I think it was more complicated than that. To become a soldier, a man signs a contract with the devil. To kill. If you are a soldier without uniform- a maquis- hiding, coming out to kill, then hiding again, things must also be done that are the acts of the devil himself. Traitors must be killed silently, without justice. An attack on the Germans will bring with it the cost of innocent people killed in reprisals. Perhaps your father was the sort of man who calculated that was a price worth paying? There were many such men hiding in France during the war, making those calculations with the lives of others. Many are heroes, with their names on monuments in the villages. It is true of all wars, is it not?"

"I don't know. I never fought in a war. But that does not make him right… because he did as others."

"No. Not right. But inevitable." She stood and walked over to the window, lifting the edge of the blind to look out on the night-lit street. "It was also why I came to Germany, at first. After the 1968 events, it was the Gaullists who march in victory down the Champs Elysées, waving the flags and singing the revolutionary songs of 1789. In Germany, the young people were burying the myths of the heroism of war. The glory of the Nation. Here war was murder, in France war was still glory. Here, the young people marched to silence the mouths of the old men and women with guilt. For what they had done in the war."

"That was with Andreas?" Jim asked, but regretted the asking.

"Yes," she said tiredly, turning back into the room. "Yes. That was with Andreas. It is over. How many times do I have to say that to you?"

"No. I was just trying to understand." Adding, without conviction, "Just what had happened."

"Well, now you know, Jim. Andreas was my past, just as Sylvie was yours. Does that make it equal? Or should I be jealous that you will get back into bed with her when you collect furniture from England?"

"I'm sorry. I didn't mean…"

She came over and ruffled his hair, a little too roughly for affection alone, "Silly boy!" Then, throwing two of the divan cushions onto the floor, "Time for sleep. Rest the bodies for the Race." Pausing halfway through bedmaking with him, she added, "Maybe we would not have met, if we had not had our lovers before. For me, Yves and Andreas. For you, Jane and Sylvie. If we had met before them, would we have been free to discover our love? Would we have been given the eyes to see each other," looking up at him, "as we see each other now?"

He could only agree that the failures of life before now made such a success for him of the present. And she was right. He was a fool to doubt it.

Chapter Thirty-nine

Saturday was glorious. It was the warm up run for the foreign runners, a celebratory jog through the Berlin streets to the Olympic Stadium to loosen the muscles for tomorrow's 42 kilometres. Singing through the echoing tunnel under the Stadium and out into the wide amphitheatre of stacked stone benches, the runners crowded in, spreading themselves in seated groups, about the grass and up the steps.

"Hitler's 1936 Games," she said to him, as they ambled to a stop. "Stolen from him, by a black American runner."

"Yes, Jesse Owen. We're reclaiming it now, just as we will reclaim the city as one."

"But easy for us. We will be on our way back to home, when they have to work with the problems of their reunification."

"Yes. Anna isn't happy about it."

"No." She pointed to soldiers handing out sandwiches to the runners. "Our second petit dejeuner, Jim. Come." As they queued, she said, "Did you hear her last night?"

"No."

"She came to bed with one of her Ossi cook boys." She shook her head, "That is not the Anna I know. She has become unsympathetic. She is losing the fun of who she was."

"I know what you mean."

"I wish to get this race over tomorrow and leave this city. It is as you said in the Dordogne last year. I am not the Gizande I was. And now, this city is no longer Berlin. For me, that is true." She put her arm round his waist, "I wish to get home. For our little family, no?" smiling up at him.

They had reached the front and took the snack and the drink each. Finding an unoccupied stretch of stone, Jim gently suggested, "I would like to see if we could visit Helena, if it's not too far off our route."

She looked at him. "Ah, the old lady. I think you are a little in love with her, no? It is a big detour from the way home."

"I would like to. She's old and it may be the last chance to see her. She said she wanted to speak to me and we never really had the chance. Both times." He looked away, reflectively, "I don't know what it is about her. She knows so much. She's lived. A bit like you, I s'pose. Getting nuggets of wisdom about life, so far on in mine." He put his arm round her shoulders, "Maybe I am a bit in love with her, but you'd be there to keep an eye on me."

"To keep an eye…?"

"To see that I behave myself."

"Okay. But remember, I am jealous of this woman who can give you wisdom I am unable to give. But first we run the race. You phone her after. We may wish to go home direct. Decide if we go to Nurnberg after." She stood up, "Now I am cold, sitting on this Nazi stone. And this sandwich is not fresh. We return to Anna."

"And perhaps she is out of bed with the chef!"

That night, after the pasta meal at Foodis, Jim and Gizande ignored Anna's warnings and caught the U-bahn across the disappearing demarcation to the East. They got out at Alexanderplatz, but it was empty, dark and as threatening as Anna had said. Racist graffiti on the walls where the hundreds of thousands had marched less than a year earlier. Distant shouts reminded Jim of some of the estates he had left behind in England. It was not what they wanted to see and they went back west on the train soon. After they went to bed, he lay awake a long time listening to the low rasp of her sleeping breath. Anna quietly came through to bed, alone, after the bar closed and he closed his eyes in assumed sleep. He finally drifted off when the first light was already washing round the edges of the blind.

She was up first and he lay there listening to her in the shower. A little frightened of what the day would do to his body. When she came out, dressed in her tracksters and teeshirt still towelling her hair, he asked, "Will we race against each other today?"

She considered this. "We will decide at the start. It is how we feel then."

Looking at her, he just wanted to let her win everything. Jumping out of bed, he pulled her into his arms, felt he should say something significant, but spoilt for choice, the moment was lost.

She disengaged from him. "This uses too much of our energy, that we require for the race." With only half a smile.

They were shepherded by stewards at the start at Charlottenburger Gate. First they stripped off down to their shorts and running vests, pinning on their numbers, then each putting the bag of their top clothes in the back of one of the trucks to collect at the finish. Given a blue balloon each, smiling foolishly at the childishness of it, they were herded through fencing to crowd together with the thousands of others, cold shoulders to strangers in the damp, misted air clattering with helicopters. Next to Jim, a middle aged German was softly singing "Deutschland uber alles" to himself, over and over again. He could hear some English voices around him and smiled at them.

"Not too fast for the baby," he smiled at her.

"For Fruhling," but she had not entirely lost her seriousness.

"Run together? Or race?" he asked.

She looked at the backs around her, too short to see across the huge crowd. "Run together to 35 kilometers. Then we see if we race."

"If we have any race left in us then!"

"Just enjoy the run, Jim."

The crowd was beginning to shuffle forward, in a surge of expectation. There was a bang as Gizande's balloon burst. The German looked at the couple with heavily ironic sorrow, "I think that is significant for you, ja? Symbolic."

Jim gave a grin he did not feel and offered his balloon to her, "Here. Have mine."

She shook her head. Then smiled, rubbed her stomach and, looking away, said, "One balloon for me is enough."

At that moment a cheer went up, the crowded heaved forward, eased back, then waited. Released balloons filled the air and Jim let his go, without watching it. And waited, toes tipped to push forward those first steps, walking, breaking into a shuffle, then a few foreshortened run paces, impatient with walking again, until at last, spaces of free roadway opened up and they were hesitantly off, dodging slower runners. Until, steady pacing at last next to each other, passing under the S-bahn bridge, the broad road of massed runners stretching ahead of them towards the east, he said to her, "At last. We're off."

"Stay with me," she said.

"Where am I going?" Getting his breath, before continuing, "It's you that can run away from me." Another pause. "Can you run slow enough to keep up with me?" An unlaughed joke.

They settled into the running and around them, the shouting at the start faded, concentration took over, with the sound of the rhythmical panting of thousands and the slap-slap of running shoes on the damp road. After fifteen minutes, through the Brandenburg Gate, still Russian guards on the monument for a few days yet, the crowds in the East had spilled half across the roadway, funnelling the runners together again, under the loud-speakered "Ode to Joy" tinnily roaring round them. He checked her from the corner of his eye several times, but she was inwardly centred on her spare and economical pacing, so he took her lead and started to settle himself, step-for-step, alongside her. Cyclists racing them along the pavements, kids running a stretch beside them, episodic knots of crowds, all receded to the very edge of vision, pushed back kilometre after kilometre, as the body sealed itself off from the discomfort, shrunk itself inwards from the ultimate, incremental and inevitable pain. The confusion and broken pace around the drinks stations, crushed plastic cups clacking underfoot, checking she was still there, but both saying nothing now. Measuring himself, and her, against those who had shaken out as the race went on to be their nameless companions. A tall thin man in red kit with a slow lope. Two men from a Berlin running club, intermittently chattering together. Two men ahead, but drawing away, wearing white *Essex Police* teeshirts, complete with little helmets. At about 25 kilometres a group of men gathered round two women came up from behind, drew alongside, wordlessly and gradually pulled away, their distance demoralisingly reminding Jim of his creeping exhaustion.

"Go, Jim," she was looking at him, reading his tiredness.

He nodded ahead at the group, "You can go if you want." A few more paces. "This is nearly as far as I've ever run."

"At 32 kilometres. Maybe."

Now in suburbia, only scattered spectators, cooling drips off the trees above the road. A sheet of numbness wrapped itself around his thighs. To keep up with her, he was having to speed up his pace, before lapsing, spurt and lapse, spurt and lapse, each time a little more distance to make up on her.

She dropped back to him, "It is the runner's wall, Jim. This is the real wall to cross."

He shook his head, "Go, Gizande. Go on," adding, "My love."

"No." She ran a few silent steps, looked at him without him looking back. Then, Jim's pace so slowed down, his body defeated, "Are you certain?"

"Yes," wanting her off and away from the dragging humiliation.

"I will wait for you at the finish." With a final, "I love you. Also," she put her face up to the road ahead and started to move away from him.

He watched her back, wanting her to give a last glance back to him. When her slight, steadily moving figure disappeared into the runners ahead, tears started to collect at the corners of his eyes and run back into his hair with his sweat. But there was still a finish to be reached. He wiped his face, sniffed hard to suck the mucus down the back of his nose, coughed the gobbet of it into his mouth and spat it out onto the roadway. The 31 kilometre marker was coming up. A bit more than six miles to go. He had done that scores of times. He mastered his legs, despite the pained stress of them, and step-by-step, got himself steadily moving forward again, the world around him sealed off in the cocoon of concentrated discomfort he drew about himself. To get himself home.

In that last interminable stretch, those who had saved something for the finish were passing him, one after another. At last the crowds started to accumulate alongside the wide road, he passed a runner, even more beaten than him, realising that he was regaining a last wind, a struggled mastery over the teetering wobble of his calves and thighs. Ahead, across the road, a structure everyone seemed to be racing for, so he set himself a last effort to reach it in some sort of battered style. But at the outer edge of all the effort he could gather, he realised they were running beneath it and beyond. He slowed for a minute, then to the gathering roar of the crowd ahead, he gritted every last shred of resource in his body, dipped his head down and forced his feet ahead again, not looking up, just getting there, accelerating a little with it, a runner in green strip out of the corner of his eye, all the venom of his energy on beating him now, a man in the road waving him across to the right, the scaffolding across the finish ahead, *4 : 2 fifty-something* on the digital clock, the green strip out of sight, he was suddenly in the funnel- there- hand on a cold metal bar, reeling, legs folding slowly beneath him, he let himself go, settling on the tarmac. All he could think was, Finished. Over and over again.

"Come on, mate," arms under his. It was the green man, behind him. English. "You okay?"

With a collection of arms to help him, he staggered to his feet again, took a few assisted steps, then shook them off. Someone hung a medal round his neck, another wrapped him in a white plastic sheet. There were camp beds lined along the roadway with masseurs working at the legs of prostrate runners, drink tables, boxes of bananas, tables full of some sort of cake, runners milling round them, some chattering together, some as bemused as Jim. When she found him, embracing him by surprise from behind.

"Oh, Jim. My love." She came round to him, unwrapped the sheet to press her damp cold body to his. "We have run through the Wall. Both of us."

But he was still too drunk with tiredness and a sort of torn and ragged elation, to say anything back to her. He let himself be led. A peeled banana into one fist. A cup of water into the other. To the truck for their bags of clothes, then to the tented showers set up in the middle of this street, everyone, men and women stripping themselves naked together, stood in the clouds of steam, waiting their turn. Jim let himself be led by her and stood motionless as she soaped him down, his mind glazed off behind the windows he looked at it all. From the distance where he was.

Going out of the finishing area later, barely able to walk, he said little, concentrating on the mechanics of moving his legs.

"What did you think, Jim? Of the experience?"

Looking at her with disbelief, "Awful. Never again."

She laughed, "The first marathon, that is always said. Tomorrow, you will think different. When the pain has gone."

"No. I will remember it. Pain like this I will always remember."

She smiled again, then wagged her finger at him, "No. I tell you. Tomorrow, you will say to yourself, only three minutes faster and I run to the finish in less than four hours. You will plan the next race."

He shook his head. "No. I will plan how to stand at the finish with Fruling- on my shoulders- to see his Mama running in less than three and a half hours." She hugged him, but, "Don't! It hurts. If you love me, find the U-bahn station."

Chapter Forty

Back at Anna's, he asked her for Helena's phone number in Nurnberg.

Gizande looked on expressionlessly, as Jim addressed Anna's surprised look, "Before I leave Germany, I must see Helena."

"Hah!" Anna snorted. "Why is this?"

"I don't know really." Jim searched around for the words, "Everything here is so… sudden… it happens, everyone has hopes- then it changes. It gets turned into something else."

"In Berlin, we call that, Life."

"No… but Helena seems to understand- the history of things," feeling foolish with the pretentiousness of it.

"Nein. History? No! She is as confused as the rest of us. You would be best going down to the Wall and paying five Deutschmarks to hire a hammer from one of the boys down there and to chip off a piece of history to take home with you in your pocket. Before it all disappears. Why travel all the long journey to Nurnberg to listen to a confused old lady?" She turned to Gizande, "Do you agree with this?" a dismissive hand towards Jim. "Do you wish to go there to see her?"

Gizande answered, her studied eyes on him, "If he does not go, he will always dream what he has missed. I know Jim. That is who he is. Better to go and be disappointed, than to not go at all."

He nodded.

Anna shrugged, "You go. I find the number. Why do I care?" He remembered the videotape and the statement he had left with her last year, but knew he would say nothing of it now. Or ever.

At first, on the phone, Helena was confused who he was. Then remembered. She sounded cautious with him, her invitation to him hedged with some reluctance. Having asked, he did not see how he could refuse. So it was agreed. Tuesday morning. She told him her address, and of a campsite close to the suburb she lived in.

They left Berlin Monday morning, Gizande leaving a note for Anna, still shut in her bedroom. Given the way of Anna now, easier than awkward goodbyes, prickly with her scepticisms. She drove, with Jim still too stiffened from the day before. The weather continued to be mild, settled and misty. They had a box of tapes and they played through them, singing along together to the ones with old sixties songs on them. She, glad to be at least on the first stage of getting back home, he, relaxed that she was indulging him with the Nurnberg diversion. Thinking through the oddness of the day before, their disengagement from each other during the race, their separation, the loss of her through the crowds of runners ahead, a potent image of her even now. A strange and private woman. A life on her terms. That he was prepared to accept.

The afternoon light was already darkening around the sombering pines and firs of the campsite, as they arrived, checked in and found a remote place under the trees. After they had made up their makeshift bed in the back, Jim pulled the doors closed and they lay together in the half-light.

She moved her head onto his shoulder. "Is this how it will always be with us?"

He hesitated, unsure what she was saying, good or bad. Finally, "What do you mean?"

"So happy. Together."

"Are you happy. Really?"

"Why do you ask? Why do you doubt?" She moved to look into his face.

He avoided this with, "It will not always be so quiet," sliding his hand over her womb. "Not after the baby comes."

He could feel her studying him. "Why do you not answer my question, Jim?"

"What?" moving his hand off her.

"Why do you have doubt? That I am happy with you," but he sensed she was also smiling.

"Do I? Maybe it's because I can't- I find it difficult to believe it."

She lay back and pulled his free arm across to place his hand over her breast. "Maybe… maybe, it is your doubt that makes me feel safe. With the doubt, you will never forget to ask yourself also, if you are doing the right- if you feel the right feelings for me. And for Fruhling, also," she added. "Without doubt arrives forgetfulness."

Moving his fingertips round on the breast. Till he felt the nipple enlargen, gently massaging it through the teeshirt between finger and thumb and she pulled at his head to guide his mouth to hers. Memory and doubt, he had plenty of that, he thought as he pulled away with wet lips to look down at her. And he spoke the thought. "I don't doubt at a moment like this, Gizande. Does this mean I won't remember it?"

"Oh! You fool! Idiot!" as she pulled at his ears to shake it out of his head, he realised that, within his sombreness, he had cracked a joke for her.

They ate at the quiet end-of-season café on the site and went to bed early. Jim was still uncomfortable with stiffness and she massaged him. Though aroused, his limbs were too inflexible and lifeless for lovemaking. She said a gentle run in the morning to loosen themselves, despite his complaint at the prospect. Before falling asleep beside him, his arm curled around her head, fingers resting with the lightest touch within the delicate undergrowth of fine hairs on the back of her neck.

When they set out the next morning, Jim, though rested, still could only run at first in a comical shuffle. She patiently stepped slowly beside, to match him. It was damp under the trees from a night shower. Out on to more open parkland with a football stadium, the road led them round until they found themselves stepping up the pace a little, passing in front of a grandiose building, tiered with rows of weeded and cracked stone steps, graffiti slogans spray painted on the back wall, some empty beer bottles clustered beside the podium that projected out towards the roadway.

"What is it?" he asked.

"I don't know. I am not certain."

Onwards, they left the road to follow a path beside a lake. Some other distant joggers. Jim feeling some of the stiffness creeping outward from his legs, picking up the pace slightly, smiling at her. "There you are-life in the old dog, and all that."

"Pardon?"

"The old dog. Me. I've still got life in me legs."

"Naturellement. Jamais doute."

He grinned, "Non. Moi, toujours doute. Oui? I wouldn't give up my doubt for anything." Remembering the night before.

She laughed, "I would not permit you to give it up."

At this point they came out onto a huge road, massive stone slabbed, stretching to left and to right. She led off down its monumental emptiness and he followed, bemused by the scale of it, the silence except for the patter of their shoes and the far hum of traffic in the city. Gradually covering the distance down to a traffic barrier at the bottom, turning together and heading back up it. The parallels of the roadway meeting in the infinity of how far it stretched ahead. Seeing the tiered building they had passed before, step-by-step emerge from behind the trees.

"I think I know where we are. I understand."

"What?"

"These are the Rally Grounds. The Nazi Rally Grounds. There!" she pointed. A sign, reading *Grosse Strasse.* "This is where they marched for Hitler."

He looked around, the parkland that had grown around it, so gentle. To set against the grubby decay of these monuments. Gravestones.

They ran on silently. Till she murmured, "Listen." Leaning her head forward, "Do you hear?"

He looked at her dumbly, then around. "What?" spoken like her, taking up her quietness.

"The sound of feet. Can you not hear it? The sound of marching feet," looking over at him.

He understood, looked down at the road in front and listened, at first only hearing the frail sound of their slapping trainers… then faintly, a backrhthym to their footsteps, loudening and ponderous, the grind of a million simultaneous boots starting to stamp across the slight reverberations of their own stride-by-stride running, thunderously resonating in their skulls, tramp-tramp-tramp. Regiment after regiment. The clatter of death, in unison… rank upon rank upon rank of young men… Till Gizande swerved off as they reached the lake, he followed and, feet back on the soft, moist path, the sound gone from their heads.

"Ghosts," was all she said. And he had nothing to add.

Helena's flat was in a modern block, looking across from the other side of the parkland they had been running in. The stone hulks were hidden amongst the trees from her window. Something faded, a little shabby anxiety about her now, she sat them down in the living room with an even older man she introduced as her brother in law, Stephan. Discovered by her in Weimar and brought here with her. While she was out in the kitchen preparing coffee, he smiled at them, then uncertainly pulled a worn and folded document from his jacket. He handed it to Jim. Opening it, he could not avoid shedding bits of the old crumbly paper onto his own lap. It was in German, but there was swastika at the top. He was about to hand it to Gizande, when Helena came in with the tray of cups.

"What's this?" offering it to her.

She took it, folded it brusquely and said some harsh words to Stephan before thrusting it back into the old man's hand. Then turned to Jim, "It is his foolishness. He always does this with a new visitor."

"What is it?"

She was reluctant to tell, almost apologetic, "His mind is fading. He is all I have remaining of family now. He was alone in a home for the old people in Weimar. I moved him to live with me, so, when I leave, I bring him with me. To here." She sat down to attend to the coffee, continuing while she poured, her eyes down to the crockery. "The paper, it was given to him by the Nazi Youth. They took his bicycle in 1945. They were taking every bicycle. To go off to fight against the Russians, with bicycles and hand bombs. Pheu! The paper is for Stephan to get his bicycle back from the Hitler Youth. Every visitor he thinks is the man to bring it back. What he saw in those years, it has made his brain untidy." She handed out the coffee, delicately china-cupped. Then turned to Jim, "You wished to visit me. For a reason."

Unsure whether it was a statement with more to follow, or a question, he waited for her. But she looked at him, forcing him to speak something at least to her and the audience of Gizande and the old man. "We had only the smallest chance to speak last year. I wanted to see you before we went back to France again." Enough of an explanation?

"I see that you and Gizi are together still." Ignoring what he had said.

"Yes." Then, checking with her, before saying to the old lady with the glow, half-shy, half-proud, whenever he said it, "We are to have a baby."

"Ah. A baby. Both French and English. Good." Said without colour.

"But we are giving it a German name. Fruhling."

She emitted a harsh laugh. The old man beside her smiled. Jim wondered what she meant by it. About being childless herself? As far as he knew. He looked at Gizande for help, but she was looking out at the vacant sky.

"Fruhling?" she finally said. "That is the spring season? Is this to memorial the new Germany?"

"No," said quietly, "Nothing like that." Unable to explain the rightness of the chosen name in words, feeling alone and washed up against the error of visiting this changed, apparently embittered old woman. Tentatively, he shifted her away from Gizande and him and the child, to engage her with herself, "How is the new Germany for you? You moved from Weimar?"

"The new Germany?" Then, with the rehearsed routine of frequent repetition, "The new Germany? What is that? More argument. More uncertainty. Again the ground moves beneath us here. What do you know?" To Jim, "From England." To Gizande, "From France. This-" pointing down through the floors of the flats below, to the earth they sat upon- "this is the country of disputed belief. In England, you unified. You had your Queen Elizabeth, you… France also." Jim looked at Gizande again, but she was determinedly faced outside the room, no recognition of what Helena was saying. "Their Revolution, a single country. Unification for us? Never. When we argue about religion then, we had Luther and Rome. But also we had Luther against Calvin. Luther against Zwingli. Dispute! Dispute! Prussia and Bavaria and Saxony. No nation, just little princes who gave themselves big titles. Who permitted the armies of Spain, of France and of Sweden to march across our lands for thirty years." She angrily forced Jim to return her gaze. "You have heard of that war?"

Jim dumbly shook his head. Alone with Helena's venom and the chaos of her saying it, the uncomprehending Stephan smiling on, Gizande away with her gaze. Why just him listening? And hearing?

"No. You would not. No one teaches the history of Germany before Hitler. The cities were burned…" Then, with restraint, looking at the tray on the table before her. "It has been the history of Germany. Our burning cities…You remember that?" challenging him, then away to herself… "I remember Berlin… at the railway station… women were arriving from Hamburg- after the Feuersturm-" grasping for the English- "the fire from the bombing?"

"Fire storm," Gizande said. Jim looked at her, but she still had her eyes out of the room.

"Yes. Firestorms. Your young men, your terror bombers. They were our Hiroshimas. The women in the station were mad with it. Crazy, dead eyes. I remember the crazy eyes. Some had children with them, hair burnt off. But one, just before me. A young woman," looking down at the place on her carpet where the memory was happening again. "She carried her case- it fell open. It was knocked by the people around her. And there… just there, it all fell onto the floor of the station, the toys, the clothes and… like a doll… mixed with them… but it was not a doll." She looked up into Jim's eyes, hers perhaps as empty for a moment as the woman's, "It was her child. Without clothes. A little boy. Naked and brown and black and yellow, from the flames. It… he, fell among the feet of strangers. He rolled a little on the marble… before everyone saw, and stood back from the sight…" The sound of her breathing in the recollection… until, "She had carried her dead child in her luggage all the way from Hamburg." Either a shrug or a shiver, she looked down again, "I have thought of that woman again. After many years. What happened to her? If she had lived, if she had survived the Russians… what would her dreams be like now. After all those years? She was of my years, I think. Or maybe younger." She sighed. "I remember these things more clearly as I am older. The years have stripped away from me the paralysis that protected me. Now I can only remember. Like Stephan, for me also it is those years that are more alive than today. Or yesterday, or tomorrow. I remember the sounds. The English bombs dropping, even distant from me, like the sound of heavy corpses being thrown down the cellar steps of the next house."

She receded into her thoughts and the room stayed still for her, Jim not moving, Gizande still motionless beside, even Stephan picking up the restraint of the moment. Then, quietly, "It is how I remember that sound." After a further pause, rising tiredly from it, "We are as disposable in the new Germany, as we were in the old. That was the German Economic

Miracle, as they call it. It was the breaking of our spirits. The National Socialists did it to us to fill the factories with good workers. The bombers did it to us after that. When the new factories were built with Yankee dollars, the good workers were ready to march back into them again." She paused, the fragility of the anger in her slight body, caved in, collapsed, for a moment. When she resumed, her voice as harsh as a rusted hinge, "Yes. We are disposable. It is only when the men of power- the politicos- give us permission, only then… Gizi?" she appealed to the other woman, who reluctantly turned from the window. "Gizi," and said a sentence in German.

Gizande nodded. Jim took this chance of re-engagement to reach his hand over to hers. Which lay limp beneath his touch.

"Yes. It is the words of Voltaire. To cultivate our gardens. Only with their permission, can we cultivate our gardens- can we do what we wish." Adding waspishly, nodding at Gizande's lap, "Even to hold hands together." Seeing Jim's shadow of a wince at this, "You came to see me. It was your wish. It was your invitation to visit this old woman. You wanted to hear what I have to say?" Then, with emphatic bitterness, "Men I have never met have determined the events of my life. They took my husband. They starved us to death after the war. They prevented me from the return to my home." With almost feeble triumph, she spelt out the words, "Now, it is too late." Jim thought for a moment that the old woman would surely fold up and surrender into sobbing. With the pain of it. But her eyes were dry, empty again.

Unable to turn to Gizande for the fragility of the moment, with the slightest pressure on the back of her hand, he sought her reassurance.

Helena reached her own hand across to Stephan and brought it into her own bony lap. The old man reached across with his other hand and sealed hers within it. She looked at him, briefly, searchingly. He just smiled back at her. Then at Gizande and Jim opposite, the two couples, hand-in-hand in the aching stillness of the room, that looked across this city. Helena took her eyes from them. "Now. Too late. My home, it is there no longer, as I knew it. Weimar. All those I knew are dead. I visited the cemetery there. It is beautiful." She paused, entering the place. "Quiet, with many trees. There are always people there to feed the flowers on the graves of their loved ones with water. It was that I visited there… that, decided me to leave. Too many dead friends and family there. Fathers and sons buried together from the two wars, both boys, marked on the same grave together, carried home from Verdun and from Russia. And the camp on the hill above the town. Where my husband and I walked in the woods there as lovers, before. And where the Russians killed him. Buchenwald."

She rolled her head slowly from side to side. "It was too painful for me. Better that the Wall had stayed- to stop me returning there." She turned to the old man next to her and, knotting her shrivelled fingers into his, exchanged a gaunt smile with his sunny one, "But I found Stephan. And there was a friend of the past in Nurnberg, who is assisting the refugee children who are coming in from East Europe- from Romanie, from Polen, from Bulgaren. So we came here. It was a way to give a little of my life that is left, with the future. With children. Not with the past and its dead."

Tears now showed at the corners of her eyes, trapped and glistening there in the webs and tangles of her lined and crumpled skin. Stephan, with immensely attentive delicacy, brought his arm round her thin shoulders and pulled her head to his, leaned slightly in upon each other, to rest temple against temple. Through watery eyes, she looked across at Gizande and Jim. "Forgive me the sentimentality. It is the way the wounds of reality so harsh, can be healed… with the tears of sentiment." She sat up again, pulled a lacy handkerchief from the sleeve of her blouse and dabbed at her eyes and the tip of her nose. "Now they stop me from being with the children. I weep too often. Now I can only work in the office, but-" holding up her hand with spread, crooked fingers - "I think these are too weak now for working on the typewriting machines."

She was finished at last, looking down at the handkerchief crushed in the pale and wrinkled hand left in her lap, resting next to Stephan's darker knuckles. Gently rubbing her own knuckles across the old man's, reassuringly. She looked up at Jim, a faint smile, "That is my life - that you wanted to hear. Can you learn wisdom from it, Englishman?"

He wanted to apologise to the old woman. For what? He cleared his throat with nervousness, then, "It must never happen again."

"It will. If the time is suitable. That is not wisdom, to wish it never again. A child would wish that, would he not?"

Gizande spoke, clear but quiet, "That is the wisdom of the child. The foolishness of the adult is to forget that wisdom, by only to think of what is possible." Jim watched the calm absoluteness of her profiled face.

Her voice unchallenged in the room for so long, Helena looked at Gizande with calculation, before speaking, almost patronisingly. "How can it be wisdom to wish for what is not possible? That is the dream of a child."

As controlled and certain as she was before, Gizande answered, "It is only when we wish for what is not possible, that we can make that which is not possible, happen." She turned her hand over and took Jim's into hers, looking at last at him. "We must depart. The journey."

Helena was not disappointed, only asking Jim, "You will come back to Germany again?"

He wanted to check with Gizande, but she had already started to stand, so he said, "I'm sure we will," doubting it as soon as said.

They shook hands with the smiling old man and out on the landing outside the door, Helena said "I hope well for the baby. I do, with my heart," as if this might be challenged.

"I hope for you and Stephan…" What could Jim hope for them? "…some peace."

"Oh, Stephan! He is my child. If they will not let me near the little Romanian gypsy children now, I have my Stephan. With his smiling and his nightmares."

A moment of awkwardness between the three of them there, how to part? Then Helena stepped back into her doorway, waving them away with the handkerchief, "Go! Go away! Depart! On your journey." Before Jim and Gizande had moved, she had turned and closed herself back in the flat, with the smiling old man.

Chapter Forty-one

They sat together back in the van for a time, before starting off. Uncertain of her, he was exhausted, wrung of what to say by all they had observed upstairs. And by the running through the tidied and sculptured rubble of those ruinous memorials that morning. Witnesses, again.

Gizande spoke at last. "She has started to remember. As old people near to death must. Either remember, or go mad with the forgetting. And as she remembers, she must explain her life. How the terrible things she saw have happened. To explain it, she cannot be a participant. She must be a victim too. As the old men of the Politburo of the DDR saw themselves. Victims of the Nazis. That all the war crimes were from the Germans in the West- the opposite side of the Great Anti-Fascist Barrier they built." She looked at Jim, inquiringly, "Is that how we live with our great disasters? We make it the fault of others?"

"I don't know." But he was so overwhelmed with the relief of being out of that flat and being with her again, he could only say, trying to retrieve something by smiling fondly to her, "And what of our successes? Are they the fault of others?"

"Successes?" she echoed, as if barely registering the eagerly uncertain boy-child beside her, who wanted so much to get on with their life together. Now. But she caught his mood for a moment and smiled, despite herself, "Successes? Ah, those are always the fault of ourselves. Naturellement! Even the ghost of your father from his grave- he bring us together, but he could not make me love you, Jim. Only you could do that." But, become serious again, she reached across her hand into his hair, her eyes intensely upon him, "We have been able to escape from that other world. That is why you have departed from England. They did not wish to hear from you that it could be different. Or from any person. It is those message carriers who are disposed. Put into exile in another land. You, Jim. But Helena cannot escape. That world is in her head… too much in her head. With its Wall, with its burning cities. With the cemeteries of her friends. Her husband and Buchenwald. There is nothing for her now, outside that world. There is no exile possible from that world in her mind." Her hand tightened on his head, almost urgent with her words, as if to press the irrevocable must-be of her words through the bone of his skull, "For us not to be a piece, a morsel of that world, we must not be in it. It does not wish for us there. Do you understand, Jim? We must be of ourselves. This is for us. And for Fruhling."

He was uncertain what she was saying and hesitated.

"Do you understand, Jim?" almost plaintively.

"I'm not sure… what does that mean? Not be in it?"

"It means to say, no. It means that we do what is the duty to ourselves. We have been fighting too many battles- you, most of all, for other people. Now, you have done enough, to find peace in your heart. With us," cupping the other hand protectively over the still small foetus inside her. Her face locking him to her. And falling either side from the moment they sat within, behind them the shaded and hidden grimnesses of all their pasts, and before them, the faintly felt and optimistic glow of Fruhling inside her.

He peeled her hand from his head and put his mouth to her palm. When he looked at her and said, "Of course," almost silently in the intimacy of the van cab, there were tears in his eyes. He thought of Helena and of sentiment, the healer. And of Tracey, that other child, to whom he had never been able to make or keep such a promise. Hoping, for this time, to get it right.

Gizande pulled him over to her and kissed, long, almost touched with desperation. After they disengaged, she said, "I will drive."

She drove it back through the parkland, back into the Rally Grounds and stopped the van in front of the tiered and decayed monument they had run past earlier. There was a coach parked up the road, with a cluster of tourists taking photographs. Herded close together, sheltering far enough away from the sinister pallor of the stained stone

"Why've we stopped here?"

She jumped down and came round to his door. "Come." He stepped down. "One last time, Jim. One last time, we will do our duty. For our world, against theirs."

She took his hand and led him up the steps, tugging him upwards, his legs still stiffened, climbing to the top, till they stood, back against the graffiti wall, exactly beneath where the huge stone swastika had once crowned it. Looking down the dozen or so steps to the podium itself. Where He had stood, face to the multitude in ranks, stretched away before Him, arrogant with the certainties the sight and sound of it all gave to Him.

She tugged his hand, whispering, "Come."

He followed her step by step downwards, hesitant. Till they stood on the last one. The cluster of empty beer bottles to his left. A wall of the history of this place, impenetrable for that moment, they stood back from it, held where they were. He was haunted by the indecision, by the awe of it, by the block-upon-block impossibility of understanding it all. The modesty of his self stood in the vast, still space of this place, swirling his head with the pandemic of events spawned from where they nearly stood, almost giddy with the thinking of it.

When she then stepped up there, almost afloat the certainty of her intent, pulling him after.

And he followed her to the plain metal balustrade, steadying himself against it, cold beneath his hand. No one there, but the two of them, hand in hand. Watching the coach load of tourists driving off and a girl, nonchalant with style, riding a bike one-handed, along the road beneath them. Weaving casually off with a clatter of her wheels. Leaving them alone. With the silence, stretched as far as they could look, even the trees unruffling, the faintest moan of life in the city behind. Together with her. Watching and being watched.

Astride exactly where that He had once stood, she braced herself and lifted her face to the grey sky. The colour of her eyes, he thought. And, barely audible, from her, "Pére saint, Dieu juste des bons esprits… ni ne doutas… dans le monde du Dieu étranger… tu connais et aimer ce que tu aimes."

The scene finally vacated, but for the two of them. And their old blue van parked beneath. He squeezed some warmth from her hand into his. Aware now that Gizande's grey eyes were upon him. With so much for him to say to her, but telling him there was so little need to say it.

That, now, at least, was the time for them to go; on their own way.

CLARA
Book Three of
The Tomorrows That Sing

...quale cum te residente ad caenum cum ducibus ac ministris tuis tempore brumali,... adveniens unus passerum domum citissime, pervolaverit; qui cum per unum ostium ingrediens, mox per aliud exierit. Ipso quidem tempore, quo intus est, hiemis tempestate non tangitur, sed tamen parvissimo spatio serenitatis ad momentum excurso, mox de hieme in hiemem regrediens, tuis oculis elabitur. Ita haec vita hominum ad modicum apparet; quid autem sequatur, quidve praecesserit, prorsus ignoramus.

...as when on a winter's night you sit feasting with your ealdormen and thanes... then a single sparrow should fly swiftly into the hall, and coming in at one door, instantly fly out through another. In that time in which it is indoors it is indeed not touched by the fury of the winter, but yet, this smallest space of calmness being passed almost in a flash, from winter going into winter again, it is lost to your eyes. Somewhat like this appears the life of a man; but of what follows or what went before, we are utterly ignorant.

The Venerable Bede, Ecclesiastical History of the English People.

Chapter One

When he had woken that morning, so certain had been the dream, he lay for a moment listening for the sound of the Algerian drug dealer's thugs outside the house. Before he realised that he was alone in the bed. Aware of her again having crept early out and away for one of her running patrols up on the mountain at the back of the farm.

Now, an hour later, his feet on the cold stone floor, he looked down at the child whose head his hand was forgetfully rested on. Drug dealers…? Where had that come from? He had only ever spoken to one Algerian, the man and his silent wife who had taken over the mini-market in Larozelle. He had seen the tough younger Africans but distantly, playing football beneath their block of flats. And their graffiti in Arab script, appearing round the town. The dream's simplicity of right and wrong, he thought ruefully, protecting his family against a criminal gang. How much more complicated was life than that, and stirred the child's soft curls in his finger tips. A remote affection, seeking her attention. The large, dark eyes looked up from the bowl, at him. As always, regarding him with that expressionless and fixed wordlessness… that he took for some unfathomable wisdom. And the child's mother took for the dumbness of some undiagnosable infirmity.

He looked away and went to the kitchen window. Peering down towards the valley, the wrong way to see her return down from the ridge, stuck with the waiting for her. As always, there was work to be done on both farms, but she understood that and he could do nothing but defer to her priorities with waiting. And to the day's mood. A visit, just him and the child, to Suzanne today. Then, the next event in his own life, not due to start for another ten days, another trip to England to shift furniture back here for one more set of hopeful and anxious exiles. That, at least, had gone well in the last two years. He had networked himself round the local estate agents, but it was the Irish couple, Theresa and James, setting up specially to find property for Brits that had been his breakthrough. Through them, almost regular work. Both a serious earning contribution and an escape from the tensions in the two farms. A geographical and an emotional escape from here. And her. And the last time, after the casual information from the English lorry driver, a sexual escape. For the four hundred francs he said the chambermaids in the cheap chain of motels he stayed in were prepared to accept for hurried sex with a guest. On the way out, the semen sucked from him between the big thighs of an African, on the way back, the pale skinned indifference of an east European to his weight on top of her. The first times he had ever paid for sex. Guilty at it, worried about infection, despite his precautions. But a secretly defiant rebuttal to her eighteen months of sudden and inexplicable remote and faintly glowering withdrawal from him and from the child.

He turned back and lifted the child from her highchair. He slipped his feet into sandals and, on his hip he took her to the door. Gizande's dog gave a single bark of recognition, then lay its jaw back between its paws. It was a second warm day in what had been a late, cold spring. The snows up above would start their retreat at last, filling the streams lower down, which was why she was out patrolling for Spanish herdsmen bringing sheep and goats from over the border onto their own high pastures so early in the year. He could not yet see her yellow waterproof descending against the mountainface. The child's hand pulled at his shirt, he looked down at her, but she sought not his attention, only an adjusted hold to look down at the dog. He lowered her and sat her on the grass across from the animal. Would she move to him? Make a sound for him? He stood back, contemplating. As if from a great distance, this strange child he spent so much time with, but felt so much another person. With the silence and the watchfulness her mother had once had, she sat still and soundless, watching the dog.

Even the name he had chosen for her snatched away before birth, in that bout of sudden anger Gizande had… He could name the day it happened. The day she came home from visiting her mother, abruptly turned against the pregnancy… Against the child herself? Yes, he had to say it, against this child. Tore the name from her, unborn. Raged suddenly at the ugliness of it all. Took down all the mirrors in both farms, leaving him a small shaving mirror in her bathroom, which she turned to the wall whenever she went in there. His request for the mirrors back after the birth was refused.

He had asked her why, desperate at her mood. "What you see is a reflection. Just the outside of us as it is."

She had looked back at him, flat at his incomprehension of her, "Is it, Jim?"

"It is for me."

"How do you know?" Then, turning away as if to be busy elsewhere, he caught indistinctly, "It shows the soul. Imprisoned behind glass."

"Not true!" he challenged. Softening, he tried to win her with, "Anyway, you have a beautiful soul."

"Do I?" she said from bleak eyes. "How do you know?" So bleakly, there was nothing he could say to match it.

So, a sort of routine after the child was born. Shaped by the farms and their seasons. Child care by him when the work was busiest for her. Sometimes jobs they could do together, where Clara could be safely watched. Such as the cheese making down in her lower farm Gizande was teaching him, cutting up the whey with the wire tool or both quietly going through each ripening cheese puncturing it to bring on the blue. When there were major outside jobs requiring them both out on the farm, she would take Clara down to her mother. He would seldom go with her and, when she returned, they would both silently work together. Pruning the vines and burning the cuttings down at her farm in the winter, planting potatoes, rebuilding the stone walls in the spring that had been toppled by frost, using mortar unlike their neighbours. Or the back breaking clearing of the gorse and heather portion by portion from La Retrait, to extend the pasture further up towards the mountains, ready to rent out to other farmers for their herds in the summer. There were moments of quiet and unspoken mutual satisfaction between them at the end of such days. But he would say nothing, neither look to her nor smile, knowing that would break the spell, before they gathered tools together and set off back to their wordless enclosure together in one or other of the farms. Or the crises, usually in the winter, of powercuts, gale damage or floods, where they worked fiercely together saving their livelihood. Either way, ending the same. Exhausted, still sharing the same beds, but turned away towards opposite walls.

So the times out of her company had become releases. He no longer ran, leaving that to her. But the visits to Suzanne, so attentive to Clara and now easier with Jim. And the furniture shifting back from over the Channel. Totally, his own thing. Solitary, between his two worlds. Her. And the place he had come from. But each vanload he negotiated, left him feeling one more trip back to Britain more foreign from the homeland he was now four years away from. Homeland, a strange concept, he had thought. Something he never knew he had till it was left behind. At the end of the untidy clutter of decisions that had brought him living here… on this mountain, with this woman, with their child.

Chapter Two

Jim sat on the bottom of her veranda steps watching, while Suzanne patiently led Clara round the pots of geraniums and the rockery of alpines beside the driveway, quietly telling the wooden-legged tottering child about each plant.

Of her own child, Jim asked, "How's Marie-Claire?"

"Oh, settled with Felipe. Like the old marriage, talking to me and Maurice of how to buy a house in Toulouse." She looked over at him, "She teaches now. Did you know that?"

"No longer the revolutionaire?"

She laughed to him and Clara looked up at her face, curious. "No. They are settled. They will not marry. That would be too bourgeois. But they will be taking a certificat- for the advantage of the tax."

"What's that?"

Clara pulled her towards the rockery and placed an uncertain foot on a large boulder at the front. "Non, non, non, ma petite…," steering the child back onto the gravel. Then, looking back at Jim, "Le certificat? Do you not know? It changes the status of your relationship. From union libre to en concubinage. Marriage without the ceremony." As the child was pulling again towards the rocks, Suzanne swept her up into her arms, shaking her head and smiling. She turned back to Jim, "Have you and Gizande not done this?"

He shrugged. "First I've ever heard of it."

She looked at him with curious surprise, "Has she never discussed this with you?" She shook her head, "Then, you will be paying much taxes that are not necessary."

Unlike Gizande, he thought, usually so precise and careful about money. But unwilling to enter a territory where he discussed with his sister what he and Gizande did and did not speak of together, he shut the door on it with an abrupt, "I will talk to her."

He looked across at the mountains to avoid Suzanne's lingering quizzical look. Until she was distracted by Clara pulling a little fistful of her dress, asking to be put down. "Naturellement, chérie," putting her on her unsteady feet. Where she squatted, grasping a cluster of gravel to let it run between her delicate fingers. Absorbed in the wonder of this Suzanne squatted beside her, smiling and murmuring to the child in the private half-language they seemed to have together. Then, turned to Jim, "She is such a beautiful little one. So good. So attentive."

"Should she not be speaking?" he asked, voicing as he spoke an edge of Gizande's harsh judgements.

"No… she is too wise to speak… until she can speak with sense… she knows. In time, she will speak." Then kissing Clara's curls, as she stood, "Until you will be wishing for her silence again."

He wished he could be as certain about Clara. His doubts, fed by Gizande's angry frustration towards the child, shored up by his own ignorance about children, were little reassured by his sister's certainties. But he was sure her unconditional love for the little girl was a beneficial antidote to his and Gizande's… what? Battles over the child? Hardly that. He had now long been too fearful of exploring whatever was at the roots of Gizande's cold anger to both him and to Clara, to put up any fight. He sought territory where they could maintain a measure of tolerance between themselves. His visits with the child to Suzanne, always just the two of them, never with Gizande, were a measure of something that might be normal for the child. He would like to have talked about his worries to his sister, but they had gone on too long and he was too fearful of what she might ask. What she might suggest. And it had been a long and difficult journey repairing his relationship with Suzanne herself, to the placidity it had now reached. Another person circumscribed by what he could not say to her. With everyone else around his life sealed off from him by his lumbering French, with her and Gizande, it was the feelings he could not express.

So, as he usually did, he lingered at Suzanne's, had lunch with her and only took Clara back in the early evening, the child asleep in her basket secured on the van's passenger seat. She woke as he carried her into the house and looked at her mother as Gizande asked him, "Has she eaten?"

"Of course. Her aunt always feeds her well."

She turned back to the stove and Jim walked far enough round the kitchen table to see what she was doing. "What's Mummy doing?" he asked the child, but his mind suddenly stuttered away to that other first night here, the woman lighting stoves and fires in the cold house, before joining him naked in the bath. Far enough away to be a story told to him about other people. And Berlin, his imprisonment, anecdotes she had told others proudly at first. In those few weeks after their return. And before her crazed anger with him that night. Heavily pregnant, angry from a row down at her mother's, Gizande had returned with accusatory fury, stripping the child of the name they had chosen. Until she was born, and at Jim's insistence, of any name at all. At one point, weeping, curled away from him in the bed, wanting her body shed of the foetus, aborted from her. Since then, the sudden and long silence. This enduring ice age of resentment.

Now he looked at the woman's back, curved over the pans, remembering her beauty. Always mysterious, inviting to seek the clues towards intimacy. But now, long since, a slammed and locked door to him.

"What do we eat tonight?"

Without looking up, "Potage. Potatoes, onions, beans."

"Can I help?"

"Take the child to bed."

"She is awake. It is still early."

Gizande looked at him, flat and expressionless, "You do it when you wish. But I am tired." Without a look at Clara, her eyes were back on the stirred pot.

"Were there any herds up on La Retrait?"

"Only some sheep alone. But they have been over on your land. There were new bootmarks in the snow. From one of their shepherds. And the cayolar has been used. There are the marks of a new fire. And broken pieces of bread."

"What will you say to them, if you meet them on the land? Will they leave if you ask?"

She shrugged, without looking at him. "Do I know? Perhaps I take a gun," with toneless sarcasm. "It is your land. You think of a plan."

Our land, he wanted to say, but would not revisit the obstinacy of her distinction between the two farms. Hers here, fruitful and productive. His, up on the mountainside, problematic and barely sustainable. "Perhaps they think it is still in Spain. Like the old map Rodruiguez sent us. Like the Mayor told you." Finally, he walked away round the table. "No. I am better at the child care," ruffling Clara's curls and smiling at her, but both father and child watching the woman. Who rattled the pot irritably, without turning round. Confronting the Spanish shepherds on the mountain? He would not know what words to say. His schoolboy French to their coarse peasant Catalan?

He sat and settled the child on his lap, giving her a spoon to play with. She examined it, then, watching her father, started to tap an uneven rhythm on the edge of the table before them. With the permission of his tolerant smile, she concentrated on the tapping tool before her, faster, slower, louder.

"Stop that noise from her." Gizande's voice froze the child.

"It's only play."

"I am tired."

Knowing he could not claim the same, with a day of visiting his sister. Wanting to plead for the child, he only repeated, "It's only play," taking the spoon gently from the little hand. Then curling the little fingers reassuringly within his.

After their dinner, the child sat beside him sucking at morsels of mashed vegetable he had cooled for her from his dish and put in her plastic bowl, then he put Clara to bed. He read her several of the nursery rhymes from the book he had bought his last visit to England. When she did speak, would it be English? Gizande had sneered at him, saying that if Clara ever did speak, she would be useless- "inutile"- in school, without French for the classes, or the local Catalan for the playground.

"Well you talk to her, then!" he had shouted.

She had looked at him and, for a moment, her eyes measured him, before she looked away, murmuring sourly, "Perhaps… perhaps, she is your child. Your child alone."

He had been sure that measurement had been significant, a crux whether he was worth what she had been about to say. But it had flickered out. And he had been left to make the impotent response, "She came from your body." Sealing the silence again between them.

Now, this night, he faced the navigation with her of what Suzanne had told him. About the civil pact and saving tax. Money was continually a problem. In general, and between them. He had cleared up the kitchen and taken her coffee into the front room, that same place where they had first made love together. Now, she was sat, with the glasses she had recently needed for reading, not raising her eyes from her book as he entered. He put the tray down on the table, then poured his own.

Sat across from her, he watched through the faint cover of the steam from his drink.

"I do still love you, you know," the saying of it as unexpected to him as hearing the sound of the words in the room.

She had stopped reading, but her eyes did not move from the page before her. Those grey eyes, he thought. So soft, but often so cold.

He continued, not to lose the moment, the lapse in distance from her, the listening, "It is true, Gizande. I do still love you."

Still without looking up, "Why say this?" clearing the rasp from her voice with a gentle cough.

"We- I need to say it." His voice made a little too precise by his watchfulness of her, "We both need to say it. To each other."

She looked at him over the rim of the glasses, "So. It is said," then stiffly back to the book.

He sat, still looking at her, the mug held motionless. Just below his eyeline to her. Taking cover behind it, he sipped, lubricating a mouth gone dry for what to say next. Hesitantly, "Suzanne says we can save tax money..."

"Pardon?" Looking up sharply.

"Suzanne... she told me we can save tax money." He put the cup aside on the table and leaned forward into the space between them.

Gizande reluctantly put her book face down, roofing the arm of her chair with it, took her glasses off and for a moment concentrated herself with balancing the folded wire and glass astride the spine. Finally, she looked back at him, as remote and uninviting as he had so often seen those eyes before. "Continue," spoken with a whisper of French.

"I do not know about it, but she said something..." He halted, looked down at his cup, uncertain. What had Suzanne said? So critical to get it right. "She called it concubinage? No... free union, that's what we need- a certificat... oh, I don't know..." Then, with feeble defiance, "She said you would know."

"Concubinage," she said quietly. "C'est concubinage."

"Yeah. Okay. Why don't we do it?"

"Non." Blunt. Final. Watching her fingers perch on the spectacles, before plucking them up, unfolding and sliding them onto her face.

"Why not?" with a touch of pleading.

"We have the free union now. This way we will stay," turning the book back into her lap.

"But the money we would save..."

She was back at her book, but he was certain she was waiting.

"Gizande," more firmly, leaned so far forward into her space, balanced unsteadily on the crouch of his legs, his buttocks almost disengaged from the chair behind. "Gizande. Listen," hands on the table rim.

She slapped the book down between them, tore the flimsy glasses off, "What do you know? You do not even know the language! What do you know, Jim?" The words were dismissive and the eyes were cold.

"I know we do not have enough money... anything - anything to get some more money!" Then pleading, to her unfathomable opposition, "It sounds so easy..."

"Easy for you. But you know nothing. Nothing."

He pushed himself up, to stand above her, thrust by the anger of his impotence, "Another thing not to tell me about. Something else you don't have to discuss with me. Explain it, then. Tell me why it's not a good idea to save on the tax we pay!"

She looked down. And he read in the back of her head, that obstinacy. Yet the nape of the neck where he had a sudden surge to place his lips, rocking him giddily with it. Then torn away by the impossibility of that, now… Ever again? "Say something. Say something to me once that's not, No!"

But her head stayed unrisen. And that first shocking row two years ago, filled his ears again. When Gizande, pregnant, seemed to turn against the child inside her.

"No, Jim," he mimicked it again, even with a fleck of the way she spoke his language. "You will not understand. The baby cannot be named Fruhling." Back into angry, male English, "Why? No answer. She would still be without a name, if I had not insisted. Esclarmonde. I finally drag it out of you, but you never use it. Clara- our little Clara- you just call her The Child." Finally, defeatedly, "Now again… something I don't know. And you won't tell me."

The bowed head motionless. Without the shake to mark a sob.

"Gizande… Gizande!" He leaned across the table, his hand hesitant to touch.

But she sensed him, flung back her neck and, full-faced, hair flicked across her eyes, challenged- "Do not touch!" Shoving back the chair with her legs, thrust and stood, furious with contempt, "You do not touch!"

He stepped back, palms raised, his eyes locked into hers. Thinking, this isn't me here. She's looking at someone else. And for a frozen moment they stilled like that. His gesture of submission. Her defiance of menace. Locked together, he thought hopelessly. Lowered his arms and slowly slumped back into his chair. She awoke, confused, from her sealed repugnance, half-folded herself back down, but stood again. Gathered her book and glasses into her numb hands, turned and left the room. He stayed and listened to her footsteps up through the house.

Chapter Three

April 10th

Dear Dad,

Long-time-no-hear? From neither end, he thought, tentative at resuming words with Tracey. The other daughter, he thought- who knows nothing of her little half-sister, Clara… as he had not known for so many years about Suzanne. Slapping down the comparison with his own father as soon as it flitted through the window opened by this letter. Read on.

You will remember Richard, though you never met. We have decided to get married. It will be on June 20th. I'm sorry that I did not consult you about the date before we set it, but Richard's Dad has to go into hospital for an operation in July and we had to have it before then- I'm sure you understand. But I would really like you to be there. True? he thought. Or just the formula of good behaviour. Would she really want him there?

I know we have always had our differences- and we've not been good at keeping in touch, but I would like you to come if you could. And would you pass on an invitation to Suzanne- after all, she is my auntie! He silently apologised to his daughter for his cynicism. *I would understand if this is too short notice to drop things and come over. But please believe- both me and Richard really would like to see you at the wedding.*

Let- me crossed out for *us- know as soon as possible.*

Love, Tracey.

P.S. I know this isn't a newsy letter, but I wanted to get this off to you as soon as possible after we set the date.

He had picked up the letter at Suzanne's and read it in the van, parked on the way back, with Clara asleep beside him. He had never given people in England any other address. La Retrait was beyond where the Poste would deliver. Gizande and her address were unknown to anyone there. And now, how did he feel about this chink through the wall he had built behind him? Cautious. Calculating the cost of every choice of response. To tell Gizande? To tell Suzanne that she was invited? Would that mean Gizande would be invited, if Tracey knew of her? Jane would be there as the mother… bringing together his past and present lives into the same room? He tried to visualise it, but could not get past the obstinate refusal Gizande faced everything with now. And Tracey herself? A stranger now? Not exactly. He remembered her patient despondency that he continued to ride a white charger, as she put it. All that pursuit of the truth. Damien. Scadding. So remote now. From the tight little life that Gizande, he and Clara were bound together in. He had even lost touch with Julian and Trish. Somewhere up at La Retrait he had some unanswered letters. He could equally not answer Tracey. Let the difficulties of the event slip away through inaction. Let all that went before, go. But he folded it back in its envelope and put it in his back pocket. Think about this one, he said cautiously to himself. As aware of the unpredictable power of doing nothing, as of making a reply.

Thinking of his father. Also come to live in this land. And die here. Also sealing himself away here from England. The foreignness of it all still to him. Had his father continued thinking in English, as he did, in this French and Catalan world? Jim had never even learnt how to eat croissants effectively. Trying to be too tidy, he always ended up with crumbs down the front of his trousers, sat in the tiny, dark bar in the village below La Retrait, when he took Clara down with him. Often only the patron reading the sports pages and the ritual of the old man with the deep and liquid cough. Counting out the pills onto the tabletop, to be taken with his beer. Watched silently for its precision by Clara sat still beside Jim.

What kept Gizande and him together. The child. Or was it what kept him from Gizande? Come between?

He thought abstractly about what if he left, taking Clara with him. Would her mother really resist? He could not imagine it, so angered had she been to the child, even long before it was born. Because of her fears, he had arranged everything for the birth with Suzanne's help. But even in that delivery suite, with its soft warm pink light, squatted in the bath, Gizande had cried out with rage. Raw and terrible fury that had pressed him away from her sight, to watch from the farthest corner of the room. And then her obsessive search for an illness in the infant, that the doctor, Dignant repeatedly refuted. The poultices of herbs, the massages with oils, sometimes in the middle of the night, Gizande having slipped from bed, Jim shuddered awake by the anxious, thin shriek of the child. Finding them together in their distress on the bathroom floor, bottles and dishes scattered across a towel, mother crouched over Clara, reaching out her tiny frightened hands towards him as he entered. Increasingly, he took the baby from her arms, often sleeping downstairs, wrapped together in a blanket on the sofa in the warmer weather that first summer. Gizande alone upstairs.

He found he was shaking his head to himself. To take Clara away? To where? Impossible to visualise. The child was what had cemented them together. His own solitary tap root here, anyway. Seeking nourishment deep down into a country that he only stiltedly understood and that only tolerated his presence, it was Clara kept him from total rootlessness. And also, perhaps, trying to make something of La Retrait. But Gizande? He feared he could never hear the voices she listened to in her head. But now, would he fear to learn whatever it was they said? To share her madness, if that was what it was.

Clearing out the tangled and rusty ancient bicycles from the barn at the back of La Retrait, he had casually asked her what she thought his father had collected them for.

She had savagely replied, "Do not ask me. Ask Suzanne. She is your father's child."

Her tone forbade further enquiry and he had ceased to speak to his sister about their father. So the bikes remained a conundrum, more grave with meaning now than his original unthinking question. Become an interrogation about Gizande herself, that he knew he would not dare to open.

He left the issue of the wedding invitation for more than a week. Until the verge of leaving back to England for the next shift of furniture. He had not left the decision drift. Indeed, he had thought of little else. How to raise it with Gizande. How she might respond. How…? Whether to tell Suzanne? The mechanics of childcare during his absence, both for this trip and for the wedding. He could not imagine Gizande agreeing to come, so did that mean he could not tell Suzanne she was invited? Going with his sister, but not with… whatever he could categorise Gizande as to others… lover no longer… the term, partner, too contractual between free parties, not messy enough for the reality… He went back to that conversation with Suzanne about saving tax. Nothing free about the union between the trapped parties the two of them were together with Clara. Concubinage? Without the sex that implied, he thought bitterly, balancing in his mind whether to buy a chambermaid again this trip or not. Or would it all be easier to keep his lives as compartmented as they had become? Say nothing to Suzanne. Give Tracey excuses for her and never mention Gizande. Or Clara. Would his English daughter ever visit here? He seemed to remember something vaguely said three years back when they had last met and separated discomfortably. The remotest likelihood.

But this? He would not be able to go to the wedding without Gizande knowing. Pretending it was only a furniture trip and he would have to produce the money earned. He would need an excuse to pack his shabby suit for the trip. Yet, with all these knotted tangles, he never doubted that, one way or another, he would be at the wedding. He owed Tracey at least his presence, even if she would not suspect whom the father at her side had become. From being the angry master of car factory politics over twenty years ago, to the solitary crusader chasing the ghost of Damien across Europe and rescuing the pathetic, cringing Stephen from behind the Berlin Wall, what had he become now? Here, a skilless farm labourer, almost dumb from the language of the land he worked. Only ever a figure of authority with the wealthy British customers he carried furniture for. As the Englishman who knew what living in France was about. Impressing those he had mild contempt for, but who paid him well.

To her turned back one evening in the kitchen, he was telling her the timetable of this next trip, when he slipped it in. "Oh, yes. You know Tracey?" Waiting. "My English daughter." For no response. "She's sent me a letter. She's getting married." Gizande continued stirring over the stove. He reflected how she still loved her cooking, but in a closed and private way that did not invite or welcome his praise. Then, stepping delicately around the next words, watchful of her, he tried to pass them off casually, "She's asked me to come- go over for it." He had considered just putting Tracey's letter in front of Gizande, but her response to the invitation to Suzanne as well seemed too much of an additional peril.

"Will you wish to go?" Without turning.

"I think I should. Do you?"

"Do I?" she said reflectively to the pot in front of her. "Do I care? Is this a thing that concerns me?"

At least not anger, he thought. Then said, "So you don't want to come."

"What will they think of me? Your family. Your daughter. Your wife will be there."

"She isn't my wife-"

But still back turned, she sharply cut in, "A wife is always a wife. For always."

"I'm divorced." Then, "You're divorced. Is Yves still your husband?" What was she saying? The back over the stove was unreadable, so he stood and went round the table. Keeping his distance, leaning against the shelves, he could see her irritated profile. Softly, "Gizande. Is it that you want us to be married?"

Her bitter cough of laughter, with a look of scorn at him, took him aback. She slid the saucepan off the heat and turned back to him. There was a calculated knowingness in her face and stance. "So that is what you wish, Jim. A new wife."

"If that's what you want," he said hopelessly. Pleading, "I want us back how we were."

"How we were? How we were? What is that? Before the child?"

"Yes," but then, untwisting the disloyalty to the sleeping Clara upstairs, he stamped out, "No! It's not about her." Grasping for it, "How you were. After..." After what, could he sum it up?

But she cut in, "Ah. How I was. It is me that am the problem. Is that what you think, Jim?"

Yes. Yes, he thought, but said, "Well, what is wrong between us?"

She turned away, idled with the spoon in the pot for a moment. Then slid it back onto the heat, with, "The food will be ruined."

He watched her, loving her how she had been, almost tearful with it and his incomprehension of how they had got to now. Finally, gauntly saying, "So you will not be coming with me."

She slammed the pot aside from the stove and faced him. "So, why do you ask my permission to attend the wedding? You have made the decision already. Me come? How can I come? I have the farms. Two farms. This. And La Retrait. And who will have the child? Do you think Gaillarde will wish to have her? For her mother to go away for the wedding of your daughter?"

"Clara could come with us," he threw in to the pause in her rant.

"The child?" with disbelief. "You would take the child all the distance in that van?"

"We could fly. It would only be a couple of days," hearing himself continue to negotiate what he knew was already lost.

"Ah. So we have the money for wedding- for flying. But we have so little money, you must be telling me your stupid ideas about the taxes." Then, savagely inspired, "This daughter of yours- she has asked you for money to pay for this wedding? You are the proud father- you will be paying for it also?"

He turned away, defeated, "No. No money. She has asked for nothing." But too quietly for her to hear.

"Pardon. What did you say?"

Forced to face her again, he spelt it out with angry emphases, "No. No money. She just asked me to be there."

"Good. That, at least…" She looked back at the pot, stirred it once, then looked up at him, a moment of examination. Showing a sliver of care for him. Before looking back down and attending to the food, again back onto the heat and turning it tiredly with the spoon.

Anger shrivelled away, he wanted to move forward to embrace her crushingly. Squeezing out from the emptiness of the last two years, from that slight body, some sort of explanation. But he always knew better than to interrupt her cooking, even in those early good days. So he drifted back round the table to his chair. Sat and toyed with his cutlery, looking down at it, but aware of every sound she made. The last scrapes of the spoon in the pot. The oven open and the clatter of hot plates. The slightest whisper of the knife slicing open the potatoes. The clip of the serving spoon gathering the served vegetables. Finally, with the soft slop of the sauce, dragged onto each potato, he allowed himself to look up at her.

He caught her own covert, simultaneous look. "Gizande…"

She turned away to put the pot behind her.

"Gizande. Do you wish to marry me?"

"No." Quietly, still back to him, "To marry you. It is impossible."

He wanted to ask why, but instead, "What do you want? You cannot want this."

"What is this? What are you saying?"

"Are you happy?"

"Huh!" She faced him a moment, her eyes shielded with bitterness. Before pushing a plateful of food towards him. "Eat. The food will be for the pig."

He reached over, but the plate was not far enough across the wide planks of the table. She had already sat, attentive to the meal before her. He walked round to collect the plate. Hot to touch, he reached for the cloth still across her shoulder. But in the handful he gathered also the loose cotton of the top of her sleeve. Accidentally or not. She looked up at him, a wisp of anxiety. He leaned down to kiss it from her lips, but she slid them away.

Still intimately close to her, he said with the patience of so many defeats, "I'm not trying to hurt you."

She pulled her shoulder free and tapped his plate with her fork, "Eat. Before it is cold."

To press himself on her? With his lips to push aside the rigid defensiveness? He stood there above her long enough for her to be forced to look up at him again. But she would not. "I'm not trying to hurt you," come out this time with nervous authority, he dared to reach out and cupped his hand under her chin. The fingers of the other knotted fiercely into the cloth to stop him shivering with the chance of the moment.

But she would not have her face turned. Eyes locked to the plate before her, hands clenched round knife and fork, she gritted out, "Eat. The food." Then shook her head free of him. "I must talk to you as a little boy? Eat."

After a hesitation, he joined the emptied hand to the other, folded the cloth round the plate's edge and returned to his side of the table.

The food was dross inside his numb mouth. Watching her. For any recognition. Any undipping of her head from her eating, the sets of cutlery unnaturally loud in the room. How had he arrived here? And in this foreign land, with this woman, somehow turned his life back into another unhappiness? Was it himself? But, rather than finding personal responsibility, he ended up blocked in with self-pity. Unable to detect where he had put a foot wrong. This time, anyway.

And he spilled this out across the kitchen, "Don't you feel lonely? Your family won't- they hardly talk to you- except to sometimes look after Clara. You won't talk to me. Now you avoid Suzanne, you don't have any friends. And Clara… you get no fun from her… We're both dead weights to you." He put his knife and fork down. "What do you want, Gizande?"

"I want to eat my food. Without your stupid talk." Looking up at him, then down again.

"God!" He shoved the plate away from him, shedding sliced beans across the table. "Bloody well say something to me for once!" He wiped a fleck of spit from his mouth. "Stop putting up barriers to every- every talk I try to have with you. You won't answer anything!" Then, with vicious calculation, what he had thought of several times, "Is this how you were with Yves?"

Her hands stilled above her plate, eyes on them. No answer.

He pushed roughly through both his and her miseries. "Was it like this with Yves? Tell me." Then, more quietly, "Tell me."

Putting down her knife and fork quietly, she looked across at him without raising her head.

Unable to read her face from its tilt, he pressed her, "I am not Yves. Tell me."

She covered her face with knuckled fists. And spoke from behind them with a wearied voice. "You are not Yves. You are Jim. Gentle man. Kind. Honest. Safe." She pulled her knuckles aside and rested her face on them, looking at him. As if at a familiar object become inexplicable, now out-of-place.

Silencing him.

"What do you want from me, Jim? Pleasantries? Jokes?"

"Jokes would be nice," he smiled. "Not many of them, these days." Then, more seriously, "I want to go away to England this trip, knowing what I'm coming back to. I don't want to worry all the way back across France, what sort of reception I'm going to get. It would be nice to get a little bit of warmth… Sometimes… It's been a long, long time, Gizande."

Flatly, without the intonation of enquiry, she said, "Is it sex that you want."

Resisting saying No, irritated at his body's arousal, he wheedled, "Not just that. That's just part of it." Then, "That would be nice," annoyed at the nervous grin he could not restrain.

The impassive face still rested on her fists, she said spiritlessly, "We can do sex together. If that is what you wish." Looking at the plates, "Now that the food has become cold."

"I want us to love each other," he entreated her. "Not just..." trailing off.

"Ah. Love. That is more difficult." She stood and leaned across to reach for his plate. He wanted to ruffle her hair, to soften and trivialise the moment from its gravity. But dared not, watching her scrape the remains into the pig bin and start to run the hot water into the sink.

After he had checked on Clara and pulled up the blanket to tuck round her small splayed legs, he cleaned his teeth and shook into his hair a little of the old aftershave he seldom used now, massaging it into his scalp and wiping the remnant onto his face. He turned the small mirror and tried to make something of the sombre face that looked back at him. Fancy your chances tonight? he silently sarcasmed back, without smiling.

She was turned away to her wall as always. His side of the bed was cold and he slowly slid himself up against her back. Before he placed his hand on her hip, he listened for her breathing. Holding back his own to hear if she was asleep. Probably not. His fingertips on the rough cotton of her pyjamas, then he slid them under and round onto the pattern of the muscles on her stomach. Her diaphragm had stopped moving. Waiting for what he did next. Up to her breasts? Or down? He moved on up, pulling the cloth free of the flesh. To search across the curve of warm skin for the nipple.

Finding it, to rub gently at its puckered pimpling, to raise it proud and stimulated. Disobedient.

She murmured a complaint, closed her elbows round herself and pushed him away. His hand limply back on her hip, he hesitated. Wanted to softly call her name. For her to answer. Over her shoulder, from her turned away mouth. Something, at least, to indicate permission. Sliding his fingers down across her buttocks, slightly feeling the curves falling away beneath cotton, but finally, without the courage. To reach inside the trousers and pull them away from her.

He waited a moment more there, at the edge of her warmth. Before rolling away his back onto the chill sheet his side, looking up into the dark. After a long and motionless wait. For her breathing to deepen slowly into sleep, he started to sluggishly massage his sex. To empty it across his belly. After mopping it with the tail of his pyjama top, he lay draggingly awake, trying to think of how she had been. But remembering only that priest. That room. That greedy tongue and stubble across his boy-belly. And he was disgusted with himself.

Chapter Four

When he went in to see Theresa to get the documents for the trip, she had another likely customer for him to shift. In addition to the London pick up.

"He lives near Birmingham. He's part of a group of friends who've bought an old castle tower. To share it out for holidays. Maybe some holiday lets through us, also. It's south of Perpignan. He said he'd like you to meet with them. They're not sure what they want to transport over and what they can get locally to get it furnished." She smiled at him impishly. As she always did to his reluctance. "I know it's not exactly on your route. But I'm sure you'll be able to hide the cost of a journey to Birmingham in your final bill when you've moved them."

"Have they guaranteed to use me to move them?" She went on smiling sweetly, without answering. "Not quite," he mimicked her accent.

"But I'm sure a visit from you, Jim, would put it in the bag. They want to move over in July. In time for the Olympics in Barcelona. He says it's cheaper to travel from France than to stay in Catalunya." He remembered Suzanne making a sour comparison between the forgotten Catalans in France and the billions being invested over the Spanish border.

"I'll think about it."

"So I can phone up Birmingham and tell them you're on your way?"

He mouthed an insult and she laughed. Warmed him, a reminder of other women. Sylvie, Gizande, even Jane… all friends once. And now Gizande. Had she ever been a friend? Was that possible between men and women? Really? He looked down at Theresa, embarrassed at his thoughts.

"Go on then, phone him. Tell him I'll phone him when I get to England and know what my schedule is. For the London job."

"I've written his name and number on the outside of the document pack," she said, pointing it out as she handed it across the desk. "When do you leave?"

"Tomorrow."

"Clara okay?"

He looked curiously at her. He could not remember ever mentioning his little daughter. "Yes. Why?"

She smiled. "I'm an Irishwoman. We always ask about the little ones. It's the Catholic in us."

He backed away from her with, "Yeah, she's fine." He met few other expatriates. There were few yet in this poor and unwelcoming corner of France. But they probably all talked about each other. At barbecues he had never been invited to, he expected. He knew nothing of her and James, just the couple he met through work. So now he asked, "Do you and James have kids?"

"Too busy." Said with a sigh of artificial regret, pushed aside with the equally false, "But we will."

He looked at her, catching this first time insight of her. Thinking what it took to decide to have a child. Or not. And how he and Gizande had reached where they were now, without decisions. Accidents.

"How is it going on at your farm?" Theresa's question made him quickly scrutinise her for what she meant.

"Oh, we're gradually clearing more of the land. For pasture. But we have to keep an eye on the Spanish, sending herds over onto the top meadows." Sounding like an expert, he thought.

She shook her head. "Well, rather you than me. James and me came here to escape from all that. We both came from the West, back home. Farming families."

Did he defend his way of life now? Indefensible. So he just said, "It's hard." Lightening with, "Makes the furniture shifts a real doddle." And disengaging from what he realised was her scrutiny by picking up the pack of documents. "Well. Be seeing you on my return. Say hello to James."

"Oh, I always do," laughing. "Drive safely. We need you, Jim."

Really? For a man who felt needed by no one. Except perhaps Clara.

The next morning, the child knew he was going away. She watched him packing and whinged quietly, just on the dry side of tears, fleetingly looking at her mother. With the eyes of both of them on him, he was hurried, made mistakes and had to unzip the case twice to stuff in forgotten items. He was always flustered, leaving. Ready for the escape from the house, yet the nagging fear of what happens when his back is turned.

He kissed Clara briefly, but said nothing under Gizande's studied onlook. And for her? She let her cheek be kissed, eyes turned away from him. Releasing him up into the van at last. The pair of them stood in the doorway, Clara clutching her mother's limp hand, he felt the sorrow, whatever the cause and wound down his window.

Eyes from Gizande to fix on the child's, "Bye-bye, darling. Look after Mummy," waggling the tips of his fingers at her. Then, back to the woman, hesitant. "And you too. Look after yourself, Gizande." Awkwardly adding, "Darling," turning away to start the motor. His eyes smart with tears, he roughly and a little angrily pulled the wheel and roared the van out of the driveway.

A retained image on the long diagonal journey across to Calais. He had not slept much in the van, somewhere near Paris, stretched in his sleeping bag across the three front seats. Avoiding company or temptation in a hotel. Stretching the cramp and the damp from his limbs, walking up and down the layby in the misty dawn.

And on to London, this first time he had come into the city with the new van, he was overcompensating for the wider, longer box behind him as he sought out a parking space in the crowded narrow roads of the northern inner suburb round the customer's address. Finally, a couple of streets away, it was late afternoon when he walked round to ring at the door.

"Jim Briggs. Removal man," he announced to the large woman, untidy in layers of bright, confused chiffony skirting.

"Oh, good!" she said, beaming. "Come in." Leading him up the stairs, she said over her shoulder, "I'm Jude. There are two of us- and the kids. We're on the two top floors. You'll probably find us mad."

He just drearily counted the number of stairs he would be working.

Through the open door of a flat, and she called, "It's Jim… the removal man!"

A woman from another room, querulously, "But he's not due yet. For two days."

Jude looked at him, "Is that right?"

He shook his head, "I'm booked to load and off tomorrow."

She called through to the other woman, "Deedee, he says it's tomorrow."

A pause. Jude smiled at him. For his indulgence of the first of many confusions with this lot, he thought, looking round at the tottering piles of books filling the hallway, still unboxed.

Deedee appeared, skinny and a touch too old for the deliberately slashed jeans. At least one gash showing an edge of red knicker. She saw his eyes, then hardened. "You're not due till the day after tomorrow."

He pulled the booking form from Theresa out of the file. "Sorry," handing it over. "You're booked for tomorrow."

Deedee looked at the paper and handed it back. "But our ferry tickets are not for tomorrow."

Jim shrugged. At the matter-of-fact. "I can go on ahead. With the furniture."

Jude said, “We were going to follow you.” Adding, smiling, “In a convoy.”

Deedee cut in, “We’re collecting the keys when we get there.”

So? he thought, but said, “I live quite close. I can turn up with your stuff when you get there.” A child of about seven was watching from round a doorway further down the corridor.

Jude laughed, “We’ll never get there without you, Jim. None of us can read a map!”

“Shut up, Jude.” Then Deedee turned to him, brusquely pleading, “Can’t you wait? Till then?”

“It’ll cost.” He thought of fitting in Birmingham and maybe getting paid twice for it. “How much stuff have you got? Let me see.”

She showed him round, with Jude following, more distantly then by the little boy and a smaller girl. Box-loads and box-loads of books, not much furniture and most of that able to be disassembled. Binbags of clothing. Plenty of stuff still unpacked. Two thirds of the van filled, maybe? Birmingham was definitely a cash-in-hand possibility, for a few bits of furniture as well.

“What time’s your ferry?” he asked Deedee.

“Late. First night, we were going to camp not far from Calais.” Seeing his puzzlement, added, “When we’ve crossed.”

“And you want me to go in convoy with you?” turning to Jude. “Camping?”

“No. We would camp and wait for you each morning. What do you do? Hotel?”

“Yes. Sometimes,” thinking that last night had been camping, without the luxury of canvas. With the unrehearsed tired patience of the pissed-about workman, he said to Deedee, “I have to make a phone call.”

She looked at him, would have questioned this, but offered reluctantly, “It’s next door. The phone.”

“Ta.” He went through. A bedroom. Dark blue with cotton wallhangings, smelling of musk. He sat on the bed edge and scowled at the little boy till he was left alone. Somewhere along the corridor, a whispered bicker between the two women.

He tapped out the Birmingham number… “I’m sorry there is no one here to take your call at present…” accent cultured, but still Brummy. He left a message, saying he would phone in the morning. The phone back in its cradle, he wondered what to do next. Where he would stay now.

He pulled his little address book from his pocket and leafed through it. No one in London. Always a remote and friendless city to him, for occasional business only. All up North or in France. He flickered back again through the pages. Four hours from his old home town? Ten o'clock or so to get there? He found the last number he had for Tracey. He had still not written back to her wedding invitation. No. Retain the intermediary cushion of a posted letter, with the chance to compose the words without the risk… of what? Saying too much or too little. Listening for the faceless words, guessing the impatience of her eyes or the shake of her head.

A few pages on, Julian and Trish. Nearly three years since they had visited? The only ones who had met Gizande. When Jim and her had been at their happiest. He had not written to them for over a year. What the hell, they had always been welcoming. Before tapping out the number, he listened, but the noises of women and kids seemed to be at the other end of the flat.

"Hello," Julian's voice.

"Hiya. Bit of a rave from the grave here."

Pleased to be recognised with, "Jim!" and the smile in Julian's voice. "Where are you calling from?"

"London. Over here for a piece of work."

"How long are you over for?"

"Only a couple of days."

"Oh. That's a real shame. Trish and I were only talking about you the other day. How's Gizande?"

Tried to say, "Fine," without tripping up. Then, "Did you know we've got a little girl now?"

"Nooo!" Then, he called aside, "Trish! It's Jim! He's a dad!" Back to the phone, "Trish wants to have a word. Here."

"Jim? Where are you?"

"London. I told Jules. I'm only here for a day or two. A job. But it's got a bit delayed."

"A dad, eh?"

"Yeah. Little girl. Clara."

"Who does she look like? You or Gizande?"

He tripped on that. Such a normal topic to have been discussed between a couple, but he and Gizande had never spoken of it. "I don't know. She's got curly hair. Dark eyes, brown. So I don't know if she looks like either of us."

"A dad, eh?" she said again. "Well, when do we see you? Can you fit in a visit?"

He paused, considering the practicalities. "I've got to be in London the day after tomorrow, back here. I also may have to drop into Birmingham."

"So what about tomorrow?" Then, "Where are you staying tonight?"

He laughed, "Funny you should ask-"

Trish interrupted, "We'll make up the divan for you. That's an order. We'll wait up. When could you get here?"

He laughed again, "It'd be after ten. At the earliest."

She said something to Julian, then, "Come on then, Jim. Stop dithering. On your way!"

Julian came back on the line, "Well, mate, I guess you've got your orders. See you later."

Smiling, with the warmth of their voices belling through his head, he could say no more than an almost shy, "Thanks," before putting the phone back in its cradle.

He stood, listened to the sounds of the flat, set himself back into the present task and went off to find where the women's voices were coming from.

Deedee was sat on her own in the living room, with Jude's voice somewhere with the children's.

"I can't get hold of Theresa, the estate agent till tomorrow," he said, adding offhandedly, "But this will cost you probably another hundred for each day. For the delay."

"I will phone the agent tomorrow," she said. Then added, "Are you alone? Won't it take another man to handle carrying some of this stuff down the stairs?"

He shrugged, "That's why we're so cheap."

"We?" she scoffed. "I only see you."

He took the challenge by looking down at her for a moment, before finally saying, "I'll see you lunchtime the day after tomorrow. Okay?" He stopped at the door. "Oh, and can you try to save me a space to park somewhere near the front door?"

"Some chance! This is London."

Chapter Five

Grinning into the successive streams of oncoming headlights, driven through the night by the sound of their friendship in his ears, it was nearly eleven when he reached Julian and Trish. The same upstairs flat. And Trish was pregnant again.

As he disengaged from her hug of welcome, Jim looked down at her and across at him. "Again?"

Julian clasped his shoulder with awkward affection, "And why not? When's your next one due?"

An answer to stumble over, "Oh, god, no. No more."

"Fatherhood not suit you?" she asked, but waved at him to sit down. "Have you eaten?"

"Not for a few hours. Not properly."

"Properly?" she crowed, smiling. "What does properly imply? Expecting a three course dinner in the middle of the night?"

Falling back onto the divan, Jim laughed, "If you're offering?" Then, "No. Honest. Anything you've got."

Going out to the kitchen, she said, "We'd better be quieter, so's not to wake Adam."

Julian sat opposite him. "It's been so long, Jim."

"Yeah. Sorry." Adding, to cover the detail of the intervening years, "You get so busy."

"Especially with kids. And I guess you're a fully fledged French paysan now, are you? Tied by the seasons?"

"Something like that. But it's not enough. That's why I come over to England. Remember that first job I did shifting your brother's stuff over to France? Well it's a little business, now. A sideline, but it pays well. It gets cash, otherwise farming down there is a bit of a cash-free way of trying to live." He was aware of wanting to talk about the difficulties of his life- probably more comfortably to Trish than to her husband- but he veered away with, "Are you still in the same job? Working for Sylvie Cathcart?"

"God, no! I've moved sideways. I manage a small voluntary project. Helps young people coming out of care to move on."

"Same sort of work then? Is it still as bad?" The question had fallen from his mouth, before the faces filled his head. "Christ! You forget it all… then it comes flooding back. Damien. Stephen. All that shit." Julian was watching him. "It must be being back here. Back in this bloody town. It's not that I really never think of it. It's just… It's so far away most of the time. Almost can't believe it ever happened." They were both silent, looking down for a minute. Before Jim asked, "Is it any better? Is it still going on?"

Julian looked back across. Measuring, before quietly reflecting, "Still going on?" He leant back in the sofa and put his hands behind his head, elbows out, eyes fixed on Jim's. "Scadding is still fighting on. He was sacked for the business about the files. Refusing to shred them. The Union dumped him. Like they did with you. But he went to an Industrial Tribunal to fight it on his own. He lost there, but I heard he's just won the right to appeal."

"What a fighter," Jim said, half admiring the precise and prickly little man he remembered. Half regretting his own distance from it. The last thing he had done really well. Trying to stand up for Damien. Berlin with Gizande and getting Stephen back. "What happened to Stephen? Do you hear?"

Julian shook his head. "Disappeared into mental health services. Locked up somewhere, out of sight. Out of his mind."

Jim shook his head. A performed gesture to cover over the obscure guilt of not having done even more than he had. Pretending to be a farmer, when his real skills were maybe riding the white chargers his eldest daughter was so dismissive of. "And Finch? He was a real villain. What happened to him?"

"I'm not sure if Finch was the real villain. They're the ones who never get touched. I heard that Finch came back and was arrested. But I don't know what happened to him. I don't even know if he was charged."

"What would they charge him with? It wasn't exactly kidnapping. After all, he had permission to be Stephen's carer- even if not to take him to Germany." But a sense that, after all, he had lost. By going back to France with Gizande, leaving the trusting boy back in the hands of Sylvie and her Social Services… "Is Cathcart still in charge?"

Julian grunted, just as Trish re-entered with a tray.

"Did I hear the Cathcart name?" she said asked sharply, looking down at her husband.

"Jim was asking."

Trish looked at him. "You never let it go, either, do you? Just like Jules. What was it about her?"

Did she know? It had been so long, that Jim could not clearly remember what he had told them and what he had not. He fumbled away from it with, "I asked about Stephen. That's all." Defensively.

"No. Cathcart's gone," Julian inserted. "Off to be an Assistant Director down south."

"Thank god," Trish said putting the tray down on the coffee table. Fried eggs on toast, beans, mug of tea, glass of red wine. Seeing him looking at the drinks, "Gave you a choice. Warmth or alcohol." Sitting beside Jim, she said firmly, "Now can we talk about something more interesting than bloody Social Services. Please." With a forkful on his way to his mouth, she asked, "How's the little one? Is she walking? We don't even know how old she is." Seeing him pause the fork, "No, go on and eat. Don't worry about me blathering."

As he chewed, it gave him time to consider his answer. He swallowed. "Clara's her name. Short for Esclarmonde. It's an old cathar name Gizande chose. Bit of a mouthful."

"It's beautiful. Esclaramonde? What does it mean?"

Mean? It was just the strange name she had used to steal from the child Fruhling. The name he had chosen and she had at first seemed delighted with. But he said, "I don't know if it means anything."

"Esclara-monde," Trish repeated. "Isn't that Light of the World?"

Jim shrugged. Neither of the parents used the full name. He had only heard Gizande's mother use it in full. "It's from some legend about witch-hunts by the Catholic Church. I just call her Clara." Avoiding the suspicion of operatic sweep in the whole name, for the sweetness of the abbreviation.

"How old is she?"

"Nearly two. She is walking well."

"Is she speaking?" Then, curious, Trish added, "What language does she speak? With you and Gizande, she'll have a choice, won't she?"

Delicate territory… "She's not a speaker. Yet." Then, lightly, "But she looks right through you. As if she knows everything you think," smiling a little too brightly from her to him. "How's Adam?"

"Terror-tot!" Julian laughed. "Into everything. Takes anything he gets in his hands to pieces. Trish thinks he'll be a car mechanic, but I think he'll be some sort of forensic investigator."

"He's a beautiful boy." Her voice was almost sombre, her eyes still penetratingly on Jim, discomforting him. He looked away from her and concentrated on his food. She had imposed a silence on them all, including her husband, leaving the scrape of his cutlery and the chomp of his jaws loud in the room.

Julian broke in with, "We'll get the divan made up when you've finished. This may be the last time you have to sleep on it like this. We're moving in just over a month. With the second babe," smiling at Trish, "we need the room. There's a spare bedroom for you on your next visit."

Next visit? Jim thought of how fortuitous this visit had been. And how comfortably welcome he felt, except when the talk touched on Gizande. Without looking at her, he sensed Trish would want to speak to him on his own. She and Gizande had got on well when they had met and she would want to know more.

Julian asked, "How long can you stay? Are you here tomorrow night?"

"I can."

"You will," from Trish, smiling at last. "Come on. Bedtime for us all." She took the untouched wineglass off the tray, leaving it on the table before Jim and cleared the rest away to the kitchen, while the two men unfolded and made the bed together.

Trish re-entered, "Night, Jim, see you in the morning."

Before Julian joined her, he said quietly, "It's been good to see you again. Reminded me how important you've been to me. To a few of us." Squeezed Jim's shoulder with a smile and a nod and went.

Leaving the visitor stood in the room by the divan. Bemused, watching the bedroom door close. Before sitting on the duvet and reflectively sipping at the rim of the wine glass.

Jim woke to the steady stare of a child's two blue eyes very close to his. Startled sudden, upright out of his sleep, sending the small boy careering off through the bedroom door shouting, "Mummy! Mummy!"

Jim lay back, drawing the blanket up about his chin, for what happened next.

After a moment, Julian came in, Adam slung against his chest peering at the stranger on the divan. "This is Uncle Jimmy." Jimmy? "He's Mummy and Daddy's friend. He lives a long way away, in another country, on a farm." The boy nuzzled shyly into his father's pyjamas. "Say hello to him, Jim- in French."

"Ola, Adam. Bon jour."

But the boy's face would not be unhidden again. Julian ruffled his hair, then looked seriously down, "I would like a word, before I get off to work. Adam goes to playgroup this morning, as Trish is lecturing." Changing tack, he suggested, "I don't know what you're doing this morning, but how about coming into the office with me?"

"Fine. I've just got to make a phone call on a job. Birmingham."

"Do that in the office. Then I'll get Trish to pick you up at lunchtime and I'll be back after work."

"You don't have to shift everything about for me. I can look after myself."

"We'll ignore that. You're our guest, unexpected or not. Jesus, Jim, we don't see you that often!" As he went back to the bedroom, he called back, "You use the bathroom first." With the afterthought, "Don't you run in the morning these days?" as he disappeared.

The office of the charity Julian now worked for was above a large, run-down ship's chandler's. Up the stairs the rooms were crowded with cheap new desks and notice boards on the walls still smelling slightly of recently painted white emulsion. They were the first to arrive.

"Just moved in?" Jim asked.

"We used to be in council offices, courtesy of Social Services. But it was too close for comfort. They treated us as their employees- which of course some of us had been. Cathcart, when she was still here, kept coming in and nosing around, making unannounced visits. I even had to tell staff to lock away papers in their desks. They refused me separate locks on our doors. Fire regs, they said."

"What was Cathcart looking for?"

"Good question. The stain of what happened to Damien Toser never entirely left her. And the Stephen Roberts mess was only just cleared up in time not to get her fingers burnt in the Court. Scadding is still battling on." But he shook his head, "However… however, it's been a long time. People lose interest. Even in murders and kidnappings. Especially with ex-care kids, where there's always a whiff of them being naughty boys who brought it on themselves."

Jim was just going to ask about Trish's brusque shut-down on talk about these things the night before, when noise on the stairs and the bang open of the door let in a woman with a shorn-short hair, a crumpled skirt and military-looking boots.

"Mornin', Jules."

"Hi. Faith, this is Jim, an old colleague."

"Colleague, eh?" she scanned Jim as if there might be something dubious about him.

"Faith suspects everyone from my past, as they must've been working for the S.S.D.- for the State!" Then turning to her, added, "Jim was sacked by them. For asking too many questions."

"And getting no bloody straight answers, I'll be bound, too."

Julian laughed, "I know the way to your heart, Faith. Jim and I'll be in my office."

"I'm out all morning. I've got a review on a new lad at the Pines. Then I'm seeing a landlord who says he's got some flats on offer."

As soon as Julian closed them into his tiny office and manoeuvred past to sit behind the desk, Jim queried, "The Pines?"

"Yes. Same place Stephen was abused at, I'm afraid. Staff have been moved on, but no-one's ever been disciplined for what went on there. It would all have been too much of a scandal."

"Trish doesn't want to talk about this- these things now, does she?"

Julian toyed with a pen, before looking up again. "It's odd working here. There's still rumours going on about what happened. I think it's mostly in the past now. There's new law that gives some better protection for kids than there used to be. But it won't go away." He sighed, "The latest thing we're sniffing around is about this charity that does runs down to the Balkans with clothes and toys donated for the kids in those terrible orphanages they've been uncovering. Have you heard about it in France?"

Jim shook his head, but his eyes filled with the trusting faces of those two Bulgarian girls in Germany. In what was it called? Hotel Youth? Just by not knowing what could have happened to them, he felt he had in some way betrayed them. Julietta? And the other one? The fragile hopefulness of them. Wanting him and Gizande to rescue them as parents, long before the insufficient parents they had now become.

Julian continued, looking back down at his fiddling hands, "There's been some link between the Pines- yes, that place again- and that charity. The Pines has got itself some good press getting its kids involved in collecting stuff to be sent to Rumania and Bulgaria. Then two of the kids went with the lorries on one of the trips…" He searched for the words to continue and, when he looked up again, the eyes looking back at Jim were moist. "One of them told us… about a goodbye party at an orphanage. The driver and the charity director who went with them... one of the kids told Pete, one of my staff, what went on… snogging with the kids in the orphanage and then they disappeared for the rest of the night- the director and the driver. It was in Rumania and the local staff just seemed to think it was all a big laugh." His voice surprisingly hardening, he ended with, "What's the point? The next time we saw the lad who'd spoken to Pete, the charity was claiming it was the lad himself who'd been having sex with the orphans and he withdrew his story. He apologised and it's all disappeared. Including him. Gone off to another home. Over in Yorkshire. With no plans for coming back."

Jim looked away, filled with a pity. Uncertain if it was for the children, or for himself. The powerlessness of his life now, enfeebled in a way he would never have been in the past when confronted with such a story. And he mumbled it, "I can't do anything…" Curtaining his immediate regret at saying this with, "What can you do, Julian?"

"Me?… Ask them uncomfortable questions. Again and again. The same questions, to the same people. Until they get promoted out of my reach."

"Like Cathcart?"

"Yes. Like your Cathcart."

He would have said, Not mine, but could not summon up even the false indignation to make it stick. Just the briefest memory of the feel of her skin folding under the stroke of his hand. To tease him.

He shrugged, struggling to say, "I…" What? Julian was looking at him, harsher than he had remembered him. A toughening, to match the softening Jim felt in himself. "I went there. Remember? Where you are now. I don't know that it did any good."

"Of course it did. At the time. You went into the East and got Stephen. That's a tremendous story, whatever you say."

Was it? He felt this man wanted him to strike some sort of valiant pose again. Alongside him to validate Julian's sour despair into something else. But Jim was far away from the person he had been in Berlin and before. He had won Gizande with how he had been then. And lost her since. He spoke it out as, "But that was then. Now I live away from all this. I have a child. I have a farm. There is nothing I can do."

Julian looked on at him reflectively. Troublingly. "Do you remember Huntley?"

"The old journalist? Is he still around?"

With a short laugh, Julian went on, "In a manner of speaking. In body, but not in soul." Jim wondered if that referred equally to him and, for the first time he felt a regret at having come on this diversionary visit. "He gave up being an independent- a freelance- and took up a job with the local rag. He admitted he was doing it to get his pension bumped up." Sneering, in way he had never heard Julian before, "You can't blame him, really, can you?" And Jim felt the "you" was really pointed at him, for an answer. Saved from that by the observation, "Of course, he had to give up all the stories he'd been trying to place about dirty councillors, lords of the manor and what-have-you. Because the Council told the editor that if any of them were published, they would only hand out the press releases to the paper's competitors- and half the paper is filled with the wonderful things the Council and its friends are doing. And most of the big ads are for Council vacancies. They can exert that power- rest of the paper is only small ads."

There were loud argumentative voices out in the office, so Julian stood wearily, adding before going out past him, "So old Huntley let himself be gagged by them."

Left in the room alone, Jim felt he had been made to feel as guilty as… who? He remembered his Disciplinary. His back to all those corrupt functionaries, watching the wind and light in the leaves outside that room. The confidence with which he had treated them. Castigating them with his charge. The appalling silence of the good. That and then Berlin and the East for Stephen, one or two martyrdoms too many. Now, sat here, one of the silent, himself.

He listened to the raised voices outside, one swearing with all the vicious vehemence it could summon, "I'm not going back to that fuckin', cuntin' shitface again! And you can't fuckin' make me!"

Julian's words indistinguishable, then, "So you fuckin' say! Every shittin' day! Arse'ole to your promises! I've fuckin' had 'em up to here! I'm off!"

"Where are you going?"

"Fuck knows. But out of here!" And the thunder of feet exiting down the stairs.

And Jim thought, while he waited for Julian to come back in, that is how Finch was once. Remembering the calculated and slick wickedness the young man had clothed himself with, in that Hotel full of children beyond the wires and walls of Germany then. And how he himself had never got to that same place as Finch. Not even close to being so corrupted by the fear and anger of the assaulted child he himself had been … He paused for the words to say what he had once been. The knight on the charger, wasn't it Tracey? Always in the right, but always knowing you had no chance of winning. With anything. Strikes, saving molested kids, marriage or love. As angry with everything then, as he felt defeated, waiting for others to make something happen, now. But it made him smile, despite everything, at the foolishness of it all.

Chapter Six

When Trish picked Jim up, with Adam sat watchfully from his booster seat in the back of the car, she drove out to show the house she and Julian were buying. It was a semi-detached in the same suburb he had visited Scadding in three years earlier. He wondered if Sydney and his wife had ever ended up living together again. Properly, as man and wife. He had thought to ask Julian what he knew, but then demurred. All this was nothing to do with him any more. They parked outside and Jim looked out through the drizzle streaked windows.

"What do you think of it?" Trish asked. Adding brightly, to fill his pause to answer, "It's not a romantic farmhouse in the Pyrenees, of course." Romantic? He compared his old life here with Jane in a similar suburban house, and living between the two farms with Gizande. How could such promise always end so sourly? Must it be himself?

"No. It's okay." He wiped away condensation from the window with his sleeve. "It's got more sense than trying to make a living off a mountainside," regetting letting this out immediately it was said.

"It's not going very well, is it?" she asked gently.

He would not turn to answer, but stared on sightlessly through the glass, feeling defeated. "It's… hard," he grudgingly admitted.

"I don't mean the farming. I mean between you and Gizande."

Deny it? And have to stonewall her enquiring disbelief. Or admit it, and have to talk about it. What could he say? He sighed. "No. It's not easy." He turned at last to face her. "She changed with the baby," and shrugged.

"How?"

He hesitated and sought the window again. He had no explanations, only descriptions. And to tell Trish of Gizande's embitterment with Clara seemed, even now, after so many months of it, a disloyalty. An unlocking of a door to their most private pain, that he had not invited anyone else into. Finally, said to the view outside, "She did not want Clara. She changed her mind." He reluctantly turned back to her, tentative for some sort of support. "While she was pregnant… she took against the child," looking down into his lap with the feebleness of his summary. Aware of the pregnancy of the woman beside him. "I don't know why."

"What's she saying about Clara?"

He was exploring how to put into her words that combination of neglect and contempt that every day brought for both the child and him, when Adam rescued him with, "Mummy! Hungry."

"Just a minute, darling," she said over her shoulder. "Go on, Jim. What does she say?"

But suddenly Trish's inquiry felt like an intrusion. Needing to be pushed away. With, "It's … difficult… to describe. Oh, I'm probably not getting it right."

"Mummy!"

"All right, darling," starting the engine, but giving Jim a last look, long enough to confirm her disbelief at his brush-off.

They drove back into town via a new dual carriageway that allowed the old estates to be bypassed. Looking through the rain at the blocks of flats, he asked, "Why're they all decorated? They've got- they used to be grey."

"Been sold off. To housing associations. They're all grilled and fortressed now, for the posher tenants. Intercoms to get in. But at least the lifts now work, so I'm told."

Jim remembered visiting them. And it was true the lifts would not come when summoned. Especially when the milkmen were using them for their deliveries, blocking open the doors at every floor. Or just unrepaired. He wondered where those he once knew had all now been herded off to. By economics. The Support the Miners Group had met in one of the flats, during the big strike. He tried to remember the names of some of those who attended, crouched on the carpet with them counting coins out of buckets while arguing over the resolution to be put to the next Trades Council meeting. What a strangely meaningless activity, when you looked back now, but he remembered they all felt that they were at the centre of the universe then. Urgent with their sense of importance. Even then, he seemed to recall the creeping impotence he had felt, that had started when he left the car plant. The impossibility of changing things. And yet… and yet, something would not let him close the door that led in to him from that outside world. Despite the hopelessness of it all, he lacked the locks and keys of selfishness… realising this, lying late into the night before, memorising Julian's words.

"How is it with you and Gizande?" Trish interrupted him. "You don't have to talk about it, but I guess you don't have many people to talk to."

He tried to laugh it off with, "True. Not with the quality of French I speak!"

"Okay. I can take a hint. I can read the sign prohibiting trespassers."

"What do you mean?" Jim asked, knowing all too well.

"You don't want to talk about it. That's okay." But clearly not okay to her.

He let it lie, looking away, out the window. But certain she would bring it up again, something he confusedly both vexed at and welcomed, the silence between them both a blockage and an invitation, the rest of the journey back to the flat.

While Trish prepared the boy's food, Adam played with a wooden train set on the far side of the lounge from where Jim sat leafing through a magazine. He became aware that the joined blocks of rail track were creeping across the carpet towards him, but each time he looked over, the child suddenly turned away and busied himself behind his determined back. Jim surreptitiously slid his bottom, cushion by cushion along the settee, until he was but two foot from the furthest reach of the tracks, steadily being clipped together towards him by the busy little pink fingers. Watching the boy, who knew he was being watched, Jim reached around him, into the cardboard box and slowly plucked out two lengths of wooden track. Adam was motionless, looking down at the last piece he held in his own hand. Without a word, Jim clipped together the two lengths and gently lay them on the carpet, six inches from the work of the boy. Who considered this new development, then pulled the new section back to clip it into the completed track. As Jim reached over for more rails, Adam pushed the box towards him, eyes still turned away. Jim fitted another section, waited, then Adam slotted in the next. Time and again, until the box was empty and the track snaked back on itself towards the entrance to his bedroom.

So concentrated had he been with the ritually performed and wordless construction between them, that Jim did not notice Trish leaning on the kitchen doorway, silently laughing. "I can see the sort of dad you are."

Looking back down at the construction he and the child had made, Jim accepted her words as praise. The watching of children, as he did with Clara, had taught him something he had never known with Tracey. Listening, outside the insistent bullying inner voice. He shrugged and smiled apologetically, "Boys. And railways."

"Do you wish you'd had a boy?"

"No," certain of that. "Clara is… Clara. It doesn't matter."

"You had another daughter, didn't you?"

"Yes. Tracey." Adam tentatively started to run the wooden train along the rail system they had built. "Yeah. She's getting married this summer."

"Are you coming over for it?"

"Yes. Maybe." Then thinking of Gizande, "If I can."

"Will Gizande come with you?" Adding, "And Clara?"

"No, probably not." Adding, "Too difficult to leave the farms."

Adam started to rush the train along the tracks, adding the growl of his throat to the clatter of its wooden wheels. As Trish came over to sit the other side of Jim.

"I won't ask again, Jim. If you don't want."

As she paused, he hesitated, watching the increasingly noisy and perilous game by Adam to keep his attention.

"Are things… difficult between you and Gizande?"

He turned, reluctantly. Perhaps the sympathetic ear of another woman? So often misled by listening to them in the past. "I said. She changed, with Clara."

"Is that it? Clara?"

"What do you mean?"

"I mean, between the pair of you. You and Gizande. Her… behaviour to Clara… doesn't it get between you both?"

"It's… It's not-" severed by the clattering crash of engine and carriages behind him, both adults forced to turn to Adam, triumphantly exploding with his mouth, tearing the rails apart with his little hands and throwing them into the air.

Trish persisted, "I mean you don't have to talk to me about it, but you have to do something about it. For Clara's sake, if Gizande is… turned against her. As well as for the pair of you."

What did he really think was going to happen? Was he just going from day to day with her and Clara? Hoping that one morning he would wake beside Gizande and she would be smiling at him? Not turned away from him, or the bed not already emptied of her? "I s'pose… Do you think she needs help?"

"Do you?"

"I don't know." He groped for an explanation. Of the feebleness of his reply. "When you live with someone, it's so easy… to just get on with the work. Especially with a little child- and the work on the farms. There's always another job to do… to stop you having the time to sit and talk. We go off to different fields. Or she goes off to do a job and I have to stay back with Clara. And then at the end of the day… you're too knackered- too exhausted for…" trying to slip away from the cluttered seriousness of it all, with the triviality of, "Owt but eat and sleep." Smiled, adding, "You know that with Adam."

And the little boy, sat amidst the ruins of his railway, watching the two adults, heard his name and shouted, "Mummy!"

Trish looked at him, then back at Jim. "You don't want to always brush it off with a joke. I can see you are worried." Then turned to her son with a studiedly patient, "Yes, Adam?"

Who had to think of something, now he had the attention he sought. "Wan' watch telly."

"Okay, my little master. Monster." And she got up, but looked at the scattered wreckage of the tracks about her feet. "But first you will put all the railway back. Back, tidy in the box. And I will bring out your tea." Going back to the kitchen.

His interview by her over, Jim stood and walked over to the window, while the boy slowly grumbled and cleared up behind him. The rain was holding off beneath a grey sky. A couple walking slowly down the pavement, he swaggering and smoking, she, her eyes turned inward and away from him. So young, he thought, to be together, but so far- a universe, apart. He thought of Gizande. And of Jane before her, thinking how you get used to the distance. How habit stops it hurting. Almost.

Chapter Seven

It was late afternoon, shortly before Julian came home, that Jim at last got an answer from the Birmingham number. The precise, posh voice at the other end explained that the job would be a complicated one. A few items of furniture to go to Perpignan from his house in Edgebaston, but most would be coming from another member of the Consortium, as he called it, from an army officer's house in Germany, near Hanover. But at a later date, because the officer was still out in Kuwait.

Jim listened to this over-long and patronisingly pronounced explanation, finally cutting across it with, "Do you want me to collect anything from you, to take to France this trip?"

There was a pause. And then, ever-so patient with the native he obviously took Jim's accent to denote, he said, "Of course. I thought you would understand. I have already explained that."

"It will have to be early tomorrow morning, then."

"How early would that be?"

After a calculating silence, Jim said flatly, "Seven thirty." Adding, "I've room for a few pieces of furniture, but not a whole load. That's what the agent told me you wanted."

"I will be discriminating, in what I let you take."

With distaste for the voice, Jim chopped off with, "Seven thirty-ish, then."

But the man stopped him replacing the phone with, "What direction will you be coming from?"

"Why?"

"Are you are using the M6, from the North, by any chance?"

"Why?"

"There are terrible roadworks. And considerable traffic, even at that time of the morning." After a pause for Jim to digest this, "So I would expect you to take account of that. We don't want to be kept waiting, do we? Either you or us?"

Jim just grunted and dropped the phone into its cradle. Supercilious prat.

Since the earlier conversation, Trish had left him alone, while she ironed in the kitchen and Adam had an afternoon sleep. Jim had sat idly watching daytime t.v. quizzes and soaps, half- irritated with himself that he would not take the opportunity of talking to her. Fearful that her common sense would come up with solutions that would require him to seriously confront Gizande when he returned. To face out her grim hostilities, alone, together, in one or other of those farmhouses.

Awful. Another in the not-very-long line of relationships left wrecked on the roadside of a life where he seemed to have blundered onwards in the sort of ignorant carelessness that ended up leaving him as alone as…? As he had always been. There was something about the abandoned child in him that never grew up, that was always blocked by his own pain from understanding the hurt of others around him. Left in an empty room, stupid with the angry tears of self-pity. His eyes even now, half glazed with them, staring blankly at the irritating trivialities on the screen before him. The residual anger against a father who was an abstraction, however Jim had tried to bring him back to life, pieced together from the rusted fragments of the dead man's half-occupation of La Retrait. The occasional archaeology of casual finds amongst the tumbled stones of the outhouses. The bikes stored in the broken barn, corroded, the boxes of old clothes in the attic, rotten. And the stories. Those of Suzanne. Against those of others, the original long tale told by old Theodor Jacob, the fragments of snide asides he could only half understand from some of the other old men who had known his father. And his father's letters to Aunt Mary, that first pieced together the truth, now too additional a perturbation since Clara, for him to get from their boxes and reread.

So, with Julian's return, Jim's mood could only sluggishly bring itself up to the other man's cheeriness. "What's with the suit?" he had asked with dragged joviality, as Julian took off his mac. He had been in court, witness for one of his young men in trouble.

"For the magistrates," he answered. Then looking at the ceiling, as if for inspiration, "To achieve change in England, wear a dark suit and think radical thoughts. Who said that?"

Trish entered from the kitchen, insignificating her husband with, "You just did, you pompous idiot." And briefly kissed him, resting her fingers inside the waistband of his trousers a little longer. Before stepping back and looking at Jim, "We've had a quiet afternoon, haven't we?"

"Yes." Reluctantly answered.

Turned to Julian, "Jim's coming over for his daughter's wedding." Then back at Jim, not entirely astonished at her theft of his decision-making like this. "Tracey, isn't she? This summer- when is it?"

"June."

"He could stay with us, couldn't he, Jules."

"If he didn't mind the mess the new house'll probably still be in."

"I haven't decided..." he faltered at first. Then with a subtled wrench of anger at them both, "I don't know if I'm coming over yet. If I can." The arid territory of his dispute over it with Gizande, reclaimed. From their generosity.

"Okay. Okay," Julian soothed. Then, "But if you do, you're welcome, you know."

"I know," he answered, a touch hopelessly.

With, "What's for dinner, darling? And how's Adam been?" they both went into the kitchen, leaving Jim sat before the telly still simpering brightly at him.

While Trish bathed the child, the two men sat across the kitchen table with the clutter of dirty plates. Silence between them at first. Jim was brooding. Julian finally rose, wiped the highchair, folded it and put it in the corner.

Jim would have offered to help wash up, but did not want to end the silence he had withdrawn into. Without watching, the plates were rattled away from before him, into the sink. Before his own frozen immobility, when to move would be to need to speak.

Finally broken, from the other man's turned and busy back above the washing up, "When've you got to leave tomorrow? To get to Brum."

"I'll have to get up at about four, at latest," and he slowly raised himself. Looked for and found a drying cloth. Picked a plate and wiped.

"Shame you can't stay longer."

Jim did not answer that.

"It's a shame you went off to France. You could have... it might have made a difference, if you'd come back to England after Berlin. There might've been a chance of getting- sorting out what was going on- Cathcart, the councillors. Even Scadding might have relented and let you help him... Who knows?"

Who indeed? He rubbed on at the pattern on the plate. He remembered with aching sharpness that first long and private journey back from Berlin, through Germany and France with Gizande. Could he have considered returning to England then? It was never even an option. The job had been done with Stephen. Northwards, back in the hands of Sylvie. And Jim travelling into the arms of Gizande. Southwards. The door back to England just as firmly closed for Jim by the last two years. A hangover buried from his morning's office conversation with Julian, the name of Vanja, the second Bulgarian girl, suddenly slipped to the front of his brain. Those bright and optimistic smiles. From where his lie was now, the irony of the girls asking him and Gizande to become their parents slugged him again.

"Do you think you will come over for your daughter's wedding?"

"Good chance of it." Jim smiled at the other man, at last able to ease off into somewhere noncommittal.

"When would you know? We mean it, when we say you can stay with us, you know."

"Sure. I know that," avoiding the question part.

After waiting for an answer, Julian asked again, "Well, when?"

Jim stacked away the last dried plate into the cupboard and, with nothing left for the cloth to do, wiped away a patch of wet on the surface before him. Had he already decided to surrender to Gizande, and not go?

He said, "I need to… work it out with Gizande. What we do with Clara… and that." But behind the feebleness of this, Jim suddenly decided. He would go. Which he affirmed with, "Make sure I've got your new address. So I can take up your offer."

"Welcome, mate. Welcome." With this rehearsed affability, Julian did not ask whether she was coming too, so Jim guessed Trish had already said something of her probings.

Adam was brought in from his bath, shy in his pyjamas, to say goodnight to his Dad and to Jim. After taking him off to bed, Trish joined them with a third glass for the opened wine bottle.

"Guess you're a wine gourmet now, Jim," a joke, but somehow with an exploratory sting in its tail.

So, defensively, "Not particularly. Gizande's farm has a few vines, but it's too high up in the mountains for decent ones."

"But you drink the stuff, don't you?"

"Oh, yes." Adding, "But only what we can afford. Cheap stuff," feeling it was a foolish admission, as soon as said.

"How do the economics work out, then?" Julian asked. "Farming down there."

"We couldn't really survive without me doing the removals. Gizande's farm is quite good, but even that needs the grants to keep going- the Brussels money. But La Retrait, my farm. It'll never give me a living on its own."

"Do you both live down at Gizande's farmhouse, then?" Trish asked and Jim knew it was not a question about farming.

"Mostly. It's only some of the best summer weather that we can stay up at La Retrait. The heating's… primitive. No hot water. Just electric for lights."

"I remember… it was lovely inside her farmhouse. The smells… beautiful."

Jim felt he was being drawn into something, but answered somewhat over-cheerily, "Oh, yes. The herbs for her oils and essences."

"And the spices. And the smell of that cooking." Looking archly into Jim's eyes, "You must be very lucky."

Jim looked away, a casual laugh become a discomforted snigger, catching Julian watching knowingly and looking away from him too. "Yes. A lot of people would give a lot… for how I live. S'pose," sounding ringingly hollow. Feeling the beginning of anger, at being forced to confront his life, before them. "But you need to live it, to know- how difficult it is."

"Life's always difficult," she said, a philosophical musing with a hard edge. "Different places make different difficulties. Living jobless down by the docks takes some beating. For difficulties." Then, reaching over to ruffle Julian's hair with an affection Jim had not seen before, "A good partner helps. Not that Jules is jobless on the docks."

"Hardly," he said, reaching for his wife's hand to kiss. "But I understand what Jim is saying. I couldn't imagine farming, in the mountains."

"Yes, but Jim made a choice. Didn't you, Jim?"

"What? What do you mean?" he asked, only too clear from Trish's sharp but not unfriendly look, where she was trying to lead him.

"Well, you didn't have to move over there, to France. You could have sold the farm- La Retrait. You could even have given it a go for a couple of years, find it wasn't working- that it wasn't viable, sell it up and come back."

He tried to keep this steered away from Gizande and just a discussion about the economic feasibility of farming in Pyreneean France, assuming the grunt of a sullen peasant. "You wouldn't get a price for it worth the taxes you'd pay in selling it," shaking his head, but watchful of her.

"So that's why you stayed in France?" she said dismissively. "Because of the size of your property taxes?"

"No. I wasn't saying that…"

"You made a choice. Didn't you, Jim?" She waited meaningfully, before continuing, "You chose Gizande. And Clara. And it looked to me, it was a choice you were bloody lucky to be offered."

Jim looked down at his fingertips and rubbed them with his thumbs. The air in the room heavy with waiting for him to reply.

Saved by Julian with, "Steady, Trish. Not so harsh on old Jim. He only said it was hard farming out there."

"You don't understand, Jules. Jim and I have been talking. Haven't we, Jim?"

Made to feel like an errant child, he could either stay looking down at his hands or look up with a foolish grin of assent. Which he did.

"The reason, Jules, I didn't want the pair of you to start on again about the boys last night- about Scadding… and Stephen Roberts… and, was it Damien? Why I didn't want you to start on that was because I know what it does to you. You'll be making plans, next thing. Getting Jim over to act as some sort of witness again in a hopeless case. Like Scadding's. You get like lads being detectives. Solving the conspiracies of the planet." With a gentler address to Jim, "And things are a bit difficult for you just now, aren't they, Jim?" Then, back to her husband, "Gizande's got some sort of post-natal depression. It isn't easy. And I know you, Jules. Down at the office this morning, I'd put money on it that you got some sort of commitment from Jim to give… some sort of help in chasing your- child abusers." Then, back at Jim, "Didn't he, Jim? Did he get you hooked on the Balkan stuff? That's the latest thing, isn't it, Jules? Isn't it?" Finalising it with, "That's why I shut you both up last night about Cathcart."

Confused between the relief Trish was offering from his reluctant commitment to past events and obscurely angry at the gift of it he was accepting from her, Jim protested feebly, "I never agreed to do anything." And saying it tasted so sour, he was forced to add, acidly, "So what if I had agreed to do something. Isn't Jules right? Not to let them get away with it." Then, with a softer caution, "You seem to have changed your tune about it, Trish… haven't you?"

"It's part of Jules' job. And yes, I am pretty pessimistic that anything can be done. And yes, I do resent it when we're not sure if our phone might be interfered with- tapped or something- because of the sort of people Jules is asking questions about." Firmly, "This is Adam's home. Why should he be… become tangled up in all this stuff, because his Dad is asking about…" Breaking off with, "Oh, you know, Jules- I've said it before." Before focussing back on Jim, "But it's got nothing now to do with you. You've got another life. What can you do about it now?"

He looked at Jules. Beneath the guarded restraint of withdrawal before his wife's challenge, Jim recognised a half-hidden appeal for him to speak out. Reminded of the almost ineffectuality Jim used to feel about this man. Facing back to the woman, he surprised himself at the retrieved gravity he spoke with. "It's not that easy. Not being able to do anything, doesn't mean it goes away. I know that."

It took her a moment to respond. "Does that mean… does that mean you are going to come back?"

He had not considered the decisions and events his words might imply, "Why should I come back? I just said it doesn't go away. Nothing's been decided. Jules hasn't really asked me to do anything." Adding, to the man, "Have you, Jules?" Watching him struggle between the wish to ask Jim and to be silent, so different from when his wife was not present.

"What are you up to, Jim?" her question drawing him back to her hawkish eyes. "What game are you playing? What are you actually trying to get out of this?"

He asserted himself, strong with denial, "I'm not getting anything! What do you mean? You don't just dump things that have happened to you. Like chasing Stephen across Germany. Like being in the room- where they murdered Damien. It's still all up there," tapping his forehead vehemently, his head actually filled with being the terrified boy pulling up his wet underpants to the crying growl from the dark of the masturbating priest. Adding hopelessly, "Even if you can't do anything about it."

The suddenness of his words filled the room then with silence.

It was a measurable stretch of time before Trish spelt out quietly, "You can't just hang on to being a victim of something that happened in the past. Unless you want it to stop you to do anything about the present."

He was sure she did not know how much of a victim he had once been. And strangely, he once would have been willing to tell her, alone. As he had once let Gizande know. But without Julian, another man, in the room. As it was now, Jim just sat unanswering in shrunken-cheeked and sullen silence. Wondering if she would be saying it the same if she knew the truth. Wayback in little Jimmy's life.

"You don't know." Jim surprised himself with the scorn he said it.

"Ach!" She stood up. "I'm going to bed." Surveying the two men, "I'll leave you two to mull over all your conspiracies. Men's work!" Then, leaning down towards Jim, "I'll tell you what I do know, Jim Briggs. You've got a wonderful woman out there. And she's hurting. I don't know why. Maybe- maybe, you don't know either. But she needs you… she and Clara need you. And they need you to be there with them, without your head filled with stuff a thousand miles away that you can't do anything about." Finally to her husband, "So you think of that, Jules. When you go on into the night, getting all self-important about your secrets- whispering them together. Both of you have your own children."

Julian's face moved to protest, but said nothing

From the doorway, she said more quietly, "I probably won't see you before you leave in the morning, Jim. Make yourself up what food you need. And keep yourself safe." Finally, seriously, with warmth, "It has been good to see you. Please come again. And bring Gizande and little Clara. Please." Closing herself into the bedroom.

The men sat for a long time, both looking down at what was left of the wine before them, whatever they would have said stolen by her.

Jim finally said, smiling slightly, "She's quite a woman."

"She certainly is." Then, smiling with tired irony, "I was going to pick your brains about- oh, I don't know… the Balkan stuff, Scadding. She was right. But…"

"You couldn't really, now?" Jim offered. "After what she's said. Yeah. I understand." Understood what? An ineffectuality in Jules? Or something about all men before wiser women? Adding darkly, "But it doesn't go away." Searching for words, "Going… getting busy with other things does not make it go away. You can't get it out of your mind." He flicked through the faces, like shuffling a pack of cards. Damien, Stephen, Vanja and Julietta, even the beautifully elfin face of Jennifer in that dirty flat of the dying Mark, his lost friend. "You can't just erase it. I can't, anyway. It's not like burning books."

Julian was looking at him. Curious at the broken and tired words of passion Jim was clunking out. Probably wanting to have been able to say them himself.

Jim released the other man with, "It's bed time," sighed out, almost with defeat.

Julian nodded. "Yeah. I suppose it is." He reached his hand over, less for a shake, than for a clutch, his fingers scrambling along the back of Jim's knuckles. Faintly desperate. At being left alone in his work with the angry and the pathetic kids? Jim wondered. And no one to share with do's and not do's of the knowledge he had? He wanted to ask Julian, what next with the Balkan story, but it would just be peepholing at something he had no part to play in. Trish had been at least right about that. Even if the children's faces would not go away from his dreams.

He gave a rough slap to Julian's hand, comradely and dismissive, "The divan. It's quieter if we both put it down and make it together."

Chapter Eight

As he approached Birmingham, lanes blocked off by grumbling lorries in a long, slow creep along the coned-off motorway, the over-pronounced voice on the phone was proving right. Although he had quietly slipped out of the flat before five, it was nearly eight o'clock when he swung in the wide gravel drive darkened by laurel bushes.

A woman in knife-edged creased slacks answered the door. "Oh. Yes," apparently knowing who he was, but preoccupied, spun on her heel and strode back up the wide hallway,

Jim hesitated, stepped inside and half closed the door to, behind him.

She had just disappeared into a side room, when he heard her say, "He's here. Your removal man."

Appearing from the room, a suave figure, elegant to the edge of effeminacy. "Ah, at last." The voice on the phone. "Insufficient notice of my warnings, I see," smiling, but without generosity. "Mr. Briggs, I assume?"

Making Jim want to exaggerate the sort of manual worker brutishness that had never been natural to him, whatever the job. "Yeah. What d'you want taken?"

"Follow me." Led into a dining room. Where the woman stood glowingly angry, her hands gripped round the carved back of a dining chair. The man gestured, "This dining table. And the chairs." He held up his hand to stop her from speaking. "The table disassembles."

"He is not taking these, Henry," she said with restraint, verged on angry tears. "You have no right. I will go to my solicitor."

"You are already going to your solicitor, my dear. Just another item she will charge you for." Then, turned from her, "Please excuse us. The table? You can manage that."

Jim cleared his throat, "It will need wrapping. To protect it." With a quick flick of his eyes at the woman, then, "If you have a blanket, I could tie it up in that."

"It's theft," she said, in bitter complaint. "What do you expect me to eat from?"

The man turned with a tired, performed tolerance, "Please excuse us?" to Jim.

Who stood, uncomprehending what was being asked.

"The hallway? Would you wait in the hallway, for a moment? Please."

Jim went and the door closed behind. He could hear the man's voice raised- something again about solicitors- and the woman sobbing. He moved away down the hall, out of hearing. Wanting to be neither here, nor at home, irritated by the demands of both. He looked away and was taking slow, restless steps across the pattern of the floor's tiling, when the man reappeared.

"Here. Please."

Jim attended, reluctant to be so summoned, but keen to be off from this place. Walking back into the dining room, but putting his hands into his pockets. The woman was sat defeatedly on one of the chairs.

"I will get you the blanket you need," the man said.

"What else am I taking?"

"I will show you. When you have dealt with this." And he left Jim alone with the woman.

He looked surreptitiously at her, but she looked up, flicking her carefully greyed hair from her face. "Does this happen to you often?" she asked, with weary challenge.

After a confused pause, "What?"

"You… becoming the agent- for theft."

"I… just do-"

"My job!" she completed, with a curl of contempt.

"Yes," he replied, quietly.

"Well? Has this happened before?"

"No."

"He got you to come so early- before my lawyer's office was open. And I suppose you will be stealing my dining room furniture straight onto a ferry to the Continent."

Jim shrugged, but said nothing.

"Men!" She looked away, scanning the contents of the room. "A conspiracy of men. Get on with it, then."

He wanted to look away from her, but could not. He cleared his throat, "Are you…? Is he leaving you?"

She was surprised at the question, as if she was for the first time aware of who Jim might be. "Of course. This-" gesturing the furniture around her, "This is being stolen from under the divorce court's nose."

He heard steps on the stairs. The man re-entered with a blanket over his arm. "Here. The top slides off and the legs unscrew from the frame," he said, leaning down to the table, ignoring his wife.

Jim looked back at her and her eyes challenged him. Inviting him to take sides. When he said, "I'll go out to the van. To get a rope. To tie the blanket round," her slight smile was an enquiry.

"Fine," the husband said from underneath.

Jim resisted smiling back at her and walked measuredly out into the hall, closing the front door and across the gravel. The drive was generous enough to allow him to swing the van round in its turning circle, without having to reverse. He checked his mirrors as he pulled away into the street, but there was no sign yet of the man. Tucked away in the laurels, half concealed by the stone gatepost, was a *For Sale* sign.

It was eleven thirty when he reached Jude and Deedee's house. No parking space outside, as he had expected. Walking himself back from parking the van two hundred yards up the street, Deedee was loading a splitting cardboard box into an old grey estate wagon.

"I'll need your parking space. For my van," he said, with a touch of expert self-satisfaction.

Which she recognised. "You're early. You said lunchtime. We don't eat lunch in London so early." Then, giving the box a last heave to squeeze it in between holdalls and binbags, she stood back and checked that the tailgate would still close over the bulge of goods. "Wanted to get this loaded before you came. Then I'll move it and you can have the space." Then, spitefully, "Will that suit you?"

He shrugged and grimaced, "Sure."

She stood to face him. "This is going to be a horrible day, as it is. Please don't make it any worse," turning on her heel and striding up the steps. At the top, in the doorway, she stopped so suddenly that, following, he almost ran into her. Close enough for a confused backing out of range of her perfume. A step back herself to keep her distance, "I was going to tell you. I phoned Theresa, the agent. She is only charging us one hundred and fifty pounds for the extra days" Ending pointedly, "Not the two hundred you said."

Jim thought, Am I that cheap? but said nothing. Following Deedee's dungareed bottom up the stairs.

Jude greeted him as they entered the flat, "Oh. Hello. We've got the kids out of the way. They're with friends, till we're all packed."

"Good," said Jim, the flat tolerance of it more for Deedee than for Jude.

He helped complete the packing of the estate. That was driven off and re-parked and Jim brought the van back outside the house. Into the afternoon, he and Deedee worked almost wordlessly together, while Jude fluttered about the flat upstairs, stuffing remaining items into bags or boxes, supplying them with mugs of tea.

At one point, after finally manoeuvring a double bed into the van together, Deedee stood back from it, "I'm not bad at this. Pretty strong. For a woman."

He smiled at her, "You said it. Not me."

And she smiled back at him, for the first time. Before jumping down into the street, away from the brief instant of comradeship. "Come on. Not time for self-congratulation." And was away upstairs again.

It was four o'clock before Jim finally slammed the back doors of the van.

Jude had gone to collect the children.

Deedee looked critically at the van, then at Jim. "Drive it carefully. That's our whole life in there. Our pasts and our futures."

He did not take it as a criticism, simply saying, with kindness at last towards this spiky woman, "I know. I understand." Recognising the risks she was taking in the weariness of her face. Taking two children. And the adult one, Jude. Into some sort of unpredictable new life. "We'll go together. I'll keep with you across France," he reassured, wondering what the relationship was between the two women. He had assumed the children were Jude's. "Plenty of stops, to give the kids a break."

She looked at him. As if she was going to make a gesture, say something, but only murmured, "I'll have a last check. For anything we've left," and went upstairs.

Jim was organising his maps and documents on the front seat and propping the bottle of water in the folds of his sleeping bag within reach, ready to go, when Jude came back, with the boy running and the girl holding her hand, snivelling tearfully.

"Oh, dear," she called to Jim cheerfully, "Not a promising start for a long journey!"

He nodded briefly and wordless. Crying children, of which he predicted to himself there would be much over the next couple of days, were something he did not want to get involved with.

Keeping together out of rush hour London was never going to be easy, but, by the time they hit the motorway to Dover, Jim could see the estate in his rearview mirror and congratulated himself on the professionalism of his driving. He had agreed with Deedee for no stops before the ferry and when they arrived there, it was still early enough in the season for Jim to get his ticket altered for the boat they were booked on, with no problems. He walked over to the estate and leaned over Deedee's open window.

"Well, that went okay. That's probably going to be the worst. There's no traffic as bad as that the way I'll take you through France."

From the front passenger seat Jude leaned over, "My god, Deedee. France! Driving on the wrong side of the road!"

Jim looked at her, glad he was not travelling in this car. "No. We're the ones who drive the wrong side." Then, to Deedee, as driver to driver, "You okay?"

Dismissed with, "Course I'm okay," Jim leaned on against the car roof for a moment before taking the hint and sauntering away. Then, remembering, sauntering back, "Oh, and don't forget, you will be leading me to the campsite the other side. I don't know where it is." She was either nervous or irritated, a finger picking at the plastic of the steering wheel. "Okay?"

"Yes. I know. You follow us there." She looked up at him impatiently. Wanting him gone. So he went again.

On the ferry, he found the table where they had started to camp out, covering the space with toys, children's books and emptied bagfuls of soft drinks and sandwiches. Uninvited to join them and keeping his distance from the children, Jim sat with a coffee at the next table and, his shoulders and legs aching from the heavy work of the day, tried to doze away the dreary repetitions of those flights of stairs.

Until being woken by a pull at his trousers. "Are you Jim?" It was the boy. Jude was smiling over towards him.

"Yes."

"Where we goin'?"

He smiled, despite himself. Looking over at Jude, "France. It's across the sea. It's… they talk a different language there. Did you know?"

"What's that?" asked softly. Then turning, with loud and whining inquiry, "Aunty Jude? What's diff'ent… sandwich?"

"Language," Jim corrected in almost a whisper.

The boy looked at him in disbelief and, had enough, went back to the other table. Deedee was reading and looked up only briefly to say, "Sit down here, Orlando."

Orlando? Jim squirmed for the boy at the consequences of such a name. Jim had always been good enough for him. As a child, James had been bad enough. But to labour under the weight of Orlando? Would wearing such a name change the child's life? Playground, or even workplace taunts? Like calling Clara her full name. Esclarmonde. Gizande now only referred to her as The Child. He looked over at the table. The little girl was curled asleep beside Deedee. So was she the mother? Of both children? With Jude, a family, of sorts. Certainly functioning better than his own. Either the present one, or the past, he thought ruefully.

"What's the girl's name?" he asked, of either adult.

Deedee answered, "Fiorella," looking at him over the top of her reading glasses. "Her father was Italian."

Was? Jim wanted to ask, but simply said, "Oh." At least it explained Orlando. Then asked, "What made you want to move to France?" Adding, "You're going for good, yeah?"

Jude replied, watched by Deedee, "We're opening a business. A centre for alternative therapies."

He knew the town where they were moving to, a small worn-out spa about twenty ks from La Retrait. He thought, how hopeless an idea, in such a remote, poor part of the country, but enquired, with polite interest, "What sort of therapies are those?"

"Aroma-massage," Jude smiled at his apparent interest. "Reflexology, crystals, meditation." He doubted their metropolitan knowledge of oils set against Gizande's.

Deedee put her book face down and half turned to square herself to him. "Well. What do you think?" Challenging him, "You know the area."

A serious response required, he could only ask, letting his scepticism leak out, with, "Who would be your customers?"

"Clients," she corrected him. "Tourists. Some of the locals, too."

Jim twisted away a smile from his face at the thought of local farmers coming for therapies. Those rough, uncared-for bodies. Gizande, with all her knowledge of oils and massage, would never think of such a possibility, without seeing the absurdity of it, like him. But he only replied to Deedee with, "There aren't many tourists. Except the skiers, but they're away over in the mountains, towards Andorra, mostly."

She picked up her book again and scanned the page, replying, without looking back at him, "The area's changing. You'll see."

Leaving Jim dismissed, to look over at Jude still smiling her bright optimism, to shrug and slide himself back into a slump for dozing.

Chapter Nine

Outside Calais, it took an hour and several false turnings before Deedee found the entrance to the campsite. She walked back to the window of Jim's van, "Sorry about getting us lost. Aren't you coming in?"

"No. I've got no tent."

"Where will you go?"

He looked along the lane they were parked on. "I'll park the van up there. See where the light from the site is." There was a widening onto the verge, surfaced with brick rubble. "I'll sleep in the van. I've got a sleeping bag."

"Are you sure?"

"Yeah. But we want to be off early. I'll be ready for seven in the morning."

"If you're sure?" He was warmed by the unaccustomed concern in the voice of this woman. "Have you eaten?"

"I ate on the ferry. I'm fine."

"Okay." She patted the van door. "See you in the morning."

As he drove up to his parking place, in his wing mirror he watched her walking back to the car. He turned the van round with difficulty in the narrow lane, so he would be facing the campsite gate for an immediate start when they emerged tomorrow.

The night had the cold of a reluctant spring and Jim knew he would only get fragmentary sleep. Getting too old for this sort of thing, he thought. His mind stirred the events of the last two days together with the prospect of what awaited him back home, for a long time…

…Before he finally realised that he was waking to a repeated tapping. Sitting up in defensive fright, he banged his shin harshly on the steering wheel. The light from the camp was gone and it was a moment before he saw Jude's face, crazily at the window, out of the dark.

"What do you want?" he grumbled, reaching over to open the door.

"Can I get in? It's freezing out here."

He put the cab light on and watched her clamber in, wrapping a bright silk robe round her.

"What do you want?" he repeated, less dourly. "No wonder you're cold, wearing that."

She grinned at him. Then seriously, looking at him with a shrewdness he would not have expected, "You don't think we're very well prepared, do you? I mean for any of this- going to live in France."

"Well, it's not for me to say." He pulled the sleeping bag up again round his chest. "I don't even know what your plans are. Not rightly." Then shook his head.

"No. I saw your face. When I said about the therapies." Then she paused. "Deedee is really worried. She's been talking about it."

"Well, why didn't she come?" regretting the coarseness of its sound as soon as said. "I mean… I didn't say anything. Only about the skiers."

"No. I left her asleep. But she's really worried. You know, that we've burnt our boats and all that. She's always had doubts, but I'm the one that rushed it all along. I just think it'll be so good for the kids, too." Then, direct to Jim, "You've made a life down there- in that part of France. It is possible, isn't it?"

An overwhelming question, that, from where his life was now.

But, before he could consider an answer, she continued, "It's not possible to live in Britain any more. The Tories back in again. It's like the old saying, if they put up a pig's bladder for election, the English would vote for it, if it looked Tory."

He laughed, aware vaguely of the election news the previous month and surprised it had not been mentioned with Trish and Julian. A measure of how far he had changed from who he had been, he thought. The irrelevance of the big events, like elections he no longer voted in. Compared to looking after Clara. And getting by, day-upon-day, with Gizande.

"France has got to be better… hasn't it?" she urgently sought for reassurance, before shivering. "It's cold," looking at him, with an exploratory meaningful smile.

It would not be unpleasant to have wrapped arms with each other just for the warmth of them, but the complications of having that in the journey ahead was too much. "There's my jacket," he offered.

She said, "Thanks," but did not move to take it. "You don't think it is a good idea- us going to live there, do you?"

"I don't know you." Then, to close it down, "Not for me to say."

"You've made a life there, haven't you? How long've you been living there?"

A life? "Four years, really."

"What made you decide? To move over and… live…"

He wondered that. Decide? Nothing so decisive. France had filled a gap that had appeared in his life. Chance. Like ending up with Gizande. Or fate, as she would once have said. Jim offered the most rational sounding explanation, "I was left some property. An old farm."

"Oh, how lovely!"

"It was a wreck. Still can't live there properly."

"What do you grow there?"

He laughed, her naivety giving him the false authority to declare, "Thorns. And rocks. So far. And a few scraggy goats."

"So how do you live?"

"I couldn't do it without this," thumping the van's steering wheel. "It your dreams that pay for my life. Trucking furniture for English people dreaming about… the so-called good life in France."

She looked at him inquisitively for a moment. "You're very bitter… cynical."

"No. Just…" and then he said the word he remembered hating from the past, "Realistic." The summary of every older man's betrayal of what they had once passionately believed. Like a gravestone weight. He would have liked to be able to take it back, but it was all too true for him now. The perishing of his belief that he could change things. That he could steer anything more significant in his life than these vanloads of other people's feeble and deceitful dreams. He looked over at this foolishly under-dressed woman and would have wished to expel her from the cab with contempt. But could only sympathise with her wish for something vaguely better and stumblingly reached out to her with, "No… you and Deedee… have the… energy, I'm sure. You'll find what you want." Then, to lighten the lack of conviction in his voice, indicating her thin clutched robe, "But you'll have to do something about getting better covered for the nights out here. Where you're going, it stays pretty cold in the winters. It's not exactly the mountains, but spring still comes pretty late."

"Thanks." She reached over and touched his shoulder. Fingertips only, she rested them there, "We could still ask your advice- when we're there. You don't live far away? Like, consult you, sort of thing?" Withdrawing her hand for his answer.

"Hah! Consult? I'm only paid to hump your boxes. And drive them." Softening for her, with, "Of course. There aren't many English down there. It's not the Dordogne. As I say, the winter's too hard. But it is beautiful." Hesitant, before finally offering, "Maybe, you and Deedee - and the kids, could come up and see my place- after you've settled in. And it's got warmer."

"Oh, thanks! That's a fine offer! Thanks, I'm sure we will."

"Come on, now. I- we all need some sleep. Long day tomorrow."

She reached over again and would have perhaps pulled him over to kiss, but he held back, smiling, and her hand turned it into a rough and friendly stroke of his cheek. Sexual or not, but affectionate. Before she opened the door behind her, stepped down and was gone into the dark.

The next morning, he was glad to be away from them, alone in his cab. The estate car kept behind him and he was careful at junctions not to let gaps and give Deedee the time to follow him. He rooted for a tape, found the one of old sixties music, something of Gizande's. Hippy-dippy music that had passed him by at the time it had been made. Something they had maybe played together, he half-listened to it anyway, calculating how far they would be able to get before tonight. In the brief early discussion he had with Deedee before they set off from the campsite, they had agreed to stop near Rouen for lunch. Jim had to take account of what the children would want. Some of the lorry drivers' cafés that he used might be a bit greasy-spoon for this journey.

He found a roadside McDonalds to stop at and again sat near but separate from the two women and the children. After eating, Jude took the kids outside onto the small play area. Deedee brought her coffee cup over to Jim's table.

"Jude told me she spoke to you. That you were not giving us much hope- in France."

"I never said that."

"I know. But Jude may seem a bit… fluffy, but she's not a fool. You may not have said it… exactly."

He was resentful of being interrogated like this, as it felt to him. "What do you want me to say? That it's like- living in some picture book?" He stared back at her. "Well it's not. Not for me. And not if you haven't got a lot of money." Adding, "Much like life anywhere, if you're not rich. It's hard work and knowing what you're doing."

"And we don't?" It was both a challenge from her and a genuine request for his opinion.

"I didn't say that!"

"No? As good as."

"Look, Deedee, I live with a French woman. I have a French sister out there. Even with all that, it's not easy. And you've the kids, too."

"So you're not alone?"

"What?" He was surprised at the personal turn of the question. "No. Why?"

She shrugged and grimaced. "Just something Jude said."

"What? What did she say?"

"It doesn't matter." She drank from her cup, before looking up, "You may be right. About us not having much chance. But if we didn't give it a go, we might always regret not knowing if we could hack it." Then, leaning back in her chair, as if to scan him, "After all, you had a go and you're still there- for all your bemoaning about winter in the mountains," giving him a grin. "After four years isn't it?"

Was that how he seemed? Moaning about the mountains? But if you lived there, it became part of the language. Like the peasants he lived amongst, nothing so sourly satisfying as measuring how bleak the prospects of the coming season. He smiled to himself, then at her, shaking his head, "You wait till you live down there. You'll get like the rest of us. Bleating on about how awful the winter has been."

"Oh no, I won't," she sat up again. "We'll be positive. We'll get something moving. Get in the tourists. Bed and breakfast. Even grow things. You watch."

Back in the van and thinking about that conversation, her tenacity had overshadowed the characteristic gloom he realised he spoke with now. But he also recognised, even without the language to really share his thoughts with his neighbours, how far he had assumed the pessimism of those about him. Reinforced by age and by his home-life.

Chapter Ten

The crash took place in the late afternoon, as they were approaching Tours. Jim did not see it in his rearview mirror and had driven a couple of hundred metres before he realised the car was no longer behind him. He pulled into the side of the road and put his flashers on, leaning out to look back. At first a string of lorries coming fast up behind obscured the view, before a break and he could see the grey motor crumpled and slewed onto the verge.

He jumped out of the passenger door and ran back up the road. Jude was dragging the children out, while Deedee stood vacant, looking down at wreckage of the car's wing and rippled bonnet, with the wheel protruding into the roadway on the naked axle, at an odd angle, sunk on its deflated tire. The small truck that had hit them was parked behind, engine still running, with the driver trying to lever the edge of his bumper away from the tyre, his only damage.

"What happened?"

Deedee looked at him, vaguely, then back at the car. "Don't know."

"You okay?"

She put the heel of her palm to her forehead and looked at him again, this time with recognition. "Yeah. Think so."

He looked over at Jude, "Are the kids okay?"

She smiled and nodded, a child's hand in each of hers, leading them back further onto the verge.

He patted Deedee on the shoulder and walked over to the driver.

While Jim still stood over him watching, the driver carried on heaving back at the bent metal, snarling, without turning round, "Qui etes vous?" He stood up, went to his passenger door, scuffled inside, before returning with a metal bar. All without looking at Jim. "Qui etes vous?"

"Un ami. Des femmes."

The man set the bar against the metal and levered it slowly back away from the tyre. He repeated, "Qui etes vous?" And again, between heaves on the bar, "Qui etes vous?"

Who am I? Jim thought, the fella who's gonna belt you one in a minute. But said in his uncertain French, "J'ai vous disé. L'ami des femmes," indicating the women and children behind him.

The driver gave a look of satisfaction at the job done on his truck and only then, looked narrowly at Jim, with, "Bien." Turned on his heel, trotted the few steps back to his cab door, hauled it open and swung himself up.

Realising, Jim stumbled forward as the engine roared. "Stop! Arretez!"

But the driver had already swerved himself out into the traffic, horns blaring and lights flashing behind him.

Jim had to jump back, furious, "BASTARD!" tumbling backwards and wrenching his ankle. To watch the truck slip between the traffic, realising he had not got the number. He pushed himself up from the muddy grass.

"Are you all right?" It was Jude, from where she had the children herded, a hand on each of their shoulders. Fiorella was quietly crying. Deedee was looking over from where she had not moved, still dumb with it all.

He shook his head and wiped his hand across the wet slime on the back of his jacket. "Did you see that?" He stepped forward, but his ankle twinged painfully. "That shitty- shitty bastard!" He limped over to Jude. "I didn't get the number. Did you?"

"Oh. No."

"Why did he try to hit you? With his lorry?" It was the boy.

Jim looked down. "Because he was a bad man. Because…" Then to Jude, nodding towards Deedee, "Is she okay?"

"Go and see."

He limped over. "Deedee?"

"What happens now?"

"The gendarmes. We wait for them- the police." He would have touched her for reassurance, but looked down at the broken car. "I didn't get that bastard's number. Did you?"

She shook her head.

He looked back at her. "We need to get this taken to a garage," knowing the car was a write-off. "You'll need to fill out the forms. The gendarmes will probably want a statement." Then, "I didn't see what happened."

"Neither did I. It was all so fast. He was next to me. Then I was off the road, here. And he was behind me." Reluctantly, he realised he would have to be in charge.

A motor cycle gendarme, all black leather with a hint of authoritarian fascism, reluctantly relented for the visibly shocked Deedee to use his radio to contact the number on her rescue insurance. Her French was surprisingly good, giving him her statement, but, man to man, he treated Jim with suspicion, as if he might have really been the driver who had escaped from the scene of the crime. Asking him questions about his business, lengthily and with suspicion scrutinising the van's documents.

Jim backed the van up nearer, so that Jude and the children could sit inside, while he and Deedee stood with the gendarme. Finally the rescue truck came, driven by a friendly elderly man, who winched the crumpled car onto the trailer and took time to be attentive to the children, as they and the women climbed into his cab. Walking round, finally testing the strapping securing the car, he looked at Jim, shook his head towards it and said sadly, "Fini. Tout fini."

At the garage, Jim told the women. The car would be left on the forecourt for the insurers to see, but it would not be leaving there. Deedee was near to tears and it was with Jude that he discussed the practicalities. The garage man phoned a small hotel in the next town and offered to drive them there. The following morning, they would return and try to pack the contents of the estate into the van and Jim would drive them on to Tours to catch a train and then deliver their possessions to them the day after tomorrow. He calculated that he would probably need another night on the road, before getting down there.

"How will we get the keys? They're with the estate agents. We were going to collect them on the way."

"Theresa?" he said. "We'll phone her tomorrow. Let's get to the hotel," aware that the garage man had been a patient onlooker to all this anxious foreign conversation.

The woman proprietor of the hotel was confused how to allocate the two rooms available between the two women, the children and Jim. After studied repetition in his plodding French, she shrugged at Jim having a double bedded room to himself and the women and children clustered together to share two single beds. To save that, he wished he had slept in the van. It was agreed that Jude stayed up in the bedroom, getting the children asleep, while Deedee ate downstairs in the little restaurant with Jim, then Deedee going up to release Jude to eat.

Deedee had said little during the meal and Jim had conceded her silence, assuming it to be the pessimism Jude had told him of, now confirmed. And there was little he believed he could say to mitigate the disaster the crash had led to. She left as soon as she could and went upstairs, having just toyed with her food.

"Deedee's very down," he said to Jude when she joined him.

"I know. It was a hell of a shock." Smiling at him, "But I don't know what we would have done without you there. It could've been worse. No injuries."

"You'll find it hard to convince Deedee of that. That it could be worse."

She gave him a brief laugh, "Or you. Even more the eternal pessimist than her."

"I didn't even get the truck's number. Think the worst and it won't surprise you when it happens," he said, unexpectedly hearing those words from his lips. Expecting the worst of others. And the events they brought with them. He realised that he would be at least a further day late home and would have to explain that to Gizande. Adjourning that problem to a phone conversation tomorrow.

Jude swallowed a mouthful from her fork. "Hah! Think of the worst and you won't see the chance of the good thing, coming along in the opposite direction. You'll miss it, if you don't have your head up to look for it."

He realised how irritating he found such sunny optimism.

Jude ate on, then looked at him, smiling, "Like you and how awful life in France is. I'll bet you get up some mornings and it's the best thing in the world, looking out there on the mountains. Don't tell me it isn't better than how we were living in London!"

He tried to feebly fend off her persuasions with, "I've never lived in London."

But she was not having it, "You know what I mean." Adding, "I've never lived in France, but I'm giving it a go. Car crashes and all. We'll get through it."

"Dragging Deedee after you?" he said, but sounding bitter rather than the intended amiable irony.

"Yes!" she theatrically stuck her chin out. "Dragging Deedee- and the kids- with me. If that's what it takes. And they'll thank me for it, in the end."

I wouldn't be so sure, he thought. But he just gave her a placidly stoical smile and stopped himself from saying anything by filling his mouth with pudding.

Next morning, back at the garage, he was able to stuff everything from the estate into crevices in the back of the van. Deedee looked at the bent metal and seemed to have lost the last night's comatose despair.

Jim went up to her. "You'll get some insurance from it. I don't suppose they're going to insist it's worth rebuilding the old thing."

"It was a good old heap. The right size for us all. Big enough."

"We'll have to look you out something else down there. Just to get around."

She looked at him. A measurement. "Thanks. For all the help."

"Jude's already thanked me. Bit useless, me not getting the other bloke's number."

She shrugged, "I don't suppose it makes a difference. In the end."

"I can put it in my statement. I'll write a witness statement to go with the claim form you'll have to send off."

As she turned away her attention to the children, "Stop it, Orlando!" she gave Jim's arm a brief squeeze. "Get over by the van! And leave your sister alone."

Jim summoned the kids and Jude from where she was trying to speak haltingly to the old garage man. "Come on! Time to get you lot off to the train!"

The two women sat in the van, each with a child on their lap. Deedee and Fiorella next to him, moving her little shoes out of the way of the gear stick. Jude, with Orlando watching the oncoming traffic out of the other window, racing at them with the growling engine noises of his mouth. They set off and just the moving off the forecourt, leaving the wreckage behind, cheered them all. Chatter started, observations about the country they were passing through, an I-Spy game that became increasingly taken over by adult silliness and laughter after Jim joined in, claiming to see increasingly absurd and bizarre things.

As they approached Tours, he said to both women, "Do you have to go by train? Why don't we give it a try going on as we are. It's tight in here, but if it gets unbearable later in the day, I can drop you off at a station somewhere nearer. Say, Limoges. Every kilometre you do with me, saves you on railfares."

"Good idea," Jude grinned keenly.

"Would we get there today?" Deedee asked.

He considered. "No. Probably not. But another night in a cheap pension would be less than all your rail fares. And you're paying for my fuel already."

"I don't know." She looked at Jude. "How would you be with Orlando on your lap all that way? He's heavier."

Before she could answer, Jim cut in, "We could stop more often. To let everyone stretch their legs. And give the kids a run-around." He really wanted them to stay in the cab with them. He felt both protective and responsible for the little family now and was aware also, of enjoying Deedee next to him, her thigh alongside his, occasionally knuckle-brushed by him as he changed gear. Telling himself that he was a sad old man and that it was going nowhere, but warming himself anyway from her closeness and the friendly gratitude that had replaced her touchiness.

"Come on, Deedee. Let's give it a try! See more of our new country high up here in Jim's van, than from rushing through it on a train. Anyway, you always see the worst of a place from a train. The back walls of factories where the rubbish is dumped!"

They all laughed at this and Deedee conceded. Jim watched for the next chance of a phone box, for them to call Theresa. And him to call Gizande.

After Deedee had spoken, Theresa wanted to speak to him.

"Sounds like you're performing quite a Sir Galahad up there, Jim. Beyond the call of business?"

He bypassed the possibility of something waspish in her words, with, "It'll be sometime tomorrow when we get down there. I'll phone you when we've got a more precise E.T.A."

"I'm sure you will. I don't know what sort of surcharge on them this will result in- with the extra days for you. And hotels. I'll see if I can claim it off their insurance."

"Great idea! Inspiration, Theresa."

"Sounds like record levels of chaos this trip. Is Gizande okay with you being late?" She jumped his hesitation to reply, "Oh, and by-the-by… I had an interesting phone call from a gentleman in Birmingham. Calling down hell and damnation on your head. In the nicest possible way, of course," she added, with an excessive Upperclass English atop her Irish. "What did you do to him?"

"Nothing. I just walked out on the job. He wasn't the nicest possible person, I can tell you. Wanted me to steal his wife's dining table, in front of her. While she still sat at it- so to speak."

"Well, what a chivalric fellow you are being! Rescuing damsels all over the place, it seems!"

"Very funny," he smiled. "I'll explain it when I get back. At least it left space for us to unload the stuff this lot had in their car, into the back of the van. Just."

"Well, you'll be pleased to know. I've saved the contract with Lord Birmingham, so you may have to go back another trip and confront him. And another pickup in Germany, he tells me?"

"Yeah. Seems so."

"Tell us when you get back." Adding, "Good work, Jim."

The phone down, before the call to Gizande, he reflected how he had never worked with women until he was middle aged. Better in some ways. Then, thinking of Sylvie, in some ways, not.

He was about to put the unanswered phone down and relieved at it, when it clicked at the other end. "Gizande?"

"Yes? You are late. I expect you home- the last night. Where are you?"

"Near Tours. There has been a crash."

"Not you? Hurt?" The slightest anxiety?

"No. I haven't crashed. It was the… family I was with."

"What is the family?"

"I have been driving them down. They were following me. In their car. And they crashed."

"Are they hurt?" sounding uncomprehending from her end of the line.

"No. No, they're not hurt. But now I've got them in the van with me."

Suddenly, she was impatient with it all. "So, you are late. Naturally. Another time. And another time, I am losing time to work on the farm."

With nothing to say to this, he waited. Thinking, you don't mind the cash this work puts in our hands.

"So. You will come home, when you will come home." She stopped for an answer.

To what? he thought, but still somehow made to feel guilty.

"When will that be?"

"When will I be home? Tomorrow. Afternoon, I think."

"You think…," left hanging there, with that intolerant defeatedness of hers. "So. You will come when you decide. And we will wait for you. Goodbye." And the phone clicked down.

Back in the van, Deedee asked simply, "Okay?"

And he would have probably said something to her, if Jude had not been there. Something disloyal to Gizande. But all he said was, "Sure." And looked out of the window while he started the engine. To hide the angry unhappiness in his face, petulant and impotent as a little boy.

Chapter Eleven

Had he been on his own, that third night he would have driven on to get home in the early hours. But, after leaving behind the hangover from the call home somewhere on the long open roads south of the Loire, they all recaptured the cheerful and playful mood of games, jokes and chatter. When the latening afternoon brought with it tiredness in the children and the decision what to do that night, he was enjoying himself too much to do anything than to agree to another hotel stop. But he recognised the dangerousness of how he felt and negotiated hard back against the reckless seeker of sexual opportunities that his feeling towards Deedee may make of him. Self pitying, as the curt call with Gizande had let him become.

So, when they found a small motel and the women climbed down to go in, he said to them, "I'm going to sleep in the van tonight."

It was Jude who said, "Oh. Why, Jim?"

He had prepared the response, "I got a bit worried about leaving the van last night. It's got all your worldly possessions inside. And I usually sleep in the cab."

"Oh, come on, Jim," Deedee said with friendly impatience. "We're paying for this. If you park it right in front of Reception, nothing's going to happen to it."

"Yes. Deedee's right. Come in with us." Even the children were smiling up appealingly at him.

He wanted to weaken. But feared to, for either the complications of what might happen, or the little humiliations, if it did not. "No. I'll come in and eat with you, but I'll stay in the van, thanks."

So, after they had booked in and taken what they needed for the night from the back of the van, he stayed outside in the cool dusk, rearranging and repacking some of the more precarious pieces of luggage and cargo in the back. Until Deedee collected him to join them for dinner. She was wearing a dress, light cotton and flowered, bare-legged and the belt at the waist drawing the material to shape round her body.

She saw him looking at her, so he said, "I've got nothing to dress for dinner in."

She laughed, "It was hot in the room. So I changed." Then, with a calculated smile, "Not what you may be thinking. Not at all." Finally, before turning to cross back into the motel, "I came to tell you we're ready for dinner. Come and join us."

This evening the children ate with them, Deedee helping Fiorella with her food. Afterwards, Jude took them upstairs, while Jim and Deedee sat finishing the wine.

"Whose are the kids? It's difficult to work out. Sometimes- mostly, I think they're Jude's. But sometimes, I'm not sure."

"Does it matter?"

"To the kids, I guess it does."

"Well, the kids know. Who their mum is. I mean does it matter to anyone else?"

Taken back by the restrained defiance of this, Jim had to acknowledge, "No. I suppose not. It was only- I only asked. I wasn't criticising- or disapproving, or anything."

"Good." Adding, now that he had made his withdrawal, "I am their biological mother. We are both their practical and emotional parents. Does that make it clear? If it seems that Jude is doing more, that's because we agreed she would do the childcare on the way down through France, while I did the driving. But we didn't account for losing the car."

"No. Bit of a blow, that."

Leaving them both silent to that. Jim eased himself back in the chair to look elsewhere. Two other solitary men eating at their tables. The young waitress looked up, expecting at first to be summoned, so he looked back to Deedee.

"Have you got kids, Jim?"

Welcomed back by her genuine enquiry, "Yes. A girl in England. Getting married in June."

"That's nothing to do with the Frenchwoman you live with now?"

The direct and inquisitorial question put him back. "No. No, we have a little girl."

She smiled at this, "Hard work, eh?"

"What d'you mean?"

"The kid. The little girl. It's hard work for you both, isn't it?"

Asking deeply enough to make him defensive? He tried to take in the meaning of her steady stare at him, but had to look away. "No. She's fine. She's a lovely little girl."

"Oh, sure. But it's still hard work." Waiting only briefly for some sort of answer, before, "It obviously doesn't make you a happy person. However lovely the little girl is. Does it?"

He gave a snort of embarrassed laughter, "Is it that obvious?" Her inquisition was less unwelcome than Trish's had been, but he still wanted to step back from her almost bullying and intrusive intimacy. Yet only stumbled with, "It's like all- like all relationships. You can't stay lovey-dovey for ever." Trailing off with, "You have to get down to the hard work of it all." Yet, left with still wanting to invite her to talk about himself, but steering away from the dangerousness of it. So, he smiled a little foolishly back at her, with nothing left to say.

"Yes. It's obvious. From the moment you looked at my crotch, when you first came to the flat."

The foolish smile stayed on his face, a vacant and wobbly screen to his embarrassment. "I'm… sorry. Did I… offend you?" Wondering why she had said it. Any more than a crude put-down?

"I was angry at first. Made you a dirty old man at first meeting," grinning with this. "But it doesn't matter now. It's a sort of compliment, I s'pose. In an animal sort of way."

He felt permitted to relax. "I never know how to behave with women. It's not really…" trailing away, as he measured how confessional he could become with her. "…It's not really that that's all I think about when I'm with women, but… I s'pose I was brought up in a man's world, with no women around." Ending ruefully, "Maybe it's too late to learn the proper manners."

She poured herself more wine, offering to top up his glass with the last from the bottle.

He nodded, "Sure," watching her hold it for the last drips.

She sipped her glass, then, "It's both. It's the way we dress too. I don't know why we do it- I mean women. I was wearing those jeans, wasn't I? I know the slit in them shows a bit of my underwear. So if I don't want a bloke to look, why do I wear them? It gets in the way. Between guys and women- being able to be friends."

Her words so blunt and candid it made him cautious. For hidden meanings.

"What d'you think, Jim?"

To this apparently simple and open question, only a straight answer could be given. "Like I said, I was brought up just with blokes. I was in a boy's orphanage. Then I worked in mills and then in a car factory. Always with men. I don't think… I think it's difficult to get to be a friend with a woman. If you've never learnt the rules. I guess it might be different if you've grown up with- the opposite sex… You know, gone to school and that, from the start with girls. But I don't know. And it was so different with people my age… everything was separate between the sexes. There were men's jobs and there were women's jobs… Even in the mills- there were plenty of women working there, but they had their jobs and the men had theirs. We even had separate rooms to have lunch and have a smoke."

"Tell me about it. Didn't you know your parents?" Then, "You don't mind me asking, do you?"

"No." He was enjoying it. The interest of her intelligence, not entirely suppressing the attractiveness of the situation, privately together, her bare arms and the dress. "No. But I'm not used to it. Talk like this."

"Like what?"

Any talk at all, in recent years, he thought. What might pass as talk. Only with other English like now, or like Trish and Julian. Maybe a full life with someone of another language could never be possible? But he recognised the dishonesty of this as an explanation of what did and did not pass between him and Gizande. "Proper grown-up conversation. You never get the chance, I think- with kids."

"Maybe. Maybe not. Depends on how you prioritise things. That's what works with me and Jude. Some people think we're dykes we're so close. But it's not that. It's just that we know how to share. We've worked out what's needed for the kids- and when it's time for the adults to have their space." She opened her hands widely to demonstrate the simplicity of it all. "It works for us both. No hassle. She gets to have kids without the problems of a relationship with a man always there. Which is what she wants. I get help with the kids. And we're both best friends. And nothing gets between us. Nothing." She gently rapped the palms of her hands back down onto the table. "Anyway. Anyway. You were going to tell me about your parents. Yeah?"

After considering how to shuffle and deal the events, he started with the death of Aunt Mary, which he now knew was the beginning of the life he led now. And she listened. The letters explaining how his father, Francis, had lived a second life. Suzanne, the discovered half-sister. The later truth about Francis, unpalatable to his daughter and denied. The gift of the farm from the step-mother he had never met. The guarded way he now spoke of his father, uncertain of which truth to believe.

After he drew to an end, Deedee said, "We were right to take you for a sad man. Jude and I talked about it."

Nervous at the image of conversation elsewhere about him, he probed with tentative and clumsy irony, "Would that be sad, as in sad, old bastard?"

"It definitely is, if you ask a question like that. If you don't want to talk about yourself, tell me." Eyebrows arched to him, "Well?"

He waved his hand ineffectually, brushing his last remark from the table, with, "Sorry." Remembering his caution with Trish.

"This is what friendship is about, Jim. I haven't got any hidden motives. You're interesting. I took it you wanted to talk. So I talked. That's what being friendly is about. That's why Jude came out to talk the night at Calais. To get what you thought about what we're doing."

"I…only met you- and Jude, two days ago."

"So? Don't be so bloody English!" she smiled at him. "Like there's some bottom limit to the time you're allowed before being friendly? Like not kissing on the first date- no, sorry, that wasn't meant- but you know what I mean."

He was not sure he did. And waited for her. To spell it out to him.

"If you like someone, you don't have to wait to start being friendly, Jim… For Christ's sake. You were willing enough to tell me about your family. All I did was sympathise. When I said we took you as sad. Okay?" She shook her head. "Maybe it's too late and it's been a long day." She drank the last from her glass, looked through it away from him out into the darkness beyond the motel forecourt. Before planting it back down on the table, with finality. "Time for me to go and see how Jude's doing with the kids."

As she left, he watched her, wishing her both the friend she spoke of, but also- the legs and the swing of the hem of the dress- that touch- any touch, so missing now between him and Gizande. And silently cursed himself for the foolishness of his hunger, knowing how pleasing it would be to have her close to him in the van tomorrow.

The next morning, Deedee appeared preoccupied and sat by the window with the boy, with Jude and Fiorella next to him. Serves you right, he thought to himself, but Jude was pleasant and talkative, wanting to know about the villages, about Larozelle, the mountains and how life was organised where they were going to live. The ways of French bureaucracy, both intimidating and funny, how the land was farmed, the taxes- and the kilometres rushed under their wheels, shrugging from him whatever had or had not happened the evening before with Deedee. Back again as only a friendly driver.

He waited outside in the van, when Deedee ran into estate agent's office to get the keys, just giving Theresa a wave as they drove off again. When they finally arrived, the receding sun was at an angle to shine away the shadows from the steep enclosing cliffs of the gorge the spa was deeply set into. Deceptively welcoming, Jim thought, but said nothing to temper the excitement of their arrival. Jude and the children rushing up the narrow stairs, from room to room, Deedee following them, smiling despite herself, while Jim started to unload the boxes and furniture into the ground floor shop. Jude came down and helped him. When they had finished, it was nearly dark. He could still hear the distant voices of the Orlando and his mother upstairs.

"I'll call Dee down."

"No. Don't bother." He did not want the awkwardness. "Theresa will do the bill for you." He held out his hand, she took it, but pulled him down to kiss his cheek.

"Thanks for everything, Jim. You've been great. And so patient, with all of us."

"No. We got here," for the want of saying anything else to cover his retreat from her gesture. Turning to leave, he remembered, "Oh, the witness statement. For the accident. I'll type one up and drop it in. Tomorrow probably."

"Any time." She was still stood in the shop doorway, when he looked back from the van. "You're welcome. Anytime."

Chapter Twelve

"Gizande? Gizaaande!" he called as he entered her farm. The dog wandered casually up, looked, then went back to the barn where her four wheel drive was parked. The kitchen was cold and empty. He felt the stove and it was low. He riddled some ash out of the bottom, opened it and threw kindling, then several logs onto the embers. Watching them catch flames, before closing it.

He went out into the yard again and looked into the barns and outbuildings, but she would have heard him from there driving up in the van. He looked into the dark, across the immediate fields and the orchard, before returning to the house. As he re-entered the kitchen, she came in from the stairs. In her coat, with bare legs and slippers. Looking sleepy.

"Where's Clara?"

"She is with my mother." She went to the stove, opened it, saw the new fire in it and closed it again. Summoning herself for the explanation he would expect, "I had been not well. Malade. Ill."

"What's wrong?" Sounding too harsh to himself in his question, he repeated, gentler, "What's wrong with you?" Adding, with a hesitation that gave it a false note, "Love?"

"I am ill. That is enough, no?"

Obviously. So he asked, "Can I do anything? Get you a warm drink?"

"No." Leaving it bluntly at that. Then, "Your brother-in law has visited. Maurice. He tells me a story that your sister has a letter. From some Russians…" She paused, corrected herself, "No. They are not Russians, but they have lived in Russia. They were from here, before the war. They say they know your…" Her voice gravelled and she looked away while she cleared her throat. Continuing, with her back to him, hands on the worktop supporting her, staring at the shelved jars of herbs a few inches from her eyes. "…Your father- Francis. They knew your father. Your sister wishes to speak with you. Maurice says that she is… very frightened. She does not know what to do."

"Who are they?" He felt the plunge of spirit he had felt before. At the revelation of other secrets of that life, of the father he had never met.

"I do not know." Her voice an almost inaudible rasp. "I tell you what Maurice say to me." After a long pause, "That is all I know."

"I'll go to see her." Then, thinking of the witness statement he had promised Jude. "Tomorrow. I will go up in the evening. When Suzanne is back from work. Can you look after Clara?"

"She can stay with my mother. One more day." She sighed, "I wish to return to my bed. The goats will need feeding tonight." And she went to the door.

"Can I get you anything?"

"No." Her look at him was the briefest glance, but he could not miss the furtiveness in it. "Tell me about your journey later. Tomorrow. Do not forget the goats." And she was gone.

He stood motionless for a long time, his eyes sightless towards the space she had occupied. Once she would have called Suzanne by her name. Once a friend, but now just his sister. As Clara was just their nameless child. A welling anxiety that he was living with a totally unknown person. As uncertain watching her now, as an exploration of blind fingertips fumbling across a stranger's face for meaning.

He had phoned, but Suzanne was already asleep, Maurice told him. So, in his ponderous French, Jim made his arrangement with her husband to visit her tomorrow. Then he brought the portable typewriter into the kitchen, as, no fires lit elsewhere, it was now the warmest room. Slowly he fingertip typed out his statement on the accident. In English. That night, he fed the goats in their shed, before he brought in his sleeping bag from the van, lit a small fire in the living room and slept fitfully on the sofa there. Gizande had still not appeared in the morning, when Suzanne phoned.

"You can come over, Jim, to see me during the day. I have told the school that I am unwell and will not be appearing for work today." So he left a note for Gizande tucked into the top of the typewriter still on the kitchen table and drove off.

Despite the drifts of drizzle, Suzanne was sat out in the glassed-in verandah when he arrived. He kissed her cheek and stood back to look at her. This woman he could have been so close to, but for their shared father. She had evidently slept poorly also.

"The letter," she said indicating it on the table.

He picked it up. It was from a notaire. "So it's not from these people themselves, it's a legal letter." He handed it over to her, "What's it say? Who are these people?"

"It says… it asks for… to have a meeting. At the notaire's office. See-"

She handed him back the letter, but he could only look at the elaborate legalese French was beyond him. He looked up at her, "Why? A meeting about what?"

"Look. It says…" Frustrated at his stupidity, she put out her hand for the letter again. "It says… a family… who have spent many years in Russia… now making a return to France… where they once had property… searching?… No, seeking information… Believe I can be of assistance..” She looked down the sheet of paper, still incredulous despite the many times she had obviously read and reread it. Before she looked up at Jim, appealing to him for understanding, “But why ask me? And why a letter from a notaire? They do not even write their name.” Flicking the letter back onto the table beside her, with distaste, “Why would they do this in such a method? What do they want?”

He could not understand her distress. “But what do you think it’s about? I mean, it may be nothing. Maybe it’s a letter that they’ve sent to a whole number of people. Looking for information. I mean, we know nothing… what it’s about.” He thought carefully and, yes, he believed the reassurance he was giving her. “Think about it, Suzanne. If they’ve been in Russia for all those years- when would that be? The war? Did they somehow end up in Russia after the war? If it’s that long ago, these people may be pretty old and they’re trying to trace their past.” Then, a minor inspiration, “Maybe they were in a concentration camp. Lots of those were liberated by the Russians. So they ended up in Russia. Could be. Who knows? And as it says, they’re only seeking information. You can only know, if you meet them.”

She stared at him, to believe his reassurances, “Is that what you believe, Jim?” but he could see that she did not. “The letter says of our father.”

“It was only a guess- as good as any other. Why do you have to believe the worst?” Wondering what that worst in her mind could be, that she was so distressed by the letter. For the first time, seeing her as pessimistic about a visitation from their father’s past as he usually was. Something she knew and he did not? “You can only know, if you reply to it.”

She looked down at it on the table, trying to see it as he did. Looking up at him, “You believe I should make a reply?”

Taken aback, “Of course.” What else?

She reached across and folded it over and over, pressing its contents out of sight, and dropped the small creased square of paper she had made of it, between them. Both watched it push against her folds, jerkily reopening like a grubby, over-fingered flower. Before giving up, still, exhausted of effort.

She drew her eyes away from it. “How is Clara?”

“She is with Gizande’s mother. Gizande has been unwell while I’ve been away.” Then, “I’ll collect Clara today. Or Gizande will. They’ll be plenty to do on the farms if she’s ill. But I’ll try to bring Clara over to see you this week.” Knowing how much Suzanne enjoyed the little girl’s quiet company. "If you stay off work-"

"No," she interrupted. "I must return to work. I will be better. You are right, Jim. I am perhaps thinking things… I do not know what I am thinking." Getting up from her chair. But not before Jim saw the ghosts in her face, whatever they were.

He knocked at the shop door window for some time, listening to music coming from somewhere up in the house. Before Jude appeared. Smiling, she threaded her arm through his and led him in.

"Welcome to our home!"

Many of the boxes were still stacked where he had left them the day before. It was dark in the shop as two large, heavy throws covered with Tibetan lettering, one mauve, the other orange, had been hung across the window.

She saw him looking at them. "Had to put them up, as there were some not very nice kids hanging about outside, watching."

He wanted to disengage from her arm, but she led him up the stairs. Calling, "Dee! Kids! We've got a vis-it-ooor!"

Orlando's face appeared through the staircase further up, smiling. Then disappeared, busy elsewhere. Into a bare room, Deedee propped on a mattress on the floor, Fiorella curled asleep, possessively content across her stomach, both half-wrapped in disorderly bedclothes. There was a fan heater humming loudly in the corner.

"Take a seat, Jim," Deedee patted the edge of the mattress. "It's what goes for a chair here, so far."

"Drinks, everyone? Tea, Jim?" Jude asked.

"Yeah. Sure. Thanks."

She patted him on the shoulder and went out.

He smiled at Deedee, "So how was the first night?"

"Oh, chaos. Took hours to get the kids down. That's why I'm still in bed. Oh, and you were right about the cold. After the sun went, the temperature plummeted."

"I know. And there's deep shadows in this valley. Once the sun gets behind the rocks. Have you got enough heating?"

"Not really. There's a central heating system of sorts. But the electrics of it need looking at. Do you know anyone?"

"Yeah. Probably. I'll have a word around." Then, remembered, "Oh, I've done my witness statement. On the accident." He pulled it from his shirt pocket and handed it over.

"Thanks, Jim." She beamed at him, "But it's brilliant. Just to be here. We will make a fist of it, you know. Do or die. Whatever you think of our chances."

"Well, if believing it is enough, I guess you've got enough of that to see you through." Warming himself from her optimism.

"Did Jude tell you about the kids outside? Last night."

"She said that's why you hung those- why you covered the windows downstairs."

"Well, I was none too pleased about that sort of welcoming." She checked that the little girl still slept, before resuming in almost a whisper, "Did Jude tell you? They had their dicks out and were wanking. Right on the street. Grinning at us."

Jim was shocked, less by the fact it had happened, as hearing it from this woman's mouth. Finally asking, "What will you do?"

"Will the police do anything?"

"What can they? They can't park a carload of gendarmes outside all night." He knew that the nearest Gendarmerie was Larozelle. "Were the kids Arab?"

"Why?"

"If they're Arab, you might get them interested."

"Why?"

"Well, they're racists, the gendarmes round here."

"Oh, great! So the only way to get protection is to appeal to the racism of the police?"

He shrugged, but was eager to differentiate himself, "Look it's not me that's saying it. It's just that's the way it is. Not how you wish it to be."

"Well, thank you, Jim. If I wanted a negative take on things here, I knew I could depend on you."

"It's not me…"

Interrupted by Jude entering with a trayful of teas and a tin box of biscuits, Orlando behind her, leaping onto the bed, waking his dreamy sister. And Jude brought in her cheerfulness, smothering the frost of Deedee's words to him.

Chapter Thirteen

He had decided to go to Tracey's wedding, whatever Gizande said. All he needed was the courage- or energy, to confront her and confirm that she would not come over to England with him. With him returned, the following day she left her bed and went back to working on the farm. Anything rather than be dependent on his administrations of care to her, he thought. With Clara returned from her grandmother, he went back to his tasks for the child. He took her up to La Retrait with him and spent a day with the old rotavator cutting up the area of rough turf they planned for vegetables. The circumstances for confrontation had not seemed quite right the previous two days, but, away from her, up beneath the mountains, he had the space to rehearse what he would say. To recognise that rather than courage, it was what he had decided he owed to Tracey that would determine, not the cowardice of getting it precisely right. Under the scrutiny of those grey eyes, he doubted he could ever do that, these days.

He waited till they were sat across from each other over dinner.

"I'm going to go to Tracey's wedding."

She went on eating.

"Will you come? With me. You and Clara?" Precise and restrained.

"Me? Come to the wedding? We have spoken of this before. No. I do not wish to come." She looked down at her food. "You go. If you know we have the money for this…"

He thought of Birmingham. "I may be able to combine it with a job in the van."

She shrugged. "I have said before. The travel to there is too far for the child."

He watched her. "For Clara, you mean."

She looked at him, curious. Then repeated, "Yes. For the child."

He needed to make the point, but only half-heartedly said, "Clara. She is called Clara." Modestly enough for her to be able to ignore it. "I stayed with Trish and Julian this last trip."

"You never told me."

Interest from her? "You never asked." He ate another spoonful. "They would like to see you. And especially Clara. Trish is having another child." Said casually, as if attentive to the food.

He caught a momentary hunted look from her, as he looked up for a response. But she was back eating.

"Will you reconsider? Think about it again?"

"I spoke already. It is too much travel for the child."

"Clara," he corrected, acidly. "She has a name." He thought of Fiorella travelling down on Deedee's lap, only a little older than Clara. "The child will be fine. The journey will be fine for her. An adventure- it'll be an adventure for her."

"I have said to you. I will not go."

"That's you. I may take Clara with me- on my own." He watched her bowed head over her bowl. For an answer. "It would let you get on with work on the farm, without worrying about caring for her."

"No." She stood, picked up her dish and turned to the sink.

To him, now, that was suddenly a gesture of contempt. Of unwarranted control. And he was seized with an angry urgency to not let it pass unmarked. "Wait!" He stood himself, gathering the words. "That's enough! Gizande. This is important. Listen to me."

She spoke from the sink. "Oh, yes. It is important for you. It is the marriage of your daughter. It is not important for me."

The width of the table between that back and him dammed his frustration. "It's here again! I'm talking to your bloody back. That bloody, fucking back, again." On the rising crest of turbulent feeling, he could fall either way. To tears or to fury. A demand, "Look at me." She did not, but she was stilled by his words, by their unexpected venom, her hands unmoving in the sink water. "Always turned to me. Always when I want us to talk about something important- always! That bloody back gets turned again. Like in bed. Face to the wall. Face to the fucking wall. Every night. It never used to be like this." From here, across the kitchen, he was a supplicant, but he knew that if the table were not between them, he would want to shake an answer from her with violence. Any answer, to anything. "Say something to me, Gizande. Say something."

She did, but it was mumbled inaudibly.

"What? What did you say?"

"I said." With patient impatience, still turned away. "I did say something. I say I do not come."

"Turn to me. I didn't hear," although he had. "Turn to me. At least give me… a face to talk to."

But she remained, her eyes locked down on her sunken hands.

He had no choice. But to go to her. He started to go round the rim of the table. Awkward with fear of what he might do. And how she might respond. But yearning to break the deadlock of the last two years, as well as her turned back now.

As he came round, she remained frozen-still, eyes downwards.

He reached out for the top of her arm. Through her sleeve, he felt the muscles contract and shrink beneath his grasp.

"Non..." It was a broken sound. The arm pulled against him, but feebly. "Non...Jiiim." Her chin to her chest, lolling her head, closing her eyes.

"Gizande..." he whispered. "What is it...?"

She pulled against him, more forcefully, her eyelids now screwed shut.

"Gizande-" gripping more tightly with his voice and his fingers. "Stop! Calm down-"

"Non!" She thrashed her arm away, spraying him with water as she pulled herself out of the sink, away from him. Confronting, desperation for a moment in her eyes, then malice.

He reached out for her again, but his hesitation let her back away. He stepped forward again, uncertain what to do, but certain he had to do it. As she stepped back again, he shot his hand out this time and caught her forearm. The cotton sleeve tore, as she shook his fingers into a tighter grip. Wordless, the pair of them, lashing at either end of each other's arm, his eyes as gripped to hers as his hand to her arm, pulled across the floor by her strength. Suddenly, there was a knife between them. Held in her other hand, her eyes defiant, animal. They were both still for a moment. She waved the point of steel towards his face. But he saw her face cloud with uncertainty. She put the blade's edge to his wrist. So gently, it was almost a kiss, so he eased his grip on her, but still held on. The knife moved away, held for a time indecisively, then placed softly back beside the sink.

He gathered her to him. And she came, limp, a carcass. So long since she had been in his arms, even like this, it was good enough for him. For moments they rested, leaned together, her face hidden in his shirtfront, arms limp, his eyes sightless across the kitchen, his head filled with the unscented smell of her. Then, his blank stare slipped into focus. On the shelved lines of little pots of spices, bottles of oils. Softly, he spoke into the ear just beneath his mouth, "Tell me what is wrong. Just tell me what I- we have done to you. Is it... is it anything to do with that old religion of yours? With your catharisme?" seeking somewhere for an explanation. Remembering the quiet enthusiasm she had once had in telling him such things. "You once told me- told me about how they became perfects- your granddad - how they gave up everything to do with animals..." He was stumbling to remember, losing his way, "They gave up everything to get to heaven..." He would have said, sex, but instead the more modest and, for him truer words came out, "As well as human love. Is that it? Becoming a perfect."

Her face, risen from his teeshirt, was wet. Immediately, in her look of hurt and curiosity, he saw her denial. Before she said it, "No," the breath of the word caught damply against his neck. "Why should you think that?"

He scanned her face. She was truthful, open to him for that moment. Before he pulled her to his chest again and said to the room behind, "Well, what is it? What have I done? What has Clara?"

Her hands pressed her away from his body, but her head still lowered away from him. "Non. Clara? Non. Pas Clara- not Esclarmonde."

The name pronounced at last, a sort of engagement with her. Pressing her, with urgency, "But… she sees you- you're so distant. Almost with disgust at her… it looks to me."

She turned to the table, propped on her arms, her head sunk between her shoulders. Her shoulder bones protruded, every vertebra above the seam of cotton countable. He moved behind her and rested a hand either side of her neck, cupping it gently. Rubbing his thumbs slowly up and down the skin above that crest of spine. Soothing himself there, his eyes curious upon the that body he had not watched from so close for so long a time. Moving the fingertips of his right hand up into the soft rough hairs, feeling the base of her skull beneath. Moving a moment beneath his touch, as if to expose more stretched skin to his soothing. Taking this as a sign, an invitation, he descended on the place with his lips…

The briefest rest there, before she shook it away from him, groaning, "Non… non…"

As she started to writhe away from beneath him, he gripped across her shoulder blades, the next thrash of her driving his nails deeper to hang on to the handle made by each collar bone.

"Non!…"

Lashing from under him as he pressed her forward, legs entrapped around hers, wordlessly urgent, forcing her downwards onto the tabletop.

"NO!"

Till her face was pushed down against the wood, his pressed into her cheek, holding her there, the pair of them panting each other's breath, his whole body locked down across her from knee to the tip of his nose. She closed her eyes, an inch from his and gradually stilled beneath him. He lay there long enough. Then kissed her ear. She was motionless. Kiss by cautious kiss. He moved into her hair and back down to her neck, as far as the edge of cotton. Releasing his grip from her shoulder, one hand pulled aside the cloth to kiss beneath, touching the skin to taste with the tip of his tongue. He leaned away from her to see. Her face still to the table, from the closed eye he could see, a tear, hesitatingly down the side of her nose. She would be able to feel his swelled sex, pressing against her buttocks. So, calculatingly vigilant for a response, he rubbed himself up and down upon her several watchful times.

Stilled upon the tabletop, only another tear.

He examined the cotton sweatsuit bottoms she was wearing. Just an elasticated waist, he delicately stretched it, bent over and started to edge them down over her hips. He restrained his breathing, as if silent, he might not be detected by her. A thief of her in the night. The waistband stuck, caught on the table's edge, beneath the weight of her body. Would she lift, to release it? He pulled gently at it. But she did not move. He considered it, then reached round her, pressing his exploring fingers into the flesh of her belly, to find the edge of material and disengage it. Once done, he slid the bottoms from the knickers underneath, far enough for them to fall around her ankles, her socks and the tops of her trainers.

Should he speak to her? She lay there. He looked from knickers, to her face then back again to knickers. He dare not say a word. So he plucked at the edge of this last piece of clothing and rolled them downwards. Far enough to uncertainly, eyes on her face for a reaction, slide his fingers to explore for the soft and wet flesh it had been so long since his body had visited. He could not find it at first between her legs, bending down, rubbing back and forth, awkwardly it was at last found. But rough and dry and uninviting. He pressed her thighs apart and tried to better open the parched lips, now unable to see her face, and hurrying with the urgent surge of his own body.

It was all too slow, she was passive, slumped and unresponsive, time was running out. Fumblingly, he started to undo his own trousers, stumbled over the belt, zipped down and dropped them, catching his penis and twisting it painfully with his pants as he pulled them away. He tried to aim it with his rushing fingers into the space, pushing aside her flesh to find it, hoisting her buttocks roughly, legs pressed apart, guiding himself in again, tugging away at the twisted knickers, pushing and jostling himself inside her, whatever the hurt to him against the shrivelled dehydration of her.

"Eurrh!" And it came, a joyless painful jerk, spattering himself at the entrance and across her legs, her clothing and the side of the table. A couple of final spasms of his body and he lurched back looking down at it, disengaged from her, drooling semen, already flopping limp. Ashamed of himself. Looking at her now. Her face still lying on the wood, but tearless now, staring across the kitchen, but seeing nothing.

He half turned away to pull up his clothing and hide himself within it. What to say? He looked at her untidily undressed body and it was the scene of a crime. The forensic photograph. To cover it up, he started to unroll her knickers to slide them up back around her.

But she stirred. "No," barely audible. Propping herself wearily upon her elbows first, then upwards, she looked down at herself and started to untangle the underwear. She paused at a glob of semen, stared at it, then smeared it into the fabric with her thumb, before pulling the knickers back over herself. She dragged the sweatsuit bottoms after.

He should apologise, but a sullenness within him would not let him do it. He stepped back from her, preoccupying himself with buckling back his belt.

Without looking at him, she went round him to the sink, looked for a moment blankly at the unfinished dishes there and said, in a blurred and husky voice, "I go to bed."

As she left the room, closing the door after her, he dare not look up to watch her. Listening to her slow sound of feet up the staircase.

Chapter Fourteen

He had waited till there was no more sound of her upstairs. Hardening and chilling himself to what had happened, his head was slopped around with a swill of self-disgust and self-justification. It was in this mood that he decided to write to Tracey and accept the invitation. A brief and factual statement that he would be there and he would arrange his own accommodation. Drinking most of a bottle of wine while he tip-tapped it out slowly on the typewriter.

The next morning, out of the house alone and on the way to see Theresa, he posted it. It was James and not her in the office. He did not know about the Birmingham job, so Jim explained and told him to book it for the week after Tracey's wedding, preferably the Monday. Just over a month away. Refreshed with the decision taken, he went to the spa on the way back to see Deedee and Jude. They were painting the walls of the shop together, the children playing together in a bad tempered way around the counter.

"How's things?" was his cheerful entrance.

"Jim! Great to see you!" from Jude. "See, we're putting down roots. Showing the town we're here for good."

Deedee shook her head with fond exasperation, "We're only painting the damn walls, Jude." And smiled at Jim.

Jude took his arm and led him to the half-painted wall. "Well. What do you think?" It was a bright lemon.

He looked round the room. "It's okay." He released his arm from her. Then, to Deedee, "There's a lot to do."

Jude grinned at him, "Well, we've got spare paint brushes." Returning with one. "Here."

He looked over to Deedee. "I haven't got long."

She shrugged with a smile, "Give us as long as you've got. If you want. Do you need an overall?"

"No. These are only work clothes." So he dipped the brush and started.

"Have you spoken to anyone about a car for us?" Deedee asked.

He had forgotten, with the tensions at home. "Sorry. Not yet. I'll speak to- there's a man runs a garage. I got both my vans from him. I'll have a word."

"Something cheap, please."

They painted on in silence for a time.

"Have those boys been back? The Arabs?"

"Yes. They're around all the time when it gets dark."

Jude said, "Anyone for tea? I'll brew a pot." No one answered, but she put down her brush and went out anyway.

"They weren't all North Africans. I never said they were," Deedee said caustically.

"I thought you said…"

"No. It was you who said about Arabs," the last word with sarcastic emphasis.

"So. Have you gone to the police about them?"

"No. If the only way to get a cop here is to play to his racism, we won't bother." She looked hard at him. "Is this what happens to you after a few years here? That you get like that. Like them. Or were you always like that?"

"Hey, easy. Back off a bit, Deedee," he protested, but he was uneasy with her words. Uncertain what he had thought about race. Mostly, in his life it had not been an issue. Few enough- not even sure what to name them- had been working in the car plant by the time he left. They both went back to painting and he was left with more doubts that he was as good a man as he had once believed.

She looked round to check that the children had gone out with Jude, then said quietly, "We didn't have them pulling their dicks out last night. They just hang about outside. They might be interested in what we're doing here. Who knows, maybe we could get some of them in, after we open up for business. They're just bored kids really."

He said nothing of his derision for such a naïve view. But passed it by with, "Oh. I've got another trip back to the UK. Next month. Combining my daughter's wedding, with a pick up in Birmingham. To Perpignan."

She said nothing.

He was left with the discomfort of how she had spoken of him. "I'll have to go soon. After a cuppa."

The return of Jude, the tray and the children swept away her silence into the corners of the room. He wanted to be away soon and parked his wet brush across the rim of the paint tin. He had expected a brief and cheerful break from home. And to tease himself a little with being near Deedee, to surreptitiously watch her neat and casual body. But not to be.

Just left with Jude's barging flirtatiousness. "You don't have sugar, do you, Jim? There I remembered."

The children argued over the biscuits and Jim watched, his mind elsewhere. He had left Clara with Gizande. He would have to return. And face up to whatever the previous night had left behind.

"What sort of car will you get us, Jim?"

He looked from this often foolish woman, over to Deedee. "What sort of car can you afford?" But she was looking away, past where the orange hanging had been pinned back to let light in, out into the street. At a youth walking past. "Is that one of them?" he asked.

"Yes," she said, almost dreamily, "I think so."

He would have offered something authoritative to say, but supped back his tea. Watching her. Till she turned. When he quickly drank the rest back, wiping his lips as he put the mug back down. "I must be going." Standing, "I'll mention about the car. And let you know."

"Oh, and the electrics- for the central heating. You said you'd ask about that too." Adding, "Have a good trip back."

At first he did not understand.

"To England."

"Oh! Are you going back already?" Jude asked.

"Next month. A job in Birmingham."

"Oh, we can give you a shopping list. Leaf tea. Leaf tea, specially. We can't get it down here, can we Dee?"

"No, Jude," smiling to Jim and rolling her eyes. "No, darling, we can't get leaf tea here."

Enough warmth by the time he had left, for him to smile about the women, as he drove home.

There was a note on the kitchen table. She had left Clara down at her mother's and had then gone up to La Retrait. To check on the Spanish herdsmen. He would be collecting the child. It was a criticism. Within the brief statement of arrangements was his departure this morning, leaving her and Clara asleep. She would be running up into the mountains, as she often did after they had argued together. Sweating the touch of him from her. Cleansing herself, he thought bitterly. He looked across at the place on the table. Where he had bent her beneath himself. And shivered. Still angry at it, both with himself and her, it now felt dangerous. Her knife. The force he had used on her.

He went out to the van and drove it up deep into the valley, climbing through the small, silent village, to the increasingly roughened road that led to La Retrait. Her four-wheeler was parked there. He wound down the window and sat listening. So far up here, except for the occasional crow, seldom a sound during the day, but the wind. Usually this tramontane, clear and cool now, but bitter death in the winter. He walked round the farm and squinted up towards the cliffed and precipiced ridges above. As he had so often, looking for her. Wanting her to descend, transformed. To the person she had once been, before Clara, when she had led him running up into the mountains with her. But least likely- impossible today, of all days, he thought. After last night.

It was still a cool wind, blowing down across from what the early summer had left of the snowfields, drifted up and icy behind the rocky walls. Quivering a clutch of bloodied poppies from the earth he had turned at the front. He started to walk upwards, across the sweet, new grass pushing from the ground they had cleared for meadowland. Ready soon for renting to other farmers' herds- before the autumn comes. Through the gap left in the repaired wall, he steered himself to the crag beyond that gave him full sight across the rough ground to the screes that propped the base of the cliffs. And up them to the edge of the sky. As he clambered to the top, he saw her. The stab of yellow tiny against the monumental landscape of grey rubble. Descending carefully and quickly between the slabs and outcrops.

He watched for a moment. To confirm. Then he scrambled back behind down the back of the crag, darting back through the wall and the outbuildings round to the front of La Retrait. He searched for the key on the ring from his pocket and unlocked the padlock to the front door. Pressing it closed behind him, he leaned against it, looking round the barely inhabited room. Still only a watchtower at the edge of his life, the rest of the large dim rooms above were still empty. He stepped forward into the room, saw on one of the chairs the neat pile of clothes she had left to change into after her run. He picked them up and buried his face into them. To smell her, but only inhaling their cool launderedness. Replacing them carefully, he stepped over to the cold stove and sat on its edge, awaiting her.

It was a long time with just the whimper of the wind round the cornices of the house, before he heard her feet crunch and stop on the rough gravel outside. His heart was beating with powerful anxiousness. At how she would be, this morning.

The door scraped open and she was shaped blackly in the opening, against the bright light outside. Breathing heavily, stood there for a moment.

"Why are you here?" A wary inquisition, fearing that somehow she was in for a sex attack now from him? The second of a series?

He cleared his throat. "We need to do something about this place- La Retrait." He drew an expansive hand across the room. "To turn it into a real place to live. To work for us."

The breathing from her exertion eased.

She continued to stand in the doorway, watching, her face hidden from him as silhouette. Ready to exit?

He continued, regardless, "We need to replace this old stove. Perhaps keep it, just for heating the room, but bring in a gas cooker. Run it off bottles. And a septic tank. A fosse septique? To replace the puisard?" She neither confirmed nor corrected his French. "Get a phone up here. A telephone? Maybe even a Minitel. We could turn this into a proper place to stay- even take in tourists- walkers in the summer, climbers- then maybe skiers in the winter. A real business. There's enough room." He was running out of ideas up against her persistent and still silence. "We could add it to the farming side…" Then a further inspiration, in his rehearsed and watchful excitement. "You - we could grow your herbs up here. For your essential oils. You said you have an old oil press - from your grandfather. We could grow lavender - rosemary and marjoram - that sage - clara sage?"

"Clary sage." Her voice was tired. "Those are the English names for it. But it will not grow here. Excessive rain. It is too wet, the earth."

"Well, what else could we grow here?" Not waiting for another defeatist answer, "We could make something really good of this place?" Unable to avoid the query in his voice, he swept it aside with, "We bloody well could! Fence off the top to stop the Spanish getting their flocks in."

Now he waited for her.

"Where is Clara -" correcting herself- "the child? Is she left with my mother?"

"I will collect her. I came up here to see you… first." Now hesitant, guarded.

"Why? What do you wish …? Why to see me?"

"Nothing wrong," he allowed himself to plead. Then unable to restrain the low hoarseness of, "Nothing like that. I promise."

"Like what?" Almost spat out of her, a challenge for him to put into words what had happened the night before.

He would like to have talked about what had happened. Close to her, holding each others' hands, genuine wish to speak to each other in their eyes. But looking at her defiance across the room, he knew it could not happen. He looked away, at the rough floor between his shoes.

"I am cold. From the running. I must change."

Meaning he must leave, so he slowly pushed himself upright. As she went to the chair for her clothes, he went round the table away from her, towards the door.

"What is that mark? On your blouson?"

He turned, "What mark?"

"Behind. A mark in yellow."

He could not see it, but knew it was the paint from Deedee and Jude's. "Don't know." He pretended to look for it over his shoulder.

"It is paint."

He shrugged, "It's only an old jacket." He was in the doorway. "I'll let you dress," and went out.

He was sat against the bonnet of her vehicle when she reappeared. "We could make something more of this place. Don't you think so, Gizande?"

She squinted at him, against the sun.

"Don't you think so? Don't you agree… we could make better use of it?"

She looked about them. "It is poor land. It will not grow much, except grass for goats and sheep. To fence? It will cost more of francs than the worth of the grass eaten by their animals. But, yes, it is beautiful in this place. Tourists may also find it beautiful. But it is very much work to make this place comfortable for them. And while we work on this, who will cultivate my farm? Where fruit and food can be growing." She looked back at him. "And you must be doing your journeys back to England also. That is money to help, which we cannot lose."

Was she saying she welcomed his absences? He had never sensed this before. "I don't like being away," he lied. Adding for the conviction of it, "Away from you and Clara."

She went round to the car door, dismissing this with, "Then you must collect her, from my mother. Already she has been there for longer time than I promised."

She started the engine with an angry rev and he stood clear of the tyres grinding across the broken stones. She wound down her window, "I said to my mother that I would see her also."

Voice raised over the engine, "Does that mean you will collect Clara?"

She shook her head, engaged the gears and bounced away in a spatter of small stones that made him put his hands before his face. He looked after her. Even though she was going to her mother's, she would not collect Clara? He and the little girl would go up to Suzanne's in the afternoon, he promised himself. Leaving Gizande to her self.

She had driven off so hard that she was out of sight by the time he set off after her, more cautiously rocking the van down the rutted track. When he arrived, he entered by the back door as submissively as he usually did. Gizande's mother had never concealed her feelings for Jim. A shift between fear and contempt he could never explain, however courteously he behaved towards her. And there was the added discomfort of a chance meeting with Gaillarde, Gizande's daughter, living in the house when home from college. Here, he always looked round a door before entering a room.

No one in the kitchen, but voices next door. Angry, Gizande's loudest, her mother a lower growl. He could not understand as it was in the Catalan dialect they always used together. He idly looked around. He hoped Clara was out of earshot of the argument. The washing up was half done in the sink. He smiled, looked towards the doorway, then rolled his sleeves up. He rinsed several plates, checking each scrupulously, then the cutlery and stacked them carefully on the drainer. Next, a saucepan. Finally a large, encrusted casserole dish. He quietly scraped away at this, chipping large black flakes from its inside, dipping and rinsing it, until the water was too murky with grease and fragments to continue. As he watched it drain away, he listened for the voices, but could no longer hear them. He pushed some of the large pieces of debris down the plughole, before starting to refill the sink, refreshing it with a long burst of washing up liquid and stirring the water into a froth, before re-immersing the pot.

He did not hear the women enter, finally looking round and smiling at them in the doorway. Gizande becoming a slighter version of her mother's suspicious and sceptical looks, he recognised. Nodding to the sink, "Just giving a hand," his grin widening vacantly, feeling a buffoon.

To the older woman's narrowing eyes at what he was doing. Then crying out, unmistakably angry, whatever she was saying. Crossing the room to him, grabbing his forearms from the water and casting him aside, she plunged her hands in the water and lifted the pot, streaming water, looking at it, running her fingers round its half-cleaned interior. Shorter than him, but threateningly close, she looked up venomously into his face. And finding there what she had expected, spelt out each contemptuous word, "Idiot! Imbécile Anglais!" Turning to her daughter, holding the pot aloft, she ran off a couple of gabbled fierce Catalan sentences.

Jim looked past her at Gizande. Appealing for a sympathetic explanation. But the mother elbowed him aside, now almost keening to the old crock cradled in her arms. Jim stepped further from her reach, looking again at Gizande, "What's up? What's wrong?"

"That was her marmite. Her special pot for cooking cassoulet. You have taken the lacquer from it. It is what gives the taste. The old people never clean the old marmite- the casserole. They say the taste is in the cooking again- repetitive, of the morsels from the dinner before… and the dinner before that." Jim looked blankly at the old woman who had pulled the plug, then at Gizande. "Do you understand?"

All too well. Another cock-up through ignorance, he thought. Would he ever be able to be a participant in this land, or ever remain some sort of oafish and inarticulate observer? He turned back to the mother. "Pardon." He never knew how to address her, this sort of nearly mother-in-law. "Pardon, madame. Je ne le connais pas." He looked down at the pot in her hands. Irreparable. He would have bought her a new one, if that was not the exact opposite of what was required. Again, and finally, "Pardon." Then, to Gizande, "Where is Clara? I will take her."

"She is asleep."

The mother said something.

"What? What did she say?" he asked.

"She say… that she put the child for a sleep, when you did not arrive to collect her. What will you do with her today?"

"I have work to do at your place. The beans. She can be with me. I will dress her warm. She will get dirty, but I will give her a bath. Then I will go to my sister. Clara enjoys that." Aware that he was spelling out his contribution to their lives, however fractured they might have become.

She seemed to have quietly acknowledged that in the way she said, "Good. Bien."

"And convince your mother that I really am sorry." He looked at Gizande, repeating, "I really am sorry," knowing the words were for her and not the mother behind him.

Chapter Fifteen

With the spring well advancing into summer, like everyone else not in the mountains, Suzanne was out in her garden when they arrived. She left her spade and came up to the van window to look in smiling, spidering her fingers at Clara. The girl smiled back and held up her arms towards her aunt.

"Hiya, Aunty Suzy!" Jim said for her, but was ignored. He climbed out and went round. Suzanne briefly and lightly greeted him with her lips to his cheeks. "Come to see her favourite relative, again!" he said and lifted Clara out.

Swept giggling into Suzanne's arms. "Ooooohh! Ma petite dame charmante !" Jigging her off for a tour of what she had been doing in the vegetable beds alongside the veranda.

Jim watched, smiling. "She does speak to you, sort of, doesn't she?" he called over. "Sort of chortles at you, doesn't she?"

Suzanne was too absorbed with the little visitor to answer. Jim went back to the veranda steps and would have sat there, but called over, "I'll make some coffee- and a drink for her," going inside. He put the percolator on and the cups out, then, waiting for it, wandered through the rooms, remembering this as his first home in France. And the welcome it had initially given him. But that he had outstayed. He heard the guttering of the coffee and crossed back towards the kitchen. He noticed some pictures, both the framed and not, on the hallway bureau, stacked face down. He had only turned over and looked at a few, recognising them as once up in the lounge, when the coffee insisted on attention.

Setting the tray of cups and a plastic mug for Clara on the table, ready to pour, he had to clear aside an untidy pile of papers, letters and documents. He found juice in the fridge, then poured out the coffees. He took it out to the veranda and set it down. Suzanne and Clara had disappeared. He went out and followed them round, finally finding them in the goat shed. Joining them to look down into a pen where two small kids were aggressively and noisily suckling from their mother. Clara watched with a serious understanding of it.

"You always say she will talk," Jim said to his sister. "I think the first words she says will be with you."

"No. The words will be with you. You will see. Her first words will be with you- English words."

"Gizande says-" then regretted opening up anything to Suzanne about her. Especially after the night before. "I worry that I will hold her back from speaking in French- and, as for Catalan…"

"It will happen. You should not worry." She smiled at him, "You always come here to ask the same question and I always respond with the same answer. You come for the reassurance from an educator and I give that to you. This is the reassurance for this visit. I have given it. You do not have to ask again." She was laughing at him and he was enjoying it. The difficulties between them had been greatly healed since Clara, but that had seemed to coincide with Gizande ceasing to be the friend she had once been with Suzanne and Maurice. Ceasing to visit. Something between these women and between himself, beyond his comprehension.

"This visit, I've asked enough. Until the next," he said and reached over to tousle Clara's curls. "I've made the coffee. It's on the veranda."

As they walked slowly round, the child still in Suzanne's arms, Jim asked, "Did you sort out that letter? From the notaire in Toulouse?"

From her silence, he sensed he had said something wrong. As they rounded the house to the front, he found he was left heading for the veranda, while she wandered away with Clara, past the van, over to the fence. Where she stood, looking over towards the broken fangs of the mountains stretching away to either end of the horizon. He was hesitant to understand, so just stood there too, looking at her back, the breeze pulling the dress around her legs her only motion.

Finally, wearily it seemed, she turned, eyes down and crossed towards him and passed up the steps, putting Clara down at the top. He followed.

"Ah. You have poured the coffee," she remarked. "It will be cold. Is there more?" Seeing him move to go, she raised her hand, "No. I will go."

He went over to the large cane chair and from behind it, pulled out the cardboard box of toys that Suzanne kept for Clara. The child followed to squat down, pulling out each familiar piece, one by one.

Suzanne returned, emptied their cups into a jug and poured the fresh coffee. "The English do not understand coffee. Our father-" she stopped. Before continuing with a false offhandedness, "He was the same…"

"I saw the photos you've taken down. And where are the albums? If you don't want them, can I take one or two pictures? I only have a few of him. From Aunt Mary."

She looked at him, then back at her coffee. "You ask about the notaire. I have written to agree a meeting." It had wearied her to say it. "It was the advice of Maurice. He will accompany me."

"It should be interesting." He tried to maintain a lightness, against whatever sombreness this seemed to bring her. To throw into her shadows, a light he did not believe in himself. "Maybe you can help them. About their past here- before they went to Russia." Feeling he was labouring heavily over this. "Do you know any more about them? Where they lived?"

"No." It was sharp and closing. "I only go to see them, because Maurice thinks it is best."

Should he press her to speak more of it? Her finality left it impossible to speak of, yet the only topic to think. He was silently over-attentive to the rim of his coffee cup with his thumb. He glanced up at her and caught her looking away from him. The sole sound was the quiet rattle of toys in the corner by Clara. Despite a modest closening with his sister, Jim knew that it was dependent on her bond with his child, not with himself.

He had finished the drink, put the cup down and leaned forward for the plastic cup of juice, "Clara. Clara… juice… jus…"

The girl looked up, stood up from her squat, took the cup into her little fingers and waddled over to Suzanne. Who looked down, smiled and took her upon her lap.

Jim watched, a mother-and-child image never seen within his own home. Aware of how many things could not be easily spoken of- both to and by this woman. Generous as she was. He wanted to ease her somehow, as a thankfulness. What he put into words was awkward, "You know, Suzanne, you shouldn't worry about… you mustn't think it's necessarily something bad, this meeting… Maurice will be with you…" She watched him, guardedly. "I'll come as well," he offered. "If you think it would help."

"You?" with a genuine disbelief. "You? You who cannot even read the letter from the notaire! Or are you able to?" She placed Clara back on her feet, a little roughly. Abandoned, bemused in the middle of the room, looking after her aunt leaving the room abruptly.

Suzanne was back, stood over him, flourishing the sheaf of letters and documents that had been on the kitchen table. On the verge of injured tears, "So, you will be of assistance? You will contribute to the disputations with the lawyer? What would you say?"

"I offered to help," he gritted the words back at her. "Why must there be a disputation? You don't know what it is about yet." With an appeal to her, "I only offered… it was support- my support. I wasn't coming as some sort of legal expert."

She sat down suddenly, the papers crumpling into the fold of her dress. She looked down at them absently, before looking back at him. "You know what this concerns, Jim, don't you? You understand? It is about our father."

As if he had known, he was unable to register surprise.

She let the papers fall on to the table, looking down at them. "I know you will believe it easily. Whatever ill deeds he may have done. It is easy for you. You never met him." Eyes now on him, "He was not ever your true father."

"I was too young. To remember. A baby. When he left for Spain." Almost as a musing to himself. "But you are right. He was truly your father, not mine. His…" he searched for what he wanted to say, but it would have been an indulgence to speak of his own hurt. In the face of her evident distress. And a childishness he should have long since come to terms with.

Suzanne's hand was suddenly across his, leaning herself at him, insistent, "You have been angry with me, I know." He would have protested, genuinely, but she pressed on. "For my own incredulité- that I did not believe the stories you were being told- and which you were bringing back in to my home. The stories of Theodor Jacob… and the other old men. Perhaps I…" Her hand released him. She looked down at little Clara, whose eyes were wondering at her aunt's face. But Suzanne's gaze was elsewhere, inside herself, steering blankly away to the view outside. The words to herself, a first understanding of something profound about whom she had been. To Jim and to everyone else. "Perhaps… I always knew those stories may be true. Veritable. I remember… arguments… un combat," drifting between the languages as she tried to fix her memories. Before waking and finding his face again. "When I was at school, there were names called in the recreation… area- the play ground? I was always angry, to fight the girls who said such things. The anger of my belief in my father- was that the anger that I must be- obliged to defend his dishonesties? Do you think that is true, Jim?"

"How can I know?" he said quietly. "Only you…"

She nodded slowly, "Yes. Only I can know." Then, "But is it not a terrible thing?" her face twisting with trying to comprehend it. "To send your child out in to the world to lie for the protection of your reputation?"

Clara, never having seen her aunt so hurt, retreated between her father's knees and Jim gathered his arms round her, his eyes still fixed on his sister.

"Now… now I have said this and you understand, you will permit Gizande to visit our house again."

Him, permit? He was taken aback with this. "What do you mean?"

"She has not visited for so long. She has been my friend. I wish for her to be a friend again."

"I have never stopped her." And seeing her quizzical face, spelt it out, "I have never said anything to stop her visiting you."

"Oh." The single sound was disappointment and regret.

What could he say now? He could see the responsibility she had assumed rested with him, somehow reversed itself into her uncomprehending self-blame. What had she done? For her friend to cut herself off? He could almost hear the words in the look of her face. The same thoughts- the same searching questions he continually asked himself about Gizande. He should share this with Suzanne, but would he dare? A sort of disloyalty in speaking openly? To talk of the lovelessness?

So, "She has not been well, Gizande," was all he could offer. Adding, "Since Clara." Who looked up at him at the sound of her name.

"You have never said this, Jim? Why not?"

He kissed the child on the top of her head and wrapped a curl round his finger, drawing it out to spring back softly against her skull. "Because… we have not been close enough to have this conversation. As you say, there has been too much suspicion." Ending bluntly with, "Our father came between us."

"You are right." She sat back in the chair, looking at the father and daughter together. "It is little Clara that has stopped us from… never seeing each other."

Jim felt profoundly relieved. However little he may yet say about his home life to her, just the removal of the obstacle between him and his sister was enough. "It's so good. I have so few people I am close to-" Correcting himself, "I'm not feeling sorry for myself. No. It's just that the long time I was staying here, in your home- I know it was too long. And then, I was being singled out by lots of the old men- especially in my early days over here- for them to tell me stories about him. I became a sort of listening fool for them. And I couldn't check them out with you, because I thought you didn't want… you didn't want to hear."

"I did not."

Then, of a sudden, the letters he had read in that widowless room in the Bradford solicitor's office. Those letters of confession from Francis to Mary. And the final and confirmatory one from Suzanne's mother. He had never spoken of them.

"I have letters from him." He watched her startled attentiveness, before continuing. "They were sent to my Aunt Mary. They were in her documents when she died. And there was a letter from your mother. To Mary, giving me La Retrait."

"Ah. I never questioned closely about that. I was never interested in the property. We received the letter from your notaire in England and it seemed sufficient justice. That you should have something from your father. I had this farm," she indicated out of the windows. "I never used a notaire myself. Perhaps I was concerned that such close examination of my father's affairs may discover things I did not wish to know." Continuing, more darkly, "That is why I fear to meet these people from Russia. I do not wish to discover things."

Patient as she was, the adult talk was clearly going on too long for Clara and from pulling at his shirt front she reached up and hit her little fist at the side of his jaw. Almost painful, he said aloud to her, "Ow! You hit me!"

But Suzanne cut in, "You say you have letters from him. Do you have them here, in France?"

"Yes. They are in Gizande's house." He hesitated whether to invite her, bringing the women together again. But steered away with, "I'll bring them over. They don't leave much doubt. About our father." Looking for her response.

"Yes." Then backing away, considering the speed of her commitment, she corrected herself, "No. Let me think about it. Let me… have this meeting in Toulouse first. Too many new things will not be good."

There was a long silence. He looked away, down at Clara, who clung to him. He feared to press Suzanne too hard. Why should he? Because his possession of the old letters became a tool to recover the lost ground of early intimacy that he had once had with this woman. After they had first discovered each other. Had he lived too long with his disbelief in their father's goodness? Become too comfortable with the dead man's deceits? Almost a corruption in itself, to lose that early anger and come to terms with whatever the shortcomings of that Francis and the painful-perhaps terrible consequences of his actions upon those around him. He covertly looked at the sister, struggling to approximate her life now with how it had been before she knew.

She was looking at the crumpled papers on the table. Without taking her eyes away from them, she put the empty cups slowly, with a dream-like care, back on the tray, then the documents. She stood, picked it up and walked out.

He listened for a moment. A muffled sound? Hesitant whether to join her, what to do with the child in his arms, he finally rose and, with Clara, went out towards the kitchen. Seeing the stacked down photographs in the hall, then the documents left on the tray on the kitchen table, as he entered, he could piece together what had been happening to her before he came today. Now caught by him, tired of it all, as she folded dried items of clothing out of a laundry basket.

"What will you do with the photos?" he asked tentatively. Wanting them for himself. To look in privacy into that face. Try to understand him.

Suzanne said nothing.

Jim offered, "You can have the letters- you can see the letters whenever you want," sounding wheedling, almost a crude attempt at bartering.

"Let us not talk of it any more," a severe stiffening in her, as she indicated Clara. "Not before the child."

Unable to cease his inquisitiveness, he pressed on creepingly, "Does Maurice know?" She looked back at him with no readable expression in her face. "How much does he know?"

Turning away with the basket, she spoke a sharp single word, "Enough!" Thumping the basket down on the sideboard, she pulled an ironing board from beside the fridge. "How much do any of us know? About him." Unwrapping the flex from round the iron. "About our father. Say no more now." Again indicating Clara, it was the signal that he was to leave now.

As he was leaving, he realised he had not told her about Tracey's wedding. He would have turned back to tell her, but he realised explanations would be needed about Gizande- about him going on his own

On the road home he realised he missed something he had not had for years. That old and simplistic comradeship of men friends. Left-footing through splattered mud along the wing of a football pitch, looking for Mark to pass to. Or pubbing it afterwards, as they had together so many years ago, arguing about trade union politics. Shared against the rest of the world, safe in your place within the tribe. United against the rest, whoever they were.

Chapter Sixteen

In that last month before the wedding, he thought about the ideas of modernising La Retrait. He had a long conversation with an old farmer he met at the bricolage about how best to manage a septic tank on such a remote site. It was explained to Jim how to feed the overflows of sewage into a reedbed, inviting him up to his farm to see such an arrangement in action. The old man was tolerant of Jim's French and he spent an afternoon walking round the fields on this farm, nearly as high up into the mountains as his own, filling his head with ideas. He also priced what it would cost to buy and install a gas cooker. Later he would realise that there was something in all this that was a preparation for perhaps leaving Gizande, an escape from his dependence on living on her farm. In her home, he was drinking more, staying up late in the kitchen with a bottle or more of wine after she had gone to bed after dinner. He did not share the bed again with her, staying every night down on the sofa in the sleeping bag. They talked between themselves of only the most functional matters, the days mostly becoming a routine of him getting Clara ready, taking her up to La Retrait, where he had started to finish and paint the walls of the long upstairs room under the huge beams. Leaving Gizande down alone on her farm.

It was hard work, harder, he realised, because of now being into his mid fifties. Guessing how long he could continue to do such things to his body. Dismissing the unfeasibility of spending winter up here and reaching spring alive. Even the last times he had run with Gizande over two years ago, recovery from every ache and every pain was taking longer, even then.

One morning, she said that she had forgotten to tell him that Theresa had phoned for him the day before. Jim called the office and James answered. He did not know what his wife had wanted, but she would be in after lunch. After a morning with Clara working at La Retrait, Jim had to go to Larozelle for some more sand, cement and plaster to repair the rough walls of the second unused downstairs room, so he called in to see Theresa, Clara perched on his hip.

"Good morning, Jim. Good morning, Clara," they were greeted with.

"Told you phoned, yesterday."

"Ah. Yes. The English women phoned. The couple you moved last month. They wished to speak to you. You had said something about helping them to get a car?"

"Oh, yes." He had forgotten again. Both the car and someone for their electrics. "Who phoned? Which one?"

She pondered. "I'm not sure. Why, does it matter?"

"No. No."

"I can't remember. I wouldn't give them your number, of course." She looked at him curiously, "All part of an after-sales service I didn't know we had been giving?"

He felt stupidly defensive and he feared it showed. So he minimised, with, "Just said I'd ask around- for an old banger. To replace the one they crashed."

"Ah, the knight and the damsels?" she teased.

"Very funny. Didn't seem unreasonable thing to do."

"No. Of course not. Most reasonable," fixing him with a mocking smile. Then, addressing Clara, "Don't let your Daddy get one of those broken-down jalopies from his disreputable French acquaintances…" back looking at Jim, "…for those nice ladies."

A denial of anything would have been an admission, so he changed the subject, maintaining a casual businesslike seriousness, "Have you spoken to Birmingham? Is he okay about the dates for me to do the pick-up?"

"He wasn't happy that it was you, again. I told him he had no choice. So I think our astonishingly cheap prices were the deciding factor. Not the manners of the driver. The other job for his friend in Germany, he wants us to get someone else to do. He wants you to phone when you get over. To fix the time."

"I'll be going over three days early. My daughter's getting wed."

"Another daughter?" she smiled at Clara.

"Yeah. Lord Birmingham is paying for the trip."

She did not ask if he was going alone. As he drove off, he wondered if she had already guessed that. Theresa and James's office was an outpost of that life he led on the roads to the UK and back, and Gizande was not part of.

The throws had gone from the shopfront, replaced by a slatted wooden blind. Jude answered.

"Who is this?" tickling Clara under her chin, making her squirm with pleasure and shyness into her father's jacket.

"Clara. My girl."

"Isn't she beautiful?"

He said nothing, looking down at the child's curls, holding her for Jude's strokes.

"Come in. Did you get our message?"

"I've seen Theresa." Then to Jude's questioning look, "The estate agent."

"Oh, yes. So you don't have to do anything about getting a car."

"What? Why not?"

"Didn't she tell you?"

"What? Tell me what?"

"We've got one. Dee phoned. She can't have said. Anyway," pulling him inside by his arm, "come upstairs. You're all part of our plan," she giggled.

He followed. The painting of the shop had been completed. Some tables and chairs had appeared. And a Gaggia coffee machine shone from the counter. Up in the same room as his last visit, now a bed had been built. Deedee was sat at a desk by the window. He walked over and looked out. A few metres from the house a precipitous sheet of weeping rock climbed into the sky. Straight out of the unkempt patch of garden, it leaned its shadow over the gorge they were in below.

"Definitely not a suburban London view," Deedee said to him. "Do you think water ever stops coming out of the rock there?"

"Probably not. Does the damp get into the back walls of the house?"

"Not that we've noticed. Yet." Only then did she notice Clara. "Hello, you. What's your name?"

"She doesn't talk yet." Rephrasing it, "She's decided not to talk till she's ready."

Addressing the child directly, "You start to speak when you decide-" A check with Jim- "What's her name?"

"Clara. Short for Esclarmonde."

"Wow!" Attentive again to the child, "Esclar-monde. What a proud name! A name for a real lady." Gently taking the small fingers in hers, "You speak when you decide. When you've decided you've got something worth saying. There's too many silly grown-ups saying too many worthless things." Turning her smile to Jim, "She's lovely. A delight."

Warmed, almost heated by the intimacy of the moment, he could only agree, "I know," almost foolishly coy with it.

As if she realised what he felt, she discomforted herself from him and the child by sitting back in the stiff and simple chair. "The car. We've got a car. That's where your other daughter comes in."

Uncomprehending, he waited.

"Well, Jude's dad's got us a car. A four-wheel drive estate- and it's left-hand drive. Trouble is, it's back in England."

He turned as Jude took up the tale. With a deliberately performed wheedling ingratiation, "Well… well… as you told us that you were going back to England for you daughter's wedding- your other daughter, of course- we wondered… we just wondered if you could take a passenger?…"

Deedee cut in with, "We'd pay, of course. Whatever."

"Could you see yourself as helping us… in that itty-bitty way?"

He put Clara down, relieved of her weight, unexpectedly commenting, "Where're your kids?" Thinking Clara might like to play- especially with the little girl- knowing how few other children she met.

Deedee said, "They're upstairs." Turning to Jude, "They're very quiet. Do you want to have a look?"

After she had gone, Deedee asked, "Would you do that for us? Give Jude a lift back to London?"

Disappointingly, Jude. All that time with him in the cab. Not a particularly attractive prospect. "I won't be going to London."

"Well you won't be going far past it, will you?"

"I'll go across to Poole. Then up through to Swindon and the Midlands."

"Oh. Well, she'll have to get a train down to London. From where you can drop her off." Somehow inferring his lack of generosity.

Correcting this with, "Yeah. I'll do it. No problem."

"Thanks." She looked down at Clara. "She's so quiet. Watching everything we do. Spends lots of time with adults?"

"Yes. Lots of time with me," wondering what insight and opinion of him that might give.

Deedee looked up at him. Then back to the papers before her on the desk. "Bloody French bureaucracy. Seems to take ten forms to do anything in this country."

"Only ten?" he said with mock disbelief. "You can't be getting it right with that few."

"Yeah. Well, my job. I've got the French, so I do all the forms. Jude cares for the kids." She considered, then, "I was thinking… While Jude's away, I thought I would do something special with them, as I've been so busy, I haven't had much time for them. Where's the best place to go- for something nice for the kids to do?"

Something nice to do with kids? He just took Clara around with him on his daily chores and she accompanied him in her passive way. He wondered what harm this life might be doing her, with no contact with the things other children did? So much time alone with him. He tried to invent something to answer her. "There's Carcassonne. With its old walls and that." He had only driven distantly past them, but never stopped there.

"Oh, yes. Maybe. 'Lando would like that."

He realised he was still standing oppressively close, above her in this corner of the room and drifted away, followed obediently by Clara.

"There you are," Deedee chuckled. "Follows you everywhere. Like a little dog."

"Is that bad?"

"No. Just unusual. Quite sweet really. Is she like that with her mum too?"

Resisting the temptation to engage her in some sympathetic way with the rotted state of his relationship with Gizande, he simply said, "No…" Then, "Just a Daddy's little girl, really." He doubted that this woman could be enticed by some sort of appeal to his unhappiness at home. Anyway, he rebuffed himself with, who are you fooling at your age?

"Wait till little Clara learns the ways of rebellion from other children", she said. "It'll come."

Jim had no memory of himself at this age, before he went to Institution. He knew he had lived with Mary for a few years, but could not remember any shred of that. Swept away by what happened later.

"Expelled from eight schools," Deedee remarked musingly. "When I really got going, I was a crazy kid…"

Expelled? Why had that never happened in the Institution? Was that even possible, to expel an orphan in those days? Afterwards, as an adult, he was expelled from nearly every job he ever had, so maybe he was just a late developer?

"What for?" he asked.

She shrugged. "Oh, all sorts. Smoking. Drinking. Boys. It wasn't that I was bad, or anything. It was just… that the rules were all so unreasonable- so easy to break." She continued to talk at the window. Out to the wall of rock. "That's why I wanted my kids away from all that. That testing, the National Curriculum, the three Rs- all the way schools are going back home. Joyless. Just learning for a job- just teaching… none of the difficult things…"

He was not certain what she meant, only offering, "There's plenty of that stuff probably in the schooling over here, too."

"Well…" She turned reluctantly round, saw him as if for the first time. "I'm sure you're right. You usually are- about the less pleasant things in this country. Like the racist police?"

"So? Was I right? Did you go to the police?"

"No. Thank God." Looking at him stubbornly, "No, thank you. We solved our problems- as you should. By talking. We had the boys in for coffee. We have to live together- next to each other, so that's what we did."

"And did it work?" unable to keep the slightest sneer of scepticism from his throat.

"Yes, it did. More than that, a couple of them are really talented singers. We played some Indian music we had and they sang us some of their Moroccan songs." She nodded, a challenge back to him, "And it was really exciting stuff. They're going to bring some of their tapes of their people's music. Who knows? Maybe we could get some music fusion going down here." Finally, to him, "A better way than getting the racist Gendarmerie to beat them up, don't you think?"

"I never said that." Defensive.

"No? Well, music is a sure certainty as a better language to speak to them."

"Are you musical, you and Jude?" A pleasantry, to change the tone.

"Yes. It's what we do. I record musicians. Ethnic music. Jude cooks for them. The therapies and the tourists'll provide the funding." She turned back to her papers.

With a finality that left him shufflingly in the centre of the room, only with Clara to attend to. Knowing he was no longer welcome to speak. "I'll call Jude. And arrange about picking her up for England."

"Yeah. You do that." Without turning round to him, as he left.

Chapter Seventeen

He was in an intolerant mood when he returned to Gizande's. She had her head under the bonnet of her vehicle.

After letting Clara out of the van, he went and leaned over to look at the engine.

She did not look up at him. "Where have you been?"

"To Theresa- and James."

"It was a long time."

"Business," was all he said tersely, realising that when Clara started to speak there would be another version of what happened when he was away from home.

"Your sister phoned." It was never now Suzanne but always his sister. "She say there is a letter for you from England."

It would be from Tracey, he thought, watching her battle her greasy forearms with a spanner on a nut. "Can I help?"

She just grunted and heaved at it. Till it slowly eased and a few turns before she could start to spin it off between her fingers. "Why do you send your letters to her home, not here?"

Where was this leading? Did she want to scrutinise the few letters he received? "Because it's your house, not mine." He understood the walls he put up between all the different parts of his lives. Between the past and the present. Between Gizande and Suzanne. France and England. Even between Deedee and Gizande. So that nobody knew the whole Jim and perhaps he was a different Jim to each person. And could stay that way.

Gizande stepped back with the nut between finger and thumb, looking at him. "Ah, La Retrait Parfaite is your real house, now. That is why you are doing so much work there now. You intend to move your life to there?"

He was taken aback by her swift recognition of what he was only dimly beginning to realise himself. "Why? Why do you ask? Is that what you would want?"

She looked at him and would have said something, but escaped from it by placing the nut on the engine head and leaning back inside.

He did not want her to answer either. "Do you want coffee?"

"Yes," through the clenched effort of starting to unlock another nut. "Bring it to me. Here."

He watched her bent there, too much a shadow of how he had bent her beneath him that night in the kitchen. And now he dared not touch. For fear of how he might want to break her again. And her want him to break her? he wondered. As proof obscurely, that he was as bad as Yves, as all the rest? As bad that night as he had never known he could have been. He wanted to reassure her, to regain from her something of the good opinion he had not had for two years. But he knew he was a long way beyond that boundary. Looking on at the pair of them from afar. Strangers, from an upstairs window.

He went in to make the coffee, deliberately leaving Clara outside in the unfamiliar company of being alone with her mother.

He picked up the letter from Suzanne that evening. The house was empty, but the envelope was where he knew it would be left for him, on the veranda table. He sat there in the dusk light and opened it.

Wedding Invitation

Mr. Richard Griffiths Everard and Miss Tracey Jane Briggs

Cordially invite.........*DAD*..

To their wedding... He smiled at the warmth of *DAD*, planted in her own capital-printed hand, amongst the curlicued silver lettering. Mrs. Everard, then. Escaping from the undecorative simplicity of Briggs. Registry, not church, he was relieved to see.

There was a second card, slid out from behind the one he was reading...

Cordially invite........*Aunty Sue*..he did not even remember ever having told Tracey Suzanne's name. What to do about that?

Behind that was a single folded sheet.

Dear Dad,

I'm so glad you can come for the wedding. You will see from the top of this that we've moved- phone on the new number and tell us whether you want somewhere to stay arranged. We can't put you up as we are having to put up Richard's family and his Dad is not very well. But I can arrange somewhere for you.

As we will be going off on honeymoon to Florida after the reception, I might not have much chance to see you. Can you come over early- so we can have a bit of time together the day before the wedding. I'm sure it'll be chaos, but Mum has got most everything in hand and I'm sure we can get some time together.

I've included an invitation to the aunt I've never met. I think I've got the name right- apologies if not. I really want to meet her- and what better time and event to do it at?

We've missed out on each other for years now, Dad, so- something illegible with crossing out, then resuming- *let's have some time just for us- pleasure with my family round me- and no business this time-*

So looking forward to seeing you.

Much Love,
Tracey.

The warmth of it overwhelmed him. Her toleration of all he felt he had failed to do for her- with her gentle stricture at the end. He read it again in the receding light, mouthing the words as he passed over them, trying to hear this daughter's voice speak them, her arm through his, so vivid to him that he wanted to sob before he reached the end. But it dried in his throat, unwhimpered, restrained by looking up from the letter and away to the precisioned silhouette of peaks lining the horizon to the west. Reflective calculation of what it would be like. Apart from Tracey, the Mum with everything in hand. Jane. First facing since their divorce. Knowing no one, who would he be to them? Father of the bride. The letter said nothing about his role, so he presumed he would not be wanted to give away the bride. Doubting that ever happened in a Registry Office. Explaining himself to strangers? As The French Farmer? he smiled to himself. Eyes back on her words, he shook his head at the generosity of them, glistened through the unwept tears.

He could phone her. Even from here, the empty house. Out of Gizande's hearing. He wiped the wet out of each eye with his knuckle and took the letter to the hall phone. He sat and opened the bureau to set the phone on it. The photos of their father they had spoken of during that painfully closening, but finally distanced afternoon, were stacked inside. Stuffed out of sight and still face down. He picked out one. The young man stood astride a bicycle, beret on head, cigarette hung from lip, pistol handle stuck out of trouser belt, grinning. The next one, of a group of men in uniform sat on the steps of a building. He immediately saw Francis, cockily swaggered in the front line. Somewhere, he had seen this before. Jim picked up the first one again, looked and would have said something to it if he could think of the right thing. But he was dumbed by the confident challenge of the face looking back at him from out of that black and white world. He tucked the picture into his shirt pocket.

After the international code, he started to dial the number. It sounded at the other end, repetitive for long enough, that he began to realise it would not be answered. Relieved and disappointed, he was about to put the phone back down when it spoke at him, "We're sorry there is no one here to answer your call. Please leave a message after the tone."

He looked at the plastic instrument in his hand and it toned back at him. He mumbled, "Tracey…" What to say? Trivial or significant, after so long without hearing each other's voices? "Tracey… it's Dad…" Why was he phoning? To talk to her and hear her voice. So, instead? "Tracey, I got your cards. Thanks. I'll be there." Suddenly, he thought of the invitation to Suzanne. To whom he would never give it. Phoning from her house. "I'll be alone. Your aunt can't come. I'll come over… early, like you asked…" Then, sweeping away all the clutter of uncertainties and hesitations in his voice, he hurriedly ended with, "I'll phone when I get across on the ferry." Clattering the handpiece back in its cradle, as if it had scorched him.

Suddenly it occurred to him that it might not be Tracey who picked up that feebly chaotic message. What would Richard make of it? Richard Griffiths Everard, whose voice he had once heard on the phone? Then he realised, you could find out the number of who had phoned. What if Tracey called this number back and spoke to Suzanne? Idiot! he cursed himself. Shit.

After a moment, he tidied the disturbed photographs back into their corner of the desk, lifted the phone back onto the top and closed the lid. He stood and replaced the chair. Looking back at things as if to check that he was leaving no evidence of his coming. He patted the shirt pocket to check the photo was there and went to leave. But stopped. Pulled it out again and looked at the man. Who seemed to be looking back at Jim with almost derision. With all that he was and what he had. And what Jim would never be. Or have.

Chapter Eighteen

The morning he left for England, he wanted to make his preparations without Gizande. He had dithered about what clothes to take with him for the wedding. And everything that might go with it. But finally, she had ironed several shirts for him, while he rushed in and out of the kitchen adding things to the contents of the case open on the table. Aware that he would be late for picking up Jude. Finally, there was only the photo to find. He had wanted it for Tracey to see her grandfather, as he had never shown her any of those photos.

"There was a photo, Gizande. I left it in my blue workshirt." She continued ironing. "In the pocket. Have you seen it?"

"What photo?" she said without looking up.

"It was of my Dad. My father. Francis."

She lifted the last shirt off the ironing board and held it up, "Bien." French, for his ears. "There." Starting to fold it.

"What have you done with it?"

"With what?"

"The photo. Have you seen it?"

She brought the folded shirt over and carefully smoothed it down into the case. "Why have I seen this photograph?"

"Because you washed the clothes."

"Maybe… the photo was in the machine. And it is lost." Almost mocking him.

"No. You are always so careful. You joke- you used to joke about what you found when you turned out my pockets for the wash. Remember?"

She returned to fold up the blanket she had used to iron on. "I know nothing. Of your photograph."

"Damn!" And he ran up to the unused room where he still had the unpacked boxes of documents and books he had first brought with him from England to Suzanne's. Aunt Mary's photos were on top. Frequently looked over, at one time. He took a couple at random, of his father. Then ran downstairs again.

She stood across the room, her back against the cooker, watching him as he closed the case.

"I'll be back in a week."

Her face denoted nothing to him.

"Okay, Gizande?"

She shrugged. "Okay? What is okay?"

He wanted to go, now. But leave on his terms, with at least some slight sense of her consent. Her permission. "I'm going. I'll bring something back for you. And for Clara."

She gave him a mirthless laugh, "Oh. Please. A gift." Then, tiredly, "Yes. You will return."

Thinking thanks for the loving farewell, he hoisted down the case and lunged out to the van. Knowing that he deserved no such fondness. Forgetting to look in on the sleeping Clara before he went. Remembering this as he drove away, trying to see Gizande in the mirror. Left her with a powerful sense above all, of the joylessness of her life. Without his escapes, back across the seas to the UK. Trapped. Without even the touch of the child he was leaving her with, in that gaunt ugly house.

Outside the shop, Jude was already waiting, with a rolled up sleeping bag, a large grip and another bag. Deedee was stood behind in the doorway, with the children. Jim went round to slide open the side door.

"Well prepared? What's the sleeping bag for?" as he started to lift Jude's luggage aboard.

"The journey."

"But I told you could sleep in the hotel- I'd drop you off, sleep in the van and come back in the morning. That's what I do." He usually only slept in the van on the home trip to protect the goods and when there was a bed awaiting him. But this time he had told Jude he had decided to sleep out both ways to save money.

She looked at him with humorous defiance, "Maybe I wanted to save money on the hotel, too. Yeah?"

He hefted the last bag aboard. He would have said something sceptical of her ability to tolerate the discomfort, but he was aware of Deedee's eyes upon them. "Okay, okay," was all he could grunt as he rumbled slam-shut the door.

Deedee called out, "Have a nice time, you two!" And Jim scowled back at her ironic smile, going round the van to throw himself sullenly into the driving seat.

Jude climbed up her side, gave him a smile and settled herself, pulling open her coat with obviousness, to the long line of buttons risen and fell down the centre line of her body, holding the flimsy pink and patterned dress around her. "Okay?" she asked, as if she was checking that her permission was understood by him.

And he could not stop himself from smiling at her. At her warm blatancy. And at the comic self-awareness with which she overplayed the part. Rinsing off immediately his petulance. "Okay, Jude," as he switched the ignition, looking past her to Deedee, certain that she understood, too.

Jude had, of course, dominated the talk throughout the day, up across western France. Talk of their life before in London, on the fringe of a world of experimental theatre, something she called "cultural politics", artists and musicians. Things Jim could offer nothing to, except establish his general Northern dislike of the capital, and listen. She had asked about his life before, but he spoke only curtly and uninviting to her about it. She had also rattled on about their plans for the shop and café, the first floor rooms they intended to turn into a holiday apartment, Deedee teaching her French and how excited they had both been about the North African boys' music.

He pulled off the Route National down a lane through a prairie of tall maize as it was becoming dusk. Parking across the turning into the overgrown forecourt of an isolated, tumbledown barn. The silence after the engine stopped, was almost oppressive. He would not look at her, as the humorous display of her body when they had started off now revisited them. He was determined to hold on to his place across the front seats of the van for the night. She could make what she could of the space in the back of the van.

"Well… is the back unlocked?"

"Yeah. The side door." He wanted to ask something like, Are you alright? just to soften the edge he felt, with a little courtesy. But he feared what alternative she might offer. "I'll open it. It's sometimes a bit stiff," and jumped out, walking round through the grass.

She was waiting, looking up at the lavender and mauve sky. "It's almost warm enough to sleep outside."

"Not recommended. The bugs," sliding back the door. "Your bedroom," indicating the interior. "There's a light, but don't leave it on all night, as it drains the battery. And attracts the mozzies." He banged the steel floor. "Have you got enough cushioning for this?"

She grinned and rolled a large breast with her hand, "I've got it built-in, thanks. No, I've got an airbed which I'll blow up." Then, looking at him, "Anything else, Jim?"

He shook his head and retreated back to his cab. Where he sat, listening to her noises through the grill above his head. At first, unpacking, then the sound of her blowing up the bed. A long series of blasts of air, weakening and less frequent. Until, "Oooh… shit!" He could hear her exhausted breathing for a time, before the sound of her putting her lips and lungs to the job again. This time, as she recovered herself, she was gasping.

Finally breaking his retreat from her. "Do you want a hand?" he called through.

"A hand?" She panted several times, before resuming, "I could do with a helping pair of lungs… Please?"

He went round. She was on her knees, astride the barely inflated bed. He climbed up, she shifted aside. "Here," wiped the valve and started to blow rhythmically into it, eyes down to the task in concentration. After a time, he broke off, dizzy with it.

Smiling, she took it off him, "Here, I'll have a few puffs." After several, her lips made a farting sound against the rubber and she sniggered with laughter. Grabbing the tube from her to close the air, he joined her, snorting at the idiocy of the pair of them doing this. Also aware of the pleasant tension of it, them together in these remote and darkening fields.

"Come on. A last drive at it," and started to pump his lungs into it again. He sealed the valve finally, knelt on the bed to test it. Then lay full length and bounced a couple of times.

She took his hand, gently yet firmly, but he could not clearly see her face with the light behind her head. She put his fingers deep between her legs, pushing aside her underwear, up to her warm moistness.

"It's the sort of underwear that stays uncomplicated," she whispered. "You can touch me without taking them off." She pressed his fingertips into her, then murmured, "And I didn't know what sort of situation we were going to be in when we did it…"

He made a fist, pulled against her and withdrew his hand out.

"Oh, go on, Jim, don't be such a pious old fraud." There was a gentle provocation in her voice. "I can see you sticking out your trousers. You know you want it. If you go off to your sleeping bag and I hear you wanking in the front later in the night, I'll be really pissed off with you."

She waited for an answer he could not give, but just lay there, looking up for signs from her face. Immobile for what next.

"I'm not a serious woman- look at the way I dress. Don't get frightened you're getting into something." She was starting to unbutton the dress, down far enough to pull it aside away to show her bra. "Having a laugh, that's what it's about. Just having a laugh." She pulled his hand up again, selecting his index and thumb and pressing them round the clip deep in her cleavage, clicked unfastened to swing the two breasts apart. "And a bit of pleasure." She unfolded his fingers to wrap his hand around her breast and sighed deeply, tilting her head back so he could see her smile for a moment. Her other hand continuing unbuttoning the dress, while he started tentatively to massage the large breast, larger than he had ever held before, the nipple beginning the push into his palm like a finger, the flush of it washing through his body to his toes. Then, the dress opened to its hem, with one shrug she freed her shoulders of it. With a second, she slipped off the bra, sat astride just in those loose and lacy French knickers. "I even brought my own protection." From somewhere she had pulled out a condom packet, waving it before him. Before starting to open his trousers, belt and zip, pressing them down and away from his underpants. Pulling those then away from him, tearing open the packet and feeling for where to roll the condom down and over him.

He jerked and whimpered, "No!" But it was too late, the rubber teat in her fingers filled and wobbling with the squirt of him, whinnying and twisting away from her.

There was a smile in her voice as she laid her hand on his groin, calming him, "It's okay. First run." She peeled away the wet condom, gathered the edge of her dress and tenderly wiped him dry. "Like wine in old bottles…" Her hair fell across his thighs and belly as she bent over him, filling his whole body it seemed within her mouth. He squirmed with the pleasure of it. Her face was suddenly close above his in the dark, grinning. "…it needs more care in the drinking of it." A second condom, still laughing- then she was sliding her full thigh across him, her smooth belly rubbing squashily over his hairy one- as she fitted his half-reawoken sex past the panties and into the drenched and dripping warmth of her, that closed around him. So that as he started to be rocked by the heaving embrace of those thighs, he could only think fleetingly of how opposite this was to how Gizande had ever been, even astride him that first and distant night, before that image was swallowed up too with everything else, his body thrashed beneath the rise and fall above of her overhanging trunk, moving meat upon his meat, as he reached up to grab and crush her pendulous, rocking breasts against his face.

Afterwards, he was wordless for a long time, only their breathing to be heard, recovering from it, lying side by side. Before he said in a hoarse whisper, still looking up into the roof, "You've given this some thought, haven't you?"

"What do you mean?"

"Like… you prepared for it. You planned?"

She giggled and sat up on her elbow to look down in his face, "I'm always prepared for it. Why not? The original Boy Scout, me. Got all my badges for getting and giving pleasure, I have." She touched her fingertips to his flaccid, exhausted sex, "Wouldn't you agree?"

"You make it a laugh." He thought of Jane, Sylvie and most of all Gizande. "You make me laugh."

"You, Jim, make me want-" stressed word- "to make you laugh. You're so serious… so sad, it makes you gentle. But it's like… you needed a bit of fun. Yeah?"

He reached into her hair and brought her lips down on his, with a kiss of thanks. For the relaxation he felt, the absence of any sense of serious cementation joining them. No obligations. Except to the funniness and the consideration she had dealt with his body that night.

Getting cold later, he collected his sleeping bag from the front and they slept separate but close together in the back until dawn. Starting up again, they stopped at a transport café, a Les Routiers, and washed as best as they could in the toilets there before a breakfast. As they set off towards the coast, they were cheerful with each other, but not intimate, Jim feeling freer to tell her of his past life than he had the day before. Taking up most of the day with his different lives, as shop steward, as social services worker, telling her about the rescue of Stephen, which impressed her, but only briefly covering his present life, mentioning Gizande but not naming her.

They caught the night ferry and they tried to sleep at a table in the bar, but the drunks were too noisy, so they ended up bedded together under their coats on the carpet of one of the unlit lounges, among the other sleepers.

It was early afternoon when he dropped her at Reading Station. He helped her down with her luggage and climbed back into the cab of the van. She leaned in the passenger door and put a folded paper bag on the seat. "Remind you of the fun we had." She grinned at him, her eyes twinkling with jokiness, "Probably never happen again, but it was a laugh." She slammed the door and he watched her scamper, almost lightly despite the bags, across the station forecourt. To disappear inside without a look back.

He reached over for the package she had left him, but a taxi behind him honked irritably, so he moved off. On the edge of town, he pulled up to make his phone calls, remembered the bag and opened it. He pulled out the French knickers. He held them up, to their full width. Then crushed them to his nose, blinding himself with the smell both of her and of him still stained into their silkiness. Reopening his eyes to the stare of an elderly couple from a bus shelter watching, probably not much older than him. She, gaping shock, he, the faintest smile beneath a white and flourished moustache.

Chapter Nineteen

Three calls and none of them whom he had expected.

Julian, rather than Trish, expecting Jim that night, signing off with, "Good timing for you to be here. Something's come up, but I've been told not to talk about it on the phone. Tell you when I see you."

Birmingham, and it was the wife. "Thank you. For refusing to take the furniture the last time. It will be Monday, this time. Is that suitable? Name a time after ten… Yes, he will be here. We will both be here, with our solicitors" –cynical laugh- "to greet you."

Tracy, and he thought it might be her at first, so long since hearing her voice. But it was Jane. "Moved in to get all the wedding sorted. How are you, Jim?" a genuine inquiry. "Should be fine to come over and see Tracy tomorrow. She's looking forward to it. Are you alone?… Fine. I'll let her know that you phoned."

Back in England again. With all the complicated networks left over from most of a life lived here. Unlike the scarcity of his relationships in France. And now, back here to perform the ritual of being important to that other daughter he had believed he had long since ceased to have any significance for. Driving back up the motorway, he felt discomfort about the weekend ahead. Anticipating meeting his ex-wife. Relieved tonight to be headed for the relatively unrehearsed climate of Julian and Trish's new house.

Julian welcomed him into a hallway in the middle of being repapered. Stepping Jim over the rolls of wallpaper and round the pasting table, he smiled, "Getting a real feel for this. It's brilliant to do a job where you see the results so clearly- up on the walls, before your eyes. If I ever give up social work, I might take up painting and decorating. Never done it before, but I feel I've got a real dab hand for it."

Jim had to stand and make admiration at the work. "Like I've had to learn how to rebuild ruined farmhouses in France," thinking how the rough old walls of La Retrait would never see a roll of wallpaper. Reflecting further, how many new layers of wallpaper now covered any identity he had left behind on the walls of the houses he had lived in with Jane. And with Tracey. Then, directly to Julian, "Why, are you thinking of leaving social work? Though this job gave you the sort of independence you wanted."

He did not answer, but led Jim through into the sitting room. French windows were opened out onto a small, neat garden. Where Trish was sat in the early evening sunlight, watching Adam play. Her pregnancy had filled her out since Jim's last visit.

"Welcome to the baby machine. Again," pulling him down to kiss his cheek.

"It suits you," he smiled.

"What I always say," Julian said. "But she won't have it!"

"Prisoner of my biology, more like."

Jim caught Adam staring at him, smiled back at the boy, who just answered with his fixed and furrowed scowl.

"What are your plans, Jim?" Trish asked. "Jules, get him a beer. And me a fruit juice."

"My plans? The wedding is the day after tomorrow- Saturday. I've got to be in Birmingham for a moving job, Monday morning. So… I'll stay till Sunday night, if that's okay?"

"Fine." Then, penetratingly, "How's Gizande?"

He sat down on a plastic chair opposite her and took his time shifting to get comfortable. Delaying the discomfort of his answer. Without looking at her, "The same."

She sighed. "I wish I could see her. Did you pass on my love to her?"

Had he been asked to that? He only remembered making a fleeting reference to staying with them. Lost in the watchful circling of each other that had ended in Gizande across the table beneath him. Still shameful. He carefully cleared his throat, "I told her I stayed with you."

Rescued by Julian's return. "A beer for Jim. A pineapple juice for you, darling." Then calling over to Adam, "Are you alright, sunshine?"

Whose answer was to turn his scowl down to two toy trucks and bash them together.

"He's not a happy bunny, at present," Trish said quietly. "He doesn't relish the idea of a little sister."

"Yeah," Julian added. "Since we've told him it's a girl."

"Yes. A friend for your little Clara," a calculated remark from her. "When we come and visit. We don't have to wait to next summer, do we? After the baby's born, I'd like us to try to get out to visit Jim and Gizande at the back end of the year- what about the winter? Snow in the mountains. Adam would love it."

"We couldn't drive out there, could we Jim? Not at that time of year?"

"No. You could fly. To Toulouse." His imagination deadened by the prospect of what such a visit would be like. Whether Gizande would be capable or willing of rising to the occasion of being hostess? He could only doubt it.

"We'll think about it," from her look at him, making it clear it was her option to invite and not Jim's.

She put Adam to bed and, after the evening meal, followed herself.

Julian locked out the mild dusk beyond the French windows and drew the curtains across them. Closing Jim in together with him in the room.

He poured out two more beers. "Trish won't have me talking about it when she's around." He sat. Remembering Trish's vehemence his last visit at the men's work, as she bitterly termed it, Jim watched his indecisive search for how to start. The first words. "It's all sort of come together, since you last came. You remember. The talk in my office." Smiling weakly, "Before we were so rudely interrupted."

Jim said nothing, but just looked back impassive. Giving nothing away.

"Well, it's all coming together in Scadding's case. He's got an appeal. Industrial Tribunal, about his sacking. And Finch has turned up as a witness. You remember Finch?"

Remember? Unforgotten, for the rest of my life, Jim thought. The clever and embittered little fixer pimp in that fake hotel, those last few days of the old East Germany. "How the hell has he turned up? Back here."

"Good question. I'd heard rumours he was back and that he was arrested. But the first we properly heard was in the local papers that he'd turned himself in and suddenly he's been sentenced for abduction- of Stephen- and the court case is all over before we knew of it. It's just a snippet in the local rag. That he's got eighteen months- only eighteen months, mind, for kidnapping a kid like he did. So, although he went down, it looked like he was protected, by someone, for such a short sentence. Trivial, compared with the sort of stuff they deal out to the lads I work with- for doing far less. Anyway, he's out and back on the streets in less than six months." Julian shook his head to himself. "Then, the next thing, I get a call from him. He's contacted Syd Scadding - and Syd's given him my number at work. I've been giving Sydney a bit of help with getting it together for his Tribunal appeal. The Union dumped him years ago and he's been soldiering on against the Council all on his own."

Jim realised he was impatient to know about Finch, hungry for understanding, "How- what does he want? Witness, you said?"

"Yeah." Julian could not help smiling at its unlikelihood, "He's offered himself as a witness for Scadding. Says he knows all about the abuse that was in the documents that Cathcart was trying to get Syd to shred. And that'd be true wouldn't it, Jim? That Finch would know about that?"

"Oh, sure. He'd know. But what's his motive? Why'd he come forward now? He's not a natural to have a conscience, you know."

"Revenge? Get back at those who let him go down?"

Jim considered. He reviewed the long day he and Gizande had spent with Finch three years ago. And the police cell. It all appeared too simple, coming from that complex and devious young man. "Maybe," was all he could offer, for revenge alone seemed too abstract a reward for the man, as Jim understood him. "Where's he been? Before he got locked up. Has he said what happened after East Germany collapsed? There's a gap, isn't there?" He thought of Julietta and the other girl, name forgotten again. "There were a load of kids in that hotel. What happened to them?"

"Steady, Jim. I've only had one phone conversation with him. About Scadding." Julian toyed with the neck of his beer bottle. "Anyway… I've taken a bit of a liberty. I knew you were coming over when I spoke to him. So I suggested you and him meet…" He waited for Jim's response.

Entrapped by both his repugnance and his fascination with Finch, he muttered, "That evil, little shit? I'll meet him. I'll meet him on home ground, without the Stasi to protect him."

"I didn't know what days you were here, except Saturday. So I arranged early Saturday morning. Is that okay?"

Jim was thinking only of Finch. Re-picturing him in his mind. "Sure. I'll meet him."

Barely hearing Julian continue, "It makes so much sense, bringing you both together for Syd. You know what the documents were and you can corroborate what Finch says was going on." Adding, with delicious malice, "Sylvia Cathcart will go ape, when she hears. She's just making her name- read she's been appointed to a Government committee to review how well the Children Act's getting on. What a joke!"

Her name bringing back Jim, "Her? That treacherous bitch? Saying what's good for kids?"

Julian laughed along with his venom, "That's how it works, isn't it? They only appoint you to look at how to protect kids, if they know what you recommend isn't going involve too many probing questions."

Jim joined him, with enjoyable contempt, "Well, you're not going to get probing questions from our Sylvie, are you? Got too much to hide herself!"

"Exactly! That's why getting you together with Finch is so right. A dream team, for Scadding's case."

Jim was inspired, "What about..." almost speechless with it. "What about calling her as a witness? Were you going to? After all, it was her who was ordering Scadding to destroy the stuff."

"Hadn't really thought that far, yet. We need a solicitor who will do it for free- on a no-win, no-fee basis. But seeing you and Finch, across the courtroom from Cathcart would be something."

They both spent a moment, each relishing their differently malicious images of the scene.

"So you'll meet Finch, Jim?"

"Sure. When is it?"

"Saturday."

His guts turned with disappointment, "Fuck! That's Tracey's wedding."

"I know. But I've arranged it early. Eight o'clock Finch's agreed to come to my office. What time's the wedding?"

"Eleven." He calculated. "That shouldn't be too much of a problem. I should make it in time." Then, to Julian, "Does Trish know all about this?"

"No. She'd probably kill me." He shrugged, "But what can I do? Leave poor old Syd in the shit? With no one else caring a fuck what happens to him. Or to the kids?" He offered, "It's being pregnant. It makes her extra cautious. Nesty, if you like," an explanation without conviction. Giving him permission to continue, man-to-man about it, with Jim.

Who studied him, surprised now, at how much persistence Julian was still pursuing this after so many years. Reassessing the man. More gripped to getting justice, than Jim himself was. Aware that the vengeance and malice that shaped his own feelings now- against Finch and, surprising himself still how strong, against Sylvie- that these had little to do with children. Or doing the right thing. Perhaps he could do just that, for his own personal and wrong reasons...

"You're working really hard on all this, aren't you, Jules."

Julian smiled, almost apologetically, "You should see the file of cuttings I keep at the office. All the trials for abuse of kids. The cases in Leicester, in Staffordshire. And, of course, the North Wales stuff. The lot. It's strictly outside my job description, but we get plenty- no, some kids in care, who come through the project and they're in a real mess. And when they trust us, they tell us some stories... Would the families they came from do worse to them?... I don't know... But I can't just ignore it all..."

"And all this without Trish knowing?"

He looked flatly down at the table and said quietly, "Yes. Without Trish knowing. At least the most of it."

As Jim himself had done it, without Jane knowing. Until Tracey had rooted through his files and sent them back to Social Services. But would Jim have ever started, without the enticement of the pretty co-conspirator Sylvie had been? An odd thought to come at this time. Tempering his embitteredness about her, with memories of their sex.

Julian took Jim's detachedness, thinking about other things, to be time to finish, and stood slowly up. "Well, we'll see what Finch has to give us on Saturday." Smiling down, "It's going to be worth it, just to see how you two deal with it. After he got you locked up in the East."

Deal with it? He supposed the situation made them allies, on the same side, witnesses for Sydney Scadding. An even odder relationship than thinking about Sylvie as she had been.

Chapter Twenty

Friday morning, Tracey arranged to come and pick Jim up from Julian and Trish's house. Jim went outside to wait in the sunshine when she was due. She pulled up unexpectedly in a red Toyota sports car with an aerofoil swaggered on its tail.

"Very posh," looking it up and down with exaggerated awe. "Is it Richard's?"

"No, Dad," she replied with arch huffiness. "Mine. All mine," patting the leather steering wheel with possessive satisfaction.

"Hi." It was Trish, come up the drive from the house, behind Jim.

"Oh. Trish. Meet Tracey. My daughter," silently saying to himself, my only daughter, please. "Tracey, this is Trish. Her and Julian are the friends I'm staying with."

"Hi. Do you mean my Dad has real friends?"

Trish laughed, "Oh, yes. An occasional letter. When he can be bothered to distract himself from the life he's living in France."

Careful, he thought. The walls between his lives were thin indeed, at this moment.

"An occasional letter?" Tracey crowed. "How occasional would that be?" giving her father a challenging look. Both women laughing together, as he went round to climb into the car. To end the scene in time.

"Good luck with the wedding," Trish offered.

"I'm sorry you weren't invited…I never knew-"

"No. No, don't be silly. We wouldn't expect that." Rubbing her swollen womb, "Anyway, I'm not too good at socialising for too long."

With a final, "Good luck with the baby," as Tracey drove them off, remarking to Jim, "Nice woman."

After they reached the main road and she let the engine out, leaving its throaty roar behind them, she turned to him. "Well, Dad. What sort of life are you living in France? Apart from Aunty Sue, who's your friends out there? What do you do?"

The echoing void of guilt he felt, at that question. Guilt that he had never told her of Gizande- or, now, of her little half-sister, Clara. Lies by omission as grave as his own father's French family, secret from Jim for forty years? Guilt, even, that this was the daughter of the woman he had left? And that he was another deserting father- somewhere in his mind would always be that, however absurd that actually was as a feeling to have. Given the confident, wry look he was getting from the smart young woman driving next to him.

He looked away shiftily, to glance at the huge, half-constructed retail park they were at that moment passing. And knew he would lie to her, "No. No friends, really. Apart from Suzanne, I live a quiet life. Putting together the old farm." Ashamed at how plausible it sounded, both the words and the quiet stoicism with which he spoke them.

"Oh, yes. I was sorry Aunt Suzanne couldn't come. I really wanted to meet her. Our family's been so lop-sided, with all Mum's relatives, and no one from your side for most of my life." Executing the junction of a roundabout, before gunning the car off competently again. "It would've been nice for her to come. She's a teacher, isn't she? Like Mum used to be."

He mumbled assent, probably unheard through the engine noise, but she chattered on anyway, "Mum can't wait to see you. She says she can't imagine you as a French peasant!"

He was able to smile back at this. "What does Mum do now, if she's not a teacher?"

"Oh, she's a big wheel in the Education Department. Up at Headquarters. She runs the in-service training courses."

"And you? Are you still in computers?"

"Well, sort of. I work for the same firm as Richard now. We set up systems for companies and organisations. We're just starting a big contract with the Police here. I'm number two on the team running that," she beamed at him.

"So that's where the flash motor comes from?"

She patted the wheel again, "It sure is." She looked across at him and smiled, "It's a shame that Aunty Sue couldn't come, but it's good for you- good to have a bit of time with you, Dad."

Not entirely certain he was back into territory safe from probing about France, he looked ahead, down the rural road they were speeding along and asked, "Where are you taking me?"

"A favourite little haunt, for lunch. And it's on me."

It was a thatched pub, deep down country lanes, past farm gates that had spilled their dirt out onto the road, crusted and dusty in the warm summer weather. They sat outside to eat, a wooden table on the grass. He encouraged her to talk about her job, but it was actually boringly technical to listen to. He realised, as he had in the past, that, but for being his daughter, he would never have anything to share with this young woman. Would probably never have even met her, so disparate were their two worlds. So they ate in silence for a time, showing all the other symbols of intimacy together, except talking. He realised he wanted this over, feeling fearfully exposed to even her most casual questions about his life. And ashamed of feeling that.

So he calculated to fill the risky silence with talking about the work he was doing and his plans for La Retrait, elaborating the reality of them as he went on.

"But how do you pay for all this?" she asked. "How do you actually have the money to live, while all this is going on?"

So he told her about the furniture moving, being awarded with the inquisitorial, "You've been coming over to England, all these times?" With the fact that he had never visited her on any trip, spoken only with the accusation of the look she gave him.

He retreated with, "It's mostly London. Never up North."

But he knew he had not pacified her criticism, from seeing the cast of her face. So he looked away, remarking, "I've got a load to pick up on Monday. From Birmingham. And that's as far north as I've had a job." She pointedly finished looking at him and concentrated back on her food. "I'm shifting the stuff to Perpignan," was his lame attempt to keep her engaged with the trivia of his job, probably as uninteresting as her work had been to him.

Finally, after a few more mouthfuls from the plate, she spelt it out. "I don't know how you can have come to England all those times and not made the effort- to come up and see me."

"There's a tight timetable on these jobs," he said feebly.

"Oh, come on, Dad!"

She had never come out to France (thank, god), but would he dare use that as a riposte? Would he even want to score points like that against her? Or risk encouraging her to visit his other life. It had been difficult enough with Trish briefly meeting her, Trish who had met and liked Gizande. Confused with the mess of dishonesties in his head, he could only look back at her, with his dumb expression.

She just shook her head at him. And looked away. "I don't understand… you…" He could not see her face, but her words were fractured with hurt. "Why've you always… avoided me? All my life- even when I was a baby, Mum told me." She turned back and shocked him that her face was fierce with trying to hold back the glitter of tears in her eyes.

"'Snot true… Tracey," in speaking her name, a slight appeal. For an understanding he did not deserve. Or for her silence.

"Isn't it, Dad?" asked with such despair, as to void any answer he might have dreamed of giving.

So he sat on, silent with the accusation. Trying to hold a passive face to the mental perturbation crawling with discomfort behind it.

"Oh, it's pointless. We always end up like this. With me upset." The next words, "Don't we, Dad?" a cross-examination that would only permit an answer. Of some sort. "Do you know, Dad? It's the only time I ever cry- it's when I'm with you." Urgent with her despairing question, "Why is it? Why is it- tell me… How do you make me turn back into being such a child?"

He carried on sitting this out in an uncomfortable silence of gradual irritation. With both himself and, selfishly, with her.

She saw the obstinacy of his wordlessness and sourly turned back to the last of the food on her plate with, "Oh, don't bother. Why should it matter? You're hardly an important part of my life any more." Adding, "Are you?" with such a dismissive accent, it forbade a reply.

Permission for him to return to toying with the last of the food on his own plate. Their cutlery's noise on the china marking the muteness between them. Wondering why he had ever come to her wedding. Simply to refute Gizande's wishes? No. The self-regard of this stung him. Pulled up sharply by it. His daughter here with him, was owed by him a duty. A duty to repair something of what he had neglected in her past. However remote her person and the type of life she lived now, was from what he would have wanted for himself.

He wiped his mouth with the napkin and cleared his throat, before speaking. "I don't see you often- that's true. I live a long way away. Let's not argue about- if you think I could have visited you more often or not. I'm here now. You are getting married tomorrow." She at last looked up at him. As surprised as he was, at the measured words he was speaking. "Lots of families split up. Lots of dads end up living a long way from their adult children. I know. I move plenty of them away from their families to end up living in France. So the time we spend together… we need to treat it… what- how would you call it? More carefully." He looked back at her and he could sense the fondness that he must be showing her in his eyes. This young woman, with whom he would never share friendship, but always share- yes, the only way to say it - blood. He smiled, "We never agree about anything, Tracey. Let's not pretend we ever will. But… we're stuck with each other - dad and daughter - whatever…"

She sniffed and smiled, dabbing the corner of each eye and looking back at the napkin to see if any mascara had come off.

He reassured, "You're all right. It's all still in place. You look… marvellous." Honouring her smartness, "As I'm sure you will tomorrow."

She shook her head. "You have changed, Dad. I don't know. Most of the time, I just think of you as you used to be. I don't see you- hardly at all." She waved a hand, "I'm not making a point about that. No, it's just that I expect you to not change at all. I guess I'm comfortable with the Dad I could argue with- when I was a kid. Then, you come at me from a completely different direction. I've never had you speak to me like that before. I guess kids always expect their parents to stay the same, don't they?"

How would he know? But avoiding the self-piteousness of that with, "Probably." Before deciding the excuse was worth saying, "I never got much practice. Having parents."

She smiled again and reached across to engage his hand, "I'm sorry. That I got upset."

"No. All right."

"I s'pose… I can't imagine what it would be like, not having parents. Do you feel angry about it? About your Dad running off to Spain like that?"

Angry? "No. Not now. I did at first. When I learnt about it all from Aunt Mary's letters. But… I don't know… you end up having no expectations of someone who behaved like that, I think. And who you never met." Then, reflectively, he squeezed her hand. "He's buried out there. In the village where your Aunt Suzanne lives. He became religious- maybe he always was. There's something on his gravestone. Something about…" And, searching up into the bright clouds, he pressed his mind to recall the words, the whole scene, stood there in the cemetery, beside his newly discovered sister five years before. "Something about… Christ could be born… a thousand times in… in Galilee," the last words coming to him suddenly, out in a rush, "But all in vain until he is born in me." He looked back at her face, so unusually engaged with him, listening. "What does it mean? What do you make of it? That anyway, was what your grandfather left us. Some… words on a tombstone."

"Does Aunty Sue know what it means?"

"It was some sort of- there was a row about it after he was dead. His widow- my step-mother- who's also dead- she discovered what it meant later. It's in English, so she didn't know till someone translated it. But it's supposed to be some sort of religious heresy." He smiled at her, "I tell you, out there, the family histories get so complicated."

"I think I know what it means." She puzzled for the right words for a moment. "It means that…it's no good just believing- no. It's like Christ doesn't exist, until- except inside someone, when they believe in him."

He looked at her and she had revealed something to him, that he had somehow always known. "Yes! That's it. D'you know, I never got that before. A person only exists- they only live as other people see them.

That's what it means. We're only what other people think we are. We're only the people others think we are."

But she was looking oddly at him. "I don't think it says that at all. How do you work that one out?" She withdrew her hand. "It's about Christ, isn't it?"

But he was suddenly zealous with the discovery. "No. It's more than that," brushing her words aside. "It's like him. Like Francis - your granddad. There's stacks of different stories about him. And different opinions to go with them. Either he's a hero- like he is - sort of, to Suzanne. Or a lot of the older locals think he was a bit of a villain. There's no right or wrong about him, maybe, but whoever he is, now he only exists- his real person can only be the opinions of those still alive- what they think of him now." He stopped to look at her and appealed for her to join him in his sudden understanding, "Do you see? I don't think it's about Christ at all. It's just about who we become. After we've… gone."

She just gave an acted shiver, "Yuk. Are we going to talk about death? About what people think about us after we're dead. Dad, it is my wedding tomorrow." Then she remarked, unexpectedly, "Anyway, you talk lots about your Dad. But you never mention your Mum. It seems it's just a boy's world in your head. What the world will think about the men. What about her?"

What a question. Dead. He had grown up so certain of her disappearance in death, just at the point of his birth, it was almost as if he had been born from the body of his father. He realised she really did not exist for him. Mary had never spoken of her. None of the documents about Francis referred to her at all. He only knew- from somewhere- that they had been married and her name had been Rosemary. He must have seen it on his birth certificate at some time. But had never reflected on who she might have been.

"What about her," he repeated slowly. "I don't know. Everything I knew about my family I learnt from Aunt Mary. And she never mentioned my mother. I didn't know much about Francis, till I got Mary's papers, after she died. She hid a lot from me about your granddad, you know. But she made sure I knew it afterwards. Like she didn't want me to have too good an opinion of him. Eventually." He thought of Rodruiguez, the solicitor and his quiet professional relish for the paper trail Mary had left him to reveal. "She wanted me to know the truth about him- her truth, at least. But nothing about my mother."

"Another invisible woman," she said cynically. "Like the history of the world when we let men write it. I bet that if you wrote your life story, it would all be what the boys did. The women would be written out."

He wanted to deny such a thing, knowing that it would be the women in his life that he reflected on. Who had been so important and whom he continually struggled to understand and give meaning to. Like Gizande. Like this daughter, sat with him now. But he simply said, "No. Not true," with a quiet authority that made her examine him for what he meant.

"What do you mean?"

He was reluctant to invite her into such a discussion of his life, so he pondered a moment. Before replying, "The women in my life have been more important. Far more important than it may seem to you." Ending with, "Don't go by appearances." Said with a finality that did not invite debate.

"Who? Mum?" she asked sharply.

He paused, knowing that she was leading him into territories of deceit. "Yes. And Aunt Mary."

"Aunt Mary? But, Dad! You hardly ever visited her," she exasperated.

But he just shook his head and tidied his knife and fork together on the empty plate.

She gave up trying to get the answers she wanted from him. Just her Dad. And left him with what she took to be silent dishonesties about his past. But was actually a wall of deceits set against her scrutiny of his present.

She drove him back to Trish's afterwards. As they were separating, Tracey reflected, "It's been an odd day. We've talked about some odd things really. We haven't talked about the wedding at all."

Jim smiled, "Well, what did you expect me to do? Advise you on the bridesmaids' dresses?"

She replied tautly, "I won't be having bridesmaids. It's a Registry Office wedding." He was getting out of the car, when she said, "You must give me Trish's number. I'd like to phone her."

No chance. But he would never speak that. As she left him on the pavement, he stood there, looking after the red car as it went away, and he remembered the discussion they had had, and about his mother. And he wondered if all the women in his life had been about filling that gap. But women who had been younger. Jane, Sylvie, Gizande. Fortunate he had been to attract younger women. Or had that been his failure? Why he could not keep them. Or had the gap been Tracey? Searching for the little girl he had lost and whom he had never really found again. Driving off in her playfully red Toyota. Turning on his heel back into the drive up to Trish's house. Firmly rejecting such speculations as fruitless, just as his pocketed hand felt the photograph of Francis he had forgotten to give her.

Chapter Twenty-one

That evening Trish took Adam on a visit to her parents, so that Julian could get on with completing the decoration of the hall. He pasted and climbed the ladder to hang the drops of wallpaper Jim measured and cut for him. They spoke little, such was the surprising precision and concentration Julian applied to the task. Trish was back late with a sleepy Adam and, after putting him to bed, she went out to bring back take away curries for them all. Watching the news about the civil war in Yugoslavia, the couple spoke with quiet disbelief that this was happening again in Europe. Jim had little to offer, barely being aware that the war had been happening from the world he had been inhabiting- without television or a newspaper he could adequately understand. As he went to bed early, Julian quietly reminded him- out of Trish's hearing - of their appointment to see Finch tomorrow, before the wedding.

He had woken up, drenched with cold sweat, his head filled with the shrieked realisation that he had not bought a wedding present. The complications to fitting that in with the meeting with Finch and getting to the registry office on time, slapped him grimly across the face. After panic, he slumped over the impossibility of it. And even if he could squeeze in a rush to the shops- what could he get? What would she want, that daughter he did not know? So shaken by the awakening, that he lay sleepless, as the light began to warm through the curtains, repeatedly going over his morose anticipations of the day ahead. Wondering if he could absent himself with a plea of illness. Then disposing of the idea, realising that meeting Finch again was too much of an excitement for him to miss. And that he would never convince Trish.

By breakfast, it was raining. Steady wavering sheets of it driven across the suburb roofs in the wind. Trish stayed in bed with Adam and Julian prepared the breakfasts.

"We're meeting Finch at eight, Jim," he said quietly.

"I know. Are there any shops near your office?" Admitting, "I realised I hadn't bought a present."

"God. No. There's a ship's chandler's. And a builder's yard. You'd have to go into town. Won't be much time. Will you fit it all in?" asking the obvious.

"Have to," replied with gloom.

"Hang on," Julian went out and returned with a piece of used wrapping paper he tried to smooth into some sort of decency. "If you get something, you can wrap it in this. Doesn't look too obviously Christmassy, does it?"

Jim took it wordlessly.

"Let's get going. Follow me to the office in your van."

Before they set off, Jim carefully hung his old suit jacket from the head rest of the passenger seat. At least being creaseless could compensate for the impoverishment of its worn cloth.

When they reached the office, the chandler's was already open, despite the large *Final Closing Down Sale Reductions On All Goods* sign filling the window. Jim took his wallet from his jacket and ran in from the rain. To wander without hope amongst the cans of deck varnish, hawsers and blocks and tackle. Finally, with a beautifully finished brass barometer mounted on a wooden plaque, that crisis was averted, despite it costing more than he would have budgeted for. Collecting the wrapping paper from the van, he ran up the stairs to Julian's office.

"It'll do," Jim said off-hand while he wrapped the purchase, but actually quite proud of it.

That done, Julian placed a ring-binder before him. "While we wait for Finch, have a look at these. They're the cuttings I told you about."

Jim opened it up. It was carefully put together, with dividers marking the sections. *Leicester. Staffs. N. Wales. N. Ireland. USA.* Jim leafed through them. Under *N.W.*, he found the Scadding cuttings. Brief and without detail, they were just bald references to an appeal against dismissal. Further on, there was a section *Cath. Church.* Several articles about priests in Ireland and USA. Then a long cutting on allegations against a priest in Yorkshire, a teacher who had run youth clubs back in the 50s. *Lent money by his diocese to "pay off" the victim.* Who denied accepting payment and was quoted as *appealing for others to come forward as witnesses.* His solicitor attacking *the confidentiality of the Confession to conceal crimes.* A spokesman for the Church referring to the victim's *history of mental illness*, but *promised a full enquiry… better procedures for listening to young people.* Jim pulled himself up, calculated the age of the victim as similar to his, then unclipped the article from the folder, as if to hold it, the cheap newsprint between his fingertips, made it more real. Before rereading the piece. Slowly, listening to the sound of his own heart. Thumping with the fear and the excitement of recognition. Julian's humming and paper rustling next door, the rain against the window, the traffic outside, all closed off from him.

The appeal for witnesses had no detail. There was no photograph and he did not recognise the priest's name. But then, he had forgotten names. Only that event itself was vivid. Visiting him less now, unannounced, but still as lucid an image when he chose to recall it. Or it chose to recall itself. Would he have anything to say? As a witness. After all those years, he was surprised there would be anyone willing to listen.

Julian was in the room, saying something. Jim dragged his attention to it. "Finch is late. What do you think of the file? Quite a collection."

Jim could only reply remotely, "Yes…" Recovering with, "Yeah… makes you realise… how widespread it is. And how long it's all been going on."

Julian came over to look over his shoulder. "Oh, the Catholic Church stuff. That hasn't even started coming out. The stories starting to come out of Ireland are horrific. And the same priests were coming over here, to take up jobs. They still are. And being covered for by the bishops, when anything comes out."

Jim would have spoken of himself and the fathers, but, waiting for Finch was the wrong time. And he still was not sure Julian would be the right person.

Saved a decision anyway, by a hammering at the door downstairs, he replaced the cutting.

"Finch," Julian muttered and went to let him in.

Jim tried to unclutter his head of what he had just read, but he was uncertain of what posture to replace it with for meeting Finch again. An abyss emptied him as he listened to the sound of feet on the stairway.

When he entered, when Jim could let himself look up into the young man's face, he knew immediately what had changed. The confidence was gone, along with the expensive cut of clothes Jim had previously seen him in. There was a furtiveness, a reluctance to be held by the eyes, immediately visible. How he was looking round the room and the cheap, casual street clothes he was concealed in. Giving Jim the confidence to hold him in his gaze.

Julian followed him into the room. "I don't have to introduce you two, do I?"

Neither answered him. So he pulled a chair for Finch to sit in, which he did suddenly. Two and a half feet across the desk from Jim. Close enough for him to count every unshaven bristle round the taut lips, catch every switch of muscle in the hooded eyelids scanning the open file between them. Jim closed it and held it out for Julian, without taking his eyes from Finch. Who flicked a glance up at the other man, as if now hesitant, uncertain why- or if, he should be here.

Jim cleared his throat and recaptured Finch's eyes. "Well, Billy. Change of fortunes, eh?"

"What?" Given the opportunity to spit back a semblance of certainty, he now scowled across.

Jim would have provoked him by a reminder of Finch's arrogance in East Germany, but in stead opted for a crude inveiglement, "Julian tells me we are to be on the same side. Witnesses for Sydney Scadding?"

"Yeah. For my own reasons."

Avoiding this invitation for argument, Jim asked, "What evidence can you give to help Mr. Scadding?" his precision a doubting sarcasm in itself.

"I know a fuck sight more than you do! You know that. I've been there!"

"I – we-" indicating Julian, "can guess what you will say. But have you got the documents to prove it? In a court of law?"

"An Industrial Appeal Tribunal," Finch bluntly corrected him.

"Yes. Okay. A tribunal. But, have you got the documentary proof? To back up what you say."

"I got plenty of proof. I got things they don't know I know. Things the pair of you wouldn't dream of. So don't get off on being the experts on what's been happening to kids. I'm the expert. I know who pays the piper." Ending with the vehemence of jabbing his finger across the desk, "Remember. I was the piper. So I know."

Julian spoke, forcing Finch to find him awkwardly over his shoulder. "Yes. We may believe what you say, but can you prove it to the Tribunal? Have you got the proof to back up what you say?"

"If it's just revenge you want…" Finch lunged back to meet Jim's words, keen to confront, "…that's a poor reason to make a witness. To make a good witness, anyway."

"Well, Mr. Briggs. What's the engine that keeps you goin'? Wouldn't that be revenge, also?" It rang Jim's memory of the cold intelligence across that conference table in the DDR.

"I have the documents. Do you?" Adding, "D'you have anything but the revenge?"

Finch tapped his temple and leaned so far across that Jim could smell the cheap alcohol on his breath. "It's all safe up here. Names. Dates. Places. Where no one can shred it." Leaning back with a performed complacency, "Don't you worry about me as a witness. I've got it under control. When the time comes, I'll know what to say. And how much. Just enough to get things running."

Jim reminded himself about the children in the hotel and the beast this young man had been. But instead of interrogation, he chose provocation, "Not a good enough witness for yourself though, were you? Didn't keep you out of nick."

"Got me only eighteen months. Out after six," said with calculation. Then, shrugging, "That wasn't a trial. That was a deal. Only six months and I'd shut up."

"So, why've you decided to talk now?"

"Maybe I've decided the deal wasn't good enough."

To remind Finch that there was a witness in the room, Jim pointedly looked at Julian, before asking, "So this is all part of you trying to get a better deal- from your old masters? And if some better deal is offered, you'd then pull out as a witness?"

"Why should I pull out? I got the sentence I wanted. Now I can sing as much as I want. Done my time. Finished with that. Done my time, so they can't sentence me again for it." Spelt out, as if he was revealing a plan that the other two men's understanding would never have reached themselves.

From behind him, Julian. "Do you really believe that getting you back in court is the only way the people you are betraying can get back at you?"

Without looking away from Jim, Finch answered, "Betrayed? What does that mean? Nothing- does it, Jim Briggs?" His eyes knowingly seeking Jim's consent. To what? Something Finch unsuspectedly knew? "Betrayal? Doesn't that mean there's got to be loyalty first? It's deals. The world keeps going with deals, not with loyalty. I made one deal with them in court. Now I'm makin' another. Right?"

"And if- half way through it all- they come up with a better deal, you'd dump Syd Scadding." Terse and quietly spoken, Jim added, "Because it suited you."

"Look, you two," Finch said with the patient impatience of his knowingness. "I've got stuff no one else can give you. Get it? I was their main organiser for…" inventorizing his authority for a moment, "…for just over two years. I got the whole business into Europe. Set up the networks, got the kids moving where the business wanted them. Not just inside Europe," nodding to Jim, "but you know, setting up deals with the communists. Tapping into the Balkans. Bringing the black kids from Africa up through from southern Italy."

Overcoming his distaste, Jim had no alternative but to ask as if Finch's trader language offered the only words to describe. "So why did they get shot of you?" With the sarcastic afterthought, "As their main man?"

"I was treading on the toes of others. Established traders, you might say. The Balkan gangs. You tasted them a little, didn't you, Jim?" Grinning briefly. "Then, of course, the Mafia. The Naples mob, the Camorristi. There, who'd've guessed a sad little care kid like me could've mixed in such circles and got to know stuff like that?" Tossed at the pair of them. To prove the worth of whom they were talking to and of the goods he had on offer. Registering the point, before moving on, "My bosses started to get cold feet. They wanted to sell the business off and I became a disposable asset." He leaned forward, keen to communicate his expertise, "But I was the specialist. Kids. Although I say it myself, no one understood that trade like me. You see, I was - I had been one of them. I understood what it took… how to bring the young ones up to standard. Without pushing them so hard you break them- burn them out, so they end up being no good for anything but the rough end of the street trade. The people my bosses wanted to bring in, they weren't specialists. They were into everything- drugs, guns, cigarettes, controlling the construction industry- which is what my bosses understood. Building and bribing their way round planning regs. That sort of thing. But the kids? They just wanted bulk. Big numbers of kids moved up from southern Europe and the Med, to the North, where the customers were. But they missed the trick. Kids were arriving in the beds of the rich with no idea what they were doing. Twenty four hours off a ferry from Tunisia, they were in a hotel in Brussels, no language, no one told them what to do. Or why they were there. And then they wondered why some big businessman ended up complaining because the hotel manager had to be called to smuggle a screaming Arab kid out of the building- and all the doors on the corridor were opening to see what was happening." He paused, for the effect of it all. Taking a look too at Julian, who was now sat backed on the edge of the table at the far end of the room. Showing the hurt in his face, that Jim hoped he was suppressing from his.

Finch continued, somehow both salacious but expert. "I knew how to bring a kid up to that level. Where the punter gets the really good experience they paid for. I used to call it silkiness. Yeah, that's right. Silkiness. It's not just how the kid's skin feels, it's something to do with the way they use it. Some kids will never have it. And they're the ones only good for the street trade. But it's the skill in seeing the ones you can really bring on. Giving them a little of what they want, so that they can dream their dreams. It's the kids you can keep believing that their dreams will come true- they're the ones who can really give the punters a good time." He sat back and, suddenly clouded, looked past Jim, "Not the terrified ones. But the gangsters who they brought in- who took my business off me- they didn't have a fuck of an idea how to do that. They had no idea of how to bring kids along for the quality trade. It was all hard facing with pimps and beatings. Like backstreet whoring, which is all they knew. To get the quality trade, you needed the time to bring the kids on. And it's the quality trade that pays."

The silence he offered to Jim and Julian, they had nothing to fill it with. Except their wordless, almost collusive nausea. Bringing Finch back to them with his smirking words, "So that's what brings us all together, yeah? Giving them back as good as we got. This Scadding guy, for what they did to him." Twisting round to Julian, "Not sure what your angle is, but I'm sure it's the same thing." Before he swung back to Jim with, "And with you, Jim, it's Sylvia Cathcart. Kicking you out of her bed. Yeah?"

An insolent wait for an answer Jim was too confused to give. Eyes locked on Finch's face. Furious with the panic at how much this vicious little pimp knew about him. The detail of it? And refusing to meet the eyes of Julian, hearing this for the first time, he was sure.

"Well?" Finch poked again for a response. "I was dead surprised when you turned up in Thuringerwald with that French number. I had expected it to be Sylvie- if it was to be anyone- panicking about getting that loony Stephen lad back and saving her bloody job for her. But the French woman? She dumped you too, old man? That why you're back in the old U of K?"

Jim cleared his throat, before squeezing the words from it, "You're just a little shit."

Finch laughed, a single dry cough of a laugh. "We all are. That's why we're here. We've all got something on the world. And we're here to use it- to get back at the world for what it's got on us. Doin' it together makes us stronger… Yeah?"

"Is this the sort of thing you've got to say in the tribunal?"

"What? About you and Sylvie?" he grinned.

"No!" Gathering himself, "No, I mean rambling on about how that trade- as you call it- that trafficking of kids is carried out. It's the Council that will be in the dock against Scadding, not the Naples Mafia or the Bulgarian gangs. What have you got that can back up what Scadding is saying? About why he was being ordered to shred those documents."

"Sure, Jim." He lounged back, with arrogant emphasis. "I've got the lot in diaries. Way back, I knew how to protect myself with writing everything down in diaries. I've got it all. Names, dates, addresses, who paid what. To who. Punters, car registrations. Goin' back six or seven years. And they're safe. Hidden away, till I decide to make a call on them."

A pause for effect. "Pretty sharp for a sixteen year old, eh? To have sussed that out back then, yeah?"

Jim finally looked over at Julian. Who raised his eyebrows and shrugged his shoulders.

Which Finch caught. "Look… a court would be the best place for me to let the stuff I know out. It gets to be part of the official record. Indestructible. But if I can't do it that way, I'll go to the press. Not the best, that, but at least it would save me the money to employ a brief."

"A brief?" Julian asked, after a moment of surprise.

"Course. You don't expect me to come without my own brief? I'm not putting my future in the hands of some no-win, no-fee backstreet solicitor from the sticks. Look at it this way. I know Scadding'll probably be strapped for cash. So, I'll bring a bit of class to the proceedings. A real lawyer to stuff whoever the Council put up there."

"They'll have a London barrister, too," Julian said. "They've had one since Scadding's disciplinary. They know how important it is."

Jim wondered what he was getting himself into. A bigger enterprise than anything intimated in the surreptitious chats he had with Julian.

Finch continued, shrewd and alert to his listeners, "Look at it this way. We was robbed. The high and mighty got too greedy. They gave up redistributing a bit of their goods and services through the likes of me and wanted to keep it to themselves. Well, that's out of order. We need to get some of that back, but doing it with a bag snatch won't do. To do it properly- to make it work- for us- against them, we need to make a little investment. Like staking out the place we plan to burgle. That's what my diaries've been. A long stakeout, before I move. So when I get to court, I've spent so much already investing in that moment, I'm not going to waste it all by getting a second rater- a loser- to represent me, am I?"

Jim could visualise Finch taking over the proceedings. The witness become the plaintiff star and Scadding shoved off stage somewhere. And how Scadding, who had refused to even use Jim himself as tainted goods, would deplore this conversation they were having on his behalf with a creature such as Finch.

With this in mind, again Jim looked over to Julian. Who took the cue, with formality, "Okay, Mr. Finch. That has been very helpful. We need to discuss what you've told us. We need to go back to Mr. Scadding… and his legal team and-"

Finch laughed, "Is this the bit in the audition, where you say, Don't call us, we'll call you?" He waved his hand and sat forward, as if to close things down, "Nah, I know. Time to go." He stood and looked hard at Julian, "Don't underestimate me. I'm serious. About getting this out. Okay?"

The two standing men seemed to be in face-to-face confrontation for a moment. Before Julian answered, with just a whisper of irony, "I'm sure you are. Serious about it." Then offered his hand for farewell.

Finch looked down and finally allowed his own hand to be shaken. Then turning round to Jim, still crouched at the desk, discouraged. "Good to see you again, Jim. In better circumstances. As they say." Offering his hand. Leaving it there long after it was clear that Jim would not respond. Only withdrawn when Jim's surly misanthropy to him had been undeniably established. Allowed Julian to see Finch out downstairs. Leaving Jim to stare into the ugly space left behind, wondering what the man really knew about him. And Sylvie. And what this all might cost him in time and revelations to others.

Time? It was getting late. Jim was already standing, when Julian re-entered. "You'll have to be getting off to your wedding. We'll talk about this tonight. Or tomorrow." Adding, searchingly, "I can see you're none too impressed with him."

"No. Look, Jules…" wanting to differentiate from Finch. But it was too complicated, with the press of time. "Yes. We'll talk about it. I must be going."

He rushed downstairs with the parcelled present. Away from Julian's questioning smile. The rain had stopped. He climbed into the van with a crunch under his foot that made him look down. The floor was covered with granules of broken glass. He looked across at the quarter light in the passenger door. Smashed. Then. His jacket gone from where he had left it hanging on the seat. His guts gaped with the shock of it. Before he realised his wallet was in his trousers. Should he go back up and tell Julian? What was the point? Making him even later. For a jacketless arrival at the wedding. Shit! Shit! Fuck! He exhaled, as he turned the ignition key. How to explain that, as the father of the bride? He could see the knowing, intolerant shake of Tracey's head.

Banging the gear stick into place, he pulled away.

Chapter Twenty-two

Late. Made later by the temporary traffic lights on the dual carriageway past where the old tanning factory was being demolished. Waiting for the long articulated lorry carrying a crane to make several attempts at backing into the site, he looked at the remains of where he had once worked, after the sack from the car plant. The stink of a century of rotten carcasses still seeped from the heaps of broken bricks. Tacked to the fencing cage round the site was a rough sign, *Pleese do not feed the men.*

He was nearly twenty five minutes late when he slewed the van up against the kerb outside the registry office. He straightened his tie before taking a deep breath and entering. The woman at reception directed him and he opened the door as little as he could to squeeze in at the back of the crowded room. Stood without a seat so that faces looked round up at him. Every one eyeing his jacketless shirt, him eyeing the suits of the men, the overdress of the women, looking for the back of a head he might recognise. Near the front, Jane and, he thought, her elderly mother. Tracey, turquoise-hatted, stood next to the tall man who was his son-in-law. Nearly, as the registrar said a last few words. The start of murmuring amongst the guests as the signing of the book was taking place. Camera flashes from the front, as the photographer took over the proceedings "Both together. Can you look into each other's eyes? Now another, with the bridegroom signing, please." Taking long enough for the audience to get restless and start talking amongst themselves.

"Doesn't she look gorgeous?"

"And such a tall couple together."

"Harry could not come. Stuck in Saudi. But I understand he really pushed the boat out when it came to a present for them."

"Bloody photographer could get on with it! I could do with a drink," which Jim could agree with, eager to escape his exposure, stood and underdressed in the formality of the setting.

Tracey stood up and, next to her new husband, smiled glowing and confident back across the crowd of guests. So that a few tentatively started clapping, before this dissolved into well-behaved laughter. Her eyes lighted on her dad, questioned briefly, before passing on. He could now see Jane staring at him and he smiled uncomfortably back at her. Before people started to stand, so he lost sight of the front of the room. He edged towards the doorway. The bride and groom were slowly making their way out, led by the photographer. Jim peered over shoulders at his daughter, watching her smile, acknowledging guests, reminding himself of how she had grown up to whom she was without him noticing, or paying much attention. Until it had become too late and they were already strangers. The confidence and poise of her, even her look to him before she left the room, smiling at the mouth, critical glance of the eyes.

The photographer called back into the room, "Please. No one leave. We will be taking the group pictures on the steps outside."

Smartly suited and smelling strongly of too much of the same perfume he remembered, Jane was beside him. "Glad you could make it. Shame you were late. Tracey wanted you up the front, next to me."

His first reply was only, "Oh," to her waspish tone. Then, with visible deceit, mumbled, "I overslept."

"And the informal dress?" scanning his shirt.

"My jacket was stolen. Broke into my van, by smashing the window." Some of the nearest guests were trying to catch what he said, above the chatter of the crowd emptying from the room.

"This morning?"

He nodded.

"Where?"

He named the street of Julian's office.

"But how were you there? Getting to here? Tracey told me where your friends live. But that's down by the docks."

"I was dropping a friend off. At his work."

"What? On a Saturday?"

"Yes," he said, but he sensed that the listeners-in around them chimed with her disbelief.

They were now out into the vestibule and the photographer was trying to marshal the crowd into manageable squads. "Family, please. Family, please, out onto the steps. Then, close friends. If you could gather inside the doors, ready for when you are called. The weather is favouring us, but please! As quick as you can, before the next shower."

Jim would have liked to drop back from Jane, become inconspicuous, but she tangled her fingers into his and drew him after her. Out into the sunlight, glittering off the wet paving stones. Squinting at the surly glance from Jane's mother, as Jane pulled him into line along from the bride and groom at the bottom of the steps.

The photographer looked up from his viewfinder. "The gentleman in the white shirt?" and Jim shrank. "Have you your jacket, please?"

He shook his head, but Jane stamped out a decisive, "No," that pulled all eyes not already there, to stare at Jim.

"Well, sir. If you could stand… somewhere behind the groom's shoulder. Please."

Jim shuffled round to where it put him amongst the groom's family. One of whom, presumably the father, raised a stick he had been leaning on and shouted harshly, "No! He's the bride's father. Can't be on our side."

Jim shuffled a few steps back, to peer numbly from between Tracey's and Richard's shoulders. Back at the evidently irritated photographer and his lens.

"No. Sir. You cannot… Move a little to your left. Behind the other shoulder of the bride." Dipping again to his viewfinder, muttering loudly, "That will have to do."

Where Jim directed his anger at the absurd situation he found himself in. Barely able to obey the oily injunction to, "Smile, please." Several clicks, before calling past them, "Close friends now, please."

And Tracey turned, "Where is your jacket, Dad?"

"Ask your mother." Adding, "Stolen. This morning."

After several photos of variants of the crowd of guests, Tracey and Richard were led off to the small formal rose garden at the side of the office for portraits of the pair of them. People broke away into chatting groups and Jim drifted over to look at the damage to his van's window. Stuck on the windscreen was a plastic envelope, with *PARKING FINE* in large red letters.

"Shit," almost caving in with the weariness of another thing going wrong today. He looked down at the chipped double yellow line his tyre squatted on, then pulled away the envelope, leaving a tacky square of gum on the screen. Taking the notification out of its envelope, he glanced at it and knew he would be out of the country before he had to pay.

As he wandered back to the guests, Jane was waiting, having seen it all. "Parking ticket as well? You haven't thought today through very well. You were planning to drive that van?" indicating the stained vehicle, for the sake of its stains. "To drive that van to the reception, and then not drink?" She let this sink in, before spelling it out, "How're you going to get back afterwards to your friends? Get a taxi and leave the van in the hotel car park all night?"

He was getting increasingly antagonised by the day. By the events, by the photographer and by Jane and his, "Probably. Why not?" came out as a surly, lumpen challenge.

Which Jane dismissed with, "I will get someone to follow you to your friends. Where you can leave the van and he can bring you back. Then you can drink without worrying. And get a taxi back afterwards." A presumption there that he would be thrown into the back seat as a drunk, at the end of the day? he thought. But she prompted his answer with, "Yes?" Like a schoolmarm bent over a child.

"Yeah. Fine," he said with marked sarcasm, as if he was back four years in a solicitor's office, arguing about divorce matters with her. Reluctantly conceding.

After the photos were over, Jane introduced him to Douglas, a silver-suited man in his thirties with a performed southern accent and unsuitably gelled and spiked hair to go with it. He would follow Jim and the van to Trish's and drive him back to the reception. When he had parked the van in the street outside the house and retrieved the scruffily packaged present, Douglas leaned over to open the passenger door of his car. A big, polished Range Rover.

Jim climbed in. "Thanks for the lift," coming out with a touch of the terseness he felt for the way he had let Jane harried him into this.

As they drove off, Douglas glanced into the mirror, "Of course. Looks like your van's taken a beating?"

"What d'you mean?" Jim listened to the unexpected surliness of his words. And the way his English loosened whenever he came back from France, freed from the need to spell himself out with precision.

"It's done some travelling, from the look of it."

A criticism of its dirt? He took it as so, "Come straight from the Pyrenees to get here." The unexpected defiance of Jim's tone making a reply uninvited. So Douglas leaned over, switched on the radio and whistled through his teeth, eyes on the road, for the rest of the journey. Even when Jim stepped down and said, "Thanks, again." Stilted with being unable to apologise.

The reception was at a large, modern hotel next to the new motorway. Jim entered, bearing his gift. He recognised some of Richard's family from the registry office and followed them through to the large dining room, where groups of guests were gathering, filling the wait with chatter. Jane was already there, at the top table, talking to a waiter.

Jim deposited the present on the table put aside for them and went over to her. Determined to be more courteous. "Hi. Where do I sit?"

She looked at him and did not at first recognise her ex-husband from the place of busy organisation where her mind was. "Ah. Jim." Waving her hand to the rest of the room. "Anywhere. Any of the other tables," before getting back to the menu card she was studying with the waiter.

Jim looked at the name cards on the top table between them, his own evidently not curlicued among them. "So I won't be expected to make a speech, then?"

Jane looked up again, surprised to see him still there. "No. Did you want to?"

"Bride's father. Thought it was… customary."

Hesitant, "But…" before she gave him her full attention. "Did you mean to give a speech, Jim?" clearly rattled by the unpredicted - and unpredictable - prospect of this interference with the plans. "Why?"

"Why not? It's customary." A woman he took to be Richard's mother was now listening to them, with a look of concern and Jim now wanted to disengage from what was turning from a tease to a goading of Jane. He put his hands up, a token of surrender, "No. It doesn't matter." Unable to resist the final, "I don't want to embarrass any one," before moving off to a nearby table and sitting himself down decisively to claim a seat among strangers. He did not know any of them and angled his chair away so that he could have a full view of the proceedings on the top table. Having to remind himself that he was here to celebrate his daughter's wedding, however distasteful he was finding some of the company and some of the duties associated with that. Deciding it was about getting through the afternoon.

During the food, he idly listened to the chatter of the others at the table. Three couples, they all seemed to know each other, more or less. The women listened to the men talking about business, and whether the current recession would turn into a full slump. He gathered one was something to do with retailing, another an accountant demonstrating his superior grasp of the wider economics of things. Until the women got bored of listening and started to talk across the men about the wedding. The guests, what they were wearing and whether they should be. What presents they had given and whether they were good enough. Overpowering the solemn tones of the men's talk, forcing them to give up and join in. Contributing their own observations about the cars others had arrived in. Refusing to be joined in, while sure he would not be invited to, Jim kept his seat half turned from the table, picking at his food with a fork, eyes elsewhere, but listening. Certain that his old van would have been the star of the husbands' derision and his jacketlessness of the wives', was he not sat there beside them.

After food, the speeches. The groom's father apologised for not standing, earning a murmur of commiseration for his visible ill-health. He spoke at length about the hard work of the newly weds being the foundation for a successful marriage, clearly implying with the shy pomposity he directed to his own wife, sat next to him, that the young couple were following their own example. Jane stood next, earning Jim some guests' glances, from her to him and back again, and why was he not making the speech. He was irritated at this implied shame and his tickled indignation muffled the first words of her speech. "…overcoming whatever difficulties she may have had as a little girl, by sheer determination and dogged ambition to do better." Better? Better than Tracey's father, was Jane saying? "…agree with Richard's father, that is the foundation for a good marriage, and, in time, a strong family," looking down at Tracey, who was holding her new husband's hand, her eyes lowered chastely at the slight ruffle of applause the last remark incited.

Conceited bloody sermonising, Jim thought. How Jane had changed, comfortable to parrot the superior complacencies of people like this. Clearly, her people now. Dogged ambition? He thought of La Retrait and the huge labours he had applied to its repairs. His hands opened before him on his lap, like two coarse flowers, with their calluses and scars. And looked around at the hands refolding themselves after the polite applause, back onto the tablecloth. The manicured whiteness of them, both men and women. Remembering, from far back, his pleasant surprise at the roughness of Gizande's palms. And felt close to her, painful for the distance he was now from her, as well as the separateness that had come between them. The woken snarl of, What do these know about work? restrained and unspoken.

"…happy to have found each other, and now ready to make a real contribution as the team they obviously are, to the lives of those about them, now and in the future." Jane sat down to acknowledge the applause. Tracey caught his eye, so Jim joined in with a few reluctant, soundless claps.

Then the best man, already florid with drink, stood up so suddenly, he lurched and there was a moment he might have fallen- before clutching Richard's shoulder. Steadying himself as he surveyed his audience, until he felt confident enough to turn the clutch into a congratulatory pat, then a couple more heftier slaps to the groom. "Richard, my old mate! Richard… and Tracey… No big speeches from me. You all know me too well for all that…" Then, meagrely inspired, "Anyway, what could I add to what's been said? Richard's dad and Tracey's mum have said it all. This is a couple who… know where they're going- yes!" Laughing at himself, "Florida!"

Jim noticed that there was beginning to be concern about where this might be going. The slightest shadow of a cloud passing across the faces at the top table.

"No, seriously. After Florida- after all that…" After almost audibly struggling to think what you did in Florida, he chose, "Disneyland! After all that Donald Duck!" bursting out with a laugh that sneezed spit across the room, repeating the lewd rhyme, "All that Donald Duck!" He teetered, tittering on at his own humour. Gradually realising how still the room had become, watching his performance, stiffening with the anxiety of what he might say next.

So he stopped to consider what that might be. Whispered the word, "Honeymoon," so quietly that only those nearest him picked up the regretful salaciousness of his tone. From which he shook himself awake. "Yes. The honeymoon that… that the honeymoon should be as happy as… the rest of their long marriage would be." The relief amongst the guests so palpable that even the best man could hear it. And he beamed with self-congratulation and boomed out, "A toast to the bride and groom!"

People raised their glasses. Some stood, then gradually, untidily, the sound of chairs as everyone stood. Including Jim. And they repeated, some murmured, some bellowed, "The bride and groom!" Jim whispered it. Suddenly, the moment the glasses were downed was a signal. The room was full of waiters hurriedly, with firm courtesy clearing, moving the guests away from the tables, which were pushed back, cleared and stacked to clear the space for dancing. The DJ appeared on the stage at the other end from the top table. And people stood around talking, chattering, while they were waiting.

When the music started, a slow ballad, the crowd had stood back for the bride and groom's first dance. Watching with held astonishment, as Tracey walked across the floor towards Jim and held out her arms for him to take her. Aware of the onlookers, Jim stepped hesitantly forward to let her take his hand and put his other to her waist. As if summoned in a dream.

They stood there looking at each other, when he said quietly, "I can't dance."

She smiled, "I know Dad." And moved them off into the first shuffling steps. "You never did do dancing, did you? I don't want Fred Astaire, you know. Dad, I saw you there in your white shirt, on your own. I knew you wouldn't have anything to talk to my friends about. I thought let's change the order of events. I just want them to see that it's my Dad and, whatever has happened, there's still a bit of me that can't help being proud of some of the things you've done, even if it's against my better judgement." She gave him a hug, continuing, "If I let myself to think like you, I suppose I understand why you've done some of the things you've done."

She turned her head with its glittering smile towards the faces of the onlooking guests, for a few steps.

Then, glitter back to warmth, she returned to him. "Thanks for the barometer as a present. It's unusual. We may get several canteens of cutlery, but I bet no one else gets us a marine barometer. I'm sure it's something you wouldn't have thought of before you went to live in France." Squinting her eyes with inquisitiveness, "Something's happened to you there. It can't be all bad."

He was not going to answer that. So she just smiled away to the guests for a few more steps, before drawing the pair of them to a stop in the middle of the floor, kissing his cheek, to step back with a slight bow to him. To which he responded, grinning as widely as he was able. To her, and to their doubting audience.

He watched her dance with Richard. Until others joined them, then he drifted over to the bar and took his drink away to a quiet corner.

Soon after, Tracey and Richard went off to change for their honeymoon flight. When they returned, Jim saw how she was flushed and looking up at Richard with fondness and he realised how important this ceremony had been for her. He waited for her to approach him through the crowds of well wishers and gave her the firmest and broadest of hugs, with no hesitations, he could summon up from the depths of his affections. For this daughter, whom he had never done enough for, but who understood him in her own way better than he would ever understand her. She unembraced him, looked him deep in the eyes for a minute, giving him the warmest smile he had ever had from her. Remembering that the photo of her grandfather he had intended to bring for her had been stolen with his jacket. And then she was gone, leaving Jim with her friends, her new relatives and his ex-wife.

Chapter Twenty-three

It was eight o'clock, before he rambled up Julian and Trish's drive from where the taxi had left him. Rambled, because that was the only way the afternoon's alcohol would let his legs move. But his mind was locked onto the loss of whom he had once been and the world that had disappeared with it. Marked by the occasion he had just left. Confronted by an even drunker man who had said he remembered Jim from working in the Council, the boozy hostility how he described Jim's past self had collected onlookers. "Veritable wrecker" was the odd phrase the man could not escape from describing Jim. Who listened from his seat, an eye to the gathered audience, for a long time thinking it worthless to answer the meandering, repetitious tirade. Until, finally wiping flecks of the man's spit from his forehead, Jim rose, taller than he had appeared and the crowd drew back, inhaling with expectation. As the drunk reeled back a couple of unsteady steps, Jim had said quietly to him and to them, "Veritable?" repeating it in French, "Veri-table? You wouldn't know truth if it slapped you in the face." Picked up his beer glass and walked away in his own uncertain step, out through the French windows onto the wide patio at the back of the hotel. To breathe in lungfulls of open air and the distant view of the Welsh hills on the western horizon.

Realising that the world he had appropriated as a young man- the car plants, docks, the old warehouses fed for their labour by the men and women from the neat terraces in their shadows- had all gone. Replaced by the first-time-buyer bright brick estates of undersized houses, the brilliantly coloured oversized tin sheds of the retail parks. Stripping him of that deceitful identity that had let him be, for a few short long-ago years, a bit of a hero to some people. And the disappointments of being that. Pondering the honesty and affection of Tracey to himself and his continual inability to be honest with her about his own life. Ashamed of how he had ended up again in a loveless home. Or created one, as the only thing he could repeatedly do, by allowing himself to fuck with other women. The only word for it. With another small child now to take the consequences, but Jim now far more knowing of the costs that could bring. The damage it could cause.

Before entering the house, and being forced to give some account of his day, especially to Trish, he wandered up to the van, slewed across the drive. Along with La Retrait, the sum of his own world. He went to the broken quarter light and picked out sharp crumbs of glass from between the lips of the rubber seal. Cutting his thumb on one. Turning away and entering the front door, sucking it.

Trish met him from the other end of the hallway, Adam behind her.

"Hi. How did it go?"

Going to speak and finding the thumb, he pulled it out and examined the small seeping wound. Looked up at her again and saw Adam, from behind her skirt, mimicking him, with all seriousness studying his own wet thumb.

"How did it go?" Trish repeated.

How to sum it all up? What to tell and what not? So he settled for, "It was okay." Then correcting himself for enthusiasm, "It went very well."

She approached. "What've you done with your thumb?"

He held it out for her to take. "Just cut it on glass. The van."

Her quizzical look at him required more.

"The window's broke. Just the quarter light."

She let go of his hand. "I'll get a plaster."

He followed her. And Adam, holding up his own thumb for his mother's attention.

Julian rose from the armchair as they entered, with a questioning look to him. And a hint of amusement? The interview with Finch forced its way to the forefront of Jim's mind, through the crowded preoccupation with the reception. He looked from Julian to Trish, going out to get his medication. Did she know about this morning's meeting? Would the two men have to wait for her to go to bed again?

Julian was shaking his head, soundlessly mouthing silence. Watched from below by Adam.

Jim broke the silence as Trish returned, by flopping back into a chair with, "I've had too much to drink!"

She came over and her knee on the arm, leaned over him to wrap the wound. Stepping back. "Okay? How did you break the glass?"

"While it was parked. Broken into. Outside the registry office." An easy lie.

Until her, "Where's your jacket?"

He looked down at his shirt sleeves, to ponder an answer and to avoid her eyes. Just offering, "Stolen." Hoping it was enough to end her questions.

She was doubtful, but offered him a coffee. While he drank this, he told them about the reception. As if it had gone well. Trish then took Adam upstairs and Julian confirmed in a whisper that she did not know about the meeting with Finch. They would talk later.

Trish fussed downstairs with minor tidying chores between the kitchen and sitting room the two men were sat in. Enforcing small talk about the wedding, rather than what they were waiting to speak of. Guiltily, he heard himself speaking of the day with increasing ridicule, self-applauding with the reckless dishonesty of the drink in him. Trish stopped to listen once or twice, but finally shook her head at his silliness and took herself off to bed.

When they were certain the footsteps had taken her finally out of hearing, Julian looked over at him. "Well, what did you think of Finch?"

"Don't trust him. He's in it for himself. Or, maybe not. How do you know he's not been sent to sniff around Scadding's case? For the other side." Proud of the cynical wisdom of that, he let himself smile inappropriately at Julian.

"I'd thought of that." He paused, reflecting. "But all that stuff about what a good pimp he'd been- that ridiculous sense of almost professional injured pride in how the new bosses were spoiling all the good work he'd done. Somehow, that rang true."

Jim grunted, unable at first to order his dulled mind to respond. Finally clutching at, "The diaries! His diaries he spoke of. You didn't believe that, did you?"

Julian spread his hands. "We'll have to see them- a sample of them, at least. I thought that would be the acid test- whether we let him aboard the case or not. Ask him to produce some of the diaries for us to see."

Us? It dawned on Jim how involved it sounded he was becoming. He blurted, "I'll be back in France," reminding of his escape.

Julian looked across, smiling and comradely, "Yes, I know. But you'll be back in the UK before the hearing. There's no date yet, just been given permission to go ahead. On one of your visits, we could set up another meeting. To really test him."

He began to realise how little he now wanted all this. Back on the treadmill of the moral expectations he was supposed to have of himself. Duty towards those who did not want him there. Scadding now, as it had once been Damien. "Have you spoken to Scadding yet? About having Finch as a witness?"

"Christ, no. You know him. His buttoned-up view of the world would be appalled. No. I wanted to be sure myself, then approach Scadding's solicitor- when we get one. Get the solicitor to sell the idea."

Jim rolled back into the cushions of the chair. "No chance. You'll never get Finch past Sydney Scadding. I'd bet money on it." Wishing to kill the idea. All of it. Closing the book finally on them all- Scadding, the Council, Whispering Pines, the boys, the Bulgarian gymnasts… and Damien. At last, closing those accusatory eyes to let the dead boy sleep. And Jim, also, closing his own eyes at that moment. Drained entirely of the will by the confusing insistentcies of the day. Of which the man sat opposite was just another he wanted to shut out. And sleep, for ever.

"Sorry. You must be tired."

Forcing Jim to awaken to blearily observe Julian's gentle consideration. "Yeah…"

"Oh, yes. The van window and your jacket. How did that happen?"

"Outside your office," Jim replied flatly.

"You don't think it was Finch, do you?"

Jim had not considered that, but the order of events was so tangled in his head and he was so tired, he could make no sense of their knottings. No longer important, he wanted bed. He shrugged. Blame was not important to him now. He wanted to sleep. Then return home to Gizande. However it had been between them, in this moment, his daze allowed him a fondness he wanted to curl up with. Away from here.

Julian recognised it, reluctantly. "Okay. Time for bed." Then, "You okay?" Waiting for an answer Jim did not offer. "Have a good sleep. Got friends coming round tomorrow. Some of them are keen to meet you."

Oh, no. Jim remained slumped. At the prospect of another day's bright chatter.

Julian hesitated. "Okay?" again.

"Yes," Jim muttered. "I'll make my own way up." Leaving his host with no doubt that he wanted to be left alone. Relieved Sylvie had not been mentioned.

The party of their friends was not what he expected. An unpleasant surprise in a different way. He had lain in bed that Sunday morning long after he was fully awake, hiding from Julian's recruitment of him to the cause and from the disapproval he was sure to expect from Trish for the groggy, shallow dishonesty of his behaviour the previous evening. Guests started arriving about three o'clock. It was an old-fashioned afternoon tea he had read the middle classes used to enjoy. He was the only one not in a couple sat around in the garden chairs. The four children were led to a picnic set out for them at the edge of the flowerbeds and intermittently supervised by Trish as she smilingly patrolled round her guests.

Jim was uncomfortable from the start. From the gushing, "Jim Briggs", he was greeted with on introduction, several people obviously knew of him. But as what? he wondered, sat apart from the gathering prattle about events and people he knew nothing of.

Julian saw this and attempted to include Jim. "Most of you don't know Jim, here. But you may have heard of him. He used to feature big in the old days of militancy in the car factories. Didn't you, Jim?"

What could you answer to that? Nothing, except the forced smile that allowed Julian to continue.

"But the finest thing he ever did, never got the headlines it should have- of course." He looked at Jim for the permission to continue that he would never give. Trish had circled round to stand behind Jim's chair, both protective of him and possessive of the assumed status of her guest. "He lost his job standing up for a kid who had been abused- raped in a children's home." The warmth of his audience jolted with discomfort at these words, giving anxious glances towards their own children at the end of the garden. "A job, I might add, working for Social Services!"

Jim felt oppressed by the cumulative praise of the narration, but Julian continued, as if what he took to be the modesty of his subject was unworthy of the great things he had done. "But… but," raising his hands to be sure of their attention, "But. Better than this, he followed a kid- another kid- who'd been kidnapped because he was witness to the abuse… Jim, here, followed him to Berlin…" pausing for effect, before ratcheting it up. "And this was when the Wall was still standing- he chased the kid and the kidnapper right into East Germany- got locked up by the Stalinist police…" He looked at Jim with real pride and affection, "And still got the kid out and back to Britain."

The silence after this was long. Jim looked round the faces, smiling at him as they were required to, then dropped his eyes to the half-eaten sandwich on the plate in his lap.

"Fabulous!" A woman's voice.

"No," Jim heard himself say.

Only the offstage sound of the children, the adults' smiles now uncertain. Waiting for him to explain.

But all he would say was to repeat, "No," shaking his head this time. Leaving them to sort out the silence for themselves, so disengaged did he feel from this sort of people.

It was Trish from behind his shoulder who broke it. "I doubt that Jim's any of those things now, Jules." She put her hand on Jim's shoulder. "He's a farmer in the Pyrenees now. And a dad."

A middle-aged woman spoke, whom Jim had noticed earlier had been giving him more particularly inquisitive looks than the others. "He can never escape from who he was in the car industry. I remember." She leaned forward. "You don't remember me, do you, Jim?" She laughed a little and looked round at the others. "It must be the ravages of my advancing years, but he doesn't recognise me." Looking back at Jim, "I'm Linda. Remember."

Stultified, he stared back. Linda?

She turned back to the spectators, "Years back- the late sixties?- we had a fling together. I was in the Young Socialists. He was my hero." She looked briefly with a coy apology at her husband next to her. "I was determined to get him. And I did." The laughter went from her face and she looked back fixedly into Jim's. "That's what he'll always be. A reminder that just because you work at a mindless job in a factory, you don't have to behave like a slave."

Jim sat on in his confusion, trying to rebuild the face of those few nights in her bedsitter, from the plump comfort of that flesh before him. But, more importantly, the person he must have seemed to her. And she still vividly remembered, but he could no longer piece together.

Trish's fingers on his shoulder squeezed him awake. "Well, who are you, Jim? The car factory hero? The hero rescuing kids from the communists? Or the French farmer?" When he did not answer, she said, "Maybe you should write a book about your life and then you could tell us who you really are."

Thankful at her rescue, he could smile up at her and escape with, "But no one'ld be interested."

Polite laughter at this allowed everyone to be released from the enforced attention to him and started to resume talking amongst themselves. Trish went off to attend to the children, but Linda came over to sit beside him.

"It's been so long, Jim."

"I'm sorry I didn't recognise you."

"That's okay. The fate of all ageing women. I now look more like my mother than myself."

"I never met your mother," making them both laugh slightly.

"No. Well you have now," framing her face with her hands and tilting it comically.

He just shook his head, at a loss what to say to her, so remote did the life when he knew her seem, how inappropriate her sudden intimacy about then.

"Farmer in France?" she asked. "Is that true?"

"Yes. I suppose so."

"And married? And a dad?"

Avoiding the complicated specifics, he replied, "Well, we're all married now, aren't we?" nodding over her shoulder towards her husband.

"And you were then, Jim. When we were getting it together." She smiled ruefully. "I know your wife, you know. Well, I suppose she's your ex-wife now. Jane. She still calls herself Briggs. Kept your name."

He wondered why Jane had never shaken him off completely. "How d'you know her?"

"I'm a teacher. She runs the training courses- Baker days and all that." She corrected herself, "I don't really know her. Like outside work. But she's sometimes a speaker at meetings we go to."

He looked at Linda without saying anything more. Thinking how little he had to connect himself to her. Sharing more with his ex-wife than she could ever again with him. How even the recalled fragments of intimacies with a lover so many years before, could not bridge the decades since of separate lives. More talk with her would be a fruitless task. Leading nowhere, except backwards to a life that was several long episodes different from who he was now.

She leaned closer to him. "But I'll never regret it," she whispered. "Between you and me. I think of it still. Often."

He moved back in his chair, away from her confiding closeness. He had not thought of Linda for years. How had he remained significant to her? He looked again at her, with different understanding. At the sincerity of her eyes looking back at him, inquiring, he was certain, if he felt the same. Of what emptiness in her life since, to make an enduring memory of such a brief affair. That she had ended, he remembered. Had he been a crossroads for this woman? The moment when she had taken the turning, since forever regretted? Barely credible, that this other person could see it so differently now, after all those years. Almost absurd enough to tempt him to the crudity of thinking of her as just a good fuck at the time. And speaking it aloud, as a way of escape from the seriousness of being whatever those eyes required of him now.

"Ah, well," he heard himself saying. "I'm back to France tomorrow."

It shook her awake from her recollections. She turned to look over at the reality of her husband to give him a checking smile. When she turned back to Jim, she was still smiling, but examining him with hurt eyes, as if for the last time. He wanted to touch her, to thank her, to reassure that her memories were well placed, but knew he would do nothing of the sort.

Maintaining his fixed half-smile, while she said hopelessly, "Yes. Of course," tidying away her moment of unwise indiscretion with this stranger behind the civility of the words. "Travel safely." She pushed herself up from the chair and, standing over him, with the sun behind her, he was uncertain if she was close to tears when she said, "It was good to meet you again."

Watching her return to her husband and turn her chair so that Jim was now out of her view. Feeling that he had somehow coarsely misused her, he looked round the crowd of guests again, confirming his disengagement from them. Comforting him that he was on the road again in the morning and that anything worthwhile left in his life would be there for him back home in the Pyrenees. Whatever the difficulties waiting to be tackled.

Chapter Twenty-four

The next morning, he crept from the house, but was unable to restrain the noises of the engine starting and his tyres on the gravel of the drive. As he drove away, a last look back caught Julian waving at him from an upstairs window. Jim pretended he had not seen.

He pulled into that other driveway in the Birmingham suburb only ten minutes before he was due, despite the extra time he had allowed for the journey from the north. A young woman in a dark trouser suit answered the door.

"The removal man?"

"Yes?" with his inquiry - who she was- unconsidered as she brusquely led him off up the hallway. Following, into the same dining room he remembered.

The wife stepped forward, "I'm so glad that it is you they could send again."

"I'm not sure I am," he said ruefully, looking over at the husband, from where he stood at the window, scowling back. "Is it properly sorted this time? Am I goin' to be doin' the move?"

"Yes." Indicating the young woman, "This is my solicitor. We're all here. We're waiting for my husband's."

Jim looked from one to the other. "Well, what happens now?"

"We wait," the husband answered tersely.

"Is there anything I could be moving… while we're waiting?" No one answered, so he spelt it out. "Anything you folks will agree goes in the move?"

The husband looked acidly at the wife. "Is that reasonable enough for you? The chairs from the front room you said I could have- can he be putting those in the van?"

She simply replied, "It's your solicitor that's missing."

The husband took his eyes sourly back outside, as if a point had been proved. Leaving the room creaking with the discomfort of their mutual contempt.

Jim finally broke the silence with, "I'll be waiting out in the van. Till you're ready to use me."

"You won't be driving off again, will you?" the wife asked, with the hint of a provocative smile.

"No." He avoided the temptation to join in the goading of the husband. "Not till I've been given something to carry."

As he turned to go, the solicitor said, "Do you have documentary proof of where you are taking the furniture?"

He turned at the doorway. "I've got an address. In Perpignan. Ask him," indicating the husband. "He knows."

The solicitor was insultingly patient with Jim, "A document. Something from your company that confirms the address where it is agreed the goods are to be deposited. As proof."

"No. I've got a scrap of paper in the cab with the address- two addresses. Where I get the key. And where I leave the furniture." Irritated with her superciliousness, he added, "We're like that down there. It's all word of mouth, done on trust. Ask him," throwing a gesture to the husband. "He'll have the documents. If you need to prove something." And left the room.

Sat back in the cab, he wanted so much to be got going. Out of the place. Proof? That the world was being taken over by lawyers. He though of Suzanne and wondered if she had yet had her meeting with the advocate and the Russians she had been so anxious about. Then of the home he had been sharing with Gizande. And her refusal to consider the legal arrangement Suzanne had suggested. Concubinage. Without that piece of paper, he supposed he had no rights to live on in Gizane's home. Maybe that was her intention. Preparing for his eviction. Backed up by the power of lawyers, if she wanted. Difficult to believe she could ever act like that? He would work on to get La Retrait more habitable, as his insurance, though he could not visualise what living alone up there would be like. Should he be worried about his situation? Go to an advocate and get advice himself? With his feeble level of understanding even street market French, he would need Suzanne to accompany him for that, but she was too preoccupied herself at present. And he did not want to share with her the broken down state of his relationship with Gizande.

He glanced back at the house and saw the husband staring back out of his window at him. Before disappearing. Jim felt a brief, unexpected sympathy for him. After twenty minutes passed and no one else having arrived, Jim re-entered the house. The three of them were still stood in the dining room, the wife and her solicitor on one side, the husband on the other, with his back to the window.

"How long d'you expect me to wait?" At first addressed to the room as a whole, he turned to the wife. "I've got a ferry to catch this evening."

She looked across at her husband, almost with triumph, "Well?"

"What do you expect me to say?"

She looked at Jim and could not keep the mischief from her eyes, beneath theatrically arched eyebrows, "What do you think, Mr. Briggs?"

"I need to be gettin' on wi' my job." Adding, "Whatever's goin' on here," retreating again behind the chopped syllables these people brought out in him.

The solicitor announced to the husband, with the restrained and knowing spitefulness of her profession, "It is you who have commissioned the removal man. I certainly cannot spend all day waiting for your solicitor to arrive. And the Court would look askance at any removal taking place without me present."

He looked from his window again, but there was still no one there. He spoke to the pane, "So… we must go ahead, I suppose."

The selection and collection of the pieces of furniture was supervised by the wife attended by the solicitor making notes, with the husband in tow behind, saying little, reluctantly helping Jim with the few bigger pieces into the back of the van, clearly finally defeated. As if Jim was no longer being employed by him and was only answerable to the women. At midday, before he finally closed the back doors of the van, he let the three of them look in and check the contents. A large space of the floor was empty.

The husband remarked, "Hardly worth your trip, Mr. Briggs," before turning bitterly back into the house.

The wife held out her hand, "Thank you, Mr. Briggs. You have been of great assistance. I will write to your employers, if I may, thanking them."

Jim wiped his hand on his overall before taking her thin bony fingers within his briefly, only offering, "If you want," in answer.

"I will," she pressed. "I will."

"Right." Uncertain what he was assenting to, he now just wanted to get off. "Goodbye," as he retreated to his cab.

As he waited in the gateway to get out into the stream of traffic, he said aloud to himself, "What the fuck was all that about?" Reflecting, as he shunted his way through the fringes of the city to reach the motorways, how the only people left in the England he visited now seemed to tangle him up in their games. Willing himself back home to Gizande and Clara, he lumped them all together, Trish and Julian, Tracey too. Adding Deedee and Jude. Them, most of all, exporting their trickiness out to the land he had once escaped into, from all that. He wanted no surprises any more and wanted to play a part in no one's games. He wanted to sort out what he had got and regretted the night in the cornfield with Jude. Yet, he surprised himself by thinking of Sylvie as they had- all too briefly- been. As they might have been… If. As he had not thought of her for a very long time. Before dismissing the spectre as simply another might-have-been escape attempt from the painful hard work of getting back to living with someone.

Chapter Twenty-five

Once he had left that sad collection of furniture in the big, empty house by the sea beyond Perpignan, and he turned for home, he thought of nothing but how he would open his arms to Gizande. A gesture of reconciliation, enwrapping the Gizande who had been missing these last two years, but whom he dare let himself believe had gone forever… Or even, who had never existed. The face inside his head looked back at him with the ironic affection she had shown him in the early days. Those last few familiar kilometres of dusk, he found himself smiling in the darkening cab, warmed with where he was going. So that when he finally saw the sharp silhouette of the dark house against the curtain of slated clouds concealing the mountain tops, no vehicle outside, he had his explanation. Down at her mother's, collecting Clara, where she would have been left for the day.

Retrieving the key from beneath the pot by the back door, he heard the dog whimpering from the barn as he went into the kitchen. The stove was cold. Opening its top door, there was no hint of warmth from the grey ash inside. It had not been lit for at least two days. Stayed down at her mother's? A stack of plates upturned on the drainer. Rubbed with his finger, they were bone dry.

Up the stairs, he found the blue overalls she had been wearing when he left, hanging over the side of the bath. The mirrored cabinet over the sink was open and empty of the few items of makeup she ever used. He rubbed his finger along one of its shelves and touched it to the tip of his nose and, as he breathed in the stale scent of her, it was the first intimation of anxiety.

He went on to the bedroom that had increasingly become only hers. There were empty hangers in the wardrobe, but he frowned to remember what clothes might be missing, so routine had been her garb of either jeans or overalls. The bag of bottles of oils and ointments gone with her, too.

He returned to the kitchen, now looking for evidence. Nothing there he could read into it. Certainly no note.

He ran back up to Clara's room. Drawers were open. The one where her little socks and underwear were kept, emptied, but for an unmatched pair. Down at her mother's for several days? He froze. The search was over. At least, that search to find them anywhere in this house. He remained squatting, staring sightlessly into the bottom of the drawer. Until his calves cramped, making him stand up and shake his legs free of it. He held back the welling anxiety with the single determination. Not tonight.

He would do nothing tonight. Until tomorrow. He would not phone the mother. He could not handle that conversation in French, without reading her face before him. He would stay the night here.

Slowly, he pushed the drawer closed with the toe of his boot and went downstairs. He returned to the kitchen. The bread crock was empty, the fridge had been cleared and was switched off at the plug. He filled the electric kettle and switched it on to boil while he went back out to the van to retrieve his sleeping bag. The dog was silent now. He thought about locking the outside door. Indeed, he looked at it for a long time as if it would give him an answer, before he decided to leave it unlocked. Waiting for her return?

He made himself a black tea with a teabag and retreated to the front room with his sleeping bag. Without undressing, he unzipped it and lay it over himself like a quilt. He saw some last, weak light coming through the window. Restlessly, he got up again, switched the room's lights off and went back to his chair, pulling the bag up over his chin, almost child-like, to let the ache of being alone again wash over him. The certainty, even the security of it, snuffling with the regret, the relief. As he knew he would not sleep that night, he let the scenes of his relationship with her- and of other relationships- flicker through his brain, drugging him to the stupor that is the edge of sleep. Then startling him awake again with a particularly stark recollection.

It was 6.30 and fully light before he finally abandoned the pretence. He sat up, head hung, slumped groggily on the edge of the sofa. He saw the untouched cup of tea on the floor and remembered indifferently that his body was hungry.

He went upstairs to wash, feeling his age. He could not continue sleeping this way for much longer, on couches and van seats. His clothes in the bedroom cupboard were untouched, just as he had left them, with the addition of a couple of shirts that she had been ironing when he had left. He took one of these, as if to clothe himself with her care. Perhaps. He chose underwear and socks and went to the bathroom.

But he closed the scent of her into the cabinet above the sink. Picking up the small shaving mirror, and turning it over to confront his face. The skin on his throat, above his adam's apple was beginning to sag with age. His eyelids were bruised with sleeplessness. Having forgotten to switch on the immersion heater, he only had a sink of cold, scummy water to make the careful preparations of his face and body for the day ahead.

The mother answered the door without surprise. "L'Anglais," she noted with indifference. Adding, "Vous n'avons pas abandonné la petite?"

"Ou est Gizande?"

As she studied his face before answering, a figure appeared in the dark corridor behind her.

Gizande? It was the daughter, Gaillarde. "Ou est ta mére?" he called to her.

She came up and examined his face over her grandmother's shoulder. "You do not know?"

Of course. She was learning English at her college. "Non. No. I return from England."

"She has left la petite with grandmother."

Who said something to the girl in Catalan.

Gaillarde's eyes back onto his face. Interrogatory, but also sympathetic, even seeking his support. "She says she has visited the police. But they know nothing."

Measuring that, before he asked, "How is Clara?"

The girl smiled. "She is asleep now."

"Does she know Gizande- does she know her mother has gone?"

Smiling again, "Who knows what Esclarmonde thinks? She continues to play."

"Can I see her?"

The girl spoke to the mother, then turned back to Jim. "Grandmother says she sleeps. Come later."

There was more talk between the women and then Gaillarde said to him, "My grandmother says come back this evening." She shrugged, as if anything else was beyond her powers, "Then you can see the little one."

He was certain she wanted to reassure, but she stepped back into the corridor shadows. As the grandmother looked away from him and closed the door. Leaving him staring at the panels, with so many other questions.

Back in Gizande's house he started to search for answers, to root them out of the fabric of the building, if need be. He went to the bedroom first. The silence of the house was full of her, her absence now merged with the quietness of when she was here. The limp clothes on the hangers could actually have been filled by her slight limbs. So that he started to speak to her as he searched through the drawers and the cupboards and the shelves, inside the books on them, in the opened boxes, murmuring his explanation to her, for every intrusion he made into the private world she had created of so much of this house- from him. Talking across the years to her, to recapture that intimacy- so brief- he believed he had with her, "…Gizande… Gizande…" repeating her name, he searched for her.

As she had left no note and no explanation with her mother, he knew he would be seeking something hidden. He conducted the search with precision. Every page of every bundle of papers that he found, back and front, then replacing them with care. As he did not know what exactly would give him his answer, he looked for signs in everything. It was well into the afternoon before he finished, not an item left to examine, he was certain.

He decided to go up to La Retrait. Maybe she had been there in his absence. As he went out to the van, he heard the dog whimpering again. Why had she locked it up? He would feed the animal when he returned.

By the time he reached the rough track up to his farm, it was raining. The wind was driving it with horizontal force up against the cab windows, flecks of it through the broken quarter light wetting his hand on the steering wheel. He crunched the tyres up as close as he could to the old wooden door. His fingers fumbled numbly in the frozen wet, as he fiddled the key into the padlock.

As always, the air inside was dank with not being enough lived in, not enough warmed by the inhalations and exhalations of people. Nothing of her there, but he took the time to stroll around this space of his. Into the second downstairs room, where he planned to open up the old fireplace. Examining the high corners of the ceiling for any signs of damp. Rubbing his hand across the surface of the early summer's plastering. If he ended up having to live here, he thought he could tolerate at least three of the four seasons on this mountain. He went on upstairs, checked that the window clasp was firmly locked against the weather, then returned downstairs to the door, to peer outside at the storm. A few shards of sunlight split through the slabs of slate-grey cloud, igniting- just for a moment- a rainbow, one foot planted in the already brightening green of the valley below, the other planted on the dark mountainside behind him.

The shepherd's hut, he thought. When the rain cleared, he would go up there.

He pulled the door half open, walked back to sit on the bed, watching the rain, some of it spattering on the large stone pavings inside the entrance. But it was soon gone, as quick as it had come. He went out, collected his waterproof, and set off up the hill at the back of the farm, against the gusts of wind working their way round and down the mountain. It was a steady climb through the rough grass, between rocks, until he came to the bottom of the slope of scree. He started to work his way around and in between the huge, tumbled, wet-black boulders, concentrating on foot and hand holds as he climbed up. He also looked over his shoulder at the clouds, watching for a return of the rain. By the time he reached the top of the scree, where it broke out into the upper meadows, his fingertips were dulled and imprecise from the cold stone and his chest was chilled by the wind through his clothing.

There were some goats there, but they were too far for him to tell if they were from the Spanish herdsmen or were wild. The hut would probably show signs if there had been any interlopers. So he steadily tramped up across the grassland. The sun came out again, shimmering and sparkling the rippling tussocks of green in the light. Stopping for breath, he looked around and back to where the escarpment plunged down towards La Retrait, hiding it from his view and he wondered that this could all be his.

He approached the hut cautiously, but as he rounded to the door side of it, he saw that the large rock they always placed against it when they left was there. With several heaves, he rolled it aside and dragged the door open. He had brought no matches for the paraffin lamp, but the bright sunlight outside threw a dim illumination into the windowless interior. There was a scorched log on the fireplace from a long-ago fire and a rusty tin on the hearth half filled with old, dried bits of dung. It smelt uninhabited- at least for the last several days.

He sat down on the stone bench and something stuck into his backside. He pulled a black plastic bag from under him and inside was a book. As he opened it, the sun disappeared from outside and he could not read from the page. He rose and went to the door. A dog-eared paperback, *Montsegur et l'énigme cathare.* He leafed through to a section of photographs. Ruined castles. There were illegible squiggles against the text that he could not understand. It was her writing. He peered into the desperate tangle of one phrase a few pages into the book and gave up, assuming it must be in Catalan. He looked for other signs of her in that dark and comfortless room, where she had probably spent so much time. But there were none.

Pocketing the book, he went outside and scanned the horizon, as if he was expecting her yellow cagoule to appear between the rocks of the peaks above. For a moment, he shivered at the thought that she might be dead. But then he remembered the carefully selected clothing taken from the empty hangers in the bedroom. Maybe driven away by his rape. He shuddered again at the memory and the chill of the wind. Pushing the door back and rolling the rock across it.

As he crossed back to the scree for the descent, he said aloud, "Sorry, Gizande… so sorry…" each word ripped away from his lips and scattered by the blast of the gusts.

Chapter Twenty-six

Back at La Retrait, he locked the door and set off in the van to her house. There, he remembered the dog and went into the barn. It barked at him, then had second thoughts and whimpered, squirming its body at the full length of the chain it was attached to, appealing to him. He had never liked the animal, but he searched for some food, not knowing what she fed it with. He edged past its snuffling at his legs into the small back tool room. He had never been in here because she always allocated him the tasks and the tools to go with them whenever he worked down at her farm, he had never had to seek them for himself. There were spades, hoes and forks dangling from nails in the wall. Two shelves, one with a sack of dog food, next to some part-used tins of paint. He reached for the sack, went next door and found the dog's dish. He filled it and the animal set to it greedily. There was another dish for water and he went to the tap outside the barn.

Putting the sack back on the shelf in the inner room, he noticed an old leather briefcase on the other shelf. He pulled it down and went outside into the light. One of its buckles broken, he undid the other, opened the flap and looked inside. A brown envelope and a ring-bound notepad. Which he pulled out, but it was awkward stood there, turning the pages with only one hand free, so he took out his keys and unlocked his way back into the house. The note book had the same desperate scribblings in Catalan as in the margins of the book he had found in the hut. He pulled that from his pocket and compared. A few of the pad's pages choked full of her writings, some with just a few lines of angry words, in between some pages carelessly bypassed, blank. He then carefully shook the contents of the envelope onto the kitchen table. There were the photos of his father that he had been searching for before he had left for England. He sorted through them several times, to check his disbelief that she had taken them. Why would she have? That man in the beret still looked back at him smiling, now it seemed almost knowingly, at his son.

He peered into the mouth of the envelope for anything more. Stuck at the bottom was a black audio cassette. He pulled it out and turned it over. On it was a label, handwritten simply *pour Gizande*. He took it over to the radio tape player on the other side of the room and snapped it in. It hummed, then a hiss, before the music started. He recognised it from the first notes… in stately repetition of those geometrics of passion, winding themselves up, diving and climbing down and up again, as if they were seeking a way of escape- from this room, and all its discomforts for him, from now into another life, past or future… it was the Bach cello. That first music of Casals that Suzanne had played to him on those discs. The old composer's gift to their father. He went back to where the photos lay and looked down at them… before he realised that this music was different… he listened… it rushed across the pauses with a glitter of reckless technique, overplaying the highest and the lowest notes… it was not the Casals he once heard and had taped for himself. A different recording? The faint groans of Casals' breathing were gone. He looked across at the machine. Different though it was, it still reminded him of the delight of those first days in France, discovering his sister, returning to England his head filled with images and expectations of Gizande.

Abruptly the music stopped. There was a sound of breathing that, at first, he was uncertain if it was his own. Then the voice cleared its throat, breathed again, as if summoning up courage, and said, "Gizande. That is your mother. I apologise for telling you this in English, but it has been hard for me to speak it at all. And for all the years I have lived in this country, as I get older, I know it is in English that is the language I reflect in. I dream still in English, the good dreams and the bad. But to speak in French, I must first shape the words in English before I make the translation. It is the realisation of all old people… that we return to who we were once, long ago when young. The memories of then become sharper than what happened this morning…"

The voice paused and Jim held his breath with it, leaning, propped on rigid arms, his head hung sightlessly above that scattering of old photographs.

"You have known me since you were a little girl… No… you have not known me. You have not known who I am… The woman you live with is not your mother… and your father was not your real father. Your true mother was American. She was very beautiful. And talented. Her father was a diplomat, for the Americans in Paris. I knew him from the work I did. After the war. After the Liberation. Your mother, I will call Elizabeth, played the cello. That was her, you have just heard on this tape. When I returned from Paris, at the end of the war, as you know, I was in the circle of Pablo Casals. It was required of me, for my work. Pau, the old man. The old genius… I promised to Elizabeth's father that I would introduce her to Pau, and perhaps the old man would listen to her music. And maybe… if she was good enough, he would give her lessons… teach her. At the time she was only twelve years old. Casals thought she was good. Every summer she would come from France to stay in Prades. And she would play there, among the old men, learning from them, sat amongst them, so pretty and so serious, leaning over that great, big instrument, one of her skinny legs either side of it… those first years… but so quickly then she became a young woman… beautiful and wise…"

There was a long reflective pause. Then a click, as the recorder had been switched off, clicking again to resume… after how long for that voice to summon back its self-control, Jim wondered.

"I could not help myself from loving her. We would meet when we could. Whenever her schedule of lessons and concerts would permit her… And we would walk into the hills. One day, all the way from Prades, up to the top of Mont Canigou. She talked of her ambitions, of her future on the concert stages of the world. I told her of the war. We walked to be alone, of course, but I also walked to be undiscovered. I so feared the old man discovering us, walking out as he did under that black umbrella to keep the sun off. He learnt everything that went on in that little town. I knew that if he saw me with Elizabeth, he would only have to see us to understand. For him, there was no recreation for his students. He would see her neglecting the music. Her parents would be told and it would be over between us and my work with the circle of Casals- all the years of trust that I had built up..."

There was a long silence. Jim listened, waited, for a denial from the voice… of it being whom he feared… anything, but confirm who he was.

"And then, of course, Gizande, it was you who gave us away." There was a fond smile in the voice. "I did not even know until Elizabeth was back in Paris. On one of my visits to the Casals house, Senora Capdevila called me into the room- that room where I had watched Elizabeth practice with the old man- and she told me I would not be welcome in the house any more. I received a letter from the American Embassy. It was written by one of their lawyers. I was told I would not see Elizabeth again. She would return to the United States. Nothing was said about the child- about you. I knew from the letter an abortion was planned. It did not say it, but there was something in the chilly words that told me you were to be killed inside your mother's womb. It was the scandal of it all, the position of her father, the promise of Elizabeth's career on the concert stage… Your abortion would be the only possibility. So, I wrote back that day. I sent copies of my letter to people I knew of importance in the British and American Embassies, in NATO, which was just setting up in Paris, even to several French Government officials. In the letter, I notified that lawyer that I would fight for your life. My words, of course were nothing so dramatic. I tried to capture the same cold legal tone of the original letter. I informed him that such an abortion was illegal in France and, should it go ahead, I would do my utmost to publicise the crime, whatever the cost to me. I agreed to never see Elizabeth again, but said that I would find a good family to adopt the child and bring her up in France." A long pause, as if breathless from the disclosure, "... That family is your mother- and your dead father. When I wrote that letter, for all its apparent calculation, after I'd posted it and all the copies, I wept with loss and defeat. I am not a man of emotion. You may agree with that. I could not have done the things I did in the war - and before and since - if I'd been a cry baby. But it had immediate effect. An official from their Embassy visited me two days later. It as an embarrassment, of course. He came unannounced and had been waiting in my house with my wife for several hours, when I returned and found him. I made excuses and told lies to her- as I had during the war- so used to not sharing my life with her. I walked the man out into the field behind the house, leaving Constancia on the veranda, looking after us -"

Constancia on the veranda... Constancia on the veranda... Constancia on the veranda... Constancia on the veranda, as if it was not a tape, but the jumping arm of a gramophone, the words of confirmation played on and on in his head, deafening him to the drone of the continued story from the other side of that kitchen... its excuses, its half-truths and its deceits. He walked slowly and leadenly across to it and switched on the silence, brooding over the machine.

How long had she known? How long had she had this tape? How many times had she forced herself to listen to it? That she had kept it hidden, he was certain indicated that it had been played again and again. He imagined her, in his absence, retrieving it from its secret place and listening, hoping each time that perhaps the voice would say something different? He knew. He understood that he, also, would have to hear every last word himself... for anything that would let him escape from this knowing.

He rewound the tape, until he found those words, "... leaving Constancia on the veranda, looking after us. I told the Embassy man that I would give them the name of a family who would adopt the child, who they could approve. But he was not interested. For the Embassy and for Elizabeth's parents, it was all a matter of burying the scandal. As I spoke to that man in the field behind the house, I had no idea who I could ask to take the child. That evening, I went up to see your grandfather. During the war, I had sometimes sought his advice. He was too wise to completely trust me, but we had worked together on the escape lines into Spain. He listened and returned a day or two later, saying that his daughter and son-in-law agreed to take you when you were born. The Americans agreed, of course. They would have agreed to anything. That is how you got the family who have been your parents for over thirty years. It was all arranged with the utmost discretion. Your parents went away for several months. Your father was given a job on an American airbase in the north. It was all arranged by the Embassy. And when they returned, they had the baby that was you. I never saw Elizabeth again. I kept the secret too. I never told Constancia. I believe she knew something. Making public your true identity would have benefited nobody-"

"Oh, no! You vile old man!" Jim spat aloud his contempt and knocked the player over, as he switched off the voice again. It would have benefited nobody? What you mean- what you mean, is that everything was for your own benefit! For your advantage - lying, holding back the truth like this, until you were too far away to be touched by it.

"… So, there you are, my daughter. How strange that it should turn out that you are half-American, when it was the Americans who you so fiercely hated during your years in Paris and Germany. You are neither Catalan, nor French. You are an Anglo-Saxon… Why have I told you this? Why? … Why have I told you now- when I kept it a secret for so many years?" There was a long pause. Then a chuckle, "It is the softening of an old man's brain, I suppose. No, it is true. The wish has now come upon me to tidy up my life- to sort out at least one of the big lies- in a life that has been- yes- untidy with so many deceptions and with so many falsehoods. I have given this to your mother, with the agreement that it is up to her how she passes this information on to you… after I am dead. And I suppose it will be her choice whether she tells you this at all. But as you are listening now, Gizande, you will know I have fulfilled my responsibility to you… finally… at last…"

The hiss of the wordless tape filled the room.

Jim stared across at the machine, waiting for a denial of all that he had listened to. Or even of a better explanation, freeing him from the weight of the liabilities left him by that man. His father. Shared with Gizande.

He must have stood there for a long time after the tape had clicked itself off the end of its length. It was the realisation of Clara that stirred him from the impotent lassitude that Francis' confession had left him with. He wanted to shake the man by the lapels of the jacket he was wearing in the photograph on the table. He wanted to tear that posturing beret from his head and to choke from his collar some sort of blubbering apology from this man who said he seldom cried. But he had escaped from Jim with his death. And from Clara. And from Gizande. When had she known? When had she first heard the tape? He could not believe that she would have knowingly- with her half-brother- had sex… that word chosen, he realised, by a brain that shrank away from the vocabulary of love -

"GOD! BASTARD!" he shouted, enraged. Even from out of his grave, that man had been able to reach out and steal from the son he had abandoned- what had been most worthwhile in Jim's life. Gizande must have learnt of it sometime… when?

A revelation. Near to Clara's birth… explaining all the maternal anxieties for the health of a child born of incest… And, before that, her cry for Clara's abortion- as nearly as her own. And only a month ago, but half a metre along the edge of the table Jim now rested his clenched knuckles on, he had forced her down in what must have become an unspeakable act of violation for her. Oh, Gizande… how sorry I am… that you could but see me now… and believe me… The urgency of finding her now shrieked at him. Where might she have gone? What might she have done to herself?

He would visit Suzanne in his search. He was sure she would not know that she too shared their father with Gizande. And Jim would not be telling her. Before he left, he carefully replaced the tape and the photographs in the briefcase and returned it to the shelf in the back room of the barn. Should Gizande return while he was away, he did not yet want her to discover what he now knew. He needed to rehearse that scene for when it came about.

Chapter Twenty-seven

As he approached Suzanne's house, the veranda where Constancia had stood that afternoon watching her husband walk off with the American visitor, took on a new meaning for him. Where Jim himself had sat so often with his sister and Maurice and Marie-Claire, or with just Suzanne and Clara, was now in the ownership of the ghosts from the story he had just listened to. Suzanne had just got back from her school. There was her case and a pile of exercise books on the kitchen table.

He called for her and she answered from upstairs, "I will be with you."

All the photographs of her father had now disappeared not just from the front room, but also from the top of the bureau in the hall.

She came down the staircase, tying up the belt of her jeans. "I wanted to speak to you, Jim. But Gizande said to me that you were in England."

"When did you speak to her?"

She paused on the bottom step to remember. "It was Thursday?"

"Has Gizande been here?"

She looked at him quizzically, "No. Of course not. I spoke by the telephone to her." She continued looking at him, but her eyes were filling with sorrow. "Oh, Jim."

Did she know then? He let them come together in an embrace, for the first time for several years.

"Ah, Jim. It has been awful."

He felt him letting himself slide towards tears, along with her. She had spoken with Gizande, but she must know she had since disappeared. Had she been told about the tape as well? He disengaged to stand back from her blurred face. "You know she has gone. Gizande has gone."

Suzanne stared at him, collecting up from her distractedness. "Oh, Jim, why are we so unfortunate? Our life just…" She let the words trail away and hugged him again, this time sobbing, slowly, between long and deep inhaled breaths, she spoke words indistinctly lost within the folds of the front of his shirt. "How could he have done it? How could he have done it?"

He listened for some confirmation that she knew. What she knew.

"How could he be such a wicked man…? It is… it is that he was two men. One who did those things. And the man who was my father, who loved me, who played with me." She pulled herself away from him again and looked up. "How could he be…?"

"I know," he replied.

But, as if suddenly awaking, she shook her head, "Ah! But you have always known, have you not, Jim. You believed those stories of Jacob and the other old men." She stood away from him and wiped dry the cheek beneath each eye. "We know now, Maurice and I. I told Gizande." She reflected on this, as if rehearing the conversation in her head. "We have been apart for some time. Perhaps it has been my foolishness. But I had become so angry with you. But when I told her- oh, she cried- she cried out, so loud- as if she had learned such a terrible thing about her own father."

Jim must have visibly shown his shock, because she looked at him. "Yes. I had forgotten what a fine woman- what a beautiful spirit your Gizande has. She is able to feel my distress- as if it was herself."

As if about her own father? So did Suzanne not know? What then was she talking about? He blurted out, "She's gone. Gizande- she's disappeared. She has left Clara with her mother and Gaillarde. She has taken clothes."

Suzanne shook her head at him, linked her arm to his, and led him out to the verandah.

"Did Gizande say anything about me?" he asked, when they were sat down.

"No. We just talked about Father and the gulags. And the house."

"The gulags?"

She sighed. "That is what they are being called already in the village. The ones from Russia. They are the children of Spanish refugees who once lived here before the war. They fled from the Germans. This was their house. This," and she vehemently pointed to the ground beneath them, her face clouding with embitterment. "They escape from the Nazis. And they run from our father. This was their house. He stole it from them."

"How do you know?"

"We had the meeting with the advocate. He had all the documents- the letters. Do you know what our father did?" She looked across at her brother, the eyes haunted with the loyalty and the disbelief… now crushed beneath the proof she had been forced to read. "Do you know what he did? He wrote to the Vichy security. He said that the Spanish were active in the Resistance. Of course they were. They were his comrades. They were with him in the taking of Jews into Spain. They were his comrades, so he had all the evidence to give to the fascist police. But he warned them- the Spanish, that the police were coming, so that they could flee- escape. He even arranged for places on a boat from Marseilles to Turkey. It is all in letters- the documents of the Vichy Government seized at the end of the war. They have been searching for more than a year in the files of Government offices in Paris, the gulags."

"What happened then?" Jim asked.

"Well of course. Our father took their house. We have been occupying their house for more than fifty years," she said sarcastically.

"What happened to the Spanish?"

"Oh! I think the name they have been given tells the story. Yes. Gulags. Their parents went to Russia. There the children were born. They are a brother and a sister- like us!" she laughed cynically. "But of course, Spanish Republicans were an embarrassment to Stalin, also, and they were swept up into his camps, during one of his great imprisonments. They grew up there. The parents naturally, are now dead. But the children knew the story. They were released, but were unable to leave Russia. Only after the perestroika- the glasnost, when the Wall fell, they came to make enquiries. They have been in France for more than a year. Maurice and I have talked and talked… every night. There is nothing else we can do. There is nothing else I can think of. He wishes to go to the court, but I am not so certain. He has been advised that- because of the many years we have lived in the house, we have legitimates. But I am not certain." She looked at him, "We talk of it every night, late into the night, and I cannot decide." Then, waking to what Jim himself had said earlier, she said, "I am so sorry. Gizande… Have you argued?"

Should he tell her about the tape? But he knew how unjust it would be to heap more of the wreckage from their father's life onto her, at this time. "No. No arguments. No new ones. Just the disagreements over Clara, that I have told you about."

Suzanne shrugged her shoulders, "I know nothing. She said nothing on the telephone when I spoke with her. When did she leave?"

"I don't know. That's what I came to ask you."

"Pauvre Jim. Will you stay to eat? Maurice works late tonight. It is the night that the pharmacy remains open."

He wanted to stay, but he feared the conversation continually turning round to their father. He did not want the dishonesty of holding back what he so wanted to speak of to someone, so he said, "No. Thank you." Thinking, against all the odds, of Gizande's empty house and the wild hope that she might be even now re-entering it. With some harmless explanation for her absence. "No. I must go."

"Why? There is no-one home to eat with."

"I know. But…" He paused.

"Go, then," she said dismissively. Then, reaching across to rest her hand on his wrist, she said again, "Go then," but in a soft voice.

Chapter Twenty-eight

Back at Gizande's, the house was of course still empty. Tiredly, he travelled aimlessly from room to room, half hoping to find just something to help him understand. He felt unwell, feverish even. He wiped cold sweat from his forehead. His guts felt turgid. He had eaten almost nothing, but his sour mouth wished for no food. His whole body felt infected by some mild but persistent poison.

Finally, he found himself in the bathroom, again with the picture of his face up against that small mirror. Sallow and drained, the two pairs of lifeless eyes peered back at each other. Was he anything of Francis- in any way? Jim had only possessed black and white photographs of his father. He tried to remember the complexion of the skin from some of the colour photos in Suzanne's, that had now disappeared.

He turned away, went to the cupboard and switched on the immersion heater. He would bathe. Downstairs to the kitchen, he found a tin of soup, opened it into a saucepan and started to heat it on the electric ring. Waiting for it, he looked over at the radio, and dared it to speak. When he sat down and started to swallow the soup, spoonful by spoonful, he stared into the half light of the room in front of him, seeking the right questions to ask, now the voice of that other man had spoken in this room of hers… so particularly hers, with its scent of herbs, its orderly little jars of oils. Now that Francis had spoken here, Jim could not get that voice to leave the room.

Between spoonfuls, as if preparing for an interview.

Did you not know how your selfishness would hurt Gizande?

But it was only Jim's own presence in her life that poisoned the knowledge of who her father really was. Maybe if Jim and her had not been the parents of Clara, if Jim had never arrived in France, if Mary had never left those letters for him- if all those things, perhaps Gizande's discovery could have been one of joy. Finding a sister in Suzanne, as he had.

Why did you never leave me the whole story also, so that I could not make that terrible mistake? Of fathering my sister's child.

But he had then sealed himself off from England, just as Jim had built that wall between life there then, and life here now. With what he had learnt today, it was now far more important to seal the knowledge here. Tracey could never be allowed to visit him here. He thought back to those shoe boxes from Mary. The photos, the letters, the detailed recording of her confessions, penances and prayers, her Hail Marys for her sins. And now this bequest from her appeared to have nothing of the generous spirit he had once seen it as. Was it a vengeance against that brother who had escaped, leaving her with the responsibility for the small child? And the guilt when she was unable to fulfil her duty to the boy. Just as his father had used the tape to Gizande as a way of settling his conscience before death. Manipulated from the grave by the letters left by his aunt as well.

By the time he returned to the last few millimetres of soup in the bottom of the bowl, they were cold. He dropped the spoon with a rattle into them and went upstairs to run his bath.

Laying in the barely warm water, his head propped back up at the ceiling, he asked aloud, "Was it the death of my mother?" Was it that so hurt you, so wounded you that you had to abandon me? He thought of the calculation such a journey would have required. The preparation to travel across Europe to Lourdes - and then into a country at civil war - could never have been the whim of a moment. Was that the first step by Francis?

Aloud again, "Was that what made you such a cold and heartless man?" Jim remembered Suzanne speak of their father as being two people. But he understood there had only been one. The father she had grown to love was but a screen for the other. He even recognised the selfish self-importance of a man in public life towards his family, remembering his own absence at the occupied car plant, while Tracey was being born.

"Am I that much of you?" he suddenly heard himself crying out, the words banged between the walls against the pipes and cupboards of the room. He closed his eyes to the despair and slid down into the water, holding his breath at first. Then gradually, opening his mouth to leak the water between his teeth, down to his lungs- but he could not. He exploded to the surface, coughing, choking and spitting the water from his throat, with grasping gasps for air. Until finally, slowly panting. He rested his slumped head on his wet knees.

There was humourless laughter, somewhere in his head. He listened, yet beyond it he could hear the dog, out in the barn, barking furiously. His ears alerted to that, he sat up still in the water. The barking went on. There was something out there.

Quietly, he stood and reached for the towel, wiping the worst of the wet from himself before stepping out and putting on his dressing gown. He went downstairs. In the kitchen, he picked up the iron coal shovel, unlocked the door and went barefoot down through the storeroom, out into the twilit yard. From the shadows of the barn, the dog was still bellowing with angry frustration, clanking his chain as he kept furiously leaping against it to full length. Stepping back against the wall, Jim watched for any movement. Nothing to be seen. But, like the dog, he could feel someone there. He waited motionless, for a long time, the voice of the animal battering round the yard. Until his damp skin became cold and he shivered. Watchfully, he crossed to the barn, silencing the barks, and gave the hound a rough and friendly rub into its long mane of fur. It whimpered, crawling back from him on its belly.

Jim took a last look around the edges of the buildings, but it really was too cold now for him and he returned and locked himself again inside the house. As he went back to the bathroom, he could still hear the frightened whimper from the yard. The water he stepped back into was tepid, but he lay back into it to wash the cold from outside off his skin.

He was still listening for the dog, when he heard a creak on the stair. He did not move, but turned his eyes to the dark hole beyond the open door. There was another squeak, the complaint of a floor board at carried weight. Jim held his breath to squeeze every fleck of sound from the silence. Fixated by the gap beyond the room, out into the unlit corridor.

"Gizande?" hoarse and barely above a whisper. He carefully cleared his throat and called, only slightly louder, "Gizande."

Making as few sounds as possible, he reached for the damp towel, slowly rose from the water, streaming it from him noisily. He wrapped it round himself and crept to the doorway. There was nothing there, but the simple chair that had always been outside. Down the staircase, there were no shadows against the light thrown from the kitchen.

He went back in and, sitting his backside on the rim of the bath, started to dry himself.

-So… you found me at last, James. It was the voice from the tape, but with a touch of wryness, even sarcasm. It did not plead for Jim's goodwill. Half unwrapped in the towel, he submitted to listening to the voice from outside the room. -You found me and now you wish to become my accuser? Briefly, that humourless laugh he had heard inside his own head. -I have been accused by professionals. The most famous advocates and judges in this land, at the time. You have no case, my son. You were not there, during the war. You would not, you could not understand. You have never fought to the death, have you?

"No." Jim's reply was a defensive whisper.

-No… you have been brought up on the rewriting of war that the journalists and historians commence on the day the victors celebrate. People like me become an embarrassment. No one will admit that the victory was finally only possible through the dirty deeds of people like me. The five-star generals who go into politics must erase the record. The bishops, the popes, God bless them, preach sermons against those they had entertained in their palaces, those whose confessions they had absolved but a few weeks before. Do you not believe me?

Believe him? Did it matter whether it was true or not, the result had been the abandonment of his children to his deceits. "Who cares… about believing you? You were a liar then. It's easy to be honest about your life… when you are dead."

-Hah! Of course, my moralising son would have been different… War makes liars of us all. In the choice between being honest in death and keeping alive with dishonesty, who chooses the first? You, James, have never had to make that choice. In France we know- men of my age learned that. Do you know why no one down here, in the old Vichy, wishes to commemorate World War One with a brass band? No? I will tell you. It is because here, to remember the glories of that war, we have to remember that its hero was Petain. A hero in one war, a villain, a war criminal, as they term it, in the next. A war criminal? There can be no such thing. Was there anyone out there between the trenches refereeing the fighting against fouls then? Handing out penalties? Never. Nor for the wars I was in. There were no heroes in either war, just villains… and fools. The voice waited, for Jim to reflect on this. - The winners of wars share the triumphs, but the responsibility for the horrors is always with the defeated. France had tried to join the winners. That was the myth of the Resistance. Of De Gaulle. That we had defeated the Nazis before the first soldier stepped ashore at Normandy. No, we were the defeated. And an occupied country just has two gangs of criminals fighting each other, one for the occupier, the other for the liberators- who become the next occupiers. There were never any heroes here, believe me. Only as an old man, did I understand this. As you get older, the past becomes more important. It occupies your thoughts more. Trying to get it right in the end. That is why I had to make the tape for Gizande. A signing off of the accounts. Are you yet old enough, James, to feel a little of this?

Jim would not answer. Everything the voice said felt like an enticement to join in its dishonesties. Gizande, Suzanne and himself, just as… what? His brain was too bruised beneath the skull to seek for a word that summarised this man's abandonment of them.

-Was I wrong? I held to my beliefs. As you did, once. You would have been my enemy, James. A consorter with communists. You have wished for everything I crusaded against in Spain and later in France. But you have never had the opportunity to see where the excesses would have led you to. I saw the burning of churches, the murder of priests. What happened in Spain could not be permitted to happen in France, when the Germans were driven out… Could it?

"So that makes everything you did…" Jim groped for an understanding. "Everything was holy, was it? The theft of the house from the Spaniards? Elizabeth… and Gizande? Leaving me? How…? How to explain you never - ever - came for me? Even after the war was over?"

-Ah. I wrote to Mary. Many times. She would not reply. I could not return to England. I still had my work in France. And enemies in England would always prevent my return there.

"I read those letters." He could not let himself call this man, Father. "I read those letters and they were…" Full of lies? "… filled with gaps. You never told her the full truth, did you? In that letter left for me- presenting yourself as some Christian saint - some sort of crusader - you never mentioned Suzanne - or Constancia! Or Gizande. You wrote it as you wished. Nothing there about how comfortable you made yourself- and how many lives you had to tread on to do it."

-Oh, James… James, you do not understand how it was. I suffered also. I was imprisoned. I risked my life so that it was only by chance that I lived.

"Yes!" Jim spat out his contempt, all the anger of the trepidation forced upon him at the mention of his father's name in a barroom conversation in the village, his own silence from Suzanne of the latest tale told by a buttonholing old peasant. "I have heard! I've heard the stories of men visited by the police who have disappeared in the night- and only you knew where they had been hiding. I have heard them so many times since I've lived here, I can only believe…"

Furious, he stood, cloaked the towel round his shoulders and strode the three strides across the bathroom floor. The corridor outside was, of course, empty, but the cushion on the chair was warm. He picked it up and pushed his face into it. To inhale whatever stink may be left of the other man and to suck back the tears from his eyes. With a defiant sneer, he cast the cushion away and it bounced twice soundlessly from the staircase walls, down towards the kitchen.

He was very cold. The bloody war! He shivered. Fifty years gone and it was just as now for the old survivors round here, just as critical as ever to shape a good name with half truths and omissions. Quivering there at the top of the stairs, he realised that the war he had been too young to endure, had brought more than deaths to this country. In the eyes of the sly old men gathering annually at the Liberation memorial in Larozelle, there was the shiftiness of preserving fragile reputation. And that man- the Francis he had never known, who had decided, for whatever reason never to know his son - retained the right from his grave - from beneath that stone etched with ambiguity - to shape the life of that son. And the lives of his sisters… those beloved, kind and wise women who had once taken Jim to their hearts. Until the dead old man had poisoned it all. Retaining some ancient paternal right to continue making choices for the three of them.

Too chilled to weep, he pulled the damp towel tighter round himself and shuffled into the bedroom. Become her room now. Kneeling on the edge of the mattress, he dragged the duvet back, shrugged off the towel, and crept naked beneath the bedding, searching for remorse in anything remaindered of her in the sheets. Anything to warm.

He was now back on the side of the house over the barns. The dog was at last silenced. Lying there, listening to the birdsong receding as the night closed in, he crawled towards sleep.

… smeared with mud, too tired to wrench at the roots that clamping themselves round his suffocating throat, dragging him back from that stone slab of a door that offered opening to some hopefulness beyond, a slit of its light towards the hooded and shadowed woman he knew was beyond in that great cold space of the room. Again and again, he almost wrenched himself free, but fell back, failing, wanting to cry out from a throat parched of all but a whisper only he could hear and the feeble, bloodied blows of his knuckles against the cold rock…

Awake. At first, it was just the dog he heard, angry yelping barks ricocheting round the yard below. Then, the hammering at the door. He lay there, still stunned with sleep, his brain half-tangled into the roots of that dream again. It was still dark round the corners of the shutters.

He rolled over and planted his feet on the cold floor. Collecting his dressing gown, he went downstairs.

"O-kay! O-kay!" he shouted at the repeated blows below. Stopping them. He switched on the store room light and opened the door.

A suited man in the dimness, another behind him. "Madame Azéma?"

"Non."

He showed an identity card. His photo and the words *Juge d'Instruction* before it was flashed back into an inside pocket. "Mister Briggs? Yes?"

"Yes."

"Has Madame Azéma returned from Germany?"

"No. Not to here."

"Not to here? Where do you say she is?"

"I say nothing. I did not know she was in Germany. Only when you said."

"You know of Germany, Mister Briggs. We know. You have been there before." He waited for an answer, which Jim was too confused to realise was being requested. "May we come in? Please," the last said with an insistent matter-of-fact lack of courtesy.

He turned and led them wordlessly in. On the way up to the kitchen, one of them tripped on a tool. Jim stood against the stove to face them, passive to whatever would come next.

"Yes, Mister Briggs, Germany. You went before to the East. You stole a video cassette. And now that cassette has disappeared." Before he could be astonished at that, "You went into East Berlin with a man who is now a fugitive from Justice. We believe that your Gizande," sneeringly said, "may have been with him. Where is she now?"

"I do not know. I'm searching myself. Her mother has spoken to the police. She's missing."

"When did she leave?"

"I don't know," irritated by this man's persistent disbelief. "I have been away myself. I've been in England."

"You went on Wednesday, we believe. With an English friend."

Jim was startled that the man should know this.

The man replied to his surprise with, "Like the father, like the son. Why must your family always meddle in the politics of other countries?" Wagging his finger close enough to Jim's eyes to force him back against the edge of the stove, "I will warn you Mister Briggs, we will be watching you. If we find that you are concealing information from us, your English passport will not protect you. You understand?"

"What information? Gizande-? Madame Azéma? If I knew where she was, I wouldn't be here now."

The man stood back and nodded to his large, silent companion. "Remember, Mister Briggs. I ask you to remember what I say. No secrets. You understand?" He dipped his fingers into the breast pocket of his jacket and took out a small card. "Any information. Any information of any type, you will telephone my office."

Jim took it and read the Paris number on the card and *Palais de Justice.* He looked up at the man's now smile. As if only an amiable conversation had passed between them. "I will say goodbye," and he left the room, followed by the watchful, younger henchman. Clattering over the fallen tool again in the store room, before the door closed. Jim stood and listened to the car start and go. Leaving just the sound of the dog. And his shaken pondering at whatever had just happened.

He realised that when he had been searching through Gizande's documents for evidence of where she had gone, an envelope sometime ago from Anna had been sorted through his fingers. He went back to the bureau and found it. The headed notepaper had the address and phone number of her latest restaurant in Berlin. He went to the phone in the front room, but saw from the clock there that it was past three o'clock. The restaurant would be closed. He would have to wait till the following day.

His sleeping bag was still tumbled on the carpet from the previous night. Wrapping the dressing gown round his legs, he awkwardly climbed inside and rolled himself up on the sofa. But he was unable to sink now below the accumulated chaos of explanations and incomprehensions of the last two days. Among the fragmentations of another night's broken sleep, he tried to piece together what his father had said. The tape and the voice from the chair in the corridor, both bleeding into each other, so that he wanted to retrieve the tape, go back to the kitchen and turn on the player again. As if that would somehow separate fact from fiction. The truth from the man's lies he could now feel slithering over the inner surface of his skull… slimy trails of overfed slugs eating away at his innermost self… But he dare not get up to hear it over again, feeling it too much like an accusation of himself.

Outside the dog was quiet again and the last before sinking into an unsatisfactory torpid coma, had been the sound of a distant owl.

Chapter Twenty-nine

The morning he lay in the damp sleeping bag a long time before his weary rise. He had nothing to do till he phoned Anna's number and he guessed he might not get her at the restaurant before eleven. He was unsure about the time zones to Berlin, but guessed that would be at least midday here.

Whatever cleansing the evening before's bath had given him, was now fouled by the night. As he washed himself in an indifferent way, disgusted at the body he saw before him and what it had done, what it had been responsible for, he muttered on at the dead old man. Provoking, enticing him to reappear. Perhaps Jim felt more certain, surer in the questions he would challenge with. But maybe it was only the defeatedness that, whoever he was speaking to, the old man was dead. Escaped from his children's righteous and confused anger, years before. Unreachable now, unable to feel the flecks of spit from his son's fury on his face. Leaving the three of them behind, to negotiate their lives out of the tangle of dishonesties he had left them strung together with. To decide what truth to tell to each other. If, and how much, and when.

He sought out some clean clothes, but was confused what he might be dressing for. Another day up the mountain? A journey to wherever he might discover Gizande was? Or, remembering the threatening words of the night before, an interview in a magistrate's office?

He thought unexpectedly of Clara. He had not seen her yet. Had not kept his promise to pick her up last night, but was now doubtful of how he felt about the child. Evidence, as she was, of wrong, however innocent she would always be of it herself. She must never know. She must never know the truth.

Who knows now, apart from Gizande and himself? He sweated at the thought.

Her mother, certainly.

Gaillarde? No. Why should she be told?

That judge? He had seemed to know everything about his father, as well as him. Was he holding that back, to use for a later squeeze on Jim? For what?

He shook from his head the impossibilities of just how far he could speculate in those directions and returned to the child herself. Fondly, of her curly seriousness, and smiled. Whatever Gizande and he could broker out of the confusions they had been left with, there was one certainty. Clara must be protected.

With that intent clear, he started to tidy the house, then went out to check what he thought might be needed outside. He fed the dog, then went out to the field at the back. The cows looked as if they had been milked recently. That was always her job and he could only guess from the size of the udders. Had her mother or Gaillarde come up while he was on the mountain yesterday? They had said nothing. It would give him a pretext to revisit them later and this time see his daughter.

But only after the call to Anna.

He was answered quickly, in a couple of rings. There was the clash of pots and people in the background. And then, a voice near the phone, which he was sure was Anna's, called out to somebody.

"Anna?"

"Ja?" It was her voice, interrupted in her busyness.

"It's Jim. Jim Briggs."

"Ah. Jim." There was no smile in her voice. "One minute. I will take the call on another phone. Wait." An electronic piece of classical music chimed in, a few bars repeated several times, before she came on the line again, with no background noise this time.

"Jim. I was expecting you."

"Is Gizande there?"

"No. Yes. Where are you?"

"Why did you not phone me? I've been looking for her."

"She told me you were in England. I do not know where. I can not phone you."

"No. I'm back home. I must speak to her."

"Of course. Of course." There was a dismissiveness there.

"Can I speak to Gizande? I must speak to her."

"I think you must come, Jim." Now a tiredness, a resignation in her voice.

"What has happened? Tell me what has happened."

"What has happened? There are difficulties here. With the police."

"I know, Anna. I've had them here. A judge - a magistrate from Paris's been here. He said something about a fugitive from justice. Gizande" Then it struck him, "It's Andreas. Is she with Andreas?"

"Not now," she said quietly.

He was confused. Had someone else come into the room with her? And she could not speak? He was irate, at his impotence, the distance things were happening from him.

"She is no longer with Andreas now."

"What happened? When did she come there? How long has this been going on?"

"Jim," she cut in. "Jim!" silencing him. "You must come here. You-must come to Berlin."

How? he thought.

"You must come immediate, now. As quick as you can."

He would have to fly. He would collect the cheque from Theresa for the Birmingham job and buy as cheap a ticket as he could. "If I come, can you meet me at the airport, Anna?"

He sensed her reluctance. "Okay. Okay. You find when you arrive in Berlin and what airport. I will meet you."

"Is Gizande alright?"

"All right?" she reflected. "She is not in hospital. She is not in prison. Is that all right?"

He refused to answer that. Stopping short of any further explanation from her.

"You telephone me when you know the time you arrive. Okay?"

Taking his silence as the end of the conversation and ringing off.

The flight was from Toulouse, changing at Charles de Gaulle for Berlin. He tried to phone Anna, but someone else told him she was not there and phone later.

Soon after he put the phone down, there was a call from the yard, "Hola? Hola!"

Jim went down. It was Gaillarde, cycled up to milk the cows. He helped her drive the five cows from the field into the shed at the back of the barn where the milking machine was kept. As she expertly linked up the animals, he watched her, reminded of her mother. She looked up, gave him a smile and continued.

"When you have finished, I will take you home to your grandmother. After. Okay?"

He had seldom spoken to these step children. To Guillem, the angry brother, still living with his father, he had not seen or spoken to for near on three years. He had seen Gaillarde at her grandmother's house several times, but his visits there were always difficult and always to do with collecting Clara or Gizande.

The girl looked as her mother must once have and he caught himself sentimentally wondering how his life may have been different if he had met Gizande then, instead of Jane. The childishness of the thought, given what he knew now, must have clouded his face at the point when Gaillarde gave him another of her glances.

"Bien?" she asked.

Touched by her concern, he shook the cloud from him. "College aujourd'hui?"

"Non. No," reverting to English, knowing how poor the French was that this man spoke. "It is the examination. To prepare what we have been instructed. Yes?"

He wondered whether to explore what she knew about her mother's whereabouts, but backed away from a question. Berlin was enough, for the time being.

With Gaillarde finished, after she had unplugged the last cow, they drove them out again into the field. They bucketed water from the yard tap to the trough, then canned the milk and put it into the tiny room that served as a cold store.

It was done wordlessly until, after loading her bike into the van, he said, "Bien."

They both climbed in and drove off. Despite the wordlessness of the encounter, as he drove down to the mother's house, he was sure this girl- this young woman- could be an ally during the present difficulties. However little she knew. And smiled over at her, in recognition of this and she smiled in return. An understanding of sorts, he felt part of her family at least.

When he parked outside the mother's house, Gaillarde said to him, "Esclarmonde?" tilting her head. "You wish to visit her?"

Jim grinned broadly, his head cleared by this girl of all the adult and serious concerns that had crowded and clouded him. "Of course. Ma fille. Naturellement."

And she laughed, whether at his warmth or at his pronunciation, he didn't care. "She demands after you."

Demands? Clara speaks? "Quoi? Elle parles?"

Still smiling, but questioning, "Oui. Of course. For her father."

Jim stared at her and something of the power of his demonstrated feelings stole Gaillarde's smile and forced her to look away, embarrassed. But she made herself face him again, "Yes. Of course. Why will a child not ask after her father?"

He shook his head awake and climbed out of the van, the young woman also. By the time he had unloaded the bike, the mother was at the door, surly to see him, as ever.

"Clara?" Jim asked.

He was led through to the back room beyond the kitchen. The child looked up from her play and smiled. "Pa-pa." Spoken so confident and clear, that Jim stepped forward and swept her up into his arms, crushing her curls to the side of his face, her little arms reached chubbily round his neck.

"Clara…"

He held her there a long time, before kissing into the ringlets. Then turned to the two women in the doorway behind him, the old one serious, the young one behind her snickering her white teeth and nodding, her point proved. He would have included Gaillarde in the embrace too, but for the old woman. Whose eyes he now looked into and, at that moment, she knew what he knew. And was there the slightest suggestion there, that the burden was off her shoulders? That the voice on the tape had spoken now to all who needed to know.

He would have to explain what had to be done next. He looked at Gaillarde for support, before he launched his leaky boat of French. "Gizande est dans l'Allemagne. Dans Berlin. Je veux aller a Berlin… pour retourne…" He ran aground and turned to the girl, "To bring your mother home. To bring Gizande home."

The old woman was nodding, understood without translation.

"Clara restes ici?" he continued. "Deux ou trois jours?"

It was Gaillarde who was troubled at what he said. "Why my mother in Berlin?"

Aware, at the corner of his eye, that Clara was listening to him as attentively as the adults, he invented the formula, "She is visiting friends."

But it was not enough for the young woman. So he added, "She will return with me. I promise." And he held Clara away from him to look at her and include her in the pledge.

Chapter Thirty

Jim remained to play with Clara for an hour. Until he overstayed his welcome with the mother. He went back to Gizande's. As he would have to leave the van at Toulouse airport, he effected a temporary repair on the broken quarter light, using some transparent plastic and tape. Cleaning out the vehicle, he found the paper bag with Jude's knickers in it. They felt stale, sharpening the shame he now felt for the selfish self-pity that had led him to that. Yet he did wonder whether to phone Deedee, just for the company… but he recognised that the worm of sexual opportunism was curled within that consideration, knowing that Deedee would probably be alone but for the kids, with Jude not yet returned from the UK. And anyway, he was far too tired. But he could not decide to throw the knickers away, so he stuffed the bag back where he found it.

Inside, he tried again Anna's number. She was there this time, but evidently busy, so he just briefly gave her the details of his arrival and she brusquely confirmed that she would pick him up. He phoned Theresa and she agreed to pay him in cash. He would pick that up the following morning before setting off to Toulouse. Then he returned to her bed. Very slowly, with numb fingers, unlaced his boots and took his trousers off. It was still mid afternoon, but he slid away beneath the duvet.

He dreamt of Francis, the meeting this time in an ambiguity of places. Now across a conference room table, then in a small, cheaply furnished office, even in a white-tiled cell like the one in East Germany. Sometimes the conversation was reasonable, almost pedantic in consideration of details. At other times, they became angry with each other, passionately dismissive of a rationalisation or a sniff of half a dishonesty. It was less the words spoken he remembered when he woke, more the mood or the setting of their speaking. Only the broken shards, unable to be fully pieced together again, could be recollected of the conversation. Somehow phrased with a wisdom the voice outside the bathroom door had not had, but just as cynical. Just as arrogantly certain of his own record.

…War lets us loose on each other and on ourselves, so it can tie us up. If we live long enough. War opens a moral trapdoor through which all of us may drop. To end up swinging on the end of a rope woven from our own doings… One man from the Foreign Office they parachuted in early forty four, told me, You have to work with disagreeable people against even more ghastly people. How very English ruling classes that was!

But who were the ghastly for you? And who were the disagreeable? The Nazis? Or the communists?

Francis smiled, What would you say? Given what we know now about the Gulag?

And Auschwitz.?…

Remorse changes nothing, it is useless. Who would it help, after the events?

But without it, can your victims ever forgive you?…

Francis mused about hiding OAS men on the run in the sixties, With Algeria, it was difficult to know who your masters were. We knew there was oil there and did we want to give it away, to the arabs? DeGaulle was selling out France's future… You can never leave you know. It was easy for the French to let a foreigner carry the blame, for all the mess of the war, for the corruption and the collaboration that they endured, did to each other, during those years. They trap you there. They won't ever let you give up. When I finally finished, after the Algerian business, they fed little morsels of information to people in the communities round here. It turned me from being the hero I had been seen as, into some sort of collaborationist traitor... Was it all worth it, the cost? I don't know. Only you can say. And Suzanne… and of course Gizande. And maybe Constancia could have said.

But Elizabeth, Gizande's mother, that wasn't political, that was just greed for a girl's body.

Defensive at this, Francis snapped, How do you know? It was love.

How can you say that when you did nothing to keep her, you let her go from your life, just like that, Gizande's mother.

Ha! You're as hypocritical as old man Casals about it! It was alright for him to take a juicy young musician for a wife a few years later, when he married Marta, a girl who played the cello without the feeling of my Elizabeth, and he went off to Puerto Rico to become the guest of Presidents. But for me, it was some form of sexual crime. Remember, James, it was me that saved Gizande's life. I stopped the abortion… Perhaps, James, we're more alike than even you think, or than you would like to believe. You say you were political, in your different way. What were the costs for your family? What were the costs for your daughter, the English one? Then, how would the world look without people like us, Jim? How would it look?…

The cruelty behind Francis's charm reminded him… Own charm? Jim's success with women won by the charm of his own vulnerability. The sadness that made him gentle, as Jude had put it. Was it that had enticed a series of younger women to mother Jim?…

It was night when he reopened his eyes. There was no clock in the room. The small travel alarm she usually kept beside her bed, he noticed was gone. But he knew from the relaxation of his limbs, spread apart beneath the bedding, that he had slept well. He felt his penis sluggishly aroused and rubbed it a few times reassuringly. How pleasant it would be to have Gizande beside him again, sharing the bed. He was doubtful that she would ever let that happen again. Or indeed, if it was right that it ever should. He speculated what life would be like with her back here. Would it only be her tolerated truce, with him permanently sleeping apart from her? Moving out to La Retrait? Or would the truth now shared between them demolish the wall? Whatever the tape had said, she would never be his sister- not how he felt now, holding himself beneath the bedding, thinking of the good times with her…

Until uninvited disgust seeped in on him. He took his hand away from himself… but then replaced it, thinking of Deedee… and women before that… he stroked himself up and down a few exploratory times, seeking the flaccid release of even a half-hearted ejaculation. But he could not do it. Not here. Not in this bed, bringing the memories of other bodies here, without her permission. So he rolled over and crushed the life out of it beneath the weight of his body, looking across longingly for her, at the empty pillow next to him. Waiting to see her as she had once been, tomorrow.

The flights were harassing. The plane to Berlin was late boarding, so he had to spend an extra hour in the crowded departure lounge at Charles de Gaulle. His nerves were exhausted from what had happened in the last few days and from what to expect when he landed. Anna's unwelcoming tone had made him feel discouragingly alone.

As he came out through the arrival gates, her smile to him was brief and perfunctory. Without the embrace she would once have offered, she led him straight off towards the car parks.

"Before you ask me, Jim, Gizi has said she will come to my flat this evening. To speak with you." Gizi. The old Berlin nickname that so trivialised the serious woman he had fallen for. Only come to speak with him? For the first time, his assumptions that they would be returning to France together sounded fragile. He said nothing, but followed Anna's clacking high heels on the marble, through the crowds, wondering if the single change of clothing he carried in his holdall would be enough.

Anna's flat was out in a leafy suburb to the west of the city, near a lake. It was furnished to impress rather than for comfort. There were modern paintings on the walls. Large, expensive books on art and cookery on the shelves, or stacked precisely on the tables.

"Coffee?" she offered, but with an automatic courtesy that made him want to refuse. He knew that if he did, she might be off and leave him here. They had not spoken in the car while she drove here irritatedly through the city's late afternoon traffic.

"When will Gizande come?"

"She says at eight o'clock. I will have to leave you here. I must work. Back in the restaurant. She will come and ring the bell- the buzzer. You see?" She led him over to a silver keyboard on the wall near the entrance door. "Her voice will speak through here. Then you will press the number buttons. Zero, five, seven, five. You remember that? Then Gizi may enter the building and she will come up on the lift." She walked back to the centre of the room, uncomfortable with him here. "We must have such security now on our homes in Berlin. Because of all the Poles and Russians here now. The tramps and the mafia." But it was said idly, a commonplace often repeated. "You will make yourself comfortable while you wait."

She said something in German, then, "A message on the telephone."

She pressed the button and he immediately recognised Gizande's voice saying, "Anna," then continuing in German, even though he could recognise the defensive anxiety in her voice.

When it ended, he asked, "What did she say?"

Anna was impatient, "It was Gizi. She now says she will not meet you here. Because she wishes not to be alone with you. She says now she will come to the restaurant. At eight. When I am at my most busy." She shrugged.

He felt required to apologise, but said nothing. She resentfully pondered him. She must have seen the troubled confusion in his eyes. Gizande did not want to see him alone?

"There. That is why," she said emphatically, as if the whole story had been explained and laid before the incoherent Jim. "I do not have the time for these problems of you and Gizi."

He was slumped inside himself, with nowhere to go with his questions. For the briefest instant he thought of asking Anna to take him straight back to the airport. To fly away from all this tumbling ambiguity. To avoid whatever confrontation tonight would bring with Gizande.

Anna finished staring at the man for the tiresome situation he had brought her, turned away, swept up her handbag and said, "I must return to my restaurant. You must come with me."

Jim stood up and picked up his holdall.

She said, "You leave your bag here. Do not take it to the restaurant."

It was another wordless drive with her back across the city. Despite his sullen inwardness, he noticed the huge construction sites of Berlin rebirthing itself as the centre of Germany again, perhaps of Europe. Anna's restaurant was now in the East in a street off the old heart of the city, across the gap left by the demolition of the Wall, the shadows of its towers and kilometres of barbed wire fences already gone. A surviving statue of Lenin still stood across from the restaurant, gesturing a hand towards the first floor windows, towards the west. Anna's place below the *3 Ls* sign was shiny, modern and smart, alien to Jim. He followed her inside. Staff were busy laying tables for the start of evening meals. She was transformed as she entered, the hard smile on her face, issuing instructions, checking with questions, as she swept through to the back, with Jim in her wake.

They were in the short corridor to the kitchen before he stopped himself. "Anna."

"Oh yes," remembering he was with her.

"There is still well over two hours till I meet Gizi," catching himself using the clipped alias. "I will come back."

She looked at him critically, making him aware of his out-of-place scruffiness. "Have you any Deutschmarks?"

He hadn't. "No."

"There is a wechsel in the main street. Go out and to the right." Clearly a solution to have him out of her footsteps.

Out in the street, it was busy, probably mostly with workers going home. He had so little to do with cities in the last few years, he found it difficult to read the signs. That people should be dressed so smartly for going to work. It had been a long time since his own work-life had been more important than home life. Since he had last suited himself up for it. Apart from overalls or jeans for a particularly dirty job, he dressed as now. Comfortable and out of place here.

He found the wechsel and coming out, wondered what to do with his money. He wandered over and looked through the grille round a building site, watching the men at work in the deep pit, pouring concrete for the foundations. Of the new Germany? Trying to get a purchase in the broken floors of the exhausted cities beneath with these concrete sheathed threads of steel. Building out of the wreckage of all the Berlins before. He remembered Anna's complaints in 1990 about the effects of the fall of the Wall. But she seemed to be doing well enough out of it now. It was like the whole world was moving on apace, except him. Was it just his age? He wished himself back with Clara. And turned away from all this.

He moved on through the new shops and offices bronzing in the early evening sun. Nothing interested him here. He could only think of what Gizande would be like. Within an hour he was back in the street of Anna's restaurant. He sat on the edge of Lenin's plinth, keeping the graffitied, sculptured trousers of the leader between him and the restaurant's front window.

He hoped she might turn up early- very early. But sat thinking about her here just made him feel defeated. So he set off to walk briskly round several of the neighbouring blocks. Head down, as if he had somewhere to go, he kept up an urgent pace, the exercise itself beginning to pump his lungs and refresh his brain just with the simplicity of doing it. Back past the restaurant in twenty minutes and with the briefest of glances in the front window, seeing some of the tables now occupied, he set off immediately on the circuit again. Timing himself to do it even quicker. The third circuit he was not far short of running it and he noticed a man in a kiosk selling newspapers and cigarettes look strangely at him. This time Jim just smiled back, a little manic. After that one he stood panting, leaning up against Lenin, recovering himself, before he went in.

A waiter came up to him.

"Anna?" Jim requested.

The waiter looked questioning.

"Anna. The boss," pointing to the rear door to the kitchen.

He followed the man and stood near the doorway, waiting for Anna to be brought back.

"You are too early. It is half of an hour before she comes."

Jim shrugged, "I will wait."

Anna looked at him, "Will you eat?"

He thought he could never afford the food at a place like this. There was a small bar at the back, with stools. It was the only thing here that reminded him of Foodi, her old bohemian café in the West. "No. I will drink."

She shrugged back at him, "Okay."

He ordered a tall beer from the barman and it was even more expensive than he could have guessed. But he could take a long time sipping it down.

Chapter Thirty-one

When Gizande arrived, she stood there in the doorway, looking round for him. Before she caught sight of him, he was astonished. She looked thin and ill. He could not believe that she had changed so much in just a few days. But then, he thought, it might have been what she was wearing. He had not seen her in anything like the leather miniskirt and the skimpy top for years, revealing how her slight body now seemed frail. Somehow unloved, in the sluttish way she appeared. She crossed the room to him. High heels and mascara as well.

With, "Hi," she sat down on the barstool beside him and looked away to the bartender to order her drink. She pulled a packet of cigarettes from the little handbag she had and lit one, still looked away, waiting for the drink. Smoking? Had she ever? he thought, but said nothing. Was it a stranger, or was it a performance? He sipped his beer until her drink returned, some strange cocktail thing.

She had her lips to her drink when he said, "I know. I found the tape," surprised at himself for saying it.

Taking the glass away from her mouth, she carefully and precisely placed it on the shiny bartop and looked down, the skin on her face as chilled as the lumps of ice floating before her. It was a long silence, enough for him to conjecture whether the muteness he had always taken to be her meditative wisdom, had actually always been fear of sharing what was inside her. With the matter-of-factness of a long anticipated defeat, she finally said, "I was not able to escape you. And your father."

Your father, he thought- our father. "Escape to Andreas?" he said, but it sounded aggressive, so he added, "I had worked it out. Before Anna told me." It was all the wrong thing to say, but this frigid, skinny doll beside him would not tolerate the embracing arm he wanted to extend, he knew. With no other customers, the barman was looking on at them from the other end of the bar.

"So. You know," still speaking down to her glass.

"Why didn't you want me to see you alone?"

Her eyes flicked once at him with menace, then away. "You know the reason."

"Why? Are you frightened of me?"

"Should I not be?" said flatly.

He thought of the rape. "I did not know then. You waved the knife at me. I was the one who should have-"

She cut across the feeble pleading with, "I should have used the knife. Why did I not?" looking away again.

He retreated to his beer, before coming back softly with, "We have a child, Gizande."

She examined his face with her eyes glittering both with restrained tears and with unleashed venom, "Ah, yes. The poison you put into my body. Did you not know then what you were doing, Jim?"

"How could I? You knew before me… about the tape. You heard it before me. And never told me."

"How do you tell such a thing?" Adding with spiteful whispered contempt, "To your brother," stated at last. A drink, then, "Why have you come here?" she asked bitterly.

"You asked me. Because you wanted to meet here and not at the flat. Why have you come?"

"No," she said. "My meaning- why have you come to Berlin?"

Astonished at the question and unsure of the answer, he could only finally say, "For you." Waiting, before he asked, "Why did you come? To Berlin?"

Underneath the brittleness of the surface she had built around herself in the last two years - perhaps even longer- he could see throbbing in the vein on her temple, the turbulent torrents of all the poisons she felt herself being destroyed by. He wanted to be gentle and strong to her, but not combative. He sat on in the silence between them, impotent at how to achieve that.

Finally, he murmured, almost fearfully, "You should come home."

Eyes fixed ahead at the shelves and bottles behind the bar, she said, "Home?," bleakly. "What is home?"

"Home is family," but he immediately regretted having said it.

She turned her embittered eyes upon him. "Family? Oh, yes. You are. You lock me in the chains of your family two times. Brother and… Two times your prisoner, yes?"

"There is-" and he stared away from mentioning Clara. "Gaillarde. And your mother. They want you home."

"My mother? The mother that knew what I was doing- with you. And she was too frightened to tell me… only when too late."

He thought of the sour face in the doorway, with Gaillarde's bright smile over its shoulder. "She can't help it. She loves Clara. Just as Gaillarde does. And Suzanne."

"Have you told Suzanne?"

"No. Of course not. She's very depressed about the gulags- those Russians who say her house is theirs."

Gizande shook her head, looking away again. Another crippled limb of this ghastly mess, too tangled for her to contemplate.

"Only your mother knows." As if keeping the cabal of secrecy between just the three of them would be as satisfactory as the denial of what had happened. Then the thought, looking round, before he whispered to Gizande, "Does Anna?"

"No."

He waited. Another long time, looking at his beer without touching it. Before he asked, "Will you - do you plan to stay in Berlin?" With Andreas.

She spoke with a quietness, not to Jim, but to some friend, a confidante only she could see in the mirror behind the bar. "It is finished here. Also, what could I do here? Anna does not wish me. C'est fini. Am Ende." Before she re-awoke to him beside her and turned, sarcastic, "What would you have me do here? Wash the plates for Anna in this place?"

So powerfully did he want touch her then, that he started to reach out. But she locked her bare, thin arm to her side and shrank away on the stool. Jim said, "I did not do it. I did nothing. I never knew till two days ago- listening to the tape."

She could no longer look at him again because of the feelings between them. "It has been done, Jim," his name for the first time. "You did it. If you knew what you did, is not important. You did it."

Two noisy young men took the stools at the bar next to him. The restaurant was beginning to fill now. Two couples were waiting by the entrance for waiters to direct them to spaces amongst the crowded tables. The increasing clatter meant he had to speak louder. "What about Clara?" he said at last, believing them protected from her most savage possible replies by the strangers now close about them.

"Clara?" she whispered, Jim leaning towards her to hear. "I cannot… I should not… she should not be alive," the last word almost strangulated by her withdrawal back inside the diseased redoubt she had built for herself.

"Look. We can't talk here," looking round him to demonstrate to her their lack of privacy. "Shall we walk? And talk that way."

"What can we talk of? There is nothing to talk of."

"We must decide about Clara. About Esclarmonde," offering her the name she had finally and reluctantly chosen.

"What decide?" she asked without a challenge- only surrender. "You decide. She is your child. You say so."

"No, Gizande," finding a little strength at last, probably from her weakness. "You are her mother. I am her father. She is our child." He took a long drink from the beer and planted it back emphatically on the bartop. “Come on. We’ll walk,” stepping off the stool and standing over her.

Sudden uncertainty at his gesture flickered in her eyes.

“We will walk. I’ll do nothing to you on the streets. Come on, Gizande.”

She hesitated. So he reached his arm out to her again, this time decisively, but stopping just short of touch. Rather than accept any offer of assistance from his proffered flesh, she slid off the other side of the stool, the leather of her skirt squeaking against the plastic.

Anna watched them as they crossed to the doorway and Jim swapped a mechanical smile with her, across the noise of the customers. At the entrance, he stood back, letting Gizande pass through untouched. Outside the twilight was barely detectable beyond the electric glitter of the city’s streets.

It was cool, so he offered, “Want my jacket?”

When she shook her head, he set them off on the circuit he had walked earlier, but at a quieter pace. The walking allowed them to face each street ahead separately, though together. Jim waited until they had turned off the main shopping boulevard, at the corner where the newspaper kiosk was now closed, before he spoke. “So it’s over with Andreas?”

She did not answer. But it was an affirmation.

“Where are you staying?”

She looked across at him. Then away, still not answering.

“Is it far away?”

She shook her head.

“Can we go there now? To get your things?” Explaining, “You must go back to Anna’s tonight. Then, tomorrow, we can return,” letting the unspoken word, home, fall between the click of her heels on the pavement.

“No. Not to Anna,” she said quietly.

“Where, then? You must-” rephrasing it, “You need to leave this place, now, Gizande.”

They walked on for a long time after this and had turned into another busy street, back towards the restaurant.

“What did you want tonight, Gizande? Why did you agree to meet me?”

She walked on, so determinedly locked away from him that finally, he stopped. And reached out, pulling her to a stop by the cold skin of her arm. She half-heartedly twisted it away, but he held on.

“What did you want to happen tonight, Gizande? Did you expect me to leave your life completely? And Clara? And your family? Gaillarde?”

She looked at him, the livid green light from a shop beside them etching the gaunt bones of her face. She then panicked and shook her eyes from him, now thrashing her arm away- as if the rape again.

"What did you expect me to say?" he repeated through gritted teeth.

A couple of bypassers looked at the raised foreign voice, glanced at the cheap-looking woman he was holding and hurried on.

"Look at you, Gizande," but the name spoken chopped itself down to the Gizi he saw before him, sullen and rebellious, the child of the woman he had loved. He reached his hand out to her other arm. To still her. "You're cold. Go. Please. Take my jacket." He was sure she was about to cry. In fact, he wanted her to, certain at that moment how paper-thin was the surface of her self-control. But she held back from the tears.

Letting go of both her arms, he started to slip the jacket off, but she shook her head. He shrugged it back onto his shoulders. Leaving them stood across from each other, deadlocked in the silent recognition that they only had each other left. As well as the child, a thousand miles away, waiting for them to take her home.

"Where will you go tomorrow?" Offering her, "Will you come with me?"

"Where will you take me, Jim?" It was softly spoken, but quivered with an almost inaudible wail twisted into his name. "Will you take me away from the police, also?"

He remembered his own short interview two nights ago.

She flapped her hand dismissively at him and started to walk away again. He took after her. "What do they want? To sign my name at the bottom of a page of lies? What do the police always want." She stopped again and confronted him, "You ask them," sweeping a pointed finger round at the passing crowds. "One will be him- a policeman. They know how to do this. Even in this New Germany," said with derision, "they will find an Ossi who learned how to spy on his friends. They will find an Ossi who is without a job and they will pay him a few pfennigs to follow me." She looked again, bitterly, at the crowd of passers. "Which one is it, Jim? Do you recognise him?"

"But why?" He was uncertain between what he knew and the crazed difference this woman had become. "Is it true?" affirming his disbelief.

"Ah. So Anna has not told you?"

"Told me what?"

"About Andreas. You said you knew about Andreas," sneering at him.

"Only that you've met him here. How long's this been going on? When did you arrange to meet?" the questions leading him into uncomfortable areas of imagination.

She blew her cheeks up and let the air seep out of them in a strangely childish gesture of boredom. "Names, places and dates, Jim? And shall I put my name at the end of the page for you also?"

"Where is Andreas now? Is that where you have been staying?"

Nothing. But she turned to walk on, leaving him to draw his own conclusions.

They were back outside the restaurant. What now? He felt the moment between them fragile enough for it to happen either way. With maybe this delicate leaf of a body before him blown away from him for ever. "You say," he started reluctantly. "You say how you want it to be… when we get back home. I will do nothing that," his mouth stumbled over trying to say it. Then said exactly what he feared, "I will do nothing you don't want me to. I'll even live in La Retrait, if you ask. But Clara must have us both. I will… I will keep my promises… Gizande."

She looked up at him and, despite her face being in the shadow of Lenin, for a brief moment he thought she had recognised the hurt it had cost him also. But she neatly tidied it away, "You will keep your promises? It is me that will have the piece of paper with your name at the bottom. La pacte," she laughed mirthlessly.

"Shall we go in?" He indicated the restaurant behind her.

"Pourquoi?"

"Do we have anywhere else to go?"

"No. I do not wish to pass the night watching Anna smiling to please her rich clients."

But he knew they had turned a corner. And it was for him to say that she knew there was only Jim. All the better options, whatever they had been, had been swept away from her. "Gizande," the warmth he felt for this woman croaking in his throat. With the sympathy he felt for her- for the both of them. And the anxiety that even now, the moment could be lost. "Let's go and collect your things. You said it's not too far. We'll get a taxi."

"Where is your van?" starting as a joke, but she thought better of. "Okay. Collect my things. Then?"

"I will ask Anna for the key to her flat. Tomorrow, we'll see the police together. Then we'll go home. To France."

"If the police…" but shrugged.

He went into the restaurant and found Anna had joined the barman, to help with the drinks. Jim leaned over, "Can I have your key, Anna?"

The man next to him, obviously a regular who knew Anna, crowed with mock salaciousness, "I also, Anna! I, also! Can I have your key?" and several people along the bar laughed.

She smiled at them, but not at Jim.

"I'm collecting Gizande's things. We'll go back to your flat after. And tomorrow, I'll- we will clear things up and go home."

She looked at him, then went off. She returned and firmly planted the key in his palm with, "One night only."

As Jim left, the man at the bar crowed again, "A key for me, Anna! And I will stay for one night only, also!"

Outside, Gizande was stood exactly where he had left her, her shoulders towards the restaurant window. Back in the main street, she called a taxi.

The place they went to had once been an office. Grand, nineteenth century commerce. As she led him up the main staircase, still ceramic tiled, it was a place where two worlds had collided. On the brightly lit lower floors, the uniform had become polished pale wood doors, with modern brass fittings and spyholes. As they climbed into the ill-lit the upper storeys, the old doors of the offices had survived, not yet replaced. Chipped and stained, some retaining the small tarnished metal frames for nameplates, long since gone. The floors were scuffed and scarred. There were clusters of posters along these upper corridors, advertising rock concerts and demonstrations. The taxi journey had disoriented Jim and he was not sure whether he was in the old East or the West of the city.

They reached the door she had the key for. The uncurtained apartment windows looked across the city. The television tower by Alexanderplatz was there, perhaps a couple of kilometres away, but still drawing him up to the window to see its full height. There were gaps on the bookshelves and, where a computer had been there were only the connectors at the end of a tangle of wires.

She had disappeared into another room and he followed her. She was packing. He wondered if she had applied the same hurried anxiety to the task at home, when she had packed to leave then. He felt intrusive there, pain at the meaning of the empty room and its bed. He wandered back to what was left on the shelves. Definitely Andreas, he thought. Despite the German, he could see titles about Hitler, about Paris '68, Engels. Kommunismus, Sozialismus, Faschismus. So predictable. He felt tired with it. He could no longer offer the passionate certainties on these shelves. That had long gone for him, years before the felling of any Walls. Leaflets crumpled up in the hands of workers passing through factory gates to get at the money for their mortgages.

She was behind him, the case in one hand, trivial little handbag in the other, the boniness of her shoulders and her ribs shown through the blouse by the light from the bedroom behind. He was unspoken as he went forward and reached for the skin above her collar bone. She let him touch it, only the fingertips, briefly. Before, "We go."

Outside, the taxi they had asked to wait, had gone. And it was a long walk to a street where another could be found. He took the case from her and she accepted his oversized jacket draped around her narrowed shoulders.

Chapter Thirty-two

He was awoken from the sofa by Anna coming in. Confused, he looked around for Gizande, but she was in the spare room. He had gone in twice to see her. The last time she had thrashed her blanket off and he was grateful for the chance to re-cover her.

"A good evening?" he asked Anna.

"Noise," she said. "And too many young people, with too much alcohol to drink."

"She's asleep," he said, as if he had been asked about the woman next door.

"Ah-ha," she answered, not looking up from the sheaf of letters she was sorting through from the small table next to the door.

On sitting up, if that would get her attention, he said, "I'm going to the police. Then we'll get a flight home- if they let us."

"Who? The police? They will permit her to go now. They have Andreas. Gizi thinks she is important. It is her drama. They have Andreas. They will let you go." All this said with her eyes still down to the letter in her fingers. She looked up at him finally, "I make a chocolate drink. Do you wish one, also?"

He nodded and followed her into the kitchen. "What's it all been about, Anna?"

"Gizi? And Andreas?" She hissed out between her teeth. "Nobody tells Jim. Huh," and grunted. "It is Gizi and Andreas, as it has always been. You saw it when you were here before. Her dangerous lover," said with the briefest sneer. "When things become difficult in the farm, the little country girl runs away to the city. What has she said to you?" The kettle having boiled, she could shrug him off and attend to stirring the hot water into the two mugs. Placing his on the table between them. "She does not want a small child."

"She wanted it! You knew how happy she was expecting it, when we came to Berlin for the marathon."

Anna shrugged again, "She wants it. She does not want it."

No further to go with her with that, "Andreas? What sort of trouble is he in?"

"Andreas plays games with people's lives. It was fun once, when Gizi was here first- the student fresh from Paris in 68… the demonstrations, the happenings. We were all making a joke on the streets- of the big capitalists. But most of us grew up - even Gizi returned to France when things started to become dangerous. She returned for her bad marriage to Yves." He waited for her to continue. She blew steam from the surface of her drink and walked to the kitchen window. "But Andreas stayed with the groups. He continued. We were his old friends and we did not really know what he was doing. He was with more dangerous people. The police say with Palestinians. And the Rote Armee Fraktion, the Baader-Meinhof people. There is accusation that he was in Munich in 1972. He was something with the Black September- when the Jewish athletes were killed. Perhaps we suspected some of this. But Gizi had gone then. I did not know. None of us knew, until she returned with you in '89, that she had kept communication with Andreas, over so many years."

Although not entirely unpredictable, Jim felt stunned by this, just as Anna turned and saw it in his face, simply saying, "Yes," from her distance. "Andreas was excitement. She had young children and talking to Andreas on the telephone, writing letters to him, was adventure for her. I think, also, it was the same with you."

He looked back at the measurement her eyes were making of him.

"You were to be a new adventure, Jim. You came with your stories of-" She searched for the word, "Kreuzzug? Crusade? Yes- for the prostitute boys. She sent me a letter about you. When the adventure took you to the DDR, she came with you. And after that, she was in love with you. You became lovers after then- am I correct?"

He nodded.

"But you no more want adventures, do you, Jim? You wish to be a father. You wish to learn as a farmer. Maybe, that is Gizi's disappointment. Andreas has known, since the fall of the Wall, that the police would be interested in him. He knew what was in the files of the DDR. He says the Stasi never paid him. Perhaps it is true. The Stasi put the weapons into the back of his car, that he took into the West- for Baader-Meinhof, that is true. You know nothing, Jim. You will not know that Andreas came to France in the summer? He visited Gizi. He was arrested by the French Police and returned to Germany. You understand that the Stasi had destroyed the files with shredding, about Andreas and the others from the West who worked with the East. We Germans can be a very patient people. Particular, we love our documents. Perhaps it is only a German folk tale, but in Bavaria, they say there is a house of women where all the plastic bags of documents that have been shredded by the Stasi are being put together again. Now, there is a job for the German women!" She smiled bitterly at the thought, "It is always the German women. After the war, they clean the bricks from the ruins for the building again of the cities. After the Wall, now perhaps they must join together the documents with glue to build again our true history from the little pieces of broken paper.

Every strip of the paper is matched to the next- the millions of little pieces of the paper put together again. To put together again the evidence. They say that is how the police arrested him. By then," she sighed, "there was only silly little Gizi left who thought Andreas was a hero. So he called her, and she came."

"What will happen now?" he asked, almost mechanically.

"He will be in prison. He tried to leave the country, so he will be in prison until his trial. They have the evidence. He will be in prison for many years. There is an appetite now in Germany for imprisoning the Stasi and their friends. He will find it difficult for any witnesses for him. Most of them are in prison or dead, who were, at that time, his comrades," a sarcastic knot tied in the last word.

"Will they let her go? Tomorrow?"

"She has done nothing. But make a fool of herself. She was not in Germany when the crimes were done."

"The French police want her," he blurted. "They came and spoke to me. That was how I knew she had come to Germany - to Berlin."

"I cannot know what the French will do, but I think it is over for her in Germany."

Absurdly, inside Jim's head, popped up the comic line, For you, Gizi, the war is over, but he puckered his mouth against it.

"So," she said directly to him. "You must go tomorrow. I do not want Gizi here in my home. I do not want the politics to interfere with my business." She drank the last from her mug. "Okay?" and went to the sink to rinse it.

He realised his had been barely drunk. "Yeah. Sure."

"I will not be awake early in the morning. Be silent, as you leave, yes?"

He nodded and she left the room, leaving him to finish the tepid chocolate.

It was seven-thirty when he went into the spare room. Gizande was lying awake, watching him cross towards her. He hesitated whether to sit on the bed edge, but decided to do it without her permission.

"When do you have to go to the police?" he asked.

"In this morning."

"What time? Where is it?"

"I know. We will take a taxi."

"Anna says she thinks there will be no problems."

"Huh! What does Anna know? She feeds police officers and politicians in her restaurant. She thinks that after the Wall, it is all democracy, democracy, democracy."

He shook his head of this and stood up. "Gizande, we must get ready. Anna asked us to be quiet, because she's sleeping. She was late from work."

"You spoke with her?" accusingly.

"We spoke. She woke me up when she came in. I'll use the bathroom first. Then I'll call you."

Afterwards, while she was in the bathroom, he wrote Anna a note.

Thanks for the help. Sorry about the trouble that we've caused. He remembered that the French Police had asked about. *The video of the boys that I stole from Billy Finch's office. Do you remember it? If you still have it, destroy it.* He knew now that he would have to leave Damien, Finch and all those children. He would send off all his documents and files to Julian to be used however he wished in helping Scadding. That little man would never have welcomed Jim as a witness anyway. He would have to give what care she would allow to Gizande. And Clara. He signed off with, *Please keep in contact with the crazy English amateur who's got himself tied up in all of this, love, Jim.* He would like to leave a touch of warmth with that hard woman Anna had become.

The taxi took them back across the city. In the police station, he was allowed to enter the interview room with Gizande only after an explanation. She was right. They did want her to put her name at the bottom of a piece of paper. She read it, looked up with one more defiant glance at the uniformed officer, before signing it.

She stood up and the policeman unexpectedly came across and shook Jim's hand.

Outside on the street, he asked her, "What did you sign? What did it say?"

"I signed to say the dates I was in Germany, living with Andreas. And the dates that I was living back in France."

"Is that all?"

"It is enough for them. It proves that I was not with Andreas at the time of the crimes they say he has." She swung away from him and walked a few uncertain paces up the street.

He took her by the shoulders and pulled her back to him, into his embrace. Unresponsively, she let him wrap himself round her and they stood there in the middle of the pavement for a moment, held together, her barely breathing detectable, the furied clatter of the city sweeping round them.

He disengaged. "Let's see if we can get some plane tickets back home."

With her signature on the police statement, Gizande's anger had gone. In the taxi to the airport, the queue for tickets, and at Departures, in the waiting lounge and on the two flights back to Toulouse, she said nothing. And he asked nothing of her. He was guiding her home. As soon as they reached the van in the Toulouse airport car park that evening, he put their baggage in the back, unlocked her door for her and went round to climb in. He looked over at her to see if it was worth offering a smile now. She was turned away, looking blindly out, her head at rest against the window. He saw she had dropped the cigarette packet into the glove compartment. It was resting on the paper bag. With Jude's knickers in it. Nothing he could do about it, but watch nervously each time she reached for another cigarette during that drive back to her farm.

Where the dog yelped and snuffled with pleasure, knowing his mistress was back home, even before she got out of the van. While he unloaded the bags, he could hear her quieten the dog with her affectionate murmur. He decided against disposing of the brown paper bag, as he might be visible in the cab light. He would do that later. He unlocked into the house and followed her through to the kitchen, watching from the doorway as she drifted round the circumference of the big central table, trailing a fingertip along its edge. A re-measurement of a place she had been long and far away from. Only when the circuit of the room brought her back face-to-face with Jim, did she lift her eyes deep from where they had been and look at him. Although only an instant, he smelt the stale smoke on her breath, before she switched away her eyes in panic. Awake to where she was, and who was with her.

"I'll sleep down stairs," he offered quickly, to reassure. He wondered whether to offer to move to La Retrait as soon as possible, but thought better of saying anything.

By the time she had already left the room, deadened by her response to coming home, the denial of any possible welcome except for the dog, he was also exhausted by the long hours of travel next to the silent woman. He listened to her feet and followed the sound of them across the floors upstairs. From her bedroom to bathroom. Then, had he heard a few steps up the corridor to Clara's room? Before finally back to the bathroom.

He dropped his bag on the sofa, next to the crumpled sleeping bag, before slowly going upstairs with her case. As he reached the top, the bolt inside the bathroom door snapped sharply shut. Leaving her case on the bed, he returned downstairs to try to sleep. Listening, he was alert to her back in the house. He heard her cross for the toilet some time in the early hours, imagining her bare legs tucked beneath her, as she sat there. As she had in the early days living with him, so naturally and without self-consciousness, sharing that bathroom as he bathed or shaved. This night, those upstairs rooms were a forbidden zone.

Chapter Thirty-three

He left early in the morning to collect Clara, leaving Gizande upstairs, as awake as he had been, he speculated. Leaving her there to avoid whatever confrontation might blow between her and her mother. He had thought better of leaving her a note of explanation, shying away from the temptation of too many difficult words

When the old woman opened the door to him, he spoke his rehearsed phrase to her, "Gizande a retourné. Avec moi." Then, her eyes still examining him, "Je veux recherché Clara." Seeking a response from her with a final, "Oui?"

Denying him even a nod of assent, he followed her through into the house.

Clara was joyed to see him. She clung to him with her small warmly-pyjamed limbs. "Papa! Ouerr! Papa." Then drawing away from his face, with a serious look, she indicated she wanted to show him something in her room. He carried her through to be shown a rickety and uncertain castle built from the coloured wooden bricks that had once been her mother's. While he dressed her, he murmured his praise for the child's hard work to her ear in a mixture of English and French.

He re-entered the kitchen holding the child's hand. He asked after Gaillarde and understood from the old woman that it was an examination day. He tried to convey his best wishes for the girl, before he left.

He drove them both down to Larozelle, where the mini-market still opens early. In the shop, he went round with Clara toddling behind, a bunch of his trousers gripped in her little fist, making him limp slowly up and down the narrow aisles as he filled his basket with milk, bread, cheese and eggs, a courgette, mushrooms and tomatoes. Added for the omelettes he planned to cook for them all when he got back.

As he crossed the square back to the van, a man beckoned to Jim. He went over, before he recognised it was old Theodor Jacob's son. And in the car sat the old man himself. Jim had not spoken to him since that day five years ago on the verandah of Suzanne's house. When the crimes of his father had first been told. And he had only seen him with his family a few times since from a distance. Looking in at the wound down car window, Jim was struck by how very much more elderly the man looked.

Clara tugged at his hand, for attention, so he lifted her up. "Ma petite. My little girl."

Jacob smiled slowly and proffered a hand to the child, but she shied away from its shrivelled scaleyness. "Monsieur Brige, it is an honour to have a child for a man of your years."

Jim nodded and smiled, his trust of the old man as instinctive as when they had first met.

"I wished to speak of…" He stopped to reorganise his thoughts. "I wish to speak with you of the troubles of your sister." Adding, "Les gulags."

Jim put Clara down onto her feet again, but held onto her hand to steady himself. He had almost let this other thing that Francis had left them, become forgotten. As the oldest brother of the three of them, did that now make him responsible for all the property of lies left to them by their father? How much more did this old man know?

Seeing the dizzy confusion of these thoughts in Jim's face, Jacob asked, "You know of the gulags? Madame Planisolles had told you of them?"

"Yes."

"I know of that time. You understand?"

"Yes. You told me before."

"I wish to speak with you, Jim," using that name for the first time. "You should know these things."

"I can't speak now. The little one…"

"Ah, yes." He waved an arm, "Do you not wish to know what I say? I will understand if it is too difficult, too painful in your family to know the true things. I will understand that the lies may be a comfort to you all." Who- or what- was the old man including there? "You may come to visit me. You know where I live?"

"I think so."

"You are welcome, whenever it is possible."

Jim stepped back, away from the car, still looking back into that pair of rheumy old eyes. "I will try," and, as he led Clara away, his other hand loaded with the carrier bag of food, he saw ahead of him, on the other side of the square, stood outside his pharmacy, Maurice watching him. As he reached the pavement, he let go of the child's hand, he gave a wave. As stunted and uncertain as he felt, being caught by Suzanne's husband talking to the enemy.

Driving back to the farm, he was inattentive to Clara, his head filled with the irate confusion of being asked to make an unreasonable choice of sides. Again. The discomfort of truth or the comfort of lies, as old Jacob had said. As he lifted Clara down, back home, he grabbed the paper bag from the glove compartment and stuffed it deep into his back trouser pocket, a place he was certain Gizande would not be touching, he thought acidly.

Inside, the kitchen was empty and as he had left it. Putting the shopping down, he led Clara through and up the stairs, saying, "Maman… Maman," to her. He turned the knob of the door, to let the little girl push it open, with so much caution and trepidation. Standing back in to the shadows of the corridor, touching the back of his knees to the chair where his father had sat those few nights before. Through the frame of the door, he could see Gizande looking at the child, her arms still hidden and unwelcoming beneath the duvet.

Clara stepped forward into the room, wordlessly, her own arms defensively restrained to her sides. Before looking over her shoulder to check that her father was still there. A couple of shuffling steps more and she was at the rim of the bed, as if standing to attention, waiting for orders.

Jim followed into the doorway, blank at what to say to make it easier. So, he spoke through the child, "Maman is home… Esclarmonde is home," leaving his own presence unspoken. He stepped forward again and lifted the child onto the bed. Surprised, she tipped forward onto her mother and, unable to do anything else, clung her little arms around Gizande's neck, burying her face into the space of pillow behind the woman's ear. The look on Gizande's face was startled and, at first, she rigidly clung back from responding to the squirming, desperately hugging thing across her breasts and shoulder, burying itself against her head. Finally, closing her eyes, shutting out the reality of who this child was- and the man stood behind- she slowly drew her bare arms from under the bedding and delicately lay the open fingers of each hand upon the back of the child, quieting her. Quieting them both. Turning towards Jim a tattoo on the back of her shoulder, of a red fist, clenched in defiance. He retreated from the room to leave them together.

Downstairs, he went through the usually tedious routine of laying and lighting the stove, this time with pleasure. Not forgetting to take the paper bag from his pocket, he opened it, looking a last time secretively at the knickers… before shoving them into the flames. And he started to prepare the omelette mixture and chop the vegetables.

Waiting for the oil in the pan on the electric ring to heat, he called up the staircase, "Nourriture! Food!"

He sliced and buttered the bread, started to fry the vegetables, then slopped the first portion of the eggy mixture into the pan. So that when they entered, Clara sat on her mother's hip, her little childish arms and legs clinging the shapes of Gizande's thinned body from the long nightshirt she was wearing. Although the woman's mouth did not move to anything of a smile, he convinced himself that there was a warmth about her eyes as she looked at the three plates of food on the table. He had arranged the places all down one side, Clara between the two adults, so that they would not have to look at each other. Sat in her highchair, the little girl chortled to herself as she started to spoon the pieces of omelette into her mouth.

After otherwise silence between the adults for an expectedly long time, Gizande broke it with, "She begins to speak."

Although she continued with her eyes away from him, down to her food, Jim smiled and answered with a thumpingly affirmative, "Yes!"

"Then we must be careful what we say in her hearing." She then said, "I will bring in the cows this morning." Relieving him that the routines of the farm were enforcing their own pattern of resumption and maybe healing.

"Gaillarde has been milking them." Adding, "She's a very nice girl. She loves Clara."

Gizande looked sharply at him, a slap-down reminder that nothing was resolved.

So he said, "Clara will help me tidy up the house and we will do the laundry- the washing."

She wiped the last from her plate with a torn knob of the bread, put it in her mouth and rose, leaving the room without further acknowledging either of them.

As he and the child moved about the house that morning, muttering between themselves, he thought that any thaw between mother and child would perhaps melt the ice between him and Gizande also. So when he called her in for lunch, he told her that he had to go to town to get the van window repaired. She was clearly reluctant to be left with the child, but did not argue.

While the garage-man was attending to the van window, Jim decided to chance his luck and walked into the centre to see Maurice. After he had asked the assistant, Maurice appeared from the back of the pharmacy.

"Est ce que Suzanne chez vous?" Jim asked hesitantly.

Maurice immediately shepherded him in round the counter to the back room. "Non. Suzanne, pas a l'école. Malade. Comprenez-vous?" He drew the imaginary tracks of tears with a fingertip down his cheeks, repeating, "Malade." Explaining all to Jim with, "C'est les gulags."

"Je veux visiter- a la?"

"Oui, oui," and Maurice smiled, somewhat wanly.

Jim wanted to mention the meeting with Jacob that Maurice had seen and hesitantly checked the man's face, but decided against it.

As he drove up the serpentine road to the plateau where Suzanne lived, he could at least be relieved the evidence of his own last troubled trip to England was gone. The window repaired and the knickers into ashes. But, as he crested the escarpment to the road rolling away before him through the fields and the patches of forest, he was back again in the land of the consequences of Francis, beautiful as it looked that day.

In the driveway, there was another car as well as Suzanne's. She came running out to him, "Jim! You did not telephone."

"No. I saw Maurice. He said you were off- sick. How are you?"

"Oh, Jim, you should not be here today."

"Why? Who's here? What's wrong?"

"It is the gulag-" but stopped herself. "It- it is the Russians. You know."

"They have come here?" indignant on her own behalf, on the wreckage of the family he now felt he was the head of. He wanted to push past her, into the house, to clear it of strangers. Of all the uninvited poisonous confusions left by Francis.

"No, Jim!" she restrained him with a hand. "I have asked them to see the house. Maurice does not know."

Jim looked over her shoulder at the two faces looking out from behind the verandah glass. What a stage that verandah had been for so many scenes of the family melodrama.

She slid her hand down to his elbow. "Come," and guided him towards the house. As they climbed the steps, she said, "They speak only a little French. But they speak Spanish, from their mother, and they are more comfortable with my bad Spanish than in French."

Jim had not overcome his surliness when he was introduced and had to shake each of their hands. They were brother and sister. And older than he expected.

There was coffee already out. Suzanne brought him a cup.

"Why are they here?" he asked her.

"To see the house." Her face appealed to him, "They have had a terrible history. All the years in Russia, in the camps. And after. From their mother and their father, before they died, they were given the dream. The dream of this house. Maurice does not know they have come. You must say nothing to him."

He looked back at the couple, guessing from what he knew that they were a few years younger than him, but looked at least ten years older. They smiled at him, not knowing his thoughts. Then the man started to speak the words to Suzanne, but his eyes continually back to examine her brother's face. Even Jim could recognise there was something halting and stilted in the Spanish that Suzanne translated to him.

She remained fixed to the face of the speaking man, even while she deciphered the words through her French, into the English for Jim. "They wish you to know the story. They were born on that journey to Russia. On the boat from Istanbul to Crimea. They are twins. At first, their father and mother thought that they will be welcome - as heroes of the war in Spain - fighting the fascism. But they did not understand. Stalin had made the pact with Hitler. Now they were enemies, every country in Europe. Their father was in prison in the north... on the canals - on the building of the canals..."

She waited for another episode of distress from the man to translate.

"At first, they were permitted to live in Leningrad. Their mother could send letters to their father. She even visited him once. But, when the Germans invaded Russia, all things changed. All foreigners were enemies. Their mother and the infants-" indicating the aged pair- "took them- to the south, near the frontier with Afghanistan. They heard no more of their father. He died – anonyme - somewhere in the north, perhaps during the war, perhaps after."

Another wait for him to add to his story.

"After, the mother died. They were nine years. They do not know, but she said to them she was going to the north, to find the father. She never returned. The children became zecs - that is the name for the prisoners in the Russian system- you see, Jim, I know the detail now of this story," her own sad insertion in the narrative. "He says they were under Article 735. They met other Spanish children of the republicans also under the same Article of the law. They were told their mother was in prison, but only much later, in 1958, they were eighteen years, they were told she died in Moscow. They believe she was taken from the train and as she speak Russian as a Spanish - as a foreigner, she was shot as a spy."

She nodded for the man to continue in his Spanish, Jim watching him with as much suspicion as a Soviet.

"That is their story. They came from the prison after the death of Stalin, when many were made free. He says their mother spoke of here as it was the Garden of Eden. Anything would grow in the soil, she said. But in Russia, it was only the dark, cold forests of the north or the rocks of Khazakstan in the south. Cutting the trees or breaking the rocks. That was the only Russia we were permitted to know," slipping into his exact words, as if Suzanne herself had undergone their life with them. "Here or Spain was nothing for us. Only an escape from Russia. And we knew there was a home here our parents had spoken of. He spoke of your father as a gentle man, who was occupying the home until our return. So we have returned."

She waited for more of the story to translate, but she knew the man had stopped, resting his hand in his sister's. In the silence of the room that followed, both Jim and Suzanne dwelled separately on the consequences of the tale that had been told.

"What do they want now, Suzanne?"

"They want… they wish for - to return to their home."

"It was never their home! They never lived here." Jim was angered.

"It is their home," defeatedly denying his doubt. "What other home have they had? You hear the story."

"What will you do? Where would you go? You cannot give away this place. You have lived here all your life. They've never lived here."

"Jim," looking directly at him. "It was a thieving. You have understood our father for longer than I have. You must then understand this crime by him."

"Will you sell it to them? The home? Do they have money? What about Maurice?" He wanted to bully her out of her beaten resignation with his inquisitions. To urge her on to resist this further bequest of deceit from their father. "What will you tell Maurice? He will never agree, surely?"

"It was my father- our father who did the crime. It was not the father of Maurice."

"Where will you live? Where will you go to?"

She shrugged. "It must be done. Do not ask me the method to do it."

Jim scrutinised the other man's face for evidence of theft. But deep as he went into the man's eyes and the eyes of the prematurely grandmotherish sister beside him, he could only find honesty looking back at him, waiting courteously for Suzanne to say something in her Spanish.

"Ask them," Jim started. "Ask them…" but the questions that preyed about his head were ones that he could only fear the answers to. "But d'you know the story is true, Suzanne? Do you know?" immediately recalling the conversation with old Jacob that morning.

"I have seen the documents- the documents they have found in Paris. They are the archives of the Vichy Government. There is a letter from our father. It is true. It is his name at the end, how he wrote it. They say there are other letters from him there, from the time of the war. He was writing to the Petainistes, at the time he said to us that he was a fighter against them, against fascism."

Again, Jim wished he could confront the man who had spoken to him from the dark in Gizande's house, and interrogate him with violence.

Looking over at Suzanne, she had shrunk with hearing the story again, a further confirmation of her father.

She looked back at him, "I saw the documents. I saw, at the advocate, the letter with my father's name at the bottom."

Jim suddenly stood, clearing his head above the oppressiveness of the three of them crouched in confrontation around the reverberations of that narrative. The brother and sister shrank back from the savagery of the scowl in Jim's face. He turned away to the window. Outside the afternoon sun gave all the colours to the delicate garden Suzanne had created beyond the driveway, as if to display what she intended to lose. He looked out beyond, to the mountains. Somewhere down there in the folds of a valley beneath them, Gizande and Clara were together, with all the consequences of that, also. Driven up against the madnesses left alive by the dead man, all of them. What had you thought you were doing? With the lies to your children.

"Pardon? Jim? You say?"

He swung round to her, realising he may have muttered his last thought aloud.

"No. Nothing. What can I do? How can I help you, Suzanne?"

"Do you think that Maurice is right? That we should go to the court? That we should…" her voice trailed off.

He wanted to say yes. He wanted to believe that the pleasant and honourable man he knew Maurice to be, was right. But he could only remain dumb, as guilty as she felt before the crimes of their father.

Suzanne took his silence for assent.

"Will they pay you money for the house? Do they have any?" he repeated.

"I do not know."

"Well, ask them," he snarled, furious at this pair of strangers bringing their appeal for justice, another disruption in the life of his family.

"No. I will not ask. That I will leave to the advocates."

"When will you tell Maurice? When will you tell him what you're doing? What you intend."

"You must say nothing, Jim. I need time to think. I need the best time to say it to him. Please… say nothing to Maurice."

"Oh, Suzanne… why us? Why did it happen to us? Did he never think? Did he never understand what his actions would…? What he would be doing to us?"

"I understand him now- as you have learned of our father. I understand our father now, as you have learned of him. He is a monster of egotism," her haunted eyes turned up to him, then looked down and away to the floor beneath her feet.

He indicated the other couple with a roughened gesture of his hand, "They must go now. If this is what you say you've got to do, Suzanne, you must now do it through an advocate. After you've told Maurice. But they must go now. You mustn't listen to them, now, and all their stories. Stop torturing yourself." If he had the Spanish to say goodbye to them and to get them moving out of the house at that moment, he would have. But he just stood waiting, to ensure she said it herself.

After a long pause, she said something quietly to them in Spanish and they immediately stood up. Jim turned away from them and looked out of the window, certain he would offer no gesture of goodbye. He watched her accompany them to their car across the drive. Parked exactly as he remembered the car with Jacob in, those years ago, when Jim had started to learn the truth about his father.

She stood and watched them go, before she returned to the house. As she sat back down, he now sat down beside her.

"I have heard the story before. In the advocate's office. It is right that you have heard it also. But it is confirmed now. The brother has told the story the second time to my ears, in the same words. I did not doubt it the first time, but now I am certain. Absolument," as if this statement could only attain the full stamp of truth, by giving it this final punctuation in her own language. How different, how thoroughly crushed by the truths was this woman, compared with the crashing lunges of Gizande to escape and to deny them.

She collected up the coffee cups and went out with them, leaving him for a time thinking of the two women as sisters. And him as their brother. The differences and the similarities. Before he shivered the idea from himself and followed her.

She was drifting round the house, from room to room purposelessly or as if she was saying goodbye to each of them, long before she had to. On the dining room table, the same one he had been sat at when Gizande had first entered that room five years ago, there was a large opened book. He idly lifted the cover to see the title. It was a Collected Works of Shakespeare.

From the window, she watched him. "Your great English poet."

"Not mine. I've never even seen one of his plays." He shook his head, "Probably wouldn't understand it. We had to read it in English lessons to one of the fathers. He kept giving me the girl parts," the trivial memory sharpening itself with, "I was always getting teased about it afterwards. By the other lads."

"I have been reading the plays. I have been searching for our father there, but I have not found him. Even the most difficult characters- those who make the worst crimes- they seem to examine their conscience. Do you think our father did?"

He wondered whether to tell her about his conversation with Francis, but it felt too foolish to explain, too likely to leak with things he did not want her to hear. So he said, "He was always someone who knew he was in the right, when he wasn't. He had an explanation for his wrongdoings."

She thought about that the other side of the room, with her back to him, looking at the titles on the spines of her books. "Yes, I believe that is so. No one does things of evil without an explanation that satisfies themselves, at least." She turned round to him, "Yes. You are a wise man, Jim."

He gave a short, dry laugh, "Living with- learning about our-" hesitating on the word- "my father leads me to a lot of wisdom. I say my father because, as I learnt things of him, I didn't tell you because it made you upset. The old men who had known him were always trying to tell me stories about him."

"Jacob and his family, eh?"

"No." He would not tell her about the conversation in the square in town that morning. He wondered whether Maurice would and should he pre-empt that? But it seemed unnecessarily cruel at this moment, piling one thing upon another. "No. Other old men, other people. Sometimes I haven't understood all their French, but…" letting it trail off, becoming restless with what he was choosing not to tell her. Too much like the way of their father. He wanted to go. Gizande and Clara awaited him with the results of his experiment in leaving them together. "I must go, now."

She woke to him, "Why did you come up here this afternoon?"

Should he say he had been sent by Maurice? Was that what happened? Or was it as the dutiful older brother, trying again to quieten the marionettes, sent wildly shaking by the dead puppet master? "I wanted to see how you were," he said carefully.

"So, you have seen me. It feels better, now that I have made the resolution."

He did not accept any invitation to talk further about it, if that was what she had just offered. "I must go."

She came across and took his arm, "Merci. For being of much help, Jim, my big brother."

The lushness was almost embarrassing him as she led him out, leaning her head on his shoulder. The affection of at least one of his sisters, he thought, nauseously, as he drove away from her to the other.

Chapter Thirty-four

After he had put Clara to bed that evening, he stopped Gizande from going upstairs, escaping into her bedroom again. "We must talk. You know that. You - we don't stop things happening by not speaking of them." He looked at her in the dark corner at the bottom of the stairs, where he had cut off her retreat.

She looked back at him, saying nothing, and went into the front room. Refolding his sleeping bag on the settee, she sat next to it.

From the doorway, he asked, "A drink?"

She shook her head, but then said, "Biere."

He brought back two bottles from the kitchen, then sat down. He started with, "He's here, you know. He's here, Francis," deliberately choosing the neutral first name. "He spoke to me the other night."

She looked up at him sharply.

"Has he spoken to you as well, Gizande?. I mean, more than the tape."

She nodded, now eyes away from him again.

"Why is he here? He's never lived here, has he?"

Nothing.

"Is it just that we can summon his spirit? Is it our anxiety that calls him to give an explanation? You understand more of this spiritual stuff. Why here?"

She spoke at last. "He knew this place. He was often here in the time of my grandfather, during the war and afterwards. He would often come to argue about God and about politics and philosophy. Even until soon before the death of my grandfather."

"It…" he was truly hesitant at what had come into his mind to say next.

She sensed it and looked over at him, with restrained fright in her face at what might be coming now.

"It must hurt you that neither of them told you the truth." Leaving her in no doubt by adding, "About Elizabeth."

She froze at the word and finally whispered, "Si."

And now those old men have unwittingly enforced the two of us as liars to Clara, he thought. To Suzanne. "For me," he said, "Francis just made excuses."

"I tried to understand..." she stumbled into words. Jim was the only person she could speak to and try to comprehend what had happened to her. "I wish to- égaler- to réconciler- to match? You understand?"

He shook his head.

"To put together what the man I knew when he was alive- he was like a generous uncle, you know? And the man I know since the tape. And it is impossible for me, Jim?" This shudder of feeling with its brief reach-out towards him with his first name, was quickly shut down by her. "No!" firmly stated.

He let the silence that left the room prickled with its discomfort for the both of them, a long time before he tried to unlock her with a simple, "Well?"

But she clasped her hands over her ears at it and at the insistent silence. He watched her face clench the muscles, sucked back around the protruding bones. Till she was utterly still, clamped between her fingers, rigidly motionless, only the minuscule throb of that vein upon the temple turned towards him. He would wait. Now he knew that and his pity for her- for them both- warmed him with love and the inevitability of them both being bound together, whatever way they worked out of it eventually. He waited for her to unclench herself, sat for so long motionless himself that he became almost hallucinogenic with staring at it, counting the pulse of the blood on the side of her forehead.

With incremental gradualness, the rigidity retreated from her limbs, the muscles on her thin arms softened and the frozen hysteria of denial started to thaw, until finally she was slumped and sagged, hung from her shoulders. And to Jim, recognisably older for the first time.

She reached over to the sleeping bag and fiddled idly with the zipper. Then inhaled and stood tiredly. "I will go to bed." And left him with the feeling that, strangely, progress of a sort had been started between them.

When he awoke, Gizande had already left for the fields. He had not heard her. He made himself a cup of coffee, then woke Clara. He phoned Suzanne and asked if he could leave Clara with her for a couple of hours. She agreed, with an unexpected warmth in her voice.

After he had dropped the little girl off, Jim drove on to the sawmill. Behind it, set aside within a large, severely formal garden of low, trimmed shrubs and hedges separating gravel paths, was the large and pompously architectured bulk of the mansion marked *Famille Jacob* by the nameplate on the gatepost.

A middle-aged woman answered the door to him. There was the sound of children in the rear rooms of the house.

"Monsieur Jacob?"

She looked quizzically at him. He was sure she knew who he was.

"Monsieur Theodor Jacob?"

She studied him, then went, without saying a word.

He waited a long time at the open door, before he heard footsteps on the gravel behind him. It was the son who had been with old Jacob yesterday.

Jim smiled at him, but the man did not smile back. "Questque c'est?" he asked abruptly. He was wearing jeans and a checked shirt that were flecked with sawdust. He was obviously irritated at being interrupted from his work.

"Je-veux-voir-votre-pére," Jim spelt out uncertainly.

The man grunted and pushed past him, into the house. It was the woman who returned, to invite Jim in with expressionless unenthusiasm.

Old Jacob sat in a wheelchair, his legs tucked beneath a blanket.

"You will excuse them, please. They do it for me. They fight the old battles that are not needed to be fought. For them, you are your father, as they can not reach the man in the tomb. So, they can not understand why I should wish to invite his son into my house, the house of the family."

"I'm not sure I understand why you wish to," Jim said, offering this with the flicker of a nervous smile.

Jacob turned to the daughter-in-law, who was still standing by the door, and issued an order dismissively. Turning to Jim as she left, "You will have a cognac?"

"No. Thanks. I'm driving."

"A biere, peut-etre?"

"Non. No."

Jacob shrugged. When the woman returned with the drinks, the old man took his and sipped it. Then sent her off.

The house had become silent, no sound of children. As if everything was listening in to what would be said in this room.

"To understand who are the gulags now, you must understand your father then. And the history of France, from the year Forty, and after." He started as if it was a matter of fact that his monologue had only undergone the briefest interruption by the serving of drinks, not that it was a resumption of yesterday in the square, or of five years ago on Suzanne's verandah. He sipped his drink again and considered Jim over the rim of the small glass, before replacing it on the tray beside him. "I commence to understand those years more easily as I become older. I have little to do now. My children are managing the timber work now. My old body will not permit me to do more than sit here - in this machine," tapping the wheelchair's armrest - "and think of the past. As we get older, it is more important. I remember things from then, that I had forgotten. Each remembrance assists in making the memory certain. It is important to have the account correct and finished, before I go. Are you yet old enough for this to have commenced with you?"

Jim was settled for listening to the old man, unprepared for being asked to take part, so he hesitated, before shaking his head. Re-familiarising himself again with reflective pace of this old man's way of telling, after the years.

"It is the survivors who are forced to live on with the shame of not dying then, with our comrades. We have been forced to remember. But, for the men who caused those dead? Those find no shame. Only the refusing… the ability to invent the excuses for what they have done." Marking this with a pause, before, "So it was, with your father," those old watery eyes not leaving Jim's face. Pressing him to minimise whatever Francis had done, as if he had somehow been a co-accused in the deeds he was about to be told of.

"I did not know your father in the very early days. I know he was rescued from the camp at Gurs through the intercession of Casals. You know the great musician from Spain?"

Jim nodded, dumbly.

"I do not know how that was, but Pau Casals was a wise man. A man of many friends still in the high positions. Because of the music." The ancient eyes across the room punctured deep into Jim's discomfort. "I told you already of the betrayal of the Republicans after the liberation? By your father?" Before nodding at the recollection, "Yes, I remember." Then resuming, the point having been made, "When I met your father, it was later. After his time in Gurs. Concerning my work on the railways. He already had the appearance of an officer of the L'Armée de l'Intérieure. Of the Resistance. He carried a Walther pistolet, for that appearance. He was not able to hit anything with the bullets, when he was able to get them. It was a joke for us, behind his back. All the world knew this. He was important because the English had made him so. They needed a fascist on their side of the war. You understand?" The bare crudity of this made Jim clench himself. Jacob saw this, "Did you not understand this of your father? To be sure that there was no revolution in this country in Forty Four. That the property was returned to the bourgeoisie. Even to the friends of Vichy." With a slight smile to himself, he added, "There was an expression we used for such people. He was the man who stayed behind to look after the furniture. You understand?"

Of course he understood. Just additions to the almost completed jigsaw he already had inside his head, Jim endured the unravelling revelations to know how much this old man knew. Even as far as who

Gizande was? Frozen in the expectation of the story moving onwards to that period. Fitting himself into the edge of the picture of Francis's deeds.

Jacob sipped again. "Are you certain you will not drink? Not a coffee?"

Jim wordlessly shook his head, his throat too parched to answer.

"But for this, your father expected a recompense. This he was able to do with his position. For assisting the escapers from France into Spain, across the mountains, he was an industry for- for the illégalisme. You understand? He was able to create the cartes d'identités to sell to Jews escaping from the arrestations for the camps. He had friends in the ministries from where he was able to get food entitlements- the tickets for food. The workers in the industries were allocated more bread and milk. With these tickets, he was able to sell for money. When the Germans came here, they demanded requisition of all bicycles. You father was able to purchase the bicycles before that, and he had the hope to sell them after the Liberation. All this was for his profit. He was even able to buy the property from the Vichy Government that had been stolen from the Jews. The farm you have, La Retrait? That is such a property. It was given to a Jew I knew for a debt. When the Jew disappeared into the camps, your father was its thief. Of course, that was permissible, because of the work he did there on the frontier, smuggling the escapers into Spain. After the war, it became a convenience for the entering and leaving Spain with the contraband. Smuggling, yes? For discovering the ways to make profit, your father was an artist. It was even said he was paid for information by the factory bosses. Who was in the Resistance, who were the militants, so that those he named could be handed over to the Gestapo. Perhaps it was so. It was possible."

The old man sighed, whether from regret for what had happened, or from satisfaction at the story told, Jim could not tell. But he felt poisoned by it. Angry at having to endure hearing it, but somehow fulfilling a duty in remaining to listen.

"As the war came back to France and the Germans and the Vichy were swept away, we believed it was the time for the revolution. It was the time I was able to return to France from England. We had the guns. The government of the towns was ours. We started l'épuration - you understand?" searching for a word. "The purification? It was the arrest of the Vichy men and the collaborateurs. Many were shot. Your father was searched for, also."

To his own surprise, Jim blurted, "Would you have? Would you've shot him, if you had the chance?"

Jacob regarded him, those weakly eyes glittering for a moment, "Would you have, had you been me? Would you have used the gun against him?"

Now? At this moment? Yes. But also against this old man and all the other story tellers about this family of his, a massacre of all those who told what he had heard. To get back where he had once been. Before this knowledge.

"Perhaps, you, like me, would have the pretext to do nothing. For the purification did not continue. De Gaulle made the compromises. He wished for no revolution. He wished for no revolutionaries in his government offices. He needed the little men who had worked for both sides. The silence of the clerks, it is called, yes? The man who puts his signature to the form placed onto his desk, whatever the form requests, whatever the government. All nations have those people. During this time, your father disappeared. For two years. It is said that even his wife did not know where he had gone. When he returned, the times had changed. The trials of the collaborationists were mostly finished. People wanted comfort again, after the hunger and the death. There was no appetite for the social transformation, for the courage and the sacrifice required for that. Your father was permitted to resume his life among us. There were those who would never speak to him again. There were certain places he could not go with safety. But he was protected by the state now. He even returned as one of the circle of Casals for a time. But the stories remained, until his death. It was the appearance of you, the son we never knew of, that gave nourishment again for us old men, who never believed that the justice had been completed. That the world had ceased to listen to our tales."

Jim felt impatient at being used, at the childish simplicity of being held responsible. Agitated at the man who had given Jim his name, to be carried like a branded scar around this patch of mountains and gorges. Shaken, that these old men saw him as fair game to pursue their vendetta, even if now it was a revenge couched in the reasonable narrative of the courteous vieillard sat across from him. So he spelt out, viperishly, "You called me here to tell me about the gulags. What has all this to do with them?"

"I call you?" a performance of mildest astonishment crossed Jacob's face. "How was that possible? No. You came, because it was necessary for you to know." Then waiting for a response that Jim was not going to give. "The gulags? The farm of your sister? That was the first occasion when your father looked after the furniture for those who left their homes by one of the necessities of war. For most of the furniture, the proprietors never returned. Only this one case have they return. Too late for your father. It is sad perhaps that it is your sister and you are to have the responsibility… but that is history. Just as the children not born in Germany when Hitler was extinguished, they must today continue to bear the cost." He shifted himself with infinite care in the wheelchair seat. The effort of it drained him and for a long moment, he remained head down, his shoulders rising and falling with the effort of recovering his breath. Finally, looking up at Jim, there was a flickering of malice in the ancient, clouded eyes as he said, "Your family has had the advantage of living in that farm for many years. Now, the return of the children to claim it… it will be justice. Perhaps the tribunal, the word of the judge will decide. Perhaps…" and he looked calculatingly at Jim, querying for some sort of confession from Jim, "…perhaps you will advise your sister of the proper route for your family to take…"

"What would that be?" asked coldly, wanting to know what Jacob and the other old men would expect, but refusing to concede anything to them.

"You will know. If the problem is taken for the consideration of the judge, there will be much publicity. If the affair is resolved privately, it will be less painful." The gently spoken words knowingly shrouding their threat. Acknowledged, as the old man added, "You do not understand how transactions are completed here. You do not have the language. You do not have the understanding of what is not said also, but is known, for it has been the way affairs have been resolved in these valleys for many generations… for many, many generations."

There, in the benign ominousness of those words, lay the impossibility of Jim responding. His long silence, considering the implications of what had been said, became a reluctant consent to what the old man had spoken. No language of any sort to answer back. Just the inevitability of taking on again the unfinished business of a dead father.

It was necessary now to leave. But he was as weighted to his chair with the inability of how to finish this with any grace, as Jacob was to his wheelchair by his infirmities. Finally, he muttered only, "I must go."

"Yes. That is true," the old man holding out his hand as Jim stood.

That, at least, could be refused. A gesture of self-respect, however feeble or ambiguous, he looked down at the offer of the liver-spotted, wrinkled fingers, faintly quivering with the effort of being offered. Before they were withdrawn by Jacob, smiling down to himself, then up at Jim, forcing him to look back. And answer with his own eyes, the old man's guile wrapped around with generosity, forced to put a brief and obligatory smile to his own lips, before turning to leave the house.

Chapter Thirty-five

Leaving the house, down the steps and crunched across the gravel, Jim felt beaten. The old man's generosity in telling the truth about his father had actually been the caning of the son, worse than any of the split bamboo thrashings he remembered from those other fathers, far greater than to enforce Jim's submission as a child. That final smile by Jacob, so reasonable, so understanding, had actually been the satisfaction of an old man at last seeing that sentence had been pronounced and justice had been delivered to its rightful and proper place.

He could not return to Suzanne. At least, not yet. He convinced himself that she would be enjoying the time with her little niece, long enough to leave Clara there longer.

Jude, dammit, he thought. And Deedee. Before setting off in the van towards the spa. The steep grey damp cliffs of the narrow defile that led there, closed themselves above him against the sun. When he parked outside the café, it was chill enough in the dank shadows of the rock to pull his coat over his shoulders as went to the door.

It was answered eventually to several knocks of his knuckles against the cold glass, by a man buttoning up his shirt.

"Jude? Is Jude in?"

"No. She's out with the children." The Englishman scanned him. "Who shall I say?"

"Just say Jim called. Is Deedee in?" he added, just as she herself appeared from behind, in a thin dressing gown that showed she had nothing on underneath.

"Jim! Have you met Charles?" Jim had barely time to glance back at the man, before she added, "Jude's feller- her husband."

He felt himself blush at Deedee, who was grinning impishly.

"Did she tell you about him?"

And he knew that she had already been told he had had sex with Jude. And that his visit had probably interrupted Deedee having sex with Charles. What another mess, he furied at himself.

"Won't you come in?"

"Yes- no. I've got to- I've got to go and collect Clara," he stumbled through the words. And the chaos of his embarrassments.

"Oh, go on! Come in. Anyway, I've got something to show you. It's from the insurance. About the crash. Just have a look at it. But… I'd like your opinion. Come on. I think they're going to settle and pay us for the old write-off." She took his wrist and pulled him in past Charles, close enough to smell her scent mixed with a bit of sweat.

And led him upstairs. Charles did not follow. Jim just felt turbulently confused and struggled against it, but let his arm be limply led. He was pulled after her into the room with the desk and the bed. The sheets were still disorderly. Dishevelled. And warm, he guessed.

"Here." She pushed a letter before his eyes. Which he took mechanically and looked at, but could not read the words of. She stood there watching him, perched like a bird, the sole of one foot against the ankle of the other, the bent knee parting the front of the dressing gown far up towards the top of her thigh. Which she knew he was watching around the edge of the letter in his hand.

But for Charles, somewhere beyond the open door and the stairway behind him, he might have attacked her at that moment, so furious with this and the other woman, so humiliated by the inabilities to control his body. He thrust the letter back at her, snarling, "Yeah. Okay."

To which, she prettily answered, "It's good, isn't it? Getting that much for that old heap being written off."

"I gotta go. I gotta collect Clara."

"Oh, little Clara. You must bring her up again. She can play with our kids."

But when she said that, he was already tumbling out of the room and down the stairs. In flight, just as Jude was shepherding the two children through the front door to Charles.

"Hello, Jim!" genuinely warm to see him. "When did- ? When did you come here? You've met Charles, have you?"

"Yeh. I'm off. To collect Clara."

She laughed and it included teasing. As he pushed past her outside, he felt her hand give a cheerful clasp of his buttock. He slammed the van door behind him and scowled back at the shop but Jude, the children and Charles had already disappeared inside and Jim could hear their laughter inside his head. He switched on the ignition, not knowing where to take his humiliated anger. Back to being as alone and untrusting as he had ever been, he finally engaged the gears and crawled away. Giggling eyes watching from the windows of the floors above, he let the van take him where the road led, down where the gorge opened into a narrow valley crowded with trees.

He passed a cluster of men with shotguns broken open over their forearms, smoking and talking together round some four-wheel drives. He realised it was Saturday. The hunters were out from behind their shop counters and office desks. What would he do himself? His preference would have been to work on his own up at La Retrait, but he needed to buy wire and plug sockets for extending the primitive electric circuitry and he had spent the cash for that on his air ticket to Berlin. He could try to return to Gizande and cheerfully build upon the tentative move she had allowed him towards her the previous night, but dare he believe in it? Feeling the slapstick oaf today was making of him so far. Only Clara, perhaps a bit of Suzanne and doubtfully Gizande defined his life now. Denied a family as such a little boy, he realised that now it was too late to learn the skills of rebuilding one from such wreckage. The denial of options crept with cold hopelessness through his whole body, enervating him of all but the ability to let the steering wheel slide through his fingers, pulling the van round the tight curves of the winding valley.

Eventually the road led him serpentining up the valley sides to the plateau, running straight from the lip of the escarpment, between fields, towards the scribbled line of the Pyrenees, beginning to smudge with the clouds of an approaching storm. Just before he turned into Suzanne's driveway, he swung the wheel over and changed route, driving round the back of the village to the cemetery. There was a young couple assisting an elderly lady up one of the paths to a graveside. He watched them from the van, before he got out, feeling it was safe to visit his father's grave without being observed, at the other end of the graveyard.

Halfway along the line of headstones, he became aware that Francis's was somehow crooked. As he came up to it, he saw the crack like a jagged lightning across the stone where it had been smashed and then daubed in black paint with the swastika and splashed letters to spell the word *Fasciste.* Jim went to touch the stone, as if to push together the two splintered edges of the crack. But he stepped back from it, distancing himself, remote at least from this consequence of the dead man's life. Nothing random about the damage. A force like a sledge hammer brought into the cemetery to do the business. He thought of the scowling eyes of Jacob's son. Perhaps. The futility of guessing about Francis, with so many enemies, Jim realised he could have struck the blow himself, for it was nothing less than the truth. Suzanne would be upset, he thought. Or would she? Would they both be able to abandon their father at last, as he had once abandoned Jim and Gizande? He shook his head. It was too complex.

He stood there a long time, before he spoke aloud. "Well, is this what you would've wished?" He listened for an answer. "It's only what you deserve." Adding a contemptuous, "Dad."

He picked the wilted flowers out of the little jar that Suzanne had used to replace every week. And cast them aside angrily, realising that

Francis had won his race, getting to the finishing line without being found out. Whatever happened afterwards was for his children to deal with.

He looked around the graveyard for anyone watching. The old lady and the young woman were at their grave. The man was carrying a can of water back from the tap, towards them. All with their backs turned to Jim, he stepped up to the stone and gave it an experimental push. Looked over his shoulder again, before giving a serious heave with his full weight. The broken edges of stone grated slightly together, but would move no further. He tried once more, but powerlessly. Standing back, panting, he read the ambiguous words again,

Christ could be born a thousand times in Galilee
But all in vain until he is born in me.

Rather than hidden wisdom, he saw them now for what they were, another layer of obscurity to conceal the truth of this man's life. He stepped up again and gave the stone an impotent kick, before turning back to the van.

Clara was eating her lunch at Suzanne's kitchen table when he arrived. He had not wanted to stay, but he had no choice, until the child had finished. Suzanne drew him almost conspiratorially into the hallway, out of Clara's sight. When she allowed her face to show its distress.

"Jim. I…" Saying no more, she pulled an envelope from her apron pocket and held it out for him.

At that moment, Clara called from the kitchen behind him, "Pa-pa! Pa-pa!"

He turned, switched on a smile and gave the child a tinkly wave with his fingertips. Before turning back to his sister. He opened the envelope and slid the photo from inside. It was black-and-white, of a group of half a dozen women, their heads shaven, with a crowd around them, each caught with a jeer and a gesticulation. One of the heads, her skull polished clean of whom she had been, had been ringed in biro with *PROSTITUÉE FASCISTE* written off away to the corner in scribbled capitals.

"What's this?" he asked Suzanne.

"It is my mother."

"When? When was this?"

"Quarante Quatre. Forty Four. C'est la coiffure de Quarante Quatre."

He frowned at her for an explanation.

"What they did to les collabos… who shared the bed with the Nazis. The shaven head. Les collaboratrices."

"Because of…?" He could not allow himself to give the man a family title. "Because of Francis?" Knowing as soon as he said it how cruelly he had distanced himself from her over the years, he reached his arm round her shoulders, but she shook herself away from any contact.

"She was not a collabo. Never! Such a person- no!"

He studied the face of the woman on the photo. It was passive, as if whatever happened next was only to be expected. "He- he sent it," he snarled. "You know. He sent it." As clearly as the tape, Jim knew this had come from that man. Whoever had actually scrawled and stuffed the photo in its envelope.

"Who? What do you know, Jim?" She grasped each of his shoulders and forced him to look her closely in the eyes. "What do you know, Jim?"

At that moment Clara, behind them, cried out, "Pa-pa! Pa-paaa!" anxious at the raised voices of her two beloved adults in the next room.

"It is him," Jim gritted out. "It is…" and halted for a way of saying it. "It's the man who says he is our father."

Suzanne looked startled for a moment. Then, dismissive, "No. He's dead."

"No, Suzanne. I spoke to him. He has returned. He was in Gizande's house. She has heard him also."

"Oh, no, Jim. No. He spoke with you and Gizande?" Disbelief, almost ridicule.

"No while she was away, he came- he came to the house."

"Jim, no!" Her hands gripped through the shoulders of his jacket, urgent to dissuade him. "It is a dream. No. You have heard too many stories."

"But," he whispered urgently, "they're true, Suzanne. All true." His eyes, almost pushing out of their sockets, stared into hers with unassailable conviction. Letting the photograph tumble from his fingers, he grabbed her wrists and forced them together, plucking them away from his shoulders, beginning to hurt her with the gripped emphasis of the gesture. "They are all true, Suzanne."

There was fear in her face and she tried to shake herself from him.

"Pa-paaaa!" came the long frightened cry from next door.

He released her, woken to it.

"Who have you spoke to, Jim?"

"Does it matter? They are all true."

"Pa-paa!" the shriek this time followed by the clatter of cutlery on the floor.

Neither of the adults moved. She waited for his answer. He waited for her acknowledgement that it was true. Gizande's tape. The photograph he had dropped on the floor. Even the broken gravestone. Were all the work of Francis. But Jim was aware how much more he knew than his sister. "You know it is true… the gulags."

"Ah… but Maurice says that it is necessary… to oppose them. I must go to the Courts." Clara had now started to sob, bereft.

"L'enfant," Suzanne said and slipped past into the kitchen.

He stood there, listening to her cooing voice calming the little girl. Setting the vengeful voice inside his head against her infant distress. Until Clara, her cheeks pink and wet, was carried through by her aunt.

"I must get home," Jim said. "Gizande doesn't know where I- where we are." And probably relieved for all that, he thought. Just to have them away from the house. But Maurice was right. They could not surrender to what their father had left behind. None of the three of them, whatever they did, however they handled it between them. Him and Gizande owed it to Clara to resist. That was the way of healing, he was now sure. To stand proud and separate from the patrimonies and the legacies left by the dead old man. And, in that way, to return him to his grave.

"What did you say, Jim?"

He must have spelt out some of his thoughts on his moving lips. "Maurice is correct. Suzanne, we must fight against him."

"Against who?" But she understood. "We fight against the brother and sister, whose house was stolen by our father? Are they the enemy? Must they take the responsibility for the acts of our father?"

Jim looked at Clara, who was seriously watching from one adult to the other. And when Jim's eyes met hers, she reached out her little fisted arms to be taken by him and Suzanne handed her over.

"No, Jim," she said. "To fight, that is the man's solution. We must consider the best way. We may fight and lose."

Jim shrugged, settling the weight of Clara onto his hip, and looked around the home where he had been first welcomed in France. "Or lose this house, without fighting. Is that a woman's solution?"

She turned away, in to the kitchen. He was angry with her, but also frustrated that he could not tell the totality of what he knew. Both angry with each other. He bent to pick up the photo from the floor and placed it on the top of the bureau. Wondering what his sister had done with the photos of their father that had been stacked there face-down on a previous visit. He remembered the gravestone. She would find that out soon enough anyway, for him to tell her now. "Suzanne."

She was at the sink, her back to him. "No. You must go. Gizande waits."

That was good enough for him to leave, without bothering.

Chapter Thirty-six

When they returned, he found Gizande in the cheese shed. She asked them nothing, but, after Jim had been stood in the doorway for a time, with Clara looking on curiously at this mother, a little hand in his for reassurance, she simply said, "The police have visited today," without pausing from cleaning and wiping down the steel equipment. "They asked for you."

"The police visited while you were away in Berlin. Then, they asked for you."

"I know. He told me."

"What did they want?"

"They have spoken with the German police. They are satisfied, now that Andreas is in prison." Flashing a look at him with, "The whole world is satisfied now that Andreas is in the prison," before resuming the cleaning.

He ignored it and simply tersely offered, "Want help here?"

"No."

He stood, waiting for anything more to be said. Then left and took Clara back into the house. He went upstairs and set the child down in her room, an encumbrance, and went through to the small third bedroom that had once been Guillem's, but had become storage. Under a stack of old farming magazines, he found the box of documents that he had brought from England. All that was left of that once importance. Kneeling over it in a clear piece of the carpet, he started to take out documents from the top. Revisiting Damien, Scadding, and Stephen, too, for a last time. In order to say goodbye. Choosing what would be useful to send to Julian, into one pile and what would be burnt, into another. Or burn the lot.

A sound behind him. He turned and Clara was at the door, upset and snuffling for his attention. She was alert to the disturbances going on in the adults around her. A moment for him to choose, but he urgently wanted to sort the documents. To clear his life of at least one thing that he had control of its disposal.

He stood, swept the child up in his arms, with, "A maman," and carried her down through the house and out to the cheese shed. Where Gizande was hosing the tile floor.

"Here. You take her," gruffly dangling out the child towards its mother.

Who looked up, confused, then with pointed irritation, back to her hosing without a word.

He put the child down. Some of the sprayed water sprinkled her bare legs and dress and she skipped backwards against him. But he pushed her forward again, "You take her this afternoon. I'm busy."

She put the hose aside. "I am occupied. It is not possible." She was watchful of him, whether this was not one of his seldom bouts of anger. Perhaps disordering into an assault again, if she was incautious in how she responded to him. Indicating the floor with an appeal for understanding from her opened, free hand. "I must make clean."

"I have work to do this afternoon. On documents." Said with dogged vehemence. "I cannot have the child. It is your responsibility also."

She was going to say something, but his face warned her off whatever it was going to be.

So he added, acidly, "I've done my shift."

"What…?" but she thought better of it. She went back to turn off the hose at the tap and returned, attentively wiping each hand on her overalls. Avoiding both his and the child's eyes. Reluctantly, reaching Clara, she looked back at her watching daughter. Deciding what to do next.

"Well, how about giving her a cuddle," he cut into the pause.

She looked over at him venomously, an easier option than the girl at her feet. "It has no meaning for you. Why? Why does it have no meaning for you? Why-?"

"Shut up! Don't dare say it in front of her!" He almost reeled with the violence swilling about inside him.

Gizande stepped back, defensive, but better placed to riposte attack. "She comprends nothing of what we say."

Thinking, what does she know? With the months of behaving as if Clara was not there. "She starts to talk." Adding sneeringly, "So she is learning to listen. You said this." Before turning back towards the house, he finalised with, "Spend an afternoon getting to know her. Maybe you can love her back." His last sight as he left, Clara's little anxious face looking after him.

Back up in Guillem's room, Jim returned to the documents. He knew he would never be returning to that world. What had happened here, Clara, the tape, the gulags, even the broken gravestone, had all made a bonfire of the bridges back to England. His duties lay here. Where he believed he was needed. Julian, even Trish and Tracey, would probably remain welcoming enough, but he did not need them. To retrieve something from the wreckage left by his father. He looked up from the sorting of sheets and bundles through his fingers. The comparison had come alive in head. Like the urban bomber, long since gone home to watch with proud excitement the ruination he has been responsible for on the television news that night. Francis sat far away in distant comfort, staring into the screen watching his children wandering stunned and bloodstained, their blundered brains in search of a fragment of rationale among the debris they were stepping through.

Stilled by the image, his eyes unseeing the wallpaper he was staring at, it was a time before Jim was certain that the voice was back, speaking to him.

-What did you expect, son? Happy families? Live in the real world. Do things that might make a difference, and there will always be places you can't return to. It was something me and old Casals had in common. We both daren't go back to Spain after the war. Both had enemies waiting for us. It was what fooled the old man for so long that he and me believed the same things. Like you and me, James. I couldn't go back to England either. My old masters in the secret service, they were now high and mighty. Ministers, senior civil servants and the like. And the story was that we had all fought an honourable war. If I had returned, there would be charges against me, trials. Embarrassments. Just as if you returned and started to shout out about those boys. Remember, the story of what happens in the world is seldom told by those who made it happen. We're too busy doing it, for that.

"Oh, sod off!" Jim snapped it down at the box before him, not looking back to where the voice had come from, somewhere over his shoulder. "Don't compare yourself to me. You profited from it. You traded in people's lives. They had no choice, but to depend on you."

-I got them what they wanted, the dead man sneered. They weren't going to be able to take the things they paid me with, over the Pyrenees, into Spain. You forget, it was also about survival. Nobody was giving me a ration card to get food. Constancia had hers taken away-

"This wasn't about food! What about all those bicycles in La Retrait?"

-Huh! Those were my income. Bicycles were gold makers in those years. I hired them out when I could. But some were transport for the Resistance.

"The Resistance? The only liberation you were doing was of other people's property."

-You forget. You forget what the total picture was. From the end of 1943, it was known that that war was won. Anyway, it was then that the new war was declared, the one they came to call the Cold War. Remember, I had seen a red republic in action. I had seen the burnt churches in Spain in 1936 and 7. France could not become communist. My duty then became to prepare for the new war.

"By betraying your comrades to the fascists, yes?"

-Who were my comrades then? asked the old man sarcastically. Who could they be?

"Well, none of them definitely were your comrades in Forty Four- when you had to run away. And leave Constancia. Of course- yes, I've seen that photograph of her. You always- you always have a good reason for saving yourself, but not those around you. Like your wife. Like your children. Why did she ever have you back?"

-Because, and there was a waspish smile in his tone, she was Spanish. She was a catholic wife and she could not return to Spain.

"Because of you. Always, always, because of you. Sod off. Go away."

And at this, Jim turned to where the last sound of the voice had come, from the doorway. There was nothing there. Kneeling and twisted round, he listened. There was no sound in the house, but his breathing. It was a time before he untwisted himself and leaned, unseeing, again over the open box. Looking down its empty liftshaft, teetering, deciding what to do with the space that dropped away below him. Leading back down to where he had come from. Once. To fill it with himself? To fling himself down into it, back into England? To become some sort of professional witness for all those victims of all those ills? Or to seal it up inside the dead and empty building that his past had become.

The paper on top was a sheet of notes he had written, back in 86 or 87. Half the page was taken up with a list of decoded initials. Letters, followed by names, and often question marks. In the middle, as if hid amongst then was *DT = Damien Toser.* With no question mark. But what he remembered from when the page had been written was the intimate excitement of conspiracy with Sylvie, often knelt close to each other on the carpet. Set among that growing ocean of such paper spread away from them, the almost pubescent simplicity of how it felt then. Before the sex in Bradford. And, after dwelling on the image long enough for it to putrefy with what had happened since, he shook it out of his head and returned it to the other documents.

Soon before he had finished, the sound of Clara's voice downstairs with her mother. At least the child was making the effort, he thought. The fifty or so pages that he was going to send to Julian he bagged up. The rest, after a nervous check through them, he boxed back for burning. He told himself it was the right thing to do. Before he descended the stairs to face whatever was going on there.

He cooked the meal from whatever there was left in the house, a sign that their domestic routines had completely broken down. Since he had returned from the UK, no proper shopping had been done. And they were left with produce from the farm and last of the tins.

After he had put Clara to bed, he found Gizande clearing up in the kitchen and said, "We must go to the market this week. The kitchen is empty."

"I will -" she started.

But he cut her off, "No. Come with me."

She glanced at him, then carried on sweeping crumbs into her hand.

He wanted to ask her whether they would ever do anything together again. But was fearful that she might answer. Big questions require big answers, so, instead, he said almost conversationally, "He was here again today. When I was upstairs."

She knew who he meant. She watched him briefly, then went back to her work.

"He was just making excuses again," Jim carried on. What about? he thought for a moment. Before he summarised, "How stealing bikes and furniture from the Jews was part of the great battle against communism."

She went over to the bin in the corner and emptied her hand of what she had collected, precisely picking off the last crumbs that had stuck to her fingers. He waited for her to turn round, to give her the chance to say anything. He watched her until she became aware and uncomfortable with his watching and her eyes sought some other task to occupy her. Other than being with him.

He could forgive her everything, except her silence. Even Andreas.

Then, she spoke. From where she was, across the room, her rigid back turned away from him. "You have been the thief of my true family."

Jim looked dumbly at her for this sudden pronouncement.

"I would today have Suzanne as my sister, if - if you…" she hesitated, stumbled, as she turned to face him, "…if you were not here." And she pointed down at the floor of the house, with that same gesture of place as Suzanne had made when she had talked about the gulags claim on her home. "Now, because you are here in my home, because I must keep it as a secret…"

"Oh, yes," Jim answered. "I s'pose that was my fault. The reason you didn't know - and the reason we fell in love," spelling out the words, "was because your mother had never told you. She had the tape and she waited until after -"

Gizande cut in, "Until after- until after I had your child in my stomach- in my body," the words whispered across the room as scattered dust.

He was trapped in anger again. Was this how it was always going to be? Her denials of the child? The blame for it only on him? "You're a fool, Gizande - a fool over this."

"Oh, yes-" she started to answer with contempt.

But he pressed on, "What I took for your intelligence - it's not, is it? It's not. All this silence, all this not answering- it's because you're terrified of life - and you always have been. Even before you knew." He pointed at his own face, "I can accept it. We were brought together and we fell in love. Maybe we fell in love because we were brother and sister and we didn't know it. But underneath it - underneath all that sitting around being silent and fooling me that you were being wise, you're really just another little catholic girl, aren't you?"

She stood there, across the room, planted to the spot, her mouth half open, making a face of fury. With hunted eyes.

"Beneath all the talk of the stranger world," he shoved his way onwards at her, "and catharism, you're actually a little girl who's never forgotten to be obedient to the priests, aren't you?"

The initial shock at his attack gone, her face began to clench.

"That's it, Gizande, isn't it? Just like Constancia. Loyal to it to the end. Remember, I know about these things. I was raised by priests. I know how they do it. You're just frightened - fear of the devil, that's what the stranger world really is, isn't it? It's just nothing more than an old fashioned catholic fear of the devil. Just like they probably drummed it into you about the fires of hell - just as they did it to me as a kid."

She now fought back. "You came here," and she took a step towards him, "and you took my life away." Another step. "So I cannot go from the house, because I do not know- what other people know with truth, about who you are." Step by step. "Now I have lost my son. I never see him. And my daughter -" As his recent meeting with Gaillarde in the cowshed was remembered, she caught a look in his face, misinterpreting it, "No! My real daughter. Gaillarde - my true daughter," said with poisoned virulence, as she reached the corner of the table, only an arm-reach away, her teeth exposed with the turn back of her lips, spittle flecking her chin, she was ugly with it. "You think nothing of my belief in the stranger world, but I know it now - I know it now. It is not a belief from the books. It is the evil we must live here. You - you," her voice a feral growl, her finger projected towards him, so savagely that he took half a step back. "You - you have brought it into my life. It is the world of the stranger god - here!"

her voice hoarse with the venom. "It is you who have been the- who have brought the message of the devil."

"What devil? There is no devil." Urgent with it, he hissed, "The only devil was the father we shared. I did nothing - I knew nothing - just as you did. It was you - it was you who gave me the permission to come to your bed. I was after it, but you gave it. That time," he said with fearsome emphasis, "there was no rape."

Trapped in their antagonism, with nowhere to go but for one of them, beyond the words to strike out at the other. For Jim, the moment passed first, as the sense of utter defeat swooned through his body. He now believed he had finally lost her. She read it in his eyes and there was no sympathy for him. Stonily, she held her gaze and in it Jim was sure he saw a glitter of triumph. He breathed out all the tension, the years of living with her. He wanted to ask, What about Clara? But knew, whatever arrangements, the child would be staying with him. He felt as he should say something. At least to denote his surrender. But the victory in her eyes prompted him to say nothing. So he looked down at his feet, which she took as his submission. And he left the room.

Afterword

She left quietly the next day. I lay in the sleeping bag, listening. Anything to avoid another confrontation in the kitchen. Only later did I discover that she had not gone to the fields, but she had taken most of her clothes with her too.

The next time I saw her, she was back living in Germany. After she had disappeared, I needed to make contact to sort out all the problems of the farm. And at least to tell her that Guillem was going to move back in as I left. Suzanne helped with all the negotiations, but it was Gaillarde who really acted as the representative of the family in these matters and I liked to think she had a little regret that she had lost me as her step father.

It was Anna, of course, who finally tracked Gizande down to where she was living, near the prison, back in Germany. She had promised Gizande not to give the address, but I was told where she worked as a waitress in a Rasthof on the nearby autobahn. It seemed logical for me to go there by van and during the long drive, I relived those two journeys I had made with her to Berlin.

She had agreed to meet me at the end of her shift. I was going to be early, so I pulled into the service area before hers to spin out the time watching the Asian and African and east European women working there. Russians? From all that I had been hearing about the history of Europe, I remembered something. Had it been Helena- or more probably, Anna who said, "The Ivans raped our women in 1945 and now their women wipe the shit from our toilets on the autobahnen." Like everything, a crude and crooked sort of justice.

Wondering whether I was there finally to triumph over the pathetic situation she had chosen for herself now, when I entered her Rasthof I saw Gizande sat in a quiet and empty corner, wearing her uniform. As I came up, she gave me a smile, slight and brief. But warm enough so that I couldn't remember which of us spoke, "Hi," first. As I sat opposite her, our knees momentarily brushed.

I thought then, where would we start? With what had happened to me? What had happened to her? Her kids? Clara? So, looking down at her uniform and looking round at the bleakness of any motorway services in any place at that time of night, I asked, "Are you okay?"

She nodded, "Ja," then smiled. "Oui. Ou, yes. Jim, which is the right language for me now?" It was said to make me smile and this slightest possibility of repair between us touched me. Before the realities plucked it away again.

I would have asked about where she lived, but I understood from the phone call from Anna, that would be forbidden ground. And I wouldn't introduce the topic of Clara. So, "I think the farm is doing well. It is Guillem's work, but I meet Gaillarde in town sometimes and she tells me about it. I think she goes up and helps her brother when she can, quite a lot."

"They were always intimate together," she reflected a little nostalgically. "They were a good brother and sister for each other."

"Huh." I allowed my thoughts on that to surface, but said no more of what was in my mind. That I had arrived in France without a family and, since then, my father had crowded my life with being a brother- or lover- to those sisters. So I continued, "She told me he is experimenting with a new strain of cattle. He hopes one day to breed." I wondered if she heard from them herself, but left the silence for her to fill.

That she was not really listening to me, her next words showed, "I failed in the traditional thing. I married Yves. I had two children, but... I had been away out in the world... and I could not submit."

I wondered if now she had found the right mix. In this solitary devotion outside the prison walls. The loyal little wife and the radical cause, without the need for sex. Almost a Virgin Mary.

As if she heard my thoughts, still without looking at me, she continued dreamily, "Now, with Andreas... I may visit him one time the month. It is all that I am permitted. I am not wife. Or sister. It is all that is permitted."

I watched the hopelessness of it in her face, all her life circumscribed by one short meeting every month with a man I doubted, from my memory of him, recognised the cost she was paying. Then, maybe that was what she had always threatened herself with. Another of a series of relationships where she had paid the cost of the man's crimes.

"Suzanne, she is well?" she unexpectedly asked.

I was circumspect in answering. "She is fine. She has come to terms with-" but I looked at her to see whether she understood the phrase. Or was detached enough to be barely aware of what I answered. But I corrected myself anyway, "She understands now the gulags." Wondering whether to tell or not. That Suzanne had restrained my offer to mediate between her and Maurice. A foolish gesture anyway, given the poverty of my French. But, as she didn't ask, I added nothing. Just as she had not really asked about her half-sister.

She was so wrapped up in that glazed dream she could see before her that when she spoke again, I was not sure if she was speaking the words of Andreas. Speaking for both of them, maybe for me also. "Maybe

I was wrong, what I have been doing. But what do I do when I know how bad the world is to the poorest people?"

I did not understand and was not going to seek an invitation to wherever she was. I tried to draw her back. From where she was, into the empty clattering room where we were. "Why does everything have to have a name? You used to say you believed in catharism. You called it the old belief. Now it is something else. Why isn't being good just enough?"

She woke to me there with her, focussing her eyes on me, before looking out at the night beyond the wet window beside her. "Before I knew, catharisme was a pretty idea. When I knew- who I am - it was possible to run up into the mountains. To reach the places of the perfect ones. But I ran to excess - to my exhaustion. The truth was that the evil of the stranger world is too big. It is so huge, it can not be moved. I was without power, when I knew of the tape. Then, when you hear the tape, you did not believe of the evil as I do. You still wished to live with me- like a husband - keeping the lie hidden. That was impossible. I now saved myself, yes. I escaped. From you and from Esclarmonde." She paused, to reflect on this. "You can only become a perfect by removing yourself from the world, from all the corruptions. Here, I can live simply. I have no relationship. Only the relationship that I am the visitor to Andreas. I am the only person who makes the visits. It is what I must do. Each life we live is a prison. I am a prisoner with him." This was said without drama, without hesitation, a modest self-definition from long meditations. Alone with her self. "Jim, I was fertilised with that child by the Devil. You were his instrument. You were not to know. But it was also necessary that I leave you. Two of you. Your saving, you must construct for yourself."

"I have nothing to save myself from," my answer sounding too smart, so I pushed aside the complacent sound of it with, "Can it be a crime - can it be a sin, if we never knew we were committing it? Now - with Clara - isn't it a crime to take away her parents? Gizande, I love Clara. Clara loves me. I told your mother that Clara-"

"She is not my mother."

"I told her that Clara deserves her continued silence. That she should die with that secret, knowing that she has kept Clara happy. And with her family. She agreed. No one will know. It is safe."

But she was shaking her head, "It is not the keeping of secrets that is important. Will that keep silent what I know within my body? For you, it was a moment, the faucet of your semen opened within me. For me, at two months, I learn that it will be the child of my brother. And I continued to permit it to grow within me for the complete nine months. For that permission… That is why I am here," a perfunctory summary of the place with a hand. Whitened and softened by too much water in the kitchens, from the gentle rasp of the touch I had once known.

That was the last time I saw her. I believe she still writes to Gaillarde, who has once or twice referred to her mother when I've met her in the town. She has her own child now and lives with a young Arab man who was with her on one occasion. She has suggested I bring Clara down to visit, but nothing has come of it. Suzanne tells me that I'm over-protective of my little girl, but Clara is now at the école maternelle and she has been bullied by some of the other children. For being the outsider, like her father. When she goes to her elementary school, it will be where her aunt now teaches. Outside Suzanne, I have few relationships. At the école gates, waiting for Clara, the other mums avoid me. I'm sure I'm the subject of their gossip. And will be, as soon as I turn my back.

I think about Gizande often. She did return once, for the funeral of her mother. Gaillarde told me with apologies, that I would not be welcome to join the family and Gizande made no attempt to make contact during the two days she was back home. With the death of the old woman, finally released from her fear of the secret of who she really was, she could return to her desolate sentinalship outside the prison walls. I know she trusts my silence about our shared father. Even from Suzanne, who has had enough consequences of the man. The Police visited once more, about a year after she went to Germany. They asked some pointless questions about my trips to England. Nothing about her or Andreas. Then I started to get some harassing letters from the French tax authorities, which Suzanne has helped me to fend off. Maybe I'm just on that list of people the authorities wish to irritate, when they've nothing more important to do.

A few letters find their way up here to me at La Retraite - or Il Refugio? Des Parfaits? What do I call it now? No longer Perfect, if it ever could have been. Earned its real name at last, whatever that is? We are, of course, beyond the delivery of the Poste, but every visit to Larozelle, I check for poste restante. I used to hope foolishly, for something from her. A letter did arrive from Germany, but it was from Vanja, one of the Bulgarian girls. I remember it was addressed to *Mister & Madame Briggs.* It thanked us for speaking to Finch, who had arranged for them to leave the hotel and found them a family in Erfurt to live with. She wrote that the two of them were now students and the awkward English of the letter sparkled with the gaiety and promise of their new lives. Could any of that have been the truth? Anyway, I have mislaid it and have never been able to write a reply.

Most recently, a letter from Julian. He is in Bosnia now, working with one of the charities to help young people repair their communities. He said Scadding finally won his case, without Finch's help, but on appeal by the Council he was not awarded his legal costs, so the precise little hero is as badly off as before. He is ill, with his wife looking after him. Perhaps some sort of resolution for the pair of them, despite their poverty? Julian wrote, *I couldn't have done any of this but for you, Jim. Your docs won Sydney's case. It was your example that I look up to in everything I do. I wouldn't be in Mostar now, but for you.* He wrote how he was working with the locals to get the Mostar Bridge rebuilt. It had been destroyed by the Serbs. Before the war, they had all been Mostarians, but the same young men who had dived together from the Bridge, were killing each other in 1993. Broken into the river, it separated the town, Serbs from Muslims, but the hope to rebuild it, he wrote, *lifting the first stones from the river bottom was like phoenix arising, joining their world together again.* I doubted it. It was too typical of Julian's naivety. I heard Anna's voice in my head. About the Berlin Wall. In that case, the illusion was that smashing it down would release the phoenix. But what they learned, really, was how different they had become, east and west. When the Bridge was rebuilt, would it not just be a symbol of the separation of the tribes, either side of the uncrossable river of the blood that had been spilt? I knew nothing of the place myself, but I understood that maybe something has been for ever lost in the destruction of its Bridge. The illusion they then had that it joined them, when now they know that it marked their separation. That cannot be rebuilt. In Berlin, they thought the Wall divided them. Until it was torn down, when they realised it had been the cement that joined them. Made them both Berliners- either side of it. When it was up it joined the town, but when it was down, it separated them. There is now an east side and a west side both in Mostar and in Berlin, in a way there never had been before. As Anna said, they have learned in Berlin not to take the past or the future for granted. Julian also wrote that he had heard of an English man called Finch operating in the local Serbian enclave, rumoured to be trading captured Muslim women and maybe guns? Too much of a coincidence? But there was no mention in the letter of Trish and the kids. I will write a reply.

The letter prompted me to think about Damien, something I do less often than I used to. I just know now how little you can do to curb the appetites of the rich, the powerful and the protected. And the appetites of those lesser monsters who procure for them. However gross those appetites may be. At least with my present life, tucked away in this remote corner of France, I don't have to deal with them, apart from shifting the occasional load of their overpriced junk from London to a second home in the Dordogne or down on the coast.

I also saw a photo of Klinsmaar in Suzanne's newspaper. Last time, my smooth interrogator in the DDR prison. He was now part of a delegation from the European Bank of Reconstruction and Development, whatever that is. They were on a visit to one of East European applicants to join the European Union. Trading like Finch in the debris of communism?

Tracey has never visited. I have kept her at arms' length, blocking any hint from her of coming in her early letters, with excusive dishonesties. It would have been too much. Despite that, I know somehow that we will never be strangers. Now we have settled into a routine of Xmas cards. I always sign it just myself. Perhaps I should ask Suzanne to sign it, the aunt she wanted at her wedding. Even get Clara to add her crude and careful tumble of the letters of her own name to the card, introducing the sisters to each other. And wait for a response? Or let it decay by distance? After all, don't we hang on too long to people, just because they happen to be related to us? Maybe I am really an embarrassment to my oldest daughter. Better remaining out at the remotest rim of the geography of her life.

I'm certain now of one thing. That there are no moral certainties. There are no simple yes/no questions to life, as I once thought. While Gizande still seeks them with her solitary vigil outside the prison walls. I still occasionally speak to Anna. We have a phone line at last up here. She sent me a mobile phone, but it is an anachronism as they have not erected any masts yet so that signals can reach this end of the valley. Maybe it will happen and it will cease to be an ornament. Anna has also dumped the moral certainties of the youth she once shared with Gizande. And Andreas, who she says will not be released for another six years. But for Anna, it has all been replaced by making money.

I would have had things different in many ways. But, faced with them again, would I have done anything different? I'm not sure. I think it's doubtful. Doubtful whether I would've been able to do anything in a different way… Truly, from where I stand now, looking out over these mountains, with the life I have, would I have wanted to do anything different? I speak French now. I have the full vocabulary, but I'm still pretty ponderous at putting the words together to make sense. At home, I now use nuggets of French increasingly buried in the English sentences between us. Suzanne is still embittered about what happened. The vicious anonymous letters, the loss of her home - the loss of her headteacher's job. But I think, most of all, more even than her severance with Maurice, it has been the loss of the father she thought she had known and had loved her without qualification. A writer from England visited me the summer before last. I was intrigued, so I did not discourage him coming when he phoned me from Larozelle, as Suzanne was away visiting Marie-Claire and Felipe in Toulouse. He was researching for a book about the war and had heard about Francis. He wanted to write about him as a war hero. I listened to him for an hour, before sending him away with nothing. From Francis himself, I've heard nothing since that last time in the box room. Suzanne and I eventually went up to clean the graffiti from the cracked headstone. The last time she's returned to that village. Perhaps he's buried back there for ever now.

At this time of my life, I understand I'm dying, little-by-little. The physician would tell me that my cells have been more dying than renewing for decades now. I can now believe him, from the slower steps and the hastier, shallower breaths I have to take climbing up this familiar mountain to the hut. It is the wisdom given by the slow approach enforced by age, that unblinds the eyes of trivial and selfish optimism for your self. We know at last that we cannot stay here ourselves, so we can only wonder if we will leave the world a little better than we found it. Remembering the past now, I try to give it meaning. A value to measure every recalled event I have taken part in. Better or worse… worse or better? Even the bad deeds, with their weight of guilt, may have shaped a way forward to better things. Didn't they? Or were they just little acts of evil on the vast panorama of the World of the Stranger God- as Gizande used to call it? Or could they have been what I learnt from? To take a better step forward, the next time? Certainly, to never despair, but never to hope too much. I look forward to fewer events. A little boredom in my life is welcome now.

I heard Deedee, Jude and Charles went back to England. I wasn't asked to shift them this time. Furniture moving is tedious now and getting too tiring for my old body. I don't know what we will do for the money it makes, when I'm too knackered to go on doing it, back and forth to England. I took a young man, Roland, with me last time to help, but his extra cut barely made the trip worthwhile for me. Theresa told me she'd also got a letter from tax authorities asking about me- so that's another reason I might have to give up. And I guess my pension prospects from the UK are probably pretty messy. I need to speak to the Consulate. Visit Toulouse myself for that, when I've got time.

Really the two of us are dependent on Suzanne's income, now that she has returned to teaching. I only play at farming. As I probably always have, since I arrived in this country. We have forty French alpine goats, giving good milk for carrying on cheese making. They seem to like the rough scrub round La Retraite, finding the sweet summer flowers amongst it to eat. The best of times is feeding the new born kids with milk from the bottle, the warmth and smell of their new bodies against me. The pleasure of Clara in helping. The worst is the fighting between them, sometimes gashing each others' udders with their horns. But I would need to sell in a dozen markets a week in the summer to make any worthwhile money out of the cheeses.

The fresh summer grass of the top meadows is now rented out each year for the sheep of one of our lower neighbours. I keep the shepherd's hut checked and tidy, since now one of the new GR walking routes comes close by. About twice a month I climb up there and fill the large plastic water bottle I put there for refreshment. And read the visitors book that I leave in an old biscuit tin on the stone bench. Even some English have passed through, signing the book. One couple writing that they were so jealous of the beauty they have found, they wish to return to live in these mountains. That was Teddy and Tamsin from Hampshire. Puffing with exertion up the hill, it's difficult to believe I ever ran a marathon. But not so hard to remember running in these hills with Gizande.

We've bought a television now. It was my idea. I watch it. I can't understand most of the French, spoken too fast for my still-pedestrian ear. She has brought her books. But I will sit there in the evenings, her beside me reading a book or marking the children's work, me idly watching, my mind really reciting over and over again all the things that have happened.

As we are the two who should never have lived together… and loved, now we find that, of all the people in the world, we both are the only two who can live with each other. Melted together in the hurt of how those who went before have scarred us. Stuck with the circumstances they have bequeathed, we have found a certain peace, a tolerance of what cannot be changed. The evidence of it is Clara and the quiet delight we draw from watching her grow. The whisper of the child's feet on the rug outside our door, as she comes to join us in bed every morning. Giving Clara what I had only been able to deny to Tracey.

I often think of all the other people who have touched my life in ways they had never intended - and perhaps would never know. Maybe that was the same for everyone. Our own failures become a success to someone else. They gain from my loss. It isn't a matter of cost. It is a matter of giving and, out of it all, my failures as a father - as my father had failed me- the drained away loves for Jane, for Sylvie - and even of forgotten Linda… they revisit me, so that sitting here now, I get some sort of sense of the generosity of things. The meanness had only been in my and others' inability to understand.

I can hear the steady clocking up across the hills from further down the valley, the sound of a neighbour's sledge hammer knocking in fencing stakes, defining the edge of his world. As he does, defining ours. I would reach over to touch your hand, but realise you are already looking at me. Any movement now, would be too much.

La Fin

Lightning Source UK Ltd.
Milton Keynes UK
23 September 2009

144103UK00001B/30/P